W9-CLR-333

Dear Hannah & Caroline —
    May you be blessed by reading
This extraordinary book —
                        Love,
                            Nini &
                        Uncle Dan

"This classic has refreshed my spirit time and again when my soul has longed for Christ-centered guidance through a maze of modern detours and diversions. I'm so grateful this special edition of *The Pilgrim's Progress* is now available to not only a new generation of Christians but to believers like myself who need direction and refreshment along our journey toward Home."

JONI EARECKSON TADA, President, Joni and Friends International Disability Center

"If any smoothing of Bunyan's seventeenth-century language plus new colored pictures can set *Pilgrim's Progress* aglow in the hearts of today's young readers, this lovely book will surely do it."

J. I. PACKER, Professor of Theology, Regent College

"Every generation is heir to John Bunyan's timeless allegory, and to each generation falls the task of commending this tale anew. The collaboration of editor C. J. Lovik and illustrator Mike Wimmer has yielded a book that could well be a classic for our time. With great care, Lovik has combined the best elements of Bunyan's rich, evocative prose with accessibility for the modern reader. And in Wimmer, Bunyan has met his illustrator for the twenty-first century. The thirty illustrations that grace this edition are a world in themselves—the equal of any that appear in J.R.R. Tolkien's books."

KEVIN BELMONTE, lead historical consultant for the motion picture *Amazing Grace*

"If you are looking for a classic edition of *The Pilgrim's Progress*, with a simplified form of Bunyan's original text, traditional color illustrations, and explanatory notes, this is undoubtedly the version for you."

TIMOTHY DOWLEY, author of *The Christians*

"For two centuries following its publication (Part 1 in 1678, Part 2 in 1684), *The Pilgrim's Progress* gained the status of best-read book (apart from the Bible). This magnificent production by Crossway with stunning illustrations by Mike Wimmer should help reinstate Bunyan's classic allegory to the status it belongs. It should be a question we ask ourselves: Have I read *The Pilgrim's Progress*? If not, repent immediately, for in taking up this volume you will find pastoral insights from a pastor of souls to help you discover the biblical way of salvation and aid you in the journey home."

DEREK W. H. THOMAS, John E. Richards Professor of Systematic Theology, Reformed Theological Seminary (Jackson)

"This is one of the best books I've ever read."

MARK DEVER, Senior Pastor, Capitol Hill Baptist Church

"C. J. Lovik's new edition of *The Pilgrim's Progress* almost takes one's breath away. The text is readable, the notes are clear, and the illustrations are absolutely beautiful. This is a book to be in everyone's library and will definitely occupy a prominent place in the libraries provided for Rafiki's children and adults in Africa. It is a joy to know that Lovik's edition of the Bunyan classic will be read by and to thousands of children throughout the world."

> ROSEMARY JENSEN, Founder and President, Rafiki Foundation;
> author of *Praying the Attributes of God* and *Living the Words of Jesus*

"*The Pilgrim's Progress* has long been a favorite of many. Now there is even more to love with this beautiful, updated edition. Editor's notes clarify the ideas in John Bunyan's classic allegory, while footnotes show where in Scripture Bunyan found them. The detailed color illustrations will delight both new readers and long-time lovers of this beloved tale."

> STARR MEADE, author of *Keeping Holiday* and *Training Hearts,*
> *Teaching Minds*

"Like countless others, I have been greatly influenced by *The Pilgrim's Progress*. Charles Spurgeon called it 'next to the Bible, the book that I value most.' It has already inspired generations, and I am confident that this new edition will inspire the rising generation. It is refreshingly readable while remaining true to this timeless classic. The illustrations, Scripture references, and study notes make it a superb resource for family devotions and study groups."

> SUSAN HUNT, author of *Spiritual Mothering*

"The longer I journey through our dear Immanuel's land, the more grateful I am for John Bunyan's 'dream' and the cruel imprisonment that occasioned it. What a gift weary travelers have been given in this precious, timeless classic—and what beauty, insight, and encouragement was borne out of his suffering! Unafraid to challenge the outward trials of moralism, materialism, and persecution, humble enough to confess his own doubts and despair, Bunyan leads us on our way to the Celestial City we long to see. And what a gift modern readers have been blessed with in C. J. Lovik's careful editing and Mike Wimmer's luminous illustrations! This book is beautiful! *The Pilgrim's Progress* has always been a cherished treasure, but this edition makes Christian's story—our story—sing! I'm so thankful for it!"

> ELYSE FITZPATRICK, author of *Because He Loves Me* and
> *Comforts from the Cross*

"If a picture truly does speak a thousand words, this version of *The Pilgrim's Progress* will be the best of all. Combining the beauty of Mike Wimmer's illustrations with this timeless classic is a stroke of genius."

> STEVE MURPHY, Publisher, *Homeschooling Today* magazine

The Pilgrim's Progress

The Pilgrim's Progress

From This World to That Which Is to Come

John Bunyan

C. J. Lovik, editor

Illustrated by Mike Wimmer

CROSSWAY

WHEATON, ILLINOIS

The Pilgrim's Progress

Updated text copyright © 2009 by C. J. Lovik

Illustrations copyright © 2009 by C. J. Lovik

Published by Crossway
1300 Crescent Street
Wheaton, Illinois 60187

All rights reserved. No part of this publication may be reproduced, stored in a retrieval system or transmitted in any form by any means, electronic, mechanical, photocopy, recording or otherwise, without the prior permission of the publisher, except as provided for by USA copyright law.

Cover design: Josh Dennis

Cover and interior illustrations: Mike Wimmer

First printing, 2009

Printed in China

Hardcover ISBN: 978-1-4335-0699-4
PDF ISBN: 978-1-4335-0700-7
Mobipocket ISBN: 978-1-4335-0701-4
ePub ISBN: 978-1-4335-1880-5

Library of Congress Cataloging-in-Publication Data

Bunyan, John, 1628–1688.
  The pilgrim's progress : from this world to that which is to come /
John Bunyan ; updated by C.J. Lovik ; illustrated by Michael Wimmer.
  — (Updated version).
      p. cm.
  Includes bibliographical references.
  ISBN-13: 978-1-4335-0699-4 (hc)
  1. Christian pilgrims and pilgrimages—Fiction. 2. Christian life—
Fiction. I. Lovik, Craig John, 1946–   . II. Title.
PR3330.A2L68   2009
823'.4—dc22   2009004765

Crossway is a publishing ministry of Good News Publishers.

OGP		24	23	22	21	20	19	18	17	16	15	14
19	18	17	16	15	14	13	12	11	10	9	8	7	6	5

Contents

LIST OF ILLUSTRATIONS

PUBLISHER'S FOREWORD

THE BUNYAN LEGACY

Except for the Bible itself, *The Pilgrim's Progress* is widely recognized as the most influential, beloved, and widely distributed book in the English language. First published in 1678, it became instantly popular throughout English culture, irrespective of education, economic status, or social class. It is widely regarded as a work of genius, though the author, John Bunyan (1628–1688), had only a limited, grade-school education and made his living at the tinker's trade, going from house to house repairing pots and pans.

Bunyan's achievement is all the more remarkable, given the fact that he was the object of extended religious persecution as a result of his call to preaching. From 1655 to 1660, Bunyan preached regularly at the local Bedford Baptist congregation and in the surrounding towns. But because he had not been licensed to preach by the established Church of England, he was imprisoned in the primitive conditions of the Bedford Jail beginning in early 1661, where he languished for the next twelve years. It is during this period, however, that Bunyan most likely wrote the original draft of *The Pilgrim's Progress*, with a copy of the Bible providing his only reference material.

Written in the form of a highly imaginative allegory, *The Pilgrim's Progress* tells the unforgettable story of Christian and the extreme, soul-threatening dangers he encounters on his journey to the Celestial City. But it is also much more than an allegory; in a sense, it is both the personal story of Bunyan and the universal story of anyone who undertakes the same eternal pilgrimage. The result is a masterpiece of literature as well as spiritual truth—a book that at one time was loved and read in nearly every home in England and North America, a book that has endured as a classic for more than three centuries.

ABOUT THIS EDITION

The purpose in publishing this edition of *The Pilgrim's Progress* is to carry forward this treasured legacy for a new generation. With this as the objective, the text of this edition has only been lightly edited. Thus the intention of both the editor and the publisher has only been to update highly archaic words and awkward sentence structure, while retaining the beauty and brilliance of the original story. Likewise, the intention of this edition has never been to simplify or to change Bunyan's original story, but to let the story unfold with all the power, truth, and remarkable creativity of the original. It is our hope and prayer, then, that the following pages will fascinate and captivate the hearts and minds of this generation today, as was the case when *The Pilgrim's Progress* was first published more than three centuries ago.

It should be noted further that this new edition has become a reality only through the vision of the editor, C. J. Lovik. As the publisher of this edition we are deeply grateful to Mr. Lovik—for his lifelong love, from the age of nine, for John Bunyan and *The Pilgrim's Progress*; for his literary skill and great care in editing the text; and for his painstaking labor of love in doing the editorial work over more than a decade. It is indeed a privilege to be entrusted with the publication of *The Pilgrim's Progress*, which we seek to carry out in a manner worthy of Bunyan's legacy.

Lastly, it is important to note the new art that was created specifically for this edition—the thirty, full-color, original paintings by the highly acclaimed artist, Mike Wimmer, which appear throughout the following pages. There is a sense in which these new paintings also carry forward the Bunyan legacy, in that many of the earliest editions of *The Pilgrim's Progress* also included original, engraved illustrations. As was the case more than three hundred years ago, these new illustrations—beautifully rendered in exquisite detail and faithfulness to the story—will delight a new generation of children and adults and will powerfully reinforce the timeless truths of Bunyan's original story.

It is with much appreciation, then—first to Bunyan for his timeless allegory of eternal realities and then to all those who have had a part in carrying forward the extraordinary Bunyan legacy—that we, as the publisher, commend this new edition of *The Pilgrim's Progress*, for the eternal benefit of all who read this work and for the glory of God alone.

Lane T. Dennis, Ph.D.
President and Publisher, Crossway

Editor's Introduction

by C. J. Lovik

The writings of John Bunyan have been an immeasurable gift to generations of English-speaking Christians. His most famous work, *Pilgrim's Progress*, has provided rich nutrients to the soil out of which practical Christianity has flourished and borne much fruit. Bunyan was the supreme Bible teacher for "everyman." To use an old illustration, it was Bunyan who placed the grain down on the barn floor where the little lambs could reach it, feast, and thrive.

There was nothing elitist or sophisticated about Bunyan, but there was something uniquely profound. Bunyan understood and expounded the timeless eternal truths of Holy Scripture—the miracle of redemptive grace and the battle every pilgrim must wage before he arrives at the Celestial City. And he did it in a way that even the simplest child could understand.

Since the age of nine years old, my appreciation and love for the works of Bunyan, especially *Pilgrim's Progress*, has grown and deepened. There was a time when I rarely heard a sermon in which some incident from *Pilgrim's Progress* was not used to illustrate a biblical truth. Many of those illustrations have guided me through my own pilgrimage. But, sadly, what was such a great benefit to me is enjoyed by only a relative few today.

In my late twenties I began teaching a class called "Pictures from *Pilgrim's Progress*," a title borrowed from Charles Spurgeon. In those days, three or four decades ago, I did not need to ask for a show of hands from those who had read *Pilgrim's Progress*, as all were familiar with the book. Even the unchurched were familiar with *Pilgrim's Progress*, as it was on the required reading list for every public high school student. Today things are much different, and you would be hard-pressed to find one in twenty Christians who have read *Pilgrim's Progress*. For those who are under thirty, the ratio would be even higher. And among those who were familiar with the book, it would typically not be the original text they had read but a children's paraphrase.

Many skilled authors have attempted to bring *Pilgrim's Progress* to modern English readers. I applaud their efforts and respect the desire to reclaim the lost readership this book once enjoyed. But it occurred to me, after reading many of these attempts, that something very important had been lost in the translation. In short, many of the truths that Bunyan so skillfully and artfully proposed had been dulled or skipped over in an attempt to keep the modern reader's interest. In addition much of the antiquity of the work had been lost, and with it was lost the voice and tenor of Bunyan himself.

For anyone who wishes to "update" the original text of *Pilgrim's Progress*, the challenge is indeed great. The English language has changed significantly in the last three hundred and fifty years. Scores of metaphors and sayings that were in common use and understood by all in the seventeenth century are now antiquated or obscure, creating a major obstacle for the modern reader. But in addition to this, the modern English reader often considers Bunyan's literary form of allegory to be antiquated and inconsequential, thereby missing the vibrant truths that are so richly illustrated in Bunyan's allegory.

The challenge of updating Bunyan's classic—in a way that preserves the author's voice and respects the antiquity of the work—was daunting and arduous. For nearly a year this was my constant focus—to prayerfully and carefully discern which stones on the path to leave untouched and which stones to adjust, however slight an adjustment may be necessary, to make the path passable once more (and glorious!) for the modern English reader. Likewise, my goal throughout has always been to respect the literary style of Bunyan and the truths he unfolded in his timeless narrative. The greatest compliment that I could receive after reading this updated edition of *Pilgrim's Progress* is that the reader would be able to honestly say that he has really read and encountered Bunyan and his classic work.

It is my hope and prayer that *Pilgrim's Progress* might once more be a blessing and inspiration to a new generation. Clearly Christians today are in great need of understanding, guidance, and encouragement. Thus it is my dream that in the pulpits of the English-speaking world *Pilgrim's Progress* might once again come into prominence and popular understanding—and likewise in the hearts of individuals and the homes of families around the world. What a tremendous thing it would be if a whole generation were to rediscover the deep, eternal truths of Bunyan's allegory—as an alternative and antidote to the lurid diet of Vanity Fair that is everywhere today in movies, videos, literature, and the Internet.

I have dedicated my efforts on this work to my gracious Lord and Savior, who is the author of all that is good and true. And having said this, I feel an obligation to add one more thing: As wonderful as *Pilgrim's Progress* is, it is not the Bible, nor is it equal to the Bible in any way except as a brilliant commentary on the only Scriptures—the Old and New Testaments. Bunyan wanted his readers to understand that fact; and so, in his absence, I am compelled to pass this along to you—the Scriptures stand alone!

Finally, one cannot read much of Bunyan without coming into contact with his poems and rhymes. When Bunyan's character Christian lost his burden at the foot of the cross, Bunyan exuberantly voiced the unimaginable joy of the event in a poem. This has inspired me to do the same. And so I offer my own poem to you, the reader, in hopes that it might be enjoyed by you and pleasing to my Lord.

The shadow of a wooden cross
A rising Son displayed.
In that place and on that day
An ancient debt was paid.

Prophetic Word merged with flesh,
With love bound to a tree.
There justice met with mercy
For all the world to see.

Divine the name of Him who hangs
With emblem wounds of glory,
Page of light that turned the night
Into a different story.

Joy was mixed with agony
That day upon the tree.
Reflecting on the Book of Life
My Savior thought of me.

Love deep and wide and full and free,
Love priceless and apart,
Love stained with crimson hues and tears
Has entered human hearts.

Look up, dear soul, and fix blind eyes
Upon the Savior's tree
And you will find as others have,
He makes the sightless see.

An unexpected resting place
Was found beneath that tree,
Where all my burdens came undone
And I found liberty.

Now, as you immerse yourself in the following pages, may Bunyan's timeless story come alive for you in all its rich allegorical power and beauty.

Christian looks for a way of escape outside the City of Destruction.

Chapter One

PILGRIM'S GREAT DISTRESS

As I walked through the wilderness of this world, I came to a certain place where there was a cave;[1] and I lay down in that place to sleep. As I slept, I dreamed a dream, and in this dream I saw a man clothed in rags,[2] standing in a place with his face turned away from his own house. He had a book in his hand and a heavy burden upon his back.[a]

I looked and saw him open the book and begin to read; and as he read, he wept and trembled. Not being able to contain himself, he cried out in a loud voice, "What shall I do?"[b3]

In this condition he went home and tried to keep to himself for as long as he could, so that his wife and children would not see him in distress. But after a short time his anguish had increased so much that he could not remain silent. So he began to share with his wife and children what was on his troubled mind; and this is what he told them:

"Dear wife and children, I am greatly troubled by this burden that torments me and grows and weighs so heavily upon me. Moreover, I have received information that the city in which we live

[a]Isaiah 64:6; Luke 14:33; Psalm 38; Habakkuk 2:2.
[b]Acts 2:36–37.

will be burned with fire from Heaven.[4] When this happens, all of us will be destroyed, unless (by a way I do not as yet see) some way of escape can be found, so that we may be delivered."

Hearing this, his family was greatly amazed, not because they believed what he said to them was true, but because they thought that he was losing his mind. So as the evening approached, hoping that sleep might settle his mind, they quickly put him to bed.

But the night was as troublesome to him as the day. Instead of sleeping, he spent the night in sighs and tears. So when morning came, his family came to find out how he was doing. "Worse and worse," he told them. He started speaking to them again about his fears and concerns, but they became cold toward him. They tried to change his outlook by treating him rudely. Sometimes they would deride, sometimes they would chide, and other times they would just ignore him.[5]

So he began retiring to his private room to pray for them and to pity them, and also to try to find consolation for his own misery. He would often walk alone in the fields, sometimes reading and sometimes praying; and for a long time this is how he spent his days.[6]

Then one day I saw the man walking in the fields (which he often did), reading in his book, and greatly distressed in his mind. As he read, he burst out, as he had done before, crying, "What shall I do to be saved?"[c][7]

I noticed that he looked this way and then that way, as if he would run; yet he stood still, because he could not decide which way to go. Just then I looked and saw someone named Evangelist coming toward him.[8] Evangelist came up to the man and asked, "Why are you crying out?"

He answered, "Sir, I understand from reading the book in my hand that I am condemned to die and after that to come to judgment.[d] I am not willing to do the first,[e] nor able to do the second."[f]

---

[c]Acts 16:31–32.
[d]Hebrews 9:27.
[e]Job 16:21–22.
[f]Ezekiel 22:14.

Evangelist points Christian to the sheep gate.

Then Evangelist asked, "Why are you not willing to die, since this life is attended with so many evils?"

The man answered, "Because I am afraid that this burden that is on my back will sink me lower than the grave, and I shall fall into Hell.[g]

"And, sir," continued the man, "if I am not ready to die, then I am not prepared to go to judgment and from there to execution. Thinking about these things distresses me greatly."

Then Evangelist said, "If this is your condition, why are you standing still?"

The man responded, "Because I do not know where to go."

Then Evangelist gave him a parchment and unrolled it so that the man could read, "Flee from the wrath to come."[h][9]

When he had read it, the man looked at Evangelist very carefully and said, "Which way should I run?"[10]

Then Evangelist, pointing with his finger to a very wide field asked, "Do you see the distant narrow gate?"[i][11]

"No," the man replied.

Then Evangelist asked, "Do you see the distant shining light?"[j]

"I think I do," the man answered.

Then Evangelist said, "Keep that light in your eye, and go up directly toward it, and soon you will see the narrow gate. And when you finally come to the gate, knock and you will be told what to do."[12]

So I saw in my dream that the man began to run. He had not run very far from his home when his wife and children, realizing what was happening, cried after him to return.[k] But the man put his fingers in his ears and ran on crying, "Life! Life! Eternal life!" So without looking back, he fled toward the middle of the valley.

The neighbors also came out to see what was going on, and when they saw who it was that was running, some mocked him, others

[g]Isaiah 30:33.
[h]Matthew 3:7.
[i]Matthew 7:13–14.
[j]Psalm 119:105; 2 Peter 1:19.
[k]Luke 14:26.

yelled out threats, and some cried after the man to return. Among those were two who decided to bring him back by force. The name of the one was Obstinate, and the name of the other was Pliable.[13]

Now by this time the man was a good distance away. But Obstinate and Pliable were determined to pursue him, which they did. Soon they caught up with him, and he asked them, "Why have you run after me?" The neighbors answered, "To persuade you to go back with us."

"But that is not possible," the man replied. "You live in the City of Destruction, the place where I was born; and I believe that if you stay in that city you will die sooner or later, and then you will sink lower than the grave, into a place that burns with fire and brimstone. Please consider, good neighbors, coming along with me."

"What!" said Obstinate. "And leave our friends and comforts behind us?"

"Yes," said the fleeing man Christian (for that was his name), "because all that you leave behind is not worthy to be compared with even a little of what I am seeking to enjoy.[l] And if you will come along with me and not give up, we will both be blessed with treasure to spare, beyond anything we can imagine.[m] Come along with me and see if what I am telling you is not true."

"What are you looking for?" Obstinate replied. "What is so valuable that you would turn your back on all the world to find it?"

"I am looking," Christian explained, "for an 'inheritance that is imperishable, undefiled, and unfading, kept in Heaven.'[n] It is kept safe there to be given at the appointed time to those who diligently seek it.[o] You can read about it in my book."

"Nonsense!" said Obstinate. "Away with your book. Will you come back with us or not?"

"No!" said Christian. "I have laid my hand to the plow and cannot look back. I have started this journey, and I must finish it."[p]

---

[l]2 Corinthians 4:18.
[m]Luke 15:17.
[n]1 Peter 1:4.
[o]Hebrews 11:16.
[p]Luke 9:62.

"Come on, Pliable," Obstinate urged his companion. "Let's turn around and go home without him. There is a group of these mixed-up lunatics who get a crazy idea in their head and are wiser in their own eyes than seven men who can render a reason."[q]

Then Pliable said, "Don't be so harsh. If what the good Christian says is true, the things he is looking for are better than anything we have. I feel like I should go along with my neighbor."

"What! More fools still?" Obstinate replied. "Do what I say, and go back. Who knows where this lunatic will lead you? Go back; go back and be wise."

"Don't listen to him," Christian urged. "Come with me, Pliable. There are things to be gained such as I was telling you about, and many more glories besides. If you don't believe me, read about it in this book; and as far as the trustworthiness of this book goes, it is all confirmed by the blood of Him who made it."[r]

"Well, neighbor Obstinate," said Pliable, "I have come to a decision. I have decided to go along with Christian and to cast in my lot with him." Pliable thought for a second and then turned to Christian and asked, "But do you know the way to the desired place?"

"I was given directions by a man whose name is Evangelist," Christian said. "He told me to go as quickly as I could to the little gate that is just up ahead, and once there we will receive instructions about the way before us."

"Come then, good neighbor," Pliable replied. "Let's be going." Then they went on together.

"And I will go back to my home," said Obstinate. "I will not be a companion of such misled fanatical fellows."

Now I saw in my dream, after Obstinate returned to the City of Destruction, that Christian and Pliable began to talk as they walked together through the middle of the valley. Thus they began to converse.

"I am glad," Christian said, "that you were persuaded to come

---

[q]Proverbs 26:16.
[r]Hebrews 13:20–21; also Hebrews 9:17–21.

along with me. I am surprised that Obstinate returned so quickly to the City of Destruction. I think if he had felt the power and terror of the unseen, as I have, he would have been persuaded to come along with us."

"Come, neighbor Christian, since it is just the two of us, tell me more about the wonderful things that await us when we arrive at the place to which we are going."

"I can better conceive of them with my mind," Christian explained, "than talk about them. But since you are interested, I will read about them from my book."

"And do you think that the words of your book are true?" Pliable asked.

"Yes, very sure, for the words were written by the One who cannot lie," Christian replied.[s]

"Well said; please tell me about the things that await us."[14]

"There is an endless Kingdom to be inhabited and everlasting life to be given to us so that we may live in that Kingdom forever," Christian explained.[t]

"Well said. What else?" Pliable asked.

"We will be given crowns of glory and clothing that will make us shine like the sun!"[u]

"This sounds very pleasant. What else?"

"There shall neither be crying nor sorrow, for He who is owner of the place will wipe all tears from our eyes."[v]

"And what company shall we have there?" Pliable asked.

"We will be with seraphim and cherubim[w] and creatures who will dazzle your eyes when you look at them. You will meet with thousands who have gone before us to that place. None of them are hurtful, but all of them are loving and holy, every one walking in the sight of God and standing in His presence with acceptance forever.

---

[s]Titus 1:2.
[t]Isaiah 65:17.
[u]John 10:27–29; 2 Timothy 4:8; Revelation 3:4; Matthew 13:43.
[v]Isaiah 25:8; Revelation 7:17; 21:4.
[w]Isaiah 6:2; 1 Thessalonians 4:16–17; Revelation 5:11.

In a word, there we will see the elders with their golden crowns.[x] There we will see the holy virgins with their golden harps. There we will see men who were cut in pieces by the world, burnt in flames, eaten by beasts, drowned in the seas, suffering all this and more for the love they have for the Lord of the place.[y] Everyone in that place is clothed with immortality, as with a robe."

"Hearing about this is enough to excite my heart," Pliable replied. "But are these things to be enjoyed by anyone? What do we have to do to share in all these things?"

"The Lord," Christian replied, "the governor of the country, has recorded in this book that if we are truly willing to have it, He will give it to us freely."[z]

"Well, my good companion, I am glad to hear about these things. Come, let's hasten our pace," Pliable replied.

"I cannot go as fast as I would like because of this burden that is on my back."

Now I saw in my dream, just as they had finished talking, that they came near to a very miry swamp that was in the middle of the valley. Then suddenly both Christian and Pliable, who were not paying attention to where they were walking, fell into the swamp. The name of the swamp was Despond. They wallowed there until they were both completely covered with mud. Christian, weighed down by the burden on his back, began to sink.

Then Pliable said, "Ah, neighbor Christian, where are you now?"

"Honestly," said Christian, "I don't know."

Christian's answer offended Pliable, who angrily said to Christian, "Is this the happiness you have been telling me about all the time we have been together? If we have this much difficulty at the beginning of our journey, what may we expect between now and the end of our journey? If I get out of this swamp alive, you can have the brave country that you're so fond of talking about without me." And with that he gave a desperate struggle or two and got out

---

[x]Revelation 4:4; 14:1–5.
[y]John 12:25; 2 Corinthians 5:2–4.
[z]Isaiah 55:1–2, 12; John 6:37; Revelation 21:6; 22:17.

Help rescues Christian from the Swamp of Despond.

of the mire on the side of the swamp that was nearest to the City of Destruction. So away he went, and Christian never saw him again.[15]

Christian was left to struggle in the Swamp of Despond alone. In spite of the difficulty, Christian still tried to get to the side of the swamp that was the furthest from the City of Destruction and nearest the narrow gate. He finally reached the edge of the swamp, but he could not, no matter how hard he tried, lift himself out of the swamp because of the heavy burden that was on his back.[16] Just then I saw in my dream that a man whose name was Help came to him and asked, "What are you doing here?"

"Sir," said Christian, "I was told to go this way by a man called Evangelist, who directed me also to the narrow gate so that I would escape the wrath to come. And as I was going there, I fell in here."

"But why didn't you look for the steps?" Help asked.[17]

"I was so frightened that I stepped the wrong way and fell into the swamp."

Then Help said, "Give me your hand." So Christian gave him his hand, and he pulled him out,[aa] set him on solid ground, and told him to go on his way.

Going over to the man who had pulled him out of the swamp, Christian asked, "Sir, since this swamp is right between the City of Destruction and the narrow gate, why hasn't someone filled this swamp so that travelers could walk over it safely?"

"This miry swamp," Help replied, "cannot be filled or repaired. It is the low spot where collects all the scum and filth that goes along with conviction for sin, and that is why it is called the Swamp of Despond. When a sinner is awakened to his lost condition, then doubts, fears, and discouraging apprehensions swell up in his soul, along with other miseries, which all get together and settle in this swamp. And that is why the ground is so bad in this place.

"It is not the pleasure of the King that this place should remain

---

[aa]Psalm 40:2.

so bad.[ab] His laborers, at the direction of his Majesty's surveyors, have been trying to repair it for sixteen hundred years. To the best of my knowledge, this place has swallowed up twenty thousand wheelbarrows of wholesome instruction brought from all corners of the King's dominion. But even after all the best material for mending this swamp has been applied, it still remains the Swamp of Despond. There are, by the direction of the Lawgiver, good solid steps placed through the middle of the swamp, but the poor weather and filth that spews from the swamp make them hard to see. Even when the weather is good and the steps plainly seen, some men are so confused and mixed-up that they miss the steps and end up in the swamp. One thing you can be sure of, though—once you go through the narrow gate, the ground is good."[ac]

[ab]Isaiah 35:3–4.
[ac]2 Samuel 7:23.

Chapter Two

THE WAY OF THE WORLD
OR THE NARROW WAY

ow I saw in my dream that by this time Pliable had returned to his home. Upon his arrival his neighbors came to visit him. Some of his neighbors called him a wise man for coming back. Some called him a fool for starting such a hazardous journey with Christian in the first place. Others mocked Pliable for his cowardliness, saying, "If we had begun such a journey, we would not have abandoned it because of a few difficulties." Embarrassed and pouting, Pliable hid himself for a time. But at last he got a little of his confidence back and joined in with the others in deriding poor Christian behind his back.

Now as Christian was walking by himself, he spied someone far-off, crossing over the field to meet him. When their paths crossed, the gentleman who met up with Christian introduced himself as Mr. Worldly-Wiseman. He lived in the town of Carnal Policy, a very great town that was near the place from which Christian had come.[1]

Mr. Worldly-Wiseman immediately suspected that Christian was the person who had set out from the City of Destruction, since news of his departure had spread as far as the cities and towns surrounding Christian's former home. As Mr. Worldly-Wiseman viewed Christian's disheveled appearance and heard his sighs and groans, he was convinced that this was the rumored man and began to talk to him.[2]

"Where are you going?" Mr. Worldly-Wiseman asked. "How did you get yourself into such bad shape, and what are you doing with this great burden on your back?"

"Indeed," Christian replied, "a burden heavy as any creature ever had! And since you ask me, 'Where are you going?' I will tell you, sir. I am going to the small sheep gate that lies ahead, for I am informed that there will I enter into a way where I will soon get rid of my heavy burden."

"Do you have a wife and children?" Worldly-Wiseman asked.

"Yes, but I am so oppressed by this burden that I cannot take pleasure in my family as I used to. I now feel as if I am a man who has no family."[a]

"Will you listen to me if I give you counsel?"

"If it is good I will, for I stand in need of good counsel," Christian replied.

"I advise you to quickly get rid of your burden," Worldly-Wiseman explained, "for you will never be settled in your mind until then, nor will you enjoy the benefits of the blessings that God has given you."[3]

"That is what I am seeking," said Christian. "I want nothing more than to be rid of this heavy burden. But I cannot free myself from it, nor is there any man in our country who can take it off my shoulders. That is why I am going toward the small gate ahead, as I told you, so that I may be rid of my burden."

"Who told you to go this way to be rid of your burden?"

Christian answered, "He was a man who appeared to be very honorable and great. His name, as I recall, was Evangelist."

"Shame on him for such counsel!" Worldly-Wiseman protested. "There is not a more dangerous and troublesome way in the world

---

[a] 1 Corinthians 7:29.

than the way he has directed you. Look at the difficulty you have experienced already. I can see that you are already covered in dirt from the Swamp of Despond. Listen to me: that swamp is only the beginning of the sorrows and troubles you will find if you follow that way. Hear what I have to say since I am older than you: if you continue on the way that Evangelist has directed, your journey will be attended by weariness, pain, hunger, perils, nakedness, sword, lions, dragons, darkness, and, in a word, death! The truth of what I am telling you has been confirmed by many testimonies. Why should a man so carelessly cast himself into such peril by giving heed to a stranger?"

"Why, sir," Christian said, "this burden upon my back is more terrible to me than all the things that you have mentioned. I do not care what I meet with on the way, as long as I can also meet with deliverance from my burden."

"How did you come to bear this burden in the first place?" Worldly-Wiseman asked.

"By reading this book in my hand."

"I thought so," Worldly-Wiseman stated softly. "What has happened to you has also happened to other weak men who meddle with things too high for them. You see," said the old gentleman, "you have suddenly been distracted from the important things that matter most to men. You have lost your proper focus on life, and the distractions that now command your attention will cause you to do desperate things in order to obtain something you do not even understand."[4]

"I know that I wish to obtain ease from my heavy burden."

Worldly-Wiseman went on, "But why do you seek ease from your burden in a way that is surrounded by so many dangers? If you only had the patience to hear me, I could direct you to a place where you could obtain your desire without the dangers you are now headed for. Listen to me, and I will show you a safe remedy. Furthermore, be assured that instead of those dangers, you will meet with much safety, friendship, and contentment."[5]

Mr. Worldly-Wiseman directs Christian out of the way.

"Sir, I beg you, share this secret with me," Christian implored.

Worldly-Wiseman told him, "You will find the relief you seek in a nearby village called Morality. In that village resides a gentleman whose name is Legality, a judicious man of very good reputation. He has the skill to help rid men of burdens like the one you have on your shoulders. To my knowledge, he has done a great deal of good in this way. He also has the skill to cure those who have become mentally unbalanced because of their burdens.[6]

"My advice is to go to him immediately so that you can be helped. His house is not quite a mile from here, and if he is not at home, then you will be helped by his son, whose name is Civility.

"Follow my instructions, and you will be eased of your burden. Rest assured that if you decide not to go back to the City of Destruction, you can send for your wife and children so that they may live with you in the village of Morality. There are many empty houses in the village, and I am sure you can live in one of them for a reasonable rate. Daily necessities are also cheap and good there, as are all the things you need to live a happier life, including honest neighbors, good credit, and fashionable surroundings. All these good things are waiting for you there."

Now Christian was rather taken aback by everything that Mr. Worldly-Wiseman told him. But he presently concluded that if what the old gentleman said was true, then his wisest course was to take his advice. After reflecting on the matter for a moment, Christian spoke up.

"Sir, which way do I go to this honest Mr. Legality's house?" Christian inquired.

"Do you see the hill in the distance?"

Christian answered, "Yes, very well."

"Go around that hill, and the first house you come to is his."

So Christian left his path to go to Mr. Legality's house for help. As Christian neared the hill, he was struck by how high and foreboding the hill appeared. One side of the hill hung precariously over the path that wound its way around it, and Christian feared that the overhanging hill would fall on him.

Filled with fear, Christian stopped his journey and stood still, wondering what he should do. His burden also now seemed heavier to him than it was just moments before he had taken this detour off the path that Evangelist had instructed him to follow.

Flashes of fire came out of the hill, and Christian was afraid that he would be burned.[b] Christian began to sweat and quake with fear.[c][7] He was sorry that he had taken Mr. Worldly-Wiseman's counsel. It was when he was thus filled with regret that he saw Evangelist coming to meet him. At the sight of him, Christian began to blush in shame.

Evangelist drew nearer and nearer to Christian, and looking at him with a severe and dreadful countenance, he began reasoning with Christian.

"What are you doing here, Christian?" he asked.

Hearing these words, Christian did not know how to answer and stood speechless before him.

Then Evangelist inquired further, "Aren't you the man whom I found crying outside the walls of the City of Destruction?"

"Yes, sir, I am the man," Christian answered.

Evangelist asked, "Didn't I direct you to the way that leads to the small sheep gate?"

"Yes, sir," said Christian.

"How is it, then, that you have so quickly turned aside? For you are no longer following the way I showed you."

Christian explained, "After I had gone over the Swamp of Despond, I met a gentleman who persuaded me that I might find relief from my burden from a certain man in the village that lies ahead."

"Who was he?"[8]

Christian went on, "He looked like a gentleman and talked much

---

[b]Exodus 19:16, 18.
[c]Hebrews 12:21.

Christian is terrified under Mount Sinai.

to me and got me at last to yield. So I came here, but when I saw this hill and how it hangs over the path, I suddenly stopped my journey, fearing this mountain would fall on my head."

"What did this gentleman say to you?" Evangelist asked.

"Why, he asked me where I was going, so I told him."

"And what did he say then?" Evangelist inquired further.

"He asked me if I had a family. I told him I did, but that I am so pressed down with the burden that is on my back that I cannot take pleasure in them as I once did."

Evangelist said, "And then what did he say?"

Christian continued, "He told me to quickly get rid of my burden, and I told him it was ease from the burden that I sought. Then I told him that I was going to the small sheep gate up ahead to receive further direction on how I might get to the place of deliverance. So he said that he would show me a better way, a shorter way, and one without the difficulties of the way on which you sent me, sir.

"He then said, 'I will direct you to a gentleman who has the skill to take off your burden.' So I believed him and turned from the way you sent me into this path, in order that I might find relief from my burden. But when I came to this place and saw how dangerous things are, I stopped in fear. Now I do not know what to do."

"Then," said Evangelist, "stand still for a while, so that I may show you the words of God." So Christian stood trembling. Then Evangelist said, "See that you do not refuse Him who is speaking. For if they did not escape when they refused Him who warned them on earth, much less will we escape if we reject Him who warns from Heaven."[d] He also said, "Now the just shall live by faith: but if any man draws back, God's soul shall have no pleasure in him."[e]

Evangelist then explained to Christian, "You are the man who is running into this misery. You have begun to reject the counsel of the Most High and to draw back your foot from the way of peace, even almost to your own destruction!"

---

[d]Hebrews 12:25.
[e]Hebrews 10:38.

Then Christian fell down at Evangelist's feet as if he were dead, crying, "Woe is me, for I am undone!"

When Evangelist saw this, he lifted him up with his right hand and said, "Every sin and blasphemy will be forgiven people.[f] Do not disbelieve, but believe."[g] Christian regained some of his strength and stood up trembling before Evangelist.

Then Evangelist proceeded, saying, "Give earnest attention to the things that I am going to tell you. I will now show you who it was that deluded you and to whom it was that he sent you.

"The man that met you is named Mr. Worldly-Wiseman, and he is well named because he loves only the doctrine of this world[h] (he always goes to the town of Morality to attend church). He loves that doctrine best because it keeps him away from the cross.[i] And because he is of this fleshly disposition, he tries to direct poor sinners away from the path to which I send them, even though it is the only right path. Now there are three things in this man's counsel that you must utterly abhor:

"1. His convincing you to leave the right path.

"2. His effort to make the cross repulsive to you.

"3. His sending you on a way that leads to death.

"First, you must abhor his turning you out of the right way and also your own willingness to consent to his counsel. You must hate it because this is to reject the counsel of God in exchange for the counsel of a Worldly-Wiseman. The Lord says, 'Strive to enter in through the narrow door,[j] the narrow door to which I send you; for the gate is narrow and the way is hard that leads to life, and those who find it are few.'[k]

"From this narrow gate, and from the way that leads to it, has this wicked man turned you, and by so doing he has almost brought you to your own destruction. You must hate that he

[f]Matthew 12:31; Mark 3:28.
[g]John 20:27.
[h]1 John 4:5.
[i]Galatians 6:12.
[j]Luke 13:24.
[k]Matthew 7:14.

turned you out of the right way and abhor yourself for listening to him.

"Secondly, you must abhor his effort to make the cross loathsome to you, for the cross is what you are to prefer above all else, even more than all the treasures of Egypt.[l] Besides, the King of glory has told you that 'whoever finds his life will lose it.'[m] And, 'If anyone comes to me and does not hate his own father and mother and wife and children and brothers and sisters, yes, and even his own life, he cannot be my disciple.'[n] Anyone who tries to persuade you otherwise is opposing the only truth by which you can have eternal life. And you must hate all such doctrines.

"Thirdly, you must hate that he directed you into a way that leads to death. You must also know about the person to whom he sent you, and how unable that person is to deliver you from your burden.

"The person to whom you were sent for relief, whose name is Legality, is the son of the slave woman who, with all her children, is still in bondage. The mountain that you feared would fall on your head is Mount Sinai. Now if the slave woman and all her children are in bondage, how can you expect them to set you free from your burden?

"This Mr. Legality is not able to loose you of your burden. No man has ever gotten rid of his burden by Mr. Legality's help, nor are any going to. You cannot be set free by the works of the Law, for by the deeds of the Law no man living is able to get rid of his burden.

"Mr. Worldly-Wiseman is an alien, and Mr. Legality is a cheat. As for his son Civility, notwithstanding his pleasant looks, he is nothing more than a hypocrite who is also unable to help you. Believe me, there is nothing in all the noise that you heard from these dull men but an intent to rob you of your salvation by turning you away from the way in which I directed you."

After this, Evangelist called aloud to the heavens for confirma-

---

[l]Hebrews 11:25–26.
[m]Mark 8:35; John 12:25; Matthew 10:39.
[n]Luke 14:26.

tion of what he had said, and with that there came words and fire out of the mountain under which poor Christian stood that made his hair stand on end. The words that Christian heard were these: "For all who rely on works of the law are 'under a curse': for it is written, 'Cursed be everyone who does not abide by all things written in the Book of the Law, and do them.'"[o]

Now Christian looked for nothing but death and began to cry out desperately, even cursing the time that he had met with Mr. Worldly-Wiseman, calling himself a thousand fools for listening to his counsel. He also was greatly ashamed to think that this gentleman's arguments, flowing only from the deception of the flesh, should have persuaded him to forsake the right way. After this, he approached Evangelist with the following words and thoughts.

Christian asked, "Sir, what do you think? Is there hope for me? May I go back to the way and up to the sheep gate? Will I be abandoned for this and sent back from where I came, disgraced and ashamed? I am sorry I listened to Worldly-Wiseman's counsel. Can my sins be forgiven?"

Then Evangelist said to him, "Your sin is very great, for by it you have committed two evils: you have forsaken the way that is good, and you have walked in forbidden paths. Yet will the man at the gate receive you, for he has goodwill for men."

Then Evangelist warned Christian to be careful and not to turn aside again, "lest you perish in the way, for His wrath is quickly kindled."[p]

Then Christian asked to go back to the way leading to the narrow sheep gate, and Evangelist, after he had kissed him, gave him a smile and bid him Godspeed.

So Christian went on with haste. He spoke to no one as he quickly returned to the path that led to the small sheep gate, and if anyone asked him a question, Christian would not even give him an answer.

---

[o]Galatians 3:10.
[p]Psalm 2:12.

Christian knocks on the sheep gate.

He went like someone who was treading on forbidden ground. He could not think himself safe until he had once again gotten back on the path he had abandoned to follow Mr. Worldly-Wiseman's counsel.

So after a little while, Christian arrived at the gate. Now over the gate there was written, "Knock and it will be opened to you."[q]

Christian knocked more than once or twice, saying, "May I now enter? Will He within open to pitiful me, though I have been an undeserving rebel? Then will I not fail to sing His lasting praise on high."

At last a very serious person came to the gate whose name was Good-Will. Good-Will asked who was there, from where he came, and what he wanted.[9]

"I am a poor burdened sinner," Christian said. "I come from the City of Destruction, but I am going to Mount Zion, so that I may be delivered from the wrath to come. I am informed that through this gate is the way to safety, and I want to know if you are willing to let me in!"

"I am willing with all my heart," said he, and with that he opened the gate.

As Christian started walking through the gate, Good-Will pulled him in roughly. Christian asked, "Why did you pull me in so forcefully?"

Good-Will told him, "A little distance from this gate there stands a strong castle, of which Beelzebub is the captain. From there, both he and those who are with him shoot arrows at travelers who come up to this gate, in order to slay poor sinners before they can enter into safety."[10]

Then said Christian, "I rejoice and tremble." So when he was safely in,[11] the man at the gate asked him who sent him.

Christian replied, "Evangelist sent me, and told me to knock at the gate (as I did); and he said that you, sir, would tell me what I must do next."

---

[q]Matthew 7:7.

Good-Will told him, "An open door is set before you, and no man can shut it."

"Now I begin to reap the benefits of all the hazards and difficulties I have come through," Christian stated.

"But how is it that only you decided to come here?" Good-Will inquired.

Christian explained, "Because none of my neighbors saw the danger they were in. But I saw it more and more clearly."

Good-Will then asked, "Did any of them know that you were coming here?"

Christian told him, "Yes, my wife and children saw me start the journey and called after me to stop and return to the City of Destruction. Also, some of my neighbors stood crying and calling after me to return, but I put my fingers in my ears and continued my journey to this place."

"But did any of them follow you to persuade you to come back?" Good-Will asked.

Christian answered, "Yes, two men named Obstinate and Pliable, but when they saw that they could not convince me to return, Obstinate went back, though Pliable came with me a little way."

"But why didn't he continue on with you?" Good-Will asked further.

Christian explained, "We traveled together until we came to the Swamp of Despond, into which we suddenly fell. It was then that my neighbor, Pliable, became discouraged and would not go further. As soon as he could get out of the swamp on the side next to his own house, he told me that I could possess the brave country without his company. So he went on his way, and I continued on mine. He followed after Obstinate while I went on to this gate."

Then said Good-Will, "Alas, poor Pliable! Is the celestial glory of so little value to him that he considers it unworthy of his hazarding a few difficulties to obtain it?"

Christian sighed. "I have told you the truth about Pliable; now I must tell you the truth about myself. I am no better than Pliable.[12]

It is true that he went back to his own house, but I also turned aside to go into the way of death, being persuaded to do so by the seductive arguments of one Mr. Worldly-Wiseman."

"Oh, was it he who ambushed you?" Good-Will asked. "I can only imagine that he tried to convince you to seek ease at the hands of Mr. Legality. They are both cheats. But did you take his counsel?"

Christian admitted, "Yes, as far and as long as I dared. I went to find Mr. Legality, until I became afraid that the mountain that stands by his house was going to fall upon my head, and I was forced to stop."

"That mountain has been the death of many and will be the death of many more," Good-Will said sadly. "It was well that you escaped being dashed into pieces by it."

Christian went on, "Truly, I do not know what would have become of me if Evangelist had not come to my rescue by that mountain as I stood paralyzed by my confused thoughts. It was God's mercy that he came to help me, or else I would not be standing here before you. So here I am, more deserving of death by that mountain than of talking with you here. Oh, what a favor you do me by admitting me entrance through the gate!"

"We make no objections to anyone, no matter what they have done before they come to the gate. They are 'never cast out,'[r] Good-Will said. "And now, Christian, come with me for a moment, and I will teach you about the way you must go. Look in front of you; do you see this narrow way? *That* is the way you must go. It was carved out by the patriarchs, prophets, Christ, and His apostles, and it is as straight as a ruler can make it. This is the way you must go."

"But," said Christian, "are there no turnings or windings by which a stranger might lose his way?"

"Yes, there are many other ways, but they are all crooked and wide. That is how you can distinguish the right way from the wrong way; the right way is always straight and narrow."[s]

---

[r] John 6:37.
[s] Matthew 7:14.

Then I saw in my dream that Christian asked Good-Will to help him remove the burden that was upon his back; for as yet he had not gotten rid of it, nor could he by any means get it off without help.

Good-Will told him, "As far as your burden, be content to bear it until you come to the place of deliverance; once you are there, it will fall from your back by itself."[13]

Christian then began to prepare himself for the journey. As he was getting ready, Good-Will told him that after he had gone a good distance from the gate he would come to the house of the Interpreter. He was told to knock at the door of that house, where he would be shown excellent things. Then Good-Will bid Christian Godspeed.[14]

After Christian departed, he went on until he came to the house of the Interpreter, where he knocked over and over. At last a man came to the door and asked who was there.

Christian told him, "Sir, I am a traveler who was told by an acquaintance of the good man of this house to come here for my profit; therefore I would like to speak with the master of the house."

So the man called for the master of the house who after a little time came to Christian, asking how He might assist him.

"Sir," said Christian, "I am a man who has come from the City of Destruction, and I am going to Mount Zion. I was told by the man who stands at the entrance gate to this way that if I called here, You would show me excellent things that would help me on my journey."

Then said the Interpreter, "Come in. I will show you those things that will be profitable to you."[15] So he commanded His servant to light the candle and then asked Christian to follow Him to a private room that, when the manservant opened the door, revealed a picture of a very grave person hanging on the wall. This is what the man in the picture looked like: he had eyes lifted up to Heaven, the best of books in his hand, the law of truth written upon his lips, the world behind his back. He stood as if pleading with men, and a crown of gold hung over his head."

Then said Christian, "What does this mean?"

"The man in this picture represents one of a thousand: he can conceive children,[t] travail in birth with children,[u] and nurse them himself when they are born. You see him with his eyes lifted up to Heaven, the best of books in his hand and the law of truth written on his lips. All this is to show you that his work is to know and unfold dark things to sinners. You see him pleading with men, the world cast behind him, and a crown hanging over his head to show you that by rejecting and despising the things of this present world for the love that he has for his Master's service, he is sure to have glory as his reward in the world to come. I have shown you this picture first because the man whom it represents is the only man authorized by the Lord of the place where you are going to be your guide in all the difficult places you will encounter on the way. So pay attention to what I have shown you, and keep this picture foremost in your mind, so that if you meet with someone who doesn't resemble this picture's likeness but who pretends to lead you in the right way, you will not follow him down to destruction."

Then the Interpreter took Christian by the hand and led him into a very large parlor that was full of dust because it was never swept. After He had reviewed it a little while, the Interpreter called for a man to come and sweep. Now when he began to sweep, the dust began to fly about so much and was so thick that Christian almost choked. Then said the Interpreter to a damsel who stood nearby, "Bring water, and sprinkle the room." When she had done as requested, it was swept and cleansed very pleasantly.

Then Christian asked, "What does this mean?"

The Interpreter answered, "This parlor is the heart of a man that has never been sanctified by the sweet grace of the gospel; the dust is his original sin and inward corruptions that have defiled the whole man. The first man that began to sweep is the Law; the damsel that brought water and sprinkled it is the gospel. You saw that as soon as the first man began to sweep, the dust filled the room

---

[t] 1 Corinthians 4:15.
[u] Galatians 4:19.

so thickly that it could not be cleansed, and you almost choked on it. This is to show you that the Law, instead of cleansing the heart from sin, actually revives, increases, and adds strength to it. Even though the Law uncovers and forbids sin, it is powerless to conquer or subdue it at all.ᵛ

"Then you saw the damsel sprinkle the room with water, after which it was pleasingly cleansed. This is to show you the way in which the gospel comes into the heart with its sweet and precious influences. You saw the damsel clear the dust from the room by sprinkling the floor with water. This shows how sin is vanquished and subdued and the soul made clean through faith and consequently fit for the King of glory to inhabit."ʷ

I also saw in my dream that the Interpreter took Christian by the hand into a little room where there sat two little children, each one in his own chair. The name of the older child was Passion, and the name of the younger was Patience. Passion seemed to be very discontent, but Patience was very quiet. Then Christian asked, "What is the reason for the discontentment of Passion?"

The Interpreter answered, "Their Guardian would have them wait for their best things until the beginning of next year. Passion wants it all now, but Patience is willing to wait."

Then I saw that someone came to Passion and brought him a bag of treasure, pouring it at his feet. Passion picked up the treasure rejoicing and laughed Patience to scorn. But as I watched for a while, all the treasure either rusted or molded away, and soon he had nothing left but rust and rags.

Then Christian asked the Interpreter to explain this more fully to him.

So he said, "These two lads are figures: Passion, of the men of this world, and Patience, of the men of that world which is to come. You saw that Passion wanted to have it all now, this year. In other words, the men of this world want all their good things now, in this

---

ᵛRomans 7:6; 1 Corinthians 15:56; Romans 5:20.
ʷJohn 15:3; Ephesians 5:26; Acts 15:9; Romans 16:25–26; John 15:13.

world, and cannot wait for their portion of good in the next world. The proverb 'A bird in the hand is worth two in the bush' is of more authority with them than are all the divine testimonies of the good that is waiting in the world to come. But as you saw, Passion had quickly wasted all his treasure away and was soon left with nothing but rags; so will it be with all such men at the end of this world."

Then said Christian, "Now I see that Patience was the wisest for several reasons: first, because he waited for the best things; second, because he will have the glory of his reward when the other has nothing but rags."

"Yes," Interpreter said, "and you may add another reason, which is that the glory of the next world will never wear out, whereas the treasure that Passion received was suddenly gone. As it turns out, Passion had no reason to laugh at Patience just because he had his good things first. In the end Patience will laugh at Passion because Patience will have his best things last; for first must give place to last. The last things will finally come, and when they do, nothing will succeed or replace them. He that has his good things in this world spends and uses them up in time, but he that has his good things last has them lastingly, for the last things go on forever. Just like it was said of the rich man, 'You in your lifetime received your good things, and likewise Lazarus evil things; but now he is comforted, and you are tormented.'"[x]

Christian said, "Now I perceive that it is not best to covet things that are in the here and now, but to wait for things to come."

"You speak truly," said the Interpreter, "'for the things that are seen are temporal, but the things that are not seen are eternal.'[y] But even though this is so, yet the things that are present are close neighbors with our fleshly appetites, while the things that are to come are strangers to these appetites. Most men will not ignore the present world that they can see in order to make the world they cannot see the object of their desires. Therefore, there is an

---

[x]Luke 16:25.
[y]2 Corinthians 4:18.

A brave pilgrim battles his way into the Celestial City.

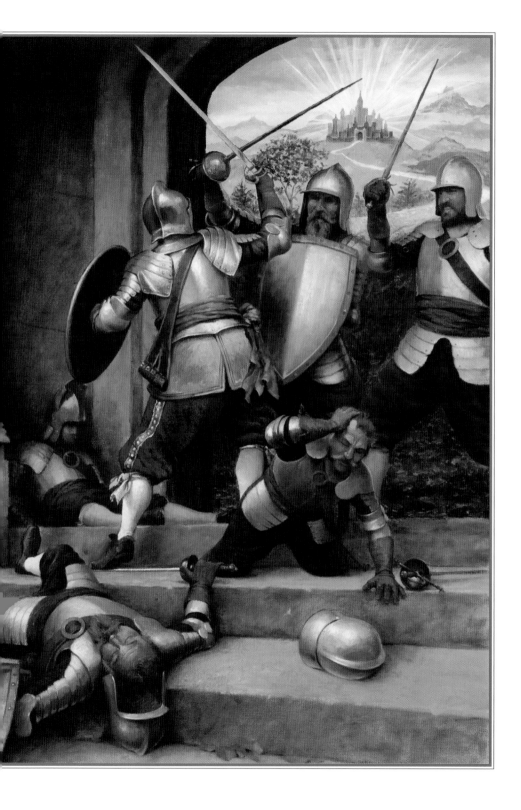

immediate friendship between this world and a man's fleshly desires and a corresponding distance between carnal man and eternal things."

Then I saw in my dream that the Interpreter took Christian by the hand and led him into a room where there was a fireplace. The flames from the fireplace grew larger and hotter even though there was someone continually throwing water on it to try to quench it.

Then said Christian, "What does this mean?"

The Interpreter answered, "This fire is the work of grace that God accomplishes in the heart; he who throws water on the flames to try to extinguish it is the Devil. But as you see, the fire burns higher and hotter despite his efforts to put it out. Now let me show the reason for that."

So the Interpreter took Christian to the other side of the wall, where he saw a Man with a vessel of oil in His hand, from which He secretly funneled oil into the fire.

Then Christian asked, "What does this mean?"

The Interpreter answered, "This is Christ who continually, with the oil of His grace, maintains the work already begun in the heart. No matter what the Devil tries to do, the gracious work that Christ is doing in the souls of His people only increases.[z] You saw that the Man stood behind the wall to maintain the fire; that is to teach you that it is hard for the one being tempted to see how this work of grace is maintained in the soul."

After this I saw that the Interpreter took Christian by the hand and led him into a pleasant place, where was built a stately palace, beautiful to behold. At the sight of it Christian was greatly delighted. He looked up and saw people clothed in gold walking on top of the thick palace walls.

Then Christian asked, "May we go into the palace?"

The Interpreter took him and led him up toward the door of the palace. There Christian saw a great company of men standing at the palace door, all desiring to go in, but few daring to. A little dis-

---

[z] 2 Corinthians 12:9.

tance from the door there was a man sitting at a table with a book open before him. He was writing the names of those who wished to enter the palace. Christian also saw in the doorway many armed men who were determined to inflict as many injuries and wounds as they could on anyone trying to enter the palace.

Christian was amazed. At last, after every man retreated back for fear of the armed men, Christian saw a man with a very determined look on his face come up to the man sitting at the table and say, "Set down my name, sir." As soon as his name was written in the book, Christian saw the man draw his sword, put a helmet upon his head, and rush toward the armed men at the door, who tried to stop him with deadly force. But the man, not at all discouraged, began cutting and hacking most fiercely at his attackers.

After he had received and given many wounds to those who attempted to keep him out, he cut his way through them all[aa] and pressed forward into the palace. Then Christian heard a pleasant voice from those who were inside the palace, even those who walked upon the top of the palace, saying, "Come in, come in; eternal glory you shall win."

So the determined man went in and was clothed with gold. Then Christian smiled and said, "I think I know what this means, and I think it is time for me to continue my journey."

"No," said the Interpreter. "Stay until I have shown you a little more, and after that you can go on your way." So he took Christian by the hand and led him into a very dark room, where a man sat in an iron cage.

The man in the cage seemed very sad. He sat with his eyes looking down to the ground, his hands folded together, and he sighed as if his heart would break. Then Christian asked, "What does this mean?" Instead of answering, the Interpreter asked Christian to talk with the man.

So Christian asked the man, "Who are you?"

The man answered, "I am not who I used to be."

[aa]Acts 14:22.

"Who did you used to be?" Christian asked.

The man said, "I was once fair and flourishing in my profession of faith, both in my own eyes and also in the eyes of others. I was, I once thought, deserving of the Celestial City and was full of joy as I considered going there."[ab]

Christian inquired, "Well, who are you now?"

The man replied, "I am now a man of despair, and it surrounds me as does this iron cage. I cannot get out. O now I cannot!"

"But how did you come to be in this condition?" Christian asked him.

He answered honestly, "I stopped being watchful and diligent. I rushed after my own lusts. I sinned against the light of the Word and the goodness of God. I have grieved the Spirit, and He is gone. I tempted the Devil, and he has come to me. I have provoked God to anger, and He has left me. I have so hardened my heart that I cannot repent."

Then Christian asked the Interpreter, "Is there no hope for such a man as this?"

"Ask him," said the Interpreter.

So Christian asked the man, "Is there no hope? Must you be kept in the iron cage of despair?"

"No hope, none at all," replied the man in the iron cage.

"But consider this: the Son of the Blessed is full of pity."

The man protested, "I have crucified Him to myself afresh;[ac] I have despised His person;[ad] I have despised His righteousness; I have 'counted His blood an unholy thing'; I have 'insulted the Spirit of grace.'[ae] Therefore, I have shut myself out of all the promises, and there now remains to me nothing but threatenings, dreadful threatenings, fearful threatenings of certain judgment and fiery indignation, which shall devour me as an adversary."

"How did you bring yourself into this condition?"

[ab]Luke 8:13.
[ac]Hebrews 6:6.
[ad]Luke 19:14.
[ae]Hebrews 10:28–29.

The man explained, "I promised myself much delight from the lusts, pleasures, and the profits of this world. But now every one of those things wounds me and gnaws at me like a burning worm."

"But can't you even now repent and turn away from those things?" Christian asked hopefully.

"God has denied me repentance," the man said. "His Word gives me no encouragement to believe. He Himself has shut me up in this iron cage, and all the men in the world do not have the power to let me out. O eternity! Eternity! How will I deal with the misery that waits for me in eternity!"

Then the Interpreter said to Christian, "Remember this man's misery, and let it be an everlasting caution to you."

"Well," Christian said, "this is fearful! May God help me to watch and be sober and pray, that I may avoid the cause of this man's misery! But, sir, isn't it time for me to go on my way?"

Interpreter added, "Stay until I show you one more thing, and then you may go on your way."

So he took Christian by the hand again and led him into a chamber, where there was a man getting out of bed; and as he dressed himself, he shook and trembled. Then Christian asked, "Why does this man tremble?"

The Interpreter then called the man over and told him to tell Christian the reason for his trembling. This is what the man told Christian:

"This night, as I was in my sleep, I dreamed and witnessed the heavens grow pitch-black. I also heard and saw the most terrible thunder and lightning; so I looked up in my dream and saw the clouds begin to roll in at an unusual rate of speed. Then I heard the great sound of a trumpet and saw a Man sitting upon a great cloud, attended by thousands from Heaven. They were all clothed in flaming fire, and the heavens were as a burning flame. I then heard a voice saying, 'Arise, you that are dead, and come to judgment.' With that the rocks split, the graves opened, and the dead who were in them came out. Some of them were extremely glad and looked upward, and some tried to hide themselves under the mountains for fear.[af] Then I saw the Man who sat upon the cloud open a book and bid the world come near. A fierce flame spewed out from before Him, creating a barrier between Him and the world of men, like the barrier between a judge and the prisoners at the bar.[ag]

"I heard the Man who sat on the cloud proclaim to the heavenly hosts who attended Him, 'Gather together the tares, the chaff, and stubble, and cast them into the burning lake.'[ah] And immediately the bottomless pit opened, just where I stood. And out of the mouth of that pit came smoke and the coals of fire, accompanied by hideous noises. Then I heard the Man who sat on the clouds proclaim to the heavenly host, 'Gather My wheat into my barn.'[ai] And with that I saw many people caught up and carried away into the clouds, but I was left behind.[aj] I tried to hide myself, but I could not, for the Man who sat upon the cloud kept his eye upon me; my sins also came into my mind, and my conscience accused me without mercy.[ak] Then I woke from my sleep."

Christian asked, "But what was it that made you so afraid of this sight?"

He explained, "Why, I thought that the Day of Judgment was come and that I was not ready for it. But what frightened me most was that the angels gathered up others but left me behind. Also the pit of Hell opened her mouth just below where I stood. My conscience also afflicted me, and I thought the Judge had His eye upon me, and I saw in His expression both anger and indignation."

Then said the Interpreter to Christian, "Have you considered all these things?"

"Yes," Christian answered, "and they cause me to both hope and fear."

Interpreter told him seriously, "Keep all these things in your

---

[af]1 Corinthians 15:52; 1 Thessalonians 4:16; Jude 14; John 5:28–29; 2 Thessalonians 1:7–8; Revelation 20:11–14; Isaiah 26:21; Micah 7:16–17; Psalm 95:1–3; Daniel 10:7.
[ag]Malachi 3:2–3; Daniel 7:9–10.
[ah]Matthew 3:12; 13:30; Malachi 4:1.
[ai]Luke 3:17.
[aj]1 Thessalonians 4:16–17.
[ak]Romans 2:14–15.

mind as a constant encouragement and warning as you journey on ahead to the Celestial City." Then Christian began to prepare himself for the journey ahead, and when he was ready to depart, the Interpreter said, "May the Comforter be with you always to guide you in the way that leads to the City."

So Christian went on his way, saying, "Here I have seen things rare and profitable, things pleasant and dreadful, things to give me stability and wisdom to deal with my tasks at hand. For showing me what I need to understand for the journey ahead, I thank You, good Interpreter."

Christian's burden comes loose at the cross.

Chapter Three

A Burden Lifted and a Journey Begun

Now I saw in my dream that the highway up which Christian was to go was fenced on each side with a wall; the wall was called Salvation.[a] Therefore, it was up this highway that Christian ran, but not without great difficulty because of the burden of the load on his back.[1]

He ran till he came to a small hill, at the top of which stood a cross and at the bottom of which was a tomb. I saw in my dream that when Christian walked up the hill to the cross, his burden came loose from his shoulders and fell off his back, tumbling down the hill until it came to the mouth of the tomb, where it fell in to be seen no more.

Then Christian was relieved and delighted and exclaimed with a joyful heart, "He has given me rest by His sorrow and life by His death." For a while he stood still in front of the cross to look and wonder; it was very surprising to him that the sight of the cross should ease him of his burden. He continued looking at the cross until tears began streaming down his cheeks.[b2] As he stood looking and weep-

---

[a]Isaiah 26:1.
[b]Zechariah 12:10.

ing, three Shining Ones came to him and greeted him with, "Peace be with you." Then the first said to him, "Your sins are forgiven."[c] The second stripped him of his rags and dressed him with new clothing.[d] The third put a mark on his forehead and gave him a scroll with a seal on it. He told Christian to review it often as he went on his way and at the end of his journey to turn it in at the Celestial Gate.[e][3] After this they went their way.

Then Christian gave three leaps for joy and went on his way singing:

> *"Thus far I did come,*
> *Burdened with my sin.*
> *Nor could I find relief*
> *From my grief within.*
>
> *Until here I came,*
> *What a place this is!*
> *Here shall be the beginning,*
> *Of full, eternal bliss!*
>
> *Now my burden falls*
> *From my back forever.*
> *From the cords that bound it,*
> *By grace my grief is severed.*
>
> *Blessed cross! Blessed tomb!*
> *Rather, most blessed be*
> *The Man who there was put to shame,*
> *A shame He took for me!"*

I saw then in my dream that Christian went on until he came to the bottom of the hill. There he saw lying by the side of the path three men fast asleep, with chains upon their feet. The name of the one was Foolish, the second Sloth, and the third Presumption.[4]

Christian went to them to see if he might awaken them and said to them, "'You will be like one who lies down in the midst of the sea,

[c]Mark 2:5.
[d]Zechariah 3:4.
[e]Ephesians 1:13.

Formalist and Hypocrisy trespass over the Wall of Salvation.

like one who lies on top of a mast,[f] though the Dead Sea is under you, a gulf that has no bottom. Wake up and get back on the path, and if you are willing, I will help you take off your iron shackles." He also told them, "If he that 'goes about like a roaring lion' comes by and finds you like this, he will destroy you with his teeth."[g] With that they looked at Christian and began to reply to him. Foolish said, "I see no danger." Sloth said, "I just need a little more sleep." And Presumption said, "Everyone needs to make his own choices. You need to mind your own business and not meddle in ours." So they all lay down to sleep again, and Christian went on his way.

Christian was troubled to think that men in such danger should have so little regard for the kindness he had extended when he awakened them, counseled them, and offered to free them of their iron shackles.[5] As he was thinking about this, he saw two men come tumbling over the wall on the left side and onto the path. They immediately came toward Christian. The name of the one was Formalist, and the name of the other was Hypocrisy. Soon they were walking with Christian on the path. Christian immediately began to engage them in conversation.[6]

Christian asked, "Gentlemen, where did you come from, and where are you going?"

Formality and Hypocrisy replied, "We were born in the land of Vain-Glory and are going to Mount Zion where we expect we will receive both praise and honor."

"Why didn't you enter by the gate that stands at the beginning of the way? Don't you know that it is written that 'he who does not come in by the door but climbs up some other way is a thief and a robber'?"[h]

Formalist and Hypocrisy answered that to go to the gate in order to enter into the way was considered by them and all their countrymen to be too inconvenient and roundabout, especially since

[f] Proverbs 23:34.
[g] 1 Peter 5:8.
[h] John 10:1.

they could shorten the journey by simply climbing over the wall, as they had done.

"But won't this be seen as trespassing?" Christian asked. "Don't you think the Lord of the City for which we are bound must count it as a violation of His revealed will?"

Formalist and Hypocrisy told Christian not to worry about it since it had been the custom of their land for more than a thousand years.

"But," asked Christian, "will your custom stand up in a court of law?"

They replied, "This custom of entering the way by taking a shortcut has been going on as a long-standing practice for more than a thousand years and would be ruled as a legal practice by any impartial judge. And besides," they added, "as long as we get into the way, what does it matter how we get in? If we are in, we are in. You came into the way through the narrow gate, and we came tumbling over the wall, and since we are both in, who is to say that your chosen path is better than ours?"

Christian told them, "I walk by the rule of my Master; you walk by the rude working of your own notions. You are condemned as thieves already by the Lord of the way; therefore, I doubt you will be found as true men at the end of the journey. You came in by yourselves, without His direction, and will go out by yourselves, without His mercy."

To this they had little to say, except to tell Christian to mind his own business. Then I saw that Formalist and Hypocrisy went along with Christian, saying only that as far as the laws and ordinances were concerned, they would obey them as conscientiously as Christian. They added that they saw no difference between themselves and Christian except for the coat he wore, which they speculated was given to Christian to hide his shame and nakedness.

Christian responded, "You will not be saved by keeping laws and ordinances. You cannot be saved, because you did not come in

Christian begins his journey up the Hill Difficulty.

by the door.[i] As for the coat that is on my back, it was given to me by the Lord of the place where I am going and is, as you say, a cover for my nakedness. I take it as a token of His kindness to me, for I had nothing but rags before. Besides, I take some comfort in the fact that when I come to the gate of the City, the Lord of that place will surely recognize me since it is His coat on my back, a coat that He gave me the day that He stripped me of my rags.

"I also have a mark on my forehead, which perhaps you have not noticed. One of my Lord's most intimate associates placed it on my forehead the day that my burden fell off my shoulders.

"Also I have been given a scroll to read as a comfort to me as I make my journey. I was also told to turn it in at the Celestial Gate as an assurance that I will be welcomed into the Celestial City. I doubt you have any interest in all these things since you did not come in at the gate."

To this, Formalist and Hypocrisy gave no reply. They just looked at each other and laughed.

Then I saw that they all kept walking along the path, except that Christian walked up ahead and had no more conversation with Formalist and Hypocrisy. He only talked with himself, sometimes sighing, sometimes encouraging himself, and often refreshing himself by reading from the scroll that one of the Shining Ones had given him.

I saw, then, that they all went on until they came to the foot of the Hill Difficulty,[7] at the bottom of which was a spring of fresh water. Here the men were faced with a choice of three paths. The path that led directly from the gate continued straight up the steep hill. Another path turned to the left and a third to the right of the hill. Christian went to the spring and drank until he was no longer thirsty[j] and then began to go up the Hill Difficulty, saying:

> *"The hill, though high, I desire to ascend,*
> *The difficulty will not me offend;*

---

[i] Galatians 2:16.
[j] Isaiah 49:10.

For I perceive the way to life lies here.
Be strong, my heart, let's neither faint nor fear;
Better, though difficult, the right way to go,
Than wrong, though easy, where the end is woe."

Formalist and Hypocrisy also came to the foot of the hill, but when they saw how steep and high it was and that there were two simpler ways to go, they chose the ways that looked easier. They supposed that the two ways would go around the hill and meet up again with the straight way that Christian was taking. Now the name of one of those ways was Danger, and the name of the other was Destruction. So Formalist took the way that is called Danger, which led him into a great wooded area; and Hypocrisy went the way to Destruction, which led him into a wide field full of dark mountains, where he stumbled, fell, and never got up.

I looked and saw Christian go up the hill, where I noticed him slowing his pace from running to walking and finally to scrambling up the path on his hands and knees because it was very steep.

Now I saw that about halfway up the hill there was a pleasant arbor built by the Lord of the hill for the refreshment of weary travelers. When Christian reached this spot, he sat down to rest.

Then he pulled his scroll out from under his coat and was comforted by what he read. He also took a fresh look at the coat that had been given to him earlier when he stood by the cross. As he entertained pleasant thoughts about the changes that had taken place in his life, he at last fell into a slumber and finally into a deep sleep, from which he did not awake until it was almost night; and in his sleep, his scroll fell out of his hand.[8]

Now, as he was sleeping, someone came to him and awakened him, saying, "Go to the ant, O sluggard; consider her ways and be wise."[k] And with that Christian sprang up and sped on his way. He had not traveled far when he came to the top of the hill.

Now, at the top of the hill, two men came running to meet him. The name of the one was Timorous and of the other Mistrust, to

[k]Proverbs 6:6.

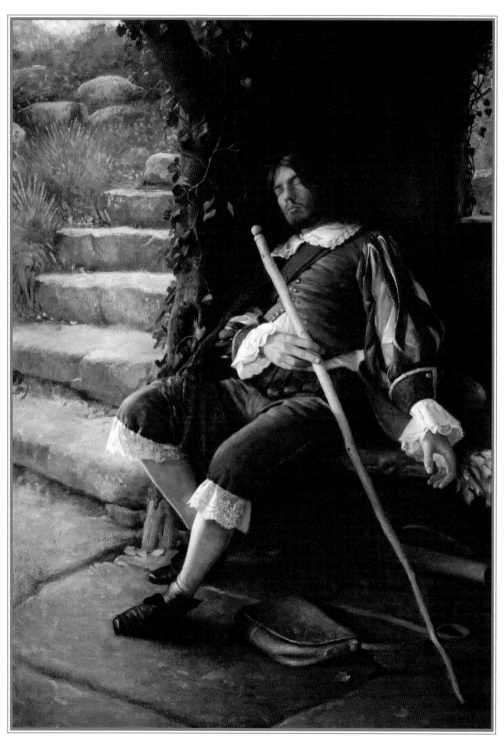

Christian sleeps in the arbor on the Hill Difficulty.

whom Christian said, "Sirs, what's the matter? You're running the wrong way."[9]

Timorous answered that they were going to the City of Zion and had climbed up the Hill Difficulty. "But," he added, "the farther we went, the more danger we encountered. So we turned around and are going back from where we came."

"Yes," said Mistrust, "for just ahead there are a couple of lions in the way—we don't know if they are sleeping or awake. But we are sure that if we came within their reach, they would pull us to pieces."

Then Christian said, "You're making me afraid. Where shall I run to be safe? If I go back to my own country, which is prepared for fire and brimstone, I shall certainly perish. If I can get to the Celestial City, I am sure to be safe. I must go forward. To go back is nothing but death; to go forward is fear of death, and life everlasting beyond it. I will go forward."

So Mistrust and Timorous ran down the hill, and Christian went on his way. But thinking again of what he had just heard from the men, he felt in his coat for his scroll so that he might read it and be comforted; but it was not there.

Then Christian was in great distress and didn't know what to do. He wanted to be comforted by the words in the scroll and also knew it was his pass into the Celestial City.

He stood still and became very perplexed and didn't know what to do. At last he remembered that he had slept in the arbor that is on the side of the hill. Falling down upon his knees, he asked God's forgiveness for his foolish act and then went back to look for his scroll.

All the way as he went back, there was a great sorrow in Christian's heart. Sometimes he sighed, sometimes he wept, and oftentimes he chided himself for being so foolish as to fall asleep in that place, which was only erected for a little refreshment for the weary. So he went all the way to the arbor, carefully looking on this side and on that, hoping he might find the scroll that had been such a comfort to him on his journey.

Finally he came within sight of the arbor where he had previously sat and slept. The sight of the place renewed his sorrow as he remembered again how wrong he had been to fall asleep.[l]

He began crying over his sinful sleep, saying, "O wretched man that I am, that I should sleep in the daytime, that I should sleep in the midst of difficulty, that I should so indulge the flesh as to use that rest to ease my flesh, which the Lord of the hill intended only for the relief of the spirits of pilgrims!

"How many steps have I taken in vain! This is what happened to Israel for their sin. They were sent back again by the way of the Red Sea. I am now retracing those steps with sorrow that I might have traveled with delight, had it not been for this sinful sleep. How far I might have been on my way by this time! I am forced to retrace those steps three times over that I should have traveled only once. Now I am about to enter the darkness of night, for the day is almost over. Oh, that I had not slept."[10]

Christian sat down in the arbor and wept, but at last looking sorrowfully down under the seat, he spied his scroll. With trembling and haste he snatched it up and put it into his coat. No one could have been more joyful than this man was after he retrieved his scroll! The scroll was the assurance of his life and acceptance at the Celestial City. He placed it carefully in his coat, gave thanks to God for directing his eyes to the place where it lay, and with joy and tears began his journey again.

Christian nimbly went up the rest of the hill. But before he reached the top of the hill, the sun went down. He recalled again the vanity of sleeping at the arbor; and so he began to talk with himself.

"O sinful sleep; for that little rest I am now making my journey in the dark of night! I must walk without the sun; darkness must cover the path of my feet; and I must hear the noise of the doleful creatures because of my sinful sleep."[m]

Just then he remembered the story that Mistrust and Timorous

---

[l] 1 Thessalonians 5:7–8; Revelation 2:5.
[m] 1 Thessalonians 5:6–7.

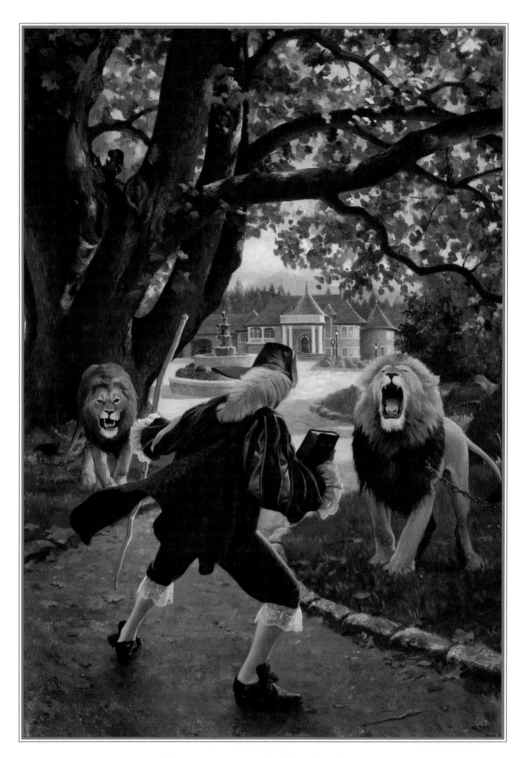

Christian is terrified by the lions.

had told him of how they were frightened by the sight of the lions. Then Christian said to himself, "These beasts prowl in the night looking for their prey, and if they should meet with me in the dark, how can I escape from them? How should I keep from being torn in pieces by them?"

With these thoughts in his mind, he went on his way. But while he was fretting over his unhappy circumstances, he lifted up his eyes and beheld a very stately palace in front of him. The name of the place was House Beautiful, and it stood by the side of the highway.[11]

So I saw in my dream that he quickly walked forward, hoping he might find lodging. But before he had gone far, he entered into a very narrow passage, which was about a furlong off the porter's lodge. Looking very carefully ahead as he went, he spied two lions in the way.

"Now," he thought, "I see the dangers that drove Mistrust and Timorous back." The lions were chained, but he did not see the chains. Then he was afraid and thought about going back, seeing nothing but death ahead of him.

Just then the porter at the lodge, whose name is Watchful, seeing that Christian had stopped his progress as if he would go back, cried out to him, asking, "Is your strength so small?[n] Don't fear the lions, for they are chained and are placed there to test your faith and to discover those who have none. Keep in the middle of the path, and no harm shall come to you.

> "*Difficulty is behind, Fear is before.*
> *Though he's got on the hill, the lions roar.*
> *A Christian man is never long at ease.*
> *When one fright's gone, another does him seize.*"

Then I saw that Christian went forward, trembling for fear of the lions, but carefully following the directions of the porter.[12] He heard them roar, but they did him no harm. Then he clapped his

---

[n]Mark 8:34–37.

hands and went on until he came and stood in front of the gate where the porter was.

Then said Christian to the porter, "Sir, whose house is this? And may I lodge here tonight?"

The porter answered, "This house was built by the Lord of the hill. He built it for the relief and security of pilgrims." The porter also asked Christian where he was from and where he was going.[13]

"I am come from the City of Destruction and am going to Mount Zion," Christian replied, "but because the sun has now set, I was hoping to lodge here tonight."

The porter inquired, "What is your name?"

"My name is now Christian, but my name used to be Graceless. I came of the race of Japheth, whom God will persuade to dwell in the tents of Shem."[o]

"But why is it that you come so late?" the porter asked. "The sun has indeed set."

Christian replied, "I would have been here sooner, but 'wretched man that I am!' I slept in the arbor that stands on the hillside, and in my sleep I lost my scroll. I traveled without it to the brow of the hill, where I searched for it but could not find it. I was then forced, with a sorrowful heart, to go back to the arbor where I had slept. It was there I recovered my scroll, and now I am here."

The porter stated, "Well, I will call out one of the virgins of this place who will, if she approves of your testimony, bring you in to the rest of the family, according to the rules of the house."

Then Watchful, the porter, rang a bell, at the sound of which a serious-looking, beautiful maiden came out of the door of the house. Her name was Discretion, and she immediately asked why she had been called.

The porter answered, "This man is on a journey from the City of Destruction to Mount Zion, but being weary and with night coming on he has asked me if he might lodge here tonight. I told him I would call for you, who, after having a conversation with

---

°Genesis 9:27.

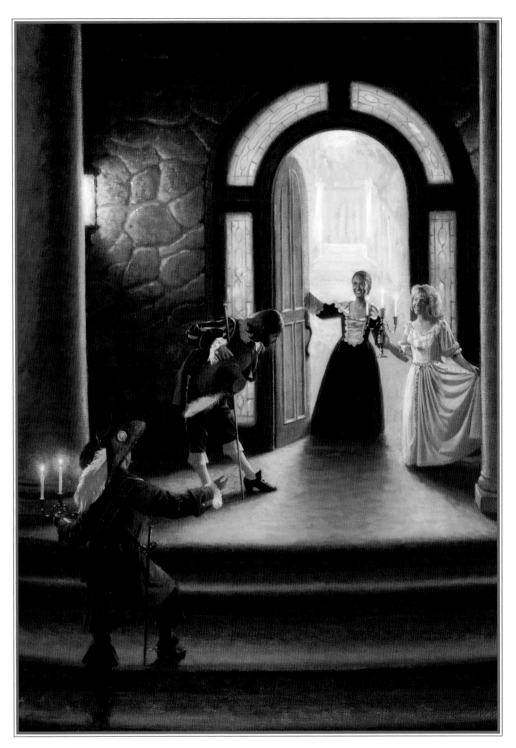

Christian is greeted outside the House Beautiful.

him, may do what seems best to you, even according to the law of the house."

Then she asked Christian where he was from and where he was going, and he told her. She asked him also how he got into the way, and he told her. Then she asked him what he had seen and met with in the way, to which he replied, "My name is Christian, and I have a very strong desire to lodge here tonight because from what I perceive, this place was built by the Lord of the hill for the relief and security of pilgrims." So she smiled, with tears in her eyes; and after a short pause, she said, "I will call for two or three more of the family."

So she ran to the door and called out for Prudence, Piety, and Charity, who after a little more conversation with him invited him to meet the family. Many of them met him at the threshold of the house. "Come in," they said, "you are blessed of the Lord. This house was built by the Lord of the hill for the purpose of showing hospitality to pilgrims such as yourself." Then he bowed his head and followed them into the house.

When he had come in and sat down, they gave him something to drink and conversed together until supper was ready. Some of them passed the time profitably with very interesting discussions. Finally they asked Piety and Prudence and Charity to converse with him.

Piety began, "Come, good Christian, since we have received you into our home with such charity this night, let's spend our time profitably by discussing all the things that have happened to you so far on your journey."

Christian responded, "I am glad you are interested in my journey and would be happy to share my adventures with you."

"What was the first thing that motivated you to become a pilgrim?" Piety asked.

"I was driven out of my native country by a dreadful message that I could not get out of my head, and the message was that destruction was unavoidable if I stayed in the place where I was."

"But how did it happen that you came out of your country by this way?" Piety inquired further.

Christian answered, "It was as God would have it. I was under the fear of destruction. I did not know where to go, but by chance I was approached by a man as I was trembling and weeping. His name was Evangelist, and he directed me to the small sheep gate, which without his direction I would never have found. And that put me on the way that led me directly to this house."

Piety then asked, "But did you not come by the house of the Interpreter?"

"Yes," Christian went on, "and while I was there I saw and heard things that I will remember forever, three things that were the most important. First, how Christ, despite Satan, maintains His work of grace in the heart. Second, the man in the iron cage who sinned himself out of the hope of God's mercy. And finally, the dream of the man who thought in his sleep that the Day of Judgment had come."

" Did he tell you about his dream?" Piety wondered.

"Yes, and it was dreadful. It made my heart ache as he was telling it; yet I am glad I heard it."

Piety inquired, "Was that all that you saw at the house of the Interpreter?"

Christian answered, "No. He took me to a stately palace where the people were dressed in gold; and it was here that I saw a brave man cut his way through the armed men who stood in the door to keep him out. Then he was invited to come in to eternal glory. Seeing these things enraptured my heart! I would have stayed at that good man's house for a year, but I knew I had further to go."

"And what else did you see in the way?" Piety wanted to know.

"See! I went a little farther, and I saw one who hung bleeding upon a tree, and the very sight of Him made my burden fall off my back (for I had groaned under a very heavy burden, but then it fell off). It was a strange thing to see, and I have never seen anything like it before. And while I stood looking up at the one hanging on the cross, three Shining Ones came to me. One of them testified that my sins were forgiven; another stripped me of my rags and gave me this embroidered coat that you see; and the third gave me the mark that you see on my forehead and gave me this sealed scroll." And with that he plucked it out of his coat.

Piety again asked, "But you saw more than this, did you not?"

Christian continued, "The things that I have told you were the best. But there were some other things I saw. Namely, I saw three men—Foolish, Sloth, and Presumption—lying asleep a little out of the way, with irons upon their ankles. But do you think I could awake them?

"I also saw Formality and Hypocrisy come tumbling over the wall with a false pretense of going to Zion, but they were quickly lost, as I warned them they would be, but they would not believe me. But the hardest thing I encountered was getting up this hill and then coming upon the lions. If it had not been for the good porter who stands at the gate, I think I might have retreated and abandoned my journey. But now I thank God I am here, and I thank you for receiving me."

Then Prudence began to ask Christian some questions.

"Do you ever think of the country you came from?"

"Yes," Christian replied, "but with much shame and detestation. 'Honestly, if I had pleasant thoughts about the country from which I have come, I might have taken the opportunity to return; but I desire a better country, one that is heavenly.'"[p]

Prudence asked further, "Do you not still carry some of the baggage from the place you escaped?"

"Yes, but against my will. I still have within me some of the carnal thoughts that all my countrymen, as well as myself, were delighted with. Now all those things cause me to grieve. If I could master my own heart, I would choose never to think of those things again, but when I try only to think about those things that are best, those things that are the worst creep back into my mind and behavior."[q]

---

[p]Hebrews 11:15–16.
[q]Romans 7:16–19.

"Don't you find that sometimes you can defeat those evil things that at other times seem to defeat you?" Prudence suggested.

Christian answered, "Yes, it happens occasionally. They are golden hours that I treasure."

"Can you remember the means by which you're able occasionally to defeat the evil desires and thoughts that assail you?"

Christian said, "Yes. When I think about what I experienced at the cross, that will do it. When I look at the embroidered coat, that will do it. When I read the scroll that I carry in my coat, that will do it. And when my thoughts turn to the place to which I am going, that will do it."

Prudence inquired, "And what is it that makes you desirous to go to Mount Zion?"

Christian replied, "Why, it is there that I hope to see alive my Savior who hung dead on the cross. It is there that I hope to be rid of all those things that to this day are an annoyance to me. They say that in that place there is no death, and I will dwell there with the company that I like best.[r] For, to tell you the truth, I love Him because He eased me of my burden. I am weary of my inward sickness. I desire to be where I will die no more, with a company that will continually cry, 'Holy, holy, holy!'"

Then Charity said to Christian, "Do you have a family? Are you a married man?"

"I have a wife and four small children."

"And why did you not bring them along with you?" Charity asked.

Then Christian wept and said, "Oh, how willingly would I have brought them along! But they were all completely against my going on this pilgrimage."

Charity urged, "But you should have talked to them and should have tried to show them the danger of being left behind."

"I did," Christian explained. "I told them what God had shown

---

[r]Isaiah 25:8; Revelation 21:4.

to me regarding the destruction of our city. But they treated me like I was jesting, and they did not believe me."[s]

Charity inquired further, "And did you pray to God that He would bless your counsel to them?"

Christian replied, "Yes, I did and with much pleading. As you can imagine, my wife and poor children are very precious to me."

"Did you tell them of your own sorrow and fear of destruction?" Charity asked. "I suppose that the coming destruction was visible enough to you."

"Yes, over and over and over," Christian reported. "They could also see the fear in my face, in my tears, and also in my trembling under the apprehension of the judgment that hung over our heads. Unfortunately, all this was not enough to convince them to come with me."

Charity inquired, "What did they say for themselves? What reason did they give for not coming with you?"

"My wife was afraid of losing this world, and my children were swayed by the foolish delights of youth. So by one thing or another they left me to make this pilgrimage on my own."

Charity asked further, "But couldn't they see the vanity of life in the City of Destruction and how your life had changed for the better as you prepared to leave? Couldn't you convince them how foolish it was to stay and how much better it would be for them to come along with you?"

Christian responded, "Yes, although I cannot commend my life, for I am conscious of my many failings. I know that a man by the witness of his life may overturn any persuasive arguments he may make. Yet I can say that I was very careful not to give them any occasion for offense by my own actions. I did nothing to give them cause for not coming on this pilgrimage. And it was for this very thing that they found fault with me. They complained that I was too precise and that I denied myself things, for their sakes, in which they saw no evil. I think I can say that what they saw in me that

---

[s]Genesis 19:14.

Christian is entertained at the House Beautiful.

hindered them was my great concern that I not sin against God or do any wrong to my neighbor."

Charity commented, "Indeed Cain hated his brother 'because his own works were evil, and his brother's righteous.'[t] And if your wife and children have been offended with you for this, they show themselves to be implacable to good, and 'you will have delivered your soul' from their blood."[u]

Now I saw in my dream that they sat talking together until supper was ready. So when all was prepared and ready, they sat down to eat. Now the table was furnished with savory foods and with wine that was well refined, and all their conversation at the table was about the Lord of the hill.

They spoke with reverence about what He had done and why He did what He did and the reason He built that house. And by the things they said, I perceived that He had been a great warrior. He had fought with and slain "him that had the power of death," but not without great danger to Himself.[v] Hearing this made me love Him even more.

They said, and I believe (as said Christian), that He did it with the loss of much blood. But what made it most glorious and gracious was that He did it all out of pure love to His country. And besides, some of the household said they had spoken with Him since He died on the cross; and they have attested that they heard it from His own lips that there is nowhere to be found, no matter how far one might travel, anyone who had a greater love for poor pilgrims than He.

They, moreover, gave an instance of what they heard Him say, which was that He had stripped Himself of His glory that He might do this for the poor. They also heard Him say and affirm "that He would not dwell in the mountain of Zion alone." They said also that He had made many pilgrims into princes, even though by nature they were born beggars, and their original dwelling had been the dunghill.[w]

---

[t] 1 John 3:12.
[u] Ezekiel 3:19.
[v] Hebrews 2:14–15.
[w] 1 Samuel 2:8; Psalm 113:7.

Christian examines the records contained in the House Beautiful.

This was the topic of their fellowship and conversation, which lasted late into the evening. After they had prayerfully committed themselves to their Lord for protection, they all went to bed. They took Christian to a large upper chamber, whose window opened toward the rising sun. The name of the chamber was Peace, and this is where he slept until the break of day. When he awoke he sang:

"Where am I now? Is this the love and care
Of Jesus for the men that pilgrims are?
Thus to provide! That I should be forgiven,
And dwell already the next door to Heaven!"

So in the morning they all got up, and after some more discourse they told him that he should not depart until they had shown him some of the treasures of that place. First they took him into the study, where they showed him records of the greatest antiquities; in which, as I remember my dream, they showed him first the pedigree of the Lord of the hill, that He was the son of the Ancient of Days and became that by eternal generation. Here also was more fully recorded the acts that He had done and the names of many hundreds whom He had taken into His service. Recorded there was how He had placed them in such habitations that could neither by length of days nor decays or nature ever be dissolved.

Then they read to him some of the worthy acts that some of His servants had done, how they had "through faith conquered kingdoms, enforced justice, obtained promises, stopped the mouths of lions, quenched the power of fire, escaped the edge of the sword, were made strong out of weakness, became mighty in war, put foreign armies to flight."[x]

Then they read, in another part of the records, where it was declared how willing their Lord was to receive anyone into His favor, even those who in time past had offered great affronts to His person and proceedings. Here also were several other histories of many other famous things that Christian was able to read. Things

---

[x]Hebrews 11:33–34.

both ancient and modern together with prophecies and predictions of things that have already occurred or soon will come to pass. Predictions and prophecies full of dread and amazement to our enemies, and comfort and solace for pilgrims.

The next day they took him into the armory, where they showed him all manner of furniture that their Lord had provided for pilgrims. There were swords, shields, helmets, breastplates, ALL-PRAYER, and shoes that would not wear out. And there was enough to dress out as many men for the service of their Lord as there were stars in the heavens.

They also showed him the instruments with which some of His servants had done wonderful things. They showed him Moses' rod; the hammer and nail with which Jael slew Sisera; the pitchers, trumpets, and lamps, too, with which Gideon put to flight the armies of Midian. Then they showed him the ox's goad used by Shamgar to slay six hundred men. They also showed him the jawbone with which Samson did such mighty feats. They showed him the sling and stone with which David slew Goliath of Gath, and the sword also with which their Lord in the final days will kill the Man of Sin. And besides all that they showed him many other excellent things, with which Christian was much delighted. Once this was done, they all went to rest.

Then I saw in my dream that the next day Christian got up to continue his journey. But before he could leave, they convinced him to stay for another day, hoping the weather would be clear so they could show him the Delectable Mountains. They told Christian that this would further encourage and comfort him since those mountains were nearer to his final destination than where he was now. So he consented to stay. When the next morning came, they took him to the top of the house and asked him to look south, which he did. Then he saw some distance away a most pleasant mountainous country, beautified with woods, vineyards, fruits of all sorts, flowers, springs, and fountains, very delectable to behold.[y]

---

[y]Isaiah 33:16–17.

Christian views Immanuel's Land from the House Beautiful.

Then he asked the name of the country. They said it was Immanuel's Land; and "like this hill it is for all the pilgrims. And when you go there, with the assistance of the shepherds who live there, you may see the gates of the Celestial City."

Now they all agreed that Christian was ready to go forward on his journey. But they wanted to visit the armory one last time before he left.

So they did, and while they were there, they covered him from head to foot with armor to protect him should he be assaulted along the way. Christian, now dressed in full armor, went with his friends to the gate.[14] When he arrived at the gate, he asked the porter if any other pilgrims had passed by. The porter answered, "Yes."

"Did you ask him his name?" Christian inquired.

The porter replied, "I asked him his name, and he told me it was Faithful."

"Oh," said Christian, "I know him. He is my townsman, a close neighbor. He comes from the place where I was born. How far ahead do you think he is?"

The porter responded, "By this time I think he should be below the hill."

"Well," said Christian, "good porter, the Lord be with you and increase your blessings for all the kindness you have shown me."

Then he began to go forward. Discretion, Piety, Charity, and Prudence accompanied him down to the foot of the hill. And they all went on together, rehearsing their former conversations until they came to the top of the hill.

Then Christian said, "It appears that going down the hill is going to be as difficult and dangerous as it was climbing up the hill."

"Yes," said Prudence, "it is a hard thing for a man to go down into the Valley of Humiliation, which is where you are headed. It is difficult to go down the hill without slipping and falling, which is why we are going to accompany you down the hill."

So he began to go down, very carefully; and even with all his caution and assistance he almost slipped a time or two.

Then I saw in my dream that they all arrived at the bottom of the hill where they gave Christian a loaf of bread, a bottle of wine, and a cluster of raisins. Then Christian went on his way.

Chapter Four

A Fierce Battle and a Dark Valley

nce he was in the Valley of Humiliation, poor Christian was immediately put to the test. He had not gone very far before he spied a foul fiend coming over the field to meet him. His name was Apollyon.[1]

Christian was afraid and struggled in his mind to know what he should do. Should he go back or stand his ground? As Christian thought about what to do, he realized that he had no armor for his back and that turning and running would give the enemy an easy target for his darts. Christian decided that standing his ground would give him the best chance of surviving Apollyon's attack.

So Christian went forward, and Apollyon met him. Now the monster was hideous to behold. He was clothed with scales like a fish (they are his pride), he had wings like a dragon, feet like a bear, a belly from which came fire and smoke, and the mouth of a lion. When he had advanced near Christian, he viewed him with a disdainful look and then began to question him.

Apollyon asked him, "Where did you come from? Where are you bound?"

"I came from the City of Destruction, which is the place of all evil, and I am going to the City of Zion," Christian answered.

"By your answer I perceive that you are one of my subjects, for all that country is mine, and I am the prince and god of it. How is it that you have run away from your king? Were it not for the fact that I wish you to enter into my service again, I would strike you to the ground with one blow."

Christian responded, "Indeed, I was born in your dominions, but your service was hard, and a man cannot live on the wages you pay, 'for the wages of sin is death.'ᵃ Therefore, when I grew into a greater understanding, I did as other thoughtful persons have done: I searched to see if there was a way to make myself into the person I should be."

To that, Apollyon protested, "There is no prince who will so easily lose his subjects, nor will I lose you. But since you complained about your service and wages, be content to go back. What our country can afford, I promise to give to you."

Christian boldly proclaimed, "But I have given myself to another, even to the King of princes, so how can I in fairness go back to you?"

"As the proverb says, you have 'changed a bad for a worse,'" Apollyon said, "but it is very common for those who have professed themselves His servants to give Him the slip after a while and return to me. And if you return to me, everything will be well with you."

Christian asserted with confidence, "I have given Him my faith and have sworn my allegiance to Him. How can I change my mind now without being hanged as a traitor?"

"You did the same to me, and yet I am willing to let it pass, if you will now turn and come back."

Christian replied, "What I promised you was done in ignorance, and besides, I believe that the Prince under whose banner I now stand is able to absolve me and to pardon me for those things I did while in your service. Besides, O you destroying Apollyon, to speak

---

ᵃRomans 6:23.

truth, I like His service, His wages, His servants, His government, His company, and His country better than yours. You can stop trying to persuade me otherwise. I am His servant, and I will follow Him."

Apollyon then boldly stated, "Consider again, when you have cooled down, what you are likely to meet up with on the way you have chosen. You know that for the most part His servants come to an ill end, because they are transgressors against me and my ways. Think how many of them have been put to shameful deaths! Besides, you count His service better than mine, and yet He has never come out of the place where He dwells to deliver from my hands any who served Him. But as for me, how many times, as the whole world very well knows, have I delivered from Him and His, either by power or fraud, those who have faithfully served me! Likewise will I deliver you."

"His present restraint not to deliver them is for the purpose of testing their love, to see if they will cling to Him to the end," Christian asserted. "As for the ill end you say they come to, that just adds glory to their account. For they do not expect deliverance now and will endure all life's trials, knowing it adds to their glory in eternal life when their Prince comes in His and the angels' glory."

"You have already been unfaithful in your service to Him—so why do you think you will receive wages from Him?" Apollyon challenged.

"How, O Apollyon, have I been unfaithful to Him?"

Apollyon accused, "You almost fainted when you first set out, when you almost choked in the Swamp of Despond. You also attempted to get rid of your burden in the wrong way, instead of patiently waiting for the Prince to take it off. You sinfully slept and lost your scroll, you were almost persuaded to go back at the sight of the lions, and when you talk of your journey and of what you have heard and seen, you inwardly desire your own glory in all you do and say."

"All this is true, and much more that you have failed to mention," Christian agreed. "But the Prince whom I now serve and honor is merciful and ready to forgive. Besides, these infirmities possessed me while I was in your country, for there I allowed them to come in. But I have groaned under them, have been sorry for them, and have obtained pardon from my Prince."

Then Apollyon broke into a hideous rage, shrieking, "I am an enemy to this Prince! I hate His person, His laws, and His people! I have purposely come here to stop you!"

"Apollyon, beware of what you do, for I am in the King's Highway, the Way of Holiness. Therefore take heed to yourself."

Then Apollyon straddled himself over the whole breadth of the way and countered, "I am void of fear in this matter. Prepare to breathe your last, for I swear by my infernal den that you will go no further. Here will I spill your soul."

And with that he threw a flaming dart at Christian's breast, but Christian had a shield in his hand by which he averted it and its danger.

Then Christian drew his sword, for he saw that it was time to make a stand. Apollyon quickly advanced on Christian, throwing darts as thick as hail. Christian did all he could to avoid being struck, yet he could not prevent Apollyon from wounding him in his head, his hand, and his foot. These wounds caused Christian to falter a little, and Apollyon advanced even more. Finally Christian found new courage and resisted as manfully as he could. This mortal combat lasted for above half a day, until Christian grew weaker and weaker because of his many wounds.

Then Apollyon, spying his opportunity, began to move closer to Christian, wrestling with him until Christian fell to the ground. With that, Christian's sword flew out of his hand. Then said Apollyon, "I have you now!" and almost crushed Christian to death, so that Christian began to despair of life.

But as God would have it, while Apollyon lifted himself up to deliver his last blow and to make a full end of this good man, Christian nimbly stretched out his hand for his sword and grabbed

Christian battles Apollyon.

it, saying, "Rejoice not against me, O my enemy: when I fall, I shall rise back up."[b2] With that, Christian gave Apollyon a deadly thrust, which made the fiend fall back as one who had received a mortal wound. Christian, seeing his advantage, thrust his sword at him again, saying, "Nay, in all these things we are more than conquerors, through Him who loved us."[c] When he heard those words, Apollyon spread out his dragon wings and flew away, and Christian saw him no more.[d3]

During this entire battle that I saw and heard in my dream, the yelling and hideous roaring from Apollyon can scarcely be imagined, resembling the voice of a dragon. Nor can the intensity of the sighs and groans that issued from Christian be fully described. Christian fought with such vigor that his countenance never once relaxed its grim expression until he perceived that he had wounded Apollyon with his two-edged sword. Only then did Christian smile and look upward, but until that point, it was the most dreadful and fierce fight I had ever witnessed.

When the battle was over, Christian said, "I will here give thanks to Him who delivered me out of the mouth of the lion, to him who helped me against Apollyon." So Christian rejoiced with this song of thanks:

> *"Great Beelzebub, the Captain of this fiend,*
> *Designed my ruin; therefore to this end*
> *He sent him harnessed with weapons and with rage*
> *That hellish was, and did fiercely me in battle engage.*
> *But God's angel Michael helped me, and I,*
> *By slash of sword, did make the fiend to fly.*
> *Therefore to my God I give my lasting praise*
> *And thank and bless His holy Name always."[4]*

Then there came to Christian a messenger with a handful of leaves taken from the Tree of Life. Christian took the leaves and applied them to his wounds, which healed immediately. He then sat

---
[b]Micah 7:8.
[c]Romans 8:37.
[d]James 4:7.

down and ate some of the bread and drank from the bottle that had been given to him by Prudence, Piety, and Charity.

After Christian had refreshed himself, he began his journey again. Not knowing whether Apollyon would come back for another skirmish or whether some other enemy might be at hand, Christian drew his sword and walked carefully through the valley, but he met with no other enemies.

Now at the end of the Valley of Humiliation there was another valley, the Valley of the Shadow of Death.[5] And since there was no other way to the Celestial City, Christian was obliged to go through it.

Now this valley was a very solitary place, and as the prophet Jeremiah described it, "a wilderness, a land of deserts, and of pits, a land of drought, and of the shadow of death, a land that no man [but a Christian] passed through, and where no one lived."[e]

Now here Christian was to be afflicted more than in his fight with Apollyon, as the following adventure will show.

When Christian came to the borders of the Valley of the Shadow of Death, I saw in my dream that he met two men coming toward him, children of those men who brought an evil report concerning the good land of Canaan.[f6] These two men were quickly retreating when Christian stopped them and asked them where they were going.

They said, "Back! back! And we would advise you to do so too, if you have any concern for your life or your peace of mind."

"Why? What's the matter?" inquired Christian.

"Matter!" said they. "We were going the same way that you are now going, and we went as far as we dared to go and almost went past the point of no return. Had we continued, we would not be here to warn you."

"But what did you encounter that made you so fearful?" asked Christian.

"Why, we were almost in the Valley of the Shadow of Death, but

[e]Jeremiah 2:6.
[f]Numbers 13.

Christian walks through the Valley of the Shadow of Death.

as our good fortune would have it, we looked ahead and saw the danger before we came to it."[g]

"But what have you seen?" persisted Christian.

"Seen!" they nearly shouted. "Why, the valley itself, which is black as pitch; yet we also saw hobgoblins, satyrs, and dragons of the pit. We also heard in the valley a continual howling and yelling that sounded like people in unutterable misery who are bound in affliction and irons. Over the valley hangs the discouraging clouds of confusion. Death also spreads his wings over it. In a word, it is dreadful and completely unruly."[h][7]

Then Christian said, "All these terrors aside, nothing that you have said so far convinces me that this is anything but the way to the Celestial City."[i][8]

"Have your own way, but we will not choose it as ours."

So they parted, and Christian went on his way, with his sword in his hand, fearing he might yet be assaulted.

Then I saw in my dream that for the entire length of the valley, there was a very deep ditch on the right side. It is into this ditch that the blind have been leading the blind since the beginning of time, to the destruction of both blind leaders and their followers.[j]

I saw also on the left side of the valley a very dangerous quagmire, in which not even a good man can find solid footing or bottom if he falls in. This is the bog King David fell into, and no doubt would have been smothered, had not He who is able pulled him out.[9]

The pathway was exceedingly narrow, and good Christian was tested to his limits. For in the dark, when he tried to avoid the ditch on the one hand, he was ready to tip over into the mire on the other. Also when he sought to escape the mire, unless he was very careful, he would almost fall into the ditch.

And so Christian went on, and I heard him sigh bitterly. For besides the dangers mentioned above, the pathway was so dark that

[g]Psalm 44:19; 107:10.
[h]Job 3:5; 10:22.
[i]Jeremiah 2:6.
[j]Psalm 69:14–15.

often when he lifted up his foot to step forward, he never was sure where his foot would land or what he would step on.

In the middle of this valley I saw in my dream the mouth of Hell, and it stood right next to the path.[10]

What shall I do now? thought Christian. Abundant flame and smoke spewed from the place, with sparks and hideous noises (things that could not be fought with a sword, as Apollyon was). Christian put his sword back in its sheath and took out another weapon, the one called All-prayer.[k]

Then I heard Christian cry out, "O Lord, I beseech You, deliver my soul!"[l] He continued in this way for a long time, but still the flames were reaching toward him. Also he heard tortured, sad voices and the sound of things rushing and scurrying back and forth, and sometimes Christian thought he was going to be torn to pieces or trampled down like mud in the streets.

Christian saw these frightful sights and heard the dreadful noises for several miles of his journey, and, adding to his troubles, he came to a place where he thought he heard a company of fiends coming forward to meet him. Christian stopped to think about how best to meet this new enemy. For a brief moment he thought about turning back but then thought that perhaps he was halfway through the valley. He also remembered how he had already vanquished many dangers and that the danger of going back might prove worse than the dangers ahead of him. So he made up his mind to continue going forward.

The fiends seemed to be coming nearer and nearer, but when they were almost upon him, Christian cried out with a most vehement voice, "I will walk in the strength of the Lord God!" So they turned around and went back from where they came.

By this time I noticed that poor Christian was so confounded that he did not recognize his own voice. Just when he came near the mouth of the burning pit, one of the wicked ones stepped up

---

[k]Ephesians 6:18.
[l]Psalm 116:4.

softly behind him and whispered many grievous blasphemies to him, which Christian truly thought had come from his own mind. It grieved Christian more than anything that he had met with before to think that he should now blaspheme Him whom he loved, though in truth Christian had not done that. He wished to stop the wicked thought but did not have the discretion to simply plug his ears to silence the lies that a wicked one spoke to him or to recognize their source.

After Christian had traveled in this disturbing condition for some time, he thought he heard the voice of a man going before him, saying, "Though I walk through the valley of the shadow of death, I will fear no evil; for You are with me."[m]

Then Christian was glad, and for good reasons. For one, Christian believed that someone who feared God was in the valley with him. Secondly, he perceived that God was with this person up ahead, even though it was dark and dismal. Christian reasoned that if God was with this fellow traveler, then He was also with him, even though the evil in this place prevented his perception of it.[n] Thirdly, Christian hoped that he could catch up with the person ahead and have a companion on his journey.

So he went forward and called out to the pilgrim ahead of him, but this fellow traveler did not know what to answer since he thought that he was alone. Finally the sun came up on a new day, and Christian rejoiced and said, "He has 'turned the shadow of death into the morning.'"[o][11]

Then Christian looked back, not out of any desire to return, but so that he could see by the light of day what hazards he had gone through in the dark. So he saw more clearly the ditch that was on the one hand and the quagmire on the other. He also saw how narrow the way was that went between them both. He saw the hobgoblins, satyrs, and dragons of the pit, but all far-off (for after the sun came up, they would not come near). But yet they were revealed to

[m]Psalm 23:4.
[n]Job 9:11.
[o]Amos 5:8.

him just as it is written, "He discovers deep things out of darkness, and brings out to light the shadow of death."[p] Christian was deeply moved by his deliverance from all the dangers of the solitary way that went through the valley, dangers that he feared more before but could only now clearly see.

In the new light of day, Christian realized how treacherous the first part of his journey through the Valley of the Shadow of Death had been. But it would not compare to the dangers that lay before him, which he had yet to travel. As Christian viewed the path ahead, he saw that it was full of pits, pitfalls, deep holes, snares, traps, and false paths that led down to the pit. Christian realized what a mercy it was to have the light of day, for had it still been dark he would never in a thousand lifetimes have been able to safely reach the end of his journey through the Valley of the Shadow of Death. So as Christian watched the sun rising he said, "His candle shines upon my head, and by His light I walk through darkness."[q] It was in this light that Christian came to the end of the valley.

Now I saw in my dream that at the end of this valley lay blood, bones, ashes, and the mangled bodies of men, even of some pilgrims who had gone this way before. While I was musing about what had caused this carnage, I spied a cave where two giants, Pope and Pagan, lived in the olden days. It was their power and tyranny that had cruelly put to death the men whose bones, blood, ashes, and mangled bodies I beheld.

Christian went by this place without much danger, which made me wonder, but I have since learned that Pagan had been dead for a long while. As for the other, even though he is still alive, his advanced age and the many skirmishes of his younger days have caused him to grow crazy and stiff in his joints. Now he can do little more than sit in his cave's mouth, grinning at pilgrims as they go by and biting his nails because he can no longer capture and destroy them.

---

[p]Job 12:22.
[q]Job 29:3.

So I saw in my dream that Christian went right past the old man sitting in the mouth of the cave. But as he passed, the old man poked his head out of his cave and snarled, "More like you must be burned." Christian held his peace and passed by the wretched old man without any difficulty. Then Christian sang:

"O world of wonders! (I can say no less)
That I should be preserved in this distress
That I have met with here! O blessed be
That hand that from it did deliver me!
Dangers in darkness, devils, Hell and sin
Encompassed me, while I this place was in:
Yea, snares and pits and traps and nets did lie
Upon my path, that worthless, foolish I
Might have been caught, entangled, and cast down;
But since I live, let Jesus wear the crown."

Chapter Five

A Faithful Friend

ow as Christian went on his way, he came to a little upward slope that had been put there for the purpose of helping pilgrims see what lay ahead of them. Christian ascended the slope, and looking from that height, he saw Faithful just ahead of him on his journey. Then called Christian aloud, "Hello, hello! Wait right there, and I will come to you and be your companion."[1] Hearing this, Faithful looked behind him and saw Christian, who cried out again, "Stay, stay, so I can catch up with you."

But Faithful answered, "No, I am fleeing for my life, and the avenger of blood is behind me!"

Hearing this, Christian gathered his strength and ran with all his might in order to catch up with Faithful. Soon he had not only caught up with Faithful but had run past him a little ways, so that the last became the first. Then he turned and proudly smiled at Faithful, feeling smug about overtaking him. At that moment Christian stumbled and fell to the ground with such force that it left him unable to rise to his feet until Faithful came and helped him up.[2]

Then I saw in my dream that they went on together with brotherly affection for each other and had many pleasant conversations about all the things that had happened to them on their pilgrimage.[3]

"My honored friend," Christian said to his beloved brother Faithful, "I am glad that I have overtaken you and that God has done a work in both our spirits, so that we can walk as companions on this pleasant path."[4]

Faithful said, "I would have liked to have enjoyed your company from the beginning of the journey, but you left earlier than I did, and I was forced to come this far all alone."

"How long did you stay in the City of Destruction before you set out after me on your pilgrimage?"

Faithful answered, "Until I could stay no longer, for there was a lot of talk after you left that our city would in a short time be burned down to the ground with fire from Heaven."

"Really? Your neighbors said that?"

"Yes, and for a while it was all anyone talked about," Faithful answered.

"Really!" Christian exclaimed. "And why are you the only one who left to escape the danger?"

Faithful went on, "Well, like I said, there was a lot of talk about it, but I don't think anyone really believed it. Even when the topic was on everyone's lips, I heard some speak deridingly of you and your desperate journey (as some derisively called your pilgrimage). But I believed it, and I still believe that our city will one day be destroyed by fire and brimstone from above, and that is why I made my escape."

"Did you hear anything about your neighbor Pliable?" Christian asked.

"Yes, Christian. I heard that he followed you until he came to the Swamp of Despond where he fell in, although he denied that part. I am sure it was true since he was soiled with the scum from that place."

"And what did his neighbors say to him?" Christian asked further.

Faithful responded, "When I left, Pliable had been the object of derision ever since he returned to the city. Many mocked and despised him and would not share his company any longer. He is seven times worse off than if he had never left the city."

Christian asked, "But why do they despise him since they also despise the way that he forsook?"

Faithful explained, "They say, 'Hang him, he is a turncoat; he was not true to his profession.' I think God has stirred up even his enemies to hiss at him and make him a proverb because he has forsaken the way."[a]

"Did you talk with him before you left on your journey?"

"I met him once in the streets," Faithful said, "but he looked the other way, ashamed of what he had done, so I did not speak with him."

Christian added, "Well, when I first started my journey, I had hopes for that man; but now I fear he will perish in the overthrow of the city. For it has happened to him according to the true proverb, 'The dog has returned to his own vomit; and the sow that was washed has returned to wallow in the mire.'"[b]

"I fear you are right. But who can prevent what is to come?" Faithful stated plaintively.

"Well, neighbor Faithful," said Christian, "let's talk of things that are of more immediate concern. Tell me, what have you met with on this journey? I would be very surprised to hear that you had undergone no adventures along the way."

"I escaped the Swamp of Despond, which I understand you fell into, and I got to the sheep gate without any danger. But I did meet with someone whose name was Wanton, who would have liked very much to harm me," Faithful reported.

"It was good you escaped her trap. Joseph was pursued by her, and he escaped her, but it almost cost him his life.[c] But what did she do to you?"

---

[a]Jeremiah 29:18–19.
[b]2 Peter 2:22.
[c]Genesis 39:11–13.

Faithful answered, "You can hardly imagine what a flattering tongue she had. She worked hard to turn me away from the path in order to go with her, promising me all sorts of fleshly pleasures and contentment."

"I am sure there is one pleasure she could not promise you—a good conscience."

"Yes, you know what I mean, all carnal and fleshly pleasures," Faithful agreed.

Christian added, "Thank God you have escaped her. The one with whom the Lord is angry will fall into her deep pit."[d]

"Well, I don't know if I completely escaped her or not."

"How is that?" Christian inquired. "I hope you did not consent to her desires."

"No," Faithful assured him, "I did not defile myself, for I remembered an old writing that I had seen that said, 'Her steps follow the path to Hell.'[e] So I shut my eyes so that I would not be bewitched with her seductive appearance.[f] Then she cursed me and abused me with her tongue, and I went on my way."

"Did you meet with any other assaults on your journey?"

Faithful recounted, "When I came to the foot of the hill called Difficulty, I met a very old man who asked me my name and destination. I told him that I was a pilgrim, going to the Celestial City. Then the old man said to me, 'You look like an honest fellow. Would you be willing to come and live with and work for me for the wages that I would be willing to give you?'

"Then I asked him his name and where he lived. He said his name was Adam the First and that he lived in the town of Deceit.[g]

"I then asked him what sort of work he had for me to do and what were the wages he would pay. He told me that his work included many delights, and for wages he would make me the heir to his estate.

---

[d]Proverbs. 22:14.
[e]Proverbs 5:5.
[f]Job 31:1.
[g]Ephesians 4:22.

"I further asked him what sort of house he lived in and what other servants he had. So he told me that his house was maintained with all the dainties in the world and that his servants were all relatives of his. Then I asked if he had any children. He said that he had but three daughters: Lust of the Flesh, Lust of the Eyes, and Pride of Life.[h] Then he told me that I could marry them all if I wished. Then I asked for how long a time he would have me live with him. And he told me that I would live with him as long as he lived."

"What was the outcome of this discussion?" Christian asked.

"Why, at first I found myself somewhat inclined to go with the man, for I thought that his offer sounded very good," Faithful said. "But as I looked at his forehead and spoke with him, I saw written, 'Put off the old man with his deeds.'"

"And then what happened?"

"Then it came rushing into my mind that despite his flattering words, he would sell me as a slave when we got to his home," Faithful said. "So I asked him to stop talking, and I told him I would not come near the door to his house.

"Then he cursed me and told me that he would send someone after me who would make my soul bitter. So I turned to go away from him, but just as I turned to go, I felt him take hold of my flesh and give me such a deadly pinch that I thought he had pulled a part of me off for himself. This made me shriek, 'Oh, wretched man!'[i] So I went on my way up the Hill Difficulty.

"Now when I had climbed about halfway up, I looked behind and saw someone coming after me, swift as the wind. Soon he overtook me just about the place where the arbor stands."

"That is the place," said Christian, "where I sat down to rest, fell asleep, and lost my scroll."

"Dear brother, hear me out," Faithful urged. "So as soon as the man overtook me, without saying a word, he struck me and knocked me down unconscious. When I came to, I asked him why he had

---

[h]1 John 2:16.
[i]Romans 7:24.

thus assaulted me. He said that it was because of my secret incli-
nation to follow Adam the First, and with that he struck me with
another deadly blow on the chest and beat me down backward, and
I lay at his feet as if I were dead. So when I came to, I cried to him
for mercy. But he said, 'I do not know how to show mercy' and with
that knocked me down again. He would have beaten me to death,
except One came by and told him to stop."

"Who was it that told him to stop?"

Faithful went on, "I did not recognize Him at first, but as He
went by I saw the wounds in His hands and in His side. Then I concluded that He was our Lord. So I continued up the hill."

Christian then explained, "The man who overtook you was
Moses. He spares no one, and he does not know how to show mercy
to anyone who transgresses his law."

"I know that very well. It was not the first time that he had met
with me. He was the one who came to me when I lived securely at
home and who told me he would burn my house over my head if I
stayed there."

Christian asked, "But didn't you see the house that stood on the
top of the hill, on the side of the hill where Moses met you?"

Faithful answered, "Yes, and I saw the lions also, before I came
near the house. But I think they were asleep, for it was about noon.
Because I had so much of the day ahead of me, I passed by the porter and came down the hill."

"Yes, the porter told me that he saw you go by," Christian said.
"I wish you had visited the house, for they would have shown you
many rarities that you would have remembered the rest of your
life. But tell me, did you meet anyone in the Valley of Humiliation?"

Faithful responded, "Yes, I met someone named Discontent who
would have gladly persuaded me to go back with him. His reasoning
was that the valley was altogether without honor. He told me that if
I went into the valley I would be disobeying all my friends, such as
Pride, Arrogance, Self-conceit, Worldly-Glory, and others he knew.

He said they would be very much offended if I made a fool of myself by wading through the Valley of Humiliation."

"Well, how did you answer him?"

Faithful replied, "I told him that even though all those he named had once been my kindred, for undeniably they were my relations according to the flesh, they had disowned me since I became a pilgrim, as I had also rejected them. Therefore they had no more claim on me than those who had never been of my lineage.

"I told him, moreover, that he had misrepresented the Valley of Humiliation, for before there is any honor there is humility; and 'a haughty spirit comes before a fall.'[j] So I told him that I would rather go through this valley to find the honor that true wise men seek than choose those things that this man and his worldly friends think most worthy of our affections."

"Did you meet anyone else in the valley?" Christian inquired.

Faithful answered, "Yes, I met with a man named Shame. However, of all the men that I met with in my pilgrimage, he, I think, bears the wrong name. The others would leave me after a little argumentation, but this bold-faced Shame would never have left me."

"Why, what did he say to you?"

Faithful said, "He objected to religion itself; he said it was a pitiful, low, sneaking business for a man to consider religion. He said that a tender conscience is an unmanly thing and that I would be the object of ridicule if I watched over my words and ways and did not allow myself the liberties to which the brave spirits of the times accustom themselves. He also observed that not many mighty, rich, or wise are of my opinion.[k] He also was quick to point out that most of the pilgrims are disreputable, powerless, and poor. He said that those who follow the way are out of step with the times in which they live, proving their ignorance and lack of understanding in all natural science.

[j]Proverbs 16:18.
[k]1 Corinthians 1:26; 3:18; Philippians 3:7–8; John 7:48.

"Yes, he railed against many things. For example, he said it was a shame to sit regretful and mournful under a sermon and a shame to come home sighing and groaning. He thought it a shame to ask my neighbor's forgiveness for petty offenses or to make restitution when I had taken away something that belonged to another. He said that religion estranges men from the company of great men, who will tolerate vices (which he called by fine, respectable names), and makes them respect base sin because of their religious fraternity. Then he asked, 'Is not this a shame?'"

"And what did you say to him?" Christian asked.

"At first I did not know what to say," Faithful recounted. "He put my mind in such a spin that the blood rushed to my head. Yes, Shame almost silenced me. But then I began to consider, 'That which is highly esteemed among men, is an abomination to God.'[l] And I began to consider that Shame was telling me what men were like, but nothing about what God or the Word of God is like.

"Moreover, I realized that on the Day of Judgment we will not be doomed to death or life according to the harassing spirits of the world but according to the wisdom and law of the Highest. Therefore, thought I, what God says is indeed best, though all the men in the world are against it, seeing that God prefers His religion and a tender conscience. I understood that He calls those people wise who make themselves fools for the Kingdom of Heaven and declares that the poor man who loves Christ is richer than the greatest man in the world who hates Him.

"So I said, 'Shame, depart, for you are an enemy to my salvation! Shall I consider your arguments, Shame, against my Sovereign Lord? If so, then how can I look Him in the face at His coming? Can I now be ashamed of His ways and servants and expect the blessing?'[m]

"Indeed, this Shame was a bold villain. I could hardly get him to leave my company. He would haunt me and continually whisper in

---

[l]Luke 16:15.
[m]Mark 8:38.

my ear about one or another of the infirmities that attend religion. At last I told him it was useless for him to attempt to persuade me further, for those things that he disdained were the very things in which I saw the most glory. So at last I was able to leave the company of this unfortunate man. And when I had finally shaken him off, I began to sing:

> *"The trials that those men do meet withal,*
> *Who are obedient to the heavenly call,*
> *Are manifold, and suited to the flesh,*
> *And come, and come, and come again afresh;*
> *That now, or sometime else, we by them may*
> *Be taken, overcome, and cast away.*
> *O let the pilgrims, let the pilgrims, then,*
> *Be vigilant, and quit themselves like men."*

"I am glad, my brother, that you stood up to this villain so bravely," Christian said. And I think you are right that he has the wrong name, for he is bold enough to follow us in the streets and attempt to put us to shame before all men, that is, to make us ashamed of that which is good. If he were not so audacious, he would never attempt to do what he does. But we will resist him, notwithstanding all his bravadoes, for he is the promoter of fools! 'The wise will inherit honor,' said Solomon, 'but fools get disgrace.'"[n]

Faithful said intently, "I think we must pray to our Lord for help in resisting and fighting Shame. For He desires us to be valiant for the truth while we go on our pilgrimage upon the earth."

"You speak the truth, but did you meet anybody else in the valley?" Christian wondered.

Faithful answered, "No I didn't, for I had sunshine all the rest of the way through the Valley of Humiliation and also through the Valley of the Shadow of Death."

"I am glad it went well for you," Christian said. It did not go so well with me. As soon as I entered the valley, I had dreadful combat with the foul fiend Apollyon. Truthfully, I thought he was going

---

[n]Proverbs 3:35.

to kill me, especially when he got me down and pressed me under his weight. I thought he was going to surely crush me to death, for when he threw me down, my sword flew out of my hand. He told me he was sure of his victory over me, but I cried to God, and He heard me and delivered me from my troubles. Then I entered into the Valley of the Shadow of Death and had no light for almost half the way. On more than one occasion I thought I was going to be killed; but at last day broke, and the sun rose, and I went through the rest of the valley with far more ease and quiet."

Chapter Six

A FAITH BEYOND WORDS

N ow I saw in my dream that as they went on, Faithful looked to one side and saw a man whose name was Talkative[1] walking beside them a short distance away. For on that part of the path there was room enough for many to walk together. Talkative was a tall man and looked more handsome at a distance than he did up close. Faithful spoke to Talkative.

"Friend, how are you?" Faithful inquired. "Are you going to the heavenly country?"

"That is exactly where I am going," Talkative replied.

Faithful responded, "Very good. I hope we may have the pleasure of your company."

"I would be happy to be your companion on the journey."

"Come then, let's go together and spend our time in conversation about things that are excellent," Faithful invited.

Talkative said, "I am glad to have met someone who realizes how profitable it is to talk about good things. To tell you the truth, there are very few of us who will spend their time during travels speaking about what is good. Most men will waste their time talking about things that are of no value, a fact that troubles me."

Faithful agreed, "Yes, that waste of time is something to regret.

Is there anything more worthy of our tongues and mouths than to speak of the things of God and Heaven?"

"I'm enjoying your company already," Talkative said warmly. "Your speech is full of conviction. And to what you said I would add that there is nothing more profitable or pleasant as talking about the things of God. Also, if a man likes to talk about history, or the mystery of things, or miracles, or signs and wonders, where would he find it recorded more sweetly than in the Holy Scripture?"

Faithful agreed, saying, "That is true. We should desire to thus be profited in our conversation by purposely talking about the things of God."

Talkative added, "Those are my thoughts also, for to talk of such things is most profitable. By so doing, a man may gain knowledge about many things, including the vanity of earthly things and the benefit of things above. To be more specific, by talking a man may learn the necessity of the new birth, the insufficiency of our works, the need of Christ's righteousness, etc.

"In addition, by talking a man may learn what it is to repent, to believe, to pray, to suffer, and the like. By talking a man may learn what are the great promises and consolations of the gospel and be comforted by those promises. Further, by talking a man may learn to refute false opinions, to defend the truth, and also to instruct the ignorant."

"All this is true, and glad am I to hear you say them," Faithful stated.

Talkative went on, "Because there is so little talk of these things, there are few who understand the need for faith and the necessity of a work of grace in their soul for the obtaining of eternal life. They still ignorantly live by the works of the Law, through which no man may by any means obtain the Kingdom of Heaven."

Faithful said, "Yes, but the heavenly knowledge of these things is the gift of God. No man can attain them by human industry or by merely talking about them."

"All this I know very well," Talkative said softly. "For a man can receive nothing unless it is given to him from Heaven: all is of grace, not of works. I could give you a hundred Scriptures to confirm this."

"Well, then," said Faithful, "what is that one thing that we should spend our time talking about?"

"Whatever you like," Talkative offered. "I will talk of things heavenly or earthly, moral or evangelical, sacred or profane, past or future, domestic or foreign, important or inconsequential, so long as it is done for our benefit."

Now Faithful began to marvel about Talkative, and stepping over to where Christian was walking, he softly said to him, "What a brave companion have we found! Do you not think that this man will make a very excellent pilgrim?"

Hearing this, Christian smiled gingerly and said, "The man with whom you are so impressed will beguile with that tongue of his twenty who do not know him."[2]

"Do you know him?" Faithful asked.

"Know him? Yes, better than he knows himself."

Faithful inquired, "Tell me, who is he?"

Christian replied, "His name is Talkative. He dwells in our town. I am surprised that he is a stranger to you, but perhaps it is understandable since our town is so large."

"Whose son is he? And where does he live?" Faithful inquired.

Christian reported, "He is the son of Mr. Say-well. He lives in Prating Row, and he is known to all who are acquainted with him by the name of Talkative. Notwithstanding his fine tongue, he is a miserable person."[3]

"Well, he seems to be a very respectable man," Faithful stated.

Christian responded, "Yes, to those who don't really know him. He is best abroad; near home, he is unseemly. Your impression of him as a respectable man brings to my mind the work of a painter whose pictures show attractively at a distance but unpleasantly up close."

"I noticed you smiled. Are you jesting with me?" Faithful wondered.

Christian protested, "God forbid that I should jest (although I did smile). I would not accuse anyone falsely! I will give you a further insight into who this man really is. This man travels with any company and talks of everything. As he is now talking with you, so will he talk when he is drinking at the pub. And the more he drinks, the more he talks. Religion has no place in his heart, his home, or his conversation. He is all talk, and his religion is to make noise with his mouth."

"Really! Then I have been greatly deceived by this man," Faithful concluded.

"Yes, you may be sure of it," Christian asserted. "Remember the proverb, 'They say and do not.'[a] But 'the kingdom of God is not in word, but in power.'[b] He talks of prayer, of repentance, of faith, and of the new birth, but he only knows how to talk about them. I have been with his family and have observed him both at home and abroad, and I know what I say about him is the truth.

"His house is as empty of true religion as the white of an egg is without flavor. In his house there is no prayer and no sign of repentance for sin. The ox of the field in his own way serves God far better than he. He is a stain, a reproach, and a shame to true religion. No one who knows him has a good word to say about him.[c]

"The common people who know him say this about him: 'a saint abroad and a devil at home.' His poor family knows what a tyrant he is. He is rude, raving at the slightest provocation, and so unreasonable with his servants that they do not know what to do or say to him. Men who have any financial dealings with him say that it is better to deal with a known cheat than with him. This man Talkative is worse than a cheat and far surpasses the worst criminal in his ability to beguile and defraud.

"To make matters worse, he is bringing up his sons to follow in his footsteps. If he sees in his own children even the slightest tendency toward a tender conscience, he calls them fools and block-

---

[a]Matthew 23:3.
[b]1 Corinthians 4:20.
[c]Romans 2:24–25.

heads, discourages it in every way he can, and makes a mockery of them before others. It is my opinion that he has, by his wicked life, caused many to stumble and fall. And unless God prevents it, he will be the ruin of many more."

"Well, my brother," Faithful said, "I am inclined to believe you, not only because you know him, but also because I cannot imagine that you would say these things slanderously or falsely out of ill will, but only because this warning is true."

Christian went on, "Had I just met him, I might have shared your good opinion of this man. Had I received a bad report about Talkative from those who are the enemies of true religion, as often happens when evil men speak of faithful men, I would have considered those reports slanderous. But based on my own knowledge of the man and the reports of good men who are ashamed of him and his company, I can assure you that he is as guilty as I am reporting."

"I can see that saying and doing are two different things," Faithful said sadly. "I will be more careful to observe the difference in the future."

Christian solemnly stated, "They are two different things indeed and are as diverse as are the soul and the body. For just as the body without the soul is a lifeless carcass, so also is saying without the doing. The soul of religion is the practiced, working part: 'Pure religion and undefiled, before God and the Father, is this, to visit the fatherless and widows in their affliction, and to keep himself unspotted from the world.'[d] Talkative is not aware of this truth. He thinks that hearing and talking will make him a good Christian, and so he deceives his own soul.

"By hearing, God's Word is indeed sown in our hearts, but talking alone in response to that Word is not enough to prove that the seed is bearing fruit in our lives. Let us be very certain that at the day of doom, men will be judged according to their fruits.[e] No one will be asked, 'Did you believe?' but instead, 'Were you doers, or only

---

[d]James 1:27; also see verses 22–26.
[e]Matthew 13, 25.

talkers?' Accordingly they will be judged. The end of the world is compared to a harvest, the harvest of our souls. As you know, men at harvesttime are only interested in fruit. This doesn't mean that we can believe anything false to true faith as long as we bear fruit. Far from it, but I say this to show you how insignificant the profession of Talkative will be on that final Day of Judgment."

Faithful added, "This brings to my mind what Moses said when he described the beast that is clean.[f] The clean beast is one that both parts the hoof and chews the cud, not the beast that is only one or the other. The hare chews the cud but is still unclean because he does not part the hoof. This truly resembles Talkative who chews upon the Word as he seeks knowledge. But he doesn't divide at the hoof. That is, he does not part with the way of sinners. Just like the hare, he has the foot of an unclean dog or bear and is therefore unclean."

"As far as I know, you have declared the true sense of those gospel texts," Christian affirmed. "And I will add one more thing: Paul calls some men, those who are great talkers, 'sounding brass and tinkling cymbals.' That is, as he explains in another place, 'things without life, giving sound.'[g] These men are without life, without the true faith and grace of the gospel, even though their talk sounds like the tongue or voice of an angel. Consequently, these are men who will never dwell in the Kingdom of Heaven among those who are the children of life."

Faithful said, "Well, I was not fond of his company when we first conversed, but now I am sick of it. What shall we do to get rid of him?"

"Take my advice, and do as I tell you, and you will find that he will soon be sick of your company also, unless God touches his heart and changes it," Christian suggested.

Faithful asked, "What would you have me do?"

Christian answered, "Go to him and enter into some serious

---

[f]Leviticus 11; Deuteronomy 14.
[g]1 Corinthians 13:1–3; 14:7.

discourse about the power of religion, which he will affirm, I assure you. Then ask him plainly whether this power is something that is truly working itself out in his heart and in his home and in his behavior."

So Faithful stepped back over to where Talkative was walking and began to converse with him. "How are you doing?" he asked.

"Very well, thank you," Talkative replied. "I thought we should have had a great deal of talk by now."

Faithful offered, "If you would like, we will continue our conversation. And when we last spoke, you left it to me to pose a topic for discussion. Here is my question: how does the saving grace of God make itself known when it is in the heart of man?"

"I see," Talkative stated. "You want to talk about the power of things. Well, that is a very good question, and I will be happy to answer you. I will make my answer brief and to the point. First, where the grace of God is at work in the heart, it causes there to be a great outcry against sin. Secondly—"

Faithful interjected, "Wait a minute. Let's consider your points one at a time. I think you should have said, 'It makes itself known by inclining the soul to abhor its sin.'"[4]

"Why, what is the difference between crying out against and abhorring sin?" Talkative inquired.

Faithful answered, "There is a great deal of difference. A man may cry out against sin out of principle, but he cannot abhor it unless he has God's own antipathy against it. For instance, I have seen many cry out against sin in the pulpit who yet abide it well enough in their own heart, home, and manner of life.

"Potiphar's wife cried out against Joseph with a loud voice, as if she had been very holy. Yet she would have gladly, despite her cries to the contrary, committed adultery with him.[h] Some cry out against sin as a mother cries out against her child, when she calls her a good-for-nothing and a naughty girl and then smothers her with hugs and kisses."

---

[h]Genesis 39:15.

"I think you're trying to trip me up with details," Talkative accused.

Faithful responded, "No, I am only trying to set things right. But what is the second way in which a work of grace makes itself known in the heart of man?"

"Great knowledge of gospel mysteries," Talkative offered.

Faithful countered, "This sign should have been first, but first or last, it is also false. For knowledge, even great knowledge, may be obtained in the mysteries of the gospel without a work of grace in the soul.[i] The truth is that a man can have an abundance of knowledge and still be nothing, and so consequently, no child of God.

"When Christ asked, 'Do you know all these things?' and the disciples answered, 'Yes,' He added, 'Blessed are you if you do them.'[j] He did not pronounce a blessing for knowing but for doing. For there is a knowledge that is not connected with doing: 'he that knows his master's will, and does not do it.' A man may know like an angel and yet not be a Christian. Therefore the point you make is not true.

"Indeed, to know is something that pleases talkers and boasters, but to do is that which pleases God. Not that the heart can be good without knowledge, for without knowledge the heart is empty. But there are two kinds of knowledge: the first is alone in its bare speculation of things, and the second is accompanied by the grace of faith and love, which causes a man to do the will of God from the heart.

"The first kind of knowledge will serve the talker. But a true Christian will not be content until his knowledge results in sincere works that please God. 'Give me understanding, and I shall keep Thy law; yea, I shall observe it with my whole heart.'"[k]

Talkative protested, "You are trying to trap me again; this is not edifying."

"Well then, tell me another way in which the saving grace of

---

[i]1 Corinthians 13.
[j]John 13:17.
[k]Psalm 119:34.

God makes itself known when it is in the heart of man," Faithful challenged.

"Not I, for I see we shall not agree."

Faithful offered, "Well, if you will not, may I have your permission to do it?"

"You are free to say whatever you want," Talkative said.

Faithful began, "A work of grace in the soul makes itself known either to the one who has it or to onlookers.

"Where God's grace is truly at work, it produces conviction of sin as the converted soul becomes aware of the defilement of his nature and the sin of unbelief (a sin that he now knows with certainty will send him to Hell unless he finds mercy at God's hand by faith in Jesus Christ).[l]

"This new awakening of the soul works in him to produce a sorrow and shame for sin, but that is not all. He also finds revealed in him the Savior of the world and realizes the absolute necessity of clinging to Him for life. When he desperately clutches onto Him, the awakened soul finds that his hunger and thirst for the Savior increases just as it is promised.[m] Now, according to the strength or weakness of his faith in his Savior, so is his joy and peace, so is his love for holiness, so are his desires to know Him more and to serve Him more single-mindedly in this present world.

"But although I say that this work of grace is partially discovered by the sinner, yet it is very seldom that he is able to conclude that this is a work of grace. Because of the corruptions of his earthly nature and the continued faultiness of his reason, he is likely to misjudge the work that is going on inside of him. Therefore, in him who has this grace, there is required very sound judgment before he can, with some assurance, conclude that this is a work of God's grace.

"To others it is made known as follows:

"1. By a confession of his faith in Christ.[n]

---

[l]John 16:8; Romans 7:24; John 16:9; Mark 16:16.
[m]Psalm 38:18; Jeremiah 31:19; Galatians 2:16; Acts 4:12; Matthew 5:6; Revelation 21:6.
[n]Romans 10:10; Philippians 1:27; Matthew 5:19.

"2. By a life that is answerable to that confession. To be specific, a life of holiness: heart-holiness, family-holiness (if he has a family), and by life and conversation sharply distinguished from the world. Such a man inwardly abhors both his sin and himself for sinning, suppresses sin in his family, and promotes holiness in the world. He does not do this by talk only, as a hypocrite or talkative person may do, but by a practical demonstration of a godly life, in faith and love, through the power of the Word.°

"If you have no objection to this brief description of the work of grace and how it evidences itself in the life of a true believer, then I will ask you a second question."

Talkative calmly stated, "My part is not to object, but to listen. Let me hear your second question."

Faithful went on, "It is this: have you experienced what I have described? Do your life and your conduct testify to prove it? Or does your religion consist of words only, without deeds to attest to the truth of them?

"Please, if you want to answer me, be careful to say no more than what you know God above will say Amen to. Say nothing that your conscience would not approve. 'For it is not the one who commends himself who is approved, but the one whom the Lord commends.'ᵖ Besides, it is great wickedness to say, 'I am such and such' when my conduct and all my neighbors say completely otherwise."

Then Talkative began to blush but quickly recovered and said, "You talk now about experience, conscience, and God. You appeal to Him for justification of what is spoken. This is not the kind of discourse I expected, nor am I disposed to give an answer to such questions, nor do I feel obligated to answer, unless you are taking on the job of a catechism teacher. Even if that is how you see yourself, I refuse to allow you to become my judge. But I would be interested in why you ask me such questions."

Faithful responded, "Because you were so anxious to talk and

°John 14:15; Psalm 1:2–3; Job 42:5–6; Ezekiel 20:43.
ᵖ2 Corinthians 10:18, ESV.

because I wanted to know if there was anything to back up your talk besides talk alone. Also, to tell you the whole of it, I have heard about you. They say that you are a man whose religion is only talk and that your conduct is at odds with what you profess with your mouth. They say you are a blemish among Christians and that true religion gets a bad reputation because of your ungodly conduct. I have heard that some have already stumbled because of your wicked ways and that even more are in danger of being destroyed by your example. Alehouses, covetousness, uncleanness, swearing, lying, bad companions, and a host of other unsavory things all keep your company. The proverb about the whore is true of you, which is that she is a shame to all women; so are you a shame to all true professing Christians."

"Since you are ready to listen to the reports of others and to make rash judgments, I conclude that you are a spiteful or melancholy man, and not a fit partner for discussion. And so, adieu," Talkative said dismissively.

Then Christian came beside Faithful and said to his brother in faith, "I told you how it would happen: your words and his lusts could not agree. He would rather leave your company than reform his life. But he has left us, as I said he would. So let him go. The loss is his own, and he has saved us the trouble of leaving him. If he had stayed with us, as I am sure he would have, he would have been a blot in our company. Besides, the apostle says, 'From such withdraw thyself.'"[q]

Faithful said, "But I am glad I had this little discussion with him. Maybe he will think about what I told him. I have dealt openly with him, and so if he perishes, I am clear of his blood."

Christian added, "You did well to talk with him so directly; there is little of this faithful dealing with men nowadays. This lack of plain speaking makes religion stink in the nostrils of many, for there are these talkative fools whose religion is only in word but whose conduct is debauched and vain. When fellows like Talkative

---

[q] 1 Timothy 6:5.

are admitted into the fellowship of the godly, the world is puzzled, Christianity is disgraced, and sincere pilgrims are grieved. I wish that all men would deal with these types as you have done. Then they would either reform their conduct or flee the company of saints since it would be too hot for them."

Then Faithful said:

> *"How Talkative at first lifts up his plumes!*
> *How bravely doth he speak! How he presumes*
> *To drive down all before him! But so soon*
> *As Faithful talks of heart-work, like the moon*
> *That's past the full, into the wane he goes.*
> *And so will all but he that heart-work knows."*

So Christian and Faithful went on their way talking about all that they had seen so far, which made the journey through the wilderness much more pleasant than it would have been had they walked it alone.[5]

Chapter Seven

On Trial for the Gospel

When Christian and Faithful had almost passed through the wilderness, Faithful looked back and saw someone coming after them whom he thought he recognized. "Oh," said Faithful to his spiritual brother, "who is that coming toward us?"

Christian looked and said, "It is my good friend Evangelist."

"Yes, and my good friend also," said Faithful, "for it was he who sent me on the way to the gate." So Evangelist came up to them and greeted them.[1]

Evangelist asserted, "Peace be with you, my dear friends, and peace be with all those who have helped you along the way."

"Welcome, Evangelist!" Christian said joyfully. "Seeing you again brings to mind all your past kindness and your faithful labor done for our eternal good."[2]

"And a thousand times welcome," said Faithful. "You have no idea how sweet and desirable is your company to poor pilgrims like us!"

Then Evangelist said, "How has it gone with you, my friends, since the last time we parted? What have you met with, and how have you conducted yourselves?"

Then Christian and Faithful told him of all the things that had

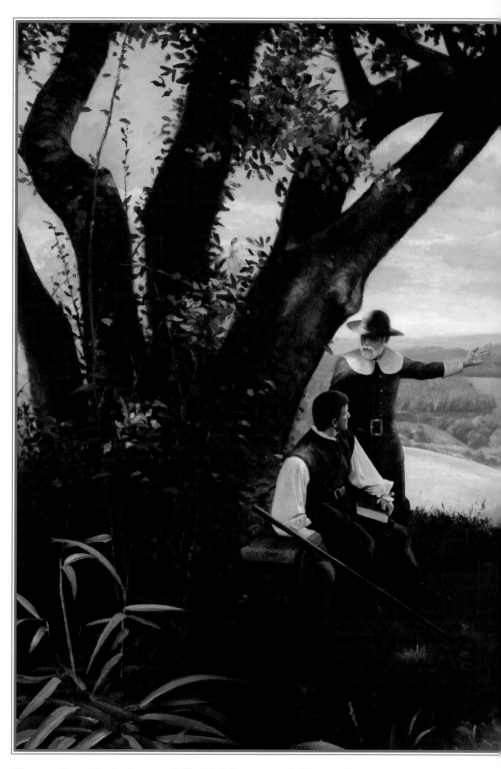

Evangelist, Christian, and Faithful approach Vanity Fair.

happened to them since they last met and of all the difficulties that had brought them to where they now were.

"I am glad," said Evangelist, "not that you have met with trials, but that you have been victors and that you have been faithful despite your many weaknesses and troubles along the way.[3] I am glad for your sakes and for mine. I have sowed, and you have reaped. The day is coming when both he who sowed and they who reaped shall rejoice together. That is, of course, if you endure to the end, 'for in due season we shall reap, if we do not give up.'[a] The crown is before you, and it is an incorruptible one; 'so run, that you may obtain' it.[b]

"Some who set out for this crown, even after they have gone quite a long ways, allow others who come along to snatch their victory from them. So hold fast to what you have, and let no man take away your crown.[c] You are not yet out of reach of the gunshot of the Devil. You have not yet resisted unto death in your striving against sin. Let the Kingdom be always before you, and believe with certainty and consistency the things that are yet unseen. Let nothing that is on this side of eternal life get inside you. Above all, take care of your own hearts, and resist the lusts that tempt you, for your hearts 'are deceitful above all things, and desperately wicked.'[d] Set your faces like a flint; you have all the power of Heaven and earth on your side."

Christian thanked Evangelist for his exhortation. Then Christian and Faithful asked him to speak of more, knowing that he was a prophet. They hoped to hear from Evangelist things that would help them resist and overcome trials they were likely to encounter as they continued their journey.

Evangelist consented to their request and began to speak to them.

"My sons, you have heard in the words of the gospel that you must go through many tribulations before you enter the Kingdom of Heaven, and also that in every city you enter, bonds and afflictions await you. Therefore, you cannot expect to travel too long on

---

[a]John 4:36; Galatians 6:9.
[b]1 Corinthians 9:24–27.
[c]Revelation 3:11.
[d]Jeremiah 17:9.

your pilgrimage without suffering tribulation. You have discovered the truth of these testimonies in the struggles you have already endured, and more will immediately follow.

"You are almost out of this wilderness and will very soon see the town you will enter next on your journey.[4] In that town you will be set upon by enemies who will be determined to kill you and who will succeed. You can be sure that one or both of you must seal his testimony with blood. So be faithful unto death, and the King will give you a crown of life. The one who dies there, although his death will be unnatural and perhaps very painful, will be better off than his companion, not only because he will arrive at the Celestial City sooner, but also because he will escape many of the miseries that the other will meet with on the rest of his journey.

"So when you come to the town and this happens to you, fulfilling what I have related, then remember me and the things that I have told you. Conduct yourselves like men, and commit the keeping of your souls to your God as you struggle to do what is right. Remember that He is your faithful Creator."

Then I saw in my dream that when they had left the borders of the wilderness, they immediately saw a town before them. The name of that town is Vanity, and in the town there is a year-round market called Vanity Fair. It bears its name because the town that hosts the fair is only concerned with things that are unimportant and vain. All that is bought and sold at the fair is likewise vain and worthless. As the ancient saying goes, 'All that cometh is vanity.'[e] This fair is no new business but has been established from ancient times. I will now explain to you its history and origins.

Almost five thousand years ago, there were pilgrims walking to the Celestial City, just as Christian and Faithful were doing. Beelzebub, Apollyon, and Legion, with their companions, seeing that the pilgrims' path went right through the town of Vanity, conspired together to set up a fair in which all sorts of vain merchandise were sold all year long. This merchandise consisted of

---

[e]Ecclesiastes 1; 2:11, 17; 11:8; Isaiah 40:17.

houses, lands, trades, places, honors, positions, titles, countries, kingdoms, lusts, pleasures, and delights of all sorts, such as whores, lewd entertainment, wives, husbands, children, masters, servants, lives, blood, bodies, souls, silver, gold, pearls, precious stones, and whatnot. Moreover, at this fair can always be seen juggling, cheats, games, plays, fools, apes, knaves, and rogues, and that of every kind. Also to be seen, and at no charge, are thefts, murders, adulteries, and false witnesses who cause death with their lies.

As in other fairs of less importance, where there are several rows and streets all properly named for the different wares that are vended, so also Vanity Fair has the proper places, rows, streets (countries and kingdoms) where the wares of this fair can be found. Here is the Britain Row, the French Row, the Italian Row, the Spanish Row, the German Row, where various sorts of vanities are to be sold. Also as in other fairs, where one particular commodity is in great demand, so it is in Vanity Fair. Here the ware of Rome is greatly promoted and desired, and only a few nations, including England, have taken a dislike to the goods of Rome.

Now as I said, the way to the Celestial City lies just through this town where this lusty fair is kept. Anyone going to the Celestial City who will not go through this town must "go out of the world."[f] The Prince of princes Himself, when He was here, went through this town to His own country. I think it was Beelzebub, the chief lord of this fair, who invited Him to buy some of his vanities. He even offered to make Him lord of the fair if only He would show him reverence as He went through the town.[g] Because the Prince was such a person of honor, Beelzebub took Him from street to street and showed Him all the kingdoms of the world in a little time in order to, if possible, allure the Blessed One to cheapen Himself and buy some of his vanities. But the Prince had no interest in the merchandise and left the town without spending so much as one penny on anything there.

[f]1 Corinthians 5:10.
[g]Matthew 4:8; Luke 4:5–7.

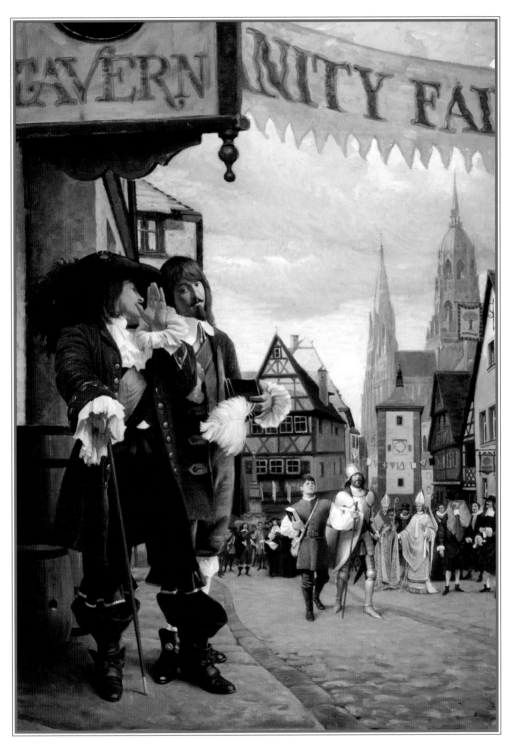

Christian and Faithful enter Vanity Fair.

This fair is a great, ancient, and long-standing place. Now these pilgrims, as I said, must pass through this Vanity Fair. And so they did, but as they entered into the fair, they created a great commotion, and all the people in the fair turned their attention to the two pilgrims.[5]

There were several reasons for this:

First, the pilgrims were dressed differently from the people trading at the fair. The people of the fair looked at them in astonishment. Some said they were fools, some said they were lunatics, and some said they were just outlandish men.[h6]

Secondly, as strange as the pilgrims' attire appeared to their onlookers, their speech was judged even stranger. Very few could even understand what the pilgrims said since they spoke the language of the promised Kingdom rather than the language of the world, which was the common language of the fair. So from one end of the fair to the other, they seemed like barbarians to the others.

Thirdly, the thing that most annoyed and puzzled the merchants was that these pilgrims put no value on the fair's goods. They did not even enjoy looking at them, and when the merchants called out to them to buy this or that, the pilgrims put their fingers in their ears and cried out, "Turn away mine eyes from beholding vanity" and looked upward, signifying that their trade and traffic was in Heaven.[i]

One merchant, observing the strange conduct of the pilgrims, mockingly said to them, "What will you buy?"

But they, looking sternly at him, answered, "We buy the truth."[j]

This caused great offense, and the merchants began to despise the pilgrims even more. Some mocked, some taunted, some spoke reproachfully, and some began to call out for others to strike them. Finally the pilgrims created so much commotion that the natural order of the fair was disrupted. The confusion was so great that word was sent to the Great One of the fair, who quickly came down

[h]1 Corinthians 2:6–8.
[i]Psalm 119:37; Philippians 3:19–20.
[j]Proverbs 23:23.

and dispatched a few of his most trusted friends to detain and question the two pilgrims.

So they were held and questioned. The men who examined them asked them where they came from, where they were going, and why they dressed in such unusual garb.

Christian and Faithful told them that they were pilgrims and strangers in the world and that they were going to their own country, which was the Heavenly Jerusalem.[k] They also told them that they had done nothing to the men or the merchants of the town that should have caused them to be so mistreated and detained from making progress on their journey. The only thing they did that caused an offense was to tell those who were trying to sell them their wares that they would only buy the truth.

The men who were appointed to examine Christian and Faithful concluded that they were either mad vagabonds or else troublemakers who had come to create confusion in the fair.

So they took them, beat them, smeared them with dirt, and then put them into a cage to be a spectacle to all the men of the fair. There they stayed for some time, the objects of ridicule, malice, or revenge for any passerby who wished to abuse them, which caused the Great One of the fair to laugh viciously at their plight.

But the pilgrims remained calm and patient. When men would come to yell and scream every sort of vile abuse at them, they responded with kind words. When men came and cursed them, they in turn blessed them, returning good words for bad and kindness for injuries.

Some men who were more thoughtful and less prejudiced than the rest began to criticize and rebuke the more brutish men of the crowd for their continual abuse of the two pilgrims. This caused a heated reaction to the pilgrims' would-be defenders who were called traitors and confederates of the caged men. Some in the mob said that those who defended the pilgrims should suffer their misfortune.

---

[k]Hebrews 11:13–16.

The more reasonable men replied that as far as they could see, the pilgrims were quiet and sober and intended nobody any harm. They also noted that many who traded in the fair were more worthy to be put into the cage than these two.

So after many angry words had passed on both sides, they began to fight among themselves, causing many injuries. While all this was happening, the two pilgrims conducted themselves with dignity and wisdom.

But after this incident the two poor pilgrims were brought before their examiners again and were charged with inciting a riot in the fair. So the authorities beat them without mercy, shackled them with irons, and led them in chains up and down the fair. This was done to frighten anyone who was thinking about speaking up on their behalf or joining their cause.

Throughout the whole spectacle, Christian and Faithful behaved themselves wisely and received the ignominy and shame that was cast upon them with so much meekness and patience that it won to their side a few men even in that fair. This put the other party into an even greater rage, so much so that they decided that the cage and the irons were not punishment enough: the two pilgrims should be put to death for all the abuse they had caused and for deluding the men of the fair. So Christian and Faithful were returned to the cage again with their feet in stocks until further plans for their execution could be made.

While enduring all this persecution, Christian and Faithful remembered what their faithful friend Evangelist had told them about the suffering that would happen to them. This strengthened their resolve to bear all the abuse and await patiently the outcome of their situation. They also reminded one another for their mutual comfort that whichever one of them suffered death would have the best outcome. Therefore each secretly hoped that he might be the one chosen for that fate. Nevertheless, each committed himself to the wise plans of Him who rules all things, and so they were content to remain in their current condition until it should please God to use them otherwise.

Then at the appointed time they were led to their trial, which was planned with only one purpose in mind—the condemnation of them both. First they were brought before their enemies and formally charged. The judge's name was Lord Hate-Good. Their indictments were the same in substance, though somewhat varying in form. The contents were as follows: "That they were enemies to, and disturbers of, trade; that they had made commotions and divisions in the town and had won a faction over to their own most dangerous opinions, in contempt of the law of the prince."

Faithful was the first to be put on trial, and he began his defense by saying that he had only set himself against the enemy of Him who is higher than the highest. And he said, "As for disturbance, I made none, for I am a man of peace. The individuals who were won over to our side were won by seeing the truth and our innocence, and they are better off for it. And as to the king you talk of, since he is Beelzebub, the enemy of our Lord, I defy him and all his angels."

Then proclamation was made that those who wished to bring accusations against the prisoners should be brought forth to present their evidence on behalf of their king.

Three witnesses came—Envy, Superstition, and Flattery. They were then asked if they knew the prisoners and what they had to say against them on behalf of the lord their king.

Then Envy stood up and said, "My lord, I have known this man a long time and will attest upon my oath before this honorable bench that he is—"

"Hold," the judge interjected. "Give him his oath." (So they swore him in.)

Then Envy continued, "My lord, this man, notwithstanding his innocent name, is one of the vilest men in our country. He does not regard prince or people, law or custom, but does all that he can to instill in others his disloyal notions, which he generally calls 'principles of faith and holiness.' In particular, I heard him with my own

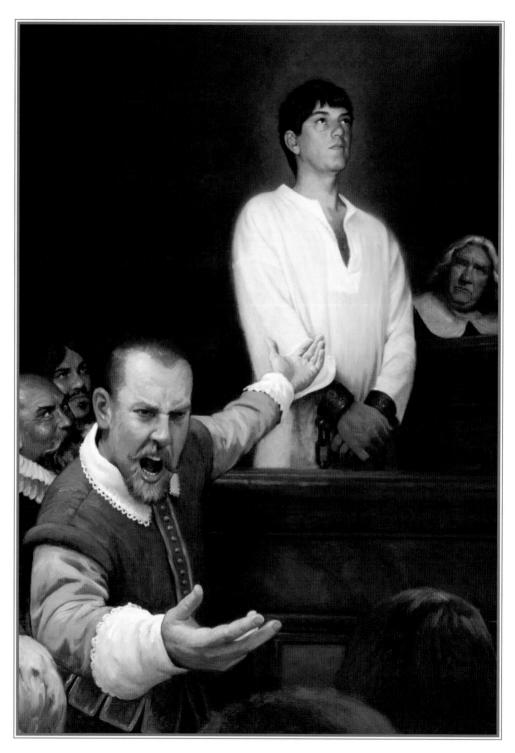

Faithful is on trial in Vanity Fair.

ears affirm that Christianity and the customs of our town of Vanity were diametrically opposed and cannot be reconciled. And by saying that, my lord, he condemns all the laudable things we do and us in the same breath."

Then the judge said to Envy, "Do you have any more to say?"

Envy loudly asserted, "My lord, I could say much more if it would not be so tedious to the court. Yet, if need be, when the other gentlemen have presented their evidence, if anything is missing that would guarantee the condemnation of the prisoners, I will enlarge my testimony against them at that time."

So he was told to stand by.

Then they called Superstition and asked him to look upon the prisoner. They also asked what he could say for their lord the king against him. After he took his oath, he began.

"My lord, I have no real acquaintance with this man, nor do I desire to have any further knowledge of him. However, after having a conversation with him the other day, I can report that he is a very dangerous fellow. I heard him say that our religion was useless and unable to show man any way to please God. We all know that this is the same as saying that we worship in vain, have no forgiveness of our sins, and face damnation. This is what I have to say to the court."

Then Flattery was sworn in and was asked to say what he knew against the prisoner, on behalf of their lord the king.

"My lord and all the rest of you gentlemen, I have known of this fellow for a long time. I have heard him say things that should not be said. He has reviled and scolded in the harshest terms our noble prince Beelzebub and has spoken contemptibly of the prince's honorable friends, whose names are the Lord Old Man, the Lord Carnal Delight, the Lord Luxurious, the Lord Desire of Vain-Glory, Lord Lechery, and Sir Greed, along with all the rest of our nobility. He has also said that if all men were of his mind, there is not one of these noblemen who would not be driven out of our town. Besides, he has not been afraid to rail against you, my lord, who are now appointed to be his judge, calling you an ungodly villain and many other such vilifying terms, with which he has sullied most of the gentry of our town."

When Flattery had finished telling his tale, the judge directed his speech to the prisoner at the bar saying, "You renegade, heretic, and traitor, have you heard what these honest gentlemen have witnessed against you?"

"May I speak a few words in my own defense?" Faithful asked.

The judge protested, "What! What! You deserve to live no longer but to be slain immediately on this very spot! But so that everyone may see our gentleness toward you, let us hear what you have to say."

Faithful began, "In the first place, in answer to what Mr. Envy has said, I never said anything but the following: whatever rules or laws or customs or peoples are contrary to the Word of God, these things are diametrically opposed to Christianity. If I have said something wrong, then convince me of my error, and I am ready here, before you all, to make my recantation.

"As to the second point that Mr. Superstition made and his charge against me, I said only this: in the worship of God there is required a divine faith that only attends a divine revelation of the will of God. Therefore, whatever things are thrust into the worship of God that are contrary to divine revelation cannot be done but by mere human faith, and human faith will not result in eternal life.

"As to what Mr. Flattery has charged, I said (without ranting) that the prince of this town, his attendants, the brutish mob, and all the rest named by Mr. Flattery are more ready for Hell than for this town and country. And so, may the Lord have mercy upon me!"

Then the judge called to the jurymen (who were standing by and had observed all that had been said and done), "Gentlemen of the jury, you see this man about whom so great an uproar has been made in this town. You have also heard what these worthy gentlemen have witnessed against him. Also you have heard his reply and confession. It is now your responsibility to hang him or save his life. But before you decide, I think I need to instruct you in our law. There was an Act made in the days of Pharaoh the Great, servant to our prince, that to prevent those of a contrary religion from multiplying and growing too strong, the male children of those troublesome people should be drowned in the river.[l]

"There was also an Act made in the days of Nebuchadnezzar the Great, another of our lord's servants, that whoever would not fall down and worship his golden image should be thrown into a fiery furnace.[m]

"There was also an Act made in the days of Darius that anyone who called upon any god except for him should be cast into the lions' den.[n] Now this rebel before you has broken the substance of these laws, not only in thought but also in word and deed. This is intolerable.

"Consider that the law made by Pharaoh was made to prevent mischief, no crime having yet been committed. But here before you is a crime apparent. As far as the second and third laws I told you of, you can see for yourself that he disputes against our religion, and for the treason he has confessed he deserves to die by execution."

After hearing all this, the jury went to private quarters to deliberate. The jurors' names were Mr. Blind-man, Mr. No-good, Mr. Malice, Mr. Love-lust, Mr. Live-loose, Mr. Hothead, Mr. High-mind, Mr. Enmity, Mr. Liar, Mr. Cruelty, Mr. Hate-light, Mr. Implacable.

Each one submitted his private verdict against Faithful to the other jurors, and after that, they unanimously concluded to bring a verdict of "guilty" against Faithful.

They went before the judge with their verdict. The first juror to speak was Mr. Blind-man, the foreman, who said, "I see clearly that this man is a heretic."

Then Mr. No-good said, "Away with such a fellow from the earth!"

"I agree," said Mr. Malice, "for I hate the very looks of him."

Then Mr. Love-lust said, "I could never stand the sight of him."

---

[l]Exodus 1.
[m]Daniel 3.
[n]Daniel 6.

"Nor I," said Mr. Live-loose, "for he would always be condemning me."

"Hang him, hang him!" said Mr. Hothead.

"A sorry vermin," said Mr. High-mind.

"My heart rises against him," said Mr. Enmity.

"He is a rogue," said Mr. Liar.

"Hanging is too good for him!" said Mr. Cruelty.

"Let us kill him quickly and get him out of the way," said Mr. Hate-light.

Then said Mr. Implacable, "Even if I was offered all the world to make peace with this man, I could not. Therefore, let us quickly bring in a guilty verdict and put him to death."

And so they did. Faithful was condemned and was taken to a place where he was put to the most cruel death they could invent. First they scourged him, then they beat him, then they lanced his flesh with knives. After that, they stoned him with stones and pierced him with their swords. Last of all, they burned him to ashes at the stake. This is how Faithful came to his end.

Now I saw in my dream that there stood behind this brutal multitude a chariot and a couple of horses, waiting for Faithful. So as soon as his adversaries had killed him, he was taken into it and was immediately carried up through the clouds, with the sound of trumpets, heading straightaway to the Celestial Gate.

But as for Christian, he had a temporary delay and was returned to prison where he stayed for some time. But He who overrules all things, having the power of even His enemies' rage in His own hand, brought about Christian's escape from their evil plans. So Christian went on his way, singing:

> "Well, Faithful, thou hast faithfully professed
> Unto thy Lord, with whom thou shalt be blessed.
> When faithless ones, with all their vain delights,
> Are crying out under their hellish plights,
> Sing, Faithful, sing, and let thy name survive;
> For though they killed thee, thou art yet alive."

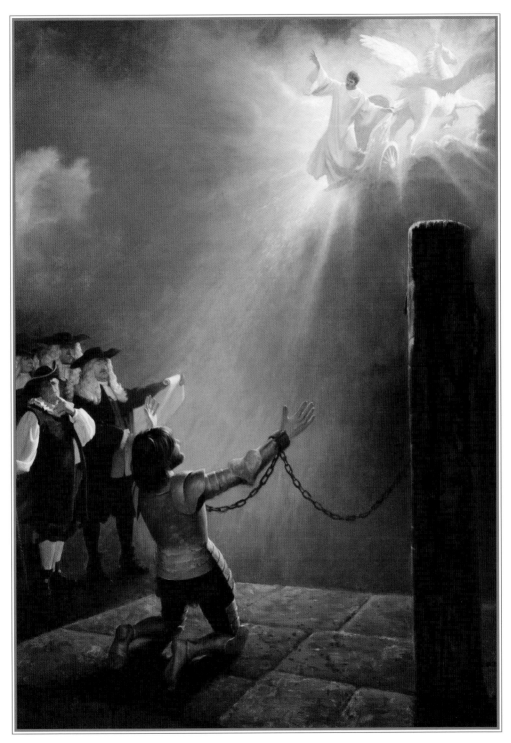

Faithful departs to the Celestial City.

Now I saw in my dream that Christian did not escape Vanity Fair by himself, for there was with him a man named Hopeful (a name he was given as he watched how Christian and Faithful in their words and in their deeds conducted themselves during all their sufferings at the fair).[7]

Hopeful had joined himself to Christian and entered into a brotherly covenant with him, promising him that he would be his companion for the rest of the journey.

So one died to bear testimony to the truth, and another rose out of his ashes to be a companion with Christian in his pilgrimage. Hopeful also told Christian there were many more men in the fair who would in due course follow after them to the Celestial City.

Chapter Eight

Confronting Worldly Attachments

So I saw in my dream that soon after they had left the fair, they overtook a man walking ahead of them whose name was By-ends. So they said to him, "What country are you from, sir, and how far you going on this way?" He told them that he came from the town of Fair-speech and that he was going to the Celestial City, but he did not tell them his name.[1]

"From Fair-speech!"[2] exclaimed Christian. "Does anything good live there?"[a]

"Yes, I hope so," said By-ends.

"Please, sir, what is your name?" inquired Christian.

By-ends answered, "I am a stranger to you, and you to me, but if you are going this way, I shall be glad of your company. If not, I must be content to walk alone."

"I have heard of this town of Fair-speech," said Christian, "and, as I remember, they say it is a wealthy place."

By-ends agreed, "Yes, I will assure you that it is, and I have many rich relatives who live there."

---

[a]Proverbs 26:25.

"May I be so bold as to ask who some of your relatives are who live there?" Christian asked.

By-ends reported, "Almost the whole town is related to me, and in particular Lord Turn-about, Lord Time-server, and Lord Fair-speech (from whose ancestors that town first took its name). Other relatives include Mr. Smooth-man, Mr. Facing-both-ways, and Mr. Anything. The parson of our parish, Mr. Two-tongues, is my uncle on my mother's side. And to tell you the truth, I have become a gentleman of good quality, even though my great-grandfather was only a ferryman, looking one way and rowing another. I earned most of my wealth by the same occupation."

Christian asked, "Are you a married man?"

By-ends replied, "Yes, and my wife is a very virtuous woman, the daughter of a virtuous woman. She was my Lady Feigning's daughter. She comes from a very honorable family and has arrived to such a pinnacle of breeding that she knows how to act cordially and respectably to all, princes and peasants alike.

"It is true that we differ in religion from those of the stricter sort, but only in two small points. First, we never strive against the wind and tide. Secondly, we are always most zealous when religion goes about in his silver slippers. We love to walk with him in the street if the sun is shining and the people are applauding him."[3]

Then Christian stepped aside to his friend Hopeful and said, "I believe this is the person they call By-ends of Fair-speech. If it is he, then we have in our company one of the most deceitful rogues who ever lived in this part of the country."[4]

Then Hopeful said, "Ask him. I do not think he should be ashamed of his name."

So Christian came up to him again and said, "Sir, you talk as if you knew more than most people in the world, and if I am not mistaken, I would guess that your name is Mr. By-ends of Fair-speech."

By-ends protested, "That is not my name, but it *is* an insulting nickname that has been given to me by those who do not care for me. I must be content to bear it as a reproach, as other good men have borne theirs before me."

"But haven't you given occasion for men to call you by this name?" Christian pressed.

"Never! Never!" By-ends protested. "The worst thing I ever did to invite such a name was to have the good luck to jump in and ride the tide of the times, profiting thereby from my skill at knowing which way the winds of change were blowing. If this is my crime, then I will count it a blessing. But I will not let the malicious load me up with reproach."

Christian responded, "Just as I thought, you are the man of whom I heard, and to tell you the truth, I fear your nickname belongs to you more properly than you would like us to think."

By-ends countered, "Well, if this is what you think, I cannot help it. Even so, you will find me to be good company if you will still allow me to travel with you."

Christian replied, "If you will go with us, you must go against wind and tide, which I believe is against your principles. You must also stand by religion in his rags as well as when he is in his silver slippers. You must stand by him when he is bound in irons as well as when he walks the streets and hears applause."

"You must not impose your faith on me. Let me have my views, and let me go with you," By-ends implored.

Christian insisted, "Not a step further unless you will do as I have just proposed, even as we do."

Then By-ends said, "I will never desert my old principles since they are harmless and profitable. If I may not go with you, then I must do what I did before you caught up to me, which is to go by myself until someone overtakes me who will be glad for my company."

Now I saw in my dream that Christian and Hopeful forsook him and kept a good distance ahead of him.

After a while Christian looked back and saw three men following Mr. By-ends. And as they came up to him, he greeted them with a low bow, and they gave him a compliment. The men's names were Mr. Hold-the-world, Mr. Money-love, and Mr. Save-all.[5] These were men with whom Mr. By-ends had formerly been acquainted, for in their youth they were schoolfellows and were taught by one Mr. Gripe-man. They had gone to school in Love-gain, which is a market town in the county of Coveting to the north.

This schoolmaster taught them the art of getting, either by violence, fraud, flattery, lying, or putting on a guise of religion. And these four gentlemen had become so proficient in the art of their master that now each of them had his own school.

When they had all greeted each other, Mr. Money-love said to Mr. By-ends, "Who are they upon the road ahead of us?" (for Christian and Hopeful were yet within view).

By-ends responded, "They are a pair from a far-off country going on pilgrimage in their own way."

Money-love asked, "Why didn't they stay with you so that we might have had their good company? For they and we, sir, are all going on a pilgrimage."

"So we are," By-ends said. "But the men before us are rigid and in love with their own notions. They disdain the opinions of others, with a superior attitude that is so narrow that if you don't agree with them in all things, they throw you out of their company."

Save-all commented, "That is bad. I have read about those who become overzealous in righteousness, judging and condemning everyone but themselves. But tell me, what were the points on which you disagreed?"

By-ends answered, "Why, they concluded that it is their duty to rush ahead on their journey in all weather, without waiting for favorable wind or tide. They would risk all in a moment for God, while I, on the other hand, am for taking advantage of all moments to secure my life and my estate. They are for holding their notions, though all other men are against them; but I am for religion so far as the times and my safety will bear it. They are for religion when in rags and contempt; but I am for religion when he walks in his golden slippers in the sunshine and with applause."

Hold-the-world agreed, "Yes, good Mr. By-ends. For my part, I count them fools who lose the things they are at liberty to keep. Let us be wise as serpents; it is best to make hay when the sun shines. You see how the bee lies still all winter and gets busy only when she can have profit along with pleasure.

"God sometimes sends rain and sometimes sunshine. If they are so foolish to go through the first, let us be content to take fair weather along with us. For my part, I like that religion best that will stand with the security of God's good blessings to us.

"Since God has given us the good things of this life, isn't it reasonable to think that He desires that we keep them for His sake? Abraham and Solomon grew rich in religion. And Job says that a good man shall lay up gold as dust. So he must not have had in mind the men who are before us, if they are as you have described them."

"I think that we are all agreed in this matter, and therefore there is no need for any more discussion about it," stated Save-all.

"You are right," Money-love said. "There is nothing more to say about this matter; anyone who does not believe Scripture or reason (and you see we have both on our side) does not know the liberties that he has to seek his own safety and security."

By-ends added, "My friends, we are all on the same pilgrimage. To help pass the time, I would like to propose a question to you: suppose a man—a minister or a tradesman or such—should have an opportunity to get a blessing and improve his station in life by becoming extremely zealous in some point of religion. Let's suppose that this religious point is something about which he has no particular interest, but by appearing to be interested he can gain an advantage, either financial or otherwise. The question I put to you is this: can he pretend to be interested and remain an upstanding, honest man?"

Money-love noted, "I see what your question is getting at, and with these gentlemen's permission I will endeavor to give you an answer. First, I will speak to your question as it concerns a minister. Suppose a minister, a worthy man, but someone with a very small income, has a desire to increase in wealth and influence. Suppose that he sees an opportunity for achieving this goal by becoming more studious, preaching more frequently and zealously, and modifying some of his principles to fit in with the preferences and temperament of his congregation. I see no reason why he cannot do this and a lot more if needed, while still remaining an honest man. And here are the reasons why:

"1. His desire of a greater income is lawful (this cannot be contradicted), since it is set before him by Providence. He should take advantage of the opportunity without questioning his conscience.

"2. Besides, his desire for more income makes him more studious, more zealous in preaching, and so on, and this makes him a better man. Yes, it makes him a better man in all aspects of his life, which also is according to the will of God.

"3. Now, as for his modifying his views and principles to make himself more acceptable to his people, this says three good things about the man. It shows that he is of a self-denying temperament, of a sweet and winning disposition, and thus more fit for ministerial duties.

"4. I conclude, then, that a minister who exchanges a small thing for a great should not be judged as covetous for doing so. Rather, since his decision results in self-improvement and industry, he should be commended as one who pursues his call, and the opportunity should be seen as something that will help him to do good.

"And now to the second part of the question, which concerns the tradesman you mentioned. Suppose this man is in a trade that makes him very little money, but by becoming religious he can improve his income, perhaps get a rich wife, and get better customers to come to his shop. For my part, I see no reason why this may not be lawfully done, and for these reasons:

"1. To become religious is a virtue, by whatever means it happens.

"2. It is not unlawful to marry a rich wife or to encourage a better class of customer to do business in his shop.

"3. Besides, the man who gets these by becoming religious gets something that is good from those who are good by becoming good himself. He gets a good wife, good customers, and a good income, and all by becoming religious, which is good. Therefore, to become religious to get all these is a good and profitable plan."

Mr. Money-love's answer to Mr. By-end's question was highly applauded by them all. They all concluded that it was such a wholesome and advantageous answer that no one would be able to contradict it. And since Christian and Hopeful were still within calling distance, they all agreed to pose these questions and answers to them, since they thought that both of them had been rude in their opposition to Mr. By-ends.

So they called after Christian and Hopeful, who stopped and waited for them to approach. As the three men drew near, they decided that Mr. Hold-the-world, and not Mr. By-ends, should propose the question to Christian and Hopeful to avoid any prejudice that might remain between Mr. By-ends and them.

So they came up to each other, and after a short salutation Mr. Hold-the-world proposed the question to Christian and Hopeful and asked them to answer it if they could.

Then said Christian, "Even a babe in religion could answer ten thousand such questions. For if it is unlawful to follow Christ for loaves, as it says in John 6, how much more abominable is it to make Him and religion into a self-serving device for getting and enjoying the world! Only heathens, hypocrites, devils, and witches are of your opinion.

"The heathens Hamor and Shechem coveted the daughters and cattle of Jacob, and when they saw that there was no way to get them but by becoming circumcised, they said to their companions, 'If every male of us be circumcised, as they are circumcised, will not their cattle and their property and every beast of theirs be ours?' Jacob's daughters and cattle were what the heathen wanted, and they used Jacob's religion as a guise to try to get it. Read the whole story.[b]

---

[b]Genesis 34:20–23.

Christian and Hopeful escape Vanity Fair.

"The hypocritical Pharisees were also of this religion. Long prayers were their pretense, but their intent was to gain the houses and property of widows, and their judgment was greater damnation from God.[c]

"Judas the devil was also of this religion, and he would rather have had the possession of the moneybag than Christ. He was lost, cast away, and the very son of perdition.

"Simon the witch was of this religion also. He wanted the Holy Ghost for the purpose of his own personal financial gain, and you can read in Acts the response of the apostle Peter to his religion.[d]

"It also occurs to me that the man who takes up religion for the world will just as easily throw away religion for the world. For just as Judas desired the world in becoming religious, so did he also sell religion and his Master for the same.

"To answer the question as you have done and to accept your answer as authentic is heathenish, hypocritical, and devilish. You will be rewarded according to your works."

Then they stood staring at one another, unable to answer Christian. Hopeful also approved of the soundness of Christian's answer. So there was a great silence among them.

So Christian and Hopeful continued their journey, but Mr. By-ends and his company stayed behind, stunned by Christian's rebuke.

Then Christian said to Hopeful, "If these men cannot stand before the sentence of men, what will they do before the sentence of God? And if they are mute when dealt with by vessels of clay, what will they do when they shall be rebuked by the flames of a devouring fire?"

---

[c]Luke 20:46–47.
[d]Acts 8:19–20.

Demas invites Christian and Hopeful into the silver mines.

Chapter Nine

REFRESHMENT AT GOD'S RIVER

hen Christian and Hopeful left them again and walked until they came to a smooth plain called Ease, where they traveled with much contentment. The plain was quite small; so they went quickly through it. Now on the far side of that plain was a little hill called Lucre, and in that hill there was a silver mine, which some of the pilgrims had turned aside to see. The ground near the brink of the pit was unstable, and many had stumbled into the pit only to suffer injuries or even death.

Then I saw in my dream that a little off the road, over by the silver mine, stood the gentlemanly Demas calling to passersby to come and see. When he saw Christian and Hopeful he shouted, "Stop! Turn aside, and I will show you something."

"What could be so interesting to see that would turn us out of our way?" Christian asked.

Demas replied, "Over here are men digging in a silver mine for treasure. If you will come and work a little, you may become rich."[1]

Then said Hopeful, "Let's go see."

"Not I," said Christian, "for I have heard of this place and of all the people who have died here digging for treasure. It is a trap that will slow pilgrims down on their journey." Then Christian called to Demas saying, "Is not this place dangerous? Hasn't it hindered many in their pilgrimage?"[a]

"Not very dangerous, except to those who are careless," Demas said, but not without blushing.

Then said Christian to Hopeful, "Let's not miss a step but keep going on our way."

Hopeful said, "I will warrant you that when By-ends comes here, and if he is given the same invitation as we, he will turn out of the way to see."

"I have no doubt you are right, for his principles lead him that way, and the odds are a hundred to one that he dies there," Christian observed.

Then Demas called again, saying, "But will you not come over and see?"

Then Christian sternly answered, saying, "Demas, you are an enemy of the ways of the Lord, and you have already been condemned by one of his Majesty's judges for turning out of the way.[b] Why, then, are you trying to bring us into similar condemnation? Besides, if we turn aside, our Lord the King will certainly hear about it, and we will be put to shame when the time comes when we ought to stand with boldness before Him."

Demas cried out again, saying that he was a brother like them on pilgrimage and that if they would wait for just a little while, he would walk with them.

Then Christian asked, "What is your name? Is it not the same by which I have called you?"

"Yes, my name is Demas. I am the son of Abraham."

Christian asserted, "I know you. Gehazi was your great-grandfather, and Judas was your father, and you have followed in their steps.[c] It is a devilish prank that you use. Your father was hanged as a traitor, and you deserve no better reward. Assure yourself that when we come to the King, we will tell him about

---

[a]Hosea 4:18.
[b]2 Timothy 4:10.
[c]2 Kings 5:20; Matthew 26:14–15; 27:1–5.

your behavior." Thus said, Christian and Hopeful continued on their way.

By this time By-ends and his companions were again within sight, and at the first invitation they went over to Demas. Now whether they fell into the pit by looking over the brink, or whether they went down to dig, or whether they were smothered in the bottom of the pit by the vapors that came up from the place, I am not certain. But this I do know: they never again were seen along the way of pilgrims.

Then Christian sang:

"By-ends and Silver Demas both agree;
One calls, the other runs, that he may be
A sharer in his lucre; so these do
Take up in this world, and no further go."

Now I saw that just on the other side of the plain, the two pilgrims came to a place in the highway where there stood an old monument. The pilgrims' attention was drawn to the monument because it looked so strange. It seemed to be in the shape of a woman.

As they looked at the statue they were puzzled and could not make sense of it until Hopeful found some strange writing at the head of the pillar. Being no scholar, Hopeful could not understand the meaning of the script. So he called Christian, who was more educated, to see if he could unlock the mystery. Christian spent some time trying to decipher the letters, and finally he understood the inscription's meaning.

Christian then read it aloud to his friend Hopeful: "Remember Lot's wife." They both concluded that the monument rested on the pillar of salt into which Lot's wife was turned after she looked back toward Sodom with a covetous heart.[d2] Seeing this amazing sight gave Christian and Hopeful occasion for the following discourse.

Christian began, "My brother Hopeful, this is a timely sight.

---

[d]Genesis 19:26.

Consider how close this monument is to the Hill of Lucre where Demas gave us the invitation to seek our fortune in the silver mines. If we had done what he enticed us to do, perhaps it would be our statues that other pilgrims would wonder at as they pass this place on the highway."

Hopeful responded, "Yes, and I am sorry that I was so foolish as to even consider it. Only now can I make out the difference between the sin of Lot's wife and my own sin. She only looked back, while I had a desire to go see. Let grace be exalted, and let me be ashamed that such a thought ever entered my heart."

Christian went on, "Let's consider what we have seen here, and let it be a reminder to us in the future. Lot's wife escaped one judgment when she fled the city of Sodom, and yet she was destroyed by another judgment and turned into a pillar of salt."

Hopeful said, "True, and she is a warning and an example to both of us, that we should avoid her sin. She is a visible sign that awaits those who do not take a lesson from this judgment. I am reminded of Korah, Dathan, and Abiram with the 250 men who perished in their sin, who also became a sign or example so that others may take heed.[e] But above all I cannot help thinking about one thing, which is how Demas and his companions can stand so confidently just a little ways from here to look for that treasure for which this woman who simply looked backwards while fleeing the destruction of Sodom was turned into a pillar of salt. It is especially perplexing since the judgment that overtook her made her an example within sight of these men. They cannot help but see her, if they would only lift up their eyes."

"It is bewildering, but it indicates that they have hardened their hearts," Christian continued. "I would compare them to those who pick pockets in the presence of the judge or empty out other people's purses while under the shadow of the gallows. It is said of the men of Sodom that they were exceptional sinners because they were sinners before the Lord. That is to say, they sinned right before His

---

[e]Numbers 26:9–10.

eyes with not enough shame even to try to hide their sin. They did this notwithstanding the kindnesses that He had shown them,[f] for the land of Sodom was like the Garden of Eden.[g] This provoked the Lord, and He made their plague of fire as hot as the Lord of Heaven could make it. The lesson is clear: those who have had examples and warnings put before them and who have received the Lord's benefits and kindness will suffer the most severe judgments if they refuse to repent and change their ways."

Hopeful agreed, "You have spoken the truth, but what a mercy is it that neither you, nor especially I, am made an example! This should give us occasion to thank God, to fear before Him, and to always remember Lot's wife."

Then I saw that they went on their way to a pleasant river that King David called "the river of God" and Saint John called "the river of the water of life."[h] Now since their path lay on the bank of this river, Christian and Hopeful walked with great delight and also drank the water of the river, which was pleasant and enlivening to their weary spirits. On either side of the banks of this river were green trees that produced all kinds of fruit, and the leaves of the trees were good for healing.

Christian and his companion were refreshed as they ate the fruit from the trees. They also ate the leaves and were healed from some of the infirmities that beset travelers in that region.

On either side of the river was a meadow, beautified with lilies and green all the year long. While in this meadow, the two pilgrims lay down and slept, for it was a pleasant and safe place. When they awoke, they gathered the fruit of the trees, drank the water of the river, and then lay down again to sleep.[i] They did this for several days and nights. Then they sang:

"Behold ye how these crystal streams do glide,
To comfort pilgrims by the highway side;

---

[f] Genesis 13:13.
[g] Genesis 13:10.
[h] Psalm 65:9; Revelation 22; see also Ezekiel 47.
[i] Psalm 23:2; Isaiah 14:30.

The meadows green, besides their fragrant smell,
Yield dainties for them: and he that can tell
What pleasant fruit, yea, leaves, these trees do yield,
Will soon sell all, that he may buy this field."

Since they had not yet arrived at their destination, they ate and drank one last time and departed.

Chapter Ten

PRISONERS OF DESPAIR

Now I saw in my dream that they had not journeyed far before the river parted away from their path. This made them a little sad, yet they dared not go out of the way. As their path proceeded away from the river, it became rough, and their feet were sore from their travels. "So the souls of the pilgrims were much discouraged because of the way,"[a] and they wished for a smoother path.

Soon they saw a little way ahead of them a pleasant-looking field called By-Path Meadow. It sat on the left side of the road, with a stile marking an entrance into it. Then said Christian to Hopeful, "If this meadow is right next to the way, let us step aside into it and walk there." Then they went to the stile to take a look and saw a path that followed alongside their rough way, just on the other side of the fence. "This is what I was hoping for," said Christian. "Here is an easier way to go. Come, good Hopeful, and let us take this smooth path that follows right next to our difficult one."[1]

"But what if this path should lead us out of the way?" Hopeful asked.

"That is not likely," said Christian. "Look, doesn't it go right

---

[a]Numbers 21:4.

next to our present path?" So Hopeful, persuaded by Christian, followed after him over the stile into By-Path Meadow.

After they had started walking on the new path, they found it very easy on their feet, and looking ahead, they saw a man walking in the same direction they were going. His name was Vain-Confidence. They called after him and asked him where the path was leading. He yelled back to them, "To the Celestial Gate."

"See," said Christian, "didn't I tell you?"

So they followed Vain-Confidence down the path, but soon the night came, darkness fell, and they lost sight of him. As for Vain-Confidence, who could not see the way ahead of him, he fell into a deep pit[b] that was put there on purpose by the prince of those grounds to catch vainglorious fools. Vain-Confidence was mortally injured when he fell into the pit.

Now Christian and Hopeful heard him fall, so they called up ahead to see if he was all right, but there was no answer except the sound of groaning.

Then Hopeful asked, "Now what should we do?" But Christian was silent, regretting that he had led him out of the way. Then began a torrential rain with fierce thunder and lightning, and the water rose. Then Hopeful groaned in himself, saying, "O that I had kept on the true way!"

"Who could have thought that this path would lead us astray?"

Hopeful continued, "I was afraid it might from the very first, and that is why I gave you that gentle caution. I would have spoken more firmly, but you are older than I."

"Good brother, don't be offended," Christian said soothingly. "I am sorry I have urged you out of the way and that I have put you into such imminent danger. Pray, my brother, forgive me. I did not do it with any evil intent."

Hopeful said warmly, "Be comforted, my brother, I forgive you, and I believe that this will work out for our good."

Christian responded, "I am glad I am traveling with a merciful

---

[b]Isaiah 9:16.

Giant Despair captures Christian and Hopeful.

brother, but we must not stand here. Let's try to get back to where we left the true path."

"But, good brother, let me lead the way."

But Christian offered, "No, if you please, let me go ahead of you so that I can be the first to meet any danger, since I am the one to blame for our present circumstances."

"No," replied Hopeful, "you should not go first. Since your mind is troubled, you might lead us in the wrong direction."

Just then they heard an encouraging voice say, "Set your heart toward the highway, even the way that you went; turn again."[c] But by this time the waters had risen, making it very dangerous to go back the way they had come.

I thought then that it is easier to go out of the way that we are on than to go back onto it when we are off the way.

But despite the risk, they began tracing their steps back to where they had first entered the wrong path. After nearly a dozen near-drownings, and because the darkness made it impossible to see anything, they decided to find a place of shelter where they could wait out the storm until daybreak. After they had found a suitable shelter they soon fell asleep in utter exhaustion.

Not far from the place where they lay sleeping stood a castle called Doubting Castle. The owner of this castle was Giant Despair, and it was on his grounds that they were now sleeping.

When Giant Despair got up in the early morning and began walking up and down in his fields, he came across Christian and Hopeful asleep on his grounds. With a grim and surly voice, he told them to awake and asked them who they were and what they were doing on his property. They told him they were pilgrims and that they had lost their way. Then said the giant, "This night you have trespassed on my property by trampling and lying on my grounds, and therefore you must come along with me." So they were forced to go because he was stronger than they. The pilgrims also had little to say for themselves, knowing that they were at fault.

---

[c]Jeremiah 31:21.

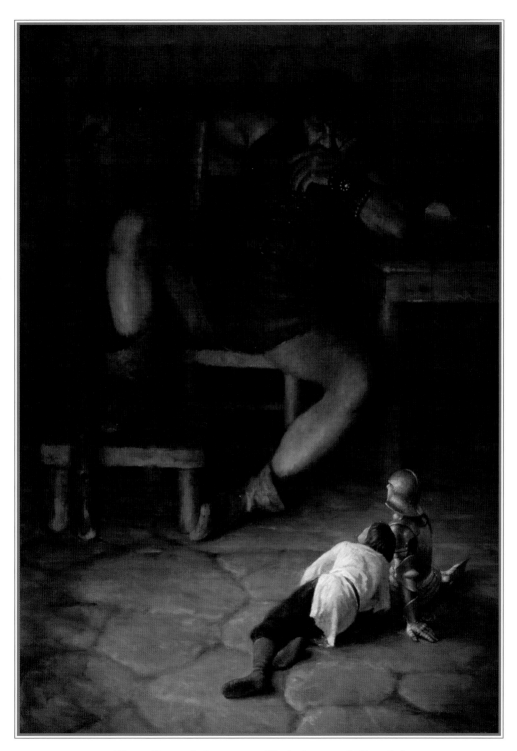

Giant Despair harasses Christian and Hopeful.

The giant therefore drove them before him and forced them into his castle, where Christian and Hopeful soon found themselves in a dark, nasty, and stinking dungeon.[d] Here they lay from Wednesday morning till Saturday night without one bit of bread or drop of water or ray of light or anyone to inquire about them. So Christian and Hopeful found themselves far from friends and acquaintances, in a hopeless and pitiable condition. Christian had double the sorrow, as he was constantly reminded that it was his ill-advised counsel that had created their present distress.

Giant Despair had a wife whose name was Distrust. When he had gone to bed, he had told his wife that he had taken a couple of prisoners and cast them into his dungeon for trespassing on his grounds. Then he asked her what she thought he should do to them. Distrust inquired about the prisoners' identities, their homeland and destination. He told her they were pilgrims bound for the Celestial City. Then she advised him to beat them without mercy when he arose in the morning.

The next morning when Giant Despair arose, he went out and found a short, thick club made from a crab tree. Then he went down into the dungeon where Christian and Hopeful were imprisoned, and there he began berating them and ranting at them as if they were dogs. Christian and Hopeful did not say a word in their defense.

Then Giant Despair pounced upon them and beat them mercilessly. The beating was so bad that when it was finally over, they were unable to help themselves or even to get up off the dungeon's cold stone floor.

Feeling satisfied with the torment he had inflicted, Giant Despair withdrew, leaving the two prisoners to console each other in their misery and to mourn the rest of the day with the sighs and bitter lamentations of their distress.

The next night, Distrust, discovering that the prisoners were still alive, advised Giant Despair to counsel them to take their own

---

[d]Psalm 88.

lives. So when morning came, the giant went to them in a surly manner as before. Seeing that they were very sore from the previous day's beating, he told them that since they were never likely to come out of that dungeon, their only way of escape would be to make an end of themselves, either with knife, rope, or poison. "For why," said he, "should you choose life, seeing it is attended with so much bitterness?"

But they asked him instead to let them go. Hearing their humble request, he scowled and rushed to make an end of them himself. However, before he could lay hands upon them he fell into one of his fits. It happened occasionally that in sunshiny weather Giant Despair lost for a time the use of his hand. Being thus affected at this time, the giant withdrew and left them to consider their predicament.

Then the prisoners considered whether it was best to take his counsel or not, and this is what they said to each other:

"Brother," said Christian, "what shall we do? The life that we now live is miserable. For my part I do not know which is best: to live like this, or to die and escape this misery. 'My soul chooseth strangling rather than life,' and the grave seems more desirable than this dungeon.[e] Shall we be ruled by the giant?"

Hopeful suggested, "Indeed, our present condition is dreadful, and death would be a relief. But still let us consider that the Lord of the country to which we are going has said, 'You shall do no murder.' And if not to another man, how much more then are we forbidden to take the giant's counsel to kill ourselves? Besides, he who kills another can only commit murder upon a body; but for someone to kill himself is to kill body and soul at the same time. Besides, my brother, you talk about the ease of the grave. But have you forgotten the Hell to which murderers go? For 'no murderer has eternal life.'[f] And let us consider again that the outcome of this is not in the hands of Giant Despair. Other prisoners like us, as far as I can tell,

---

[e]Job 7:15.
[f]1 John 3:15.

who have been captured by the giant, have managed to escape. Who knows but that God, who made the world, may soon cause Giant Despair to die? Or that the giant may forget to lock us in? Or that he may have another one of his fits and lose the use of his limbs? If that ever happens again, I am determined to gather all my courage and try my utmost to escape. I was a fool not to attempt an escape during the first fit. So, my brother, let us be patient and endure for a while longer. The time may come when we have an opportunity to escape, but let's not murder ourselves."

Hopeful's words helped calm Christian's mind, and so they continued together (in the dark) that day in their sad and doleful condition.

That evening the giant went down into the dungeon again to see if his prisoners had taken his counsel, but he found them still alive, though barely. Since the prisoners had had no bread or water and were badly wounded from their beating, they could do little but breathe. Their weak breath was all the sign of life needed to send the giant into a frenzy of rage, and he told them that since they had disobeyed his counsel, it would be worse with them than if they had never been born.

At this they trembled greatly, and Christian fell into a faint. When he recovered, they renewed their discourse about the giant's counsel and whether they should take it or not. Christian seemed inclined toward accepting the giant's advice, but Hopeful was not willing and made his second reply to Christian as follows:

"My brother," he said, "don't you remember how valiant you have been in the past? Apollyon could not crush you, nor were you defeated by all the things you heard, saw, or felt in the Valley of the Shadow of Death. Consider all the hardship, terror, and bewilderment you have already gone through! And now you are full of fear! Don't you see that though I am a far weaker man than you by nature, I inhabit this dungeon with you? The giant has wounded me as well as you and has cut off my bread and water as well as yours. I also mourn without the light. But let us exercise a little more patience. Remember how you conducted yourself in front of the men in Vanity Fair and were afraid neither of the chain, nor the cage, nor even of a bloody death. So let us (at least to avoid this shame that is unbecoming of a Christian) bear this with patience as well as we can."[2]

That same night as Giant Despair went to bed, his wife asked him about the prisoners and if they had taken his counsel. He replied, "They are sturdy rogues, and they would rather endure tremendous hardship than to do away with themselves."

Distrust replied, "Take them into the castle-yard tomorrow, and show them the bones and skulls of those whom you have already killed. Make them believe that before the week's end you will tear them in pieces just as you have done to their fellows before them."

So when the morning came, the giant took his prisoners into the castle-yard and showed them the bones and skulls according to his wife's instructions. "These," said he, "were pilgrims just as you are, and they trespassed on my grounds just as you have done. When I saw fit, I tore them in pieces. I will do the same to you within ten days. Go now, get back down to your den." With that, he beat them all the way down to the dungeon where they lay all day that Saturday in their misery, as they had before.

Now when night had fallen, and when Distrust and her husband had gone to bed, they resumed their conversation about the prisoners. The old giant wondered why he could not by his blows or his counsel bring Christian and Hopeful to an end. His wife replied, "I fear that they live in hope that someone will come to rescue them, or perhaps they have picklocks hidden, by which they hope to escape."

"Do you think so, my dear?" asked the giant. "I will search them in the morning."

Around midnight Christian and Hopeful began to pray and continued till almost the break of day. Shortly before the sun came up, good Christian, as one half-amazed, broke out in this passionate speech: "What a fool I am to lie in a stinking dungeon when I might instead walk at liberty! I have a key in my bosom called Promise that I believe will open any lock in Doubting Castle!"[3]

Hopeful responded, "That is good news, good brother. Take it out, and let's try it."

Then Christian pulled it out of his bosom and began trying to unlock the dungeon door. The door's bolts (as he turned the key) came loose, and the door flew open with ease. Christian and Hopeful both came out. Then Christian went to the outer door that leads into the castle-yard and with his key opened that door also. After that he went to the iron gate, for that also had to be opened. Though that lock was very hard, the key still opened it. Then they thrust open the gate to make a speedy escape, but that gate, as it opened, made a loud creaking noise that awakened Giant Despair. He rose hastily to pursue his prisoners but just then suffered another of his fits, which made his limbs fail and ended his pursuit. Then Christian and Hopeful pressed on eagerly and came to the King's Highway where they were safe because they were out of Giant Despair's jurisdiction.

When they had gone back over the stile, they began to consider what they should do to warn other pilgrims after them who might enter the stile and be taken prisoner by Giant Despair. They agreed to erect a pillar, engraving it with this sentence: "Over this stile is the way to Doubting Castle, which is kept by Giant Despair, who despises the King of the Celestial Country and seeks to destroy His holy pilgrims." Many, therefore, who followed after read what was written and escaped the danger. Having done this, Christian and Hopeful sang as follows:

> *"Out of the way we went, and then we found*
> *What 'twas to tread upon forbidden ground;*
> *And let them that come after have a care,*
> *Lest heedlessness makes them as we to fare.*
> *Lest they for trespassing his prisoners are*
> *Whose castle's Doubting and whose name's Despair."*

Chapter Eleven

SHEPHERDS' WARNINGS, DANGERS AVOIDED

They continued on their path until they came to the Delectable Mountains, which belong to the Lord. Once they arrived, they climbed the mountains to see the gardens, orchards, vineyards, and fountains. From the fountains they drank the water and washed themselves, and they freely ate from the vineyards.[1] Now on the top of these mountains shepherds were feeding their flocks, and they stood by the side of the highway. The pilgrims went to them, and leaning on their staves (as is common with weary pilgrims when they stand to talk), they asked, "Whose Delectable Mountains are these? And whose sheep are these that are pasturing on the mountain?"

A shepherd answered, "These mountains are Immanuel's Land, and they are within sight of His City. The sheep are also His, and He laid down His life for them."[a]

"Is this the way to the Celestial City?" Christian asked.

The shepherd replied, "You are going in the right direction."

"How far is it to get there?" Christian inquired further.

---

[a]John 10:11.

Shepherds comfort Christian and Hopeful.

One of the shepherds said, "Too far for anyone, except those who shall arrive there."

"Is the way safe or dangerous?" Christian wanted to know.

"Safe for those for whom the way is made to be safe, but the transgressors will fall off along the way."[b]

Christian asked, "Is there in this place any relief for pilgrims who are weary and faint in the way?"

A shepherd explained, "The Lord of these mountains has given us a charge not to be 'forgetful to entertain strangers';[c] therefore the benefits of the place are here for you."

I saw also in my dream that when the shepherds perceived that Christian and Hopeful were on pilgrimage, they started asking them questions such as where they had come from and by what means they had entered the way and found strength to persevere. "For few," they said, "who begin the journey make it this far."

When the shepherds heard Christian's and Hopeful's answers, they were pleased and, looking lovingly upon them, warmly welcomed them to the Delectable Mountains.

The shepherds, whose names were Knowledge, Experience, Watchful, and Sincere,[2] took them by the hand and led them to their tents where a meal had been prepared for them. They asked the pilgrims to stay there a while, to get acquainted, and to refresh themselves with all the good things of the Delectable Mountains.[3] Christian and Hopeful told them that they were happy to stay. They then went to rest that night because it was very late.

Then I saw in my dream that in the morning the shepherds called Christian and Hopeful to them and asked them to walk with them upon the mountains. So they went with them and walked a while, having a pleasant view all around them.

Then the shepherds said to one another, "Shall we show these pilgrims some wonders?" So after they had agreed to do it, they took them first to the top of the hill called Error, which was very

---

[b]Hosea 14:9.
[c]Hebrews 13:2.

steep on the far side, and asked them to look down to the bottom. So Christian and Hopeful looked down and saw at the bottom several men dashed to pieces by a fall. Then Christian asked, "What does this mean?"

The shepherds answered, "Haven't you heard of those who fell into error by listening to Hymenaeus and Philetus who denied the faith by refusing to believe in the resurrection of the body?"[d] When they answered that they had, the shepherds continued, "Those whom you see dashed in pieces at the bottom of this mountain are they, and they have continued to this day unburied, as you see, for an example to others to take heed not to clamber too high or come too near the brink of this mountain."

Then I saw that the shepherds took them to the top of another mountain named Caution and asked them look far off. When they did, they saw what they thought were several men walking up and down among the tombs there. They perceived that the men were blind because they stumbled upon the tombs and because they could not get out from among them. Then Christian asked, "What does this mean?"

The shepherds answered, "Do you see a little below these mountains a stile that leads into a meadow on the left hand of this way?" When they spotted it, the shepherds said, "From that stile there is a path that leads directly to Doubting Castle, which is kept by Giant Despair, and these," said the shepherds, pointing to those who were stumbling among the tombs, "were once on pilgrimage just as you are. But when they came to that same stile where the true way was rough, they chose to go out of it into that meadow. Once in the meadow they were taken by Giant Despair and cast into Doubting Castle. After they had been kept in the dungeon for a while, he at last put out their eyes and led them among those tombs where he left them to wander to this very day. The saying of the wise man is fulfilled, 'He that wanders out of the way of understanding shall remain in the congregation of the

---

[d] 2 Timothy 2:17–18.

dead.'"[e] Then Christian and Hopeful looked at one another with tears streaming down their faces, but they said nothing to the shepherds.

Then I saw in my dream that the shepherds took them to another place in the bottom of a ravine, where there was a door in the side of the hill. The shepherds opened the door and asked them to look in. They looked and saw that it was very dark and smoky. They also thought they heard a rumbling noise like that of a fire and the cries of someone being tormented, and they smelled the scent of brimstone.

Then Christian asked, "What does this mean?"

The shepherds told them, "This is a byway to Hell, a way that hypocrites enter by doing such things as selling their birthright, like Esau, or selling their master, like Judas, or blaspheming the gospel, like Alexander, or lying and dissembling, like Ananias and Sapphira, his wife."

Then said Hopeful to the shepherds, "I perceive that all of these people you have mentioned had the appearance of being pilgrims, just as we do, did they not?"

"Yes, and for a long time too," a shepherd replied.

Hopeful inquired, "How long did they appear to go on their pilgrimage before they were miserably cast away?"

A shepherd answered, "Some came as far as these mountains, some even farther, and some were lost long before they ever got here."

Then the pilgrims said to one another, "We need to cry to the Strong One for strength."

"Yes," a shepherd agreed, "and you will have need to use that strength when you get it."

By this time all agreed that the pilgrims should continue their journey, so they walked together toward the end of the mountains. Then the shepherds said to one another, "Let us show the pilgrims the gates of the Celestial City, if they have skill to look through

---

[e]Proverbs 21:16.

our telescope." The pilgrims consented eagerly to the idea. So they took them to the top of a high hill called Clear and gave them their telescope, which the pilgrims carefully looked through. But their recollections of all that the shepherds had just shown them made them tremble a little, causing their hands to shake and making it difficult to see clearly through the glass. But they thought they saw something like a gate and also some of the glory of the place. As they prepared to depart these mountains, they sang this song:

"Thus by the shepherds secrets are revealed,
Which from all other men are kept concealed.
Come to the shepherds, then, if you would see
Things deep, things hid, and that mysterious be."

Before they departed, the shepherd Knowledge gave them a map of the way. Another shepherd, Experience, told them to beware of the Flatterer. The third, Watchful, warned them not to sleep on the Enchanted Ground. And the fourth, Sincere, bid them Godspeed. So I awoke from my dream.[4]

Christian and Hopeful gaze at the Celestial City.

Chapter Twelve

Faith under Attack

I slept again, and I dreamed I saw the same two pilgrims going down the mountains along the highway toward the Celestial City. Now a little below these mountains on the left-hand side lies the country of Conceit.[1] From this country meandered a twisting but pleasant green lane that joined the pilgrims' highway. It was here that Christian and Hopeful met a very brisk lad who was coming out of that country. His name was Ignorance. Christian asked him where he came from and where he was going.

"Sir, I was born in the country that lies off to the left, and I am going to the Celestial City."

Christian asked, "But how do you think you will enter in at the Celestial Gate? I think you may find some difficulty there."

"As other good people do," said he.

Christian asked again, "But what have you to show at the gate that will cause it to be opened to you?"

"I know my Lord's will, and I have lived a good life," Ignorance said confidently. "I pay every man what I owe him; I pray and fast; I pay tithes and give alms; and I have left my country to go to the Celestial City."[2]

Christian challenged, "But you did not enter at the narrow

sheep gate at the beginning of this way. Instead, you have come into the way through a crooked lane. Therefore, I am afraid that whatever you think of yourself, you will be accused of being a thief and a robber on the day of reckoning, gaining no admittance to the Celestial City."

"Gentlemen, you are complete strangers to me. I do not know you," Ignorance stated. "Be content to follow the religion of your country, and I will follow the religion of mine. I hope that all will be well. And as for the narrow sheep gate that you talk of, the entire world knows that it is far away from our country. I cannot imagine that anyone in these parts even knows how to find it, nor do they need to bother since, as you can see, we have a fine, pleasant, green lane that comes down from our country and joins the way directly."

When Christian saw that the man was "wise in his own conceit," he said to Hopeful, whisperingly, "'There is more hope for a fool than for him.'"[a] And he also said, "'When he that is a fool walketh by the way, his wisdom faileth him, and he saith to everyone that he is a fool.'[b] What do you think?" continued Christian. "Should we continue walking with him, or should we walk away from him and give him time to think about what we have told him? We could stop and wait for him later and see if by degrees we can do him any good."

Then said Hopeful:

> "Let Ignorance a little while now muse
> On what is said, and let him not refuse
> Good counsel to embrace, lest he remain
> Still ignorant of what's the chiefest gain.
> God saith, those that no understanding have
> (Although He made them), them He will not save."

He further added, "I do not think it is a good idea to tell him everything at once. Let's pass him by for now, and if you would like, we will talk to him later. Perhaps he will be better able to consider what we've told him if he is given some time to do so."[3]

---

[a]Proverbs 26:12.
[b]Ecclesiastes 10:3.

So Christian and Hopeful both went on ahead, and Ignorance remained behind them. After a little while they entered into a dark lane where they saw a man whom seven demons had bound with seven strong cords. The demons were carrying him back to the door that Christian and Hopeful had seen with the shepherds on the side of the hill.[c]

Now good Christian and Hopeful began to tremble as the devils led the man away. Christian looked to see if he knew the man who was bound, and he thought he recognized him as one Turn-Away who lived in the town of Apostasy.[4] But he could not clearly see his face, for the bound man hung his head like a captured thief. Once they had passed, Hopeful looked after him and saw on his back a paper with the inscription, "Wanton professor and damnable apostate."[5]

Then said Christian to his friend Hopeful, "Now I remember something I was told about a good man who once lived in these parts. The name of the man was Little-Faith.[6] He was a good man, and he lived in the town of Sincere. The story I was told was as follows:

"Upon a part of this highway near us, Little-Faith encountered a road called Dead Man's Lane, which joins the highway from Broad-Way Gate. It is called Dead Man's Lane because of all the murders that are commonly done there. This man Little-Faith, who was going on his pilgrimage just as we are now, happened to sit down and fall asleep close by this dangerous lane. Now it just so happened that around the same time, three sturdy rogues named Faint-Heart, Mistrust, and Guilt (three brothers) were coming down the lane from Broad-Way Gate. They saw Little-Faith and came galloping up to him at full speed just as Little-Faith was awakening from his sleep and was preparing to continue his journey. Being taken thus by surprise, Little-Faith was powerless to run and, being outnumbered, was powerless to fight. The rogues demanded with threatening language that he stand up and hand over his wallet and money. White as a cloud with fear, Little-Faith

---

[c]Matthew 12:45; Proverbs 5:22.

stood up but was slow to hand over his money, reluctant to part with it. So Mistrust ran up to him, thrust his hand into his pocket, and pulled out a bag of silver.

Then Little-Faith cried out, "Thieves! Thieves!" But Guilt struck Little-Faith on the head with a club, knocking him flat to the ground where he lay bleeding profusely.[7] Heedless of the wounded man, the thieves just stood by, counting the stolen silver. But finally they heard someone approaching on the road, and fearing it might be Great-Grace who dwells in the city of Good Confidence, they ran off and left Little-Faith to tend to himself. After a while, Little-Faith came to and, gathering what strength he had left, got up and tended his wound as best he could and hobbled on his way.[8] This was the story I was told."

"Did the three thieves steal everything he had?" Hopeful asked.

Christian reported, "No, they did not find his jewels that he had hidden. But as I said, the good man suffered for his loss, since the thieves stole most of his spending money. And even though they did not find his jewels, he was still left with barely enough money to finish his journey.[d] Unless I am misinformed, he was forced to beg for enough food to sustain himself as he went on the rest of his pilgrimage. He did not sell his jewels, so he was left to beg and do what he could as he went on his way. I am told that he was hungry and malnourished for most of the rest of his journey."[9]

"Isn't it amazing that the thieves did not steal his certificate by which he was to receive his admittance at the Celestial Gate?" Hopeful wondered.

Christian commented, "It is a wonder that they missed it, although it was not through any cunning on the part of Little-Faith. He was caught off guard by them and had neither the power nor the skill to hide anything from them. It was more by God's gracious providence than by Little-Faith's own endeavors that they missed his certificate."[e]

---

[d]1 Peter 4:18.
[e]2 Timothy 1:14; 2 Peter 2:9.

Hopeful added, "But it must have been a comfort to him that they did not get this particular jewel, this certificate, from him."

"It might have been great comfort to him if he had used it as he should; but those who told me the story said that he made little use of this treasure for all the rest of the journey. I was told that because of the trauma he experienced at the hands of the thieves, he seemed to almost forget that he possessed the certificate. On the few occasions when he remembered it and might have been relieved by the thought of still having it, the memory of his loss would rush upon him and swallow up all hope and reason."

"Alas! Poor man!" Hopeful exclaimed. "This must have been a great grief to him."

Christian echoed, "Yes, grief indeed. What if we had been robbed and wounded while traveling in a strange place? It is a wonder he did not die with grief, poor heart! I was told that he spent almost all the rest of the way bitterly complaining, telling everyone he met on the way about every detail of how he was robbed, wounded, and left for dead."

Hopeful continued, "But what surprises me is that in his desperate situation he did not sell or pawn some of his hidden jewels, which may have given him some relief on his journey."

"What, do you really mean this?" Christian challenged. "Then you don't see the full picture, like a newborn bird with its shell still on its head. For what should he pawn them, or to whom should he sell them? In the country where he was robbed, his jewels were not considered valuable. Nor did he seek the kind of relief that anyone of that country could give. Besides, had his jewels been missing at the gate of the Celestial City, he would have been excluded from his inheritance (a fact of which he was well aware). Had he parted with his jewels, he would have been in worse shape than if he had been attacked by ten thousand thieves."

"Why are you so harsh, my brother?" Hopeful protested. "Esau sold his birthright for a mess of pottage, and that birthright was his greatest jewel; and if Esau could sell his jewel, then why couldn't Little-Faith do the same?"[f]

Christian asserted, "Esau did sell his birthright indeed, and so do many others, and by so doing exclude themselves from the chief blessing. But you must understand the difference between Esau and Little-Faith and also the difference between their estates. Esau's birthright was the shadow, but Little-Faith's jewels were the substance. Esau's belly was his god, but Little-Faith's belly was not. Esau's interests were in his fleshly appetite, but Little-Faith's were not. Esau could see no further than the fulfilling of his lusts. 'Behold, I am at the point to die (he said), and what profit shall this birthright do me?'[g] But Little-Faith, though it was his lot to have only a small portion of faith, was made to see and prize his jewels by faith and not to sell them, as Esau did his birthright. You do not read anywhere that Esau had faith, not even a little. So it is not a surprise that a man who is ruled by his fleshly passions and appetites is willing to sell his birthright and his soul to the Devil who resides in Hell. He is like the donkey that stubbornly goes in the wrong direction.[h] When such persons' minds are set upon their lusts, they will have them whatever the cost.

"But Little-Faith was of another temperament. His mind was fixed on things divine; his interests were upon things that were spiritual and from above. What would be the purpose for someone of Little-Faith's character to sell his spiritual treasure (had there been any who would have bought them) in order to possess the empty things of this world? Will a man pay to fill his belly with hay? Or can you persuade the turtledove to live upon carrion like the crow? Faithless ones can sell, pawn, or mortgage what they have, and themselves in the bargain, for carnal lusts; but those who have faith, saving faith, even though it is little, cannot do so. That is where you made your mistake, my brother."

---

[f]Hebrews 12:16.
[g]Genesis 25:32.
[h]Jeremiah 2:24.

Hopeful stated, "I acknowledge my mistake, but your abrupt response nearly made me angry."

Christian explained, "Why, I simply compared you to some newly hatched birds of a brisker variety that will run without thinking to and fro in unfamiliar paths, with part of their remaining shell still upon their heads. But get over that and consider the matter under debate, and all shall be well between you and me."[10]

Hopeful went on, "I am persuaded that these three fellows who attacked Little-Faith are a company of cowards. Why else would they have run when they heard the noise of someone coming down the road? Why then did Little-Faith lack courage? He might have stood his ground against them and yielded only after exhausting all other remedies."

Christian suggested, "Many have said that the three thieves were cowards, but few in the time of trial have withstood them courageously. As far as more courage, Little-Faith had none to spare. I understand that you recommend a brief brush with the rogues before yielding. This is your recommendation when they are far away from us, but I wonder if you would not have second thoughts if they were to come rushing unexpectedly on you? Also consider that they are journeymen thieves and that they serve under the king of the bottomless pit. If they called on him, he would come immediately to their aid, and he has a voice like a roaring lion.[i]

"I have been in a situation similar to that of Little-faith, and I found it a terrible thing. These three villains once attacked me, and like a courageous Christian, I resisted at first. Then they called to their master who joined them in the attack. I would, as the saying goes, have given my life for a penny, but as God would have it, I was clothed with proven armor that protected me, yet also made it difficult to stand up and fight like a man. No one can know the risks and hazards of a battle unless he has been in the battle himself."

"Yes," Hopeful somewhat agreed, "but they still seem to me to be cowards, for they ran away when they thought Great-Grace was on the way."

"True, they have often fled, both they and their master, when Great-Grace has appeared," Christian acknowledged. "That is not a surprise, for he is the King's Champion. I think you must make a distinction between Little-Faith and the King's Champion. Not all the King's subjects are His champions, nor can they all do such feats of war as a champion. Do you think that a little child could handle Goliath as David did? Or does a wren possess the strength of an ox? Some are strong, some are weak; some have great faith, some have little. This man was one of the weak, and therefore he was overcome by the thieves' evil designs."

Hopeful said, "I wish it had been Great-Grace whom the thieves had met."

"If it had been, he might have had his hands full with the three of them," Christian asserted. "Even though Great-Grace is excellent with his weapons, he does well only when he can keep them at the end of his sword point. But if Faint-Heart or Mistrust or Guilt should get close to him and knock him down, what then? If you look upon Great-Grace's face, you will see scars and cuts there that demonstrate what I have been saying. I have heard that he has despaired even of life when in combat. Didn't these same sturdy rogues and their companions make David groan, moan, and roar? Heman and Hezekiah, who were champions in their day, were severely tested when assaulted by these same rogues. Peter, who some say is the prince of the apostles, was so put to the test that by the time they were through with him he was afraid of a servant girl. And remember, these villains' king is at their beck and call. He is never out of earshot; and whenever they begin to have a difficult time, he comes in to help them if he can.

"But as for footmen like you and me, let us never desire to meet with the enemy or presume ourselves able to do better when we hear about the struggles of others. When we hear of others who have been sorely tested, let's not be deluded by thoughts of our own manhood, for those who do so are often the ones who have the worst time of it when they are tested.

"Witness Peter, of whom I made mention before. He would swagger indeed, and his vain mind prompted him to say that he would stand up for his Master when all others fled for fear. But who was it who fled in fear when these villains arrived on the scene? When we hear that such robberies are done on the King's Highway, there are two things we should do:

"1. To go out armed, being sure to take our shield with us. The Devil has no fear of us at all if he finds us without our shield. Remember what we learned? 'Above all, taking the shield of faith, wherewith ye shall be able to quench all the fiery darts of the wicked.'[j]

"2. It is also a good idea to travel in a convoy and request that the Lord go with us Himself. This made David rejoice when he was in the Valley of the Shadow of Death, and Moses would rather have died where he stood than to go one step without his God.[k] O my brother, if He will go along with us, then we need not fear even if tens of thousands set themselves against us.[l] But without Him the proud pilgrims 'fall among the slain.'[m]

"As for my part, I have been in the battle before, and I cannot boast of my own strength or courage. I stand before you alive because of the grace and goodness of my Lord. I would be very glad to never go through another such time of testing and danger. However, since the lion and the bear have not as yet devoured me, I hope God will also deliver us from the next uncircumcised Philistine."

Then sang Christian:

> *"Poor Little-Faith! Have you been among the thieves?*
> *Were you robbed? Remember this, whosoever believes*
> *And gets more faith shall then a victor be*
> *Over ten thousand, else scarce over three."*

---

[j]Ephesians 6:16.
[k]Exodus 33:15.
[l]Psalm 3:5–8; 27:1–3.
[m]Isaiah 10:4.

So Christian and Hopeful continued on their journey, with Ignorance following behind them. They continued on until they came to a place where there was a fork in the road. As they looked down each path, both appeared to be as straight as the other. They did not know which way to go.

Chapter Thirteen

FLATTERING ENEMIES AND RENEWED TRUST

As they were deciding which of the two paths to take, a man of dark complexion, covered by a white robe, came to them and asked with a very pleasant demeanor why they were standing there. They answered that they were going to the Celestial City but did not know which of the paths to take. "Follow me," encouraged the man agreeably, "for that is where I am going."[1]

So they followed him, and the way he took them turned by degrees until they were walking in a direction away from the Celestial City. Despite this bend in the road, the pilgrims were not alarmed and continued to follow the man.[2]

But by and by, before they were aware of it, he had led them both within the range of a net in which they were suddenly so entangled that they knew not what to do. With that the white robe fell off the dark man's back. Then they saw that they had been led into a trap, and there they lay weeping for some time, for they could not get themselves untangled from the net.[3]

Then Christian said to Hopeful, "Now I see my error. Didn't the shepherds tell us to beware of the Flatterers? We have discovered for ourselves the meaning of the wise man's saying, 'A man that flattereth his neighbor spreadeth a net for his feet.'"[a]

Hopeful reminded him, "They also gave us a map so we could avoid the paths of the Destroyer, but we forgot to look at it. On this matter David was indeed wiser than we, for he said, 'Concerning the works of men, by the word of Thy lips I have kept myself from the paths of the destroyer.'"[b]

While they lay hopelessly tangled in the net, chiding themselves for their error, they saw a Shining One coming toward them. He had a whip of small cords in his hand.

When he had come up to them, he asked them where they came from and what they were doing there. They told him that they were poor pilgrims going to Zion but had been led out of their way by a dark, deceptive man clothed in white who had asked them to follow him, pretending to be a pilgrim bound for Zion.

Then the Shining One with the whip said, "It is the Flatterer, a false apostle who has transformed himself into an angel of light."[c] So he tore open the net and let them out. Then he said to them, "Follow me, and I will take you back to the right way." So he led them back to the way that they had left to follow the Flatterer.

Then he asked them, "Where did you spend last night?" They said that they had been sheltered by the shepherds on the Delectable Mountains. He then asked them if the shepherds had given them a map with directions, which they affirmed. The Shining One continued, "When you came to the other path that crossed the way, did you take out your map and read the directions?" When they admitted that they hadn't because they had forgotten, the Shining One asked them if the shepherds had warned them to beware of the Flatterer.

"Yes," they answered, "but we did not imagine that this fine-spoken man was he."[d]

Then I saw in my dream that he commanded them to lie down.

---

[a]Proverbs 29:5.
[b]Psalm 17:4.
[c]Daniel 11:32; 2 Corinthians 11:13–14.
[d]Romans 16:18.

When they did, he chastised them with his whip till they were sore in order to teach them to walk only in the good way.[e] As he chastised them, he said, "As many as I love, I rebuke and chasten; be zealous, therefore, and repent."[f] After this he sent them back on their way with instructions to pay attention to the map and the directions given to them by the shepherds. So they thanked him for all his kindness and went meekly along the right way, singing:

> "Come hither, you that walk along the way;
> See how the pilgrims fare that go astray!
> They are caught in an entangling net,
> 'Cause they good counsel lightly did forget:
> 'Tis true, they were rescued, but yet you see,
> They're scourged to boot. Let this your caution be."

Now after a while, they saw a man afar off coming toward them. He was traveling alone. Then Christian said to Hopeful, "Look, a man with his back toward Zion is coming to meet us."

"I see him," Hopeful said. "Let us be careful that he is not another Flatterer."

So he drew nearer and at last met up with them. His name was Atheist, and he asked them where they were going.

"We are going to Mount Zion," Christian announced.

At this answer Atheist began to laugh uncontrollably.[4]

"Why are you laughing?" inquired Christian.

Atheist answered, "I am laughing at how ignorant you are to endure such a tedious journey and get nothing for your trouble but all the pain that goes along with such a journey."

"Why, do you think we won't be received at the Celestial City?" Christian asked.

"Received where?" Atheist asked in turn. "There is no such place as the Celestial City in all this world!"[5]

"But there is in the world to come."

Atheist continued, "When I was at home in my own country, I

heard about the Celestial City and went to find it for myself. I have spent the last twenty years seeking this city and am not any closer to finding it than the day I began looking for it."[g]

"We have both heard and believed that there is such a place to be found," Christian remarked.

Atheist asserted, "If I had not believed it existed, I would not have spent all this time looking for it. Having spent more time looking for it than you have, I can certainly assure you that the place does not exist, and so it cannot be found. I am now on my way back to get my share of those pleasures I denied myself in my useless journey to find something that does not exist."[6]

Then Christian asked Hopeful, "Is this man speaking truthfully?"

Hopeful warned, "Take heed; he is one of the Flatterers. Remember what it has cost us once already for listening to men such as this. What, no Mount Zion? Didn't we see the gates of the Celestial City from the Delectable Mountains? Also, aren't we in this present time to walk by faith?[h] Let's go on," said Hopeful. "If we do not continue on our way, the man with the whip may overtake us again. You should be the one teaching me the lesson that I will now say to you: 'Cease, my son, to hear the instruction that causeth to err from the words of knowledge.'[i] I say, my brother, cease to hear him, and let us 'believe to the saving of the soul.'"[j]

Christian explained, "My brother, I did not put the question to you because I doubted the truth, but to test you and to pull out of your own heart an honest expression of your faith. As for this man, I know that he is blinded by the god of this world.[k] Let us go on, knowing that we have believed the truth, 'and no lie is of the truth.'"[l]

"Now I rejoice in the hope of the glory of God,"[m] Hopeful said.

---

[g]Jeremiah 22:13; Ecclesiastes 10:15.
[h]2 Corinthians 5:7.
[i]Proverbs 19:27.
[j]Hebrews 10:39.
[k]1 John 2:11.
[l]1 John 2:21.
[m]Romans 5:2.

So they turned away from the man, who laughed and went on his way.[7]

Then I saw in my dream that they continued their journey until they came into a region where the air naturally induced sleepiness if one was not acclimated to it. Here Hopeful began to grow very sluggish and sleepy. He said to Christian, "I am starting to grow drowsy and can scarcely keep my eyes open. Let's lie down and take a nap."

"By no means," said Christian. "We might fall asleep and never wake up."

"Why so, my brother?" Hopeful asked. "Sleep is sweet for the travel-weary man, and a little nap would be refreshing."

"Do you recall that one of the shepherds told us to beware of the Enchanted Ground?" Christian inquired. "He meant that we should beware of sleeping. 'Therefore let us not sleep, as do others, but let us watch and be sober.'"[n][8]

Hopeful agreed, "You're right, and had I been here alone I would be asleep by now and in danger of death. What the wise man says is true, 'Two are better than one.'[o] Your company has been God's mercy to me, and 'you shall have a good reward for your labor.'"[p]

"Now then," said Christian, "to prevent us from becoming drowsy in this place, perhaps we should have a good discussion."[9]

"I wholeheartedly agree," said Hopeful.

"Where shall we begin?"

"Where God began with us,"[10] Hopeful suggested. "But you begin, if you please."

Christian said, "First I will sing you this song:

"When saints do sleepy grow, let them come hither
And hear how these two pilgrims talk together.
Yea, let them learn of them, in any wise,
Thus to keep open their drowsy slumbering eyes.
Saints' fellowship, if it be managed well,
Keeps them awake, and that in spite of Hell."

---

[n]1 Thessalonians 5:6.
[o]Ecclesiastes 4:9.
[p]Ecclesiastes 4:9.

Then Christian began, saying, "I will ask you a question. What made you decide to begin this journey?"

"Do you mean to ask how I first become concerned about the condition of my soul?" Hopeful questioned.

"Yes, that is what I mean."

Hopeful began, "For a very long time I was delighted with all the things you could see and buy at Vanity Fair. I am certain that had I continued in this way I would have been drowned in perdition and destruction."

"What kinds of things are you talking about?" Christian wondered.

"All the treasures and riches of the world," Hopeful said. "Also I delighted in rioting, reveling, drinking, swearing, lying, uncleanness, Sabbath-breaking, and all the other things that destroy the soul. But one day I began to hear and consider things that are divine, which I heard from you and the beloved Faithful, who was put to death for his faith and the testimony of his good life in Vanity Fair. I was convicted that 'the end of these things is death'[q] and that for these things' sake 'cometh the wrath of God upon the children of disobedience.'"[r]

"And did you immediately come under the power of this conviction?" Christian questioned further.

Hopeful acknowledged, "No, I was not immediately willing to acknowledge the evil of sin or the damnation that follows sinning. When my mind began to be stirred up by the Word, I tried to shut my eyes to the truth of it."

"What kept you from understanding that God was working through His blessed Spirit to bring you to Himself?"

Hopeful explained, "The reasons were as follows. First of all, I was ignorant that this was the work of God in my life, since I never imagined that God begins His work of conversion in a sinner's life by awakening him to his sin. Then there was the appeal that sin

---

[q]Romans 6:21–23.
[r]Ephesians 5:6.

still held over my flesh, and I was reluctant to abandon it. Another reason I refused then to repent is that I did not want to part ways with my old companions whose company and entertainments were very desirable to me. Finally, the times in which I came under the conviction of sin were so troublesome and frightening that I did everything I could to try to cast these times out of my memory."

"Then there were times when you were not troubled in your mind and soul?" Christian queried.

"Yes," Hopeful said, "that is true, but it would creep back into my mind, and then my soul would be as troubled as it was before, or even worse."

"What was it that brought your sins to mind again?"

Hopeful answered, "Many things, such as the following:

"1. If I met a good man in the streets; or,

"2. If I heard the Bible being read; or,

"3. If my head ached; or,

"4. If I was told that some of my neighbors were sick; or,

"5. If I heard the bell toll for the dead; or,

"6. If I thought of dying myself; or,

"7. If I heard about someone's sudden death,

"8. And lastly, the thing that brought my sin to mind and troubled my soul worse than all of these things was when I thought to myself that I must quickly come to judgment."

"And when these things reminded you of your sin," Christian stated, "could you find relief from the sense of guilt that your sin caused?"

"No, I could not," Hopeful said. "If I even thought about returning to one of my previous sins, my conscience would torment me."

"And then what did you think?" Christian asked.

Hopeful went on, "I thought about changing my ways, afraid that if I did not, I would be damned."

"And did you try to change your ways?"

Hopeful answered, "Yes. Not only did I flee from my sin, but from sinful company also; and I took up religious duties such as prayer, Bible reading, weeping for my sin, speaking the truth to my neighbors, and so on. I did all these things and many others too numerous to relate."

"And did this give you peace of mind?" Christian inquired.

"Yes, for a while," Hopeful reported. "But in the end my trouble came tumbling back upon me again, despite all my reformations."

"How did that come about since you were now reformed?" Christian wondered.

Hopeful continued, "Several things brought it about. I began to read in my Bible where it said things like 'All our righteousness is as filthy rags'[s] and 'By the works of the law shall no flesh be justified'[t] and 'When ye shall have done all those things, say, "We are unprofitable"'[u] and many other such sayings. Then I began to reason with myself: If all my righteousness is as filthy rags, if by the deeds of the Law no man can be justified, and if when we have done all we can do, we remain still unprofitable, then it is folly to think that I will enter Heaven by keeping the Law. It also occurred to me that if a man runs a hundred pounds into debt with a shopkeeper and then begins to pay cash for everything else he purchases, while leaving the old debt unpaid, the shopkeeper can rightfully sue him and cast him into prison until he pays all his past debt."

"Well, how did you apply this to yourself?" Christian asked further.

Hopeful explained, "Why, I thought about how great a debt of sin I had run up in God's book and how even if I reformed myself, I could not pay off this past debt. So how could I be freed from the damnation that I have brought upon myself by my former transgressions?"

Christian affirmed, "A very good application, but go on."

Hopeful added, "Another thing that troubled me is that when I carefully looked into my new best efforts, I saw that they were

[s]Isaiah 64:6.
[t]Galatians 2:16.
[u]Luke 17:10.

mixed up with sin. I was forced to conclude that even if I could conceivably ignore all past sins, including the sin of pride and conceit I had in myself because of my former 'good' deeds, I have committed enough sin in one of my most recent good duties to send me to Hell, even if my former life had been somehow found faultless."

"And what did you do then?" Christian asked.

"Do!" Hopeful exclaimed. "I couldn't figure out what to do until I shared my concerns with Faithful, for he and I were well acquainted. He told me that unless I could obtain the righteousness of a Man who never had sinned, neither my own righteousness nor all the righteousness of the world could save me."

"And did you think he spoke the truth?" Christian questioned.

Hopeful answered, "Had he told me this when I was pleased and satisfied with my reformed life, I would have called him a fool for his pains. But since I was now aware of my own weakness and the sin that cleaves to my best performance, I was forced to believe his opinion."

"But did you think, when he suggested it to you, that there was a Man of whom it might justly be said that He never committed sin?" Christian offered.

Hopeful said, "I must confess that the words sounded strange at first, but after keeping company and talking with Faithful, I fully believed that there was such a Man."

"And did you ask him who this Man was and how you could be justified by Him?" Christian queried.

"Yes," Hopeful replied, "and he told me it was the Lord Jesus, who sits on the right hand of the Most High. And he told me that I could be justified by Him if I would trust in what He Himself had done in the days when He lived on earth, when He suffered and hung on the tree. I asked him how that Man's righteousness could be effective to justify another before God. Faithful replied that Jesus was the mighty God, having done what He did and dying the shameful death not for Himself but for me who deserved it instead.

If I would believe in Him and what He had done for me, then His worthiness would be imputed to me."[v]

"What did you do then?"

Hopeful said, "I objected to his argument because I thought that Man was not willing to save me."

"So how did Faithful reply to that?" Christian questioned.

Hopeful recounted, "He told me to go to Him and see for myself. Then I objected that it would be presumptuous; but he said it would not be, for I had been invited to come.[w] Then he gave me the Book of Jesus to encourage me more freely to come. Faithful told me that the words in this book, including the smallest detail, stood firmer than Heaven and earth.[x]

"Then I asked him, 'What must I do when I come to Him?' He answered that I must plead upon my knees, with all my heart and soul, that the Father reveal Him to me.[y] Then I asked him further how I must make my supplication to Him. And he said that if I go to Him I would find Him upon a mercy-seat, where He sits all the year long to give pardon and forgiveness to all those who come.

"I told him that I didn't know what to say when I came. Then Faithful told me to say words to this effect: 'God, be merciful to me a sinner, and make me to know and believe in Jesus Christ. For I see that if His righteousness had not been offered, or if I have no faith in that righteousness, I am utterly cast away. Lord, I have heard that You are a merciful God and have ordained that Your Son Jesus Christ should be the Savior of the world. Moreover, You are willing to give Him for a poor sinner like me (and I am a sinner indeed). Lord, take therefore this opportunity, and magnify Your grace in the salvation of my soul, through Your Son Jesus Christ. Amen.'"[z]

"So did you do as you were asked?" Christian wondered.

"Yes," Hopeful replied, "right then and many times over."

---

[v]Hebrews 10; Romans 4; Colossians 1; 1 Peter 1.
[w]Matthew 11:28.
[x]Matthew 24:35.
[y]Psalm 95:6; Daniel 6:10; Jeremiah 29:12–13.
[z]Exodus 25:22; Leviticus 16:2; Numbers 7:89; Hebrews 4:16.

"And did the Father reveal His Son to you?" Christian inquired further.

"Neither at the first, nor second, nor third, nor fourth, nor fifth, no, nor at the sixth time," Hopeful answered honestly.

Christian asked, "What did you do then?"

Hopeful responded, "Why, I didn't know what to do."

"Did you think that you might stop praying?" Christian asked softly.

"Yes, a hundred times," Hopeful confessed.

"And what was the reason you did not?" Christian questioned.

Hopeful told him, "I believed that what Faithful told me was true and that without the righteousness of this Christ, all the world could not save me. Therefore, I thought to myself, if I stop praying I will die, and I only wish to die at the throne of grace. And with these words came into my mind, 'Though it tarry, wait for it; because it will surely come, it will not tarry.'[aa] So I continued praying until the Father showed me His Son."

"And how was He revealed to you?" Christian asked.

Hopeful explained, "I did not see Him with my bodily eyes, but with the eyes of my understanding,[ab] and it happened like this: One day I was very sad, probably sadder than ever before, and this sadness resulted from a fresh glimpse of the great depth and vileness of my sins. I was expecting nothing but Hell and the everlasting damnation of my soul. Suddenly I saw the Lord Jesus look down from Heaven upon me and say, 'Believe on the Lord Jesus Christ, and you will be saved.'[ac]

"'But,' I replied, 'Lord, I am a great, a very great, sinner.'

"He answered, 'My grace is sufficient for you.'[ad]

"Then I said, 'But, Lord, what is believing?'

"Then I understood from the Scripture that believing and coming were the same thing: 'He that cometh to Me shall never hunger,

---

[aa]Habakkuk 2:3.
[ab]Ephesians 1:18–19.
[ac]Acts 16:31.
[ad]2 Corinthians 12:9.

and he that believeth on Me shall never thirst.'[ae] Thus, those who have come to Jesus, who have run wholeheartedly to Christ for salvation, have indeed believed in Christ. Then I wept, and I asked again, 'But, Lord, will You indeed accept and save even such a great sinner as I?'

"And I heard Him say, 'He that cometh to Me, I will in no wise cast out.'[af]

"Then I asked, 'But how can I know that my faith is truly placed upon You?'

"Then He said, 'Christ Jesus came into the world to save sinners.'[ag] 'He is the end of the law for righteousness to every one who believes.'[ah] 'He died for our sins, and rose again for our justification.'[ai] 'He loved us and washed us from our sins in His own blood.'[aj] 'He is mediator between God and man.'[ak] 'He ever lives to make intercession for us.'[al]

"From all this I understood that I must look for righteousness in His person and for satisfaction for my sins by His blood. I must believe that what He did in obedience to His Father's law, in submitting to the penalty for sin, was not for Himself but for him who will accept it for his salvation and be thankful. Finally my heart was full of joy, my eyes full of tears, and my affections running over with love for the name, people, and ways of Jesus Christ."

"This was a revelation of Christ to your soul indeed," Christian confirmed. "But tell me also what particular effect this had upon your spirit."

Hopeful said, "It made me consider that this world, notwithstanding all the good things and noble deeds in it, is in a state of condemnation. It made me see that God the Father, though He is perfectly just and thus must punish all sin, can rightly justify the

---

[ae]John 6:35.
[af]John 6:37.
[ag]1 Timothy 1:15.
[ah]Romans 10:4.
[ai]Romans 4:25.
[aj]Revelation 1:5.
[ak]1 Timothy 2:5.
[al]Hebrews 7:25.

sinner who comes to Him in His Son. It made me greatly ashamed of the vileness of my former life and confounded me with the sense of my own ignorance, for until that moment I had never once been filled with thoughts of the beauty of Jesus Christ. It made me love a holy life and long to do something for the honor and glory of the name of the Lord Jesus. Yea, I thought that if I had now a thousand gallons of blood in my body, I could spill it all for the sake of the Lord Jesus."

Chapter Fourteen

STUBBORN IGNORANCE

I then saw in my dream that Hopeful looked back and noticed Ignorance, whom they had left behind, still following them. "Look how far the youngster follows behind us," he said to Christian.

"Yes, I see him," said Christian, "but he does not care for our company."

Hopeful added, "Yet I don't think it would have hurt him if he had walked along with us all this time."

Christian said, "That is true. Our companionship might have done him well, but I am sure he thinks otherwise."

"I think you are right," Hopeful stated. "However, let's wait for him."

So they did.

Then Christian said to Ignorance, "Hurry up, man. Why do you lag behind?"

Ignorance answered, "I take pleasure in walking alone and enjoy it more than traveling in the company of others, unless I really like the particular members of such company."

Then Christian said to Hopeful, softly, "Didn't I tell you he cared not for our company?" Then, turning to Ignorance, Christian said to him, "Come along with us, and let us spend our time talking as we walk through this solitary place." Then he inquired of Ignorance, saying, "How are you doing? How stands it between God and your soul now?"

Ignorance replied, "I hope well, for I am always full of good thoughts and intentions that come into my mind that comfort me as I walk."[a]

"What good thoughts and intentions?" Christian inquired. "Please, tell us."

"Why, I think of God and Heaven."

"So do the devils and damned souls," Christian pointed out.

Ignorance added, "But I think of them and also desire them."

Christian asserted, "So do many who are never going to make it to Heaven. 'The soul of the sluggard desires, and hath nothing.'"[b]

"But I think of them and leave all that I possess and enjoy that I might gain them," Ignorance claimed.

"I doubt that," Christian exclaimed, "since leaving all is a hard matter. It is a much harder matter than many are aware of. But what is it that persuades you that you have left all for God and Heaven?"

"My heart tells me so."

Christian challenged, "The wise man says, 'He that trusts his own heart is a fool.'"[c]

"This is spoken of an evil heart, but mine is a good one," Ignorance insisted.

Christian quickly asked, "But how can you prove that?"

Ignorance asserted, "It comforts me with hopes of Heaven."

"That may be your heart deceiving you," Christian warned. "A man's heart may comfort him with hopes of things that, in all truth, he has no reason to hope for."

Ignorance insisted, "But my heart and life agree together, and therefore my hope is well-grounded."

[a]Proverbs 28:26.
[b]Proverbs 13:4.
[c]Proverbs 28:26.

"Who told you that your heart and life agree together?"

"My heart tells me so," Ignorance claimed strongly.

Christian suggested, "Then ask your heart if I am a thief. Your heart may tell you that I am, but that does not make it so. Unless the Word of God bears witness in this matter, no other testimony is of value."

"But is it not a good heart that has good thoughts?" Ignorance questioned. "And isn't a good life one that is lived according to God's commandments?"

"Yes, a good heart has good thoughts, and a good life is one lived according to God's commandments," Christian agreed, adding, "But it is one thing, indeed, to have these and another thing only to think you do."

Ignorance said, "Please tell me what you consider to be good thoughts and a life lived according to God's commandments."

Christian replied, "There are good thoughts pertaining to different things, some with respect to ourselves, God, Christ, and other things."

"What do you think are good thoughts in relation to ourselves?" Ignorance inquired.

Christian answered, "Such as agree with the Word of God."

"What kind of thoughts about ourselves agree with the Word of God?" Ignorance asked further.

Christian explained, "We think rightly of ourselves when we pass the same judgment upon ourselves that the Word passes. To explain myself more fully, the Word of God says of persons in a natural condition, 'There is none righteous, there is none that doeth good.'[d] It also says that 'every imagination of the heart of man is only evil, and that continually.'[e] And again, 'The imagination of man's heart is evil from his youth.'[f] Now then, when we think these thoughts of ourselves, our thoughts are good ones because they agree with the Word of God."

[d]Romans 3:10, 12.
[e]Genesis 6:5.
[f]Genesis 8:21.

Ignorance insisted, "I will never believe that my heart is that bad."

"Therefore you have never had one good thought concerning yourself in your entire life," Christian exclaimed. "But let me go on. As the Word passes judgment upon our heart, so it passes judgment upon our ways. When the thoughts concerning our hearts and ways agree with the judgment that the Word gives of both, then are both thoughts good, because they agree with the Word."

"Tell me what you mean," Ignorance urged.

Christian went on, "Why, the Word of God says that man's ways are crooked ways; not good, but perverse.[g] It says that man is naturally opposed to the good way and cannot know it.[h] Now, when a man knows in his head and humbly believes with all his heart that the Word is right and that his ways are not good, then he has good thoughts regarding his own ways because his thoughts now agree with the judgment of the Word of God."

"What are good thoughts concerning God?"

Christian went on, "Just as our thoughts of ourselves are good when they agree with the Word of God, so are they good thoughts concerning God when they agree with what the Word says of Him. We must agree with the Word when it teaches us about the attributes of God, which are too large a subject to talk about right now. In reference to ourselves, we have right thoughts about God when we understand that He knows us better than we know ourselves and can see the sin in us when we can see none. Our thoughts concerning God are good when we understand that He knows our inmost thoughts and that our heart, with all its depths, is always clearly seen by Him. Our thoughts about God are good when we think that all our righteousness stinks in His nostrils and that therefore He cannot stand to see us come before Him in our own confidence, even with all our best performances."

Ignorance asked, "Do you think that I am such a fool as to think

---

[g]Psalm 125; Proverbs 2:15.
[h]Romans 3.

God can see no further than I? Or that I would come to God in the confidence of my best performances?"

"So what do you think on this matter?" Christian asked back.

Ignorance replied, "To be short, I think I must believe in Christ for justification."

"How is it that you think you must believe in Christ when you do not see your need for Him?" Christian questioned. "You neither see your original nor actual infirmities. You have an opinion of yourself and of your deeds that puts you in a category of man who sees no necessity for Christ's personal righteousness to justify you before God. How can you say that you believe in Christ?"

Ignorance insisted, "In spite of what you say, I believe."

"But what do you believe?" Christian inquired.

Ignorance asserted, "I believe that Christ died for sinners and that I shall be justified before God from the curse through His gracious acceptance of my obedience to His law. I believe that Christ makes my religious duties acceptable to His Father, by virtue of His merits, and so shall I be justified."

"Let me discuss your confession of faith," Christian offered. "First, you believe with a fantasy faith, for this faith is nowhere described in the Word. You also believe with a false faith that takes justification away from the personal righteousness of Christ and credits it to you. The faith you describe makes Christ a justifier of your actions, not of your person. Thus, according to this faith, you are justified by your actions, which is false. Therefore, this faith is deceitful and will leave you under God's wrath in the Day of Judgment.

"True justifying faith makes the soul aware of its lost condition under the Law. The soul that comes to the righteousness of Christ for refuge understands that it is Christ's righteousness alone that is acceptable to God. It is not a mixture of both Christ's obedience and our attempts at obedience that justify us to God. Your obedience is worthless and full of sin, and it is only the obedience of Jesus Christ that God accepts as payment for your sin. True faith causes the

soul to flee underneath the righteousness of Christ for relief from
the condemnation that we deserve, and it is Christ's righteousness
alone that will be presented as spotless before God and accepted by
Him as payment for our debt of sin."

"What!" Ignorance exclaimed. "Would you have us trust in what
Christ alone has accomplished without adding our own accomplishments? Believing in Christ and His righteousness would give us
complete abandon to live as we choose the moment we believed it.
This way of thinking would loosen the reins of our lust and permit
us to disobey God's commands to our heart's content."

"Ignorance is your name, and as your name is, so are you,"
Christian exclaimed. "Your answer demonstrates what I say. You
are ignorant of what justifying righteousness is, and you are ignorant of how to secure your soul through faith from the heavy wrath
of God. Yes, and you are also ignorant of the true effects of saving
faith in the righteousness of Christ, the effects of which are to bend
and win over the heart to God in Christ. The heart won over to Him
will love His name, His Word, His ways, and His people. Saving
faith will not, as you ignorantly imagine, give license to do evil but
will instead give the earnest desire and power to do good."

Hopeful added, "Ask him if he ever had Christ revealed to him
from Heaven."

"What! You are a man who believes in revelations?" Ignorance
protested. "I believe that what both of you, and all the rest of your
kind, say about that matter is the fruit of a distracted brain."

Hopeful went on, "Why, man? Christ is so hidden in God from
the natural apprehensions of the flesh that He cannot by any man
be rightly and savingly known unless God the Father reveals Him
to them."

"That is your faith, but not mine," Ignorance asserted. "I believe
that my faith is as good as yours, although it does not fill my head
with so many whimsical ideas as your faith does."

Christian spoke up. "Give me a moment to put in a word. You
ought not to speak so lightly of this matter. For this I will boldly

affirm, even as my good companion has done, that no man can know Jesus Christ except by the revelation of the Father.[i] Even faith also, by which the soul lays hold upon Christ, if it is right and good faith, must be wrought by the exceeding greatness of His mighty power. I perceive, poor Ignorance, that you are also ignorant of how true saving faith works its effects in the life of a true believer.[j] Wake up, see your own wretchedness, and fly to the Lord Jesus. He is the righteousness of God, for He Himself is God. Only by believing in His righteousness will you be delivered from condemnation."

"You are going too fast," Ignorance complained. "I cannot keep pace with you. You go on ahead. I must stay behind for a while."

Then they said, "Well, Ignorance, will you remain foolish? Will you ignore the good counsel given to you over and over again? And if you still refuse it, you shall know before very long the evil of your doing so. Remember, good counsel that is taken can save you, so listen to us. But if you disregard it, you will be the loser, Ignorance. We promise you that."

Then Christian addressed Hopeful. "Come, my good Hopeful. I perceive that you and I must walk by ourselves again."

So I saw in my dream that they went on ahead, and Ignorance came hobbling after them. Then Christian said to his companion, "I pity this poor man; it will not go well for him in the end."

"What a shame!" Hopeful lamented. "There is an abundance of people in our town in his same condition, entire families and even entire streets, and some are pilgrims. And if there are so many in our town, just think how many there must be in the place where Ignorance was born!"

Christian added, "Indeed, the Word says, 'He has blinded their eyes, lest they should see.'[k] But now that we are by ourselves, tell me what you think of such men. Do you think that they have ever felt the weight of conviction of their sin and the consequent fear that they might be in a dangerous state?"

---

[i] Matthew 11:27.
[j] 1 Corinthians 12:3; Ephesians 1:18–19.
[k] John 12:40.

"I would prefer you answer the question yourself, since you're my elder and more experienced," Hopeful stated.

Christian continued, "I believe that they may sometimes come under the conviction of sin; but being naturally ignorant, they do not understand that such conviction is for their good. Therefore they desperately seek to stifle them and presumptuously continue to flatter themselves that their way of thinking in their own hearts is correct."

"I believe that you are right and that fear would do these men much good in truly preparing them to go on this pilgrimage," Hopeful agreed.

Christian said, "Without a doubt the right fear can be a good thing, for as the Word says, 'The fear of the Lord is the beginning of wisdom.'"[1]

"How would you describe right fear?" Hopeful inquired.

Christian explained, "True or right fear can be known by three things. First, by what causes it: the right kind of fear is caused by saving conviction of sin. Secondly, a good fear drives the soul to quickly lay hold of Christ for salvation. And thirdly, this fear begins and sustains in the soul a great reverence for God, His Word, and His ways. It keeps the soul tender, making it afraid to turn right or left from His Word and ways. It makes the soul sensitive to anything that might dishonor God, grieve the Spirit, or cause the enemy to speak against God."

Hopeful stated, "Well said. I believe you have told the truth. Are we almost past the Enchanted Ground?"

"Why, are you tired of this discourse?"

"No," Hopeful said, "truly I just wanted to know where we are."

"We have a little over two miles farther to go. But let's get back to our conversation." Christian continued, "Now the ignorant do not understand that the conviction of sin that makes them fearful is for their own good, and so they try to stifle all such fears."

"How do they try to stifle them?" Hopeful asked.

[1]Proverbs 1:7; 9:10; Psalm 111:10; Job. 28:28.

Christian answered, "First of all, they think that those fears are caused by the Devil (even though they are caused by God); and so they resist them as they would anything else they consider destructive. Secondly, they also think that these fears would spoil their faith, when the truth is that these poor men have no real faith to spoil. So they harden their hearts against all such fears. Thirdly, they presume they ought not to fear; and therefore despite their fear they behave in willful self-confidence. Last of all, they see that those fears tend to take away their own personal merit that they imagine they have as a result of their pitiful old self-holiness, and therefore they resist them with all their might."

Hopeful stated, "I know something of this myself, for before I knew better, it was so with me."

"Well, we will leave the topic of our neighbor Ignorance for the time being and discuss another profitable question," Christian suggested.

"Gladly," Hopeful agreed, "but you begin."

"Did you know a man named Temporary who lived in your parts about ten years ago?" Christian asked. "He was a devoutly religious man back then."

Hopeful replied, "Oh, yes, I did know him. He lived in the town of Graceless about two miles away from the town of Honesty. He lived next to Mr. Turnback."

"Right," Christian said. "Those two lived under the same roof. Well, that man was at one time much awakened to the seriousness of his own sin and of the wages that were due them."

"I think you are right," Hopeful confirmed, "for my house was only three miles from him, and he would often come to visit me when in distress and full of tears. Truly I pitied the man and was not altogether without hope for him. But then again, not every one who cries, 'Lord, Lord' . . ."

Christian went on, "He told me once that he was resolved to go on pilgrimage as we are now. But all of a sudden he grew acquainted with Mr. Save-Self, and then he became a stranger to me."

"Since we are talking about him, let's discuss the reasons why he and others like him suddenly backslide," Hopeful suggested.

"That would be a profitable discussion. You begin."

"Well then, there are in my judgment four reasons for it," Hopeful asserted. "The first reason would be that though the consciences of such men are awakened, their minds are not changed. Thus when the power of guilt fades away and those things that provoked them to be religious stop, they naturally turn to their own course again. It is like the sick dog who vomits what he has eaten and casts it all out, not because he has a mind to do so, but only because his stomach is upset. When the upset stomach goes away, the dog returns to his vomit and licks it up, and so it is true, as is written, 'The dog is turned to his own vomit again.'[m] I conclude that if they long for Heaven only by virtue of their fear of the torments of Hell, then as their sense of Hell and the fears of damnation chill and cool, so do their desires for Heaven and salvation cool also. So then it comes to pass that when their guilt and fear are gone, their desires for Heaven and happiness die, and they return to their former ways again.

"A second reason for backsliding is that they have slavish fears that control them. I am talking about the fears that they have of men, for 'the fear of man brings a snare.'[n] So then, though they seem to long earnestly for Heaven while the flames of Hell are about their ears, yet when that terror is over, they have second thoughts. They begin to think that it is good to be 'wise' in the worldly sense and not run the hazard of losing it all, or at the very least of bringing themselves into avoidable and unnecessary troubles. Because of their fear of what man might do to an honest pilgrim, they fall in with the world again.

"The next reason for backsliding is the shame that attends true religion, which makes it a stumbling block to them. They are proud and haughty and consider true religion to be low and contemptible.

---

[m]2 Peter 2:22.
[n]Proverbs 29:25.

When they have lost their sense of Hell and wrath to come, they return to their former course.

"Lastly, the guilt and terror that come to mind as they consider their own miserable condition is something that grieves them. But it does not cause them to fly to Christ for safety; no, instead it causes them to try to avoid all such terrible thoughts. When their awakening to the terrors and wrath of God fade away, then they choose ways that will harden them to any such awakening in the future."

Christian said, "You have summed it up well. At the bottom of it all is the simple truth that these men never change their will or their mind. That is, they never truly repent. They are like the criminal who stands before the judge quaking and trembling. He seems to genuinely repent, but at the bottom of it all is a fear of prison, not any real remorse for his crimes. If he is set free, he will return to his criminal activity. If his mind had truly been changed, he would stop being a criminal."

"Now that I have shown you the reasons for their backsliding, you show me the manner in which they do it," Hopeful challenged.

"I will," Christian agreed. "First of all, the backsliders resist all thoughts of God, death, and the judgment to come. Thus, to continue this resistance, they begin by degrees to cast off private duties such as closet prayer, curbing their lusts, watching their souls, grieving over their sin, and the like. They also begin to shun the company of lively and warm Christians.

"After this mostly private resistance, they then grow cold to their public duties such as hearing God's Word preached, reading the Bible, and assembling together with other Christians. They start to abandon the assembly of believers, finding fault with other Christians, often naming them hypocrites, in order to provide an excuse for leaving them.

"Having abandoned the fellowship of the saints, they then begin to draw close to and associate themselves with fleshly, loose, greedy, lewd, and unruly men. This new company tempts them to give way to fleshly and lewd practices, at first in secret. They are glad if they can find any fault or sin in those they once considered honest, using them as an excuse and example to justify their own sins.

"After this season of private sin, they begin to play with certain sins openly. Finally then, being hardened, they show themselves for what they are. Then they are launched again into the gulf of misery, and unless a miracle of grace prevents it, they perish forever in their own deceit."

Chapter Fifteen

Home in the Celestial City

Now I saw in my dream that by this time the pilgrims had passed over the Enchanted Ground and entered into the country of Beulah, whose air was very sweet and pleasant.¹ Since the way went directly through Beulah, the pilgrims found comfort and relief as they traveled through this country.ª Here they heard the continual singing of birds, saw flowers appear on the earth, and heard the voice of the turtledove in the land.ᵇ In this country the sun shone night and day.² Beulah was beyond the Valley of the Shadow of Death and also out of the reach of Giant Despair, nor could they even see Doubting Castle from this place.

Here they were within sight of the City to which they were going. They also met some of the inhabitants of the country, for in this land the Shining Ones commonly walked because it was upon the borders of Heaven.³ In this land also the contract between the bride and the Bridegroom was renewed: "As the bridegroom rejoiceth over the bride, so did their God rejoice over them."ᶜ Here they had no lack of bread or wine, for in this place they met with an abundance of

---

ªIsaiah 62:4.
ᵇSong 2:10–12.
ᶜIsaiah 62:5.

what they had sought during all their pilgrimage.[d] Here they heard voices from outside the City, loud voices proclaiming, "Say ye to the daughter of Zion, 'Behold, thy salvation cometh! Behold, His reward is with Him!'"[e] Here all the inhabitants of the country called them "the holy people, the redeemed of the Lord, those sought out."[f][4]

Now as they walked in this land, they rejoiced more than they had in any other part of the journey. And as they came near the Celestial City, they could see that it was built of pearls and precious stones and that the streets were paved with gold. The natural glory of the City and the sunbeams' reflection on it made Christian feel sick with desire. Hopeful also had a few bouts of the same sickness. The sickness was so great that they had to rest from their journey while crying out because of the deep pangs of desire: "If ye find my Beloved, tell Him that I am sick with love."[g]

Finally they got some of their strength back and were able to bear their sickness. As they walked on their way, coming even nearer to the City, they came upon orchards, vineyards, and gardens that were opened to the highway. It was there that they saw a gardener standing in the path. The pilgrims asked him, "Whose lovely vineyards and gardens are these?"

He answered, "They are the King's and are planted here for His own delight, and also for the solace of pilgrims." So the gardener invited them into the vineyards and told them to refresh themselves.[h] He also showed them the King's favorite walkways and the arbors; and here they tarried and slept.

Now I beheld in my dream that during this time Christian and Hopeful talked more in their sleep than they ever did during the entire journey. The reason for this is that the grapes of these vineyards go down so sweetly that they cause the lips of those who sleep to speak.

So I saw that when they awoke, they prepared to go up to the

[d]Isaiah 62:8.
[e]Isaiah 62:11.
[f]Isaiah 62:12.
[g]Song 5:8.
[h]Deuteronomy 23:24.

City.[5] But the reflection of the sun upon the City (for "the city was pure gold"[i]) was so extremely glorious that they could not behold it without covering their eyes. They could only see it by looking through an instrument made for just that purpose.[j] So I saw that as they went on, they met two men whose raiment shone like gold and whose faces shone as the light.

These men asked the pilgrims where they came from, and they told them. They also asked them where they had lodged, what difficulties and dangers, what comforts and pleasures they had met on the way. After listening to their answers, the men who met them said, "You have only two more difficulties to overcome, and then you are in the City."

Then Christian and his companion asked the men to go along with them, so they told them they would. "But," they said, "you must enter the City by your own faith." So I saw in my dream that they went on together until they came within sight of the gate.

Now between them and the gate was a river, but there was no bridge to go over, and the river was very deep. At the sight of this river, the pilgrims were stunned. Then the men who went with them said, "You must go through the river or you cannot enter into the City at the gate."

The pilgrims then began to inquire if there were no other way to the gate, to which they answered, "Yes, but there have only been two, Enoch and Elijah, permitted to tread that path since the foundation of the world. And no one else will be permitted to go that way until the last trumpet shall sound."[k6]

Then the pilgrims, especially Christian, began to despair in their minds. They looked this way and that, but no way could be found to escape the river.

Then they asked the men if the waters were deep everywhere all the time. They told them that sometimes the water was shallow, but that they could not guide them in that matter since the

---

[i]Revelation 21:18.
[j]2 Corinthians 3:18.
[k]1 Corinthians 15:51–52.

waters were deep or shallow depending upon their faith in the King of the place.

Then they waded into the water, and upon entering, Christian began to sink. He cried out to his good friend Hopeful, saying, "I am sinking in deep waters; the billows are going over my head, all his waves go over me! Selah."[l]

Then Hopeful said, "Be of good cheer, my brother. I feel the bottom, and it is good."

Then Christian cried out, "Ah, my friend! 'The sorrows of death have compassed me about.'[m] I shall not see the land that flows with milk and honey."

With that a great darkness and horror fell upon Christian, so that he could not see ahead.

It was then that Christian lost his senses, and his memory failed him, and he could not talk in an orderly fashion of any of those sweet refreshments that he had met with in the way of his pilgrimage.

All the words that he spoke were filled with horror, and he feared that he should die in that river and never obtain entrance at the gate. He was greatly troubled by thoughts of his past sins, committed before and during his pilgrimage. It was also observed that he was troubled with apparitions of hobgoblins and evil spirits, which he continually spoke about.

It was everything that Hopeful could do to keep his brother's head above water. Sometimes Christian, despite all Hopeful's help, would slip down into the waters and rise up again half-dead.

Hopeful continually tried to comfort him, saying, "Brother, I see the gate, and men standing by to receive us."

But Christian would answer, "It is you, it is you they wait for. You have been Hopeful ever since I knew you."

"And so have you," Hopeful said to Christian.

---

[l]Psalm 69:2.
[m]Psalm 18:5.

Christian and Hopeful cross over the River of Death.

Christian answered, "If things were right with me, He would now come to help me, but because of my sin He has brought me to this snare, and He will leave me here."

Then said Hopeful, "My brother, you have forgotten the text where it is said of the wicked, 'There are no bands in their death; but their strength is firm. They are not in trouble as other men, neither are they plagued like other men.'[n] These troubles and distresses that you are going through in these waters are not a sign that God has forsaken you but are sent to try you, to see if you will call to mind all the goodness that you have received from Him. You are being tested to see if you will rely on Him in your distress."

Then I saw in my dream that Christian was in a bewildered stupor for a while. Hopeful spoke to Christian, encouraging him to "Be of good cheer," reminding him that Jesus Christ would make him whole.

With that Christian shouted out with a loud voice, "Oh, I see Him again, and He tells me, 'When you pass through the waters, I will be with you; and through the rivers, they will not overflow you.'"[o8]

Then they both took courage and crossed the river, and the enemy was as still as a stone. Christian soon found solid ground to stand on, and the rest of the river was shallow. So Christian and Hopeful crossed over the river and arrived on the other side. As soon as they came out of the river, they saw the two shining men again waiting for them. The men saluted the two pilgrims saying, "We are ministering spirits, sent here to minister to those who shall be heirs of salvation."[p] Then they all went along together toward the gate.

Now though the City stood upon a mighty hill with its foundations higher than the clouds, the pilgrims went up with ease, agility, and speed because the ministering spirits supported their arms as they led them. Also, they had left their mortal garments behind

---

[n]Psalm 73:4–5.
[o]Isaiah 43:2.
[p]Hebrews 1:14.

them in the river, for though they had gone in with them, they had come out without them.

They went up through the regions of the air, sweetly talking as they went, being comforted because they had safely crossed over the river and had such glorious companions to assist them.

They spoke about the glory of the place with the Shining Ones, who replied that the beauty and glory of it was inexpressible.[9] Then they said that it was "'Mount Zion, the heavenly Jerusalem, the innumerable company of angels, and the spirits of just men made perfect."[q] "You are going now," they said, "to the Paradise of God, wherein you shall see the tree of life and eat of its never-fading fruits. When you come there, you shall have white robes given to you, and you shall walk and talk every day with the King, even all the days of eternity.[r] There you shall not see again such things as you saw when you were in the lower region upon the earth. You will not see sorrow, sickness, affliction, and death, 'for the former things are passed away.'[s] You are now going to Abraham, Isaac, and Jacob and to the prophets, men whom God has taken away from the evil to come and who are now resting upon their beds, each one walking in his righteousness."[t]

Christian and Hopeful asked, "What must we do in the holy place?"

The Shining Ones answered, "You must receive the comforts of all your toil and have joy for all your sorrow; you must reap what you have sown, even the fruit of all your prayers, tears, and sufferings in your journey for the King. In that place you must wear crowns of gold and enjoy the perpetual sight and vision of the Holy One, for 'there you shall see Him as He is.'[u] There also you shall serve Him continually with praise, shouting, and thanksgiving, Him whom you desired to serve in the world, though with much difficulty, because of the infirmity of your flesh. There your eyes shall

[q]Hebrews 12:22–24.
[r]Revelation 2:7; 3:4; 22:5.
[s]Revelation 21:4.
[t]Isaiah 57:1–2; 65:17.
[u]1 John 3:2.

be delighted with seeing, and your ears with hearing the pleasant voice of the Mighty One. There you shall enjoy your friends again, those who have gone before you, and there you shall with joy receive all those who follow you to this holy place.

"You shall also be clothed with glory and majesty and ride with the King of glory in His royal carriage. When He shall come with the sound of the trumpet in the clouds, as upon the wings of the wind, you shall also come with Him. And when He shall sit upon the throne of judgment, you shall sit by Him. Yea, and when He passes sentence upon all the workers of iniquity, whether angels or men, you also shall have a voice in that judgment, because they were His and your enemies.ᵛ Also when He shall again return to the City with the sound of the trumpet, you shall go too and be ever with Him."

Now while they were thus drawing toward the gate, a company of the heavenly host came out to meet them, to which the Shining Ones who attended Christian and Hopeful said, "These are the men who have loved our Lord when they were in the world and who have left all for His holy name. He has sent us to fetch them, and we have brought them to the very place they have desired to be, that they may go in and look their Redeemer in the face with joy."

Then the heavenly host gave a great shout, saying, "Blessed are they who are called unto the marriage supper of the Lamb."ʷ There came out also at this time to meet them several of the King's trumpeters, clothed in white and shining raiment. They made loud, melodious noises that made the heavens echo with their sound. With shouting and the sounds of trumpets, these trumpeters saluted Christian and his companion with ten thousand welcomes.

After this they surrounded them on every side. Some went before, some behind, some on the right hand, some on the left (so as to guard them through the upper regions), continually making majestic sounds as they went, with melodious noise, in notes on

---

ᵛ1 Thessalonians 4:13–17; Jude 14; Daniel 7:9–10; 1 Corinthians 6:2–3.
ʷRevelation 19:9.

high. To anyone looking, it would have appeared that Heaven itself had come down to meet them.

And so they walked on together, and as they walked, the trumpeters mixed their joyful music with looks and gestures that signified to Christian and Hopeful how welcome they were in their company. They never stopped telling them how glad they were to meet them.

As the two pilgrims approached Heaven, it seemed to them that they were being swallowed up with the sight of angels and the sound of their melodious music. And it was then that the City itself came into their view, and they thought they heard all the bells in the City ringing to welcome them. But above all, they had warm and joyful thoughts about living there with such company, and that forever and ever. O by what tongue or pen can their glorious joy be expressed! And so they came up to the gate.

Now, when they had come up to the gate, they saw written over it in letters of gold, "Blessed are they who do His commandments, that they may have the right to the tree of life and may enter in through the gates into the City."[x]

Then I saw in my dream that the shining men told them to call at the gate. When they did, Enoch, Moses, and Elijah looked down from over the gate. It was then that someone said to those great men of God, "These pilgrims have come from the City of Destruction for the love that they have for the King of this place." Then Christian and Hopeful gave them their certificates that they had received in the beginning.

The certificates were carried in to the King, who, when He had read them, said, "Where are these men?"

"They are standing outside the gate," came the answer.

The King then commanded them to open the gate, "that the righteous nation," said He, "which keepeth the truth may enter in."[y]

Now I saw in my dream that Christian and Hopeful went in

---

[x]Revelation 22:14.
[y]Isaiah 26:2.

through the gate, and as they entered, they were transfigured and clothed with raiment that shone like gold. There they were met by others with harps and crowns, who gave them harps with which to praise and crowns in token of the King's honor.

Then I heard in my dream all the bells in the City ringing out for joy. Then Christian and Hopeful were told, "Enter ye into the joy of your Lord."

I also heard Christian and Hopeful sing with a loud voice, "Blessing and honor and glory and power be unto Him that sitteth upon the throne, and unto the Lamb, forever and ever."[z]

Now just as the gates were opened to let them in, I looked in myself, and I saw the City shining like the sun. The streets were paved with gold, and on them walked many men with crowns on their heads, palms in their hands, and golden harps to sing praises. There were also among them winged angels, and they shouted to one another continually, proclaiming, "Holy, holy, holy, is the Lord."[aa] And after that, they shut up the gates. Having seen what was inside the gates, I wished that I could join them.

Now while I was looking at all these things, I turned my head to look back and saw Ignorance approaching the river. He crossed without any of the difficulty that Christian and Hopeful had since there was a ferryman named Vain-Hope ready to take him across in his boat.

Once Ignorance arrived on the other side of the river, he ascended the hill just like Christian and Hopeful, except that no one had come to meet him or give him any encouragement as he made his way to the City. When he had come up to the gate, he looked up and read what was written above it. He then began to knock, supposing that he would quickly be invited in.

But instead of the gates opening, he was asked by the men who looked over the top of the gate, "Where did you come from? What do you want?"

---

[z]Revelation 5:13.
[aa]Revelation 4:8.

Ignorance is deposited in Hell.

Ignorance answered, "I have eaten and have drunk in the presence of the King, and He has taught in our streets." Then they asked him for his certificate, so that they might go in and show it to the King. Ignorance fumbled in his pockets but found nothing. Then they asked, "Don't you have a certificate?" Ignorance made no reply, not a word.

So they told the King, but He would not come down to see him. He commanded the two Shining Ones who had conducted Christian and Hopeful to the City to go out and take Ignorance away, binding him hand and foot. Then they took him up and carried him through the air to the door that I saw in the side of the hill, and in there they put him.

Then I saw that there was a way to Hell from the gates of Heaven as well as from the City of Destruction![10]

So I awoke, and behold, it was a dream.

THE CONCLUSION

Now, Reader,
I have told my dream to thee;
See if you can interpret it to me,
Or to yourself, or to your neighbor; but take heed
Of misinterpreting; for that, instead
Of doing good, will but thyself abuse:
By misinterpreting, evil ensues.

Take heed also, that thou be not extreme,
In playing with the outside of my dream:
Nor let my figure or similitude
Put thee into laughter or a feud.
Leave this for boys and fools; but as for thee,
Do thou the substance of my matter see.

Pull aside the curtains, look within my veil,
Turn over my metaphors, and do not fail;
There, if thou seekest them, such things thou wilt find,
As will be helpful to an honest mind.

What of my dross thou findest there? Be bold
To throw away, but yet preserve the gold;
What if my gold be wrapped up in ore?
None throws away the apple for the core.
But if thou cast all away as vain,
I know not but it will make me dream again.

EDITOR'S NOTES

Chapter One: Pilgrim's Great Distress

1. With all its temporary delights and momentary distractions, to Bunyan the world was a *wilderness*. This is an allusion to the dismal wanderings of Israel in the Sinai desert, where the soul became parched in the withering heat of unbelief. The *cave* was Bedford County Jail, where Bunyan spent twelve long years of his life because of his ardent stand against the stifling authoritarianism of the church-state, which returned in 1660 under the rule of Charles the Second.

2. His clothing of *rags* illustrates that his own righteousness was no better than filthy rags. *His face turned away from his own house* teaches us that the man is looking for help, but this help will not come from his family or from anyone in the city from which he seeks to escape.

3. The *book* the man is reading is the Word of God, the Bible. It has become both the focus of and the reason for his current state of perplexity and distress. The *heavy burden* on his back is his awakened knowledge and sense of his own sin. The man discovers the frightful condition of his heart, which provokes genuine and constant fears of damnation. These fears are an ever-present weight upon his entire person.

4. Christian's first reference to *Heaven* is fearsome and foreboding—the place from which fire falls. He is certain this fire will someday consume and destroy his city, his family, and himself. No promise is found in the book he reads, only certain doom—unless, by a way yet hidden to him, he might escape.

5. Christian's family is confused and alarmed by what they consider the eccentric and unwarranted concerns that Christian now has for the condition and final destination of his eternal soul. They think he has caught some "religious disease" and *is losing his mind*.

6. Christian's first mention of *praying* forecasts the genuineness of the work being done in his heart. To be sure, he is praying for relief from his own misery, but only after he prays for his wife and children. Christian is full of pain but also full of pity. "Graceless" has already begun to fade as "Christian" emerges.

7. Christian's first question, *"What shall I do?"* now flowers into the only question that can successfully launch his journey, *"What shall I do to be saved?"* This question is predicated by his impending sense of danger, his humbled posture under the burden of sin, and his deep desire to receive guidance that will result in both deliverance and peace. If he seeks God's face, it is a muted desire, temporarily overshadowed by his preoccupation with the tragic condition that fills his consciousness with fear and dread.

8. Then Christian meets *Evangelist*. Our current notion of an evangelist probably does not match what Bunyan had in mind. The model for this character was probably Pastor John Gifford of Bedford, an earnest and faithful minister of the gospel. Evangelist is a pastor with compassion for lost souls. He is well-instructed in the saving truths that are only found in God's Word. He does not press unbelievers for a quick decision based on an emotional appeal. Evangelist is a serious man, determined to perform the task of directing sinners to the Savior with a solemn clarity informed only by the "best of books," as it is referred to later, the very Bible that Christian holds in his hands.

9. Evangelist unrolls and reads from the *parchment* the only message that will successfully direct Christian to the Celestial City. The parchment represents the Bible, and in particular those truths in it that implore sinners to repent of their sins and *"Flee from the wrath to come."* Evangelist is imploring Christian to escape by the only way prescribed by God and available to poor sinners, Jesus Christ the Savior. It is He alone who rescues sinners from the wrath of God. Unfortunately, Christian is still blind to this truth.

10. We can imagine Evangelist asking Christian if he understands the good news. Does Christian understand the mystery of the saving work accomplished on the cross of Christ? Does he see, even when squinting, the relief that can be found in Christ alone? The answer is no.

11. When Evangelist asks Christian, *"Do you see the distant narrow gate?"* he is asking Christian if he understands that Jesus Christ is the only way by which people can enter the place where they will find rest for their souls, forgiveness of sins, and the certain hope of eternal life. In short, does he understand the good news revealed in the book he holds?

Christian again answers, "No." The mercy found only in Christ could not be seen or understood by poor Christian. The door that one must enter in order to find peace with God was outside the realm of his understanding. Christ, the only way to God the Father, is a narrow gate that most men will never find or enter. Without further revelation Christian is left with a desire to flee from certain wrath, yet with no place of safety to which he can retreat.

Evangelist is not discouraged by Christian's answer and quickly asks Christian, *"Do you see the distant shining light?"* Evangelist is asking if Christian perceives any glimmer of hope as he reads the illuminating Word of God. The answer Christian gives is the first encouraging sign as Christian responds, "I think I do."

12. Christ cannot be found without the Word, and so Evangelist tells Christian to *"Keep that light in your eye, and go up directly toward it, and soon you will see the narrow gate."* In other words, keep reading the Bible until in it the Son of God is revealed to you.

How could Evangelist be sure that Christian would find Christ as the reward for his faithful and urgent reading of God's Word? The answer is not presumptuous but rather that Evangelist, being a doctor of the soul, recognized in Christian the genuine working of the Holy Spirit, who had already enlightened poor Christian to his miserable and dangerous condition.

Evangelist did not try to interfere with Christian's struggle or attempt to end his misery. Instead he recognized the good work that had begun in Christian, and with reverence for God's perfect way of dealing with sinners, he simply encouraged Christian to keep reading the very book that had awakened him to his dark and desperate condition.

13. The actions of *Obstinate* and *Pliable* confirm the simple lesson that the world does not easily or readily give up its citizens. Obstinate represents the intolerant class of people who think it foolish and senseless to give up all the comforts of this world for what they are convinced is nothing more than a fanciful delusion and a waste of time. According to Obstinate, our loyalties should be only to this world—its friendships, opportunities, riches, security, and approval. Obstinate believes the Word of God is unreliable and misleading and pleads for Christian to put his trust in the wisdom that comes from this world rather than in the wisdom that comes from Heaven.

Pliable represents a different class of people. He is a rudderless ship, a man with mush for a backbone and a faltering will. He has no sense of his own moral failings and lacks anything that would act as a compass for his soul. He is windswept and wave-tossed. He is moved by the moment like butter on a hot plate—easily persuaded and just as easily offended.

14. As Pliable and Christian find themselves walking together toward the narrow gate, we see the stark contrast between the two pilgrims. One is burdened; the other is not. One is clutching a book that is a light to his path. The other is guideless. One is on the journey in pursuit of deliverance from besetting sins and rest for his soul. The other is on the journey in order to obtain future delights that temporarily dazzle his mind. One is slow and plodding because of his great weight and a sense of his own unrighteousness; the other is light-footed and impatient to obtain all the benefits of Heaven. One is in motion because his soul has been stirred up to both fear and hope; the other is dead to any spiritual fears,

longings, or aspirations. One is seeking God; the other is seeking self-satisfaction. One is a true pilgrim; the other is false and fading.

15. It is not surprising that a simple test would separate these two pilgrims forever. Pliable is like the seed that falls on rocky ground in which there is no root or hope of persistence. When the sun blazes hot or the cold winds blow, this rootless plant will wither and blow back to the weed patch that first cradled it.

The opportunity to test these two pilgrims comes in the form of a great miry patch of unsolid ground called the *Swamp of Despond*. After a time of wallowing in this bog and becoming completely shamed by the filth and dirt that polluted that place, Pliable comes to the end of his patience. His dignity disturbed and in a bad temper, Pliable rebukes Christian and struggles out of the mire on the side closest to his own house and nearest to the City of Destruction.

The Swamp of Despond is that place set before the narrow gate where true and false pilgrims alike are assaulted by their own internal corruption and pollution. The dirt and scum that has attached itself to our hearts and minds is agitated and revealed by both the workings of a guilty conscience and the devouring avarice of the enemy of our souls.

The purpose of the Swamp of Despond is to discourage the pilgrim from going forward by putting him in a place that is so vile as to persuade the pilgrim that going forward is too humiliating and ultimately futile. The Swamp of Despond is there to cause despair and shake any conviction that our hope lies just ahead.

The great enemy of grace is the strict accounting of our sin and corruption that when added up totals such a staggering debt that no person without faith in the sure promises of God would ever dare calculate that anything good awaits him and would further be convinced that all that does lie ahead is a complete foreclosure of his soul and all its contents.

Pliable, forced to do the sums while ankle-deep in the Swamp of Despond, is immediately offended by the prospect of his own wickedness and guilt. If the journey begins with this bitter and reprehensible sort of self-disclosure, he calculates it will end only in failure and humiliation.

16. Christian sinks deeper and deeper into the Swamp as he struggles with all his might to get to the side of the Swamp farthest away from the City of Destruction and closest to the narrow gate. Seeing himself as God sees him leaves him deeply discouraged. But even in this hopeless and sinking condition, a glimmer of promise encourages him to move in the direction of the God whose verdict upon his life he now accepts.

17. *Help* arrives on the solid ground outside the swamp with a question and a helping hand: *"Why didn't you look for the steps?"* With fear's full fury blurring Christian's vision, he could not see the steps. What are the steps? They are nothing other than the astounding promises of God. Christian's heart is so filled to overflowing with the fog of fear that he cannot discern the mighty promises that God has made to sinners. Help represents those faithful followers of Christ who strategically station themselves to encourage those seeking to enter the narrow gate. He is the experienced Christian who says with certainty and conviction that you can trust your life to the God who has made solid and trustworthy saving promises to sin-sick sinners. God's promises are always to be relied upon and will always provide a solid footing that keeps the bubbling and belching lies of Satan under feet shod with faith!

Chapter Two: The Way of the World or the Narrow Way

1. Delivered from the Swamp of Despond and on his way to the narrow gate, Christian now crosses paths with *Mr. Worldly-Wiseman*. We discover that Mr. Worldly-Wiseman is from the town of *Carnal Policy*, which further helps clarify the person Bunyan had in mind.

2. A current version of Mr. Worldly-Wiseman is any liberal, broad-minded, and compromising person who has no regard for the atoning work of Jesus Christ and would rather

believe a "gospel" advancing morality and social reform. Note how he relishes and makes sport of undermining the biblical convictions that Christian has come so recently to rely on.

3. While Obstinate was brash and coarse in his criticism of the beliefs held by Christian, Mr. Worldly-Wiseman is much more civil and polished in his attack. He pretends sympathy when his real motivation is a hatred for all things touching on the saving work of Christ. His advice is aimed at the temporal and sensory felt needs of Christian, who is persuaded that the removal of his burden is the main aim of his pilgrimage. Mr. Worldly-Wiseman's goal is to focus on the newly awakened feelings that trouble Christian. His goal is to persuade Christian that the elimination of his sense of burden is all that stands between him and a happy ending to his misbegotten journey.

4. Christian is advised not to probe too deeply into the Word of God or to pay any heed to men such as Evangelist, since men who do are often unnecessarily awakened and alarmed to perils that Mr. Worldly-Wiseman waves off as the over-imaginings of a weak mind. All his carnal advice reflects a deep hatred for the saving work of Christ. If he is successful, Christian will loathe the cross of Christ and will be permanently inoculated from the luminous truth about both his condition and eternity.

5. The charm and subtle, seductive manners of Mr. Worldly-Wiseman quickly disarm Christian who is too inexperienced and inattentive to realize that he is being prepared to abandon God altogether and replace Him with idols of morality and legality.

6. When the desire to get rid of the sensory symptoms of sin so that one can live a life of peace and safety is the only goal, and that goal is achieved by a work other than the work of Christ, the end may be peace in this life but God's certain wrath in the world to come. Mr. Worldly-Wiseman is a friend to sinners who want to lose their sense of sin, but the sworn enemy to all who desire lasting peace and eternal life.

7. The hill represents Mt. Sinai where all the demands of the Law, including perfect obedience to them, is required in order to escape the impeccable wrath of God. Christian has already been awakened to the true sense of his own condition. As a result of the inner work of God's convicting Spirit, there is no possible way that Christian can ever again fall into a self-delusion regarding his own righteousness or ability to merit the favor of God.

8. Mr. Worldly-Wiseman is not an ancient relic of the past. He is everywhere today, disguising his heresy and error by proclaiming the gospel of contentment and peace achieved by self-satisfaction and works. If he mentions Christ, it is not as the Savior who took our place, but as a good example of an exemplary life. Do we need a good example to rescue us, or do we need a Savior? If Christian had considered this question carefully earlier, he might have avoided the nearly deadly detour that Mr. Worldly-Wiseman so confidently and cunningly recommended.

9. Who is *Good-Will*? He is a picture of Jesus Himself—God's own goodwill toward sinners—Jesus who welcomes burdened sinners with grace and mercy. It is Jesus who rescues sinners. Jesus pulls them to Himself to protect them from the *arrows* of Satan.

10. Charles Spurgeon considers the fiery arrows to include the satanic suggestion that the magnitude and nature of our sins are so egregious as to disqualify us in particular from the mercy offered in general, that the Holy Spirit has been offended too many times by our past refusals, and that too many invitations to experience grace have been mocked for us to now expect salvation.

Satan suggests that perhaps we are not one of God's elect, a weed seed that has taken root and infected many with its prickly thorns of doubt. Or perhaps we have committed the unpardonable sin. Maybe we are too insignificant to warrant the merciful attentions of the Savior. Satan has an arsenal of lies each fashioned like arrows to delay, pierce, pain, and discourage the sinner from ever seeking the Savior. The Lord Jesus invites *all* who are weary and heavy-laden to come to Him and find rest for the soul.

11. There is no question that Bunyan means for us to understand that Christian is converted upon entering the narrow gate, which is a picture of Christ. So why does Christian not lose his burden? This answer is important. Remember that the burden is not sin but Christian's sense of it.

Christian has upon entering into Christ, receiving Him with faith and trust, been legally delivered from the consequences of sin. That being an established fact does not mean that he has been delivered from his own sense of sin, and as a matter of fact Christian remains sensible to it all the same. He has a saving understanding of the work Christ did on the cross, but not a sensible experience of that work done on his behalf. In time Christian will lose his burden, but only after he, in a fuller revelation of the meaning of the cross, comes to more completely understand and apprehend the grace of God.

12. Bunyan tells the truth here. Many come to Christ with little faith and are received by Christ and are forgiven for all their sins; yet they remain in a perplexed state of guilt and shame until the day they fully grasp the grace of God. Others know and experience salvation by forgiveness and all its sensible implications without any delay.

God's grace is the most incredible and insurmountable truth ever to be revealed to the human heart, which is why God has given us His Holy Spirit to superintend the process of more fully revealing the majesty of the work done on our behalf by our Savior. He teaches us to first cling to, and then enables us to adore with the faith He so graciously supplies, the mercy of God. This mercy has its cause and effect in the work of Jesus on the cross.

13. We can thank Bunyan for telling the truth here, as many have been encouraged to know that the God who instantly justifies us is also in the process of perfecting our faith. He has begun a work, and He will complete that work in His perfect time.

14. Christian is now directed by Good-Will to the *house of the Interpreter*. By this Bunyan shows the regenerative work of the Holy Spirit who shines light on things that were previously darkened. Christian will soon receive understanding about the gospel that will fill his soul with wonder, warnings, amazement, and praise.

15. After interviewing Christian and investigating the genuineness of his conversion, the Interpreter gives Christian insight into seven profitable images of truth.

   1. A *picture* of a solemn and serious person hanging on the wall. This is the picture of a true gospel pastor. The elements of the picture are there for us to contemplate the marks of a true and faithful pastor.
   2. A *parlor* full of dust—a lesson about the difference between the Law and the gospel. One stirs up the noxious reality of sin, while the other cleanses us from its power and presence in our life.
   3. Two children named *Passion* and *Patience*. This is instruction to point out the eternal virtue of patience and the calamitous end of passion.
   4. A *fireplace*. This teaches us that the grace of God, though often hidden and out of sight, will overcome the assaults of Satan and the world.
   5. *Entering into the palace*. This is a picture of a victorious pilgrim who is preserved and given victory and entry into God's Kingdom by the grace of God.
   6. The *iron cage* is a warning to all who would make light of God's promises. This man has made an idol of remorse, despair, and bitterness, never truly crying out to the Lord for mercy because he has decided that God will not hear him or respond to him favorably. He worships his sorrow and has elevated his unbelief above the promises of God. He cannot truly repent because God withholds His mercy from those who make an idol out of unbelief.
   7. A *trembling* man. The crisp and indisputable lesson here is: be prepared for the final judgment!

All these illuminations encourage Christian to both hope and fear. As a pilgrim on the King's Highway to the Celestial City, Christian must be ready and alert.

Chapter Three: A Burden Lifted and a Journey Begun

1. The *highway* is walled on both sides to indicate that for Christian, the way forward is secure and certain. After experiencing all the uncertainties and spiritual upheaval surrounding his conversion, the path ahead is well-defined and clear. Christian is about to experience deliverance and relief from the burden that has so grieved his soul. Christian fixes his eyes on the *cross* of Christ, and his burden falls off his back.

2. Christian now perceives the atonement and knows without any doubt that Christ's redemptive work on the cross is completely sufficient to satisfy the righteous wrath of God. Christian has come to understand the heart of the gospel. The Savior's blood has accomplished for him what nothing else could—deliverance from the burden and penalty of sin.

3. For the sake of Christ, God has made peace with the pilgrim, Christian. Christian is justified and is forgiven of all his sins. Christian is stripped of his rags and is given a robe of righteousness, which represents the imputed righteousness of Jesus Christ. Christian is given a *mark* on his forehead that sets him apart from the world and marks him as a true child of God who will be preserved from divine judgment. Christian is given a *scroll* with a seal on it, which represents his temporal assurance of his new life and acceptance into the Celestial City.

4. Loosed of his burden, Christian makes his way to the bottom of the hill where he finds three men fast asleep. *Foolish* represents spiritual dullness and ignorance. *Sloth* represents spiritual laziness. *Presumption* represents spiritual pride and arrogance. The consequences of all three conditions are self-inflicted incarceration and lack of progress on the King's Highway.

5. Christian's attempt to help remedy the perilous condition of these three sleeping pilgrims is met with indifference, indolence, and intolerance. Christian, troubled by the lack of spiritual concern in the "religious" world, does his best to bring about a change, but all his efforts are scorned and rebuffed. Lesson one for the new Christian—many a careless and indifferent traveler will not survive the pilgrimage.

6. Christian meets two more ill-fated pilgrims as he continues his expedition down the King's Highway. His ability to discern a false pilgrim has been advanced since his experience with Simple, Sloth, and Presumption.

Christian immediately focuses on three things that seem out of place. First, the tumbling over the wall called Salvation without coming through Christ, the narrow gate, or experiencing any illumination by the Holy Spirit immediately warns Christian that these are trespassers. Second, their testimony of having come from the land of *Vain-Glory* warns Christian that they are neither humble nor burdened by sin. Third, their wish to arrive at Mt. Zion to *receive* praise rather than to *give* praise to the only one worthy of praise alarms Christian. Christian quickly discerns that the motives of *Formalist* and *Hypocrisy* are unworthy and contemptuous.

Formalist represents the man who performs many outward religious duties but lacks any inward conviction. The condition of his heart is of little concern to Formalist; everything is external pomp and circumstance.

Hypocrisy represents the man who has persuaded others and perhaps even himself that he is righteous. He revels in deception and making false appearances. His is a fancy religion when he is in church or among other Christians but ungodly and devilish when out of their sight—all light without any heat.

Christian notices the differences between the nature of his pilgrimage, which is accredited by the Word of God, and theirs, which is not. He is different than Formalist and Hypocrisy in how he thinks, what he loves, and what he purposes in his heart to do.

And finally Christian is uniquely different because he does not boast in his own righteousness but only in the righteousness of Christ as represented by the coat on his back. He is marked out as a child of God by the mark on his forehead and is assured of his good standing by the scroll he was given by the three Shining Ones.

7. Christian, Formalist, and Hypocrisy soon arrive at the foot of the *Hill Difficulty*. Three pilgrims, three decisions.

Formalist, facing the steepness of the Hill Difficulty, chooses the path to the left around the mountain. The path is named *Danger*. Its name indicates that this is not the straight way but is a way of great variety and many religious philosophies.

Hypocrisy, seeing that the Hill Difficulty will require more commitment than he is willing to make, chooses the path to the right, a path named *Destruction*. This pathway also represents a way that is not the straight way, also a way with a wide variety of many other religious and social philosophies.

Danger and Destruction together represent all the ways that are not the straight way, the righteous way, the Lord's way. Today they might be the ways of Socialism, New Age religions, prosperity teachings, Darwinism, Fascism, Capitalism, Self-enlightenment, materialism, hedonism, Communism, Humanism, asceticism, or anything that is not the Lord's way. These all look like shortcuts, but the end result is utter and complete destruction of the soul.

8. Running, then walking, and finally crawling, Christian arrives at a place that is meant to be a temporary resting place. Here he stops and begins to read the *scroll* for encouragement and considers the *coat* given to him. He begins to contemplate the grace he has received in the middle of great difficulties. He reviews the precious promises of God in the middle of his struggles. And then he falls into a deep sleep. The simple lesson here is that a respite should never turn into a place of retirement. God gives us seasons of rest so we can gain the refreshment needed to push forward and strive with all our might toward the prize. A simple rest can become a long slumber, which may turn into a habitual lifestyle of self-indulgence and shirking. The result is the loss of the scroll, which represents a loss of assurance of salvation.

9. *Timorous* and *Mistrust* represent fair-weather pilgrims who are anxious to reach the Celestial City until they encounter persecution. The *lions* they report represent the wicked people of this world, animated by the wicked princes of the invisible realm who are dedicated to the destruction of anything genuinely godly, those who devise plans to obstruct the cause of Christ and His gospel from outside and from inside the visible church. They persecute the saints of God with whatever means they have at hand. In some ages they have been armed with the instruments of death. In other ages they can only intimidate and cause fear and confusion.

10. During this brief trial, Christian realizes that he has lost his *scroll*. In other words, he has lost his assurance of entering into the Celestial City. He painfully retraces his steps until he finds the scroll again. The cost of indolence and carelessness is driven hard and fast into the heart of Christian, who now is forced to travel over the same ground not once but three times.

11. Christian arrives at the *House Beautiful*, which represents the true church of Christ, whether it be stationed strategically in some large stone cathedral or in the humble home of a true believer.

12. The true Christian will persevere and move forward, even when filled with fear and trepidation. Christian comes close to the lions and is fearfully frozen for a moment. But then the *porter* of the House Beautiful, named *Watchful*, representing a church leader or pastor who shepherds believers through difficulty, encourages Christian to move forward without fear since the lions are chained. In other words, there was at that time a limit on the persecution of the true church of Christ. While persecution was frightening, sometimes leading to imprisonment and financial ruin, it was rarely deadly in Bunyan's day if one kept to the path. Other generations of Christians were not so fortunate, although in the end those who have suffered deadly persecution for the sake of the gospel will be favored by the Lord.

13. Five people who question the legitimacy of his Christian testimony now interview Christian. Watchful inquires regarding his beliefs and his experience. *Discretion*, *Prudence*, *Piety*, and *Charity* all take slightly different paths of investigation. Christian is approved, and all deem his testimony genuine. His admittance into the true church of Christ is based on regeneration, not merely on an affirmation of a creed or doctrine. The new convert is tested to see if the words he professes are justified with corresponding fruit in his life. Christian's testimony has all the earmarks of an authentic conversion, and the church receives him joyfully.

14. Christian is armed for the battle ahead, all through the testimony of God's Word. The preeminent job of the church is to equip Christian for life's challenges. This requires the emphasis on being fitted with tested armor. He is tutored in the Word of God. He is encouraged to rely on the Lord alone through faith in His promises and providence. He is drilled in the doctrines of salvation and is encouraged to allow these truths to work themselves deep into his soul. He is encouraged to live righteously by having within him a righteous mind soaked in Scripture and demonstrated in right living. He is taught how to pray. He is encouraged to share his faith with those who do not have peace with God.

Chapter Four: A Fierce Battle and a Dark Valley

1. Christian is immediately put to the test by the foul fiend *Apollyon*, who is the Destroyer. Christian is about to go through a process of intense humiliation. First he is encouraged to give up his pilgrimage by a series of arguments meant to shame and discourage him; then he is enticed to retreat by the powers of intimidation and accusations. When Apollyon cannot re-conquer Christian by defeating him with strategic discussion and attacking his mind, he becomes sensual and carnal in his attacks. Apollyon's true nature emerges without any further charade as he continues the attack, provoked by his hatred for the King of the Highway.

2. Christian receives many wounds and stumbles backwards as he struggles with his own imperfections and remaining unbelief. He despairs as he is tested beyond his limits, but God intervenes. The Word of God is freshly and graciously put within Christian's mind, and believing these truths with renewed faith he is spared again by God's grace alone.

3. The Word of God gives wounded Christian the victory. God renews his hope with His own promises, and Christian gives the Destroyer a deadly thrust resulting in a mortal wound to the enemy of the pilgrim's soul. Christian on his own could not defeat Apollyon. The sword of the Word of God is the only instrument that can accomplish such a task.

4. Christian may have entered the Valley of Humiliation overconfident and puffed up with false pride, but he departs with humble reliance on the Word of God and prayerful gratitude to the Lord of the Highway who has come to his aid and saved him from the Destroyer. He goes forward with his sword drawn. He has learned his lesson and now relies consciously on God's Word for protection.

5. No sooner has Christian departed from the Valley of Humiliation than he enters *the Valley of the Shadow of Death*. This represents the counterpoint to all the excitement of the conflict in the Valley of Humiliation. It is a place of depression and solitude. It is a dark place full of moody and morbid thoughts. Everything that accompanies death fills the atmosphere of this place and stifles the soul with darkness. It is the primer for Hell, a foretaste of the doom that awaits the unfaithful and unbelieving. Everything in this place cries out in protest against the best hopes and aspirations of a believer. Why is it necessary for Christian to pass through this dismal valley?

This place is meant for Christian's growth, although at the time it is hard to see the purpose of such a place. It is always hard to see the purpose in wilderness wanderings until after they are over.

6. Christian meets two *men* who report to Christian that they have given up the pilgrimage to the Celestial City and are fleeing for their lives, in the face of hobgoblins, dragons,

satyrs, unspeakable misery, howling, yelling, and other unspeakable horrors. They are like the ten spies who returned to the children of Israel with an evil report about the Land of Promise. They are motivated by what they see and what they hear and are not persuaded of better things by the Word of God. Their final punishment will be the very misery they seek to avoid. The final end of a Christian will be peace and security, no matter what temporary trials lay just ahead.

7. We should not take lightly the horrible thoughts this place of death and destruction are meant to unveil. We are warned about the misery of death and Hell and should reflect upon its timeless torments and endless darkness in which men grope hopelessly for some relief that they are fully persuaded no longer exists.

8. Christian is certainly not unaffected by this gloomy, depressing, and frightening place, but he is determined to move through it with great care.

9. Christian chooses his steps carefully, as there was a deep *ditch* on his right side and a very dangerous *quagmire* on his left. The ditch on his right side represents error in doctrine. The quagmire on his left side represents the danger of moral failings.

10. Christian comes to the very mouth of *Hell* where he is forced to seriously consider the plight of the damned. It is here that Christian feels himself overwhelmed by all the demons of Hell. He feels fear, as he believes the devils are drawing nearer, but it is a fear that causes reflection and ultimately his defiant proclamation, *"I will walk in the strength of the Lord God."* Only then do the enemies retreat.

11. A new day comes, and with it Christian is able to clearly see the perils and hazards he has passed through. The new light also gives Christian much to be thankful for, as he views ahead with clear vision the second half of his journey. It is filled with pits and snares, traps and other perils that would have made safe passage in the dark almost impossible. This is a picture of God's perfectly timed mercies, without which no pilgrim would ever safely complete the journey.

Chapter Five: A Faithful Friend

1. Christian is about to experience fellowship with *Faithful*. The faith and hope they hold in common draws them together in a lifelong relationship. Faithful and Christian are very different in a number of ways. Faithful represents a simple, more common man than Christian. He is less complicated, less fearful, and more humble. The carnal traps of this world tempt Faithful, while Christian is more easily bent toward morbid fearfulness about his own guilt. Faithful receives the promises of God without staggering at them and thereby escapes being mired in the Swamp of Despond. But he does confess to being tempted by *Madam Wanton*, revealing a more base nature. Apollyon does not attack Faithful, but Faithful is troubled by the appeals of *Discontent* and *Shame* whose attack is aimed at his abandonment of more conventional mores.

Christian and Faithful face different challenges and difficulties in this life, Bunyan's way of kindly reminding us that God's children are not stamped out of a cookie cutter, nor are they all equally tempted and tested in the same way. They are united by the fact that they are sinners saved by grace, but the application of grace upon the hearts of men is efficient no matter how different are the scars and weaknesses that sin has shaped in the individual heart.

2. The friendship between Christian and Faithful is sealed with a helping compassionate hand, which reminds us that many of the stumbles in life are preceded by pride and vainglory, and this is precisely when the helping firm hand of friendship and concern is the most needed.

3. Faithful and Christian have at the very root of their friendship a common story of receiving grace and mercy. The textures of both testimonies are meant to intertwine, encourage, and instruct. Both pilgrims learn valuable lessons as they recount to each other the distinctive experiences that bring both personal and common enlightenment and blessing.

Declaring what God has done in the soul is the common ground that unites all Christians, no matter their background. This fellowship that has at its base the wonder and constant amazement at the gracious provision and mercy of God is unique to Christians, and proof of hearts that have been humbled by grace and rightly motivated by a wholesome fear of the Lord. The exercise is soothing, refreshing, instructive, and beneficial to both pilgrims. It is also Bunyan's way of rehearsing the basic principles of Christian discipleship and biblical truth.

4. Faithful is also a reminder of how important companionship is to the Christian walk, but not more important than the desire for eternal life that motivated Faithful to keep fleeing for his life, no matter how strong the desire for friendship.

Chapter Six: A Faith Beyond Words

1. *Talkative* represents the man or woman who delights in talking about divine things but has only theoretical knowledge of such things. No actual personal heart experience correlates to the matters they love to discuss so eloquently. They are often highly esteemed by others, but those closest to them would quickly betray a life out-of-sync with their words. The mask fashioned by fluency with all subjects divine hides their real life.

2. Talkative is not easily unmasked since he loves to discuss all that is good, biblical, and supernatural. Faithful, the less discriminating of the two genuine pilgrims, is at first taken in by the silky words and orthodoxy of Talkative. But after a little instruction by Christian, Faithful investigates the life of Talkative more closely. Once the layers of religious talk are peeled off, the exposed surface turns out to be unmarked by any genuine repentance. Talkative in the end is all vaporous talk, coexisting with a life that is unconverted and graceless.

There is a warning here for true pilgrims. Beware of the talker, but also be careful not to judge too quickly those whom God has blessed with both genuine grace and a fluency to speak of divine mercy in ways more eloquent than others. The proof is in the life—not a perfect life, but a life that both delights in divine truth and magnifies God, the only giver of the sovereign grace that always produces the truly fruitful, fragrant life.

3. Bunyan helps us further shape the character of Talkative when he tell us that he lives in *Prating-Row* with his father *Say-well*. The entire family's reputation is one of spiritual impoverishment in which there is much talk about working for the Kingdom, while nothing is actually ever accomplished. The theoretical talk is one dimension that is in constant contrast and disharmony with the behavior. The real life of Talkative is a display of brutishness, ruthlessness, stinginess, and dishonesty. The bothersome noise of religious talk grows irksome when laid upon the living score of discordant behavior. Talkative's life can be read with little confusion when the high-sounding rhetoric is set alongside the double-dealing, deceitful, self-centered, and abusive behavior that litters the path down which he has trod.

4. The conversation between Faithful and Talkative ends when Faithful challenges Talkative to show in his life the fruits of the truths he so easily talks about. This conversation exposes the matter, and the false pilgrim is soon separated from the true pilgrim.

To cry out against sin but to tolerate it comfortably in the heart is an equation that sums up the false pretense of Talkative. The work of grace in the heart offers proofs that cannot be denied. The eloquent Talkative simply lacks the experiential work of grace in his heart.

Again, Christians should be warned not to judge too quickly, since many Christians struggle with sin and surrender in the battlefield of life and often fail. The important thing to understand is that God will always produce a fruitful life in those He has conquered and occupies. The same Lord will disqualify those whose religion is only talk by ordaining that their life lacks the abundance of genuine good fruit while bad fruit abounds.

5. Christian and Faithful who are now passing through a *wilderness* are left alone to continue encouraging each other. What Bunyan may have in mind is a sense of dryness

and discouragement that comes after any lengthy encounter with ones such as Talkative. After all was said, it was a dry and weary experience. Dry conversation depresses the soul.

Chapter Seven: On Trial for the Gospel

1. *Evangelist* returns to the sides of the two pilgrims both to investigate and to encourage them to faithfully endure what lies ahead.

2. Evangelist is pictured as an astute doctor of the soul. His pastoral inquiries are motivated by a genuine interest in the well-being of the two pilgrims, and his duty is to warn and instruct them as they make the treacherous journey to the Celestial City. He is joyful about their achievements and adds perspective to their trials, which are meant to both strengthen and humble the two pilgrims.

3. His basic message is meant to put steel in their backbone and to encourage them to run the race and seek the prize of Heaven. He comes to remind them that they have an enemy who seeks to destroy them.

4. Ahead, warns Evangelist, lies *Vanity Fair*. It is a place they must go through, although dangers and tribulation await all pilgrims who enter. And, prophesies Evangelist, one of them will arrive at the Celestial City before the other. Evangelist directs Christian's and Faithfull's gaze toward the incorruptible crown that is set before them.

5. Christian and Faithful have fled the City of Destruction, only to now enter Vanity Fair. What is the difference? The answer is that Christian and Faithful have changed. They now see with Heaven's eyes the schemes, traps, enticements, and entertainments of the world in a new way. So far the journey has brought us into individual contact with the likes of Mr. Worldly-Wiseman, Obstinate, Pliable, and Madam Wanton. Now Christian and Faithful must encounter the corporate system that animates all the forces who would block the progress of a true pilgrim bound for the Celestial City. Vanity Fair is the City of Destruction, the world, dressed in its best party dress. It is the place where the most seductive attractions of the world take center stage in an attempt to steal our gaze, cool our resolve, and shake our confidence, which is to be in the God who is the maker and builder of the yet unseen city.

6. In Vanity Fair live the broad-minded, who hate the narrow and old-fashioned. It is a place where Christians are invited to rest from what is commonly seen as the over-stringent demands of Jesus Christ, where Christians are lulled into ever more carnal amusements. All of these distractions are meant to dull the sense of sin and seduce the pilgrim into becoming lukewarm in both his confession and his walk. Making concessions to sin in Vanity Fair is applauded as a sign of maturity and a pre-condition of fellowship and acceptance.

Everything in Vanity Fair is designed to detour the journey to the Celestial City by whatever means are most agreeable to the fallen heart of man. If pandering does not work, then direct attacks will accomplish the same thing in Vanity Fair.

7. No longer bewitched by the seductive enticements of Vanity Fair, *Hopeful* is convinced of the gospel's truth because of Christian and Faithful's behavior and testimony while under severe persecution. He then joins Christian on his pilgrimage. Is it not a strange matter that out of all the torment, maligning, and martyrdom designed to overwhelm and destroy Faithful, Hopeful emerges? Hopeful is first and foremost the product of the genuine testimony of the two other pilgrims. Secondly, he is the picture of his very name, Hopeful. The gospel produces hope.

Chapter Eight: Confronting Worldly Attachments

1. As Christian and Hopeful begin their journey together, they soon meet up with a character who will not immediately divulge his name. He is in fact ashamed of his name because it identifies him with the world, and he has not been able to obtain a new name, which would recommend him as a genuine pilgrim.

2. *By-ends*, we learn, is from the town of *Fair-speech* and is a nephew of *Rev. Two-tongues*. By-ends by his own confession is schooled in religious duplicity and exists on the edges of the religious establishment best known for its modern, nuanced views that keep it safe with the world while pretending to have religious affections.

3. By-ends represents the kind of man who has lifted himself up through craft and manipulation, loves all that is sophisticated and refined, and uses his religious affiliation to advance his own career. His earthy bank account is all that matters. He has no account in Heaven and no checkbook backed by true faith upon which to draw.

4. By-ends is a religious charlatan whose only purpose is to aggrandize himself, guard his worldly reputation, and gain as much vainglory as this world has to offer. He is the personification of evil motives wrapped in the robe of good intentions and charitable causes, a double-minded man.

5. The introduction of *Mr. Hold-the world*, *Mr. Money-love*, and *Mr. Save-all*, whose names describe them without need for further explanation, round out the picture of the fashionable religious frauds that should be avoided by true pilgrims at all costs.

Chapter Nine: Refreshment at God's River

1. Christian and Hopeful retire to a plain called *Ease* where *Demas*, the mine-keeper, attempts to persuade them to turn out of the way to mine for silver. Great wealth for little effort is promised. Demas represents the temptation to make a lifestyle of covetousness while still holding religious convictions. It is the idea that you can hold on to comfort and self-satisfaction in one hand with your religious principles balanced nicely in the other.

2. By-Ends, Demas, and the salt pillar of Lot's wife provide a trilogy of warnings against the perils of loving this world.

Chapter Ten: Prisoners of Despair

1. Christian, who showed good judgment in his encounter with By-ends, carelessly slips over into *By-Path Meadow* to avoid the rocky path leading to the Celestial City. What starts out as a thoughtless accommodation to sore feet and the desire to avoid small difficulties ends in near-tragedy.

2. It is not an accident that just before Christian rediscovers the *key called Promise*, Hopeful glimmers with new hope. This prompts Christian to remember how faithfully and lovingly God has preserved him in the past.

In our own circumstances, the first steps back from our doubt and despair are often gilded with the memories of how God has preserved us and kept us in the past. He who began the good work, will He not finish it? Oh, yes, a thousand times yes!

3. *Giant Despair*, his wife *Distrust*, and *Doubting Castle* can all be understood in light of the key called Promise. That key represents all the promises of God directed toward sinners who belong to His Son. But in a broader light, these promises are all God's good plans for fallen sinners revealed in His Word. In a practical sense this key epitomizes all the promises that the Holy Spirit has deposited into the heart and mind of a Christian. When a Christian devalues, ignores, depresses, or otherwise despises by neglect the sure promises of God, the seeds of doubt find a welcome place to ripen into all sorts of toxic and malicious fruit. For some it is doubts about being God's elect; for others it is the tormenting thought that they are no longer able to receive God's mercy; others begin to question God's motives and character. At the extreme, some even entertain thoughts of suicide in order to escape the overwhelming cloud of anguish and hopelessness enveloping them. All these conditions and a thousand more are symptoms that can overtake us when we ignore or neglect the mighty promises of God and His great goodness while seeking ease from the many challenges of the narrow path. God is to be worshiped, not our doubts and fears. Our doubts and fears are to be overcome by the good and sure Word of God.

Chapter Eleven: Shepherds' Warnings, Dangers Avoided

1. The *Delectable Mountains* are a type of the church, which can only be appreciated after the experiential development of spiritual maturity.

2. The shepherds are pastors, and the pastoral gifts are represented by their names *Watchful, Experience, Sincere,* and *Knowledge.* The gardens, vineyards, fountains, and bountifully textured terrain are metaphors for the richness of spirit that comes with experience in the Christian walk. They also describe the contemplation of heavenly delights that are shadows of the splendor just ahead.

3. The Delectable Mountains represent the comfort of the local church and also the place where true pilgrims are constantly cautioned about the perils that lie ahead. The *hill called Error, the mountain called Caution*, Doubting Castle, the *byway to Hell*, and finally the hill called *Clear* are all metaphors designed to both caution and to give hope to weary pilgrims.

The Delectable Mountains are also the place where Christians may reflect on past perils and on the goodness of God whose saving hand has plucked them from the pitfalls that have assailed them in the past. What better place to contemplate both the goodness and severity of the gospel.

4. The respite in the Delectable Mountains concludes with special sendoffs from the shepherds. One encouraged them to heed the exposition of God's Word by God's faithful ministers, as pictured by *a map of the way*. The second warned the pilgrims to beware of the *Flatterer*—a picture of all that deludes us and appeals to our vanity. The third warned against falling asleep on the *Enchanted Ground*. This is a constant reminder that we need to humbly keep watch over our own souls. The great danger in this place is the gradual and almost imperceptible temptation to slumber and become drowsy in the care of our heart and soul. The fourth shepherd bid them Godspeed, a genuine prayer for both safety and a speedy journey to the Celestial City.

Chapter Twelve: Faith under Attack

1. Upon continuing the pilgrimage, Christian and Hopeful soon meet *Ignorance* from the country of *Conceit*. Since the opposite of ignorance is knowledge, and the opposite of conceit is humility, an important point is about to be made. But first it must be understood that Bunyan has in mind a certain type of ignorance.

It is not an all-pervasive ignorance, as illustrated by newborn chicks that carry around with them on their heads the blinding half shell out of which they were born. Bunyan is not alluding to the ignorance of the inexperienced or dull-minded person but rather a very specific self-willed ignorance—a deliberate and willful ignorance of the saving gospel truths.

2. Bunyan shows allegorically the complete blindness and particular ignorance of the false pilgrim who seems headed for the Celestial City, ignorance buffered and encapsulated with pride and conceit. This ignorance is unassailable and cannot be penetrated with the truths of the Holy Scriptures.

3. Ignorance represents the condition of one of the largest groups of false pilgrims. This malady can be diagnosed by its outcome in the deeds and words of those afflicted. The ignorant have no need to ask directions or ever feel a twinge of doubt about their condition. Ignorance holds to everything that is good and has convinced himself of the merits of his deeds and the personal goodness of his character. As such, his journey out of the country of Conceit is not motivated by thoughts of destruction or judgment but rather the desire to exchange a good place for a better one. For Ignorance, the journey from Conceit to the Celestial City is like a pleasant walk in the park, with grassy knolls and soft turf underfoot.

We must rely only on Christ who died to deliver us from the wrath of God. It is He alone who secures us to a life that is eternal with Him. It is Christ alone in our hearts who produces humility, deep contrition, and unspeakable joy. It is Christ in us who is constantly disqualifying our pride and conceit and helps us see them as the filthy rags they are. It is through Christ that all our knowledge has its full and complete purpose. Christ alone!

4. Next we meet *Turn-Away*. After exploring the confident Ignorance, we are now directed to consider the false pilgrim in the *dark lane*. Clearly *dark lane* is a metaphor for an unenlightened soul.

5. Turn-Away is considered to be a nominal Christian, but when stripped of his exterior religiosity and piety, what lies behind the mask is an apostate, ungodly, and disloyal pilgrim who has abandoned his previous gospel confession. The fickleness and abandonment are not meant to convey the loss of true gospel conviction but rather the fact that it was never present. This is a soul that has never been illuminated by the Holy Spirit, and in the end we see hellish spirits who are about to claim their prize and occupy the temple of this poor soul. Beware of gospel pretense!

6. We are meant to compare *Little-Faith* with Turn-Away. Little-Faith is the picture of a true but sadly weak Christian. Close examination of this character is meant to caution us about making too harsh a judgment about the Christian who has found himself suffering the consequences of a weak faith, guilt, and unbelief. He is the picture of the Christian who fails to be alert and watchful, is allured by the ways of the world, and falls under the tyranny and into the traps of Satan.

7. Little-Faith loses his courage to *Faint-Heart*, is robbed by *Mistrust*, and is clubbed nearly to death by *Guilt*. The lesson is clear, and the outcome seems certain. Everything points to the total abandonment that comes with mistrust and the loss of Heaven.

8. Our salvation, for those who have come the way of the cross to Christ, is sealed by the Holy Spirit. Those redeemed by a sinless substitute may at times lose all self-confidence and may on occasion feel themselves stumbling hopelessly into *Dead Man's Lane*. The sword of protection is lost, the breastplate of righteousness battered, the shield of faith knocked from our trembling hands and unreachable, the helmet of salvation sideways on our head restricting all vision. In a word, we may find ourselves altogether hopeless.

But wait! One promise remains unassailable by the enemies of our soul. One promise is far out of our enemies' reach and towers over them like a mighty fortress. Only one promise is left, but that promise is good enough! The Lord of the Highway who has begun a good work in the soul of even the weakest, most crippled pilgrim will *never* abandon him to the enemy. Little-Faith belonged to the King, and the King is greater than all the enemies of our soul combined. He will never leave us or forsake us. In this we can have *Good Confidence* and *Great-Grace* that is greater than all our sins. Little-Faith is miraculously rescued, as are we all, by the matchless grace of God.

9. Some few may confidently march up to the gates of the Celestial City and be welcomed with much joy. Others may feebly and haltingly approach the same gate overcome with the true sense of their failings and infirmities. But for them the gates will also open, and all the tears will turn to unending praise for the Christ who came to save unworthy sinners.

We are warned by the story of Little-Faith to stay alert and vigilant, but also to remain humble. The story of Little-Faith could just as easily be our story. We should avoid any self-confidence or vain pride in our spiritual accomplishments. These achievements are *jewels* that remain in our possession only by the grace of God. Comparing ourselves confidently to the sorry likes of Little-Faith may soon cause our own humiliating defeat. As Jesus told Peter in Luke 22:31–32 (*English Standard Version*), "Simon, Simon, behold, Satan demanded to have you that he might sift you like wheat, but I have prayed for you that your faith may not fail." Our confidence must remain exclusively in the Lord!

10. Christian and Hopeful have theologically solved the problem of Little-Faith and tested the testimony of Ignorance. Nevertheless Hopeful has bouts with smugness, while Christian becomes testy and a little arrogant in his treatment of Hopeful.

Chapter Thirteen: Flattering Enemies and Renewed Trust

1. What follows now is instructive. It is often when considering the failings of others that we come the closest to failing ourselves. While congratulating ourselves for our orthodoxy and spiritual discernment, we can easily wander ever so slightly off the straight path. *The Flatterer* appears in robes of light, is disingenuously full of congratulations for the good and steady progress made by Christian and Hopeful, and offers to guide them to the Celestial City.

2. The Flatterer is a picture of a smooth-talking false teacher. He is sly and deceptive, easily taking Christian and Hopeful on a meandering path that is meant to distance them from the Celestial City. All this is birthed by spiritual pride.

3. The *net* represents teachings not in line with Scripture. The litany of false teachings that are ensnaring mature Christian pilgrims has grown in these last days.

4. Christian and Faithful now meet *Atheist*. The most important thing to notice about Atheist is that *"his back [is] toward Zion."* The second thing we notice is the mocking laughter and belittling attitude toward anything but the tiny material world he has circumscribed with his small sensual mind. Atheist is the type that despises the Bible and the faith and hope it produces. He doesn't understand those sinners who have had the Son of God and His gracious purpose revealed to them in the pages of that most royal book.

5. Atheist is the naturalist, the humanist, the Darwinist, the scientist of unbelief, and the blasphemer. He represents that class of men that has been well instructed in the unbelief of the world and holds to it firmly and boastfully.

6. Atheist has a superior and callous spirit, always ready to debate and rebuke those of faith. His contempt for the unseen world is great and fixed. Any word of faith or hope unleashes in him a barrage of filthy bombast and prideful pronouncements. He is intolerant of anything that is spiritual and contemptuous of anyone whose faith directs them to the Celestial City. He is the very picture of the false professors who teach nothing but a hopeless, deterministic naturalism.

7. Christian soon produces the best remedy for such fellows as the self-worshiping Atheist. Distance is the remedy, and the more of it, the greater the wisdom. A word of reason is given to Atheist, the reason for the hope that presses them forward to the Celestial City. But once given, the heavenward mind should quickly seek to be about the journey toward Heaven, unbothered by the foolishness of all those who say there is no God. God is not glorified by anyone who makes an idol of unbelief and is certainly not going to promote in his true pilgrims the temptation to judge between our doubts, whether homegrown or imported from the University of Atheism, and his most Holy and Glorious Person. Let God be God and every man a liar!

8. Next we travel across the *Enchanted Ground*. This represents those periods of temporary peace and tranquility in our pilgrimage that are meant to enlarge our capacity to contemplate on the goodness of God. This time often results in the relaxation of spiritual effort, resulting in unholy indulgences and ultimately in a disability of our spiritual health, or worse. The signs that one is falling asleep on the plains of the Enchanted Ground are lukewarmness, inactivity, spiritual laziness, slothfulness, and sinking into doctrinal simplemindedness—in a word, slumbering while the spiritual house so patiently and painfully constructed burns down around one's ears.

9. This anecdote pictures vigorous interaction with spiritual truth, especially those truths that warn and caution us to run the race with patience and endurance. We are to keep awake with lively thoughts of the loving-kindness of our Lord and to keep strong ties with men and women who are the most likely to encourage and strengthen our faith, while avoiding the sleeping saints who seem to be able to snooze in a hurricane and sleep through an earthquake.

10. Recount the journey of God's special goodness to you on your pilgrimage to the Celestial City. "Awake, my soul, awake and hear my Savior's plea. Come to the living fountain and drink large drafts of the Savior."

Chapter Fifteen: Home in the Celestial City

1. On the horizon is *Beulah Land* with all its sweet and pleasant delights. Beulah Land is beyond the dark reach of all ill places, which are now simply faded, muted memories. What the Christian now affirms is God's keeping power and love for poor pilgrims.

2. This most wonderful place is where the sunshine appears to lighten the pilgrims' earthly concerns and illuminate the destination lying just ahead. Heaven's lights now beckon with a simple power that draws the soul into an indescribable panting for Paradise. This is the place where the final groaning—the constant noise of this temporal existence—is made silent by the unspeakable light and life that emanates from the shining city, whose maker and builder is God. Just a few breaths more of this temporal air, and soon the lungs will be filled with the light-infused atmosphere of the Celestial City.

3. Beulah Land is that place reserved for every Christian just before he enters the Celestial City, although many forego the glorious experience for reasons of spiritual destitution. But for the seasoned pilgrim in the sunset of his pilgrimage, Beulah Land looms lush and large with spiritual and heavenly graces.

4. This is blood-bought expectation, glory-filled anticipation, and Spirit-sealed transportation to a better country. Here all your desires are to do what will make you most ravenously happy, to glorify God with a new heart, your focus now fixed on the One whose wounds have certified your passage to Heaven. Heaven is Christ, and Christ is Heaven!

5. Without any thought of future difficulties, Christian and Hopeful seem ready to climb toward the Celestial City. With a zealous sense of their own sufficiency they move toward the Celestial City and the River of Death.

6. It is easy for us to forget that the last great enemy is death. All the vain methods to try and gloss over this great opponent are simply vain and unhelpful. We should not deceive ourselves as to the ferociousness of this last and final obstacle to the soul. Death *is* the final enemy.

7. We should not think that death will be free from trouble or pain. God is faithful in the deaths that are painless and peaceful, as well as in the ones that are full of final suffering and horror. The true believer has no guarantee that his death will be a painless slipping away. It may be anything but painless. Death is the last trial, and for some the experience will be a horrific affliction, while for others it may be a quick and relatively painless departure. In either case we can trust that the God who raised Jesus from the dead is the same God who will deliver us.

8. We who observe death will one day be called to encounter the final enemy with no way of escape, unless the Lord comes first. Christian gives us all hope that even in the River of Death, when thoughts of our own unrighteousness overwhelm and assail us for the last time, though we seem to almost drown in hopelessness, we are not without comfort or assistance.

Death is not a shallow trickling stream over which we can leap with light-footed abandon. Death is a meandering, dark, and sometimes treacherous river that seeks at every turn to interfere with our future hope. Death is the last chasm over which the soul must cross. It is the end of this life and all the hopes and dreams of this life. For those who have only dreamed dreams of this life, death is a stunning and fearful place unlike any other. No wonder the world so willfully ignores or shrouds death in fanciful language in its attempt to render it obscure and benign. We should not expect to escape the fear that death brings, but we may expect to meet those fears with faith as God gives it.

Christian faces death with despair and great anxiety, as Satan and his own memory of past sins flood his mind for the final attack on his soul. Christian finds the waters chilling, deep, and treacherous, slipping beneath them with despondency, only to be lifted up by God's gentle but firm grace.

When all seems lost, the Lord Himself through the testimony of Hopeful firmly but gently reminds Christian that he is redeemed, called by His name, that God is present in his circumstances and able to save to the utmost.

Hopeful approaches death with more cheer and courage. For him the final journey as he walks through on firm ground is less sorrowful and more peaceful.

Likewise, we should not forget Faithful whose journey through the dark river was glorious.

9. Earlier in his journey, when Pliable asked, "What company shall we have in the Celestial City?" Christian, who with little light and only an inkling of the realities of Heaven, had proclaimed, "We will be with seraphim and cherubim and creatures who will dazzle your eyes when you look at them. You will meet with thousands who have gone before us to that place. None of them are hurtful, but all of them are loving and holy, every one walking in the sight of God and standing in His presence with acceptance forever. In a word, there we will see the elders with their golden crowns. There we will see the holy virgins with their golden harps. There we will see men who were cut in pieces by the world, burnt in flames, eaten by beasts, drowned in the seas, suffering all this and more for the love they have for the Lord of the place. Everyone in that place is clothed with immortality, as with a robe."

10. Finally we are shown the frightening and sobering conclusion of the life of Ignorance. This dreary picture of Ignorance being cast into Hell is meant to add a final caution and warning to all who would seek the Celestial City. Heaven is not for everyone. It is not for those who, like Ignorance, have rejected the true gospel and substituted a gospel of self-righteousness and personal attainment. If you remain self-sufficient, then you have no hope of being received into the Celestial City but should expect Hell as your final destination.

Hell is a shocking and unpopular topic for Christians in this present age. It is no accident that Bunyan concludes *The Pilgrim's Progress* with this sobering warning to the unbeliever.

As certainly as there is a Heaven, there is a Hell. A Hell to be avoided at all costs. All worldly enterprises, ventures, trophies, offices, lands, riches, accomplishments, accommodations, powers, entertainments, applause, approval, and vanities turn to dust when weighed against the prospect of Heaven.

Finally, for those who ignore the proclamation of the gospel, a Christless eternity in Hell awaits them as certainly as God's Word is always true. Bunyan's final word is a carbon copy of our Lord's word. Repent and believe! Believe the gospel of Jesus Christ!

May you be a true pilgrim with a courageous testimony that Christ was crucified for sinners and is their Savior.

Our hope is Christ, our narrow but sure path to the Celestial City. Seek no other!

GREAT BOOKS OF THE WESTERN WORLD

28. GILBERT
    GALILEO
    HARVEY

29. CERVANTES

30. FRANCIS BACON

31. DESCARTES
    SPINOZA

32. MILTON

33. PASCAL

34. NEWTON
    HUYGENS

35. LOCKE
    BERKELEY
    HUME

36. SWIFT
    STERNE

37. FIELDING

38. MONTESQUIEU
    ROUSSEAU

39. ADAM SMITH

40. GIBBON I

41. GIBBON II

42. KANT

43. AMERICAN STATE
    PAPERS
    THE FEDERALIST
    J. S. MILL

44. BOSWELL

45. LAVOISIER
    FOURIER
    FARADAY

46. HEGEL

47. GOETHE

48. MELVILLE

49. DARWIN

50. MARX
    ENGELS

51. TOLSTOY

52. DOSTOEVSKY

53. WILLIAM JAMES

54. FREUD

GREAT BOOKS
OF THE WESTERN WORLD

ROBERT MAYNARD HUTCHINS, *EDITOR IN CHIEF*

13.

VIRGIL

MORTIMER J. ADLER, *Associate Editor*
Members of the Advisory Board: STRINGFELLOW BARR, SCOTT BUCHANAN, JOHN ERSKINE,
CLARENCE H. FAUST, ALEXANDER MEIKLEJOHN, JOSEPH J. SCHWAB, MARK VAN DOREN.
Editorial Consultants: A. F. B. CLARK, F. L. LUCAS, WALTER MURDOCH.
WALLACE BROCKWAY, *Executive Editor*

THE POEMS OF

VIRGIL

Translated into English Verse by JAMES RHOADES

WILLIAM BENTON, *Publisher*

ENCYCLOPÆDIA BRITANNICA, INC.

CHICAGO · LONDON · TORONTO · GENEVA · SYDNEY · TOKYO · MANILA

FERNALD LIBRARY
COLBY-SAWYER COLLEGE
NEW LONDON, N. H. 03257

By arrangement with OXFORD UNIVERSITY PRESS

AC
1
.G72
Vol. 13
Copy2

AC
1
G7
Vol. 13

THE UNIVERSITY OF CHICAGO

The Great Books
is published with the editorial advice of the faculties
of The University of Chicago

No part of this work may be reproduced or utilized in any form or by any means, electronic or mechanical, including photocopying, recording, or by any information storage and retrieval system, without permission in writing from the publisher.

1952
BY ENCYCLOPÆDIA BRITANNICA, INC.

COPYRIGHT UNDER INTERNATIONAL COPYRIGHT UNION

ALL RIGHTS RESERVED UNDER PAN AMERICAN AND UNIVERSAL COPYRIGHT CONVENTIONS BY ENCYCLOPÆDIA BRITANNICA, INC.

Library of Congress Catalog Card Number: 55–10322

68571

BIOGRAPHICAL NOTE

VIRGIL, 70–19 B.C.

PUBLIUS VERGILIUS MARO was born October 15, 70 B.C., on a farm on the banks of the Mincio, near Mantua in the region north of the Po. Although the province did not obtain the rights of Roman citizenship until 51 B.C., Virgil's father was of old Latin stock and already a citizen. The owner of a farm and pottery-works, he had acquired sufficient wealth to provide Virgil with the best available education.

Somewhere between the ages of ten and twelve he was sent to school at Cremona, which was then serving as winter headquarters for Caesar's armies; and Virgil was probably there when the *Gallic Wars* first appeared. After he had received the *toga virilis,* he continued his studies briefly at Milan before proceeding to Rome for the study of rhetoric, the traditional preparation for political life. He entered the school of Epidius, who also had as pupils the young Octavian and Mark Antony. But Virgil did not find rhetoric congenial, and, after pleading one case before the courts, he abandoned the forensic life for philosophy.

Virgil left Rome and became associated with "the Garden," a school of philosophy at Naples directed by Siron the Epicurean. He remained under his tutelage until the philosopher's death and is said to have inherited his villa. Poetry as well as philosophy was discussed at "the Garden," and many of the rising generation of poets gathered there to read Catullus and Lucretius and to write verses modeled upon the Alexandrians. A number of Virgil's minor poems, included in the *Appendix Vergiliana,* are thought to have been written during his student days.

There is little evidence of Virgil's activities during the tumultuous years of the Civil War. His health was never robust, and, if he was conscripted into Caesar's army, it was for a very brief period. In 42 B.C., the year of the battle of Philippi, it is known that he was "cultivating his woodland Muse." The year following, his father's land and his home were involved in the confiscations made for the benefit of the soldiers of the triumvirs. He is thought to have used his influence with powerful friends to obtain their restitution, although it is not known whether he succeeded. The event figures prominently in Virgil's first published work, the *Eclogues.*

These pastoral poems, which had been commenced at his home in the country, were completed and published in Rome when he was about thirty. They immediately established him as the most celebrated poet of the day, and Tacitus records that on one occasion when Virgil was present at a theatre where the *Eclogues* were recited, the audience arose and acclaimed him as they did the Emperor. He enjoyed the friendship and protection of powerful patrons and in addition to an income was given a house on the Esquiline near the garden of Maecenas. Here he made the acquaintance of Horace, Varius, the epic poet, and other men of letters and became the head of the group, which, under the patronage of Octavian and Maecenas, functioned as a kind of semi-official committee on literature for promoting the peace and well-being of the Empire.

The life of the city did not appeal to Virgil, and he soon withdrew to the seclusion of Campania, where he continued his writing. He may have begun the *Georgics* at the suggestion of Maecenas, who in his official capacity was interested in reviving agriculture and commending to the soldiers newly settled on the land the traditional virtues associated with the farm. Virgil worked for seven years on the 2,188 lines that compose the *Georgics*. He completed them in 30 B. C., and in the following year read the poem to Augustus on his return from Asia. The remaining years of his life were spent on the composition of the *Aeneid*.

In the *Eclogues* there is already a hint that Virgil was thinking of writing an epic: "When I tried to make a poem of warring kings, Apollo twitched my ear . . ." Even earlier, if the poems in the *Appendix Vergiliana* are his work, he had handled epic material and pondered the pre-eminence of the Julian line. And in the *Georgics* he tells of the temple he will build with Caesar "in the middle," and how he will sing of Caesar's battles and bring him lasting fame. By 25 B. C. he was at work upon his epic poem, for in that year Augustus, although involved with the campaign in Spain, wrote to Virgil requesting to see selections from it. Virgil replied: "Regarding my *Aeneas,* if I had anything worth your hearing, I would gladly send it, but the thing is so inchoate that it almost seems to me that I must have been out of my mind to have started such a work." The selections were provided two or three years later when Virgil read from the *Aeneid* to Augustus and Octavia; he was famed for his beautiful reading voice, and Octavia fainted when he recited the passage from the Sixth Book relating the death of her son, Marcellus.

In 19 B.C. the *Aeneid* was finished although not corrected, and Virgil set out for Athens, intending to pass three years in Greece and Asia, to visit the places described in the poem, and to perfect his work. At Athens he met Augustus and was persuaded to accompany him back to Italy. While visiting Megara under a burning sun, he was seized with illness, which grew rapidly worse as he continued his voyage. Realizing that death was imminent, he asked for his manuscripts which he wished to destroy. The poem was saved, it is said, only by the intervention and command of Augustus; it was published within a year of his death by Varius and Tucca, the two friends he had designated as his literary executors.

On September 21, a few days after landing at Brindisi, in Calabria, Virgil died, being then in his fifty-first year. He was buried at his own request near his villa in Naples, beneath the epitaph: *Mantua me genuit; Calabri rapuere; tenet nunc Parthenope; cecini pascua, rura, duces—* "Mantua gave me birth, Calabria took me away, and now Naples holds me; I sang of pastures, farms, leaders."

CONTENTS

THE ECLOGUES

ECLOGUE I

MELIBOEUS

You, Tityrus, 'neath a broad beech-canopy
Reclining, on the slender oat rehearse
Your silvan ditties: I from my sweet fields,
And home's familiar bounds, even now depart.
Exiled from home am I; while, Tityrus, you
Sit careless in the shade, and, at your call,
"Fair Amaryllis" bid the woods resound.

TITYRUS

O Meliboeus, 'twas a god vouchsafed
This ease to us, for him a god will I
Deem ever, and from my folds a tender lamb
Oft with its life-blood shall his altar stain.
His gift it is that, as your eyes may see,
My kine may roam at large, and I myself
Play on my shepherd's pipe what songs I will.   *10*

MELIBOEUS

I grudge you not the boon, but marvel more,
Such wide confusion fills the country-side.
See, sick at heart I drive my she-goats on,
And this one, O my Tityrus, scarce can lead:
For 'mid the hazel-thicket here but now
She dropped her new-yeaned twins on the bare flint,
Hope of the flock—an ill, I mind me well,
Which many a time, but for my blinded sense,
The thunder-stricken oak foretold, oft too
From hollow trunk the raven's ominous cry.
But who this god of yours? Come, Tityrus, tell.   *18*

TITYRUS

The city, Meliboeus, they call Rome,
I, simpleton, deemed like this town of ours,
Whereto we shepherds oft are wont to drive
The younglings of the flock: so too I knew
Whelps to resemble dogs, and kids their dams,
Comparing small with great; but this as far
Above all other cities rears her head
As cypress above pliant osier towers.

MELIBOEUS

And what so potent cause took you to Rome?

[3]

ECLOGUE I

TITYRUS

Freedom, which, though belated, cast at length
Her eyes upon the sluggard, when my beard
'Gan whiter fall beneath the barber's blade—
Cast eyes, I say, and, though long tarrying, came,
Now when, from Galatea's yoke released,
I serve but Amaryllis: for I will own,
While Galatea reigned over me, I had
No hope of freedom, and no thought to save.   *32*
Though many a victim from my folds went forth,
Or rich cheese pressed for the unthankful town,
Never with laden hands returned I home.

MELIBOEUS

I used to wonder, Amaryllis, why
You cried to heaven so sadly, and for whom
You left the apples hanging on the trees;
'Twas Tityrus was away. Why, Tityrus,
The very pines, the very water-springs,
The very vineyards, cried aloud for you.

TITYRUS

What could I do? how else from bonds be freed,
Or otherwhere find gods so nigh to aid?   *41*
There, Meliboeus, I saw that youth to whom
Yearly for twice six days my altars smoke.
There instant answer gave he to my suit,
"Feed, as before, your kine, boys, rear your bulls."

MELIBOEUS

So in old age, you happy man, your fields
Will still be yours, and ample for your need!
Though, with bare stones o'erspread, the pastures all
Be choked with rushy mire, your ewes with young
By no strange fodder will be tried, nor hurt
Through taint contagious of a neighbouring flock.   *50*
Happy old man, who 'mid familiar streams
And hallowed springs, will court the cooling shade!
Here, as of old, your neighbour's bordering hedge,
That feasts with willow-flower the Hybla bees,
Shall oft with gentle murmur lull to sleep,
While the leaf-dresser beneath some tall rock
Uplifts his song, nor cease their cooings hoarse
The wood-pigeons that are your heart's delight,
Nor doves their moaning in the elm-tree top.

TITYRUS

Sooner shall light stags, therefore, feed in air,   *59*
The seas their fish leave naked on the strand,
Germans and Parthians shift their natural bounds,

ECLOGUE I

And these the Arar, those the Tigris drink,
Than from my heart his face and memory fade.
    MELIBOEUS
But we far hence, to burning Libya some,
Some to the Scythian steppes, or thy swift flood,
Cretan Oaxes, now must wend our way,
Or Britain, from the whole world sundered far.
Ah! shall I ever in aftertime behold
My native bounds—see many a harvest hence
With ravished eyes the lowly turf-roofed cot
Where I was king? These fallows, trimmed so fair,
Some brutal soldier will possess, these fields
An alien master. Ah! to what a pass
Has civil discord brought our hapless folk!
For such as these, then, were our furrows sown!   72
Now, Meliboeus, graft your pears, now set
Your vines in order! Go, once happy flock,
My she-goats, go. Never again shall I,
Stretched in green cave, behold you from afar
Hang from the bushy rock; my songs are sung;
Never again will you, with me to tend,
On clover-flower, or bitter willows, browse.
    TITYRUS
Yet here, this night, you might repose with me,
On green leaves pillowed: apples ripe have I,
Soft chestnuts, and of curdled milk enow.   81
And, see, the farm-roof chimneys smoke afar,
And from the hills the shadows lengthening fall!

[5]

ECLOGUE II

ALEXIS

THE shepherd Corydon with love was fired
For fair Alexis, his own master's joy:
No room for hope had he, yet, none the less,
The thick-leaved shadowy-soaring beech-tree grove
Still would he haunt, and there alone, as thus,
To woods and hills pour forth his artless strains.
"Cruel Alexis, heed you naught my songs?
Have you no pity? you'll drive me to my death.
Now even the cattle court the cooling shade
And the green lizard hides him in the thorn:
Now for tired mowers, with the fierce heat spent,
Pounds Thestilis her mess of savoury herbs,
Wild thyme and garlic. I, with none beside,
Save hoarse cicalas shrilling through the brake,
Still track your footprints 'neath the broiling sun.   *13*
Better have borne the petulant proud disdain
Of Amaryllis, or Menalcas wooed,
Albeit he was so dark, and you so fair!
Trust not too much to colour, beauteous boy;
White privets fall, dark hyacinths are culled.
You scorn me, Alexis, who or what I am
Care not to ask—how rich in flocks, or how
In snow-white milk abounding: yet for me
Roam on Sicilian hills a thousand lambs;
Summer or winter, still my milk-pails brim.   *22*
I sing as erst Amphion of Circe sang,
What time he went to call his cattle home
On Attic Aracynthus. Nor am I
So ill to look on: lately on the beach
I saw myself, when winds had stilled the sea,
And, if that mirror lie not, would not fear
Daphnis to challenge, though yourself were judge.
Ah! were you but content with me to dwell.
Some lowly cot in the rough fields our home,
Shoot down the stags, or with green osier-wand
Round up the straggling flock! There you with me
In silvan strains will learn to rival Pan.   *31*
Pan first with wax taught reed with reed to join;
For sheep alike and shepherd Pan hath care.

[6]

Nor with the reed's edge fear you to make rough
Your dainty lip; such arts as these to learn
What did Amyntas do?—what did he not?
A pipe have I, of hemlock-stalks compact
In lessening lengths, Damoetas' dying-gift:
'Mine once,' quoth he, 'now yours, as heir to own.'
Foolish Amyntas heard and envied me.
Ay, and two fawns, I risked my neck to find
In a steep glen, with coats white-dappled still,
From a sheep's udders suckled twice a day—
These still I keep for you; which Thestilis
Implores me oft to let her lead away;   *43*
And she shall have them, since my gifts you spurn.
Come hither, beauteous boy; for you the Nymphs
Bring baskets, see, with lilies brimmed; for you,
Plucking pale violets and poppy-heads,
Now the fair Naiad, of narcissus flower
And fragrant fennel, doth one posy twine—
With cassia then, and other scented herbs,
Blends them, and sets the tender hyacinth off
With yellow marigold. I too will pick
Quinces all silvered-o'er with hoary down,
Chestnuts, which Amaryllis wont to love,
And waxen plums withal: this fruit no less
Shall have its meed of honour; and I will pluck
You too, ye laurels, and you, ye myrtles, near,
For so your sweets ye mingle. Corydon,
You are a boor, nor heeds a whit your gifts
Alexis; no, nor would Iollas yield,
Should gifts decide the day. Alack! alack!
What misery have I brought upon my head!—
Loosed on the flowers Siroces to my bane,
And the wild boar upon my crystal springs!   *59*
Whom do you fly, infatuate? gods ere now,
And Dardan Paris, have made the woods their home.
Let Pallas keep the towers her hand hath built,
Us before all things let the woods delight.
The grim-eyed lioness pursues the wolf,
The wolf the she-goat, the she-goat herself
In wanton sport the flowering cytisus,
And Corydon Alexis, each led on
By their own longing. See, the ox comes home
With plough up-tilted, and the shadows grow
To twice their length with the departing sun,
Yet me love burns, for who can limit love?
Ah! Corydon, Corydon, what hath crazed your wit?   *69*

ECLOGUE II

Your vine half-pruned hangs on the leafy elm;
Why haste you not to weave what need requires
Of pliant rush or osier? Scorned by this,
Elsewhere some new Alexis you will find." 73

[8]

ECLOGUE III

MENALCAS   DAMOETAS   PALAEMON

MENALCAS

Who owns the flock, Damoetas? Meliboeus?

DAMOETAS

Nay, they are Aegon's sheep, of late by him
Committed to my care.

MENALCAS

           O every way
Unhappy sheep, unhappy flock! while he
Still courts Neaera, fearing lest her choice
Should fall on me, this hireling shepherd here
Wrings hourly twice their udders, from the flock
Filching the life-juice, from the lambs their milk.

DAMOETAS

Hold! not so ready with your jeers at men!
We know who once, and in what shrine with you—
The he-goats looked aside—the light nymphs
    laughed—

MENALCAS

Ay, then, I warrant, when they saw *me* slash   *10*
Micon's young vines and trees with spiteful hook.

DAMOETAS

Or here by these old beeches, when you broke
The bow and arrows of Damon; for you chafed
When first you saw them given to the boy,
Cross-grained Menalcas, ay, and had you not
Done him some mischief, would have chafed to death.

MENALCAS

With thieves so daring, what can masters do?
Did I not see you, rogue, in ambush lie
For Damon's goat, while loud Lycisca barked?
And when I cried, "Where is he off to now?
Gather your flock together, Tityrus,"
You hid behind the sedges.   *20*

DAMOETAS

           Well, was he
Whom I had conquered still to keep the goat.
Which in the piping-match my pipe had won!
You may not know it, but the goat was mine.

ECLOGUE III

MENALCAS

You out-pipe *him?* when had you ever pipe
Wax-welded? in the cross-ways used you not
On grating straw some miserable tune
To mangle?

DAMOETAS

             Well, then, shall we try our skill
Each against each in turn? Lest you be loth,
I pledge this heifer; every day she comes
Twice to the milking-pail, and feeds withal
Two young ones at her udder: say you now
What you will stake upon the match with me.   *31*

MENALCAS

Naught from the flock I'll venture, for at home
I have a father and a step-dame harsh,
And twice a day both reckon up the flock,
And one withal the kids. But I will stake,
Seeing you are so mad, what you yourself
Will own more priceless far—two beechen cups
By the divine art of Alcimedon
Wrought and embossed, whereon a limber vine,
Wreathed round them by the graver's facile tool,
Twines over clustering ivy-berries pale.
Two figures, one Conon, in the midst he set.
And one—how call you him, who with his wand
Marked out for all men the whole round of heaven,
That they who reap, or stoop behind the plough,
Might know their several seasons? Nor as yet
Have I set lip to them, but lay them by.   *43*

DAMOETAS

For me too wrought the same Alcimedon
A pair of cups, and round the handles wreathed
Pliant acanthus, Orpheus in the midst,
The forests following in his wake; nor yet
Have I set lip to them, but lay them by.
Matched with a heifer, who would prate of cups?

MENALCAS

You shall not balk me now; where'er you bid,
I shall be with you; only let us have
For auditor—or see, to serve our turn,
Yonder Palaemon comes! In singing-bouts
I'll see you play the challenger no more.   *51*

DAMOETAS

Out then with what you have; I shall not shrink,
Nor budge for any man: only do you,
Neighbour Palaemon, with your whole heart's skill—

For it is no slight matter—play your part.

PALAEMON

Say on then, since on the greensward we sit,
And now is burgeoning both field and tree;
Now is the forest green, and now the year
At fairest. Do you first, Damoetas, sing,
Then you, Menalcas, in alternate strain:
Alternate strains are to the Muses dear.

DAMOETAS

"From Jove the Muse began; Jove filleth all,   60
Makes the earth fruitful, for my songs hath care."

MENALCAS

"Me Phoebus loves; for Phoebus his own gifts,
Bays and sweet-blushing hyacinths, I keep."

DAMOETAS

"Gay Galatea throws an apple at me,
Then hies to the willows, hoping to be seen."

MENALCAS

"My dear Amyntas comes unasked to me;
Not Delia to my dogs is better known."

DAMOETAS

"Gifts for my love I've found; mine eyes have marked
Where the wood-pigeons build their airy nests."

MENALCAS

"Ten golden apples have I sent my boy,   70
All that I could, to-morrow as many more."

DAMOETAS

"What words to me, and uttered O how oft,
Hath Galatea spoke! waft some of them,
Ye winds, I pray you, for the gods to hear."

MENALCAS

"It profiteth me naught, Amyntas mine,
That in your very heart you spurn me not,
If, while you hunt the boar, I guard the nets."

DAMOETAS

"Prithee, Iollas, for my birthday guest
Send me your Phyllis; when for the young crops
I slay my heifer, you yourself shall come."

MENALCAS

"I am all hers; she wept to see me go,
And, lingering on the word, 'farewell' she said,
'My beautiful Iollas, fare you well.' "

DAMOETAS

"Fell as the wolf is to the folded flock,   80
Rain to ripe corn, Sirocco to the trees,
The wrath of Amaryllis is to me."

MENALCAS

"As moisture to the corn, to ewes with young
Lithe willow, as arbute to the yeanling kids,
So sweet Amyntas, and none else, to me."

DAMOETAS

"My Muse, although she be but country-bred,
Is loved by Pollio: O Pierian Maids,
Pray you, a heifer for your reader feed!"

MENALCAS

"Pollio himself too doth new verses make:
Feed ye a bull now ripe to butt with horn,
And scatter with his hooves the flying sand."

DAMOETAS

"Who loves thee, Pollio, may he thither come
Where thee he joys beholding; ay, for him
Let honey flow, the thorn-bush spices bear."

MENALCAS

"Who hates not Bavius, let him also love   *90*
Thy songs, O Maevius, ay, and therewithal
Yoke foxes to his car, and he-goats milk."

DAMOETAS

"You, picking flowers and strawberries that grow
So near the ground, fly hence, boys, get you gone!
There's a cold adder lurking in the grass."

MENALCAS

"Forbear, my sheep, to tread too near the brink;
Yon bank is ill to trust to; even now
The ram himself, see, dries his dripping fleece!"

DAMOETAS

"Back with the she-goats, Tityrus, grazing there
So near the river! I, when time shall serve,
Will take them all, and wash them in the pool."

MENALCAS

"Boys, get your sheep together; if the heat,
As late it did, forestall us with the milk,
Vainly the dried-up udders shall we wring."

DAMOETAS

"How lean my bull amid the fattening vetch!   *100*
Alack! alack! for herdsman and for herd!
It is the self-same love that wastes us both."

MENALCAS

"These truly—nor is even love the cause—
Scarce have the flesh to keep their bones together
Some evil eye my lambkins hath bewitched."

DAMOETAS

"Say in what clime—and you shall be withal

My great Apollo—the whole breadth of heaven
Opens no wider than three ells to view."
    MENALCAS
"Say in what country grow such flowers as bear
The names of kings upon their petals writ,
And you shall have fair Phyllis for your own."
    PALAEMON
Not mine betwixt such rivals to decide:
You well deserve the heifer, so does he,
With all who either fear the sweets of love,
Or taste its bitterness. Now, boys, shut off
The sluices, for the fields have drunk their fill.   *III*

ECLOGUE IV

POLLIO

Muses of Sicily, essay we now
A somewhat loftier task! Not all men love
Coppice or lowly tamarisk: sing we woods.
Woods worthy of a Consul let them be.
   Now the last age by Cumae's Sibyl sung
Has come and gone, and the majestic roll
Of circling centuries begins anew:
Justice returns, returns old Saturn's reign,
With a new breed of men sent down from heaven.   7
Only do thou, at the boy's birth in whom
The iron shall cease, the golden race arise,
Befriend him, chaste Lucina; 'tis thine own
Apollo reigns. And in thy consulate,
This glorious age, O Pollio, shall begin,
And the months enter on their mighty march.
Under thy guidance, whatso tracks remain
Of our old wickedness, once done away,
Shall free the earth from never-ceasing fear.   14
He shall receive the life of gods, and see
Heroes with gods commingling, and himself
Be seen of them, and with his father's worth
Reign o'er a world at peace. For thee, O boy,
First shall the earth, untilled, pour freely forth
Her childish gifts, the gadding ivy-spray
With foxglove and Egyptian bean-flower mixed,
And laughing-eyed acanthus. Of themselves,
Untended, will the she-goats then bring home
Their udders swollen with milk, while flocks afield
Shall of the monstrous lion have no fear.   22
Thy very cradle shall pour forth for thee
Caressing flowers. The serpent too shall die.
Die shall the treacherous poison-plant, and far
And wide Assyrian spices spring. But soon
As thou hast skill to read of heroes' fame,
And of thy father's deeds, and inly learn
What virtue is, the plain by slow degrees
With waving corn-crops shall to golden grow,
From the wild briar shall hang the blushing grape,
And stubborn oaks sweat honey-dew. Nathless

Yet shall there lurk within of ancient wrong
Some traces, bidding tempt the deep with ships,
Gird towns with walls, with furrows cleave the earth.   *33*
Therewith a second Tiphys shall there be,
Her hero-freight a second Argo bear;
New wars too shall arise, and once again
Some great Achilles to some Troy be sent.
Then, when the mellowing years have made thee
　　man,
No more shall mariner sail, nor pine-tree bark
Ply traffic on the sea, but every land
Shall all things bear alike: the glebe no more
Shall feel the harrow's grip, nor vine the hook;
The sturdy ploughman shall loose yoke from steer,
Nor wool with varying colours learn to lie;
But in the meadows shall the ram himself,
Now with soft flush of purple, now with tint
Of yellow saffron, teach his fleece to shine.
While clothed in natural scarlet graze the lambs.   *45*
"Such still, such ages weave ye, as ye run,"
Sang to their spindles the consenting Fates
By Destiny's unalterable decree.
Assume thy greatness, for the time draws nigh,
Dear child of gods, great progeny of Jove!
See how it totters—the world's orbèd might,
Earth, and wide ocean, and the vault profound,
All, see, enraptured of the coming time!
Ah! might such length of days to me be given,
And breath suffice me to rehearse thy deeds,   *54*
Nor Thracian Orpheus should out-sing me then,
Nor Linus, though his mother this, and that
His sire should aid—Orpheus Calliope,
And Linus fair Apollo. Nay, though Pan,
With Arcady for judge, my claim contest,
With Arcady for judge great Pan himself
Should own him foiled, and from the field retire.
　　Begin to greet thy mother with a smile,
O baby-boy! ten months of weariness
For thee she bore: O baby-boy, begin!
For him, on whom his parents have not smiled,
Gods deem not worthy of their board or bed.   *64*

ECLOGUE V

MENALCAS MOPSUS

MENALCAS

Why, Mopsus, being both together met,
You skilled to breathe upon the slender reeds,
I to sing ditties, do we not sit down
Here where the elm-trees and the hazels blend?

MOPSUS

You are the elder, 'tis for me to bide
Your choice, Menalcas, whether now we seek
Yon shade that quivers to the changeful breeze,
Or the cave's shelter. Look you how the cave
Is with the wild vine's clusters over-laced!

MENALCAS

None but Amyntas on these hills of ours
Can vie with you.

MOPSUS

          What if he also strive
To out-sing Phoebus?   9

MENALCAS

            Do you first begin,
Good Mopsus, whether minded to sing aught
Of Phyllis and her loves, or Alcon's praise,
Or to fling taunts at Codrus. Come, begin,
While Tityrus watches o'er the grazing kids.

MOPSUS

Nay, then, I will essay what late I carved
On a green beech-tree's rind, playing by turns,
And marking down the notes; then afterward
Bid you Amyntas match them if he can.

MENALCAS

As limber willow to pale olive yields,
As lowly Celtic nard to rose-buds bright,
So, to my mind, Amyntas yields to you.
But hold awhile, for to the cave we come.   19

MOPSUS

"For Daphnis cruelly slain wept all the Nymphs—
Ye hazels, bear them witness, and ye streams—
When she, his mother, clasping in her arms
The hapless body of the son she bare,
To gods and stars unpitying, poured her plaint.

[16]

Then, Daphnis, to the cooling streams were none
That drove the pastured oxen, then no beast
Drank of the river, or would the grass-blade touch.
Nay, the wild rocks and woods then voiced the roar
Of Afric lions mourning for thy death.   *28*
Daphnis, 'twas thou bad'st yoke to Bacchus' car
Armenian tigresses, lead on the pomp
Of revellers, and with tender foliage wreathe
The bending spear-wands. As to trees the vine
Is crown of glory, as to vines the grape,
Bulls to the herd, to fruitful fields the corn,
So the one glory of thine own art thou.
When the Fates took thee hence, then Pales' self,
And even Apollo, left the country lone.
Where the plump barley-grain so oft we sowed,
There but wild oats and barren darnel spring;
For tender violet and narcissus bright
Thistle and prickly thorn uprear their heads. *39*
Now, O ye shepherds, strew the ground with leaves,
And o'er the fountains draw a shady veil—
So Daphnis to his memory bids be done—
And rear a tomb, and write thereon this verse:
'I, Daphnis in the woods, from hence in fame
Am to the stars exalted, guardian once
Of a fair flock, myself more fair than they.'"

  MENALCAS
So is thy song to me, poet divine,
As slumber on the grass to weary limbs,
Or to slake thirst from some sweet-bubbling rill
In summer's heat. Nor on the reeds alone,
But with thy voice art thou, thrice happy boy,
Ranked with thy master, second but to him. *49*
Yet will I, too, in turn, as best I may,
Sing thee a song, and to the stars uplift
Thy Daphnis—Daphnis to the stars extol,
For me too Daphnis loved.

  MOPSUS
       Than such a boon
What dearer could I deem? the boy himself
Was worthy to be sung, and many a time
Hath Stimichon to me your singing praised.

  MENALCAS
"In dazzling sheen with unaccustomed eyes
Daphnis stands rapt before Olympus' gate,
And sees beneath his feet the clouds and stars.
Wherefore the woods and fields, Pan, shepherd-folk,

And Dryad-maidens, thrill with eager joy; 59
Nor wolf with treacherous wile assails the flock,
Nor nets the stag: kind Daphnis loveth peace.
The unshorn mountains to the stars up-toss
Voices of gladness; ay, the very rocks,
The very thickets, shout and sing, 'A god,
A god is he, Menalcas!' Be thou kind,
Propitious to thine own. Lo! altars four,
Twain to thee, Daphnis, and to Phoebus twain
For sacrifice, we build; and I for thee
Two beakers yearly of fresh milk afoam,
And of rich olive-oil two bowls, will set; 68
And of the wine-god's bounty above all,
If cold, before the hearth, or in the shade
At harvest-time, to glad the festal hour,
From flasks of Ariusian grape will pour
Sweet nectar. Therewithal at my behest
Shall Lyctian Aegon and Damoetas sing,
And Alphesiboeus emulate in dance
The dancing Satyrs. This, thy service due,
Shalt thou lack never, both when we pay the Nymphs
Our yearly vows, and when with lustral rites
The fields we hallow. Long as the wild boar
Shall love the mountain-heights, and fish the streams,
While bees on thyme and crickets feed on dew,
Thy name, thy praise, thine honour, shall endure.
Even as to Bacchus and to Ceres, so
To thee the swain his yearly vows shall make;
And thou thereof, like them, shalt quittance claim." 80

MOPSUS

How, how repay thee for a song so rare?
For not the whispering south-wind on its way
So much delights me, nor wave-smitten beach,
Nor streams that race adown their bouldered beds.

MENALCAS

First this frail hemlock-stalk to you I give,
Which taught me "Corydon with love was fired
For fair Alexis," ay, and this beside,
"Who owns the flock?—Meliboeus?"

MOPSUS

But take you
This shepherd's crook, which, howso hard he begged,
Antigenes, then worthy to be loved,
Prevailed not to obtain—with brass, you see,
And equal knots, Menalcas, fashioned fair! 90

ECLOGUE VI

First my Thalia stooped in sportive mood
To Syracusan strains, nor blushed within
The woods to house her. When I sought to tell
Of battles and of kings, the Cynthian god
Plucked at mine ear and warned me: "Tityrus,
Beseems a shepherd-wight to feed fat sheep,
But sing a slender song." Now, Varus, I—
For lack there will not who would laud thy deeds,
And treat of dolorous wars—will rather tune
To the slim oaten reed my silvan lay.   8
I sing but as vouchsafed me; yet even this
If, if but one with ravished eyes should read,
Of thee, O Varus, shall our tamarisks
And all the woodland ring; nor can there be
A page more dear to Phoebus, than the page
Where, foremost writ, the name of Varus stands.
    Speed ye, Pierian Maids! Within a cave
Young Chromis and Mnasyllos chanced to see
Silenus sleeping, flushed, as was his wont,
With wine of yesterday. Not far aloof,
Slipped from his head, the garlands lay, and there
By its worn handle hung a ponderous cup.
Approaching—for the old man many a time
Had balked them both of a long hoped-for song—
Garlands to fetters turned, they bind him fast.   19
Then Aeglë, fairest of the Naiad-band,
Aeglë came up to the half-frightened boys,
Came, and, as now with open eyes he lay,
With juice of blood-red mulberries smeared him o'er,
Both brow and temples. Laughing at their guile.
And crying, "Why tie the fetters? loose me, boys;
Enough for you to think you had the power;
Now list the songs you wish for—songs for you,
Another meed for her"—forthwith began.
Then might you see the wild things of the wood,
With Fauns in sportive frolic beat the time,
And stubborn oaks their branchy summits bow.   28
Not Phoebus doth the rude Parnassian crag
So ravish, nor Orpheus so entrance the heights

[19]

Of Rhodope or Ismarus: for he sang
How through the mighty void the seeds were driven
Of earth, air, ocean, and of liquid fire,
How all that is from these beginnings grew,
And the young world itself took solid shape,
Then 'gan its crust to harden, and in the deep
Shut Nereus off, and mould the forms of things
Little by little; and how the earth amazed
Beheld the new sun shining, and the showers
Fall, as the clouds soared higher, what time the woods
'Gan first to rise, and living things to roam
Scattered among the hills that knew them not.　　40
Then sang he of the stones by Pyrrha cast,
Of Saturn's reign, and of Prometheus' theft,
And the Caucasian birds, and told withal
Nigh to what fountain by his comrades left
The mariners cried on Hylas, till the shore
Re-echoed "Hylas, Hylas!" Then he soothed
Pasiphaë with the love of her white bull—
Happy if cattle-kind had never been!—
O ill-starred maid, what frenzy caught thy soul
The daughters too of Proetus filled the fields
With their feigned lowings, yet no one of them
Of such unhallowed union e'er was fain
As with a beast to mate, though many a time
On her smooth forehead she had sought for horns,
And for her neck had feared the galling plough.　　51
O ill-starred maid! thou roamest now the hills,
While on soft hyacinths he, his snowy side
Reposing, under some dark ilex now
Chews the pale herbage, or some heifer tracks
Amid the crowding herd. Now close, ye Nymphs,
Ye Nymphs of Dicte, close the forest-glades,
If haply there may chance upon mine eyes
The white bull's wandering foot-prints: him belike
Following the herd, or by green pasture lured,
Some kine may guide to the Gortynian stalls.　　60
Then sings he of the maid so wonder-struck
With the apples of the Hesperids, and then
With moss-bound, bitter bark rings round the forms
Of Phaëthon's fair sisters, from the ground
Up-towering into poplars. Next he sings
Of Gallus wandering by Permessus' stream,
And by a sister of the Muses led
To the Aonian mountains, and how all
The choir of Phoebus rose to greet him; how

The shepherd Linus, singer of songs divine,
Brow-bound with flowers and bitter parsley, spake:
"These reeds the Muses give thee, take them thou,
Erst to the agèd bard of Ascra given,
Wherewith in singing he was wont to draw
Time-rooted ash-trees from the mountain heights.   *71*
With these the birth of the Grynean grove
Be voiced by thee, that of no grove beside
Apollo more may boast him." Wherefore speak
Of Scylla, child of Nisus, who, 'tis said,
Her fair white loins with barking monsters girt
Vexed the Dulichian ships, and, in the deep
Swift-eddying whirlpool, with her sea-dogs tore
The trembling mariners? or how he told
Of the changed limbs of Tereus—what a feast,
What gifts, to him by Philomel were given;
How swift she sought the desert, with what wings
Hovered in anguish o'er her ancient home?   *81*
All that, of old, Eurotas, happy stream,
Heard, as Apollo mused upon the lyre,
And bade his laurels learn, Silenus sang;
Till from Olympus, loth at his approach,
Vesper, advancing, bade the shepherds tell
Their tale of sheep, and pen them in the fold.   *86*

ECLOGUE VII

Daphnis beneath a rustling ilex-tree
Had sat him down; Thyrsis and Corydon
Had gathered in the flock, Thyrsis the sheep,
And Corydon the she-goats swollen with milk—
Both in the flower of age, Arcadians both,
Ready to sing, and in like strain reply.
Hither had strayed, while from the frost I fend
My tender myrtles, the he-goat himself,
Lord of the flock; when Daphnis I espy!
Soon as he saw me, "Hither haste," he cried,
"O Meliboeus! goat and kids are safe;   9
And, if you have an idle hour to spare,
Rest here beneath the shade. Hither the steers
Will through the meadows, of their own free will,
Untended come to drink. Here Mincius hath
With tender rushes rimmed his verdant banks,
And from yon sacred oak with busy hum
The bees are swarming." What was I to do?
No Phyllis or Alcippe left at home
Had I, to shelter my new-weanèd lambs,
And no slight matter was a singing-bout
'Twixt Corydon and Thyrsis. Howsoe'er,
I let my business wait upon their sport.
So they began to sing, voice answering voice
In strains alternate—for alternate strains
The Muses then were minded to recall—
First Corydon, then Thyrsis in reply.   20
    CORYDON
"Libethrian Nymphs, who are my heart's delight,
Grant me, as doth my Codrus, so to sing—
Next to Apollo he—or if to this
We may not all attain, my tuneful pipe
Here on this sacred pine shall silent hang."
    THYRSIS
"Arcadian shepherds, wreathe with ivy-spray
Your budding poet, so that Codrus burst
With envy: if he praise beyond my due,
Then bind my brow with foxglove, lest his tongue
With evil omen blight the coming bard."

[22]

CORYDON

"This bristling boar's head, Delian Maid, to thee,
With branching antlers of a sprightly stag,
Young Micon offers: if his luck but hold,
Full-length in polished marble, ankle-bound
With purple buskin, shall thy statue stand."   *32*

    THYRSIS

"A bowl of milk, Priapus, and these cakes,
Yearly, it is enough for thee to claim;
Thou art the guardian of a poor man's plot.
Wrought for a while in marble, if the flock
At lambing time be filled, stand there in gold."

CORYDON

"Daughter of Nereus, Galatea mine,
Sweeter than Hybla-thyme, more white than swans,
Fairer than ivy pale, soon as the steers
Shall from their pasture to the stalls repair,
If aught for Corydon thou carest, come."   *40*

    THYRSIS

"Now may I seem more bitter to your taste
Than herb Sardinian, rougher than the broom,
More worthless than strewn sea-weed, if to-day
Hath not a year out-lasted! Fie for shame!
Go home, my cattle, from your grazing go!"

CORYDON

"Ye mossy springs, and grass more soft than sleep,
And arbute green with thin shade sheltering you,
Ward off the solstice from my flock, for now
Comes on the burning summer, now the buds
Upon the limber vine-shoot 'gin to swell."

    THYRSIS

"Here is a hearth, and resinous logs, here fire   *49*
Unstinted, and doors black with ceaseless smoke.
Here heed we Boreas' icy breath as much
As the wolf heeds the number of the flock,
Or furious rivers their restraining banks."

CORYDON

"The junipers and prickly chestnuts stand,
And 'neath each tree lie strewn their several fruits,
Now the whole world is smiling, but if fair
Alexis from these hill-slopes should away,
Even the rivers you would see run dry."

    THYRSIS

"The field is parched, the grass-blades thirst to death
In the faint air; Liber hath grudged the hills
His vine's o'er-shadowing: should my Phyllis come,

Green will be all the grove, and Jupiter
Descend in floods of fertilizing rain."   60

CORYDON

"The poplar doth Alcides hold most dear,
The vine Iacchus, Phoebus his own bays,
And Venus fair the myrtle: therewithal
Phyllis doth hazels love, and while she loves,
Myrtle nor bay the hazel shall out-vie."

THYRSIS

"Ash in the forest is most beautiful,
Pine in the garden, poplar by the stream,
Fir on the mountain-height; but if more oft
Thou'ldst come to me, fair Lycidas, to thee
Both forest-ash, and garden-pine should bow."

MELIBOEUS

These I remember, and how Thyrsis strove
For victory in vain. From that time forth
Is Corydon still Corydon with us.   70

ECLOGUE VIII

Of Damon and Alphesiboeus now,
Those shepherd-singers at whose rival strains
The heifer wondering forgot to graze,
The lynx stood awe-struck, and the flowing streams,
Unwonted loiterers, stayed their course to hear—
How Damon and Alphesiboeus sang
Their pastoral ditties, will I tell the tale.
   Thou, whether broad Timavus' rocky banks
Thou now art passing, or dost skirt the shore
Of the Illyrian main,—will ever dawn
That day when I thy deeds may celebrate,
Ever that day when through the whole wide world
I may renown thy verse—that verse alone
Of Sophoclean buskin worthy found?   *10*
With thee began, to thee shall end, the strain.
Take thou these songs that owe their birth to thee,
And deign around thy temples to let creep
This ivy-chaplet 'twixt the conquering bays.
   Scarce had night's chilly shade forsook the sky
What time to nibbling sheep the dewy grass
Tastes sweetest, when, on his smooth shepherd-staff
Of olive leaning, Damon thus began.

DAMON

"Rise, Lucifer, and, heralding the light,
Bring in the genial day, while I make moan
Fooled by vain passion for a faithless bride,
For Nysa, and with this my dying breath
Call on the gods, though little it bestead—
The gods who heard her vows and heeded not.
   "Begin, my flute, with me Maenalian lays.   *21*
Ever hath Maenalus his murmuring groves
And whispering pines, and ever hears the songs
Of love-lorn shepherds, and of Pan, who first
Brooked not the tuneful reed should idle lie.
   "Begin, my flute, with me Maenalian lays.
Nysa to Mopsus given! what may not then
We lovers look for? soon shall we see mate
Griffins with mares, and in the coming age
Shy deer and hounds together come to drink.

[25]

"Begin, my flute, with me Maenalian lays.
Now, Mopsus, cut new torches, for they bring
Your bride along; now, bridegroom, scatter nuts:
Forsaking Oeta mounts the evening star!

"Begin, my flute, with me Maenalian lays.   *31*
O worthy of thy mate, while all men else
Thou scornest, and with loathing dost behold
My shepherd's pipe, my goats, my shaggy brow,
And untrimmed beard, nor deem'st that any god
For mortal doings hath regard or care.

"Begin, my flute, with me Maenalian lays.
Once with your mother, in our orchard-garth,
A little maid I saw you—I your guide—
Plucking the dewy apples. My twelfth year
I scarce had entered, and could barely reach
The brittle boughs. I looked, and I was lost;
A sudden frenzy swept my wits away.

"Begin, my flute, with me Maenalian lays.   *42*
Now know I what Love is: 'mid savage rocks
Tmaros or Rhodope brought forth the boy,
Or Garamantes in earth's utmost bounds—
No kin of ours, nor of our blood begot.

"Begin, my flute, with me Maenalian lays.
Fierce Love it was once steeled a mother's heart
With her own offspring's blood her hands to imbrue:
Mother, thou too wert cruel; say wert thou
More cruel, mother, or more ruthless he?
Ruthless the boy, thou, mother, cruel too.

"Begin, my flute, with me Maenalian lays.   *51*
Now let the wolf turn tail and fly the sheep,
Tough oaks bear golden apples, alder-trees
Bloom with narcissus-flower, the tamarisk
Sweat with rich amber, and the screech-owl vie
In singing with the swan: let Tityrus
Be Orpheus, Orpheus in the forest-glade,
Arion 'mid his dolphins on the deep.

"Begin, my flute, with me Maenalian lays.
Yea, be the whole earth to mid-ocean turned!
Farewell, ye woodlands! I from the tall peak
Of yon aerial rock will headlong plunge
Into the billows: this my latest gift,
From dying lips bequeathed thee, see thou keep.
Cease now, my flute, now cease Maenalian lays."   *61*
Thus Damon: but do ye, Pierian Maids—
We cannot all do all things—tell me how
Alphesiboeus to his strain replied.

ECLOGUE VIII

ALPHESIBOEUS

"Bring water, and with soft wool-fillet bind
These altars round about, and burn thereon
Rich vervain and male frankincense, that I
May strive with magic spells to turn astray
My lover's saner senses, whereunto
There lacketh nothing save the power of song.
    "Draw from the town, my songs, draw Daphnis
      home.
Songs can the very moon draw down from heaven
Circe with singing changed from human form
The comrades of Ulysses, and by song
Is the cold meadow-snake asunder burst.   *71*
    "Draw from the town, my songs, draw Daphnis
      home.
These triple threads of threefold colour first
I twine about thee, and three times withal
Around these altars do thine image bear:
Uneven numbers are the god's delight.
    "Draw from the town, my songs, draw Daphnis
      home.
Now, Amaryllis, ply in triple knots
The threefold colours; ply them fast, and say
This is the chain of Venus that I ply.
    "Draw from the town, my songs, draw Daphnis
      home.
As by the kindling of the self-same fire
Harder this clay, this wax the softer grows,
So by my love may Daphnis; sprinkle meal,
And with bitumen burn the brittle bays.
Me Daphnis with his cruelty doth burn,
I to melt cruel Daphnis burn this bay.   *83*
    "Draw from the town, my songs, draw Daphnis
      home.
As when some heifer, seeking for her steer
Through woodland and deep grove, sinks wearied
    out
On the green sedge beside a stream, love-lorn,
Nor marks the gathering night that calls her
    home—
As pines that heifer, with such love as hers
May Daphnis pine, and I not care to heal.
    "Draw from the town, my songs, draw Daphnis
      home.   *90*
These relics once, dear pledges of himself,
The traitor left me, which, O earth, to thee

Here on this very threshold I commit—
Pledges that bind him to redeem the debt.
 "Draw from the town, my songs, draw Daphnis
  home.
These herbs of bane to me did Moeris give,
In Pontus culled, where baneful herbs abound.
With these full oft have I seen Moeris change
To a wolf's form, and hide him in the woods,
Oft summon spirits from the tomb's recess,
And to new fields transport the standing corn.
 "Draw from the town, my songs, draw Daphnis
  home.   *100*
Take ashes, Amaryllis, fetch them forth,
And o'er your head into the running brook
Fling them, nor look behind: with these will I
Upon the heart of Daphnis make essay.
Nothing for gods, nothing for songs cares he.
 "Draw from the town, my songs, draw Daphnis
  home.
Look, look! the very embers of themselves
Have caught the altar with a flickering flame,
While I delay to fetch them: may the sign
Prove lucky! something it must mean, for sure,
And Hylax on the threshold 'gins to bark!
May we believe it, or are lovers still
By their own fancies fooled?
       Give o'er, my songs,
Daphnis is coming from the town, give o'er."   *109*

ECLOGUE IX

LYCIDAS   MOERIS

LYCIDAS
Say whither, Moeris?—Make you for the town,
Or on what errand bent?
　　　MOERIS
　　　　　　　　　　　　O Lycidas,
We have lived to see, what never yet we feared,
An interloper own our little farm,
And say, "Be off, you former husbandmen!
These fields are mine." Now, cowed and out of heart,
Since Fortune turns the whole world upside down,
We are taking him—ill luck go with the same!—
These kids you see.
　　　LYCIDAS
　　　　　　　　　　But surely I had heard
That where the hills first draw from off the plain,
And the high ridge with gentle slope descends,
Down to the brook-side and the broken crests
Of yonder veteran beeches, all the land
Was by the songs of your Menalcas saved.　　　　　*10*
　　　MOERIS
Heard it you had, and so the rumour ran,
But 'mid the clash of arms, my Lycidas,
Our songs avail no more than, as 'tis said,
Doves of Dodona when an eagle comes.
Nay, had I not, from hollow ilex-bole
Warned by a raven on the left, cut short
The rising feud, nor I, your Moeris here,
No, nor Menalcas, were alive to-day.
　　　LYCIDAS
Alack! could any of so foul a crime
Be guilty? Ah! how nearly, with thyself,
Reft was the solace that we had in thee,
Menalcas! Who then of the Nymphs had sung,
Or who with flowering herbs bestrewn the ground,
And o'er the fountains drawn a leafy veil?—　　　*20*
Who sung the stave I filched from you that day
To Amaryllis wending, our hearts' joy?—
"While I am gone, 'tis but a little way,
Feed, Tityrus, my goats, and, having fed,

Drive to the drinking-pool, and, as you drive,
Beware the he-goat; with his horn he butts."
    MOERIS
Ay, or to Varus that half-finished lay,
"Varus, thy name, so still our Mantua live—
Mantua to poor Cremona all too near—
Shall singing swans bear upward to the stars."
     LYCIDAS
So may your swarms Cyrnean yew-trees shun,   *30*
Your kine with cytisus their udders swell,
Begin, if aught you have. The Muses made
Me too a singer; I too have sung; the swains
Call me a poet, but I believe them not:
For naught of mine, or worthy Varius yet
Or Cinna deem I, but account myself
A cackling goose among melodious swans.
     MOERIS
'Twas in my thought to do so, Lycidas;
Even now was I revolving silently
If this I could recall—no paltry song: *38*
"Come, Galatea, what pleasure is 't to play
Amid the waves? Here glows the Spring, here earth
Beside the streams pours forth a thousand flowers;
Here the white poplar bends above the cave,
And the lithe vine weaves shadowy covert: come,
Leave the mad waves to beat upon the shore."
     LYCIDAS
What of the strain I heard you singing once
On a clear night alone? the notes I still
Remember, could I but recall the words.
     MOERIS
"Why, Daphnis, upward gazing, do you mark
The ancient risings of the Signs? for look
Where Dionean Caesar's star comes forth
In heaven, to gladden all the fields with corn,
And to the grape upon the sunny slopes
Her colour bring! Now, Daphnis, graft the pears;
So shall your children's children pluck their fruit."   *50*
    Time carries all things, even our wits, away.
Oft, as a boy, I sang the sun to rest,
But all those songs are from my memory fled,
And even his voice is failing Moeris now;
The wolves eyed Moeris first: but at your wish
Menalcas will repeat them oft enow.
     LYCIDAS
Your pleas but linger out my heart's desire:

Now all the deep is into silence hushed,
And all the murmuring breezes sunk to sleep.
We are half-way thither, for Bianor's tomb
Begins to show: here, Moeris, where the hinds
Are lopping the thick leafage, let us sing.   *61*
Set down the kids, yet shall we reach the town;
Or, if we fear the night may gather rain
Ere we arrive, then singing let us go,
Our way to lighten; and, that we may thus
Go singing, I will ease you of this load.
    MOERIS
Cease, boy, and get we to the work in hand:
We shall sing better when himself is come.   *67*

ECLOGUE X

GALLUS

This now, the very latest of my toils,
Vouchsafe me, Arethusa! needs must I
Sing a brief song to Gallus—brief, but yet
Such as Lycoris' self may fitly read.
Who would not sing for Gallus? So, when thou
Beneath Sicanian billows glidest on,
May Doris blend no bitter wave with thine,
Begin! The love of Gallus be our theme,
And the shrewd pangs he suffered, while, hard by,
The flat-nosed she-goats browse the tender brush.   *7*
We sing not to deaf ears; no word of ours
But the woods echo it. What groves or lawns
Held you, ye Dryad-maidens, when for love—
Love all unworthy of a loss so dear—
Gallus lay dying? for neither did the slopes
Of Pindus or Parnassus stay you then,
No, nor Aonian Aganippe. Him
Even the laurels and the tamarisks wept;
For him, outstretched beneath a lonely rock,
Wept pine-clad Maenalus, and the flinty crags
Of cold Lycaeus. The sheep too stood around—
Of us they feel no shame, poet divine;
Nor of the flock be thou ashamed: even fair
Adonis by the rivers fed his sheep—   *18*
Came shepherd too, and swine-herd footing slow,
And, from the winter-acorns dripping-wet
Menalcas. All with one accord exclaim:
"From whence this love of thine?" Apollo came;
"Gallus, art mad?" he cried, "thy bosom's care
Another love is following." Therewithal
Silvanus came, with rural honours crowned;
The flowering fennels and tall lilies shook
Before him. Yea, and our own eyes beheld
Pan, god of Arcady, with blood-red juice
Of the elder-berry, and with vermilion, dyed.
"Wilt ever make an end?" quoth he, "behold
Love recks not aught of it: his heart no more
With tears is sated than with streams the grass,
Bees with the cytisus, or goats with leaves."   *30*

ECLOGUE X

"Yet will ye sing, Arcadians, of my woes
Upon your mountains," sadly he replied--
"Arcadians, that alone have skill to sing.
O then how softly would my ashes rest,
If of my love, one day, your flutes should tell!
And would that I, of your own fellowship,
Or dresser of the ripening grape had been,
Or guardian of the flock! for surely then,
Let Phyllis, or Amyntas, or who else,
Bewitch me—what if swart Amyntas be?
Dark is the violet, dark the hyacinth—
Among the willows, 'neath the limber vine,
Reclining would my love have lain with me,
Phyllis plucked garlands, or Amyntas sung.   *41*
Here are cool springs, soft mead and grove, Lycoris;
Here might our lives with time have worn away.
But me mad love of the stern war-god holds
Armed amid weapons and opposing foes.
Whilst thou—Ah! might I but believe it not!—
Alone without me, and from home afar,
Look'st upon Alpine snows and frozen Rhine.
Ah! may the frost not hurt thee, may the sharp
And jaggèd ice not wound thy tender feet!   *49*
I will depart, re-tune the songs I framed
In verse Chalcidian to the oaten reed
Of the Sicilian swain. Resolved am I
In the woods, rather, with wild beasts to couch,
And bear my doom, and character my love
Upon the tender tree-trunks: they will grow,
And you, my love, grow with them. And meanwhile
I with the Nymphs will haunt Mount Maenalus,
Or hunt the keen wild boar. No frost so cold
But I will hem with hounds thy forest-glades,
Parthenius. Even now, methinks, I range
O'er rocks, through echoing groves, and joy to launch
Cydonian arrows from a Parthian bow.—
As if my madness could find healing thus,
Or that god soften at a mortal's grief!   *61*
Now neither Hamadryads, no, nor songs
Delight me more: ye woods, away with you!
No pangs of ours can change him; not though we
In the mid-frost should drink of Hebrus' stream,
And in wet winters face Sithonian snows,
Or, when the bark of the tall elm-tree bole
Of drought is dying, should, under Cancer's Sign,
In Aethiopian deserts drive our flocks.

[33]

68571

FERNALD LIBRARY
COLBY-SAWYER COLLEGE
NEW LONDON, N. H. 03257

Love conquers all things; yield we too to love!"   *69*
   These songs, Pierian Maids, shall it suffice
Your poet to have sung, the while he sat,
And of slim mallow wove a basket fine:
To Gallus ye will magnify their worth,
Gallus, for whom my love grows hour by hour,
As the green alder shoots in early Spring.
Come, let us rise: the shade is wont to be
Baneful to singers; baneful is the shade
Cast by the juniper, crops sicken too
In shade. Now homeward, having fed your fill—
Eve's star is rising—go, my she-goats, go.   *77*

THE GEORGICS

GEORGIC I

What makes the cornfield smile; beneath what star
Maecenas, it is meet to turn the sod
Or marry elm with vine; how tend the steer;
What pains for cattle-keeping, or what proof
Of patient trial serves for thrifty bees;—
Such are my themes.
                O universal lights
Most glorious! ye that lead the gliding year
Along the sky, Liber and Ceres mild,
If by your bounty holpen earth once changed
Chaonian acorn for the plump wheat-ear,
And mingled with the grape, your new-found gift,
The draughts of Achelous; and ye Fauns
To rustics ever kind, come foot it, Fauns
And Dryad-maids together; your gifts I sing.
And thou, for whose delight the war-horse first
Sprang from earth's womb at thy great trident's
     stroke,
Neptune; and haunter of the groves, for whom
Three hundred snow-white heifers browse the brakes,
The fertile brakes of Ceos; and clothed in power,
Thy native forest and Lycean lawns,
Pan, shepherd-god, forsaking, as the love
Of thine own Maenalus constrains thee, hear
And help, O lord of Tegea! And thou, too,
Minerva, from whose hand the olive sprung;
And boy-discoverer of the curvèd plough;
And, bearing a young cypress root-uptorn,
Silvanus, and Gods all and Goddesses,
Who make the fields your care, both ye who nurse
The tender unsown increase, and from heaven
Shed on man's sowing the riches of your rain: 23
And thou, even thou, of whom we know not yet
What mansion of the skies shall hold thee soon,
Whether to watch o'er cities be thy will,
Great Caesar, and to take the earth in charge,
That so the mighty world may welcome thee
Lord of her increase, master of her times,
Binding thy mother's myrtle round thy brow,
Or as the boundless ocean's God thou come,

Sole dread of seamen, till far Thule bow   *30*
Before thee, and Tethys win thee to her son
With all her waves for dower; or as a star
Lend thy fresh beams our lagging months to cheer,
Where 'twixt the Maid and those pursuing Claws
A space is opening; see! red Scorpio's self
His arms draws in, yea, and hath left thee more
Than thy full meed of heaven: be what thou wilt—
For neither Tartarus hopes to call thee king,
Nor may so dire a lust of sovereignty
E'er light upon thee, howso Greece admire
Elysium's fields, and Proserpine not heed
Her mother's voice entreating to return—
Vouchsafe a prosperous voyage, and smile on this
My bold endeavour, and pitying, even as I,
These poor way-wildered swains, at once begin,
Grow timely used unto the voice of prayer.   *42*
    In early spring-tide, when the icy drip
Melts from the mountains hoar, and Zephyr's breath
Unbinds the crumbling clod, even then 'tis time;
Press deep your plough behind the groaning ox,
And teach the furrow-burnished share to shine.
That land the craving farmer's prayer fulfils,
Which twice the sunshine, twice the frost has felt;
Ay, that's the land whose boundless harvest-crops
Burst, see! the barns.
               But ere our metal cleave
An unknown surface, heed we to forelearn
The winds and varying temper of the sky,
The lineal tilth and habits of the spot,
What every region yields, and what denies.   *53*
Here blithelier springs the corn, and here the grape,
There earth is green with tender growth of trees
And grass unbidden. See how from Tmolus comes
The saffron's fragrance, ivory from Ind,
From Saba's weakling sons their frankincense,
Iron from the naked Chalybs, castor rank
From Pontus, from Epirus the prize-palms
O' the mares of Elis.   *59*
           Such the eternal bond
And such the laws by Nature's hand imposed
On clime and clime, e'er since the primal dawn
When old Deucalion on the unpeopled earth
Cast stones, whence men, a flinty race, were reared.
Up then! if fat the soil, let sturdy bulls
Upturn it from the year's first opening months,

And let the clods lie bare till baked to dust
By the ripe suns of summer; but if the earth
Less fruitful be, just ere Arcturus rìse
With shallower trench uptilt it—'twill suffice;
There, lest weeds choke the crop's luxuriance, here,
Lest the scant moisture fail the barren sand.   70

    Then thou shalt suffer in alternate years
The new-reaped fields to rest, and on the plain
A crust of sloth to harden; or, when stars
Are changed in heaven, there sow the golden grain
Where erst, luxuriant with its quivering pod,
Pulse, or the slender vetch-crop, thou hast cleared,
And lupin sour, whose brittle stalks arise,
A hurtling forest. For the plain is parched
By flax-crop, parched by oats, by poppies parched
In Lethe-slumber drenched. Nathless by change
The travailing earth is lightened, but stint not
With refuse rich to soak the thirsty soil,
And shower foul ashes o'er the exhausted fields.
Thus by rotation like repose is gained,
Nor earth meanwhile uneared and thankless left.   83
Oft, too, 'twill boot to fire the naked fields,
And the light stubble burn with crackling flames;
Whether that earth therefrom some hidden strength
And fattening food derives, or that the fire
Bakes every blemish out, and sweats away
Each useless humour, or that the heat unlocks
New passages and secret pores, whereby
Their life-juice to the tender blades may win;
Or that it hardens more and helps to bind
The gaping veins, lest penetrating showers,
Or fierce sun's ravening might, or searching blast
Of the keen north should sear them. Well, I wot,
He serves the fields who with his harrow breaks
The sluggish clods, and hurdles osier-twined
Hales o'er them; from the far Olympian height
Him golden Ceres not in vain regards;   96
And he, who having ploughed the fallow plain
And heaved its furrowy ridges, turns once more
Cross-wise his shattering share, with stroke on stroke
The earth assails, and makes the field his thrall.

    Pray for wet summers and for winters fine,
Ye husbandmen; in winter's dust the crops
Exceedingly rejoice, the field hath joy;
No tilth makes Mysia lift her head so high,
Nor Gargarus his own harvests so admire.

Why tell of him, who, having launched his seed,
Sets on for close encounter, and rakes smooth
The dry dust hillocks, then on the tender corn
Lets in the flood, whose waters follow fain;
And when the parched field quivers, and all the blades
Are dying, from the brow of its hill-bed,
See! see! he lures the runnel; down it falls,
Waking hoarse murmurs o'er the polished stones,
And with its bubblings slakes the thirsty fields?   *110*
Or why of him, who lest the heavy ears
O'erweigh the stalk, while yet in tender blade
Feeds down the crop's luxuriance, when its growth
First tops the furrows? Why of him who drains
The marsh-land's gathered ooze through soaking sand,
Chiefly what time in treacherous moons a stream
Goes out in spate, and with its coat of slime
Holds all the country, whence the hollow dykes
Sweat steaming vapour?   *117*
                    But no whit the more,
For all expedients tried and travail borne
By man and beast in turning oft the soil,
Do greedy goose and Strymon-haunting cranes
And succory's bitter fibres cease to harm,
Or shade not injure. The great Sire himself
No easy road to husbandry assigned,
And first was he by human skill to rouse
The slumbering glebe, whetting the minds of men
With care on care, nor suffering realm of his
In drowsy sloth to stagnate. Before Jove
Fields knew no taming hand of husbandmen;
To mark the plain or mete with boundary-line—
Even this was impious; for the common stock
They gathered, and the earth of her own will
All things more freely, no man bidding, bore.   *128*
He to black serpents gave their venom-bane,
And bade the wolf go prowl, and ocean toss;
Shook from the leaves their honey, put fire away,
And curbed the random rivers running wine,
That use by gradual dint of thought on thought
Might forge the various arts, with furrow's help
The corn-blade win, and strike out hidden fire
From the flint's heart. Then first the streams were
          ware
Of hollowed alder-hulls: the sailor then
Their names and numbers gave to star and star,
Pleiads and Hyads, and Lycaon's child

Bright Arctos; how with nooses then was found
To catch wild beasts, and cozen them with lime,
And hem with hounds the mighty forest-glades.   *140*
Soon one with hand-net scourges the broad stream,
Probing its depths, one drags his dripping toils
Along the main; then iron's unbending might,
And shrieking saw-blade,—for the men of old
With wedges wont to cleave the splintering log;—
Then divers arts arose; toil conquered all,
Remorseless toil, and poverty's shrewd push
In times of hardship. Ceres was the first
Set mortals on with tools to turn the sod,
When now the awful groves 'gan fail to bear
Acorns and arbutes, and her wonted food
Dodona gave no more. Soon, too, the corn
Gat sorrow's increase, that an evil blight
Ate up the stalks, and thistle reared his spines
An idler in the fields; the crops die down;
Upsprings instead a shaggy growth of burrs
And caltrops; and amid the corn-fields trim
Unfruitful darnel and wild oats have sway.
Wherefore, unless thou shalt with ceaseless rake
The weeds pursue, with shouting scare the birds,
Prune with thy hook the dark field's matted shade,
Pray down the showers, all vainly thou shalt eye,
Alack! thy neighbour's heaped-up harvest-mow,
And in the greenwood from a shaken oak
Seek solace for thine hunger.   *159*
                    Now to tell
The sturdy rustics' weapons, what they are,
Without which, neither can be sown nor reared
The fruits of harvest; first the bent plough's share
And heavy timber, and slow-lumbering wains
Of the Eleusinian mother, threshing-sleighs
And drags, and harrows with their crushing weight;
Then the cheap wicker-ware of Celeus old,
Hurdles of arbute, and thy mystic fan,
Iacchus; which, full tale, long ere the time
Thou must with heed lay by, if thee await
Not all unearned the country's crown divine.   *168*
While yet within the woods, the elm is tamed
And bowed with mighty force to form the stock,
And take the plough's curved shape, then nigh the
          root
A pole eight feet projecting, earth-boards twain,
And share-beam with its double back they fix.

For yoke is early hewn a linden light,
And a tall beech for handle, from behind
To turn the car at lowest: then o'er the hearth
The wood they hang till the smoke knows it well.
   Many the precepts of the men of old
I can recount thee, so thou start not back,
And such slight cares to learn not weary thee.   *177*
And this among the first: thy threshing-floor
With ponderous roller must be levelled smooth,
And wrought by hand, and fixed with binding chalk,
Lest weeds arise, or dust a passage win
Splitting the surface, then a thousand plagues
Make sport of it: oft builds the tiny mouse
Her home, and plants her granary, underground,
Or burrow for their bed the purblind moles,
Or toad is found in hollows, and all the swarm
Of earth's unsightly creatures; or a huge
Corn-heap the weevil plunders, and the ant,
Fearful of coming age and penury.   *186*
   Mark too, what time the walnut in the woods
With ample bloom shall clothe her, and bow down
Her odorous branches, if the fruit prevail,
Like store of grain will follow, and there shall come
A mighty winnowing-time with mighty heat;
But if the shade with wealth of leaves abound,
Vainly your threshing-floor will bruise the stalks
Rich but in chaff. Many myself have seen
Steep, as they sow, their pulse-seeds, drenching them
With nitre and black oil-lees, that the fruit
Might swell within the treacherous pods, and they
Make speed to boil at howso small a fire.   *196*
Yet, culled with caution, proved with patient toil,
These have I seen degenerate, did not man
Put forth his hand with power, and year by year
Choose out the largest. So, by fate impelled,
Speed all things to the worse, and backward borne
Glide from us; even as who with struggling oars
Up stream scarce pulls a shallop, if he chance
His arms to slacken, lo! with headlong force
The current sweeps him down the hurrying tide.   *203*
   Us too behoves Arcturus' sign observe,
And the Kids' seasons and the shining Snake,
No less than those who o'er the windy main
Borne homeward tempt the Pontic, and the jaws
Of oyster-rife Abydos. When the Scales
Now poising fair the hours of sleep and day

Give half the world to sunshine, half to shade,
Then urge your bulls, my masters; sow the plain
Even to the verge of tameless winter's showers
With barley: then, too, time it is to hide
Your flax in earth, and poppy, Ceres' joy,   *212*
Aye, more than time to bend above the plough,
While earth, yet dry, forbids not, and the clouds
Are buoyant. With the spring comes bean-sowing;
Thee, too, Lucerne, the crumbling furrows then
Receive, and millet's annual care returns,
What time the white bull with his gilded horns
Opens the year, before whose threatening front,
Routed the dog-star sinks. But if it be
For wheaten harvest and the hardy spelt,
Thou tax the soil, to corn-ears wholly given,
Let Atlas' daughters hide them in the dawn,
The Cretan star, a crown of fire, depart,
Or e'er the furrow's claim of seed thou quit,
Or haste thee to entrust the whole year's hope
To earth that would not. Many have begun
Ere Maia's star be setting; these, I trow,
Their looked-for harvest fools with empty ears.   *226*
But if the vetch and common kidney-bean
Thou'rt fain to sow, nor scorn to make thy care
Pelusiac lentil, no uncertain sign
Boötes' fall will send thee; then begin,
Pursue thy sowing till half the frosts be done.
    Therefore it is the golden sun, his course
Into fixed parts dividing, rules his way
Through the twelve constellations of the world.
Five zones the heavens contain; whereof is one
Aye red with flashing sunlight, fervent aye
From fire; on either side to left and right
Are traced the utmost twain, stiff with blue ice,
And black with scowling storm-clouds, and betwixt
These and the midmost, other twain there lie,
By the Gods' grace to heart-sick mortals given,
And a path cleft between them, where might wheel
On sloping plane the system of the Signs.   *238*
And as toward Scythia and Rhipaean heights
The world mounts upward, likewise sinks it down
Toward Libya and the south, this pole of ours
Still towering high, that other, 'neath their feet,
By dark Styx frowned on, and the abysmal shades.
Here glides the huge Snake forth with sinuous coils
'Twixt the two Bears and round them river-wise—

The Bears that fear 'neath Ocean's brim to dip.
There either, say they, reigns the eternal hush
Of night that knows no seasons, her black pall
Thick-mantling fold on fold; or thitherward
From us returning Dawn brings back the day;
And when the first breath of his panting steeds
On us the Orient flings, that hour with them
Red Vesper 'gins to trim his 'lated fires.   251
Hence under doubtful skies forebode we can
The coming tempests, hence both harvest-day
And seed-time, when to smite the treacherous main
With driving oars, when launch the fair-rigged fleet,
Or in ripe hour to fell the forest-pine.
Hence, too, not idly do we watch the stars—
Their rising and their setting—and the year,
Four varying seasons to one law conformed.
    If chilly showers e'er shut the farmer's door,
Much that had soon with sunshine cried for haste,
He may forestall; the ploughman batters keen
His blunted share's hard tooth, scoops from a tree
His troughs, or on the cattle stamps a brand,
Or numbers on the corn-heaps; some make sharp
The stakes and two-pronged forks, and willow-bands
Amerian for the bending vine prepare.   265
Now let the pliant basket plaited be
Of bramble-twigs; now set your corn to parch
Before the fire; now bruise it with the stone.
Nay even on holy days some tasks to ply
Is right and lawful: this no ban forbids,
To turn the runnel's course, fence corn-fields in,
Make springes for the birds, burn up the briars,
And plunge in wholesome stream the bleating flock.
Oft too with oil or apples plenty-cheap
The creeping ass's ribs his driver packs,
And home from town returning brings instead
A dented mill-stone or black lump of pitch.   275
    The moon herself in various rank assigns
The days for labour lucky: fly the fifth;
Then sprang pale Orcus and the Eumenides;
Earth then in awful labour brought to light
Coeus, Iapetus, and Typhöeus fell,
And those sworn brethren banded to break down
The gates of heaven; thrice, sooth to say, they strove
Ossa on Pelion's top to heave and heap,
Aye, and on Ossa to up-roll amain
Leafy Olympus; thrice with thunderbolt

Their mountain-stair the Sire asunder smote.
Seventh after tenth is lucky both to set
The vine in earth, and take and tame the steer,
And fix the leashes to the warp; the ninth
To runagates is kinder, cross to thieves.　　　286
　　Many the tasks that lightlier lend themselves
In chilly night, or when the sun is young,
And Dawn bedews the world. By night 'tis best
To reap light stubble, and parched fields by night;
For nights the suppling moisture never fails.
And one will sit the long late watches out
By winter fire-light, shaping with keen blade
The torches to a point; his wife the while,
Her tedious labour soothing with a song,
Speeds the shrill comb along the warp, or else
With Vulcan's aid boils the sweet must-juice down,
And skims with leaves the quivering cauldron's wave. 296
　　But ruddy Ceres in mid heat is mown,
And in mid heat the parchèd ears are bruised
Upon the floor; to plough strip, strip to sow;
Winter's the lazy time for husbandmen.
In the cold season farmers wont to taste
The increase of their toil, and yield themselves
To mutual interchange of festal cheer.
Boon winter bids them, and unbinds their cares,
As laden keels, when now the port they touch,
And happy sailors crown the sterns with flowers.
Nathless then also time it is to strip
Acorns from oaks, and berries from the bay,
Olives, and bleeding myrtles, then to set
Snares for the crane, and meshes for the stag,
And hunt the long-eared hares, then pierce the doe
With whirl of hempen-thonged Balearic sling,
While snow lies deep, and streams are drifting ice.　　310
　　What need to tell of autumn's storms and stars,
And wherefore men must watch, when now the day
Grows shorter, and more soft the summer's heat?
When Spring the rain-bringer comes rushing down,
Or when the beards of harvest on the plain
Bristle already, and the milky corn
On its green stalk is swelling? Many a time,
When now the farmer to his yellow fields
The reaping-hind came bringing, even in act
To lop the brittle barley stems, have I
Seen all the windy legions clash in war
Together, as to rend up far and wide

The heavy corn-crop from its lowest roots,
And toss it skyward: so might winter's flaw,
Dark-eddying, whirl light stalks and flying straws.   *321*
    Oft too comes looming vast along the sky
A march of waters; mustering from above,
The clouds roll up the tempest, heaped and grim
With angry showers: down falls the height of heaven,
And with a great rain floods the smiling crops,
The oxen's labour: now the dikes fill fast,
And the void river-beds swell thunderously,
And all the panting firths of Ocean boil.
The Sire himself in midnight of the clouds
Wields with red hand the levin; through all her bulk
Earth at the hurly quakes; the beasts are fled,
And mortal hearts of every kindred sunk
In cowering terror; he with flaming brand
Athos, or Rhodope, or Ceraunian crags
Precipitates: then doubly raves the South
With shower on blinding shower, and woods and
       coasts
Wail fitfully beneath the mighty blast.   *334*
This fearing, mark the months and Signs of heaven,
Whither retires him Saturn's icy star,
And through what heavenly cycles wandereth
The glowing orb Cyllenian. Before all
Worship the Gods, and to great Ceres pay
Her yearly dues upon the happy sward
With sacrifice, anigh the utmost end
Of winter, and when Spring begins to smile.
Then lambs are fat, and wines are mellowest then;
Then sleep is sweet, and dark the shadows fall
Upon the mountains. Let your rustic youth
To Ceres do obeisance, one and all;
And for her pleasure thou mix honeycombs
With milk and the ripe wine-god; thrice for luck
Around the young corn let the victim go,
And all the choir, a joyful company,
Attend it, and with shouts bid Ceres come
To be their house-mate; and let no man dare
Put sickle to the ripened ears until,
With woven oak his temples chapleted,
He foot the ruggèd dance and chant the lay.   *350*
    Aye, and that these things we might win to know
By certain tokens, heats, and showers, and winds
That bring the frost, the Sire of all himself
Ordained what warnings in her monthly round

The moon should give, what bodes the south wind's fall,
What oft-repeated sights the herdsman seeing
Should keep his cattle closer to their stalls.
No sooner are the winds at point to rise,
Than either Ocean's firths begin to toss
And swell, and a dry crackling sound is heard
Upon the heights, or one loud ferment booms
The beach afar, and through the forest goes
A murmur multitudinous. By this
Scarce can the billow spare the curvèd keels,
When swift the sea-gulls from the middle main
Come winging, and their shrieks are shoreward borne,
When ocean-loving cormorants on dry land
Besport them, and the hern, her marshy haunts
Forsaking, mounts above the soaring cloud.   364
Oft, too, when wind is toward, the stars thou'lt see
From heaven shoot headlong, and through murky
          night
Long trails of fire white-glistening in their wake,
Or light chaff flit in air with fallen leaves,
Or feathers on the wave-top float and play.
But when from regions of the furious North
It lightens, and when thunder fills the halls
Of Eurus and of Zephyr, all the fields
With brimming dikes are flooded, and at sea
No mariner but furls his dripping sails.
Never at unawares did shower annoy:
Or, as it rises, the high-soaring cranes
Flee to the vales before it, or, with face
Upturned to heaven, the heifer snuffs the gale
Through gaping nostrils, or about the meres
Shrill-twittering flits the swallow, and the frogs
Crouch in the mud and chant their dirge of old.   378
Oft, too, the ant from out her inmost cells,
Fretting the narrow path, her eggs conveys;
Or the huge bow sucks moisture; or a host
Of rooks from food returning in long line
Clamour with jostling wings. Now mayst thou see
The various ocean-fowl and those that pry
Round Asian meads within thy freshet-pools,
Cayster, as in eager rivalry,
About their shoulders dash the plenteous spray,
Now duck their head beneath the wave, now run
Into the billows, for sheer idle joy
Of their mad bathing-revel. Then the crow
With full voice, good-for-naught, inviting rain,

Stalks on the dry sand mateless and alone.
Nor e'en the maids, that card their nightly task,
Know not the storm-sign, when in blazing crock
They see the lamp-oil sputtering with a growth
Of mouldy snuff-clots.   *392*
          So too, after rain,
Sunshine and open skies thou mayst forecast,
And learn by tokens sure, for then nor dimmed
Appear the stars' keen edges, nor the moon
As borrowing of her brother's beams to rise,
Nor fleecy films to float along the sky.
Not to the sun's warmth then upon the shore
Do halcyons dear to Thetis ope their wings,
Nor filthy swine take thought to toss on high
With scattering snout the straw-wisps. But the clouds
Seek more the vales, and rest upon the plain,
And from the roof-top the night-owl for naught
Watching the sunset plies her 'lated song.   *403*
Distinct in clearest air is Nisus seen
Towering, and Scylla for the purple lock
Pays dear; for whereso, as she flies, her wings
The light air winnow, lo! fierce, implacable,
Nisus with mighty whirr through heaven pursues;
Where Nisus heavenward soareth, there her wings
Clutch as she flies, the light air winnowing still.   *409*
Soft then the voice of rooks from indrawn throat
Thrice, four times, o'er repeated, and full oft
On their high cradles, by some hidden joy
Gladdened beyond their wont, in bustling throngs
Among the leaves they riot; so sweet it is,
When showers are spent, their own loved nests again
And tender brood to visit. Not, I deem,
That heaven some native wit to these assigned,
Or fate a larger prescience, but that when
The storm and shifting moisture of the air
Have changed their courses, and the sky-god now,
Wet with the south-wind, thickens what was rare,
And what was gross releases, then, too, change
Their spirits' fleeting phases, and their breasts
Feel other motions now, than when the wind
Was driving up the cloud-rack. Hence proceeds
That blending of the feathered choirs afield,
The cattle's exultation, and the rooks'
Deep-throated triumph.   *423*
              But if the headlong sun
And moons in order following thou regard,

Ne'er will to-morrow's hour deceive thee, ne'er
Wilt thou be caught by guile of cloudless night.
When first the moon recalls her rallying fires,
If dark the air clipped by her crescent dim,
For folks afield and on the open sea
A mighty rain is brewing; but if her face
With maiden blush she mantle, 'twill be wind,
For wind turns Phoebe still to ruddier gold.   431
But if at her fourth rising, for 'tis that
Gives surest counsel, clear she ride thro' heaven
With horns unblunted, then shall that whole day,
And to the month's end those that spring from it,
Rainless and windless be, while safe ashore
Shall sailors pay their vows to Panope,
Glaucus, and Melicertes, Ino's child.
    The sun too, both at rising, and when soon
He dives beneath the waves, shall yield thee signs;
For signs, none trustier, travel with the sun,
Both those which in their course with dawn he brings,
And those at star-rise. When his springing orb
With spots he pranketh, muffled in a cloud,
And shrinks mid-circle, then of showers beware;
For then the South comes driving from the deep,
To trees and crops and cattle bringing bane.   444
Or when at day-break through dark clouds his rays
Burst and are scattered, or when rising pale
Aurora quits Tithonus' saffron bed,
But sorry shelter then, alack! will yield
Vine-leaf to ripening grapes; so thick a hail
In spiky showers spins rattling on the roof.
And this yet more 'twill boot thee bear in mind,
When now, his course upon Olympus run,
He draws to his decline: for oft we see
Upon the sun's own face strange colours stray;   452
Dark tells of rain, of east winds fiery-red;
If spots with ruddy fire begin to mix,
Then all the heavens convulsed in wrath thou'lt see—
Storm-clouds and wind together. Me that night
Let no man bid fare forth upon the deep,
Nor rend the rope from shore. But if, when both
He brings again and hides the day's return,
Clear-orbed he shineth, idly wilt thou dread
The storm-clouds, and beneath the lustral North
See the woods waving. What late eve in fine
Bears in her bosom, whence the wind that brings
Fair-weather-clouds, or what the rainy South

Is meditating, tokens of all these
The sun will give thee. Who dare charge the sun
With leasing? He it is who warneth oft
Of hidden broils at hand and treachery,
And secret swelling of the waves of war.   465
He too it was, when Caesar's light was quenched,
For Rome had pity, when his bright head he veiled
In iron-hued darkness, till a godless age
Trembled for night eternal; at that time
Howbeit earth also, and the ocean-plains,
And dogs obscene, and birds of evil bode
Gave tokens. Yea, how often have we seen
Etna, her furnace-walls asunder riven,
In billowy floods boil o'er the Cyclops' fields,
And roll down globes of fire and molten rocks!
A clash of arms through all the heaven was heard
By Germany; strange heavings shook the Alps.   475
Yea, and by many through the breathless groves
A voice was heard with power, and wondrous-pale
Phantoms were seen upon the dusk of night,
And cattle spake, portentous! streams stand still,
And the earth yawns asunder, ivory weeps
For sorrow in the shrines, and bronzes sweat.
Up-twirling forests with his eddying tide,
Madly he bears them down, that lord of floods,
Eridanus, till through all the plain are swept
Beasts and their stalls together. At that time
In gloomy entrails ceased not to appear
Dark-threatening fibres, springs to trickle blood,
And high-built cities night-long to resound
With the wolves' howling. Never more than then
From skies all cloudless fell the thunderbolts,
Nor blazed so oft the comet's fire of bale.   488
Therefore a second time Philippi saw
The Roman hosts with kindred weapons rush
To battle, nor did the high gods deem it hard
That twice Emathia and the wide champaign
Of Haemus should be fattening with our blood.
Ay, and the time will come when there anigh,
Heaving the earth up with his curvèd plough,
Some swain will light on javelins by foul rust
Corroded, or with ponderous harrow strike
On empty helmets, while he gapes to see
Bones as of giants from the trench untombed.   497
Gods of my country, heroes of the soil,
And Romulus, and Mother Vesta, thou

[50]

Who Tuscan Tiber and Rome's Palatine
Preservest, this new champion at the least
Our fallen generation to repair
Forbid not. To the full and long ago
Our blood thy Trojan perjuries hath paid,
Laomedon. Long since the courts of heaven
Begrudge us thee, our Caesar, and complain
That thou regard'st the triumphs of mankind,
Here where the wrong is right, the right is wrong,
Where wars abound so many, and myriad-faced
Is crime; where no meet honour hath the plough;
The fields, their husbandmen led far away,
Rot in neglect, and curvèd pruning-hooks
Into the sword's stiff blade are fused and forged.   *508*
Euphrates here, here Germany new strife
Is stirring; neighbouring cities are in arms,
The laws that bound them snapped; and godless war
Rages through all the universe; as when
The four-horse chariots from the barriers poured
Still quicken o'er the course, and, idly now
Grasping the reins, the driver by his team
Is onward borne, nor heeds the car his curb.   *514*

GEORGIC II

Thus far the tilth of fields and stars of heaven;
Now will I sing thee, Bacchus, and, with thee,
The forest's young plantations and the fruit
Of slow-maturing olive. Hither haste,
O Father of the wine-press; all things here
Teem with the bounties of thy hand; for thee
With viny autumn laden blooms the field,
And foams the vintage high with brimming vats;
Hither, O Father of the wine-press, come,
And stripped of buskin stain thy barèd limbs
In the new must with me.   *8*
     First, nature's law
For generating trees is manifold;
For some of their own force spontaneous spring,
No hand of man compelling, and possess
The plains and river-windings far and wide,
As pliant osier and the bending broom,
Poplar, and willows in wan companies
With green leaf glimmering gray; and some there be
From chance-dropped seed that rear them, as the tall
Chestnuts, and, mightiest of the branching wood,
Jove's Aesculus, and oaks, oracular
Deemed by the Greeks of old. With some sprouts
 forth
A forest of dense suckers from the root,
As elms and cherries; so, too, a pigmy plant,
Beneath its mother's mighty shade upshoots
The bay-tree of Parnassus. Such the modes
Nature imparted first; hence all the race
Of forest-trees and shrubs and sacred groves
Springs into verdure.   *21*
    Other means there are,
Which use by method for itself acquired.
One, sliving suckers from the tender frame
Of the tree-mother, plants them in the trench;
One buries the bare stumps within his field,
Truncheons cleft four-wise, or sharp-pointed stakes;
Some forest-trees the layer's bent arch await,
And slips yet quick within the parent-soil;
No root need others, nor doth the pruner's hand

Shrink to restore the topmost shoot to earth
That gave it being. Nay, marvellous to tell,
Lopped of its limbs, the olive, a mere stock,
Still thrusts its root out from the sapless wood,
And oft the branches of one kind we see
Change to another's with no loss to rue,
Pear-tree transformed the ingrafted apple yield,
And stony cornels on the plum-tree blush.   *34*

   Come then, and learn what tilth to each belongs
According to their kinds, ye husbandmen,
And tame with culture the wild fruits, lest earth
Lie idle. O blithe to make all Ismarus
One forest of the wine-god, and to clothe
With olives huge Tabernus! And be thou
At hand, and with me ply the voyage of toil
I am bound on, O my glory, O thou that art
Justly the chiefest portion of my fame,
Maecenas, and on this wide ocean launched
Spread sail like wings to waft thee. Not that I
With my poor verse would comprehend the whole,
Nay, though a hundred tongues, a hundred mouths
Were mine, a voice of iron; be thou at hand,
Skirt but the nearer coast-line; see the shore
Is in our grasp; not now with feignèd song
Through winding bouts and tedious preludings
Shall I detain thee.   *46*

           Those that lift their head
Into the realms of light spontaneously,
Fruitless indeed, but blithe and strenuous spring,
Since Nature lurks within the soil. And yet
Even these, should one engraft them, or transplant
To well-drilled trenches, will anon put off
Their woodland temper, and, by frequent tilth,
To whatso craft thou summon them, make speed
To follow. So likewise will the barren shaft
That from the stock-root issueth, if it be
Set out with clear space amid open fields: *54*
Now the tree-mother's towering leaves and boughs
Darken, despoil of increase as it grows,
And blast it in the bearing. Lastly, that
Which from shed seed ariseth, upward wins
But slowly, yielding promise of its shade
To late-born generations; apples wane
Forgetful of their former juice, the grape
Bears sorry clusters, for the birds a prey.

   Soothly on all must toil be spent, and all

Trained to the trench and at great cost subdued.   *62*
But reared from truncheons olives answer best,
As vines from layers, and from the solid wood
The Paphian myrtles; while from suckers spring
Both hardy hazels and huge ash, the tree
That rims with shade the brows of Hercules,
And acorns dear to the Chaonian sire:
So springs the towering palm too, and the fir
Destined to spy the dangers of the deep.
But the rough arbutus with walnut-fruit
Is grafted; so have barren planes ere now
Stout apples borne, with chestnut-flower the beech,
The mountain-ash with pear-bloom whitened o'er,
And swine crunched acorns 'neath the boughs of
    elms.   *72*
    Nor is the method of inserting eyes
And grafting one: for where the buds push forth
Amidst the bark, and burst the membranes thin,
Even on the knot a narrow rift is made,
Wherein from some strange tree a germ they pen,
And to the moist rind bid it cleave and grow.
Or, otherwise, in knotless trunks is hewn
A breach, and deep into the solid grain
A path with wedges cloven; then fruitful slips
Are set herein, and—no long time—behold!
To heaven upshot with teeming boughs, the tree
Strange leaves admires and fruitage not its own.   *82*
    Nor of one kind alone are sturdy elms,
Willow and lotus, nor the cypress-trees
Of Ida; nor of self-same fashion spring
Fat olives, orchades, and radii
And bitter-berried pausians, no, nor yet
Apples and the forests of Alcinous;
Nor from like cuttings are Crustumian pears
And Syrian, and the heavy hand-fillers.
Not the same vintage from our trees hangs down,
Which Lesbos from Methymna's tendril plucks.   *90*
Vines Thasian are there, Mareotids white,
These apt for richer soils, for lighter those:
Psithian for raisin-wine more useful, thin
Lageos, that one day will try the feet
And tie the tongue: purples and early-ripes,
And how, O Rhaetian, shall I hymn thy praise?
Yet cope not therefore with Falernian bins.
Vines Aminaean too, best-bodied wine,
To which the Tmolian bows him, ay, and king

Phanaeus too, and, lesser of that name,
Argitis, wherewith not a grape can vie
For gush of wine-juice or for length of years.   *100*
Nor thee must I pass over, vine of Rhodes,
Welcomed by gods and at the second board,
Nor thee, Bumastus, with plump clusters swollen.
But lo! how many kinds, and what their names,
There is no telling, nor doth it boot to tell;
Who lists to know it, he too would list to learn
How many sand-grains are by Zephyr tossed
On Libya's plain, or wot, when Eurus falls
With fury on the ships, how many waves
Come rolling shoreward from the Ionian sea.
    Not that all soils can all things bear alike.   *109*
Willows by water-courses have their birth,
Alders in miry fens; on rocky heights
The barren mountain-ashes; on the shore
Myrtles throng gayest; Bacchus, lastly, loves
The bare hillside, and yews the north wind's chill.
Mark too the earth by outland tillers tamed,
And Eastern homes of Arabs, and tattooed
Geloni; to all trees their native lands
Allotted are; no clime but India bears
Black ebony; the branch of frankincense
Is Saba's sons' alone; why tell to thee
Of balsams oozing from the perfumed wood,
Or berries of acanthus ever green?   *119*
Of Aethiop forests hoar with downy wool,
Or how the Seres comb from off the leaves
Their silky fleece? Of groves which India bears,
Ocean's near neighbour, earth's remotest nook,
Where not an arrow-shot can cleave the air
Above their tree-tops? yet no laggards they,
When girded with the quiver! Media yields
The bitter juices and slow-lingering taste
Of the blest citron-fruit, than which no aid
Comes timelier, when fierce step-dames drug the cup
With simples mixed and spells of baneful power,
To drive the deadly poison from the limbs.   *130*
Large the tree's self in semblance like a bay,
And, showered it not a different scent abroad,
A bay it had been; for no wind of heaven
Its foliage falls; the flower, none faster, clings;
With it the Medes for sweetness lave the lips,
And ease the panting breathlessness of age.
    But no, not Mede-land with its wealth of woods,

Nor Ganges fair, and Hermus thick with gold,
Can match the praise of Italy; nor Ind,
Nor Bactria, nor Panchaia, one wide tract
Of incense-teeming sand. Here never bulls
With nostrils snorting fire upturned the sod
Sown with the monstrous dragon's teeth, nor crop
Of warriors bristled thick with lance and helm;   *142*
But heavy harvests and the Massic juice
Of Bacchus fill its borders, overspread
With fruitful flocks and olives. Hence arose
The war-horse stepping proudly o'er the plain;
Hence thy white flocks, Clitumnus, and the bull,
Of victims mightiest, which full oft have led,
Bathed in thy sacred stream, the triumph-pomp
Of Romans to the temples of the gods.
Here blooms perpetual spring, and summer here
In months that are not summer's; twice teem the
    flocks;
Twice doth the tree yield service of her fruit.
But ravening tigers come not nigh, nor breed
Of savage lion, nor aconite betrays
Its hapless gatherers, nor with sweep so vast
Doth the scaled serpent trail his endless coils
Along the ground, or wreathe him into spires.   *154*
Mark too her cities, so many and so proud,
Of mighty toil the achievement, town on town
Up rugged precipices heaved and reared,
And rivers undergliding ancient walls.
Or should I celebrate the sea that laves
Her upper shores and lower? or those broad lakes?
Thee, Larius, greatest and, Benacus, thee
With billowy uproar surging like the main?
Or sing her harbours, and the barrier cast
Athwart the Lucrine, and how ocean chafes
With mighty bellowings, where the Julian wave
Echoes the thunder of his rout, and through
Avernian inlets pours the Tuscan tide?   *164*
A land no less that in her veins displays
Rivers of silver, mines of copper ore,
Ay, and with gold hath flowed abundantly.
A land that reared a valiant breed of men,
The Marsi and Sabellian youth, and, schooled
To hardship, the Ligurian, and with these
The Volscian javelin-armed, the Decii too,
The Marii and Camilli, names of might,
The Scipios, stubborn warriors, ay, and thee,

Great Caesar, who in Asia's utmost bounds
With conquering arm e'en now art fending far
The unwarlike Indian from the heights of Rome.   *172*
Hail! land of Saturn, mighty mother thou
Of fruits and heroes; 'tis for thee I dare
Unseal the sacred fountains, and essay
Themes of old art and glory, as I sing
The song of Ascra through the towns of Rome.
　　Now for the native gifts of various soils,
What powers hath each, what hue, what natural bent
For yielding increase. First your stubborn lands
And churlish hill-sides, where are thorny fields
Of meagre marl and gravel, these delight
In long-lived olive-groves to Pallas dear.   *181*
Take for a sign the plenteous growth hard by
Of oleaster, and the fields strewn wide
With woodland berries. But a soil that's rich,
In moisture sweet exulting, and the plain
That teems with grasses on its fruitful breast,
Such as full oft in hollow mountain-dell
We view beneath us—from the craggy heights
Streams thither flow with fertilizing mud—
A plain which southward rising feeds the fern
By curvèd ploughs detested, this one day
Shall yield thee store of vines full strong to gush
In torrents of the wine-god; this shall be
Fruitful of grapes and flowing juice like that
We pour to heaven from bowls of gold, what time
The sleek Etruscan at the altar blows
His ivory pipe, and on the curvèd dish
We lay the reeking entrails. If to rear
Cattle delight thee rather, steers, or lambs,
Or goats that kill the tender plants, then seek
Full-fed Tarentum's glades and distant fields,
Or such a plain as luckless Mantua lost,
Whose weedy water feeds the snow-white swan: *199*
There nor clear springs nor grass the flocks will fail,
And all the day-long browsing of thy herds
Shall the cool dews of one brief night repair.
Land which the burrowing share shows dark and rich,
With crumbling soil—for this we counterfeit
In ploughing—for corn is goodliest; from no field
More wains thou'lt see wend home with plodding
　　steers;
Or that from which the husbandman in spleen
Has cleared the timber, and o'erthrown the copse

That year on year lay idle, and from the roots
Uptorn the immemorial haunt of birds;
They banished from their nests have sought the skies; *210*
But the rude plain beneath the ploughshare's stroke
Starts into sudden brightness. For indeed
The starved hill-country gravel scarce serves the bees
With lowly cassias and with rosemary;
Rough tufa and chalk too, by black water-worms
Gnawed through and through, proclaim no soils
    beside
So rife with serpent-dainties, or that yield
Such winding lairs to lurk in. That again,
Which vapoury mist and flitting smoke exhales,
Drinks moisture up and casts it forth at will,
Which, ever in its own green grass arrayed,
Mars not the metal with salt scurf of rust—
That shall thine elms with merry vines enwreathe;
That teems with olive; that shall thy tilth prove kind
To cattle, and patient of the curvèd share. *223*
Such ploughs rich Capua, such the coast that skirts
Thy ridge, Vesuvius, and the Clanian flood,
Acerrae's desolation and her bane.
How each to recognize now hear me tell.
Dost ask if loose or passing firm it be—
Since one for corn hath liking, one for wine,
The firmer sort for Ceres, none too loose
For thee, Lyaeus?—with scrutinizing eye
First choose thy ground, and bid a pit be sunk
Deep in the solid earth, then cast the mould
All back again, and stamp the surface smooth. *232*
If it suffice not, loose will be the land,
More meet for cattle and for kindly vines;
But if, rebellious, to its proper bounds
The soil returns not, but fills all the trench
And overtops it, then the glebe is gross;
Look for stiff ridges and reluctant clods,
And with strong bullocks cleave the fallow crust.
Salt ground again, and bitter, as 'tis called—
Barren for fruits, by tilth untamable,
Nor grape her kind, nor apples their good name
Maintaining—will in this wise yield thee proof:
Stout osier-baskets from the rafter-smoke,
And strainers of the winepress pluck thee down; *242*
Hereinto let that evil land, with fresh
Spring-water mixed, be trampled to the full;
The moisture, mark you, will ooze all away,

In big drops issuing through the osier-withes,
But plainly will its taste the secret tell,
And with a harsh twang ruefully distort
The mouths of them that try it. Rich soil again
We learn on this wise: tossed from hand to hand
Yet cracks it never, but pitch-like, as we hold,
Clings to the fingers. A land with moisture rife
Breeds lustier herbage, and is more than meet
Prolific. Ah! may never such for me
O'er-fertile prove, or make too stout a show
At the first earing! Heavy land or light
The mute self-witness of its weight betrays.
A glance will serve to warn thee which is black,   255
Or what the hue of any. But hard it is
To track the signs of that pernicious cold:
Pines only, noxious yews, and ivies dark
At times reveal its traces.
                         All these rules
Regarding, let your land, ay, long before,
Scorch to the quick, and into trenches carve
The mighty mountains, and their upturned clods
Bare to the north wind, ere thou plant therein
The vine's prolific kindred. Fields whose soil
Is crumbling are the best: winds look to that,
And bitter hoar-frosts, and the delver's toil
Untiring, as he stirs the loosened glebe.   264
But those, whose vigilance no care escapes,
Search for a kindred site, where first to rear
A nursery for the trees, and eke whereto
Soon to translate them, lest the sudden shock
From their new mother the young plants estrange.
Nay, even the quarter of the sky they brand
Upon the bark, that each may be restored,
As erst it stood, here bore the southern heats,
Here turned its shoulder to the northern pole;
So strong is custom formed in early years.   273
Whether on hill or plain 'tis best to plant
Your vineyard first inquire. If on some plain
You measure out rich acres, then plant thick;
Thick planting makes no niggard of the vine;
But if on rising mound or sloping hill,
Then let the rows have room, so none the less
Each line you draw, when all the trees are set,
May tally to perfection. Even as oft
In mighty war, whenas the legion's length
Deploys its cohorts, and the column stands

In open plain, the ranks of battle set,
And far and near with rippling sheen of arms
The wide earth flickers, nor yet in grisly strife
Foe grapples foe, but dubious 'twixt the hosts
The war-god wavers; so let all be ranged
In equal rows symmetric, not alone
To feed an idle fancy with the view,
But since not otherwise will earth afford
Vigour to all alike, nor yet the boughs
Have power to stretch them into open space.   287

    Shouldst haply of the furrow's depth inquire,
Even to a shallow trench I dare commit
The vine; but deeper in the ground is fixed
The tree that props it, aesculus in chief,
Which howso far its summit soars toward heaven,
So deep strikes root into the vaults of hell.
It therefore neither storms, nor blasts, nor showers
Wrench from its bed; unshaken it abides,
Sees many a generation, many an age
Of men roll onward, and survives them all,
Stretching its titan arms and branches far,
Sole central pillar of a world of shade.   297

    Nor toward the sunset let thy vineyards slope,
Nor midst the vines plant hazel; neither take
The topmost shoots for cuttings, nor from the top
Of the supporting tree your suckers tear;
So deep their love of earth; nor wound the plants
With blunted blade; nor truncheons intersperse
Of the wild olive: for oft from careless swains
A spark hath fallen, that, 'neath the unctuous rind
Hid thief-like first, now grips the tough tree-bole,
And mounting to the leaves on high, sends forth
A roar to heaven, then coursing through the boughs
And airy summits reigns victoriously,
Wraps all the grove in robes of fire, and gross
With pitch-black vapour heaves the murky reek
Skyward, but chiefly if a storm has swooped
Down on the forest, and a driving wind
Rolls up the conflagration. When 'tis so,
Their root-force fails them, nor, when lopped away,
Can they recover, and from the earth beneath
Spring to like verdure; thus alone survives
The bare wild olive with its bitter leaves.   314

    Let none persuade thee, howso weighty-wise,
To stir the soil when stiff with Boreas' breath.
Then ice-bound winter locks the fields, nor lets

The young plant fix its frozen root to earth.
Best sow your vineyards when in blushing Spring
Comes the white bird long-bodied snakes abhor,
Or on the eve of autumn's earliest frost,
Ere the swift sun-steeds touch the wintry Signs,
While summer is departing. Spring it is
Blesses the fruit-plantation, Spring the groves;
In Spring earth swells and claims the fruitful seed.   *324*
Then Aether, sire omnipotent, leaps down
With quickening showers to his glad wife's embrace,
And, might with might commingling, rears to life
All germs that teem within her; then resound
With songs of birds the greenwood-wildernesses,
And in due time the herds their loves renew;
Then the boon earth yields increase, and the fields
Unlock their bosoms to the warm west winds;
Soft moisture spreads o'er all things, and the blades
Face the new suns, and safely trust them now;
The vine-shoot, fearless of the rising south,
Or mighty north winds driving rain from heaven,
Bursts into bud, and every leaf unfolds.   *335*
Even so, methinks, when Earth to being sprang,
Dawned the first days, and such the course they held;
'Twas Spring-tide then, ay, Spring, the mighty world
Was keeping: Eurus spared his wintry blasts,
When first the flocks drank sunlight, and a race
Of men like iron from the hard glebe arose,
And wild beasts thronged the woods, and stars the
          heaven.
Nor could frail creatures bear this heavy strain,
Did not so large a respite interpose
'Twixt frost and heat, and heaven's relenting arms
Yield earth a welcome.   *345*
                              For the rest, whate'er
The sets thou plantest in thy fields, thereon
Strew refuse rich, and with abundant earth
Take heed to hide them, and dig in withal
Rough shells or porous stone, for therebetween
Will water trickle and fine vapour creep,
And so the plants their drooping spirits raise.
Aye, and there have been, who with weight of stone
Or heavy potsherd press them from above;
This serves for shield in pelting showers, and this
When the hot dog-star chaps the fields with drought.   *353*
    The slips once planted, yet remains to cleave
The earth about their roots persistently,

And toss the cumbrous hoes, or task the soil
With burrowing plough-share, and ply up and down
Your labouring bullocks through the vineyard's
    midst,
Then too smooth reeds and shafts of whittled wand,
And ashen poles and sturdy forks to shape,
Whereby supported they may learn to mount,
Laugh at the gales, and through the elm-tops win
From story up to story.   *361*
                Now while yet
The leaves are in their first fresh infant growth,
Forbear their frailty, and while yet the bough
Shoots joyfully toward heaven, with loosened rein
Launched on the void, assail it not as yet
With keen-edged sickle, but let the leaves alone
Be culled with clip of fingers here and there.
But when they clasp the elms with sturdy trunks
Erect, then strip the leaves off, prune the boughs;
Sooner they shrink from steel, but then put forth
The arm of power, and stem the branchy tide.   *370*
    Hedges too must be woven and all beasts
Barred entrance, chiefly while the leaf is young
And witless of disaster; for therewith,
Beside harsh winters and o'erpowering sun,
Wild buffaloes and pestering goats for ay
Besport them, sheep and heifers glut their greed.
Nor cold by hoar-frost curdled, nor the prone
Dead weight of summer upon the parchèd crags,
So scathe it, as the flocks with venom-bite
Of their hard tooth, whose gnawing scars the stem.   *379*
For no offence but this to Bacchus bleeds
The goat at every altar, and old plays
Upon the stage find entrance; therefore too
The sons of Theseus through the country-side—
Hamlet and crossway—set the prize of wit,
And on the smooth sward over oilèd skins
Dance in their tipsy frolic. Furthermore
The Ausonian swains, a race from Troy derived,
Make merry with rough rhymes and boisterous mirth,
Grim masks of hollowed bark assume, invoke
Thee with glad hymns, O Bacchus, and to thee
Hang puppet-faces on tall pines to swing.   *389*
Hence every vineyard teems with mellowing fruit,
Till hollow vale o'erflows, and gorge profound,
Where'er the god hath turned his comely head.
Therefore to Bacchus duly will we sing

Meet honour with ancestral hymns, and cates
And dishes bear him; and the doomèd goat
Led by the horn shall at the altar stand,
Whose entrails rich on hazel-spits we'll roast.

This further task again, to dress the vine,
Hath needs beyond exhausting; the whole soil
Thrice, four times, yearly must be cleft, the sod
With hoes reversed be crushed continually,
The whole plantation lightened of its leaves.
Round on the labourer spins the wheel of toil,
As on its own track rolls the circling year.   *402*
Soon as the vine her lingering leaves hath shed,
And the chill north wind from the forests shook
Their coronal, even then the careful swain
Looks keenly forward to the coming year,
With Saturn's curvèd fang pursues and prunes
The vine forlorn, and lops it into shape.
Be first to dig the ground up, first to clear
And burn the refuse-branches, first to house
Again your vine-poles, last to gather fruit.
Twice doth the thickening shade beset the vine,
Twice weeds with stifling briers o'ergrow the crop;   *411*
And each a toilsome labour. Do thou praise
Broad acres, farm but few. Rough twigs beside
Of butcher's broom among the woods are cut,
And reeds upon the river-banks, and still
The undressed willow claims thy fostering care.
So now the vines are fettered, now the trees
Let go the sickle, and the last dresser now
Sings of his finished rows; but still the ground
Must vexèd be, the dust be stirred, and heaven
Still set thee trembling for the ripened grapes.

Not so with olives; small husbandry need they,   *420*
Nor look for sickle bowed or biting rake,
When once they have gripped the soil, and borne the
        breeze.
Earth of herself, with hookèd fang laid bare,
Yields moisture for the plants, and heavy fruit,
The ploughshare aiding; therewithal thou'lt rear
The olive's fatness well-beloved of Peace.

Apples, moreover, soon as first they feel
Their stems wax lusty, and have found their strength,
To heaven climb swiftly, self-impelled, nor crave
Our succour. All the grove meanwhile no less
With fruit is swelling, and the wild haunts of birds
Blush with their blood-red berries. Cytisus

Is good to browse on, the tall forest yields
Pine-torches, and the nightly fires are fed
And shoot forth radiance. And shall men be loath
To plant, nor lavish of their pains? Why trace
Things mightier? Willows even and lowly brooms
To cattle their green leaves, to shepherds shade,
Fences for crops, and food for honey yield.   *436*
And blithe it is Cytorus to behold
Waving with box, Narycian groves of pitch;
Oh! blithe the sight of fields beholden not
To rake or man's endeavour! the barren woods
That crown the scalp of Caucasus, even these,
Which furious blasts for ever rive and rend,
Yield various wealth, pine-logs that serve for ships,
Cedar and cypress for the homes of men;
Hence, too, the farmers shave their wheel-spokes, hence
Drums for their wains, and curvèd boat-keels fit;   *445*
Willows bear twigs enow, the elm-tree leaves,
Myrtle stout spear-shafts, war-tried cornel too;
Yews into Ituraean bows are bent:
Nor do smooth lindens or lathe-polished box
Shrink from man's shaping and keen-furrowing steel;
Light alder floats upon the boiling flood
Sped down the Padus, and bees house their swarms
In rotten holm-oak's hollow bark and bole.
What of like praise can Bacchus' gifts afford?
Nay, Bacchus even to crime hath prompted, he
The wine-infuriate Centaurs quelled with death,
Rhoetus and Pholus, and with mighty bowl
Hylaeus threatening high the Lapithae.   *457*
    Oh! all too happy tillers of the soil,
Could they but know their blessedness, for whom
Far from the clash of arms all-equal earth
Pours from the ground herself their easy fare!
What though no lofty palace portal-proud
From all its chambers vomits forth a tide
Of morning courtiers, nor agape they gaze
On pillars with fair tortoise-shell inwrought,
Gold-purfled robes, and bronze from Ephyre;
Nor is the whiteness of their wool distained
With drugs Assyrian, nor clear olive's use
With cassia tainted; yet untroubled calm,
A life that knows no falsehood, rich enow
With various treasures, yet broad-acred ease,
Grottoes and living lakes, yet Tempes cool,
Lowing of kine, and sylvan slumbers soft,

They lack not; lawns and wild beasts' haunts are
    there,
A youth of labour patient, need-inured,
Worship, and reverend sires: with them from earth
Departing Justice her last footprints left.   *474*
   Me before all things may the Muses sweet,
Whose rites I bear with mighty passion pierced,
Receive, and show the paths and stars of heaven,
The sun's eclipses and the labouring moons,
From whence the earthquake, by what power the seas
Swell from their depths, and, every barrier burst,
Sink back upon themselves, why winter-suns
So haste to dip 'neath ocean, or what check
The lingering night retards. But if to these
High realms of nature the cold curdling blood
About my heart bar access, then be fields
And stream-washed vales my solace, let me love
Rivers and woods, inglorious. Oh for you
Plains, and Spercheius, and Taygete,
By Spartan maids o'er-revelled! Oh, for one,
Would set me in deep dells of Haemus cool,
And shield me with his boughs' o'ershadowing
    might!   *489*
Happy, who had the skill to understand
Nature's hid causes, and beneath his feet
All terrors cast, and death's relentless doom,
And the loud roar of greedy Acheron.
Blest too is he who knows the rural gods,
Pan, old Silvanus, and the sister-nymphs!
Him nor the rods of public power can bend,
Nor kingly purple, nor fierce feud that drives
Brother to turn on brother, nor descent
Of Dacian from the Danube's leaguèd flood,
Nor Rome's great State, nor kingdoms like to die;
Nor hath he grieved through pitying of the poor,
Nor envied him that hath. What fruit the boughs,
And what the fields, of their own bounteous will
Have borne, he gathers; nor iron rule of laws,
Nor maddened Forum have his eyes beheld,
Nor archives of the people. Others vex
The darksome gulfs of Ocean with their oars,
Or rush on steel: they press within the courts
And doors of princes; one with havoc falls
Upon a city and its hapless hearths,
From gems to drink, on Tyrian rugs to lie;   *506*
This hoards his wealth and broods o'er buried gold;

One at the rostra stares in blank amaze;
One gaping sits transported by the cheers,
The answering cheers of plebs and senate rolled
Along the benches: bathed in brothers' blood
Men revel, and, all delights of hearth and home
For exile changing, a new country seek
Beneath an alien sun. The husbandman
With hookèd ploughshare turns the soil; from hence
Springs his year's labour; hence, too, he sustains
Country and cottage homestead, and from hence
His herds of cattle and deserving steers.   515
No respite! still the year o'erflows with fruit,
Or young of kine, or Ceres' wheaten sheaf,
With crops the furrow loads, and bursts the barns.
Winter is come: in olive-mills they bruise
The Sicyonian berry; acorn-cheered
The swine troop homeward; woods their arbutes
      yield;
So, various fruit sheds Autumn, and high up
On sunny rocks the mellowing vintage bakes.
Meanwhile about his lips sweet children cling;
His chaste house keeps its purity; his kine
Drop milky udders, and on the lush green grass
Fat kids are striving, horn to butting horn.   526
Himself keeps holy days; stretched o'er the sward,
Where round the fire his comrades crown the bowl,
He pours libation, and thy name invokes,
Lenaeus, and for the herdsmen on an elm
Sets up a mark for the swift javelin; they
Strip their tough bodies for the rustic sport.
Such life of yore the ancient Sabines led,
Such Remus and his brother: Etruria thus,
Doubt not, to greatness grew, and Rome became
The fair world's fairest, and with circling wall
Clasped to her single breast the sevenfold hills.   535
Ay, ere the reign of Dicte's king, ere men,
Waxed godless, banqueted on slaughtered bulls,
Such life on earth did golden Saturn lead.
Nor ear of man had heard the war-trump's blast,
Nor clang of sword on stubborn anvil set.
   But lo! a boundless space we have travelled o'er;
'Tis time our steaming horses to unyoke.   542

GEORGIC III

Thee too, great Pales, will I hymn, and thee,
Amphrysian shepherd, worthy to be sung,
You, woods and waves Lycaean. All themes beside,
Which else had charmed the vacant mind with song,
Are now waxed common. Of harsh Eurystheus who
The story knows not, or that praiseless king
Busiris, and his altars? or by whom
Hath not the tale been told of Hylas young,
Latonian Delos and Hippodame,
And Pelops for his ivory shoulder famed,
Keen charioteer? Needs must a path be tried,
By which I too may lift me from the dust,
And float triumphant through the mouths of men.
Yea, I shall be the first, so life endure,
To lead the Muses with me, as I pass
To mine own country from the Aonian height;   *11*
I, Mantua, first will bring thee back the palms
Of Idumaea, and raise a marble shrine
On thy green plain fast by the water-side,
Where Mincius winds more vast in lazy coils,
And rims his margent with the tender reed.
Amid my shrine shall Caesar's godhead dwell.
To him will I, as victor, bravely dight
In Tyrian purple, drive along the bank
A hundred four-horse cars. All Greece for me,
Leaving Alpheus and Molorchus' grove,
On foot shall strive, or with the raw-hide glove;   *20*
Whilst I, my head with stripped green olive crowned,
Will offer gifts. Even now 'tis present joy
To lead the high processions to the fane,
And view the victims felled; or how the scene
Sunders with shifted face, and Britain's sons
Inwoven thereon with those proud curtains rise.
Of gold and massive ivory on the doors
I'll trace the battle of the Gangarides,
And our Quirinus' conquering arms, and there
Surging with war, and hugely flowing, the Nile,
And columns heaped on high with naval brass.   *29*
And Asia's vanquished cities I will add,
And quelled Niphates, and the Parthian foe,

Who trusts in flight and backward-volleying darts,
And trophies torn with twice triumphant hand
From empires twain on ocean's either shore.
And breathing forms of Parian marble there
Shall stand, the offspring of Assaracus,
And great names of the Jove-descended folk,
And father Tros, and Troy's first founder, lord
Of Cynthus. And accursèd Envy there
Shall dread the Furies, and thy ruthless flood,
Cocytus, and Ixion's twisted snakes,
And that vast wheel and ever-baffling stone. 39
Meanwhile the Dryad-haunted woods and lawns
Unsullied seek we; 'tis thy hard behest,
Maecenas. Without thee no lofty task
My mind essays. Up! break the sluggish bonds
Of tarriance; with loud din Cithaeron calls,
Steed-taming Epidaurus, and thy hounds,
Taygete; and hark! the assenting groves
With peal on peal reverberate the roar.
Yet must I gird me to rehearse ere long
The fiery fights of Caesar, speed his name
Through ages, countless as to Caesar's self
From the first birth-dawn of Tithonus old. 48
    If eager for the prized Olympian palm
One breed the horse, or bullock strong to plough,
Be his prime care a shapely dam to choose.
Of kine grim-faced is goodliest, with coarse head
And burly neck, whose hanging dewlaps reach
From chin to knee; of boundless length her flank;
Large every way she is, large-footed even,
With incurved horns and shaggy ears beneath.
Nor let mislike me one with spots of white
Conspicuous, or that spurns the yoke, whose horn
At times hath vice in't: liker bull-faced she,
And tall-limbed wholly, and with tip of tail
Brushing her footsteps as she walks along. 59
The age for Hymen's rites, Lucina's pangs,
Ere ten years ended, after four begins;
Their residue of days nor apt to teem,
Nor strong for ploughing. Meantime, while youth's
        delight
Survives within them, loose the males: be first
To speed thy herds of cattle to their loves,
Breed stock with stock, and keep the race supplied.
Ah! life's best hours are ever first to fly
From hapless mortals; in their place succeed

Disease and dolorous eld; till travail sore
And death unpitying sweep them from the scene.
Still will be some, whose form thou fain wouldst
  change;
Renew them still; with yearly choice of young
Preventing losses, lest too late thou rue.   *71*

   Nor steeds crave less selection; but on those
Thou think'st to rear, the promise of their line,
From earliest youth thy chiefest pains bestow.
See from the first yon high-bred colt afield,
His lofty step, his limbs' elastic tread:
Dauntless he leads the herd, still first to try
The threatening flood, or brave the unknown bridge,
By no vain noise affrighted; lofty-necked,
With clean-cut head, short belly, and stout back;
His sprightly breast exuberant with brawn.
Chestnut and grey are good; the worst-hued white
And sorrel. Then lo! if arms are clashed afar,
Bide still he cannot: ears stiffen and limbs quake;
His nostrils snort and roll out wreaths of fire.   *85*
Dense is his mane, that when uplifted falls
On his right shoulder; betwixt either loin
The spine runs double; his earth-dinting hoof
Rings with the ponderous beat of solid horn.
Even such a horse was Cyllarus, reined and tamed
By Pollux of Amyclae; such the pair
In Grecian song renowned, those steeds of Mars,
And famed Achilles' team: in such-like form
Great Saturn's self with mane flung loose on neck
Sped at his wife's approach, and flying filled
The heights of Pelion with his piercing neigh.   *94*

   Even him, when sore disease or sluggish eld
Now saps his strength, pen fast at home, and spare
His not inglorious age. A horse grown old
Slow kindling unto love in vain prolongs
The fruitless task, and, to the encounter come,
As fire in stubble blusters without strength,
He rages idly. Therefore mark thou first
Their age and mettle, other points anon,
As breed and lineage, or what pain was theirs
To lose the race, what pride the palm to win.   *102*
Seest how the chariots in mad rivalry
Poured from the barrier grip the course and go,
When youthful hope is highest, and every heart
Drained with each wild pulsation? How they ply
The circling lash, and reaching forward let

The reins hang free! Swift spins the glowing wheel;
And now they stoop, and now erect in air
Seem borne through space and towering to the sky:
No stop, no stay; the dun sand whirls aloft;
They reek with foam-flakes and pursuing breath;
So sweet is fame, so prized the victor's palm.　　*112*
'Twas Ericthonius first took heart to yoke
Four horses to his car, and rode above
The whirling wheels to victory: but the ring
And bridle-reins, mounted on horses' backs,
The Pelethronian Lapithae bequeathed,
And taught the knight in arms to spurn the ground,
And arch the upgathered footsteps of his pride.
Each task alike is arduous, and for each
A horse young, fiery, swift of foot, they seek;
How oft so-e'er yon rival may have chased
The flying foe, or boast his native plain
Epirus, or Mycenae's stubborn hold,
And trace his lineage back to Neptune's birth.　　*122*
　　These points regarded, as the time draws nigh,
With instant zeal they lavish all their care
To plump with solid fat the chosen chief
And designated husband of the herd:
And flowery herbs they cut, and serve him well
With corn and running water, that his strength
Not fail him for that labour of delight,
Nor puny colts betray the feeble sire.
The herd itself of purpose they reduce
To leanness, and when love's sweet longing first
Provokes them, they forbid the leafy food,
And pen them from the springs, and oft beside
With running shake, and tire them in the sun,
What time the threshing-floor groans heavily
With pounding of the corn-ears, and light chaff
Is whirled on high to catch the rising west.　　*134*
This do they that the soil's prolific powers
May not be dulled by surfeiting, nor choke
The sluggish furrows, but eagerly absorb
Their fill of love, and deeply entertain.
　　To care of sire the mother's care succeeds.
When great with young they wander nigh their time,
Let no man suffer them to drag the yoke
In heavy wains, nor leap across the way,
Nor scour the meads, nor swim the rushing flood.
In lonely lawns they feed them, by the course
Of brimming streams, where moss is, and the banks

With grass are greenest, where are sheltering caves,
And far outstretched the rock-flung shadow lies.   *145*
Round wooded Silarus and the ilex-bowers
Of green Alburnus swarms a wingèd pest—
Its Roman name Asilus, by the Greeks
Termed Oestros—fierce it is, and harshly hums,
Driving whole herds in terror through the groves,
Till heaven is madded by their bellowing din,
And Tanager's dry bed and forest-banks.
With this same scourge did Juno wreak of old
The terrors of her wrath, a plague devised
Against the heifer sprung from Inachus.   *153*
From this too thou, since in the noontide heats
'Tis most persistent, fend thy teeming herds,
And feed them when the sun is newly risen,
Or the first stars are ushering in the night.

But, yeaning ended, all their tender care
Is to the calves transferred; at once with marks
They brand them, both to designate their race,
And which to rear for breeding, or devote
As altar-victims, or to cleave the ground
And into ridges tear and turn the sod.
The rest along the greensward graze at will.
Those that to rustic uses thou wouldst mould,
As calves encourage and take steps to tame,
While pliant wills and plastic youth allow.   *165*
And first of slender withies round the throat
Loose collars hang, then when their free-born necks
Are used to service, with the self-same bands
Yoke them in pairs, and steer by steer compel
Keep pace together. And time it is that oft
Unfreighted wheels be drawn along the ground
Behind them, as to dint the surface-dust;
Then let the beechen axle strain and creak
'Neath some stout burden, whilst a brazen pole
Drags on the wheels made fast thereto. Meanwhile
For their unbroken youth not grass alone,
Nor meagre willow-leaves and marish-sedge,
But corn-ears with thy hand pluck from the crops.
Nor shall the brood-kine, as of yore, for thee
Brim high the snowy milking-pail, but spend
Their udders' fullness on their own sweet young.   *178*

But if fierce squadrons and the ranks of war
Delight thee rather, or on wheels to glide
At Pisa, with Alpheus fleeting by,
And in the grove of Jupiter urge on

The flying chariot, be your steed's first task
To face the warrior's armèd rage, and brook
The trumpet, and long roar of rumbling wheels,
And clink of chiming bridles in the stall;
Then more and more to love his master's voice
Caressing, or loud hand that claps his neck.
Ay, thus far let him learn to dare, when first
Weaned from his mother, and his mouth at times
Yield to the supple halter, even while yet
Weak, tottering-limbed, and ignorant of life.   *189*
But, three years ended, when the fourth arrives,
Now let him tarry not to run the ring
With rhythmic hoof-beat echoing, and now learn
Alternately to curve each bending leg,
And be like one that struggleth; then at last
Challenge the winds to race him, and at speed
Launched through the open, like a reinless thing,
Scarce print his footsteps on the surface-sand.
As when with power from Hyperborean climes
The north wind stoops, and scatters from his path
Dry clouds and storms of Scythia; the tall corn
And rippling plains 'gin shiver with light gusts;
A sound is heard among the forest-tops;
Long waves come racing shoreward: fast he flies,
With instant pinion sweeping earth and main.   *201*
    A steed like this or on the mighty course
Of Elis at the goal will sweat, and shower
Red foam-flakes from his mouth, or, kindlier task,
With patient neck support the Belgian car.
Then, broken at last, let swell their burly frame
With fattening corn-mash, for, unbroke, they will
With pride wax wanton, and, when caught, refuse
Tough lash to brook or jaggèd curb obey.
    But no device so fortifies their power
As love's blind stings of passion to forefend,
Whether on steed or steer thy choice be set.   *211*
Ay, therefore 'tis they banish bulls afar
To solitary pastures, or behind
Some mountain-barrier, or broad streams beyond,
Or else in plenteous stalls pen fast at home.
For, even through sight of her, the female wastes
His strength with smouldering fire, till he forget
Both grass and woodland. She indeed full oft
With her sweet charms can lovers proud compel
To battle for the conquest horn to horn.
In Sila's forest feeds the heifer fair,

While each on each the furious rivals run;
Wound follows wound; the black blood laves their
    limbs;
Horns push and strive against opposing horns,
With mighty groaning; all the forest-side
And far Olympus bellow back the roar.   223
Nor wont the champions in one stall to couch;
But he that's worsted hies him to strange climes
Far off, an exile, moaning much the shame,
The blows of that proud conqueror, then love's loss
Avenged not; with one glance toward the byre,
His ancient royalties behind him lie.
So with all heed his strength he practiseth,
And nightlong makes the hard bare stones his bed,
And feeds on prickly leaf and pointed rush,
And proves himself, and butting at a tree
Learns to fling wrath into his horns, with blows
Provokes the air, and scattering clouds of sand
Makes prelude of the battle; afterward,
With strength repaired and gathered might breaks
    camp,
And hurls him headlong on the unthinking foe: 236
As in mid ocean when a wave far off
Begins to whiten, mustering from the main
Its rounded breast, and, onward rolled to land
Falls with prodigious roar among the rocks,
Huge as a very mountain: but the depths
Upseethe in swirling eddies, and disgorge
The murky sand-lees from their sunken bed.
   Nay, every race on earth of men, and beasts,
And ocean-folk, and flocks, and painted birds,
Rush to the raging fire: love sways them all.
Never than then more fiercely o'er the plain
Prowls heedless of her whelps the lioness:
Nor monstrous bears such wide-spread havoc-doom
Deal through the forests; then the boar is fierce,
Most deadly then the tigress: then, alack!
Ill roaming is it on Libya's lonely plains.   249
Mark you what shivering thrills the horse's frame,
If but a waft the well-known gust conveys?
Nor curb can check them then, nor lash severe,
Nor rocks and caverned crags, nor barrier-floods,
That rend and whirl and wash the hills away.
Then speeds amain the great Sabellian boar,
His tushes whets, with forefoot tears the ground,
Rubs 'gainst a tree his flanks, and to and fro

Hardens each wallowing shoulder to the wound.
What of the youth, when love's relentless might
Stirs the fierce fire within his veins? Behold!
In blindest midnight how he swims the gulf
Convulsed with bursting storm-clouds! Over him
Heaven's huge gate thunders; the rock-shattered main
Utters a warning cry; nor parents' tears
Can backward call him, nor the maid he loves,
Too soon to die on his untimely pyre.   263
What of the spotted ounce to Bacchus dear,
Or warlike wolf-kin or the breed of dogs?
Why tell how timorous stags the battle join?
O'er all conspicuous is the rage of mares,
By Venus' self inspired of old, what time
The Potnian four with rending jaws devoured
The limbs of Glaucus. Love-constrained they roam
Past Gargarus, past the loud Ascanian flood;
They climb the mountains, and the torrents swim;
And when their eager marrow first conceives
The fire, in Spring-tide chiefly, for with Spring
Warmth doth their frames revisit, then they stand
All facing westward on the rocky heights,
And of the gentle breezes take their fill;
And oft unmated, marvellous to tell,
But of the wind impregnate, far and wide
O'er craggy height and lowly vale they scud,
Not toward thy rising, Eurus, or the sun's,
But westward and north-west, or whence up-springs
Black Auster, that glooms heaven with rainy cold.   279
Hence from their groin slow drips a poisonous juice,
By shepherds truly named hippomanes,
Hippomanes, fell stepdames oft have culled,
And mixed with herbs and spells of baneful bode.
    Fast flies meanwhile the irreparable hour,
As point to point our charmèd round we trace.
Enough of herds. This second task remains,
The wool-clad flocks and shaggy goats to treat.
Here lies a labour; hence for glory look,
Brave husbandmen. Nor doubtfully know I
How hard it is for words to triumph here,
And shed their lustre on a theme so slight:
But I am caught by ravishing desire
Above the lone Parnassian steep; I love
To walk the heights, from whence no earlier track
Slopes gently downward to Castalia's spring.   293
    Now, awful Pales, strike a louder tone.

First, for the sheep soft pencotes I decree
To browse in, till green summer's swift return;
And that the hard earth under them with straw
And handfuls of the fern be littered deep,
Lest chill of ice such tender cattle harm
With scab and loathly foot-rot. Passing thence
I bid the goats with arbute-leaves be stored,
And served with fresh spring-water, and their pens
Turned southward from the blast, to face the suns
Of winter, when Aquarius' icy beam
Now sinks in showers upon the parting year.   *304*
These too no lightlier our protection claim,
Nor prove of poorer service, howsoe'er
Milesian fleeces dipped in Tyrian reds
Repay the barterer; these with offspring teem
More numerous; these yield plenteous store of milk:
The more each dry-wrung udder froths the pail,
More copious soon the teat-pressed torrents flow.
Ay, and on Cinyps' bank the he-goats too
Their beards and grizzled chins and bristling hair
Let clip for camp-use, or as rugs to wrap
Seafaring wretches. But they browse the woods
And summits of Lycaeus, and rough briers,
And brakes that love the highland: of themselves
Right heedfully the she-goats homeward troop
Before their kids, and with plump udders clogged
Scarce cross the threshold. Wherefore rather ye,
The less they crave man's vigilance, be fain
From ice to fend them and from snowy winds;
Bring food and feast them with their branchy fare,
Nor lock your hay-loft all the winter long.   *321*
     But when glad summer at the west wind's call
Sends either flock to pasture in the glades,
Soon as the day-star shineth, hie we then
To the cool meadows, while the dawn is young,
The grass yet hoary, and to browsing herds
The dew tastes sweetest on the tender sward.
When heaven's fourth hour draws on the thickening
          drought,
And shrill cicalas pierce the brake with song,
Then at the well-springs bid them, or deep pools,
From troughs of holm-oak quaff the running wave: *330*
But at day's hottest seek a shadowy vale,
Where some vast ancient-timbered oak of Jove
Spreads his huge branches, or where huddling black
Ilex on ilex cowers in awful shade.

[75]

Then once more give them water sparingly,
And feed once more, till sunset, when cool eve
Allays the air, and dewy moonbeams slake
The forest glades, with halcyon's song the shore,
And every thicket with the goldfinch rings.
   Of Libya's shepherds why the tale pursue?
Why sing their pastures and the scattered huts
They house in? Oft their cattle day and night
Graze the whole month together, and go forth
Into far deserts where no shelter is,
So flat the plain and boundless. All his goods
The Afric swain bears with him, house and home,
Arms, Cretan quiver, and Amyclaean dog;   *345*
As some keen Roman in his country's arms
Plies the swift march beneath a cruel load;
Soon with tents pitched and at his post he stands,
Ere looked for by the foe. Not thus the tribes
Of Scythia by the far Maeotic wave,
Where turbid Ister whirls his yellow sands,
And Rhodope stretched out beneath the pole
Comes trending backward. There the herds they keep
Close-pent in byres, nor any grass is seen
Upon the plain, nor leaves upon the tree:
But with snow-ridges and deep frost afar
Heaped seven ells high the earth lies featureless: *355*
Still winter! still the north wind's icy breath!
Nay, never sun disparts the shadows pale,
Or as he rides the steep of heaven, or dips
In ocean's fiery bath his plunging car.
Quick ice-crusts curdle on the running stream,
And iron-hooped wheels the water's back now bears,
To broad wains opened, as erewhile to ships;
Brass vessels oft asunder burst, and clothes
Stiffen upon the wearers; juicy wines
They cleave with axes; to one frozen mass
Whole pools are turned; and on their untrimmed
    beards
Stiff clings the jaggèd icicle. Meanwhile
All heaven no less is filled with falling snow;   *367*
The cattle perish: oxen's mighty frames
Stand island-like amid the frost, and stags
In huddling herds, by that strange weight
    benumbed,
Scarce top the surface with their antler-points.
These with no hounds they hunt, nor net with toils,
Nor scare with terror of the crimson plume;

But, as in vain they breast the opposing block,
Butcher them, knife in hand, and so dispatch
Loud-bellowing, and with glad shouts hale them
    home.
Themselves in deep-dug caverns underground
Dwell free and careless; to their hearths they heave
Oak-logs and elm-trees whole, and fire them there,
There play the night out, and in festive glee
With barm and service sour the wine-cup mock.   *380*
So'neath the seven-starred Hyperborean wain
The folk live tameless, buffeted with blasts
Of Eurus from Rhipaean hills, and wrap
Their bodies in the tawny fells of beasts.
    If wool delight thee, first, be far removed
All prickly boskage, burrs and caltrops; shun
Luxuriant pastures; at the outset choose
White flocks with downy fleeces. For the ram,
How white soe'er himself, be but the tongue
'Neath his moist palate black, reject him, lest
He sully with dark spots his offspring's fleece,
And seek some other o'er the teeming plain.   *390*
Even with such snowy bribe of wool, if ear
May trust the tale, Pan, God of Arcady,
Snared and beguiled thee, Luna, calling thee
To the deep woods; nor thou didst spurn his call.
    But who for milk hath longing, must himself
Carry lucerne and lotus-leaves enow
With salt herbs to the cote, whence more they love
The streams, more stretch their udders, and give back
A subtle taste of saltness in the milk.
Many there be who from their mothers keep
The new-born kids, and straightway bind their mouths
With iron-tipped muzzles. What they milk at dawn,
Or in the daylight hours, at night they press;
What darkling or at sunset, this ere morn
They bear away in baskets—for to town
The shepherd hies him—or with dash of salt
Just sprinkle, and lay by for winter use.   *404*
    Nor be thy dogs last cared for; but alike
Swift Spartan hounds and fierce Molossian feed
On fattening whey. Never, with these to watch,
Dread nightly thief afold and ravening wolves,
Or Spanish desperadoes in the rear.
And oft the shy wild asses thou wilt chase,
With hounds, too, hunt the hare, with hounds the doe;
Oft from his woodland wallowing-den uprouse

[77]

The boar, and scare him with their baying, and drive,
And o'er the mountains urge into the toils
Some antlered monster to their chiming cry.   *413*
   Learn also scented cedar-wood to burn
Within the stalls, and snakes of noxious smell
With fumes of galbanum to drive away.
Oft under long-neglected cribs, or lurks
A viper ill to handle, that hath fled
The light in terror, or some snake, that wont
'Neath shade and sheltering roof to creep, and shower
Its bane among the cattle, hugs the ground,
Fell scourge of kine. Shepherd, seize stakes, seize
      stones!
And as he rears defiance, and puffs out
A hissing throat, down with him! see how low
That cowering crest is vailed in flight, the while,
His midmost coils and final sweep of tail
Relaxing, the last fold drags lingering spires.   *424*
Then that vile worm that in Calabrian glades
Uprears his breast, and wreathes a scaly back,
His length of belly pied with mighty spots—
While from their founts gush any streams, while yet
With showers of Spring and rainy south-winds earth
Is moistened, lo! he haunts the pools, and here
Housed in the banks, with fish and chattering frogs
Crams the black void of his insatiate maw.
Soon as the fens are parched, and earth with heat
Is gaping, forth he darts into the dry,
Rolls eyes of fire and rages through the fields,
Furious from thirst and by the drought dismayed.   *434*
Me list not then beneath the open heaven
To snatch soft slumber, nor on forest-ridge
Lie stretched along the grass, when, slipped his
      slough,
To glittering youth transformed he winds his spires,
And eggs or younglings leaving in his lair,
Towers sunward, lightening with three-forkèd
      tongue.
   Of sickness, too, the causes and the signs
I'll teach thee. Loathly scab assails the sheep,
When chilly showers have probed them to the quick,
And winter stark with hoar-frost, or when sweat
Unpurged cleaves to them after shearing done,
And rough thorns rend their bodies. Hence it is
Shepherds their whole flock steep in running streams,
While, plunged beneath the flood, with drenchèd fell,

The ram, launched free, goes drifting down the tide.　*447*
Else, having shorn, they smear their bodies o'er
With acrid oil-lees, and mix silver-scum
And native sulphur and Idaean pitch,
Wax mollified with ointment, and therewith
Sea-leek, strong hellebores, bitumen black.
Yet ne'er doth kindlier fortune crown his toil,
Than if with blade of iron a man dare lance
The ulcer's mouth ope: for the taint is fed
And quickened by confinement; while the swain
His hand of healing from the wound withholds,
Or sits for happier signs imploring heaven.　*456*
Aye, and when inward to the bleater's bones
The pain hath sunk and rages, and their limbs
By thirsty fever are consumed, 'tis good
To draw the enkindled heat therefrom, and pierce
Within the hoof-clefts a blood-bounding vein.
Of tribes Bisaltic such the wonted use,
And keen Gelonian, when to Rhodope
He flies, or Getic desert, and quaffs milk
With horse-blood curdled.

　　　　　　　　　Seest one far afield
Oft to the shade's mild covert win, or pull
The grass tops listlessly, or hindmost lag,
Or, browsing, cast her down amid the plain,
At night retire belated and alone;
With quick knife check the mischief, ere it creep
With dire contagion through the unwary herd.　*469*
Less thick and fast the whirlwind scours the main
With tempest in its wake, than swarm the plagues
Of cattle; nor seize they single lives alone,
But sudden clear whole feeding grounds, the flock
With all its promise, and extirpate the breed.
Well would he trow it who, so long after, still
High Alps and Noric hill-forts should behold,
And Iapydian Timavus' fields,
Ay, still behold the shepherds' realms a waste,
And far and wide the lawns untenanted.　*477*
　Here from distempered heavens erewhile arose
A piteous season, with the full fierce heat
Of autumn glowed, and cattle-kindreds all
And all wild creatures to destruction gave,
Tainted the pools, the fodder charged with bane.
Nor simple was the way of death, but when
Hot thirst through every vein impelled had drawn
Their wretched limbs together, anon o'erflowed

A watery flux, and all their bones piecemeal
Sapped by corruption to itself absorbed.
Oft in mid sacrifice to heaven—the white
Wool-woven fillet half wreathed about his brow—
Some victim, standing by the altar, there
Betwixt the loitering carles a-dying fell: 488
Or, if betimes the slaughtering priest had struck,
Nor with its heapèd entrails blazed the pile,
Nor seer to seeker thence could answer yield;
Nay, scarce the up-stabbing knife with blood was
        stained,
Scarce sullied with thin gore the surface-sand.
Hence die the calves in many a pasture fair,
Or at full cribs their lives' sweet breath resign;
Hence on the fawning dog comes madness, hence
Racks the sick swine a gasping cough that chokes
With swelling at the jaws: the conquering steed,
Uncrowned of effort and heedless of the sward,
Faints, turns him from the springs, and paws the earth
With ceaseless hoof: low droop his ears, wherefrom
Bursts fitful sweat, a sweat that waxes cold
Upon the dying beast; the skin is dry,
And rigidly repels the handler's touch. 502
These earlier signs they give that presage doom.
But, if the advancing plague 'gin fiercer grow,
Then are their eyes all fire, deep-drawn their breath,
At times groan-laboured: with long sobbing heave
Their lowest flanks; from either nostril streams
Black blood; a rough tongue clogs the obstructed jaws.
'Twas helpful through inverted horn to pour
Draughts of the wine-god down; sole way it seemed
To save the dying: soon this too proved their bane,
And, reinvigorate but with frenzy's fire,
Even at death's pinch—the gods some happier fate
Deal to the just, such madness to their foes—
Each with bared teeth his own limbs mangling tore. 514
See! as he smokes beneath the stubborn share,
The bull drops, vomiting foam-dabbled gore,
And heaves his latest groans. Sad goes the swain,
Unhooks the steer that mourns his fellow's fate,
And in mid labour leaves the plough-gear fast.
Nor tall wood's shadow, nor soft sward may stir
That heart's emotion, nor rock-channelled flood,
More pure than amber speeding to the plain:
But see! his flanks fail under him, his eyes
Are dulled with deadly torpor, and his neck

Sinks to the earth with drooping weight. What now
Besteads him toil or service? to have turned
The heavy sod with ploughshare? And yet these
Ne'er knew the Massic wine-god's baneful boon,
Nor twice replenished banquets: but on leaves
They fare, and virgin grasses, and their cups
Are crystal springs and streams with running tired,
Their healthful slumbers never broke by care.   530
Then only, say they, through that country side
For Juno's rites were cattle far to seek,
And ill-matched buffaloes the chariots drew
To their high fanes. So, painfully with rakes
They grub the soil, aye, with their very nails
Dig in the corn-seeds, and with strainèd neck
O'er the high uplands drag the creaking wains.
No wolf for ambush pries about the pen,
Nor round the flock prowls nightly; pain more sharp
Subdues him: the shy deer and fleet-foot stags
With hounds now wander by the haunts of men.   540
Vast ocean's offspring, and all tribes that swim,
On the shore's confine the wave washes up,
Like shipwrecked bodies: seals, unwonted there,
Flee to the rivers. Now the viper dies,
For all his den's close winding, and with scales
Erect the astonied water-worms. The air
Brooks not the very birds, that headlong fall,
And leave their life beneath the soaring cloud.
Moreover now nor change of fodder serves,
And subtlest cures but injure; then were foiled
The masters, Chiron sprung from Phillyron,
And Amythaon's son Melampus. See!
From Stygian darkness launched into the light
Comes raging pale Tisiphone; she drives
Disease and fear before her, day by day
Still rearing higher that all-devouring head.   553
With bleat of flocks and lowings thick resound
Rivers and parchèd banks and sloping heights.
At last in crowds she slaughters them, she chokes
The very stalls with carrion-heaps that rot
In hideous corruption, till men learn
With earth to cover them, in pits to hide.
For e'en the fells are useless; nor the flesh
With water may they purge, or tame with fire,
Nor shear the fleeces even, gnawed through and
        through
With foul disease, nor touch the putrid webs;

But, had one dared the loathly weeds to try,
Red blisters and an unclean sweat o'erran
His noisome limbs, till, no long tarriance made,
The fiery curse his tainted frame devoured.   566

GEORGIC IV

Of air-born honey, gift of heaven, I now
Take up the tale. Upon this theme no less
Look thou, Maecenas, with indulgent eye.
A marvellous display of puny powers,
High-hearted chiefs, a nation's history,
Its traits, its bent, its battles and its clans,
All, each, shall pass before you, while I sing.
Slight though the poet's theme, not slight the praise,
So frown not heaven, and Phoebus hear his call.
    First find your bees a settled sure abode,
Where neither winds can enter (winds blow back
The foragers with food returning home)
Nor sheep and butting kids tread down the flowers,
Nor heifer wandering wide upon the plain
Dash off the dew, and bruise the springing blades.   *12*
Let the gay lizard too keep far aloof
His scale-clad body from their honied stalls,
And the bee-eater, and what birds beside,
And Procne smirched with blood upon the breast
From her own murderous hands. For these roam wide
Wasting all substance, or the bees themselves
Strike flying, and in their beaks bear home, to glut
Those savage nestlings with the dainty prey.
But let clear springs and moss-green pools be near,
And through the grass a streamlet hurrying run,
Some palm-tree o'er the porch extend its shade,
Or huge-grown oleaster, that in Spring,
Their own sweet Spring-tide, when the new-made chiefs
Lead forth the young swarms, and, escaped their
      comb,
The colony comes forth to sport and play,
The neighbouring bank may lure them from the
      heat,
Or bough befriend with hospitable shade.   *24.*
O'er the mid-waters, whether swift or still,
Cast willow-branches and big stones enow,
Bridge after bridge, where they may footing find
And spread their wide wings to the summer sun,
If haply Eurus, swooping as they pause,
Have dashed with spray or plunged them in the deep.

And let green cassias and far-scented thymes,
And savory with its heavy-laden breath
Bloom round about, and violet-beds hard by
Sip sweetness from the fertilizing springs.
For the hive's self, or stitched of hollow bark,
Or from tough osier woven, let the doors
Be strait of entrance; for stiff winter's cold
Congeals the honey, and heat resolves and thaws,   36
To bees alike disastrous; not for naught
So haste they to cement the tiny pores
That pierce their walls, and fill the crevices
With pollen from the flowers, and glean and keep
To this same end the glue, that binds more fast
Than bird-lime or the pitch from Ida's pines.
Oft too in burrowed holes, if fame be true,
They make their cosy subterranean home,
And deeply lodged in hollow rocks are found,
Or in the cavern of an age-hewn tree.
Thou not the less smear round their crannied cribs
With warm smooth mud-coat, and strew leaves above;
But near their home let neither yew-tree grow,
Nor reddening crabs be roasted, and mistrust
Deep marish-ground and mire with noisome smell,
Or where the hollow rocks sonorous ring,
And the word spoken buffets and rebounds.   50
     What more? When now the golden sun has put
Winter to headlong flight beneath the world,
And oped the doors of heaven with summer ray,
Forthwith they roam the glades and forests o'er,
Rifle the painted flowers, or sip the streams,
Light-hovering on the surface. Hence it is
With some sweet rapture, that we know not of,
Their little ones they foster, hence with skill
Work out new wax or clinging honey mould.
So when the cage-escapèd hosts you see
Float heavenward through the hot clear air, until
You marvel at yon dusky cloud that spreads
And lengthens on the wind, then mark them well;
For then 'tis ever the fresh springs they seek
And bowery shelter: hither must you bring
The savoury sweets I bid, and sprinkle them,
Bruised balsam and the wax-flower's lowly weed,
And wake and shake the tinkling cymbals heard
By the great Mother: on the anointed spots
Themselves will settle, and in wonted wise
Seek of themselves the cradle's inmost depth.   66

But if to battle they have hied them forth—
For oft 'twixt king and king with uproar dire
Fierce feud arises, and at once from far
You may discern what passion sways the mob,
And how their hearts are throbbing for the strife;
Hark! the hoarse brazen note that warriors know
Chides on the loiterers, and the ear may catch
A sound that mocks the war-trump's broken blasts;
Then in hot haste they muster, then flash wings,
Sharpen their pointed beaks and knit their thews,
And round the king, even to his royal tent,
Throng rallying, and with shouts defy the foe.   76
So, when a dry Spring and clear space is given,
Forth from the gates they burst, they clash on high;
A din arises; they are heaped and rolled
Into one mighty mass, and headlong fall,
Not denselier hail through heaven, nor pelting so
Rains from the shaken oak its acorn-shower.
Conspicuous by their wings the chiefs themselves
Press through the heart of battle, and display
A giant's spirit in each pigmy frame,
Steadfast no inch to yield till these or those
The victor's ponderous arm has turned to flight.
Such fiery passions and such fierce assaults
A little sprinkled dust controls and quells.   87
And now, both leaders from the field recalled,
Who hath the worser seeming, do to death,
Lest royal waste wax burdensome, but let
His better lord it on the empty throne.
One with gold-burnished flakes will shine like fire,
For twofold are their kinds, the nobler he,
Of peerless front and lit with flashing scales;
That other, from neglect and squalor foul,
Drags slow a cumbrous belly. As with kings,
So too with people, diverse is their mould,
Some rough and loathly, as when the wayfarer
Scapes from a whirl of dust, and scorched with heat
Spits forth the dry grit from his parchèd mouth:
The others shine forth and flash with lightning-
   gleam,
Their backs all blazoned with bright drops of gold
Symmetric: this the likelier breed; from these,
When heaven brings round the season, thou shalt
   strain
Sweet honey, nor yet so sweet as passing clear,
And mellowing on the tongue the wine-god's fire.   102

But when the swarms fly aimlessly abroad,
Disport themselves in heaven and spurn their cells,
Leaving the hive unwarmed, from such vain play
Must you refrain their volatile desires,
Nor hard the task: tear off the monarchs' wings;
While these prove loiterers, none beside will dare
Mount heaven, or pluck the standards from the camp.
Let gardens with the breath of saffron flowers
Allure them, and the lord of Hellespont,
Priapus, wielder of the willow-scythe,
Safe in his keeping hold from birds and thieves.   *111*
And let the man to whom such cares are dear
Himself bring thyme and pine-trees from the heights,
And strew them in broad belts about their home;
No hand but his the blistering task should ply,
Plant the young slips, or shed the genial showers.

   And I myself, were I not even now
Furling my sails, and, nigh the journey's end,
Eager to turn my vessel's prow to shore,
Perchance would sing what careful husbandry
Makes the trim garden smile; of Paestum too,
Whose roses bloom and fade and bloom again;
How endives glory in the streams they drink,
And green banks in their parsley, and how the gourd
Twists through the grass and rounds him to a
       paunch;
Nor of Narcissus had my lips been dumb,
That loiterer of the flowers, nor supple-stemmed
Acanthus, with the praise of ivies pale,
And myrtles clinging to the shores they love.   *124*
For 'neath the shade of tall Oebalia's towers,
Where dark Galaesus laves the yellowing fields,
An old man once I mind me to have seen—
From Corycus he came—to whom had fallen
Some few poor acres of neglected land,
And they nor fruitful 'neath the plodding steer,
Meet for the grazing herd, nor good for vines.
Yet he, the while his meagre garden-herbs
Among the thorns he planted, and all round
White lilies, vervains, and lean poppy set,
In pride of spirit matched the wealth of kings,
And home returning not till night was late,
With unbought plenty heaped his board on high.   *133*
He was the first to cull the rose in spring,
He the ripe fruits in autumn; and ere yet
Winter had ceased in sullen ire to rive

The rocks with frost, and with her icy bit
Curb in the running waters, there was he
Plucking the rathe faint hyacinth, while he chid
Summer's slow footsteps and the lagging West.
Therefore he too with earliest brooding bees
And their full swarms o'erflowed, and first was he
To press the bubbling honey from the comb;
Lime-trees were his, and many a branching pine;
And all the fruits wherewith in early bloom
The orchard-tree had clothed her, in full tale
Hung there, by mellowing autumn perfected.   *143*
He too transplanted tall-grown elms a-row,
Time-toughened pear, thorns bursting with the plum
And plane now yielding serviceable shade
For dry lips to drink under: but these things,
Shut off by rigorous limits, I pass by,
And leave for others to sing after me.
   Come, then, I will unfold the natural powers
Great Jove himself upon the bees bestowed,
The boon for which, led by the shrill sweet strains
Of the Curetes and their clashing brass,
They fed the King of heaven in Dicte's cave.   *152*
Alone of all things they receive and hold
Community of offspring, and they house
Together in one city, and beneath
The shelter of majestic laws they live;
And they alone fixed home and country know,
And in the summer, warned of coming cold,
Make proof of toil, and for the general store
Hoard up their gathered harvesting. For some
Watch o'er the victualling of the hive, and these
By settled order ply their tasks afield;
And some within the confines of their home
Plant firm the comb's first layer, Narcissus' tear,
And sticky gum oozed from the bark of trees,
Then set the clinging wax to hang therefrom.
Others the while lead forth the full-grown young,
Their country's hope, and others press and pack
The thrice repurèd honey, and stretch their cells
To bursting with the clear-strained nectar sweet.   *164*
Some, too, the wardship of the gates befalls,
Who watch in turn for showers and cloudy skies,
Or ease returning labourers of their load,
Or form a band and from their precincts drive
The drones, a lazy herd. How glows the work!
How sweet the honey smells of perfumed thyme

Like the Cyclopes, when in haste they forge
From the slow-yielding ore the thunderbolts,
Some from the bull's-hide bellows in and out
Let the blasts drive, some dip i' the water-trough
The sputtering metal: with the anvil's weight
Groans Etna: they alternately in time
With giant strength uplift their sinewy arms,
Or twist the iron with the forceps' grip—
Not otherwise, to measure small with great,
The love of getting planted in their breasts
Goads on the bees, that haunt old Cecrops' heights,
Each in his sphere to labour. The old have charge
To keep the town, and build the wallèd combs,
And mould the cunning chambers; but the youth,
Their tired legs packed with thyme, come labouring
    home
Belated, for afar they range to feed
On arbutes and the grey-green willow-leaves,
And cassia and the crocus blushing red,
Glue-yielding limes, and hyacinths dusky-eyed.   *183*
One hour for rest have all, and one for toil:
With dawn they hurry from the gates—no room
For loiterers there: and once again, when even
Now bids them quit their pasturing on the plain,
Then homeward make they, then refresh their
    strength:
A hum arises: hark! they buzz and buzz
About the doors and threshold; till at length
Safe laid to rest they hush them for the night,
And welcome slumber laps their weary limbs.
But from the homestead not too far they fare,
When showers hang like to fall, nor, east winds nigh,
Confide in heaven, but 'neath the city walls
Safe-circling fetch them water, or essay
Brief out-goings, and oft weigh-up tiny stones,
As light craft ballast in the tossing tide,
Wherewith they poise them through the cloudy vast. *196*
This law of life, too, by the bees obeyed,
Will move thy wonder, that nor sex with sex
Yoke they in marriage, nor yield their limbs to love,
Nor know the pangs of labour, but alone
From leaves and honied herbs, the mothers, each,
Gather their offspring in their mouths, alone
Supply new kings and pigmy commonwealth,
And their old court and waxen realm repair.
Oft, too, while wandering, against jaggèd stones

Their wings they fray, and 'neath the burden yield
Their liberal lives: so deep their love of flowers,
So glorious deem they honey's proud acquist.
Therefore, though each a life of narrow span,
Ne'er stretched to summers more than seven, befalls,
Yet deathless doth the race endure, and still
Perennial stands the fortune of their line,
From grandsire unto grandsire backward told.   *209*
Moreover, not Aegyptus, nor the realm
Of boundless Lydia, no, nor Parthia's hordes,
Nor Median Hydaspes, to their king
Do such obeisance: lives the king unscathed,
One will inspires the million: is he dead,
Snapt is the bond of fealty; they themselves
Ravage their toil-wrought honey, and rend amain
Their own comb's waxen trellis. He is the lord
Of all their labour; him with awful eye
They reverence, and with murmuring throngs
    surround,
In crowds attend, oft shoulder him on high,
Or with their bodies shield him in the fight,
And seek through showering wounds a glorious
    death.   *218*
    Led by these tokens, and with such traits to guide,
Some say that unto bees a share is given
Of the Divine Intelligence, and to drink
Pure draughts of ether; for God permeates all—
Earth, and wide ocean, and the vault of heaven—
From whom flocks, herds, men, beasts of every kind,
Draw each at birth the fine essential flame;
Yea, and that all things hence to Him return,
Brought back by dissolution, nor can death
Find place: but, each into his starry rank,
Alive they soar, and mount the heights of heaven.
    If now their narrow home thou wouldst unseal,
And broach the treasures of the honey-house,
With draught of water first foment thy lips,
And spread before thee fumes of trailing smoke.   *230*
Twice is the teeming produce gathered in,
Twofold their time of harvest year by year,
Once when Taygete the Pleiad uplifts
Her comely forehead for the earth to see,
With foot of scorn spurning the ocean-streams,
Once when in gloom she flies the watery Fish,
And dips from heaven into the wintry wave.
Unbounded then their wrath; if hurt, they breathe

Venom into their bite, cleave to the veins
And let the sting lie buried, and leave their lives
Behind them in the wound. But if you dread
Too rigorous a winter, and would fain
Temper the coming time, and their bruised hearts
And broken estate to pity move thy soul,
Yet who would fear to fumigate with thyme,
Or cut the empty wax away? for oft
Into their comb the newt has gnawed unseen,
And the light-loathing beetles crammed their bed,
And he that sits at others' board to feast,
The do-naught drone; or 'gainst the unequal foe
Swoops the fierce hornet, or the moth's fell tribe;
Or spider, victim of Minerva's spite,
Athwart the doorway hangs her swaying net.   247
The more impoverished they, the keenlier all
To mend the fallen fortunes of their race
Will nerve them, fill the cells up, tier on tier,
And weave their granaries from the rifled flowers.
  Now, seeing that life doth even to bee-folk bring
Our human chances, if in dire disease
Their bodies' strength should languish—which anon
By no uncertain tokens may be told—
Forthwith the sick change hue; grim leanness mars
Their visage; then from out the cells they bear
Forms reft of light, and lead the mournful pomp;
Or foot to foot about the porch they hang,
Or within closed doors loiter, listless all
From famine, and benumbed with shrivelling cold.   259
Then is a deep note heard, a long-drawn hum,
As when the chill South through the forests sighs,
As when the troubled ocean hoarsely booms
With back-swung billow, as ravening tide of fire
Surges, shut fast within the furnace-walls.
Then do I bid burn scented galbanum,
And, honey-streams through reeden troughs instilled,
Challenge and cheer their flagging appetite
To taste the well-known food; and it shall boot
To mix therewith the savour bruised from gall,
And rose-leaves dried, or must to thickness boiled
By a fierce fire, or juice of raisin-grapes
From Psithian vine, and with its bitter smell
Centaury, and the famed Cecropian thyme.   269
There is a meadow-flower by country folk
Hight star-wort; 'tis a plant not far to seek;
For from one sod an ample growth it rears,

Itself all golden, but girt with plenteous leaves,
Where glory of purple shines through violet gloom.
With chaplets woven hereof full oft are decked
Heaven's altars: harsh its taste upon the tongue;
Shepherds in vales smooth-shorn of nibbling flocks
By Mella's winding waters gather it.
The roots of this, well seethed in fragrant wine,
Set in brimmed baskets at their doors for food.   *280*
    But if one's whole stock fail him at a stroke,
Nor hath he whence to breed the race anew,
'Tis time the wondrous secret to disclose
Taught by the swain of Arcady. even how
The blood of slaughtered bullocks oft has borne
Bees from corruption. I will trace me back
To its prime source the story's tangled thread,
And thence unravel. For where thy happy folk,
Canopus, city of Pellaean fame,
Dwell by the Nile's lagoon-like overflow,
And high o'er furrows they have called their own
Skim in their painted wherries; where, hard by,
The quivered Persian presses, and that flood
Which from the swart-skinned Aethiop bears him
      down,
Swift-parted into sevenfold branching mouths
With black mud fattens and makes Aegypt green,
That whole domain its welfare's hope secure
Rests on this art alone. And first is chosen
A strait recess, cramped closer to this end,
Which next with narrow roof of tiles atop
'Twixt prisoning walls they pinch, and add hereto
From the four winds four slanting window-slits.   *298*
Then seek they from the herd a steer, whose horns
With two years' growth are curling, and stop fast,
Plunge madly as he may, the panting mouth
And nostrils twain, and done with blows to death,
Batter his flesh to pulp i' the hide yet whole,
And shut the doors, and leave him there to lie.
But 'neath his ribs they scatter broken boughs,
With thyme and fresh-pulled cassias: this is done
When first the west winds bid the waters flow,
Ere flush the meadows with new tints, and ere
The twittering swallow buildeth from the beams.   *307*
Meanwhile the juice within his softened bones
Heats and ferments, and things of wondrous birth,
Footless at first, anon with feet and wings,
Swarm there and buzz, a marvel to behold;

And more and more the fleeting breeze they take,
Till, like a shower that pours from summer-clouds,
Forth burst they, or like shafts from quivering string
When Parthia's flying hosts provoke the fray.
   Say what was he, what God, that fashioned forth
This art for us, O Muses? of man's skill
Whence came the new adventure? From thy vale,
Peneian Tempe, turning, bee-bereft,
So runs the tale, by famine and disease,
Mournful the shepherd Aristaeus stood
Fast by the haunted river-head, and thus
With many a plaint to her that bare him cried: *320*
"Mother, Cyrene, mother, who hast thy home
Beneath this whirling flood, if he thou sayest,
Apollo, lord of Thymbra, be my sire,
Sprung from the Gods' high line, why barest thou me
With fortune's ban for birthright? Where is now
Thy love to me-ward banished from thy breast?
O! wherefore didst thou bid me hope for heaven?
Lo! even the crown of this poor mortal life,
Which all my skilful care by field and fold,
No art neglected, scarce had fashioned forth,
Even this falls from me, yet thou call'st me son.   *328*
Nay, then, arise! With thine own hands pluck up
My fruit-plantations: on the homestead fling
Pitiless fire; make havoc of my crops;
Burn the young plants, and wield the stubborn axe
Against my vines, if there hath taken thee
Such loathing of my greatness." But that cry,
Even from her chamber in the river-deeps,
His mother heard: around her spun the nymphs
Milesian wool stained through with hyaline dye,
Drymo, Xantho, Ligea, Phyllodoce,
Their glossy locks o'er snowy shoulders shed,
Cydippe and Lycorias yellow-haired,
A maiden one, one newly learned even then
To bear Lucina's birth-pang. Clio, too,
And Beroe, sisters, ocean-children both,
Both zoned with gold and girt with dappled fell,
Ephyre and Opis, and from Asian meads
Deiopea, and, bow at length laid by,
Fleet-footed Arethusa. But in their midst
Fair Clymene was telling o'er the tale
Of Vulcan's idle vigilance and the stealth
Of Mars' sweet rapine, and from Chaos old
Counted the jostling love-joys of the Gods.   *347*

Charmed by whose lay, the while their woolly tasks
With spindles down they drew, yet once again
Smote on his mother's ears the mournful plaint
Of Aristaeus; on their glassy thrones
Amazement held them all; but Arethuse
Before the rest put forth her auburn head,
Peering above the wave-top, and from far
Exclaimed, "Cyrene, sister, not for naught
Scared by a groan so deep, behold! 'tis he,
Even Aristaeus, thy heart's fondest care,
Here by the brink of the Peneian sire
Stands woebegone and weeping, and by name
Cries out upon thee for thy cruelty."   356
To whom, strange terror knocking at her heart,
"Bring, bring him to our sight," the mother cried;
"His feet may tread the threshold even of Gods."
So saying, she bids the flood yawn wide and yield
A pathway for his footsteps; but the wave
Arched mountain-wise closed round him, and within
Its mighty bosom welcomed, and let speed
To the deep river-bed. And now, with eyes
Of wonder gazing on his mother's hall
And watery kingdom and cave-prisoned pools
And echoing groves, he went, and, stunned by that
Stupendous whirl of waters, separate saw
All streams beneath the mighty earth that glide,
Phasis and Lycus, and that fountain-head
Whence first the deep Enipeus leaps to light,
Whence father Tiber, and whence Anio's flood,
And Hypanis that roars amid his rocks,
And Mysian Caicus, and, bull-browed
'Twixt either gilded horn, Eridanus,
Than whom none other through the laughing plains
More furious pours into the purple sea.   373
Soon as the chamber's hanging roof of stone
Was gained, and now Cyrene from her son
Had heard his idle weeping, in due course
Clear water for his hands the sisters bring,
With napkins of shorn pile, while others heap
The board with dainties, and set on afresh
The brimming goblets; with Panchaian fires
Upleap the altars; then the mother spake,
"Take beakers of Maeonian wine," she said,
"Pour we to Ocean." Ocean, sire of all,
She worships, and the sister-nymphs who guard
The hundred forests and the hundred streams;

Thrice Vesta's fire with nectar clear she dashed,
Thrice to the roof-top shot the flame and shone:
Armed with which omen she essayed to speak: *386*
"In Neptune's gulf Carpathian dwells a seer,
Caerulean Proteus, he who metes the main
With fish-drawn chariot of two-footed steeds;
Now visits he his native home once more,
Pallene and the Emathian ports; to him
We nymphs do reverence, ay, and Nereus old;
For all things knows the seer, both those which are
And have been, or which time hath yet to bring;
So willed it Neptune, whose portentous flocks,
And loathly sea-calves 'neath the surge he feeds.   *395*
Him first, my son, behoves thee seize and bind,
That he may all the cause of sickness show,
And grant a prosperous end. For save by force
No rede will he vouchsafe, nor shalt thou bend
His soul by praying; whom once made captive, ply
With rigorous force and fetters; against these
His wiles will break and spend themselves in vain.
I, when the sun has lit his noontide fires,
When the blades thirst, and cattle love the shade,
Myself will guide thee to the old man's haunt,
Whither he hies him weary from the waves,
That thou mayst safelier steal upon his sleep.   *404*
But when thou hast gripped him fast with hand and
    gyve,
Then divers forms and bestial semblances
Shall mock thy grasp; for sudden he will change
To bristly boar, fell tigress, dragon scaled,
And tawny-tufted lioness, or send forth
A crackling sound of fire, and so shake off
The fetters, or in showery drops anon
Dissolve and vanish. But the more he shifts
His endless transformations, thou, my son,
More straitlier clench the clinging bands, until
His body's shape return to that thou sawest,
When with closed eyelids first he sank to sleep."   *414*
    So saying, an odour of ambrosial dew
She sheds around, and all his frame therewith
Steeps throughly; forth from his trim-combèd locks
Breathed effluence sweet, and a lithe vigour leapt
Into his limbs. There is a cavern vast
Scooped in the mountain-side, where wave on wave
By the wind's stress is driven, and breaks far up
Its inmost creeks—safe anchorage from of old

For tempest-taken mariners: therewithin,
Behind a rock's huge barrier, Proteus hides.
Here in close covert out of the sun's eye
The youth she places, and herself the while
Swathed in a shadowy mist stands far aloof.   424
And now the ravening dog-star that burns up
The thirsty Indians blazed in heaven; his course
The fiery sun had half devoured: the blades
Were parched, and the void streams with droughty
      jaws
Baked to their mud-beds by the scorching ray,
When Proteus seeking his accustomed cave
Strode from the billows: round him frolicking
The watery folk that people the waste sea
Sprinkled the bitter brine-dew far and wide.
Along the shore in scattered groups to feed
The sea-calves stretch them: while the seer himself,
Like herdsman on the hills when evening bids
The steers from pasture to their stall repair,
And the lambs' bleating whets the listening wolves,
Sits midmost on the rock and tells his tale.   436
But Aristaeus, the foe within his clutch,
Scarce suffering him compose his agèd limbs,
With a great cry leapt on him, and ere he rose
Forestalled him with the fetters; he nathless,
All unforgetful of his ancient craft,
Transforms himself to every wondrous thing,
Fire and a fearful beast, and flowing stream.
But when no trickery found a path for flight,
Baffled at length, to his own shape returned,
With human lips he spake, "Who bade thee, then,
So reckless in youth's hardihood, affront
Our portals? or what wouldst thou hence?"—But he,
"Proteus, thou knowest, of thine own heart thou
      knowest;
For thee there is no cheating, but cease thou
To practise upon me: at heaven's behest
I for my fainting fortunes hither come
An oracle to ask thee." There he ceased.
Whereat the seer, by stubborn force constrained,
Shot forth the grey light of his gleaming eyes
Upon him, and with fiercely gnashing teeth
Unlocks his lips to spell the fates of heaven: 451
    "Doubt not 'tis wrath divine that plagues thee thus,
Nor light the debt thou payest; 'tis Orpheus' self,
Orpheus unhappy by no fault of his,

[95]

So fates prevent not, fans thy penal fires,
Yet madly raging for his ravished bride.
She in her haste to shun thy hot pursuit
Along the stream, saw not the coming death,
Where at her feet kept ward upon the bank
In the tall grass a monstrous water-snake.
But with their cries the Dryad-band her peers
Filled up the mountains to their proudest peaks:
Wailed for her fate the heights of Rhodope,
And tall Pangaea, and, beloved of Mars,
The land that bowed to Rhesus, Thrace no less
With Hebrus' stream; and Orithyia wept,
Daughter of Acte old. But Orpheus' self,
Soothing his love-pain with the hollow shell,
Thee his sweet wife on the lone shore alone,
Thee when day dawned and when it died he sang.   *465*
Nay to the jaws of Taenarus too he came,
Of Dis the infernal palace, and the grove
Grim with a horror of great darkness—came,
Entered, and faced the Manes and the King
Of terrors, the stone heart no prayer can tame.
Then from the deepest deeps of Erebus,
Wrung by his minstrelsy, the hollow shades
Came trooping, ghostly semblances of forms
Lost to the light, as birds by myriads hie
To greenwood boughs for cover, when twilight-hour
Or storms of winter chase them from the hills;
Matrons and men, and great heroic frames
Done with life's service, boys, unwedded girls,
Youths placed on pyre before their fathers' eyes.
Round them, with black slime choked and hideous
      weed,
Cocytus winds; there lies the unlovely swamp
Of dull dead water, and, to pen them fast,
Styx with her ninefold barrier poured between.   *480*
Nay, even the deep Tartarean Halls of death
Stood lost in wonderment, and the Eumenides,
Their brows with livid locks of serpents twined;
Even Cerberus held his triple jaws agape,
And, the wind hushed, Ixion's wheel stood still.
And now with homeward footstep he had passed
All perils scathless, and, at length restored,
Eurydice to realms of upper air
Had well-nigh won, behind him following—
So Proserpine had ruled it—when his heart
A sudden mad desire surprised and seized—

Meet fault to be forgiven, might Hell forgive.
For at the very threshold of the day,
Heedless, alas! and vanquished of resolve,
He stopped, turned, looked upon Eurydice
His own once more. But even with the look,
Poured out was all his labour, broken the bond
Of that fell tyrant, and a crash was heard
Three times like thunder in the meres of hell.   *493*
'Orpheus! what ruin hath thy frenzy wrought
On me, alas! and thee? Lo! once again
The unpitying fates recall me, and dark sleep
Closes my swimming eyes. And now farewell:
Girt with enormous night I am borne away,
Outstretching toward thee, thine, alas! no more,
These helpless hands.' She spake, and suddenly,
Like smoke dissolving into empty air,
Passed and was sundered from his sight; nor him
Clutching vain shadows, yearning sore to speak,
Thenceforth beheld she, nor no second time
Hell's boatman brooks he pass the watery bar.
What should he do? fly whither, twice bereaved?
Move with what tears the Manes, with what voice
The Powers of darkness? She indeed even now
Death-cold was floating on the Stygian barge!   *506*
For seven whole months unceasingly, men say,
Beneath a skyey crag, by thy lone wave,
Strymon, he wept, and in the caverns chill
Unrolled his story, melting tigers' hearts,
And leading with his lay the oaks along.
As in the poplar-shade a nightingale
Mourns her lost young, which some relentless swain,
Spying, from the nest has torn unfledged, but she
Wails the long night, and perched upon a spray
With sad insistence pipes her dolorous strain,
Till all the region with her wrongs o'erflows.
No love, no new desire, constrained his soul: *516*
By snow-bound Tanais and the icy north,
Far steppes to frost Rhipaean forever wed,
Alone he wandered, lost Eurydice
Lamenting, and the gifts of Dis ungiven.
Scorned by which tribute the Ciconian dames,
Amid their awful Bacchanalian rites
And midnight revellings, tore him limb from limb,
And strewed his fragments over the wide fields.
Then too, even then, what time the Hebrus stream,
Oeagrian Hebrus, down mid-current rolled,

Rent from the marble neck, his drifting head,
The death-chilled tongue found yet a voice to cry
'Eurydice! ah! poor Eurydice!'
With parting breath he called her, and the banks
From the broad stream caught up 'Eurydice!' "   *527*
   So Proteus ending plunged into the deep,
And, where he plunged, beneath the eddying whirl
Churned into foam the water, and was gone;
But not Cyrene, who unquestioned thus
Bespake the trembling listener: "Nay, my son,
From that sad bosom thou mayst banish care:
Hence came that plague of sickness, hence the
     nymphs,
With whom in the tall woods the dance she wove,
Wrought on thy bees, alas! this deadly bane.
Bend thou before the Dell-nymphs, gracious powers:
Bring gifts, and sue for pardon: they will grant
Peace to thine asking, and an end of wrath.   *536*
But how to approach them will I first unfold—
Four chosen bulls of peerless form and bulk,
That browse to-day the green Lycaean heights,
Pick from thy herds, as many kine to match,
Whose necks the yoke pressed never: then for these
Build up four altars by the lofty fanes,
And from their throats let gush the victims' blood,
And in the greenwood leave their bodies lone.
Then, when the ninth dawn hath displayed its beams,
To Orpheus shalt thou send his funeral dues,
Poppies of Lethe, and let slay a sheep
Coal-black, then seek the grove again, and soon
For pardon found adore Eurydice
With a slain calf for victim."   *547*
          No delay:
The self-same hour he hies him forth to do
His mother's bidding: to the shrine he came,
The appointed altars reared, and thither led
Four chosen bulls of peerless form and bulk,
With kine to match, that never yoke had known;
Then, when the ninth dawn had led in the day,
To Orpheus sent his funeral dues, and sought
The grove once more. But sudden, strange to tell!
A portent they espy: through the oxen's flesh,
Waxed soft in dissolution, hark! there hum
Bees from the belly; the rent ribs overboil!
In endless clouds they spread them, till at last
On yon tree-top together fused they cling,

And drop their cluster from the bending boughs.   *558*
   So sang I of the tilth of furrowed fields,
Of flocks and trees, while Caesar's majesty
Launched forth the levin-bolts of war by deep
Euphrates, and bare rule o'er willing folk
Though vanquished, and essayed the heights of
    heaven.
I Virgil then, of sweet Parthenope
The nursling, wooed the flowery walks of peace
Inglorious, who erst trilled for shepherd-wights
The wanton ditty, and sang in saucy youth
Thee, Tityrus, 'neath the spreading beech tree's
    shade.   *566*

THE AENEID

BOOK I

Of arms I sing, and of the man who first
From Trojan shores beneath the ban of fate
To Italy and coasts Lavinian came,
Much tossed about on land and ocean he
By violence of the gods above, to sate
Relentless Juno's ever-rankling ire,
In war, too, much enduring, till what time
A city he might found him, and bear safe
His gods to Latium, whence the Latin race,
And Alba's sires, and lofty-towering Rome.
   Say, Muse, what outrage to her power the cause,
Or angered why, the Queen of Heaven constrained
A man, so marked for goodness, still to ply
The round of peril, bear the brunt of toil:
In heavenly breasts do such fierce passions dwell?   *11*
   There was an ancient city, the abode
Of Tyrian settlers, Carthage, far to sea
Facing Italia and the Tiber-mouths,
Wealthy of substance, and in war's pursuit
None fiercer, far beyond all lands, 'tis said,
To Juno dearest—Samos' self less dear.
Here were her arms, her chariot here; that this
Should, fate consenting, a world-empire be,
Even then the goddess aimed with fond desire.
Nathless she had heard that from the blood of Troy
A race was rearing, destined to o'erthrow
Her Tyrian towers; that issuing hence should come
A people of wide empire, lords of war,
To ravage Libya: such the round of fate.   *22*
Moved by this fear, Saturnia, and therewith
Still mindful of the former strife, which erst
At Troy for her dear Argos she had waged—
Nor were the quarrel's causes and fierce pangs
Yet banished from her soul; in memory's depth
Lie stored the doom of Paris, and the affront
Of her spurned beauty, and that loathèd stock,
And the high prize of ravished Ganymede—
Fired with these thoughts besides, the Trojan few,
'Scaped from the Danai and Achilles fell,
Still must she keep upon wide ocean tossed

[103]

Aloof from Latium; and for many a year
They roamed, fate-driven, through all the circling seas:
So vast the toil to found the Roman race.   *33*
   Scarce out of sight of the Sicilian land
To seaward they were sailing cheerily,
Tilting the salt foam with each brazen beak,
When Juno, nursing in her bosom's depth
The undying wound, thus with her own soul spake:
"I to shrink foiled from my design, too weak
To ward the Teucrians' king from Italy,
Because the fates forbid! Could Pallas then
Burn up the Argive galleys, and their crews
Drown in the deep, for one man's mad offence,
Ajax, Oileus' son? With her own hand
She, hurling from the clouds Jove's nimble fire,
Scattered their barks, with winds upheaved the sea,
And him, his riven breast panting forth the flames,
Upwhirled and staked upon a pointed rock: *45*
But I, who walk the queen of heaven, at once
Sister and spouse of Jove, with one weak race
These many years must war; and is there left
Still who to Juno's godhead bows the knee,
Or lays a suppliant's offering on her shrine?"
   Such thoughts revolving in her fiery breast,
Lo! to the storm-clouds' home, Aeolia, tracts
Teeming with furious gales, the goddess came.
Here in a vast cave Aeolus, their king,
The wrestling winds and roaring hurricanes
Bends to his sway and curbs with prison-bonds;   *54*
They, with a mighty rumbling of the hill,
Growl chafing round their barriers; on the height,
Sceptre in hand, aloft sits Aeolus,
And sleeks their passions and allays their ire;
Else would they hale sea, land, and vaulted heaven
In their wild flight, and sweep them into space.
But with this fear the Sire omnipotent
Penned them in caverns dark, and o'er them piled
The bulk of lofty mountains, and a king
He gave them, who by settled bond should know
To grip the reins, or slacken, at his word.
Him Juno then with suppliant voice addressed: *64*
   "Aeolus, for to thee the Sire of gods
And King of men hath given to soothe the waves
Or lift them with his wind, a race to me
Hateful, now sailing o'er the Tuscan deep,
Bears Ilium and her conquered household gods

To Italy: strike wrath into the winds,
Sink and o'erwhelm their barks, or sunder far
And broadcast fling their bodies on the deep.
Twice seven fair nymphs of matchless mould have I,
Of whom Deiopea, fairest-formed,
In lasting wedlock will I knit with thee,
And dedicate her thine, that all her years
She for such service at thy side may spend,
And make thee father of a race as fair." 75
    Then answered Aeolus: "Thy task, O queen,
Is to search out thy pleasure, mine to do
Thy bidding: of thy grace is all I own
Of power, this sceptre, and consenting Jove;
Thou set'st me in the banquet-hall of heaven,
And mak'st me ruler of the clouds and storms."
    So having said, his spear he turned and thrust
Against the hollow mountain-side: the winds
As in compact array, where vent is given,
Rush forth and with tornado scour the world,
Swoop on the sea, and from its sunken bed
Upheave it whole in one wild onset, east,
South, and southwester with thick-coming squalls,
And roll huge billows to the shore. Anon
Rises the creak of cables, cry of men: 87
Clouds in a moment from the Trojans' eyes
Snatch heaven and day; black night broods o'er the
    deep:
Skies thunder; the air lightens, flash on flash;
No sign abroad but bodes them instant death.
Straight are Aeneas' limbs with shuddering loosed;
He groans, and, stretching his clasped hands to heaven,
Thus cries aloud: "O thrice and four times blest
Who won to die beneath Troy's lofty towers
Under their kinsmen's eyes! O Tydeus' son,
Bravest of Danaan blood! to think that I
On Ilium's plains was suffered not to fall,
Nor at thy hand let forth my life-breath, where
Fierce Hector by the son of Aeacus
Lay stricken low, where huge Sarpedon, where,
Caught down beneath his current, Simois rolls
Shields, helms, and bodies of the countless brave!" 101
    Such words out-tossing, a loud blast from the north
Strikes him full-sail, and lifts the floods to heaven:
Crash go the oars, then swerves the prow and gives
The waves her broadside: on rolls, heaped and sheer,
A watery mountain: on the wave-tops some

[105]

Hang poised; to some the sea deep-yawning shows
Bare ground amid the billows, surge with sand
Raving; three ships the south wind's sudden clutch
Hurls upon hidden rocks—Italian folk
Name them the Altars rising 'mid the waves—
A vast ridge on the sea-top: three the east
Drives on to banks and shallows from the deep,
A piteous sight, and breaks them on the shoals,
And heaps the sand about them: one which bore
The Lycians and Orontes true of heart,
Even as he gazes, a huge sea astern
Strikes from above: dashed headlong from on board
Down goes the helmsman: her, spun whirling thrice
Even where she lies, the eddying gulf devours.   117
Here and there scattered on the weltering waste
Swimmers are seen, and heroes' arms, and planks,
And Trojan wealth upon the waters strewn.
Now the stout ship of Ilioneus, and now
Of brave Achates, that which bare on board
Abas, and that too of Aletes old,
The storm hath quelled; with rib-joints loosened, all
Let in the watery foe, and gaping split.
    Meanwhile of ocean made one roaring mass,
And a storm launched, and all his water-floods
Wrung from their lowest deeps, was Neptune ware,
And sorely chafed he: o'er the deep he peered,
Above the billow lifting a calm brow: 127
Far scattered over all the main he sees
Aeneas' fleet, he sees the Trojans whelmed
Beneath the waters and the fallen sky,
Nor from her brother's heart were hid the wiles
And spite of Juno: to his side he bids
Eurus and Zephyr, and bespeaks them thus:
"Hold you such blind reliance on your birth?
So! dare ye now without my fiat, winds,
Mix earth and heaven, and mass these mountain-
    heights?
Whom I——but best the uproared floods appease:
Not all so lightly shall ye answer me
Your trespasses hereafter. Speed betimes!
And say ye to your king, not his, but mine
The empire and fell trident of the sea
By lot assigned. He sways the savage rocks,
Of thee, O Eurus, and thy tribe the home:
Let Aeolus hold court and vaunt him there,
And rule close-barred the prison of the winds."   141

So saying, and swifter than that word, he smoothes
The swelling waters, routs the banded clouds,
Brings back the sun. Cymothoe therewithal
And Triton lend their shoulders to thrust off
From the sharp rock their vessels; he himself
Upheaves them with his trident, clears a way
Through the vast quicksands, and allays the flood,
And skims the wave-top lightly charioted.
And as when oft in some vast throng hath risen
A tumult, and the base herd waxeth mad,
And brands and stones, wrath-furnished weapons, fly,
Then, if some hero chance upon their sight,
Of weight for worth or exploit, they are hushed
And stand, all ear, to listen; with his words
He sways their passion, soothes their ruffled breasts;   *153*
So all at once the roar of ocean died,
What time, forth peering o'er the main, the Sire
Borne on a cloudless heaven his coursers drove,
And flying gave his willing chariot way.

   Toil-worn the children of Aeneas strive
To make what shores are nearest, and at length
To Libya's coast they come. There is a spot
Deep in a cove's recess: an isle there makes
A harbour with the barrier of its sides,
'Gainst which no deep-sea billow but is dashed,
And sundered far into sequestered creeks.
On either side huge cliffs, a towering pair,
Frown up to heaven; sheer down in shelter sleep
Broad waters, while, a scene of waving woods,
Black shaggy groves hang beetling from above.   *165*
Under the cliff's face is a crag-hung cave;
Within, fresh springs and seats in the living rock
Nymph-haunted: the tired ships, to moor them here,
No cables need, nor hookèd anchor's fang.
Here, mustering seven from all his tale of ships,
Aeneas enters; yearning sore for land,
Outleap the Trojans, gain the wished-for beach,
And lay their brine-drenched limbs upon the shore.
Achates from a flint first struck the spark,
And nursed the fire in leaves, and, heaping round
Dry fuel, on tinder quickly caught the flame.
Then, weary of fate, their sea-marred corn they fetch,
And gear of the corn-goddess, and prepare
The rescued grain to parch, and pound with stone.   *179*
   Meanwhile Aeneas scales a crag, to scan
In one wide survey all the sea, if aught

Of Antheus and the Phrygian biremes there
Wind-drifted he may spy, or Capys, or
Caicus' arms upon the lofty stern.
Vessel in sight is none, on shore he sees
Three stags before him ranging; in their rear
The whole herd follow, and in long array
Wind feeding through the valleys. Then he stopped,
Seized in his clutch a bow and wingèd shafts—
Weapons which true Achates chanced to bear—
And first themselves the leaders, holding high
Their heads with branchy antlers, he lays low,
And then the herd, and all the rout pell-mell
Plies with his arrows through the leafy brakes,
Nor stays his hand till seven huge frames on earth
He casts in triumph, to match the tale of ships.   *193*
Thence to the port he hies, gives all their share,
And next the wine, which on Trinacria's shore
In casks Acestes had in bounty stowed—
A hero's gift at parting—he metes out,
And with this utterance soothes their troubled
    breasts:
  "O comrades, for not all unlearned of ills
Are we already—O schooled to worser woes
Than these, of these too heaven will grant an end.
Even Scylla's fury and deep-bellowing rocks
Have ye drawn nigh, and proved the Cyclop-crags:
Courage recall; dull fears forgo; belike
This too with joy will be remembered yet.   *203*
Through shifting perils, by many a brink of death,
Toward Latium are we faring, where the fates
Portend us quiet resting-places: there
The realm of Troy must from her ashes rise:
Endure, and hoard yourselves for happier days."
  So spake his lips, while, sick with extreme woe,
Hope's mask he wears, and chokes the anguish down.
They to the spoil, the feast that is to be,
Address them, flay the ribs, the flesh lay bare;
Part cleave it into pieces, and on spits
Still quivering-fresh impale them; other some
Set cauldrons on the shore, and tend the fires.   *213*
Then with the food they summon back their strength,
And stretched upon the greensward take their fill
Of old wine and fat venison. When good cheer
Had banished hunger, and the board was cleared,
In endless talk for their lost mates they yearn,
'Twixt hope and fear uncertain whether still

Among the quick to deem them, or even now
Suffering the worst, and deaf to their last cry.
And chiefly good Aeneas, now the fate
Of keen Orontes, now of Amycus,
And inly, Lycus, thine untimely doom,
And for brave Gyas, brave Cloanthus, mourns.   222
    And now they had ended, when from heights of air
Down-glancing on the sail-flown sea, and lands
With shores and widespread peoples stretched below,
Jupiter thus upon the cope of heaven
Made pause, and fixed his eyes on Libya's realm.
Him then, such cares revolving in his breast,
Sadder than wont, her bright eyes brimmed with tears,
Venus bespake: "O thou who swayest the tides
Of men and gods with sovereign power eterne,
And scar'st them with thy bolt, what crime so dire
Can my Aeneas, what the sons of Troy
Have wrought to-thee-ward, that against them now,
By death so minished, the whole world stands barred,
And all for Italy? Surely that from these
Should one day issue with revolving years
The Romans, ay, from these the warrior-chiefs
Of Teucer's blood requickened, born to rule
All-potent sea and land, thou promisedst:
What purpose, Sire, has warped thee? I indeed
Hereby, with counter-fate requiting fate,
Oft solaced me for Troy's sad overthrow;
But the same fortune, that pursued so long,
Still dogs them with disaster. Mighty king,
What end dost thou vouchsafe them of their toils?   241
Antenor, from the Achaean midst escaped,
Could thrid Illyria's windings all unscathed,
Far inward to Liburnian realms, and pass
The well-springs of Timavus, whence the sea
Bursts through nine mouths 'mid thunder of the
      rocks,
And whelms his fields beneath the roaring main.
Yet here Patavium's city founded he,
To be his Teucrians' dwelling-place, and named
The nation, and hung high the arms of Troy;
Now rests he tranquil, lulled in calm repose:
But we, thine offspring, whom thy nod assigns
The height of heaven, our ships—O misery!—lost,
To slake one wrathful spirit are forsook,
And sundered far from the Italian coast.
Is this the good man's guerdon? Dost thou so

Restore us to our empire?"
              Upon her
Smiling with that regard, wherewith he clears
Tempestuous skies, the Sire of men and gods
His daughter's lips touched, and bespake her thus: 256
"Truce, Cytherea, to thy fears, and know
Unshaken stand thy children's destinies:
Lavinium's city and predestined walls
Thou shalt behold, and in thine arms up-bear
High-souled Aeneas to the stars of heaven;
Nor hath my purpose warped me. This thy son—
For I, to ease thy gnawing care, will speak,
From fate's dark roll her inmost secrets wring—
Shall wage a mighty war in Italy,
Crush the proud folk, and for his warriors found
A city and a system, till the third
Summer hath seen him lord in Latium,
Three winters o'er the vanquished Rutules sped.
But young Ascanius, newly now surnamed
Iulus—Ilus was he while enthroned
Stood Ilium's State—shall compass in his reign
Thirty great cycles with revolving months,
And from Lavinium shift his empire's seat,
And Alba Longa's ramparts rear with power: 271
Here now shall reign full thrice a hundred years
Great Hector's line, till Ilia, royal maid
And priestess, shall twin offspring bear to Mars,
Their sire; then glorying in the tawny hide
Of the she-wolf, his nurse, shall Romulus
Take up the nation, build the war-god's town,
And call them Romans after his own name.
For these nor goals of power, nor times I fix—
Grant them a boundless sway. Fierce Juno too,
Who now with terror scares earth, sea, and heaven,
Shall turn to kinder counsels, and with me
Cherish the Romans, masters of the world,
The toga'd nation. So hath heaven decreed.
A time shall come with gliding lustres, when
The house of Assaracus to her yoke shall bow
Phthia and famed Mycenae, and bear sway
O'er conquered Argos. From that glorious line
Of Troy descending, Caesar shall be born,
Destined to bound with ocean his domain,
As with the stars his glory, Julius,
A name bequeathed from great Iulus. Him,
Laden with eastern spoils, shalt thou one day

Hold safe in heaven: to him too prayers shall rise.   *290*
Then wars shall cease, the rugged times grow mild;
Hoar Faith, and Vesta, and Quirinus then
Yoked with his brother Remus, shall give laws;
Grim-knit with bolts of iron, War's temple-gates
Shut fast shall be, while hellish Rage within
High on a grisly pile of arms, his hands
Brass-bound behind him with a hundred knots,
Shall roar terrific from blood-boltered mouth."
   So saying, he sends down Maia's son from heaven,
That Carthage her new towers and lands might ope
To greet the Teucrians, lest, unlearned of fate,
Dido repel them. Through the vast of air
His plumèd oars he plies, on Libya's strand
Has swift alighted; ay, even now he is
About his errand; the god wills, and lo!
Those haughty hearts the Punic folk put by;
Their queen in chief toward the Teucrian host
Now harbours gentle thoughts and kind desires.   *304*
   But good Aeneas, all night long perplexed
With many a care, when first the genial boon
Of light was given, resolved to issue forth,
Search out the new land, and what shores he hath
    gained
By the wind's grace, whether by man or beast—
So savage seem they—tenanted, then bear
Back to his friends the tidings of his quest.
In woody creek beneath a hollow rock
His fleet he hides, by trees and bristling shades
Closely embosomed, then himself strides forth,
Achates sole beside him, in his hand
Two javelins brandishing broad-tipped with iron.
Him, half the wood-way through, his mother met,
In face and garb a maiden, armed with gear
Of Spartan damsel, or like her of Thrace,
Harpalyce, what time she tires her steeds,
Outspeeding arrowy Hebrus in her flight.   *317*
For from her shoulders huntress-wise was slung
A shapely bow; her tresses she let trail
Upon the winds, bare-kneed, her flowing folds
Close gathered in a knot. Ere he could speak,
"Ho!" cried she, "youths, if ye have chanced to spy
One of my sisters, tell me where she strays,
With quiver and spotted lynx-skin girt, or else
Hard on the track of foaming boar, full cry."   *324*
   So Venus, and in answer Venus' son:

[111]

"None of thy sisters have I seen or heard,
O—damsel must I name thee? for thy face
Nor mortal seems, nor human rings thy voice:
O goddess surely, or Phoebus' sister thou,
Or of the blood of nymphs, whoe'er thou art,
Be kind, uplift the burden of our woe,
And deign to say what heaven bends over us,
Cast on what borders of the world: for here
Witless of country or of folk we roam,
By winds and mighty billows hither driven.
So on thine altars at our hand shall fall
Full many a victim."   *334*
                    Then spake Venus: "Nay,
Not mine to claim such worship; Tyrian maids
Wont thus to wear the quiver, and bind their limbs
High with the purple buskin. Here thou seest
The Punic realm, a Tyrian people, this
Agenor's city, but all the borderland
Libyan, a race untamable in war.
Dido, whom erst from Tyre a brother's fear
Banished, now reigns their empress; 'tis a long
And tangled tale of outrage, but the main
Threads I will trace. Sychaeus was her spouse,
In all Phoenicia lord of widest lands:
Fondly, poor heart, she loved him, by her sire
A virgin given, and in first bridal yoked.
But reigned o'er Tyre a monster-king of crime,
Pygmalion, her brother, and there came
Fury between them. At the household shrine,
Impious and blinded by the lust of gold,
With stealthy stroke at unawares he slays
Sychaeus, all reckless of his sister's love.
Long he concealed the deed, by many a base
Dissimulation with illusive hope
Fooling the love-sick bride. But in her sleep
Uprose the form of her unburied lord,
That, lifting a face pale in wondrous wise,
Laid bare the ruthless altar, and therewith
His steel-pierc'd bosom, and unveiled to view
All the dark horror of the household crime.   *356*
Then from her home at swiftest speed to hie
He bids her, and for aid upon the way
Old treasures hid within the earth reveals,
Store known to none of silver and of gold.
Scared at the tale, Dido her flight prepares
And friends to fly with: round her throng whom fierce

Hate for the tyrant, or keen terror, filled;
Chance-proffered ships they seize, and lade with gold:
Pygmalion's treasures from his gripe are borne
O'er seas, a woman piloting the way.
So to the place they came, where now thou spyest
The lofty walls and rising citadel
Of new-built Carthage, and of land they bought—
Called Byrsa from their bargaining—so much
As with a bull's hide they might compass round.   368
But who are ye, sirs, from what shores arrived,
Or on what journey bound?" So questioned, he
With accents from his deepest heart-springs drawn,
Sighing, replied:
           "Goddess, should I recount
From their first source, and wert thou free to hear,
Our sorrow's sad recital, eve would first
Put day to sleep, and shut the gates of heaven.
From ancient Troy, if haply through thine ears
Troy's name has entered, borne o'er many a main,
The wind's whim drave us to the Libyan shores.   377
Men call me good Aeneas; in this fleet
Snatched from the foe my household gods I bring,
In fame extolled above the stars. My goal
Is Italy, my country, and a race
Sprung from high Jove. With twice ten ships I
    climbed
The Phrygian main, by fate's clear promise led,
My goddess-mother pointing me the way;
Scarce seven remain, by winds and waters riven.
Myself the while, a beggar and unknown,
Range here the Libyan waste, an outcast banned
From Europe and from Asia." His sad plaint
Venus could bear no longer, but broke in
Thus on his grief's mid utterance: 387
                  "Whosoe'er
Thou art, not all unloved, methinks, of heaven
Draw'st thou the breath of life, who thus hast reached
Our Tyrian city: but go forward still,
And hence to the queen's palace win thy way;
For news I bring thee of thy friends' return,
Thy fleet in harbour, by the shifting gales
To shelter driven; or idly and for naught
My parents schooled me in prophetic lore.
See yonder swans twice six in jubilant line,
Which from the skiey region with his swoop
Jove's bird was routing o'er the plains of heaven:

Now in long train they seem some lighting-ground
To choose, or, chosen, scan it from above:
As these, returned, with hurtling pinions play,
Wheel in one flock through heaven, and utter songs,
So, of thy ships and friends aboard them, some
Are safe in port, and some with swelling sails
Now make the harbour: only do thou still
Go forward, follow where the pathway leads."   *401*
   She spake, and turning shone with rosy neck;
Her head's ambrosial locks breathed scent divine;
And, as her robe flowed downward to her feet,
She stepped no doubtful goddess. When he knew
His mother, her fleeting form he thus pursued,
Crying, "Ah! cruel thou too, wherefore mock
Thy son so oft with semblances untrue?
Why may I never clasp thy hand in mine,
Or hear unfeignèd accents and reply?"
So chiding, toward the town he wends his way.   *410*
But Venus with a dark haze hedged them in,
As on they strode, and a thick mantling mist
Miraculous shed over them, that none
Might see, or touch, or compass their delay,
Or ask their cause of coming. She herself
Aloft to Paphos hies, her loved abode
Blithe to revisit, where her temple stands,
And with Sabaean incense ever smoke
A hundred altars, fragrant with fresh flowers.
   Meanwhile, where points the track, they speed their
     way,
And now the hill they climb, that o'er the town
Hangs huge, and frowns above the opposing towers.   *420*
Aeneas marvels at the mighty mass,
Mere huts of yore, he marvels at the gates,
The busy din and paving of the ways.
The Tyrians in hot haste are building walls,
Rearing a citadel, and uprolling rocks
By toil of hand; some choose a dwelling-site,
And with a trench surround it: they appoint
An awful senate, laws, and magistrates.
Here these are digging harbours, yonder those
Lay deep foundations for a theatre,
And hew gigantic columns from the rocks,
Lofty adornments of a stage to be.   *429*
Such toil in early summer as keeps the bees
Busy in sunshine amid flowery fields,
When forth they lead the ripe youth of their race,

Or pack the amber-dripping honey, and stretch
Their cells to bursting with the nectar sweet,
Or ease returning labourers of their load,
Or form a band, and from their precincts drive
The drones, a lazy herd: how glows the work!
How sweet the honey smells of perfumed thyme!
"O happy ye, whose walls already rise,"
Exclaims Aeneas, toward the city-roofs
Upgazing, and so enters through their midst,
Hedged in with darkness, marvellous to tell,
And mingles with the folk, unseen of all.   440
    Within the city's midst a grove there stood
Bounteous of shade, where first the Punic host,
'Scaped from the brunt of whirlwind and of wave,
Dug forth, as queenly Juno had foreshown,
The symbol of a fiery horse's head:
For so, said she, their race should ever prove
Peerless in war and with abundance blest.
Sidonian Dido here a mighty fane
To Juno's praise was rearing, rich with gifts
And with the indwelling goddess: see! of brass
High on ascending steps the threshold lay,
And clenched with brass the lintels, of brass too
The doors on creaking hinges. In this grove
A strange sight met him, that first soothed his fear;
Here first Aeneas dared for safety hope,
And in his broken fortunes firmlier trust.   452
For 'neath the mighty fane while he surveys
Point after point, still waiting for the queen,
And marvels to behold what fortune crowns
The city, and her craftsmen's emulous hands
And toil of labour, there set forth he sees
The battlefields of Ilium, and the war
By fame now bruited over the whole world,
Priam and Atreus' sons, and, bane of both,
Achilles. With arrested steps he cries
Weeping, "What place, Achates, or what clime
But with the story of our grief o'erflows?
See Priam! even here, too, honour hath its meed,
And there are tears for what befalls, and hearts
Touched by the chances of mortality.   462
Fear naught, and thou shalt find this fame will bring
Some safety with it." He spake, and feasts his soul
Upon the empty picture, sighing sore,
His face all bathed with grief's abundant flow.
For, as they fought round Pergamus, behold!

Here fled the Greeks, Troy's bravest at their heels,
The Phrygians here, Achilles in his car
With crested helm pursuing. Nor far aloof
With tears he knew the snowy-canvassed tents
Of Rhesus, which, in the first sleep betrayed,
Red Tydeus' son was deluging with blood,
Who campward now drives off the fiery steeds,
Or e'er on Trojan pastures they have browsed,
Or drunk of Xanthus. Elsewhere was portrayed,
His arms in flight flung from him, Troilus:
Poor boy! for with Achilles overmatched,
Dragged by his steeds to the void car he clings,
Thrown backward, and yet grasping still the reins:
Neck, see! and hair are trailed along the ground,
And his reversed spear scribbles in the dust.   478
Meanwhile the Trojan women to the shrine
Of unregardful Pallas passed along
Bearing the peplus, all their tresses loosed,
As suppliant mourners with hand-bruisèd breasts;
On earth the goddess with averted gaze
Her eyes was fixing. There Achilles too
Had thrice dragged Hector round the walls of Troy,
And now was bartering his dead corse for gold.
Then from the bottom of his heart he heaved
A mighty groan, when he beheld the spoils,
The chariot, nay, the body of his friend,
And Priam outstretching his defenceless hands.   487
Himself too there among the Achaean chiefs
He recognized, and dusky Memnon's arms
And eastern warriors. With their moonèd shields
Penthesilea like a fury leads
The Amazonian ranks, and blazes forth
Amid her thousands, one protruding breast
Looped with a golden girdle—warrior-queen,
Who dares the shock of battle, maid with men.
    Now while Aeneas the Dardan at this sight
Marvels, beholding, while amazed he stands
In one fixed gaze immovable, the queen,
Dido, in matchless beauty, to the fane,
Thronged with a mighty company, has come.   497
As by Eurotas' banks, or on the heights
Of Cynthus, when Diana plies the dance—
A thousand Oreads upon either side
Massed in her train—she on her shoulder bears
A quiver, and as she treads o'ertops them all—
A secret rapture thrills Latona's breast—

Such Dido seemed, so moved she through their midst
Rejoicing, busied with her realm to be.   *504*
Then in the sacred portals and beneath
The mid vault of the temple, hedged with arms,
Propped high upon a throne, her seat she took.
There laws and judgements gave she to her folk,
Now meting forth their tasks in equal shares,
Now doling them by lot: when suddenly
'Mid a great throng Aeneas sees approach
Antheus, Sergestus, and Cloanthus brave,
And other Teucrians whom the black typhoon
Had scattered o'er the main, or swept afar
To alien shores. Achates and his chief,
Thrilled and bewildered betwixt joy and fear,
Yearn eagerly to clasp their hands, but still,
By the strange fact confounded, make no sign,
And from their cloudy covering watch to learn
The heroes' fortunes, on what shore their fleet
They are leaving, with what hope arrived, for lo!
From all the ships came envoys craving grace,
And with loud clamour making for the shrine.   *519*
   So when they had entered and gat leave to speak,
Their eldest, Ilioneus, thus took the word
With heart unruffled: "O queen, whom Jove assigns
To found a virgin city, and curb in
Unbending nations with the reins of law,
We Trojans, tempest-driven from sea to sea,
In bitter case implore thee, from our ships
Ward off the unutterable doom of fire:
Spare us, a pious race, and on our plight
Look with no distant eyes. We have not come
To harry with the sword your Libyan homes,
Or seize the spoil, and drive it to the shore:
Such lawlessness we like not, nor so prone
Are conquered men to insolence. There is
A spot, by Greeks Hesperia named, a land
Of old renown, mighty in arms, in soil
Prolific, where the Oenotrian heroes dwelt,
Now by a later race named Italy,
If rumour lie not, from their leader's name.   *533*
Thither our course we held, when, big with storm,
Orion, rising with a sudden sea,
Drave us on hidden shoals, and scattered us
Far athwart billows of o'ertoppling brine
And pathless rocks, before the headstrong south:
Hither we few have floated to your shores.

What race of men is this? What land allows
Custom so cruel? The welcome of the shore
Denied, they dare us at sword's point set foot
Upon the utmost margin of their land.
If men and mortal arms ye hold so light,
Yet look for gods mindful of right and wrong.   543
Aeneas was our king, none juster, none
More famed for goodness, or for feats of war.
If fate still spare that hero, if he still
Feeds on the air of heaven, nor yet is laid
In cruel darkness, naught have we to fear;
No, nor wouldst thou repent thee to have been
His challenger in kindness. Cities too
And arms to aid in Sicily have we,
And famed Acestes, sprung from Trojan blood.
Let us but haul our battered fleet ashore,
Fit planks in the forest, and trim oars, that if
Vouchsafed us still to make for Italy,
Comrades and king restored, with hearts elate
To Italy and Latium we may go;
But if cut off our safety, and if thee,
Best father of the Teucrians, Libya's deep
Holds in its keeping, and no hope is now
Left in Iulus, we at least may seek
Sicania's strait from whence we sailed, the homes
There waiting, and Acestes for our king."   558
So Ilioneus; and instant with one mouth
Clamoured assent the sons of Dardanus.
    Then briefly Dido speaks with drooping eyes:
"Cast fear adrift, ye Teucrians, shut the doors
On doubt: the hard conditions of the time
And raw youth of my kingdom to this push
Compel me, and to guard my frontiers round.
The comrades of Aeneas, and Troy's town,
Her heroes and their heroisms, and all
Her war's vast conflagration, who is there
That knows not? Not so dull indeed the hearts
We bear in Punic bosoms, nor so far
Out of the sun's track in his charioting
Our Tyrian town. The great Hesperian land
And Saturn's realm, or Eryx and the tract
That bows to king Acestes—choose ye which;
Safeguarded I will speed you on your way,
With stores to boot. Or would ye in this realm
Sit down beside me? yours the town I build:
Haul up your ships: Trojan and Tyrian

Without distinction shall be held by me.   *574*
And would that by the selfsame tempest driven
Your king himself Aeneas had been here!
For my part, I will send through all my coasts
Sure scouts, and bid them traverse Libya's land
From end to end, if haply cast ashore
Forest or city holds him wandering."
    Fired by these words long since Achates bold
And Prince Aeneas burned to break their cloud.
Achates first gat utterance: "Goddess-born,
Say now what purpose rises in thy heart?
Thou seest all safe, comrades and fleet restored,
One only lacking, whom our own eyes saw
Gulfed in mid-ocean: with thy mother's words
Else all things tally." Scarcely had he spoke,
When suddenly the cloud that wrapped them round
Sunders, and melts into the open heaven.   *587*
Forth stood Aeneas in the clear sunlight
Resplendent, face and shoulders like a god:
For she who bare him on her son had breathed
A glory of hair, and ruddy light of youth,
And on his eyes glad lustre—such a grace
As artist's hand to ivory lends, or like
Silver or Parian chased with yellow gold.
Then to the queen, by all unlooked for, thus
Sudden he speaks: "I, whom ye seek, am here,
Trojan Aeneas, snatched from Libyan waves.   *596*
Thou, who alone the unutterable woes
Of Troy hast pitied, and dost impart to us—
Sole remnant by the Danai left, fordone
With all mischances both of land and sea,
Beggared of all—a city and a home,
Dido, to yield thee worthy thanks stands not
Within our means, nor theirs who else survive
Of Dardan blood, scattered the wide world o'er.
May heaven, if any powers regard the good,
If justice and the self-approving mind
Weigh aught in the world, return thee guerdon due!
What age so blest as to have borne thee? What
Parents so noble as to call thee child?   *606*
While rivers still shall run into the sea,
While shadows sweep the mountain-sides, while
    heaven
Shall feed the stars, thy glory, name, and praise,
What land soe'er me summon, shall remain."
So saying, his right hand he reached forth to greet

Friend Ilioneus, Serestus with his left,
Then others, bold Gyas and Cloanthus bold.
Astounded by the hero's presence first,
Then at his vast misfortune, thus outspake
Sidonian Dido: "Through such mighty perils,
O goddess-born, what fate pursues, what force
To barbarous shores impels thee? Art thou that
Aeneas, whom kindly Venus by the wave
Of Phrygian Simois to the Dardan bare,
Anchises? I myself remember well
When Teucer, from his own home ousted, came
To Sidon, seeking a new realm to win
By Belus' aid: my father Belus then
Was harrying Cyprus, whose rich soil he swayed
With conquering sceptre. From that time to this
Troy's chequered fortune hath been known to me,
And thine own name, and the Pelasgian kings.   *624*
Even he, their foeman, with high praise would laud
The Teucrians, from the Teucrian's ancient stock
Claim to be sprung. Then enter, sirs, our house.
Me also, tossed from toil to toil, like chance
Suffers at length to make this land my home:
Nor all unlessoned in calamity
Learn I to aid the wretched." With such words
She to her palace leads Aeneas in,
And for the temples of the gods proclaims
Due honour. For his comrades therewithal
Down to the beach she sends a score of bulls,
A hundred bristling backs of burly swine,
Fat lambs a hundred, with their dams to boot,
Glad gifts for the glad day. Meanwhile, within,
The palace is set forth in all the pomp
Of royal splendour, and amidst the hall
A feast are they preparing—coverlets
Wrought deftly of proud purple, on the boards
Ponderous silver, and, embossed in gold,
The brave deeds of her sires, an endless-long
Array of exploits traced from chief to chief
Down from the earliest dawning of her race.   *642*
　　Aeneas, for a father's love forbade
His mind to rest, sends forward to the ships
Achates, bidding him with speed acquaint
Ascanius, and conduct him to the town—
Upon Ascanius a fond father's heart
Is wholly set—and presents he bids bring
Snatched from the wreck of Ilium, a long robe

Stiff with embroidered gold-work, and a veil
Purfled with yellow-flowered acanthus, worn
By Argive Helen, and from Mycenae brought,
What time to Troy she sailed, a bride forbid—
Her mother Leda's marvellous gift; therewith
A sceptre which erewhile had known the grasp
Of Priam's eldest daughter Ilione,
A pearl-strung necklet, and a double crown
Of gems and gold. Upon this errand sped,
Achates now was hastening to the ships.   *656*

    But Cytherea in her breast revolves
New wiles and new devices, that, for sweet
Ascanius, Cupid, changed in face and form,
May come, and with his gifts inflame the queen
To frenzy, and wrap all her frame in fire.
Ay, for in sooth she fears the treacherous house
And double-spoken Tyrians: Juno's hate
Sears her, and trouble at nightfall returns.
Thus, therefore, she bespeaks her wingèd Love:
"Son, my sole strength and mighty power, O son,
Who laughest even at the Typhoïan bolts
Of the great Father, to thy feet I fly,
And suppliant sue thy godhead. How Aeneas,
Thy brother, is buffeted from shore to shore
Over the main by Juno's rancorous spite—
These things are known to thee, and with our grief
Oft hast thou grieved. Phoenician Dido now
Holds and enchains him with her flattering words;
And much I fear where Juno's welcome tends;
She will not idle where such hopes are hinged.   *672*
So to prevent the queen with guile, and gird
With fire I purpose, that no power may change,
But strong love for Aeneas fix her mine.
Next how to achieve it hearken my device:
The royal boy, my chiefest care, e'en now
To the Sidonian town sets forth to go
At his loved father's bidding—in his hand
Gifts that escaped Troy's burning and the sea.
Him will I hide upon Cythera's height,
Or on Idalium in my sacred seat,
Lulled in deep slumber, that my stratagems
He may not know nor intervene to mar.   *682*
Then for one night—no more—feign thou his form,
And don the well-known features, boy for boy,
That when with rapture at the royal board,
The wine-god brimming, Dido to her breast

Shall take thee and embrace, and on thy lips
Imprint sweet kisses, with the subtle fire
Thy breath may poison her at unawares."
Obedient then to his dear mother's words,
Love doffed his wings, and with Iulus' step
Walked gaily forth. Meantime Ascanius,
While gentle slumber o'er his frame she pours,
Venus, to her immortal bosom clasped,
Bears upward to Idalia's wooded heights,
Where soft amaracus enfolds with flowers,
And fans him with the breath of odorous shade.   *694*

   And now, all joy, Achates for his guide,
Cupid the royal gifts obediently
Came bearing for the Tyrians. Entering,
He sees the queen set in their midst, reclined
Upon a gold couch proudly canopied.
Now Prince Aeneas, now the Trojan men
Gather, and stretch them on strewn purple. Slaves
Pour water on their hands, and proffer bread
From baskets, and bring towels with shorn pile.
Within are fifty handmaids, charged in course
To heap continuous store, and magnify
With fire the hearth-gods; and a hundred more,
With men as many and of like age, to load
The boards with viands, and set the winecups on.   *706*
The Tyrians also, through the festive hall
Gathered in crowds, are bidden to recline
On broidered couches. At Aeneas' gifts
They marvel, marvel at Iulus too—
The god-light in his face, the well-feigned words—
And at the robe, and veil embroidered-fair
With yellow-flowered acanthus. Most of all,
Ill-starred, and destined to the coming bane,
The fair Phoenician cannot gloat her fill,
But feeds the flame with gazing, by the boy
Ravished no less than by the gifts. But he,
When he had clasped Aeneas, and hung close
About his neck, sating the hungry love
Of his pretended sire, moves toward the queen.
She with her eyes, and she with all her heart
Cleaves to him, and fondles at her breast anon—
Dido, all witless of how great a god
Is her poor bosom's burden. He the while,
His Acidalian mother heeding well,
Slowly begins to blot Sychaeus out,
And with a living passion to forestall

[122]

A heart long stagnant and to love unused.   *722*
   When the first hush upon the banquet fell,
The board removed, they set on mighty bowls,
And crown the winecups. Loud the rafters ring,
As through the wide hall rolls the roar of tongues;
Down from the gilded roof hang lamps ablaze,
And flambeaux flaring put the night to rout.
And now a cup heavy with gems and gold
The queen bade bring, and filled it with pure wine,
As Belus used, and all from Belus sprung;
Then through the hall fell silence: "Jupiter,
Of hospitable laws, men say, the giver,
To Tyrians and to travellers from Troy
Grant that this day propitious be, and that
Our children's children may remember it.   *733*
Let Bacchus, source of merriment, be near,
And bounteous Juno; and, ye Tyrians too,
Grace ye our gathering with goodwill." She spake
And on the table poured the votive wine,
And, having made libation, with lip's edge
Herself first touched it, then to Bitias
Passed with a merry taunt; he, nothing loth,
Drank of the foaming goblet, and dived deep
Into the brimming gold; then other lords
In turn. Iopas of the flowing hair
Makes the hall echo with his gilded lyre,
Once taught of mightiest Atlas: and his song
Is of the wandering moon, the toiling sun,
Whence human kind and cattle, whence rain and
    fire;   *743*
Arcturus, and the showery Hyades,
And the twin Bears; why winter suns so haste
To dip themselves in Ocean, or what check
Retards the lingering nights. With shout on shout
Applaud the Tyrians, and the sons of Troy
Make answer: therewithal in varied talk
Unhappy Dido still spun out the night,
Drinking deep draughts of love; and much she asked
Of Priam, much of Hector, with what arms
Aurora's son came girded to the fray,
How fair the steeds of Diomede, or how vast
Achilles. "Nay, but, O my guest," said she,
"Come, tell us from the first the Danaan plots,
Thy comrades' woes, and thine own wanderings:
For lo! the seventh returning summer now
Bears thee a wanderer over land and wave."   *756*

BOOK II

All lips were hushed, all eyes attentive fixed:
Then Prince Aeneas from his lofty couch
Addressed him thus to speak:
                    "Unutterable,
O queen, the grief thou bid'st me to revive,
How Troy's magnificence and royal power,
Woe worth the day! the Danai overthrew;
Thrice piteous scenes which I myself beheld,
And was a mighty part of! Such a tale
Who or of Myrmidons or Dolopes
Or stern Ulysses' soldiery could tell,
And hold from weeping? Now, too, dewy night
Adown the sky falls headlong, and the stars
Sinking invite to sleep. But if to learn
Our woes such longing take thee, and to hear
Brief-told Troy's dying anguish, though my mind
At the remembrance shudders, from the grief
Recoils, I will attempt it.
                    "Broken in war   13
And baffled by the fates, the Danaan chiefs,
Now that so many grew the gliding years,
By Pallas' aid, artificer divine,
Build up a horse of mountain bulk, the ribs
Of pine-planks interwoven, feigning it
A votive offering for their home-return;
So runs the rumour. Into its dark side
Picked warriors stealthily by lot they stow,
And fill the deep vaults of its mighty womb
With arm`e`d soldiery.
                    "There lies in sight
An isle, fame-bruited, Tenedos, full-fraught
Of power, while yet stood Priam's empire—now
Mere bay and roadstead, ill for keels to trust.   23
Hither they sail, and on the barren shore
Lie hid. We deem them far upon their way,
Bound for Mycenae with a favouring gale.
Thereat all Teucria shuffles off the load
Of her long mourning. Wide are flung the gates;
Whence issuing forth with rapture we behold
The Dorian camp, the haunts now tenantless,

The shore left void: here the Dolopian band,
Here fierce Achilles pitched; here lay the fleet;
Here were they wont to meet us, host to host.
Some gape at Maid Minerva's doom-fraught gift,
And marvel at the monster-horse; and first
Thymoetes urged it within walls be haled,
And lodged in the fortress, or through treachery, or
That thither now the fates of Troy were set.   34
But Capys and the minds of saner bent
Bid either hurl it headlong in the sea—
This Danaan ambush, their suspicious gift—
Or fire it from beneath, or pierce and probe
The womb's dark hollows. With fierce party-cries
This way and that the wavering crowd is torn.
    "First of a mighty throng, outspeeding all,
Laocoon from the citadel's steep height
Comes running in hot haste, and cries from far,
'Alack! so mad, my masters! do ye think
The foe departed? deem ye any gift
Of Danaans can lack guile? have ye so learned
Ulysses? or within this timber caged
Achaeans lurk, or 'tis an engine framed
Against the walls, to spy into our homes
And pounce upon the city from above,
Or else some trickery lurks therein; trust not
The horse, ye Trojans; whatsoe'er it be,
Even gift in hand, I fear the Danai still.'   49
So saying, with main strength a huge spear he hurled
At the brute's flank, and where the framework bulged
To belly: it stood there quivering; the womb shook;
The vaults rang hollow and gave forth a groan:
And had the powers above, had our own wit
Not turned awry, he had prevailed to sack
The Argives' den; Troy still were standing; thou,
Priam's tall citadel, unshaken still.   56
    "Meanwhile a youth, his hands behind him bound,
See! Dardan hinds come haling to the king,
Loud-clamouring, who, to shape it even so,
And let the Achaeans into Troy, had thrust
A stranger's wilful presence on their path,
Dauntless of soul, and armed for this or that—
His wiles to ply, or fall on certain death.
Eager to see, Troy's sons from every side
Rush round him like a torrent, each with each
Vying to mock their captive. Come now, hear
How Danaans can deceive, and learn from one

The villainy of all. For as he stood
Helpless, confused, a target for all eyes,
And gazed around upon the Phrygian ranks,   68
'Alas!' he cried, 'what land, what ocean now
Can harbour me? or what last hope have I—
The wretch, alike from Danaan earth debarred,
And for whose blood the Dardans howl no less,
To quit their hatred?' By that burst of grief
Changed was our humour, checked each rude assault;
We urge him speak, relate from whence he sprang,
His errand what, and why, a thrall, so bold.
Then, fear abandoned, thus at length he speaks:
'All will I truly tell thee, King,' quoth he,
'Betide what may; my Argive birth I own: 78
This at the outset; nor, if Fortune shaped
Sinon for misery, shall her spite, beside,
Shape him to fraud and falsehood. It may be,
Borne on men's voices, to thine ear hath sped
Some sound of Palamede from Belus sprung,
A name world-famous, whom by lies betrayed,
Guiltless, and on a villain's charge, because
The war he gainsaid, the Pelasgian lords
Once did to death, now, lorn of light, deplore.
To him as comrade and near kinsman I
Was by a needy sire in earliest youth
Sent hither to the field. While yet enthroned
Scathless he stood, and at kings' councils throve,
I in some sort held rank and honour too:
But when Ulysses' treacherous spite, I speak
No secret, drave him from the realms of day,
Downcast and darkling my sad life dragged on,
With inward wrath for my friend's guiltless fate.
Nor—madman—could I hold my peace, but vowed,
Should chance but offer, to my Argive home
If e'er returned in triumph, to wreak his fall,
And, thus outspoken, stirred the goads of hate.   96
Thence my first slip to ruin, Ulysses thence
Ceased not to scare me with new charges, thence
To sow dark rumours in the common ear,
And hunt for armed accomplices. Indeed
No rest he took till, Calchas at his side—
But why the unwelcome record do I thus
Vainly unroll? or why the tale prolong?
If all the Achaeans in one class ye file,
And hearing that suffices, take, 'tis time,
Your vengeance; this the Ithacan would wish,

And this the Atridae grudge no gold to buy.'
  "Then truly burn we to search out and learn
The why and wherefore, strangers as we were
To guilt so monstrous and Pelasgian guile.
He, quaking, with false heart his speech renews: *108*
  " 'Oft were the Danai fain to take their flight,
Leave Troy behind, and quit the weary war;
And would they had done so! the rough sea as oft
Opposed its stormy barrier, and the south
Scared them from going. Chiefly when yon horse,
Of maple-beams compacted, stood erect,
With bellowing storm-clouds the whole welkin rang.
Doubtful, we send Eurypylus to ask
The oracle of Phoebus: from the shrine
This dolorous word he brings. "It was with blood
Of a slain virgin ye appeased the winds,
When, Danai, first ye made for Ilium's shore: *117*
With blood no less must your return be sought,
And expiation of an Argive's life."
  " 'When to the people's ears this utterance came,
Numbed were all hearts, and through their inmost
      bones
Ran a chill shudder—who was he by fate
Predestined thus? Apollo's victim who?
Then he of Ithaca with blusterings loud
Drags forth into their midst Calchas the seer;
Hotly demands, what is this will of heaven.
Nor lacked there who even then foretold to me
The schemer's cruel outrage, or who saw
The end, yet spake not. Twice five days the seer
In silence hides him, vows no word of his
Shall denounce any, or to death consign.   *127*
Scarce driven at length by the Ithacan's loud cries,
To crown their compact, he breaks forth in speech,
And dooms me to the altar. All approved,
And turned what each was fearing for himself
To one poor soul's destruction. Now drew near
The unutterable day; for me were now
The altar-rites preparing, the salt cakes
And brow-encircling fillets. I confess
I plucked me from perdition, brake my bonds,
In miry pool all night sedge-sheltered lay,
Till they should sail, if haply sailed they had.   *136*
Nor longer my old country may I hope,
Or children sweet, or longed-for sire, to see,
Of whom far likelier they for my default

Will claim the forfeit—with their death, poor souls!
Atone my trespass. But I thee implore
By the high Gods, and powers that know the truth,
By what remains to mortals anywhere
Of faith untarnished, pity woes like mine,
Pity a soul with unjust burdens bowed.'   *144*
    "Life to his tears we grant and pity too:
Priam's own voice first bids the man be loosed
From grip of gyve and fetter, and thus speaks
With kindly word: 'Whoe'er thou art, henceforth,
As for the Greeks, forget them and forgo:
Ours shalt thou be, and to my questioning
Unfold true answers: this huge monster-horse
Why built they? by whom fathered? to what end?
A sacred symbol? or some tool of war?'
He had said: the other, well equipped with guile
And craft Pelasgian, to the stars upturned
His hands now fetterless: 'You, quenchless fires,
And your inviolable majesty
I call,' quoth he, 'to witness, and you too,
Altars and heinous swords which I escaped,
And garlands of the gods, my victim-gear;   *156*
Lawful it is for me to break my vows
Of fealty to the Greeks, lawful to hate
The men themselves, and bring to the light of day
Whate'er they shroud in darkness, nor am I
Holden by any of my country's laws:
Only do thou stand by thy plighted word,
Troy, and, safeguarded, guard thy promise safe,
If truth I tell, if richly thee repay.
    " 'All hope and courage for the war's emprise
On Pallas' help the Danaans ever stayed:
But from what time, with Tydeus' impious son,
Ulysses, crime-contriver, dared to rend
Doom-fraught Palladium from its hallowed shrine,
And slew the watchmen of her castled height,
And snatched the sacred image, and feared not
With hands blood-reeking to contaminate
Her godhead's maiden fillets, from henceforth
The Danaans' hope in ebb slid ever back,
Crushed was their strength, the goddess' heart
      estranged.   *170*
Nor doubtful the dread signs Tritonia gave;
Scarce was her semblance lodged within the camp,
When from the upturned eyes shot quivering flames,
A salt sweat coursed along the limbs, and thrice—

Wondrous to tell—of her own self she sprang
From earth shield-laden, and with spear that shook.
Calchas at once with prophet-voice bids brave
Ocean in flight, for that no Argive arms
Could uptear Pergamus, except they seek
At Argos for new omens, and bring back
That will of heaven, which erst they bare away
O'er ocean with them in their curvèd keels.   *179*
And now that homeward-wafted they have sought
Mycenae, 'tis to get them arms, and gods
For their way-fellows, and, the sea recrossed,
They will be here unlooked for. In such wise
Doth Calchas sort the omens. Warned by him
They reared this image in Palladium's place,
For outraged godhead, their dark crime to quit.
But to this monstrous height of woven planks
Calchas bade lift it and upbuild to heaven,
Lest through your gates it be received, or drawn
Within the ramparts, and so shield your folk
Beneath their ancient worship. For if hand
Of yours had wronged Minerva's offering,
Mighty destruction then—which augury
May heaven first turn upon himself!—would fall
On Priam's empire and the Phrygians; but
If by your hands your city it should scale,
Asia herself should in a mighty war
Assail the walls of Pelops, and such doom
Remain in store for our posterity.'   *194*
　　"By such decoys of Sinon's art forsworn
The tale gat credence, and by craft were caught
And forcèd tears, whom neither Tydeus' son,
No, nor Achilles of Larissa, nor
Ten years had conquered, nor a thousand keels.
　　"A mightier portent and more fearful far,
Poor souls! here bursts upon them, and confounds
Their blinded senses. For Laocoon,
The priest of Neptune, as by lot assigned,
Was sacrificing at the wonted shrine
A mighty bull, when, lo! from Tenedos,
Over the tranquil ocean serpents twain—
I shudder to recount it—with huge coils
Cumbering the deep, ply shoreward side by side;   *205*
Reared on the surge their breasts and blood-red
　　　manes
O'ertop the billows; the remaining bulk
Skims ocean aft in labyrinthine folds:

Hark! how the brine seethes audibly! and now,
Their glowing eyes with blood suffused and fire,
The shore-fields they were gaining, and their chaps
Hissed, as with flickering tongues they licked them; we
Pale at the sight fly scattered; they with line
Unwavering at Laocoon aim, and first
His two sons' slender bodies either snake
Embraces and enfolds, and gnawing feeds
Upon the hapless limbs; then him they seize
Up-hurrying armed to aid them, and bind fast
With mighty spires, and now—their scaly length
Twice wreathed about his waist, twice round his
    neck—
With heads o'ertop him and high-towering throats.   *219*
He, while to rend their knots he strives amain,
His fillets with black venom drenched and gore,
Uplifts to heaven heart-piercing shrieks; as when,
'Scaped from the altar, bellows a maimed bull,
That from his neck shakes off the erring axe.
But to the temple's height that dragon pair
Gliding escape, and seek the citadel
Of fell Tritonia, to find covert close
Under the goddess' feet and orbèd shield.
Then through the trembling hearts of all there crept
Strange fear; and 'rightly hath Laocoon
Paid for his crime,' they cry, 'with point of spear
Wounding the hallowed wood, what time he hurled
His guilty lance against the flank.' Then all
Shout that the image to her shrine be drawn,
And supplication to the goddess made.   *233*
We cleave the city-walls, the ramparts ope;
All gird them to the task, beneath the hoofs
Set wheels a-gliding, and around the neck
Stretch hempen hawsers; with war-laden womb
The doom-fraught engine scales the walls: around
Boys and unwedded girls sing litanies,
And joy to touch the cable with their hands.
And so it enters, and glides threateningly
Into the city's midst. Land of my birth!
O Ilium, home of gods, and, famed in war,
Ye Dardan battlements! four times it stopped
At the gate's very threshold, and four times
From out its entrails came a clash of arms.   *243*
But frenzy-blinded we press heedless on,
And in our hallowed citadel uprear
The luckless prodigy. Then, even then,

Cassandra for the coming doom unlocks
Those lips ne'er trusted by the sons of Troy—
So heaven decreed it: we, that day our last,
Fond wretches! range the city, and festoon
With gala-boughs the temples of the gods.
   "Meanwhile the face of heaven is turned, and night
Comes up from ocean, in its mighty shade
Both earth and sky, and Myrmidonian wiles
Enveloping: stretched silent on the walls
The Teucrians lay; sleep held their weary limbs.   253
Even now the Argive host from Tenedos
With vessels in array was wending on,
Through the kind stillness of the silent moon
Seeking the well-known shore, when sudden, lo!
The royal galley reared her signal-fires,
And, shielded by the gods' unequal doom,
Sinon by stealth lets loose the pinewood bolts,
And womb-imprisoned Danai. Them the horse
Restores, thrown open, to the light of day,
And from the hollow frame exultant leap
Thessander, Sthenelus, those lords of war,
And dread Ulysses, by the lowered rope
Down-gliding; Acamas, and Thoas, and
Son's son of Peleus, Neoptolemus,
And first Machaon, Menelaus too,
Ay, and Epeus, framer of the fraud.   264
These storm the town, buried in sleep and wine;
The guards are slain; through the wide portals all
Let in their friends, and join the federate band.
   "It was the time when the first slumber falls
On suffering mortals, by the high God's gift
Then sweetliest stealing o'er them: lo! in sleep
Hector before mine eyes, all woe-begone,
Seemed then to stand, and shower down floods of
      tears;
Torn by the dragging chariot, as of old,
And black with blood-stained dust,—his swollen feet
Pierced with the thong. Ah! what a sight he was!
How all unlike that Hector, who returned
Clad in Achilles' arms, the spoils of war,
Or fresh from hurling on the Danaan decks
The fires of Phrygia! now with draggled beard,
And hair blood-clotted, wearing all those wounds
So thickly dealt him round his native walls!
Weeping myself, I first, methought, addressed
The hero, and drew forth these sorrowing words: 280

'Light of the Dardan land, O staunchest hope
Of Teucria's sons, say why this long delay?
Or from what borders, Hector, art thou come,
Much looked for? is it thus that, wearied out
With all the myriad slaughters of thy friends,
City and townsmen's ever-changing woes,
Our eyes behold thee? What unseemly cause
Hath marred thy cloudless features? or what mean
These wounds I gaze on?' Not a word spake he,
Nor recked mine idle questioning, but groan
On laboured groan from out his bosom's depth
Upheaving, 'Ah! fly, goddess-born,' he said,
'And snatch thee from the flames: the foemen hath
Our walls, and Troy from her proud summit sinks.   *290*
Enough to king and country hath been given:
If any hand could Pergamus have saved,
Then mine had saved it: Troy commits to thee
Her worship and her household gods; these take
As comrades of thy destinies; for these
Seek out a mighty city thou at length
Shalt rear thee, having roamed wide ocean o'er.'
Such words he spake, and in his hands bare forth
The sacred fillets from the inmost shrine,
And Vesta's might, and her undying fire.
      "Meantime the walls grow one confusèd scene
Of widespread anguish; and, though far withdrawn
My sire Anchises' palace amid trees
Lay sheltered, ever louder and more loud
Surges the din, swells out the alarm of war.   *301*
I start from sleep, to the high roof-top mount,
And stand, all ear, to hearken: as, when fire
Falls on the corn beneath the furious south,
Or ravening torrent from a mountain flood
Lays low the fields, lays low the laughing crops,
The oxen's labour, and drags forests down
Headlong, the hind from some tall craggy peak
Mute with amaze stands listening to the roar.
Then is the bare truth self-attested, then
The Danaan wiles unmask them; see e'en now
The house of Deiphobus a vast ruin yawns
O'ertopped by Vulcan! see his neighbour too
Ucalegon in flames! Sigeum's gulf
Reflects the blaze afar. Up goes to heaven
Shouting of men, and clarion's bray; distraught
I seize mine arms, though arms lack argument;
But my heart burns to mass a warrior-band,

And with my comrades hasten to the hold:
Frenzy and anger urge my headlong will,
And death methinks how comely, sword in hand! *317*
 "But Panthus, from the Achaean darts escaped,
Panthus, the son of Othrys, see! and priest
Of Phoebus on the height, in his own hand
The sacred emblems of the vanquished gods,
And dragging his young grandchild after him,
Nigh at wits' end comes hurrying to my door.
'Panthus, how stands the fortune of the day?
What point of vantage seize we?' Scarce had I
Uttered the words when, groaning, he replies:
'The latest day, the inevitable hour,
Has dawned on Dardan land; we, Trojans once,
And Ilium, and the Teucrians' giant fame
Have been, and are not; Jove's remorseless will
From us to Argos hath borne all away;
Our town's a-flame; the Danaans lord it there. *327*
Towering amidst the city-walls erect
The horse rains armèd warriors! far and near
Sinon with victor-insolence spreads wide
The conflagration. Through the folding gates
Some enter, myriads countless as e'er came
From great Mycenae; some, to bar our path,
With weapons have beset the narrow ways,
A wall of steel-blade edges flashing bare,
For death-blow dight: scarce seek the foremost guards
To hold the gates against them, or maintain
The blindfold conflict.' At such words as these
From Othrys' son, and at the doom of heaven,
I rush into the midst of fire and fray,
Where the grim Fury, where the battle-din
Me summons, and the shouts uptossed to heaven. *338*
Then, lo! by moonlight borne across my path,
Rhipeus, and Epytus, right brave in arms,
And Hypanis and Dymas join with me,
And gather to my side, and Mygdon's child,
The youth Coroebus. In those days it chanced
He, with mad passion for Cassandra fired,
Had come to Troy, and as a son was now
To Priam and the Phrygians lending aid,
Unhappy, not to heed the warning voice
Of his heaven-frenzied bride. Whom when I saw
Close-banded and with stomach for the fray
I thus the more exhort them: 'Warrior-hearts,
Dauntless in vain, if your desire be set

On following one who dares the bitter end,
Our fortune's plight how desperate, ye may see: 350
Gone are the gods, from shrine and altar fled,
Aye, one and all, by whom this empire stood:
The town ye seek to succour is in flames;
Then die we, plunging into the battle's midst;
One safety hath defeat—to hope for none!'
Thus were the warriors' souls to frenzy wrought.
Then like to ravening wolves in a black mist,
Whose belly-rage unbridled drives them forth
To grope for prey—their cubs left lone the while
With droughty jaws await them—on we press
Through darts, through foemen, to no doubtful
 doom,
Thridding the city's midst: Night's ebon wings
Float round us with their overarching shade. 360
Who could unfold the havoc of that night,
Tell o'er the slain, or match our teen with tears?
Stoops to her fall our ancient city, she
The empress of the ages. Through her streets
And homes, and hallowed thresholds of the gods,
Heap upon heap the dead lie strewn and stark;
Nor Teucrians only pay the bloody debt;
Sometimes, though vanquished, to their heart returns
Valour, and down the conquering Danai go.
Look where you will, heart-rending agony
And panic reign, and many a shape of death. 369
 "First to confront us, with a mighty band
Of Danai backed, behold Androgeos,
Who, all unconscious, taking foes for friends,
Thus as a comrade hails us: 'Haste, my men!
What laggard sloth retards you? others, see!
Amid her flames are plundering Pergamus,
While ye from your tall ships are newly come.'
He said, and, greeted with no sure reply,
Knew in a moment fallen amid foes.
Staggered, both foot and voice he backward drew.
As one, who, struggling with rough briars, hath trod
At unawares a serpent underfoot,
Starts back in sudden terror, as it rears
Its wrath on high, and puffs a purple throat,
Not otherwise, confounded at the sight,
Androgeos was retreating. On we rush,
With serried arms enclose them, and on ground
They knew not, and with terror ta'en aback,
Slay them on every side. So fortune's breath

Fans our first effort. Here Coroebus cries,
Waxed jubilant with courage and success: 386
'Where fortune at the outset, comrades mine,
With such clear signs of friendship points the path,
Be ours to follow: change we shields and don
The Danaan emblems. Craft or prowess, which,
Who cares to ask in dealing with a foe?
Themselves shall furnish us with arms.' So saying,
The plumèd helmet of Androgeos
He next puts on, with buckler blazoned fair,
And girds an Argive sword upon his thigh.
The like does Rhipeus, ay and Dymas too,
And all our youth exulting; every man
Arms him from out the recent spoil; then on
We press, commingling with the Danaan ranks,
Led by no god of ours, and hand to hand
Through the blind night wage many a battle-bout,
Send many Danaans to the shades below. 398
This way and that they fly, some to the ships,
Seeking at headlong speed the trusty shore;
Some clambering up the monster-horse again,
Vile dastards, hide them in the well-known womb.
Ah! not for men to trust, if gods be loath!
See where, with locks that stream upon the wind,
Maiden Cassandra, Priam's daughter, comes
Haled from the temple and Minerva's shrine;
Vainly to heaven her burning eyes she casts—
Eyes, for her tender hands are locked in chains.
This sight Coroebus brooked not; mad with rage
He hurled him on their very midst, to die.
We following all in close array rush on. 409
Here first from the high temple's top o'erwhelmed
With friendly darts, most piteous slaughter falls
Upon us, through the aspect of our arms,
And lying semblance of our Grecian crests.
Then too the Danai, with a groan of wrath
For the maid's rescue, mustering from all sides,
Fall on—impetuous Ajax, and the twin
Atridae, and all the host of Dolopes;
Even as at times, when a tornado bursts,
Winds meet in shock of battle, West, and South.
And East exulting in his orient steeds;
The forest creaks, and Nereus, all a-foam,
Storms with his trident, from its lowest depth
Upchurning all the ocean. Such beside
As through the darkness in the gloom of night

We routed by our stratagem, and chased
The city's length, appear, and first are they
Our shields and lying weapons to discern,
And mark the incongruous accent of our tongues.   *423*
Straightway we are outnumbered and o'erwhelmed;
And first Coroebus at the altar-steps
Slain of the warrior-goddess, by thy hand,
Peneleos, bites the dust: falls Rhipeus too,
Of all the Teucrians foremost without peer
For justice and fast-cleaving to the right:
The gods willed otherwise: next, pierced by friends,
Both Hypanis and Dymas are laid low;
Nor all thy goodness, Panthus, no, nor could
Apollo's fillet shield thee in thy fall.
Ashes of Ilium, and ye funeral-fires
Of my lost friends, witness, when ye went down,
I shunned no Danaan missiles, and no chance
Of blow for blow, that, had fate willed my fall,
This arm had earned it. Sundered from the rest
With me are Iphitus and Pelias,
Iphitus age-encumbered, Pelias
Sore-wounded by Ulysses. Straight we hie
Toward Priam's palace, by the shouting led.   *437*
But here a giant conflict we behold,
As warring else were nowhere, none beside
Dying the city through; so stubborn raged
The war-god, while the Danai roofward rush,
And the shield-tortoise driven besets the door.
Close cleave their ladders to the walls, and nigh
The very entrance up the rungs they press,
With left hands shielded intercept the darts,
And with the right clutch fast the battlements.
Meanwhile the Dardans, see! upwrench amain
Turret and roofing-tile; with these for darts,
Seeing the end, in death's extremity,
They stand on their defence; some topple down
August ancestral splendours—gilded beams;
Others with drawn blades block the doors below,
And guard them densely massed; fresh heart I take
To aid the palace, ease with help our men,
Add vigour to the vanquished.   *452*
                      "There was set
An entrance by a hidden door that led
From hall to hall of Priam, posternwise
Left rearward of the palace, by the which
While yet the empire stood, Andromache,

Poor heart! would ofttimes unattended seek
Her royal kinsfolk, to his grandsire's knee,
Leading her little son Astyanax.
Mounting, I gain the summit of the pile,
From whence the wretched Teucrians hurled amain
Their ineffectual darts. A turret stands
On the sheer edge, with its high pinnacle
Reared to the stars, whence Troy would oft be
    viewed,
The Danaan ships too, and the Achaean camp: *462*
This, armed with tools, assail we round about,
Where the high floor-joists lend a tottering hold,
And from its deep bed wrench, and hurl it: lo!
Suddenly with a crash down, down it goes,
Trailing wild havoc on the Danaan ranks:
But up come others, and meanwhile the storm
Of stones and motley missiles knows no stay.
Hard on the threshold, by the very door,
Pyrrhus exults, flashing in armèd sheen:
As when a serpent fed on poisonous weeds,
By winter-frosts kept swollen underground,
Fresh from the shedding of his slough, with youth
New-burnished, rolls his slippery length to light,
And, sunward towering with uplifted breast,
Flickers the three-forked lightning of his tongue.   *475*
With him huge Periphas, and Automedon,
Achilles' charioteer, who bare his arms,
And all the flower of Scyros, storm the walls,
And at the roof fling fire. In front of all,
Gripping a two-edged axe, himself is there,
Bursting the tough doors through, and from their
    hinge
The brass-bound valves divorcing: see! even now
He has hewn a beam out, scooped the stubborn oak,
And made a monstrous and wide-yawning breach.
The inner palace and far-lengthening halls
Ope and lie bare, the secret sanctuary
Of Priam and the kings of long ago;
And standing on the threshold's edge they see
Arm'd warriors.   *485*
           "But confusion reigns within,
Wild shrieks and piteous uproar; far-withdrawn
The hollow chambers, hark! with woman's plaints
Are wailing: the cry strikes the golden stars.
Then through the wide halls trembling matrons
    stray,

And, fondly clinging, clasp the doors and kiss.
On presses Pyrrhus with his father's might;
Nor barriers, no, nor guards his onset brook;
With quick blows of the battering-ram the door
Totters, the valves fall forward from the hinge:
Force cleaves a way: the Danaans flooding in
Burst them a passage, cut the foremost down,
And fill the wide space with their soldiery: 495
Not all so madly doth a foaming flood
Burst through the barrier of opposing banks
With conquering swirl, then, raging on an heap,
O'er-ride the country, and through all the plain
Sweep byre and herd before it. I myself
Saw mad with slaughter Neoptolemus,
And both the Atridae on the threshold; aye,
And Hecuba with daughters and sons' brides
A hundred, and, along the altar stretched,
Priam, polluting with his own heart's blood
The fires himself had consecrated. All
Those fifty bridal chambers, the rich hope
Of children's children, portals proudly dight
With trophies and barbaric gold, lie low;
And still the Danai swarm where fails the fire.   505
    "Haply of Priam's fate would'st also hear.
Soon as he saw the city stormed and fallen,
His palace doors wrenched open, and the foe
Amid his inmost chambers, the old man
About his shoulders, palsied now with age,
Binds, unavailing, long-forgotten arms,
Then girds him with his helpless sword, and,
        where
The foe throngs thickest, turns his steps to die.
Midmost the palace, under heaven's bare vault,
Stood a huge altar, and a bay-tree near,
Of immemorial age, drooped over it,
Embracing in its shade the household gods.   514
Here round the unavailing altar-stone,
Like doves swept headlong by a murky storm,
Hecuba and her daughters huddling cowered,
Clasping the sacred images. But when
Priam she saw in arms of youth arrayed,
'Ah! my unhappy lord, what thought so dire
Pricked thee to don this battle-gear?' she cried,
'And whither bound so hotly? Not for such
Succour or such defenders craves the time,
No, not were my own Hector now at hand.

Enough, withdraw thee hither: all shall be
Saved by this altar, or thou slain with us.'
So spake she, and drew towards her, and set down
Her aged lord upon the hallowed seat.   525
   "But lo! from Pyrrhus' slaughtering sword
     escaped,
Polites, one of Priam's sons, through darts,
Through foemen, the long corridors adown
Comes flying, and traverses the empty court,
Wounded. Him Pyrrhus with pursuing stroke
Plies hotly, and all but within his grasp
Holds even now, and pricks him with his spear:
Bursting at length upon his parents' view,
Before their very eyes prostrate he fell,
And poured his life out in a rush of blood.
Then Priam, though fast within the net of death,
Brake all restraint, nor voice nor passion spared.   534
'For crime so shameless may the gods,' he cries,
'If justice be in heaven such deeds to mark,
Pay thee due thanks, fair meed requite thee, who
Hast forced mine own son's murder on my sight,
And with his death profaned a father's eyes:
But he—thou liest to call thyself his son—
Achilles, erst with Priam, though a foe,
Dealt otherwise; with kindling shame he owned
A suppliant's rights and honour, rendered up
The bloodless corse of Hector for the tomb,
And sent me to my realm again.' So saying,
The old man heaved a weak and woundless spear,
Which, straightway by the clanging brass repelled,
From the shield's outer boss-rim harmless hung.   546
'Therefore,' said Pyrrhus, 'shalt thou bear the news,
And to my sire the son of Peleus go:
Look that thou tell him of my sorry deeds,
And how degenerate Neoptolemus;
Now die.' So speaking, to the altar's self
He haled him trembling, slipping in a pool
Of his son's blood, and wreathing in the hair
His left hand, with the right flashed out his sword,
And plunged it in his body to the hilt.
Such was the goal of Priam's destinies;
Such end befell him, with his eyes to see
Troy burnt, and Pergamus to ruin fallen,
Erewhile o'er many nations, many lands,
The haughty lord of Asia. There he lies
A vast trunk stretched along the sand, a head

Shorn from the shoulders, and a nameless corse.   *558*
  "Then first fell horror closed me round; I stood
Amazed: uprose the form of my loved sire,
As I beheld the king, in age his peer,
Cruelly wounded, gasping out his life.
Rose to my mind Creüsa too, left lone,
And my house plundered, and the plight of young
Iulus. I look back to scan what force
Is yet around me: one and all worn out
Have vanished from my side, cast them to earth
Headlong, or, fainting, dropped into the flames.   *566*
  "Now was I left alone, when I discern
Clinging to Vesta's shrine, and silently
Lurking within her solitary cell,
The daughter of Tyndareos: the fierce glare
Of conflagration lends me light to stray,
And cast my eyes o'er all things, far and near.
She, with a dread foreboding in her heart
Of Teucrian hate for Pergamus o'erthrown,
And Danaan retribution, and the wrath
Of her forsaken lord—she, common fiend
Of Troy and her own country, hidden close,
Couched by the altar from the scorn of men.   *574*
At once my soul caught fire, and rising wrath
Prompts to avenge my country, and exact
The wage of wickedness. Shall she forsooth
Live to see Sparta, and her native town
Mycenae? in the triumph she has won
Walk as a queen, and with her eyes behold
Husband and home, her parents and her sons,
Thronged round with Ilian women, and a train
Of Phrygian bondsmen? What! with Priam slain,
Troy burnt to ashes, and the Dardan shore
Bedewed so often with the sweat of blood!   *582*
Not so: albeit no memorable name
By woman's death be won, nor triumph yield
Such victory, yet to have wiped out a pest,
Wreaked worthy punishment, shall be my praise,
My joy to surfeit in avenging fire,
And to have slaked the ashes of my friends.
Such words outflinging, and by rage of heart
Transported, sudden to my sight is borne,
Never till now so dazzling to behold,
And in pure radiance beaming through the night,
My gentle mother—goddess undisguised—
Such and so stately as her form appears

To sons of heaven: she held me by the hand,
And thus, moreover, spake with rosy lips.   *593*
'Son, what fierce anguish in thy bosom stirs
Ungovernable wrath? why ragest thou?
Thy care for me fled whither? Wilt thou not
See first where thou hast left thine age-worn sire,
Anchises, whether still survive thy wife
Creüsa and Ascanius thy child?
Whom all ere this, encompassed every side
By prowling Greeks, did not my care prevent,
Or flames had snatched, or foeman's sword devoured.
Think not it is the hated face of her,
The Spartan daughter of Tyndareos,
No, nor much blamèd Paris, but the gods,
The gods, whose unrelenting hate o'erturns
This empire, and Troy's loftiness brings low.   *603*
Look—for the cloud which, o'er thy vision drawn,
Dulls mortal sight, and spreads a misty murk,
I will snatch from thee utterly: but thou
Fear not thy mother's bidding, nor refuse
Her hests to hearken—here where thou but seest
Huge shattered fragments and stone rent from stone,
And dust and smoke blent in one surging sea,
Neptune with his vast trident shakes the walls,
And heaves the deep foundations, from her bed
O'ertoppling all the city. Juno here
Storms at the entrance of the Scaean gate,
Implacable, and raging, sword on thigh,
Summons her armed confederates from the ships.   *614*
Now backward glance, and on the embattled height
Already see Tritonian Pallas throned,
Flashing with storm-cloud and with Gorgon fell.
The Sire himself each Danaan heart imbues
With courage and victorious might; himself
Against our Dardan power stirs up the gods.
Son, snatch at flight, and let thine efforts end:
Nowhere will I forsake thee till set safe
Upon thy father's threshold.' She had said,
And vanished in thick shadows of the night.
Dread forms appear, and mighty potentates
Of heaven, at feud with Troy.
                              "Ah! then mine eyes
Beheld all Ilium settling into flame,
Troy, Neptune's city, from her base o'erthrown;   *625*
As some hoar ash-tree on the mountain-tops,
Which eager husbandmen make haste to fell,

With steel and showering axe-strokes hacked and
    hewn,
Threatens and ever threatens, and nods on
With quaking foliage, rocking crest, until,
Little by little, 'neath the wounds o'erpowered,
One dying groan it utters, and falls stretched
Along the hillside, a root-severed wreck.
I get me down, and with the god to guide
Through fire and foes win unimpeded way;
Weapons give place to me, and flames retire.   *633*

    "So when at last my father's door was gained,
And the old home, my sire, whom first I seek—
My first thought now to bear him to the hills—
Refuses to live on, Troy laid in dust,
Or stoop to exile. 'Ye, whose blood,' he cried,
'Hath yet youth's freshness, and whose strength
    stands whole
In native vigour, do ye speed your flight;
Me had the high gods destined to survive,
They would have spared my home. Enough and
    more
That I have seen one downfall, and outlived
The capture of our city: here, even here,
Lay out my body, and bid farewell, and go.   *644*
This hand shall find out death: the foe will take
Pity on me, and hunger for my spoil.
Light is the loss of burial. Long ago
Hateful to heaven and useless, I drag on
My lingering days, e'er since the Sire of gods
And King of men breathed on me with the blast
Of his winged bolt, and touched me with his fire.'
    "So spake he, and stood firm, persisting; we,
My wife Creüsa, and Ascanius,
And the whole house, beseech him, bathed in tears,
Not to whelm all in his own ruin, nor add
Weight to the push of doom: he spurns our prayer,
Stands rooted to his purpose and the spot.   *654*
Once more I turn to arms, and long for death
To end my misery; for what counsel now,
What fortune was vouchsafed me? 'Didst thou
    think
That I could leave thee, sire, and go my way?
Fell word so monstrous from a father's lips?
If it be writ in heaven that naught remain
Of all this city, and thy fixed purpose hold,
So fain to heap upon Troy's funeral-pyre

Thyself and thine, death opes thee wide the door:
And, fresh from bathing in the blood of Priam,
Soon Pyrrhus will be here, who butchers son
In face of sire, and sire at altar-side.
For this then, gentle mother, did thy hand
Pluck me from sword and flame, that I might see
The foe upon my hearth-stone, see my sire,
Ascanius and Creüsa at his side,
Slaughtered and weltering in each other's blood?   *667*
Arms, arms, my men! their last reveillé calls
The vanquished. To the Danai give me back:
Let me revisit and renew the fight:
Ne'er shall we all die unavenged to-day.'
   "Therewith once more I gird my sword on, brace
And fit my left arm to the shield, and forth
Was hurrying from the house, when lo! my wife
Clasping my feet upon the threshold clung,
Held forth the young Iulus to his sire.   *674*
'If bound for death, speed us with thee through all;
But if past effort teach thee still to place
Some hope in arms, then first defend our home.
Bethink thee to whose hand thou leavest us,
Thy sire, and young Iulus, and myself,
Once called thy wife.' So loudly pleading she
Filled all the house with moans, when lo! there falls
A sudden portent marvellous to tell!
For, as betwixt their gaze and their embrace
His sorrowing parents held him, on the crown
See! of Iulus' head a tongue of fire
Light-hovering shone, and, harmless to the touch
Licked his soft locks, and round his temples fed.   *684*
We in a flutter of alarm shake out
The blazing hair, and with spring water strive
To quench the sacred flame; but joyfully
My sire Anchises with a starward gaze
Lifted his voice and upturned hands to heaven.
'Almighty Jupiter, if any prayer
Can bend thee, look upon us—only this;
And, if our goodness earn it, Sire, henceforth
Grant us thine aid, and ratify this sign.'
Scarce had the old man spoken, when there pealed
A sudden crash of thunder on the left;
And, gliding through the darkness from on high,
Shot with a torch-like trail of rushing light
A star; we mark it o'er the roof-top glide,
A fiery path displaying, and at length

Bury its brightness beneath Ida's wood:
Then lo! a long-drawn furrow-line of light!
And o'er the region hangs a sulphurous smoke.   *698*
Conquered at last my sire uplifts his head,
Invokes the gods, adores the sacred star.
'Up, up! no tarriance more! I follow, and where
Ye lead, am with you. Gods that guard our land,
Preserve my house, preserve my grandchild: yours
This omen, in your holy keeping Troy.
Son, I submit, content with thee to go.'
    "He said; and through the streets more loudly now
Is heard the fire, and nearer roll the tides
Of conflagration. 'Come then, father mine,
Mount thee upon my neck; these shoulders, see!
Shall bear thee up, nor feel that task a toil.   *708*
Come what come may, one peril both shall share,
Or one deliverance. Hand in hand with me
Let walk the child, Iulus, and my wife
Follow our footsteps from behind. And ye,
Servants, be mindful; heed what I shall say.
Quitting the city to a mound ye come
And ancient fane of Ceres in the waste:
Hard by, an aged cypress, by our sires
With holy awe regarded years on years.
To this one goal by divers tracks we'll wend.
Father, do thou the sacred emblems take,
Our country's household gods, within thy hand: *717*
Fresh from the slaughter of so fierce a strife,
For me 'twere sin to touch them, till I wash
Me clean in running water.' So I spake
And, over my broad shoulders and bowed neck
Donning for robe a tawny lion's hide,
Stoop to the burden; twines his hand in mine
The child Iulus, with unequal steps
Following his sire: my wife comes on behind.
Forth fare we through the shady ways, and me
Whom erst no showering missiles could make blench,
Nor banded Greeks in hostile ranks arrayed,
Now every breeze affrights, and every sound
Startles, so tremulous am I, at once
Fearful for my companion and my load.   *729*
    "And now, nearing the gates, the journey's length
Methought I had o'erpast, when suddenly
A sound of hurrying footsteps to mine ear
Seemed borne, and, peering through the dark, my sire
Exclaims: 'They are upon us: fly, son, fly!

I see their glowing shields and glittering arms.'
Then, in the scare, some Power that loved me not
Snatched my bewildered sense. For as I thrid
Untrodden paths, the wonted track forgo,
Alas! my wife Creüsa, now by fate
Torn from me, to my sorrow, either stopped,
Or missed her way, or weary sat her down—
I know not—to our eyes restored no more.
Nor did I once look back to learn my loss,
Nor turn my thoughts upon her, till we reached
The mound of ancient Ceres and the shrine.
Then, then, of all our gathered forces, she
Alone was wanting to the way-fellows,
Slipped from the sight of husband and of son.   *744*
Whom in my frenzy did I not upbraid
Of men and gods? Or what more cruel hap
Saw in the falling city? Ascanius,
My sire Anchises, and Troy's household gods
I give into my comrades' care, and lodge
Safe in the winding vale, then seek once more
The city, and gird me in my glittering arms,
Steadfast to re-encounter every risk,
All Troy retraverse, and expose my life
Anew to every peril. I repair
First to the walls, and that dark portal, whence
My feet had issued, trace and follow back
Each step in the dark, and scan with searching eye.   *754*
The horror round, the very silence too
Scares me; then home I turn, if haply—ah!
If thither haply she had bent her steps.
The Danai had rushed in, filled all the house.
Speeds the devouring fire before the wind,
Rolled to the roof-top; now the flames outsoar it;
The billowy heat goes raging up to heaven.
Thence I pass onward, and cast eyes again
On Priam's palace and the citadel.
Even now within the empty corridors
Of Juno's sanctuary, as chosen guards,
Phoenix and dread Ulysses watch the spoil.
Hereinto gathered from her burning shrines,
Troy's plundered treasure—tables of the gods,
Cups all of gold, and captive raiment, lie
Massed in a heap. About it in long line
Stand boys and trembling matrons. Nay, I dared
Even to launch my shouts into the dark,
Making the streets re-echo, as I called

'Creüsa' and 'Creüsa,' cry on cry,
With mournful iteration, but in vain.   770
Searching the city thus from house to house,
And raving without end, the hapless shade
And spectre of Creüsa's self appeared
Before me, statelier than the form I knew.
I stood aghast; my hair rose, and the voice
Stuck in my throat. Then thus, methought, she spake,
And with such words allayed my trouble: 'Why
To frantic sorrow give such wanton way,
O my sweet lord? Without the nod of Heaven
These things befall not; at thy side to bear
Creüsa hence—nor fate decrees, nor he
The lord of high Olympus suffers it.
Lo! exile long awaits thee, and to cleave
A vast expanse of ocean: then shalt thou
Arrive Hesperia, where with gentle march
Through their rich fields the Lydian Tiber flows.   782
High fortune here, a throne, a royal bride,
The Fates assign thee. Banish now thy tears
For loved Creüsa: I shall never look
Upon the proud homes of the Myrmidons
Or Dolopes, ne'er go to be the slave
Of Grecian dames, a Dardan woman I,
Wed to the son of Venus the divine.
But me the mighty mother of the gods
Holds on this shore. And now adieu! Guard well
The love we cherished for thy child and mine.'
So saying, she left me weeping, yearning sore
To speak, and vanished into empty air.   791
Thrice, as she stood, my arms I would have flung
About her neck, and thrice my baffled hands
Closed upon nothing, and a form that fled,
Like to light breezes, one with wingèd sleep.
So passed the night, and so at length I turn
Back to my friends, and here with wonder find
New comrades, a vast concourse, matrons, men,
An army massed for exile—piteous throng!—
From all sides gathered, armed in heart and gear,
Where'er I list to lead them over sea.
And now o'er Ida's topmost ridge the star
Of dawn was rising, bringing back the day:
The Danaans had beset and held the gates,
Nor hope of help was offered: I gave o'er,
Took up my sire and for the mountains made."   804

BOOK III

"When Asia's realm and Priam's guiltless race
The high gods doomed to overthrow, when fell
Proud Ilium, and all Neptune's city Troy
In dust lay smoking, we are driven to seek
By auguries from heaven far outland homes
And lands unpeopled, and a fleet we build
Close underneath Antandros and the heights
Of Phrygian Ida, doubtful whither fate
Dooms us to journey, where vouchsafes to stay;
And men we muster. Scarce had summer dawned
When, as my sire Anchises now bade hoist
Sail to the breath of fate, with tears I quit
My native shores, the harbours, and the plains
Where once was Troy. An exile forth I fare
Upon the deep with comrades and with son,
My hearth's Penates, and the mighty gods.   *12*
    "There lies a land afar with widespread plains
Dear to the war-god, which the Thracians till,
Once swayed by fierce Lycurgus, from of old
With hospitable hearth-ties knit to Troy,
While yet her fortune stood. Hither I sail,
And, with fate frowning on my first essay,
Upon the winding shore trace city walls,
And, from my own name, name them Aeneadae.
    "Unto Dione's child, my mother, I,
And to the gods, was doing sacrifice,
As prosperers of our toil, to heaven's high king
Slaughtering a sleek bull on the shore: hard by
A hillock stood with cornel-coppice crowned,
And myrtles bristling thick with spear-shaft wands.   *23*
Approaching, by main force I strove to pluck
The greenwood from the ground, that I might deck
With leafy boughs the altar, when a sight
Portentous meets my gaze, and strange to tell.
For from the first tree, torn with severed roots
From out the soil, trickle black gouts of blood,
That stain the earth with gore. My limbs quake,
    chilled
With horror, and cold fear congeals my blood.
A second stubborn wand once more I turn

To pluck me, and probe deep the hidden cause;
And black blood follows from the bark once more.   *33*
Much pondering in my heart, I 'gin to pray
The forest-nymphs and sire Gradivus too,
Guardian of Getic land, to prosper well
The vision, and make light the omen; but,
When for the third time, and with mightier heft,
The spear-wands I assail, and tug and strain
With bent knees 'gainst the opposing sand—should I
Speak or be silent? from the mounds' recess
A piteous groan is heard, and to mine ears
An answer borne: 'Why rendest thou a wretch
Like me, Aeneas? At last within my grave
Spare me, and spare those righteous hands to stain.
Troy-born am I, no alien to thee,
Nor from a mere log flow these blood-drops: ah!
Fly, fly the ruthless land, the shore of greed;   *44*
For I am Polydorus, here transfixed
And overwhelmed by crop of iron spears
With pointed pikes upspringing.' Then, indeed,
Quelled with distracting fear I stood amazed:
My hair rose, and the voice stuck in my throat.
   "This Polydorus, with vast weight of gold,
Unhappy Priam erst had secretly
To care of Thracia's king consigned, when now
Misdoubting of the Dardan arms, he saw
His city girdled by the leaguers' ring.   *52*
But Teucria's power once crushed, her fortune fled,
The Thracian, following the victorious arms
And star of Agamemnon, snaps all ties
Of honour, and, Polydorus done to death,
Lays his rude gripe upon the gold. To what
Drivest thou not man's heart, O lust of gold
Accursèd? When the trembling left my frame,
To chosen heads of the people I recount—
My sire in chief—the portents of the gods,
Demand their judgement. All are of one mind
To quit the land of crime, fly friendship stained,
And give our fleet the south wind. So we pay
The rites of death to Polydorus, heap
A huge mound o'er him: altars to his shade
Sad with blue fillets and black cypress stand,
And round them, with locks loosed in wonted wise,
The Ilian women: cups of milk a-foam
Yet warm, and bowls of consecrated blood
We offer, and lay the spirit in the tomb,

And with loud voices raise the farewell cry.   *68*
   "Soon as the deep gave promise fair, and winds
Had lulled the main, and Auster soughing low
Gave seaward summons, to the beach my crews
Haul down the ships, and throng the shore. Then
    forth
From harbour fare we; lands and cities fade.
In the mid main a sacred home there lies,
Unto the Nereids' mother dearer none,
Nor to Aegean Neptune: this of old
Around the shores and sea-rims wandering
With filial love the Bearer of the bow
To Myconos high-cragged and Gyarus bound,
And steadfast planting taught to laugh at storms.
Hither I sail; a safe port's halcyon calm
Here greets the weary crews; to land we leap,
Worship Apollo's town. King Anius—
King among men, and priest of Phoebus too—
Brow-bound with fillets and the sacred bay,
Speeds towards us; in Anchises an old friend
He knows; so, clasping hospitable hands,
His roof we enter.   *83*
           "I was worshipping
The antique stone-built temple of the god:
'Give us a home that shall be ours, O lord
Of Thymbra; ramparts to the way-worn give,
A breed of sons, a lasting city: keep
Unscathed Troy's second bulwark, what remains
'Scaped from the Danai and Achilles fell.
Whom must we follow? whither bid'st us go?
Where fix our habitation? Father, grant
A sign from heaven, and sink into our souls.'
   "Scarce had I spoke when suddenly meseemed
All things 'gan tremble, doors and sacred bay;
And the whole mountain moves; the shrine flies ope,
The cauldron rumbles. Prone to earth we fall,
While to our ears is borne a voice: 'O sons
Of Dardanus long-suffering, that same land,
Which bare you first from your ancestral stem,
Shall to her fertile bosom welcome back:
Seek out your ancient mother; there shall reign
The house of Aeneas o'er the world's wide shores,
And her sons' sons, and all their seed to be.'   *98*
So Phoebus: and a mighty joy arose
Confused, tumultuous; with one voice they cry,
'What is this city whither Phoebus now

Summons the wanderers, bids them to return?'
Then, pondering records of the men of old,
Thus spake my sire: 'Hearken, ye lords of Troy,
And learn what hopes are yours: amidst the main
Lies Crete, of mighty Jove the island, where
Mount Ida, and where the cradle of our race;   *105*
There in a hundred mighty towns folk dwell,
A realm most fertile, whence our earliest sire
Teucer, if rightly I recall the tale,
Was wafted first to the Rhoetean shore,
And chose a site for sovereignty; as yet
Nor Ilium nor the towers of Pergamus
Had stood: men dwelt in the low valleys; hence
The Mother, haunter of Mount Cybele,
The Corybantian cymbals, Ida's grove;
Hence the close secret of her rites, and those
Yoked lions harnessed to her queenly car.   *113*
Up therefore! hie we where Heaven's bidding leads,
Appease the winds, and seek the Gnosian realm:
Nor is't a long course thither; Jove to aid,
The third dawn lands us on the Cretan shore.'
So saying, due offerings at the shrine he slays,
A bull for Neptune, a bull too for thee,
O fair Apollo, a lamb black for storm,
White for the favouring Zephyrs.   *120*
                      "Rumour flies
That Prince Idomeneus, a banished man,
Hath quit his father's realm, the shores of Crete
Abandoned, that her hearths are void of foes,
Homes empty for our advent. Straight we leave
Ortygia's harbour, and o'er ocean fly,
Past Naxos with her Bacchant-haunted heights,
And green Donysa, past Olearos,
And snowy Paros, and the Cyclades
Sprent o'er the main, and thrid we seas that race
By crowded islands: high the seamen's shout
Rises amid their changeful toil: the crews
Bid make for Crete and for our sires: a breeze
Springing astern convoys us, and at length
To the Curetes' ancient shores we glide.   *131*
So eagerly my chosen city's walls
I 'gin to build, Pergamea calling it,
And bid my people glorying in the name
Cleave to their hearths, and rear a roofèd hold.
Scarce were the ships hauled dry ashore, the youth
Busied with marriage and new fields to till—

I laws and homes assigning—when there fell
Upon men's limbs from heaven's infected arch
A sudden wasting, and on trees and crops
Piteous contagion—a year fraught with death.
They left their pleasant lives, or dragged about
Sick bodies; Sirius too baked bare the fields;
Grass withered; the sick crop denied her food.   *142*
Back to Ortygia's oracle my sire
Bids us retraverse Ocean, and implore
The grace of Phoebus; to our weary plight
What end vouchsafes he, whence would have us seek
Aid for our trouble, whither steer our course?
  " 'Twas night: sleep held all creatures upon earth,
When lo! the sacred emblems of the gods,
The Phrygian Penates, out of Troy
Borne with me from amidst the blazing town
Seemed, as I lay in slumber, to stand forth
Before mine eyes, clear in a flood of light,
Where streamed the full moon through the casement-
        shaft,
Then thus to address me, and with these words allay
My trouble: 'That which from Apollo's lips,
Once wafted to Ortygia, thou shouldst learn,
Lo! here he utters, unsolicited
Sending us to thy very threshold. We,
Who from Dardania's burning have thyself
And thine arms followed, in the fleet thou led'st
Crossing the swollen deep—even we no less
Will lift to heaven thy sons that shall be born,
Grant empire to thy city. But do thou
Found mighty ramparts for the mighty, nor
Shirk the long toil of flight. Shift hence thy home:
Not these the shores portended, nor in Crete
Doth Delian Apollo bid thee dwell.   *162*
There is a spot, by Greeks Hesperia named,
A land of old, mighty in arms, in soil
Prolific, which the Oenotrian heroes tilled,
Now by a later race called Italy,
If rumour lie not, from their leader's name.
There is our sure home; hence sprang Dardanus,
And sire Iasius, founder of our race.
Arise, be glad, and to thy father old
Bear this no doubtful mandate, that he seek
Corythus and Ausonia's land; the fields
Of Dicte Jove denies thee!' Sore amazed
By such a vision and the voice of gods—

Nor was that slumber: face to face I seemed
Their mien, their wreathèd locks to recognize,
And their divine regard, while a chill sweat
Over my whole frame ran—from bed I leap,
And raising voice and upturned hands to heaven,
Pour unpolluted offerings on the hearth.
That homage paid, exulting I make known
All to Anchises, point by point revealed.   *179*
The twofold line, the double stock, himself
Fooled by a new confusion of old lands,
He owns, then cries aloud, 'Son, long the sport
Of Ilium's fate, Cassandra erst alone
Chanted this hap to me: I now recall
She thus foretold our destiny, and oft
Invoked Hesperia, oft the Italian realm.
But that the Teucrians to Hesperia's shore
Should come indeed, who could have thought it?
    whom
Then would Cassandra's prophecies have swayed?
Yield we to Phoebus' warning, and pursue
The wiser course.' He spake, and all with joy
His word obey; this second home we quit,
Leaving some few behind, and with sails set
Scour the waste ocean in our hollow barks.   *191*
  "Soon as our galleys gained the open deep,
And now no longer land appeared, but lo!
Ocean on all sides, and on all sides sky,
There stood a dark-blue storm-cloud o'er my head
Laden with night and tempest, and the wave
Shuddered beneath the gloom. At once the winds
Roll up the sea, and mighty billows rise:
Scattered, we toss upon the weltering waste:
Clouds wrapped the daylight, dank night stole the
    sky,
And fire burst through the welkin, flash on flash.
We are hurled from out our course, and wander on
O'er the blind waters. Palinurus even
Vows he discerns not day from night in heaven,
Nor in mid-wave can mind him of the track.   **202**
For three full days dim with blind mist we drift
Upon the deep, as many starless nights.
On the fourth day at length land first was seen
To crown the horizon, opening out afar
Mountains and wreathèd smoke. Down drop the
    sails,
We rise upon our oars; with eager strain

The seamen churn the foam, and sweep the blue.   208
   "Saved from the waves, me first the Strophad shores
Receive; the Strophades—their Grecian name—
Lie in the great Ionian, island-haunts
Of fell Celaeno and her Harpy crew,
Since Phineus' door closed on them, and they fled
Scared from their former board. More foul than they
No portent, and no fiercer plague or wrath
Of heaven e'er rose from out the Stygian wave,
Birds maiden-faced, their belly's excrement
Most noisome, and with hookèd hands and cheeks
Blanched with eternal famine.   218
                         "Hither then
Borne safe, and entering harbour, lo! we spy
Rich herds of oxen scattered o'er the plain,
And flocks too of the goat-tribe on the grass
Untended; we rush on them with the sword,
And call upon the gods and Jove himself
To share the spoil, then on the winding shore
Pile couches up, and feast on the rich fare.
But sudden from the hills with fearful swoop
The Harpies are upon us, and clap loud
Their hurtling wings, and snatch the food away,
Polluting all things with their filthy touch;
Fearful at once their cry, and foul their smell.   228
In deep recess beneath a hollow rock,
Curtained with trees and bristling shade, once more
We lay the board, renew the altar-fires:
When from a diverse point of heaven once more
Out of some hidden lair the clamorous rout
Come winging round the prey with hookèd feet,
And taint the food with tasting. Then I charge
My comrades seize their weapons and make war
On the fell brood. As bidden they do, range swords
In the grass-covert, and hide shields from sight.   237
So when along the winding shore their swoop
Sounded, Misenus from his lofty watch
With hollow brass gives warning: to the assault
My comrades rush, and a strange warfare try—
To harry with the sword these ominous birds
Of ocean. But their feathers take no hurt,
Their flesh no wound, and, soaring swift on high,
They leave behind them the half-eaten prey
And their foul traces. One, Celaeno, perched
On a tall crag, ill-boding prophetess,
Breaks into heart-wrung utterance: 'Is it war

For our kine slaughtered and our bullocks felled,
Sons of Laomedon—war, ye would wage
Against us, and the blameless Harpies drive
Forth from their father's realm? Take then to heart
My words, and write them there: what prophecies
The Sire Omnipotent taught Phoebus once,
Phoebus Apollo me, I, mightiest
Of Furies, now make known to you: the goal
Ye seek is Italy; to Italy,
The winds invoking, shall ye come, be free
Her ports to enter: but your destined town
With walls ye shall not gird, till famine dire
And your outrageous onslaught upon us
Drive you to gnaw your tables and devour.'   257
She spake, and to the forest winged her way.
As for my comrades, a quick chill of fear
Curdled the blood within them; their hearts fell;
No more with arms, but vows and prayers they now
Bid sue for grace, or be they goddesses,
Or dread ill-omened birds: aye, and my sire
Anchises from the shore with outspread hands
Calls on the mighty ones of heaven, proclaims
Due sacrifice: 'Ye gods, avert their threats,
Such evil hap forfend, and with your peace
Preserve the good.' Then bids he rend away
The rope from shore, uncoil and ease the sheets.   267
The south winds stretch our canvas: fast we fly
Over the foaming waters, borne along
As wind and helmsman summoned. Now appears
In the sea's midst Zacynthus and her woods,
Dulichium, Samë, and the towering cliffs
Of Neritos; we hurry by the rocks
Of Ithaca, Laertes' realm, and curse
The land that gave to fell Ulysses birth.
Soon too Leucate's stormy peaks, and lo!
Apollo, feared of seamen, heaves in sight:
Weary, for him we make, and enter so
The little town: our anchor from the prow
Is cast, the sterns stand ranged along the shore.   277
So beyond hope at length achieving land,
To Jove we purify us, with our vows
Kindling the altar, and crowd Actium's shore
With Ilian games: my comrades strip, and ply,
All smooth with oil, their native wrestling-bouts,
Glad to have 'scaped so many Argive towns,
And through the midst of foes our flight pursued.

Meanwhile the sun rolls round the mighty year,
And winter's icy north-winds fret the sea.
A shield of hollow brass, great Abas erst
Had wielded, on the portals' front I fix,
And with this line commemorate the deed:
'Aeneas' spoil, from Danaan conquerors won,'
Then bid them quit the harbour, man the thwarts.   *289*
With eager zeal my comrades lash the sea,
And sweep the watery floor. Anon we let
Phaeacia's airy summits drop from view,
And skirt Epirus' shore, till entering
The harbour of Chaonia, we draw nigh
Buthrotum's high-built city. Here a tale
Of things incredible assails our ears,
That Helenus, Priam's son, was reigning now
O'er Grecian cities, master of the bride
And crown of Pyrrhus, son of Aeacus,
And that Andromache had thus once more
Passed to a lord of her own race. Amazed
I stood, and my heart burned with strange desire
To accost the hero, from his lips to learn
Fortunes so strange. On from the port I fare,
Leave fleet and shore behind me, when it chanced
That nigh the city, in a grove, where flowed
A mimic Simois, Andromache
Her yearly feast was offering, gifts of grief,
Unto the ashes, summoning the shade
To Hector's tomb, which with green turf, though
    void,
She had hallowed, and twin altars, where to weep.   *305*
Soon as her wildered eyes my coming saw,
With Trojan arms about me, scared at such
A portent, her limbs stiffen in mid gaze,
Warmth left her frame, she swoons, and scarce at
    length
Breaks the long silence: 'Is't thy very face?
Com'st thou indeed with tidings, goddess-born,
A living man? or if the genial light
Hath faded from thee, where is Hector?' So
With showers of tears she spake, and all the place
Filled with her shrieking. To that passionate cry
Scarce can I frame brief answer, and, much moved,
Gasp out in faltering accents: 'I indeed
Live, and my life through all extremes drag on: *315*
Doubt not, thine eyes see truly: ah! what chance
Hurled from that height of wedded love receives,

What fortune worthy of her past hath found,
Hector's Andromache? art still the wife
Of Pyrrhus?' With downcast eyes and bated breath
She spake: 'O blest beyond all women else
The maiden child of Priam, bidden to die
'Neath Troy's tall ramparts, at the foeman's tomb,
She who ne'er brooked the casting of the lot,
Nor, captive, touched a conquering master's bed!   *324*
We, our home burnt, o'er distant oceans borne,
Have from Achilles' heir endured the pride
Of youthful insolence, borne him a son
In slavery: he, wooing afterward
Leda's Hermione, and nuptial ties
With Lacedaemon, me to Helenus,
Bondmaid to bondsman did consign. But him
Orestes, with fierce love for his stol'n bride
Fired, and still goaded by the fiends of crime,
At his ancestral altars unaware,
Waylaid and slaughtered. Neoptolemus
Thus dying, a portion of the realm he swayed
Passed o'er to Helenus, who called the fields
Chaonian, and Chaonia all the land,
From Trojan Chaon, and topped the heights with
    this
New Pergamus and Ilian citadel.   *336*
But thou—what winds, what fates have shaped thy
    course?
Or what god driven unwitting to our shores?
How fares the boy Ascanius? lives he yet
And drinks the air of heaven?—whom while in Troy . . .
But still to his lost mother doth he yearn
With boyish love? Aeneas for his sire,
Hector his uncle—do these kindle him
To antique prowess, and mettle of a man?'
So poured she forth her sorrow, and long she wept
Idly, when lo! advancing from the walls,
The hero-son of Priam, Helenus,
Comes with a mighty train, and his old friends
He knows, and leads them to his home with joy,
But all his utterance broke with bursting tears.   *348*
At every forward step I recognize
Troy, but in little, here a Pergamus,
The model of the mighty, there, though parched,
A river that from Xanthus takes its name,
And clasp the portals of a Scaean gate.
Along with me the Teucrians too enjoy

The friendly city; the king welcomed them
In spacious cloisters; midmost of the court
They poured out wine-libations, the meats set
On golden platters, goblets in their hand.   *355*
   "And now a day and yet another day
Has come and gone; the breeze invites our sails;
The south wind swells, and puffs the canvas out,
When, with these words approaching, I thus seek
An answer from the seer: 'Thou son of Troy,
Interpreter of heaven, who dost the will
Of Phoebus know, the tripods, and the bays
Dear to the Clarian god, the stars, and tongues
Of birds, and omens of the flying wing,
Come tell me—for the favouring voice of heaven
Hath my whole course declared, and one and all
The gods with power divine urged me to make
For Italy, and distant lands explore;
Only Celaeno with her Harpy voice
Chants a strange portent horrible to tell,
Boding fierce wrath and hideous famine—say
What perils first am I to shun, or by
What clue surmount such heights of suffering?'   *368*
Then with due sacrifice of slaughtered steers
First Helenus implores the grace of heaven,
Unbinds the fillets from his sacred brow,
And with his own hand to thy temple-gates,
O Phoebus, leads me, wildered with excess
Of godhead, then at last with priestly lips
Chants this prophetic utterance: 'Goddess-born—
For that thou journeyest over sea, led on
By mightier omens, plain the proof, so draws
The king of gods thy destinies, and turns
The shifting changes; such their circling course—
Few things of many, that thou may'st safelier track
Strange seas, and settle in Ausonia's port,
I will unfold thee: what remains to know
The sister-fates from Helenus withhold,
Saturnian Juno to his tongue denies.   *380*
First, Italy, which e'en now thou deemest near,
Fain blindly to attempt the neighbouring ports,
Long tracts of country, a long pathless way,
Divide from thee: aye, in Trinacrian waves
First must thine oar be bent, and thy ships pass
The salt Ausonian main, the infernal lakes,
Aeaean Circe's isle, ere thou may'st found
Upon safe shore thy city. And tokens I

Will give thee; do thou keep them stored in mind.
When by the wave of a sequestered stream
Thine anxious eye lights on a monstrous sow,
Under the holm-oaks on the margin laid,
With thirty head of swine new-littered, white,
Stretched out along the ground, white too the young
About her udders, know that there shall be
Thy city's site, there a sure rest from toil.   393
And shudder not, though ye be doomed to gnaw
Your tables; for the Fates will find a way,
Apollo hear and aid you; but these shores,
This border of the Italian coast, that lies
Nearest, by waves of our own ocean washed,
Fly, for in all their towns dwell evil Greeks.   398
Here have the Locri from Narycia built
Cities, and Lyctian Idomeneus
Filled the Sallentine fields with soldiery.
Here stands Petelia, propped upon its wall,
The tiny town of Philoctetes, lord
Of Meliboea. Nay, when o'er the main
Wafted, thy fleet hath anchored, and ashore
On new-built altars thou shalt pay thy vows,
First with a purple robe o'er-veil thy locks,
Lest in mid-worship, while the sacred fires
Yet burn, a foeman's face meet thine, and mar
The omens. And this ceremonial rite
So let thy comrades, as thyself, observe,
And in its holy use thy sons abide
Blameless. But when, departing thence, the wind
Shall waft thee nigh Sicilia's coast, and when
Pelorum's narrow bars asunder draw,
Cleave to the leftward land, the leftward sea,
Though long the circuit; shun the right, both shore
And water. For this region once, 'tis said,
By violence and huge convulsion torn—
Such power of change is in long lapse of time—
Leapt into twain, that were one land before,
Continuous; and amidst them broke the sea,
That with its waves cut off Hesperia's side
From Sicily's, and flowed, a narrow firth,
'Twixt fields and cities sundered, shore from shore.   419
The right side Scylla doth beset, the left
Implacable Charybdis, aye and thrice
In the deep whirl of her abyss sheer down
She sucks huge billows, and anon to heaven
Rears them in turn, and whips the stars with spray.

But Scylla, penned in a blind cave's recess,
Thrusts forth her mouth, drags vessels on the rocks—
Upward, of human visage, and a maid
Fair-breasted to the waist, beneath, a fish
Of bulk portentous, and with dolphin's tail
Joined to wolf's belly. Better to lag round
Trinacrian Pachynus as your goal,
The long slow circuit fetch, than once have seen
Deformèd Scylla in her cavern vast,
And rocks that to her dark blue sea-dogs ring.   *432*
Aye, and if Helenus foreknoweth aught,
And as a seer win credence, if his soul
Brim with Apollo's truth, one prescient word,
For all will I vouchsafe thee, goddess-born,
And urge the admonition o'er and o'er;
Great Juno's godhead honour first with prayer;
To Juno chant thy willing vows, and quell
With suppliant gifts the mighty queen: for so
Victor at last, Trinacria left behind,
Shalt thou to Italy's far bourne be sped.   *440*
Here landed, when to Cumae's town thou comest,
The holy lakes, Avernus' echoing groves,
Thou shalt the frenzied prophetess behold,
Who in a rock's deep hollow chants the Fates,
To leaves committing characters and names.
All prophecies upon the leaves impressed
The maid in order ranges, left to lie
Shut up within the cavern: they remain
Unmoved in place, nor from their order stir,
But none the less, when with the turning hinge
A draught of air strikes, and the open door
Unsettles the light leaves, ne'er heeds she then
To catch them, as they flutter round the cave,
Restore their places, or fit line to line: *451*
Men go their ways uncounselled, and detest
The Sibyl's seat. There count no loss of time
Too dear, though comrades chide thee, though the
        voyage
Press and provoke thy sails to sea, and thou
Might'st fill their favouring hollows, but approach
The prophetess, and with thy prayers implore
Herself to chant the oracles, and unlock
Her willing lips in speech. She will unfold
The tribes of Italy, and wars to be,
How best to shun or suffer every toil,
And to thy prayer vouchsafe a prosperous voyage.   *460*

Thus far my voice may warn thee: up, away!
And by thy deeds lift Troy in might to heaven.'
  "So spake the seer with kindly word, then gifts
Heavy with gold and carven ivory
Bids to the ships be brought, massed silver stows
And Dodonean cauldrons in our keels,
A ring-wrought hauberk triple-twilled with gold,
And superb helmet, cone and flowing crest,
The arms of Neoptolemus. My sire
Has gifts too of his own: horses beside
And guides he sends with us, fills up the tale
Of oarsmen, and equips the crews with arms.   *471*
  "Meanwhile Anchises bids rig out the fleet
Nor longer dally with the wafting wind.
Him the interpreter of Phoebus then
With high regard addressed: 'Anchises, deemed
Meet for the holy hand of Venus, loved
Of heaven, twice rescued from Troy's falling towers,
There lies Ausonia's land: make sail and seize it;
Yet hold the deep, pass by the nearer coast,
Needs must thou; of Ausonia, see, the tract
Apollo doth reveal lies yonder far.   *479*
Go forth,' said he, 'in thy son's goodness blest!
Why lengthen words, delaying while I speak
The rising gales?' Nor less Andromache,
Sad at the final parting, brings forth robes
With gold woof broidered for Ascanius,
And Phrygian scarf, nor scants the guerdon due,
But loads him with her loom-gifts, and thus speaks:
'These too, as tokens of my hand, receive,
Dear boy, in witness of the lasting love
Of Hector's wife Andromache; aye, take
The last gifts of thy kin, sole likeness thou
Still left me of my own Astyanax!
Such eyes, such hands, such looks he wore; his youth
Had now been ripening to like years with thine.'
I, as I left them, spake with rising tears: *492*
'Live, and be happy, ye, whose destined course
Is now accomplished; we from fate to fate
Must still be summoned, but your rest is won:
No plain of ocean need ye plough, pursue
No still-retreating far Ausonian fields.
A copy here of Xanthus, and a Troy
Do ye behold which your own hands have made,
I trust with happier omen, and less apt
For Grecian inroad. But if ever I

To Tiber come, and Tiber's bordering fields,
And see the ramparts to my race assigned,
Our sister cities and their kindred folk,
Here in Epirus, in Hesperia there,
Who boast the self-same founder, Dardanus,
The self-same fortunes, we will yet some day
Take, and of twain create one Troy in heart:
That task be left to our posterity.'   505
   "On through the deep we speed, and skirt the near
Ceraunians, whence the way to Italy,
And shortest passage o'er the waves. Meanwhile,
The sun drops, and the hills are veiled in gloom.
On the earth's welcome bosom, meting out
The oars by lot, we stretch us by the wave,
And, on the dry beach scattered, court repose;
Slumber bedews our weary limbs. Nor yet,
Driven by the Hours, was Night to her mid course
Attaining, when, no sluggard, from his couch
Springs Palinurus, every wind explores,
Catching the breeze with listening ears: he marks
All stars that swim the silent sky, surveys
Arcturus, and the showery Hyades,
The Twin Bears, and Orion armed in gold.   517
Seeing a set calm in a cloudless heaven,
Loudly he signals from the stern; our camp
Is broken up; we venture on the voyage,
Spreading our sail-wings. And Aurora now
Was reddening, and the stars were put to flight,
When in the distance we descry dim hills,
And Italy's low coast-line. 'Italy!'
First cries Achates; Italy our crews
Hail with a shout of triumph. Then my sire
Anchises wreathed a mighty bowl with flowers,
And filled with wine, and called upon the gods,
Standing upon the lofty stern. 'Ye gods,
Lords both of land and ocean with their storms,
Waft us a fair course, and breathe favouring gales.'   529
The wished-for breezes freshen, and the port
Widens with narrowing distance, and clear seen
The temple of Minerva tops the height.
My comrades furl the sails, and shoreward steer.
The harbour there by eastern waves is bent
Bow-wise; with salt spray foam the barrier cliffs;
The port itself lies hidden; the towered rocks
Lower their arms, on either side a wall;
The temple from the shore retires. Four steeds

Here on the grass, first omen, I beheld,
Grazing the plain at large, and white as snow.   538
Then Prince Anchises: 'War it is thou bringest,
O stranger-country! Steeds are armed for war,
And war these herds portend us. Yet at times
The same beasts use to bow them to the car,
And, yoked together, bear the friendly rein;
Yea, there is hope of peace too.' Then we pray
To sacred Pallas, queen of clanging arms,
Who first with joy received us, and with heads
Before the altar veiled in Phrygian robe,
As Helenus had so straitly charged us, pay
To Argive Juno the full rites prescribed.   547
Then without stay, each solemn vow performed,
Shifting the sail-yard horns, we quit the homes
Of Greek-born folk, and their suspected fields.
Next, known to Hercules, if true the tale,
Tarentum's gulf is sighted, while in front
Rises Lacinium's goddess, Caulon's heights,
Ship-wrecking Scylaceum. Then, far off
Out of the deep comes looming into sight
Trinacrian Aetna, and a mighty moan
Of ocean hear we, and rocks buffeted
Afar, and broken sounds upon the beach;
The shoals leap up, and sand and surges mix.   557
Then Prince Anchises: 'Doubtless this is that
Charybdis, these the crags and fearful rocks
That Helenus foretold. Rescue, my friends!
Rise on your oars together.' Nought they fail
To do his bidding, and Palinurus first
To the waves leftward turns her groaning prow;
Leftward the whole fleet strain with oar and breeze.
On the arched billow we mount up to heaven,
And once more, as the floods fail under us,
Sink to the shades below. Thrice roared the rocks
Amid their craggy hollows, thrice we saw
The foam dashed up, and the stars raining spray.   567
Meanwhile, outwearied, wind and sun alike
Failed us, and, all unwitting of the track,
To the Cyclopes' shores we drift.
                              "There lies
A harbour sheltered from the wind's approach,
Spacious itself; but Aetna hard at hand
With hideous ruin thunders, and anon
Shoots a dark cloud to heaven of whirling smoke
Pitch-black, with glowing ashes, and aloft

Heaves balls of fire, and licks the stars, anon
Rocks and the uptorn entrails of the hill
Spews forth, and heaps the molten stones in air
Booming, and from his lowest depth upboils.   577
'Tis said the huge frame of Enceladus,
Half-burnt by lightning, 'neath this mountain mass
Lies buried, while giant Aetna, piled above,
Bursts into channels, and breathes forth the fire:
Oft as he shifts his side for weariness,
Trinacria's whole bulk with the rumbling quakes,
And curtains heaven with smoke. Screened by the
    woods,
That night the monstrous portent we endure,
Yet cause of sound discern not: for no stars
Were burning, nor the vault was bright above
With constellations, but a dark pall hid
The heavens, and dead night held the moon in cloud. 587
    "And now the next dawn in the utmost east
Was breaking, and Aurora had dispelled
Dank shadows from the sky, when suddenly
Out of the woods, by extreme hunger worn,
Stalks the strange figure of an unknown man,
In piteous plight, and stretching suppliant hands
Toward the shore. We turn to gaze on him.
Ghastly his squalor, with a beard grown wild,
A garb thorn-fastened: in all else a Greek,
And in his country's arms once sent to Troy.
He when our Dardan guise, our Trojan arms,
Far off he saw, a little at the sight
Hung back afeared, and stayed his steps, but soon
With tears and prayers ran headlong to the shore:
'Now, by the stars, and by the gods above,
Aye, and this light of heaven we breathe, take me,
Ye Teucrians, I conjure you; bear me hence
To whatso land ye will; it shall suffice.
One of the Danaan fleet am I, I know it,
Own I assailed your Ilian hearths with war: 603
Wherefore, so heinous if my crime's offence,
Fling me piecemeal into the waves, or drown
In the vast ocean. If I die, 'twill be
Joy to have died by human hands.' So saying,
He clasped our knees, to our knees, writhing, clung.
We urge him say what, and from whence, he is,
Next, how by fortune bandied, to confess.   609
My sire Anchises, with no long delay,
Himself extends his right hand to the youth,

And with the ready pledge assures him; he,
Fear banished, speaks at length: 'An Ithacan
By birth am I, and comrade of ill-starred
Ulysses; Achaemenides my name;
Since poor my father Adamastus—would
That fortune still were mine!—I came to Troy.
Here in their haste these cruel doors to quit,
My friends forgot, and in the monstrous cave .
Of Cyclops left me. 'Tis a house of gore
And bloody banquetings, huge, dim within;
Himself, uptowering, strikes the stars on high—
Ye gods, rid earth of such a plague!—by none
To be eyed lightly, or in speech addressed.   *621*
On wretches' flesh and their dark blood he feeds.
I myself saw of our own number twain,
In the cave's midst as he lay backward, clutched
By his huge hand, and dashed against the rock,
And the floor drenched and swimming with their
        blood—
Saw, when their limbs, all dripping with black gore,
He munched, the warm joints quivering 'twixt his
        teeth;
But not, I trow, unpunished: nor such things
Ulysses brooked, nor was the Ithacan
In that sore strait forgetful of himself.   *629*
For when, with feasting gorged, and drowned in wine,
The monster dropped his lolling neck, and lay
Along the cave, disgorging as he slept.
Man's blood, and morsels mixed with gory wine,
We, the lots drawn, and the great powers implored,
Surge round him in one flood on every side,
And with a whetted brand bore out his eye,
Monstrous, hid sole beneath the scowling brow,
Like Argive shield or lamp of Phoebus, glad
Thus to avenge at length our comrades' shades.   *638*
But fly, ye hapless, fly, rend rope from shore:
For such, so vast, as Polyphemus here
Penning in hollow cave his fleecy flocks,
Or wringing dry their udders, a hundred more
House them at large along this winding coast,
Fell Cyclops-crew, and roam the mountain-tops.
Thrice hath the moon now filled her horns with light,
While with the beasts, in the lone forest-lairs
They haunt, I drag my life on, from the rock
Peering the vast Cyclopes to behold,
Or trembling at their voices and their tread.   *648*

Berries and stony cornels from the boughs
And uptorn herb-roots yield me sorry fare.
All quarters scanning I at last beheld
This fleet of yours stand shoreward, and to this,
Prove what it might, consigned me: 'tis enough
To have escaped the monster-brood: do ye
Rather, by any death, cut short my days.'
   "Scarce had he spoke, when on the mountain-top
Himself, in mighty bulk among his flocks
Moving, and making for the well-known shore,
The shepherd Polyphemus we descry—
Monster fell, shapeless, vast, of eyesight reft.   659
Lopped by his hand a pine tree guides his steps
And steadies; his woolly sheep beside him stray,
Sole pleasure, these, and solace of his ill.
Soon as he touched the deep waves, reached the main,
He laves therewith the flow of gore from out
His eyeless socket, and gnashing with his teeth
Groans, and through ocean now at midmost wades;
Nor wetted yet the flood his towering sides.
Trembling we speed our flight afar, take up—
Meed well deserved—our suppliant, silently
Cut loose the rope, and bending forward sweep
With emulous oars the ocean. He perceived,
And turned his steps toward the sound: but when
No power is his to reach us with his hand,
Nor skill to match the Ionian waves in chase,
A boundless roar he raises, that the sea
And all its billows trembled, and, far in,
Affrighted was the land of Italy,
And Aetna bellowed through his winding caves.   674
Thereat the race of Cyclops, from the woods
And lofty mountains startled, to the port
Rushes, and throngs the shore. We see them stand,
Each with vain-lowering eye, that brotherhood
Of Aetna, and with heads upborne to heaven,
Grim conclave: as on some tall mountain-top
When skyey oaks, or cone-hung cypresses—
Jove's lofty forest, or Diana's grove—
Stand clustering: us keen terror headlong goads,
Whithersoever to slack out the sheets,
And spread our canvas to the following breeze.   683
But Helenus' late warning bids them not
'Twixt Scylla and Charybdis hold their course—
On this or that side but a step from death:
Backward to steer the purpose holds; when lo!

The north wind from Pelorum's narrow home
Is launched upon us: I am wafted by
Pantagia's mouth of living rock, the bay
Of Megara, and low-lying Thapsus. Such
The shores he showed, unthridding all the track
Of his past wanderings—Achaemenides,
Ill-starred Ulysses' comrade.   691
        "An isle lies
Stretched full in front of the Sicanian bay,
Wave-washed Plemmyrium, called by men of old
Ortygia. Hither, the tale runs, Alpheus,
River of Elis, worked his hidden way
Beneath the sea, now, issuing at thy mouth,
Blends, Arethusa, with Sicilian waves.
The mighty guardians of the spot, as bidden,
We worship; then the o'er-fertile soil I pass
Of marshy-banked Helorus. Hence we skirt
Pachynum's lofty cliffs and jutting crags;
Far off shows Camarina, fate-ordained
To be molested never, and Gela's fields,
And Gela, from its furious river named;   702
Thence towering Acragas displays afar
Her mighty walls, once breeder of brave steeds:
Thee too I leave behind me, with sails spread,
Palmy Selinus, and I thrid the shoals
Of Lilybaeum, with blind rocks beset.
Anon the harbour and the joyless shore
Of Drepanum receives me. Here alas!
So many ocean-storms o'er-blown, I lose—
Lightener of every chance and every care—
My sire Anchises. Best of fathers, here
Thou leav'st me to my weariness, alas!
Snatched from those mighty perils all in vain.   711
Nor did the prophet, Helenus, 'mid all
His fearful bodings, of this grief foretell,
Nor dire Celaeno. My last trouble this,
And this the goal of my long voyaging.
Departing hence, heaven drave me to your shores."
  Thus Prince Aeneas, 'mid the hush of all,
Alone rehearsed the destinies of heaven,
And taught them of his wanderings, then at length
Ceased, made an end of speaking, and was still. 718

BOOK IV

But stricken long since with anguish deep, the queen
Feeds at her veins the wounds, whose hidden fire
Consumes her. To her heart comes surging back
Full oft the manhood of the man, full oft
The lustre of his line: his looks, his words,
Cling rooted fast within her bosom's core,
And anguish to her frame calm sleep denies.
Now, with the torch of Phoebus, next day's dawn
Was traversing the world, and had from heaven
The dewy shade dispelled, when, ill at ease,
Thus, heart to heart, her sister she bespeaks: *8*
"Anna, my sister, say what dreams are these
Perplex me and affright? what wondrous guest
Hath entered 'neath our portals? what a mien
He bears! what strength of breast and shoulder! I
Deem him—no idle fancy—sprung from gods:
Fear proves the base-born spirit. Ah me! what
    shocks
Of fate he sang, what draughts of battle drained!
Were not my heart's resolve set firm and fast,
With none to yoke in wedlock-bands, since he,
My first love, tricked me and betrayed by death—
Irked me not bridal torch and bridal bed—
To this one weakness I perchance had stooped.   *19*
Anna, for I will own it, since the doom
Of my poor lord Sychaeus, and the hearth
Stained by a brother's blood-guilt, only he
Hath swayed my sense, my tottering heart o'er-
    thrown.
Traces of that old flame I recognize:
But first I would that earth yawn deep for me
Or that the Sire Almighty with his bolt
May to the shades, pale shades of Erebus
And night abysmal, hurl me, before thee,
O Shame, I outrage, or thy laws relax.
He, who first joined me to himself, hath borne
My heart away with him; his only be it
To hold and guard within the grave." So saying,
Her bosom filled she with o'er-brimming tears.   *30*
   "O dearer to thy sister than the light,"

Anna replies, "wilt thou, till youth be done,
Still waste in lonely widowhood, nor e'er
The joy of children or love's guerdon know?
Think'st this to dust and buried shades a care?
Albeit I trow no suitors heretofore
Swayed thy sick heart,—no, nor in Libya's land,
Nor erst in Tyre—Iarbas thus was scorned,
And other lords to boot, whom Afric land
Rich in war's triumph rears—wilt brave no less
A love that likes thee? dost not call to mind
Within whose borders thou art planted? here
Gaetulian cities hem thee in, a race
In war untamable, and therewithal
Numidia's reinless riders, and the shoals
Of barbarous Syrtis: yonder lies a tract
Barren with drought, and the wide-raging sons
Of Barce. Wherefore tell of war's alarms
Rising from Tyre, and thine own brother's threats?   *44*
With gods to guide, methinks, and Juno's aid,
This man sailed hither in his Ilian keels.
Think what a city, sister, here thou'lt see,
Aye, what a realm, arise, so husbanded!
With Teucria's arms beside her, to what pitch
Will soar the Punic glory! only thou
Sue grace of heaven, and, expiation made,
Be lavish of good cheer, and interweave
Fresh pleas for tarriance, while on sea the storm
Still blusters, and Orion's watery star,
'Mid shattered barks, and skies implacable."   *53*
    So saying, she set the love-lit heart ablaze,
Made bold the wavering mind, and banished shame.
First they approach the shrines, and pardon seek
Amid the altars, duly-chosen ewes
To Ceres, lawgiver, and Phoebus slaying,
And sire Lyaeus—Juno before all,
Mistress of wedlock-bands. Dido herself
In peerless beauty, with her right hand grasps
A cup, and pours it full betwixt the horns
Of a white gleaming heifer, or moves on
Majestic, in the presence of the gods,
To the rich altars, and with sacrifice
Inaugurates the day, then, all agape,
Peering into the victims' cloven breasts,
Consults the quivering entrails. Ah! how blind
The eyes of seers! love-frenzied, what can vows
Or shrines avail her? Ever the flame eats

Her tender heartstrings, and the wound is there
Silent, yet quick within her bosom's core.   67
So, all on fire, unhappy Dido roams
Raging throughout the city, as some hind
Shaft-stricken, at unawares 'mid Cretan groves,
Which from far off a shepherd, with his darts
Chasing, hath pierced, and left the wingèd barb
Not knowing; through Dicte's woody glades in flight
She scours, the death-reed sticking in her side.
Now through the city's midst she with her leads
Aeneas, displaying her Sidonian wealth
And town built ready: she essays to speak,
And in mid-utterance stops; now, as day falls,
Seeking the selfsame board, poor fool! she asks
Once more to hear the tale of Ilium's woe,
And hangs upon the speaker's lips once more.   79
Then, when the guests have parted, when in turn
The low moon hides her radiance, and the stars
Sinking invite to sleep, in the void hall
With lonely grief, on his abandoned couch
She casts her, and, though sundered each from each,
Hears him and sees, or to her bosom clasps
Ascanius, ravished by his father's look,
Her tyrant passion haply to beguile.
The half-reared turrets rise not, the youth ply
No martial exercise, nor harbours build,
Nor bastions for defence in war; the works
Break off suspended, the high-threatening bulk
Of walls, and engines that uptower to heaven.   89
     Her when the well-loved spouse of Jove beheld
By such a plague possessed, and her good name
No bar to madness, thus to Venus then
Spake Saturn's daughter: "Peerless is the praise,
Ample the booty ye bear off, I wot,
Thou and thy boy, a great and famous name—
One woman by two gods o'ermatched with guile!
Me, soothly, it escapes not that thou fear'st
These walls of ours, tall Carthage and her homes
Eyeing askance; but what shall be the end?
Or whereto serves this mighty conflict now?   98
Why rather work we not a lasting peace,
And plighted spousal-troth? that, thy whole heart
Desired, thou hast. Dido with love's ablaze,
And through her frame the tide of frenzy spreads.
Rule we as one then, and with equal powers,
This people; let her own a Phrygian lord,

And yield her Tyrians to thy hand as dower."   *104*
 Perceiving that in guile of heart she spake,
To shift Rome's empire to the Libyan shore,
Venus in turn addressed her: "Who so fond
As to reject such offers, or make choice
With thee to strive for mastery, so success
Wait on thy word's accomplishment? but I
Drift doubtful of the fates, if Jupiter
To Tyrian folk and travellers from Troy
Wills but one city, or would have them blent
Nation with nation, or firm league be joined.   *112*
Thou art his wife; for thee 'tis meet to probe
His heart with supplication; do thou lead,
I follow." Then royal Juno took the word:
"Leave me that task; now, mark, I'll briefly show
How the main purpose may be compassèd.
Aeneas, unhappy Dido at his side,
Goes forth to hunt amid the forest, when
Titan to-morrow's dawn shall first display,
And with his beams lay bare the world; then I,
While huntsmen hurry, and hem the wood with
  snares,
Will a black storm of mingled hail and rain
Pour down, with thunder the whole welkin wake.   *122*
Far will their train be sundered, by thick gloom
Enveloped; Dido and the Trojan prince
To the same cave shall come. I will be there
To knit the twain, so stead me thy goodwill,
In wedlock sure and seal her for his own.
Such shall their spousal be." To her request
She of Cythera nodded, nothing loth,
And laughed at revelation of the guile.
 Meanwhile Aurora rising left the sea.
With dayspring from the gates a chosen band
Go forth; mesh-woven toils, nets, hunting-spears
Broad-tipped with iron, Massylian horsemen too,
Speed onward, and the dogs' keen-scented might.   *132*
The queen still loiters in her bower, the while
Her Punic lords beside the portal wait;
See, housed in gold and purple her steed stands,
And fiercely champs the foaming bit. At length,
Thronged with a mighty concourse, forth she comes,
Clad in Sidonian scarf with broidered hem—
Gold quiver, and locks up-knotted into gold,
Gold too the brooch that clasps her purple robe!
Here 'mid the Phrygian train Iulus rides

Exulting. Comelier than all else himself
Aeneas moves to meet them, joins the troop.   142
As when Apollo quits his winter-home,
Lycia, and Xanthus' floods, his mother's isle
Delos to visit, and renews the dance,
While round the altar in a motley throng
Shout with one voice Cretans and Dryopes,
And painted Agathyrsi; he himself
Walks over Cynthus' height, his flowing hair
Trimmed with a wreath's soft pressure, twined
      with gold;
Clatter the shafts about his shoulders; so,
Nor tardier-limbed than he, Aeneas strode;
Such beauty from his peerless face outshone.   150
Now to the heights and pathless coverts come,
Mark, how the wild goats from the crag-top scared
Run down the ridges! yonder see the stags
Scour through the open in close-huddling herds,
Dust in their wake, and leave the hills behind.
But in the glen's heart young Ascanius
Joys in his fiery steed, now these, now those
Out-galloping, and, 'mid the timorous game,
Prays heaven a foaming boar his vows may bless,
Or tawny lion from the height come down.   159
     Meanwhile with mutterings loud a mighty broil
Begins in heaven: rain follows, mixed with hail.
The Tyrian train and Trojan youth pell-mell,
With Venus' grandson, the Dardanian boy,
Dismayed, seek various shelter through the fields;
Streams from the hillside race. The Trojan prince
And Dido to the self-same cavern come.
Earth first, and bridal Juno, gave the sign;
Flashed at the nuptials fire and conscious air,
And shouted from their topmost peak the nymphs.
First day of death was that, first cause of ill;
Swayed nor by outward show, nor rumour's tongue,
Dido of secret passion dreams no more:
Marriage she calls it—name to mask her fall.   172
     Anon flies fame through Libya's mighty towns,
Fame, whom no other evil can outrun;
Motion her might, strength gains she as she goes.
Small first through fear, soon mounts she up to
      heaven,
Plants foot on earth, and hides her head in cloud.
Her once, provoked to wrath against the gods,
Earth bare, the latest of her brood, they say,

Sister to Coeus and Enceladus,
Swift-footed, fleet-winged, monster dreadful, vast,
Who, for each plume her body bears, beneath
Hath watchful eyes as many, strange to tell,
As many tongues, as many sounding mouths,
Pricks ears as many: by night 'twixt earth and heaven
She cleaves the darkness, hissing as she flies,
Nor ever droops her eyelids in sweet sleep: *185*
By day she sits perched like a sentinel,
Or on high roof-top, or on lofty tower,
And scares great cities, prone to grip as fast
False tales and baseless, as bear tidings true.
She now with manifold discourse had joy
Folks' ears to fill, now fable and now fact
Rehearsing: that Aeneas has arrived,
Sprung from the blood of Troy, with whom for lord
Fair Dido deigns to wed: now, each with each,
They lap the livelong winter in soft ease,
Heedless of empire, by base love enthralled.
Such tidings the foul goddess far and wide
Scatters from mouth to mouth: then straightway
    bends
Her course to king Iarbas, and inflames
His heart with rumour, and heaps high his wrath.   *197*
  He, sprung from Ammon and his ravished bride
A Garymantian nymph, to Jove had reared
Through his broad realms a hundred mighty fanes,
A hundred altars, and had hallowed there
Fire, the gods' sleepless sentry, to keep watch
For ever, a floor fat with blood of beasts,
And portal with gay blossoms garlanded.
He, soul-distraught, fired with the bitter tale,
Is said, before the altars, and amidst
The majesties of heaven, to have implored
Jove fervently with suppliant hands upturned.   *205*
"Almighty Jove, to whom the Moorish race
On broidered couches feasting pour as now
The offering of the wine-god, seest thou this?
Or is't for naught we dread thee, Sire, when thou
Hurlest thy thunderbolts, and do blind fires
Affright our spirit in the clouds, and brew
But empty rumblings? lo! a woman here,
Who wandering in our realm gat leave for gold
To found a paltry city, to whom we gave
Coastland to till, and laws of tenure—she
Hath our alliance spurned, and ta'en instead

Aeneas to lord, and partner of her throne.
And now that Paris, with his emasculate train,
Chin and oiled hair with Lydian headgear propped,
Enjoys the spoil: we to thy fanes, aye thine,
Bring gifts forsooth, and nurse an empty tale."   *217*

    As thus he prayed and clasped the altar, lo!
Him the Almighty heard, and turned his eyes
Towards the queen's palace, and the lovers there
Of nobler fame forgetful. Thereupon
He thus addresses Mercury, and withal
On such an errand sends him: "Hie thee forth,
Invoke the Zephyrs, son, glide on the wing,
And to the Dardan chief who loiters now
In Tyrian Carthage, and regards no whit
His fate-assignèd city, speak, bear safe
Through the swift winds my word. Not such the
     man
His beauteous mother to our hopes foretold,
Twice therefore rescued from the hosts of Greece,
But one to rule o'er Italy, a land
Teeming with empires, turbulent with war,
Hand on the race from Teucer's blood derived,
And to law's bidding make the whole world bow.   *231*
If by such high renown he be not fired,
Nor for his own fame brace him to the toil,
Yet to Ascanius can his sire begrudge
Rome's ramparts? what designs he? with what aim
Lags amid folk unfriendly, nor regards
Ausonia's race and the Lavinian fields?
Let him aboard! this is the sum in brief;
Hereof be thou my herald."   *237*
                        He had said:
Anon the other made ready to obey
His mighty sire's behest, and first he binds
About his feet the golden anklets, which
Wing-wafted bear him high o'er land and sea
Swift as the hurrying breeze, then grasps his wand,
Wherewith from Orcus the pale ghosts he bids,
Others to gloomy Tartarus sends below,
Gives or bereaves of slumber, and unseals
The eyes in death: on this relying, he drives
The winds along, and skims the weltering clouds.
Now 'mid his flight the crest and towering sides
He sees of stubborn Atlas, who bears heaven
Upon his peak, Atlas whose pine-clad head
Girt round about for ever with dark clouds,

By wind and rain is buffeted; shed snow
Mantles his shoulders, while from his hoar chin
Streams tumble, and an ice-beard bristles stiff.   *251*
Here, poised on level pinions, stayed him first
The god Cyllenian, to the waves from hence
Plunged with his whole frame headlong, like a bird
Which round the shores, round the fish-haunted
    rocks,
Flies low beside the sea-marge: thus he flew
'Twixt earth and heaven o'er Libya's sandy shore,
And clove the winds, leaving his mother's sire,
Cyllene's nursling. Soon as his winged feet
Had gained the huts, Aeneas he discerns
Building new homes, and founding towers, and lo!
A sword he wore, with yellow jasper starred,
And from his shoulders hung a cloak that burned
With Tyrian purple, wealthy Dido's gift,
Wrought by her hand, and tissued with fine gold.   *264*
Forthwith he thus assails him; "Art thou now
Of lofty Carthage the foundations laying,
And rearing a fair city, wife-enthralled?
Ah! lost to thine own kingdom and its cares!
From bright Olympus lo! the lord of heaven,
Who with his deity sways earth and sky,
Sends down, and through the swift breeze bids me
    bear
This message: What design'st thou? with what aim
Wastest in Libya's land the idle hours?
If by such high renown thou be not stirred,
Nor for thine own fame brace thee to the toil,
Yet of Ascanius springing into man,
Thine heir Iulus, and his hopes, have heed,
To whom are owed the realm of Italy,
The land of Rome." So saying, Cyllene's god
Passed, while yet speaking, from the eyes of men,
And into thin air vanished out of sight.   *278*
    But at the vision stunned and speechless stood
Aeneas: his hair with horror rose, the voice
Stuck in his throat: he burns to get him gone,
And quit the pleasant land, dazed by so dread
A warning, and the sovereign voice of heaven.
What can he do? Ah! with what words approach
The impassioned queen? what opening prelude try?
Hither and thither his swift mind he parts,
Speeds it all ways, and sweeps the round of thought,
Till, wavering long this counsel pleased him best.   *287*

Mnestheus, Sergestus, and Serestus bold
He summons all silently to trim the fleet,
Gather the crews on shore, and muster arms,
And of his altered purpose hide the cause.
Meanwhile, since gracious Dido knows not, nor
Looks for so strong a passion to be snapped,
He will try access, and what hour for speech
Most tender, and what fashion fits the need.
Right swiftly one and all his sovereign word
With joy obey, and do his bidding.   295
                              But
The queen—for who can lover's heart beguile?—
Divined it, caught at once the coming change,
Fearful where all was safety. Fame again,
Fiendish as ever, in her maddened ear
Cries that the fleet is rigging, ripe for sea.
Bankrupt at heart she rages, and on fire
Through all the city, like some Maenad, storms,
Roused by the shaken emblems, when with shout
Of Bacchus the triennial orgies goad,
And loud Cithaeron summons her by night.   303
Then she took up the word, and thus bespake
Aeneas: "False heart, didst even think to hide
So foul a wrong, and from my land depart
In silence? Can our love, and hand once joined
In hand, not hold thee, nor the cruel death
In store for Dido? Nay, beneath the sky
Of winter even dost thou fit out thy fleet,
And 'mid the north wind's blustering haste to go,
O heartless, over-sea? Why, wert thou not
Bound for strange fields and unknown homes, and
        were
Troy, as of old, still standing, would'st thou steer
Even for Troy across yon billowy deep?   313
Is it from me thou fliest? by these tears,
By thy right hand, since naught beside, alas
Myself have left me, by our love's embrace,
And marriage-rites begun, if ever I
Did thee fair service, or if aught I am
Was dear to thee, pity a falling house,
And, if prayers yet have place, I thee conjure,
Cast the thought from thee. For thy sake the tribes
Of Libya hate me, and the nomad chiefs,
And Tyrians turn to foes: for thy sake, too,
Quenched is my honour and good name of old,
By which alone I had access to heaven.

[175]

To whom dost thou abandon me to die,
O guest, since even to this has shrunk the name
Of husband? Wherefore do I linger on?
Is't that Pygmalion, my brother, may
Pull down, the while, my battlements, or me
Gaetulian Iarbas make his thrall?   326
If only, if before thy flight, my arms
Had clasped a child of thine, if in my hall
Some tiny-limbed Aeneas played, to bring
Thee back at least in feature, I had then
Not seemed so wholly captive and forlorn."
  She had said: the other by command of Jove
Kept his eyes fixed, and struggling deep at heart
To smother down the anguish, thus at length
Returns brief answer: "Naught that thou canst plead
Of all thy countless benefits, O queen,
Shall e'er by me be gainsaid, nor shall I
Tire of Elissa's memory, while of self
Still mindful, while the life-breath guides my limbs.
Brief be my words to meet the need: I ne'er
Took thought—suppose it not—to veil my flight
In secrecy, nor e'er before thee held
The bridegroom's torch, or to such compact came.   339
Had fate vouchsafed me at mine own free will
Life's course to shape, and, as my own heart prompts,
Make truce with trouble, my first fond care had been
Troy's city, and the dear ashes of my friends;
Priam's tall roof were standing, and this hand
Had, for her vanquished children, from the dust
Requickened Pergamus. But Apollo now,
The lord of Grynium, to great Italy,
To Italy the Lycian oracles,
Bid me repair: this is my love, and this
My country. If, Phoenician as thou art,
The towers of Carthage and a Libyan town
Hold thine eyes gazing, wherefore grudge, I ask,
To Teucrian settlers an Ausonian home?
We too may quest for outland kingdoms: me,
Oft as the night with dewy shade enfolds
The world, oft as the starry fires arise,
My sire Anchises' spirit warns in sleep,
And with its troubled look affrights, me too
The thought of young Ascanius, and the wrong
To that dear head, from whom my fault withholds
Hesperia's empire and predestined fields.   355
Now too the interpreter of heaven, by Jove

Himself sent down—thy head and mine I call
To witness—through the flying air has brought
A mandate: I myself beheld the god
Entering the city in clear light of day,
And with these ears drank in his accents. Cease
With thy complaints to fire thy soul and mine;
Not self-impelled steer I for Italy."
   On him, thus speaking, she was all the while
Glaring askance, and rolling to and fro
Her eyes, surveying with their silent looks
The whole man through, then thus blazed out in
     words: *364*
"No goddess was thy mother, nor Dardanus,
False man, the founder of thy line, but thee
Jaggèd with hard rocks, Caucasus begat,
And to thy lips Hyrcanian tigresses
Their udders set, since why the truth disguise?
For what worse ills restrain me? Did he moan
Over my weeping? did he bend his eyes,
Pay toll of tears, show pity for his love?
What first, what next to say? Now, now no more
Juno, great queen, nor the Saturnian Sire
Looks on these things with equal eyes. Nowhere
Can faith be trusted. Cast upon my shore
A beggar, I welcomed him, and, mad the while,
Set on my throne to share it; his lost fleet,
His crews, from death I rescued. Ah! the fires
Of frenzy toss me! Now Apollo too
Soothsayer, now the Lycian oracles,
Yea, the god's mouthpiece, sent by Jove himself,
Now through the breezes his grim bidding bears.   *378*
Such doubtless is the task of gods above,
Such care disturbs their rest. I keep thee not,
Nor would rebut thy words; go, with the winds
Chase Italy, seek realms beyond the wave.
I hope indeed that on the mid-sea rocks,
If aught the good powers can, thy lips will drain
The cup of suffering, and oft cry aloud
On Dido's name: with murky firebrands I
Will follow thee, though far, and, when cold death
Has severed soul and limbs, in every place
My shade shall haunt thee. O graceless, thou shalt
     rue it,
And I shall hear thereof, yea, for the tale
Will reach me, even among the nether dead."   *387*
   So saying, her speech broke off; she, sick at heart,

Flies from the light, and, turning from his glance,
Flings forth and leaves him with fear-palsied tongue,
Though words throng thick for utterance. Her the
    slaves
Uplift, and to a marble chamber bear,
And lay her fainting limbs upon the bed.
    But good Aeneas, though he yearns to assuage
And soothe the sufferer, with his words ward off
Her sorrow, deeply groaning and with heart
That tottered 'neath the bulk of love, nathless
Obeys heaven's bidding, to his fleet repairs.   *396*
Then fall the Teucrians to the work, and all
Along the shore drag down their lofty ships:
The pitched keel floats, and leafy oars they bring,
And timber from the woods unwrought, for flight
So eager: you may mark them on the move,
At every outlet hurrying from the town!
As when ants plunder a huge heap of corn,
Of winter ware, and house it in their store;
Moves a black column o'er the plain, the spoil
In narrow path along the grass convoying;
Some set their shoulders to the ponderous grains,
And push them, some drive up the rearward ranks,
Chiding delay; the whole track seethes with toil.   *407*
At such a sight what feelings then were thine,
Dido, or what groans utter'dst, to behold
From lofty tower the wide beach boil with men,
And the whole sea beneath thy gazing eyes
Maddened with their loud shouting? Tyrant love,
To what dost thou not drive the hearts of men?
To tears once more must she betake her now,
Once more with prayer assail him, and bow down
Her pride, a suppliant at the throne of love,
Lest she die vainly, leaving aught untried.   *415*
    "Anna, this hurrying over the whole shore
Thou seest; from all sides they are met; the sail
Now courts the breeze, the seamen in their joy
Have crowned the sterns with flowers. If strength was
    mine
Such grief to anticipate, I shall no less
Have strength to bear it, sister. This one boon,
Anna, nathless perform for wretched me.
For thee alone yon traitor made his friend,
To thee would e'en his secret moods confide;
Thou only knewest the tender ways and hours
Of access to the man: go, sister mine,

And suppliant-wise entreat our haughty foe: *424*
I never with the Danaan host conspired
At Aulis to cut off the race of Troy,
Nor sent a fleet to Pergamus, nor uptore
His sire Anchises' buried dust or shade,
That to those obdurate ears he should debar
My words from entrance. Whither hastes he so?
This last boon let him grant his hapless love,
And wait for a kind voyage and carrying winds.
For our old marriage-bond, by him betrayed,
I ask no more, no, nor that he should lack
Fair Latium, or resign his realm; I seek
An empty hour of time, respite and room
For madness to have play, till fortune tame
And school me unto grief. 'Tis the last grace
I ask—pity thy sister; grant but this,
In death I will requite it o'er and o'er." *436*
  Such was her prayer, and such the tearful tale,
Her dolorous sister bears and bears again.
But by no tearful tale will he be swayed,
Nor any words heed, to be bent thereby;
Fate hinders, heaven shuts fast his willing ears.
Even as a sturdy and time-timbered oak,
Which Alpine north winds with their fitful blasts
Strive emulous to o'ertopple: loud it creaks,
The stem rocks, and the leaves strew deep the
  ground;
Itself clings to the crag, and, howso' far
The summit soars toward the airs of heaven,
So deep strikes root into the vaults of hell.
E'en thus, with ceaseless, ever-shifting cries
The hero's heart is buffeted; he feels
The deep grief through his mighty bosom thrill;
The mind stands firm, and tears are showered in
  vain. *449*
  Then ill-starred Dido by her fate dismayed
Cries upon death: it irks her to behold
The arch of heaven. The more to goad her on
Her purpose to fulfil, and quit the light,
She saw—fearful to tell!—while offering gifts
Upon the incense-kindled altars—saw
The sacred juice darken, the outpoured wine
To loathsome gore transmuted: but to none,
Not even her sister, spake she of the sight.
Moreover in the palace was a shrine
Of marble to her former lord, which she

With wondrous honour tended, wreathed about
With snow-white fleeces and with festal boughs.   *459*
Hence fell upon her ears accents and words
As of her husband calling her, when night
Held the world darkling, and the owl alone
On roof-top uttered with funereal note,
Moan upon moan, her long-drawn wailing cry;
And many a presage of the seers of old
With omen dire affrights her. Then in sleep
Aeneas himself all fiercely goads her on
To frenzy; and ever being left alone
She seems, and evermore companionless
Pacing a weary journey, while she seeks
Her Tyrians in a land untenanted: *468*
As maddened Pentheus sees the Furies' troop,
A double sun, a twofold Thebes appear,
Or, on the stage, as Agamemnon's child,
Orestes, hunted, flies his mother armed
With firebrands and black serpents—at the door,
Vassals of vengeance, the grim sisters sit.
  So when, by grief o'erpowered, she had conceived
The frenzy, and resolved to die, alone
She weighs with her own heart the hour, the means,
And her sad sister thus bespeaks, with face
That masks her purpose, and hope-brightened brow: *477*
"Child of my sire, I have found out a way—
Give thou thy sister joy—to win him back,
Or loose me from his love. Near ocean's bound
And sunset is the far-off Aethiop land,
Where mightiest Atlas on his shoulder turns
The pole, with fiery stars bestudded: thence
Was shown me a priestess of Massylian race,
And temple-warder of the Hesperides,
Who erst with dainties to the dragon given
Kept safe the sacred boughs upon the tree,
Sprinkling moist honey and slumberous poppy-seed. *486*
She with her spells takes on her to unbind
What hearts she will, on others launch shrewd pangs,
Stop rivers in their flow, turn back the stars:
She summons ghosts at midnight; thou shalt see
Earth bellowing 'neath thy feet, and from the heights
Ash-trees descending. But I call the gods,
Thee, sister dear, and thy belovèd head,
To witness, that unwillingly I gird
The magic arts upon me. Do thou rear
In the inner court, all secretly, a pyre

To heaven, and let the hero's arms, which he,
Godless, left hanging in the chamber, all
His empty raiment, and the bridal bed,
That was my bane—let these be piled above:
To wipe out every record of the wretch,
Such is my pleasure, and thus the priestess bids."   498

So spake she, and was silent; pallor then
O'er-spreads her features. Anna none the less
Thinks not her sister by these novel rites
Weaves but a cloak for death, nor can her heart
Conceive such frenzy, nor aught worse she fears
Than when Sychaeus died: so sets about
Her errand.

But the queen, when now the pyre
Rose huge to heaven amid her hall's recess,
Of pine and cloven ilex, hangs the place
With garlands, and festoons with funeral boughs.
High over all upon the couch she lays
His empty raiment, and the sword he left,
Aye, and his image, knowing what should come.   508
Altars stand round, and with dishevelled hair
The priestess thunders forth three hundred gods,
Erebus, Chaos, and triple Hecate—
Three-visaged maid Diana. Water too
She had sprinkled, from Avernus' fountain feigned;
And downy herbs with brazen sickles shorn
By moonlight, milky with black bane, are sought,
Sought too a love-charm torn from brow of colt,
Newborn, ere dam could snatch it. She herself
With salt cake and pure hands, the altar nigh,
One foot unsandalled, and with garb ungirt,
Calls on the gods, and stars that wot of doom,
Or ere she die; aye, and if any powers
Righteous and unforgetful have in charge
Lovers ill-mated, unto these she prays.   521

'Twas night, and weary limbs o'er all the earth
Quaffed quiet slumber; forest and wild waves
Had sunk to rest; when stars with gliding orbs
Wheel midway, and when all the field is still,
Cattle, and painted birds, that haunt the breadth
Of limpid lakes, or the rough bosky wold—
Beneath night's silence laid to sleep, their cares
Awhile were lulled, their hearts forgot to ache.
Not so the spirit-vexed Phoenician queen,
Nor ever does she sink dissolved in sleep,
Nor draw the night into her heart or eyes:

Her pangs redouble, and raging love once more
Surges and swells with the high tide of wrath.   532
Thus then begins she, thus with her own heart
Revolves: "Lo! what have I to do? once more
Make trial of former suitors to my scorn?
Beg on my knees with nomad lords to mate,
Whose proffered nuptials I have spurned so oft?
Well, shall I follow, therefore, Ilium's fleet,
The Teucrians' utmost bidding? Because they
Are fain of my past succour, and the grace
Of former kindness in their hearts lives on?
Nay, if I would, who'll suffer me, or take
The hated woman to their haughty ships?
Ah! lost one, know'st not, nor perceivest yet
The perjured race of false Laomedon?   542
What then? in lonely flight shall I attend
The triumph of their seamen? or, girt round
With Tyrians and the host of all my friends,
Rush forth, and these, from their Sidonian town
Whom hardly I uptore, drive back to sea,
And bid spread canvas to the gale? Nay, die
As thou deserv'st; end sorrow with the sword.
Thou, sister, vanquished by my tears, thou first
Didst load my frantic spirit with these ills,
And thrust me on the foe. Why could I not,
Like a wild creature, free from wedlock, live
Blameless, and meddle not with woes like these?
Broken is my honour, and ill-kept the faith
Vowed to the ashes of Sychaeus!" Such
Bitter complaints kept bursting from her heart.   553
   On the high stern Aeneas, fixed to go,
His gear in order trim, now slumbering lay,
When the god's phantom with the self-same face
Returning, brake upon his sleep, and thus
Seemed to admonish him once more, in all
Like unto Mercury, both voice and hue,
And yellow locks, and youthful grace of limb:
"O goddess-born, at such a time canst thou
Sleep on? what perils compass thee about
Perceiv'st not, madman, nor canst hear the breath
Of favouring Zephyrs? In her bosom she
Craft and dire crime revolving, fixed on death,
Lashes to storm the fitful tides of wrath.   564
Why fliest not headlong hence, while headlong flight
Is in thy power? Anon the main thou'lt see
Crowded with craft, and with fierce brands aglow,

[182]

Anon the shore one fiery blaze, if dawn
Still find thee on these shores a loiterer. Up!
Break off delay! a shifting, changeful thing
Was woman ever." So he spake, and passed
Into the blackness of the night.

                          Forthwith
Aeneas, by the sudden phantom scared,
Upleaps from slumber, and plies hard his crew: 572
"Wake in hot haste, my friends, and man the thwarts;
Trim the sails quickly! sent from heaven on high,
A god, see! once again comes goading me
To speed our flight, and cut the twisted ropes.
Hail, holy among gods, we follow thee,
Whoe'er thou art, and once again obey
Thy bidding gladly. O be near with grace
To aid, and bring propitious stars in heaven."
He spake, and from the scabbard plucked his sword
Flashing and cut the cable with bare blade.
All, in one moment, the same ardour seized;
They hale, they hurry; deserted stands the shore,
The deep lies hid beneath their galleys; see!
Straining they churn the foam, and sweep the blue.   583
   Now with new ray young Dawn was sprinkling earth
Leaving Tithonus' saffron couch. The queen,
When first from her high tower she saw the light
Whiten, and all the ships with sails arow
Stand out to sea, and shore and harbour void,
With ne'er an oarsman, thrice and four times o'er
Smote with her hand the lovely breast, and rent
The yellow locks: "O Jupiter," she cries,
"Shall he then go, my kingdom put to scorn,
This stranger? will they not bring arms apace,
Pursue from all the city, and some tear loose
The ships from dock? away with speed, fetch fire,
Deal weapons out, ply oars!—what do I say?
Where am I? or what madness warps my wit?   595
Unhappy Dido! do thine impious deeds
Now touch thee home? it had been seemlier then
When thou wast offering him thy sceptre. Lo!
His hand and word of honour, who, they say,
Carries his country's home-gods where he goes,
And bowed the shoulder to his age-worn sire!
Ah! might I not have seized and rent his limbs,
Cast them piecemeal upon the wave, cut down
His friends—his own Ascanius—and served up
The son for banquet at his father's board?

But doubtful would have proved the chance of war;
Be it so: whom had I to fear, death-doomed?
I to their camp should have borne firebrands, filled
Their decks with flame, and, child and sire and race
Wiped out together, myself have crowned the pile.   *606*
O Sun, that with thy torch encompassest
All earthly deeds, and Juno, messenger
And witness of my woes, and Hecate,
Name in the city crossways yelled by night,
And dread avenging sisterhood, and gods
Of dying Elissa, heed ye this, and turn
Your power to ills that earn it, and give ear
Unto my prayers. If that accursèd life
Must reach the harbour, and float safe to shore,
If thus Jove's doom require, here stand the goal,
Yet by the sword of a brave race beset,
Outcast from home, and from Iulus' arms
Torn, let him sue for succour, and behold
His friends slain miserably, and when to terms
Of wrongful peace he yields him, let him not
His kingdom or the pleasant light enjoy,
But in the bare mid-plain, before his hour,
Fall and unburied lie. For this I pray,
And this last utterance with my life-blood pour.   *621*
And ye, O Tyrians, the whole stock and race
Dog with your hate for ever; to my dust
This boon bequeath ye. Let there be no love,
No league between the nations. O arise,
Unknown avenger, from my tomb, to chase
With fire and sword the Dardan settlers, now,
Hereafter, whensoe'er the strength is given.
Betwixt them, shore with shore, billow with wave,
And host with host, I call down enmity;
Be they themselves, and their sons' sons at war!"   *629*
    So saying, on every side she turned her thought,
Seeking how soonest to break off the life
She loathed, then briefly unto Barce spake,
Nurse of Sychaeus, for the grave's black dust
In the old country held her own: "Dear nurse,
Fetch me my sister hither, bid her haste
With water from the stream her limbs to lave,
And beasts, and expiating rites prescribed
Bring with her, and so come; and thou thyself
With a pure fillet veil thy brows. My mind
Is bent this sacrifice to Stygian Jove,
Which duly I have ordered and begun,

To consummate, and put an end to grief,
And give to flame the Dardan's funeral pyre."   640
She spake: the other with an old wife's zeal
Hurried her footstep. But, in trembling haste
And fierce with her wild purpose, Dido now,
Rolling a bloodshot eye, her quivering cheeks
Flecked with bright spots, and blanched with coming
    death,
Bursts through to the inner court, and madly mounts
The death-pyre, and unsheathes the Dardan's sword—
Boon never asked for such a need as this.
Here, when the Trojan garments she beheld,
And the familiar bed, a little while
Pausing for tears and thought, she cast herself
Upon the couch, and spake her latest words: 650
"Relics once dear, while fate and heaven allowed,
Take this my spirit, and loose me from these woes.
My life is lived; the course by fortune given
I have fulfilled, and now the shade of me
Passes majestic to the world below.
I have built a noble city, mine own walls
Beheld, avenged my husband, and therewith
Wreaked on my brother the reward of hate;
Happy, ah! all too happy, if only—if
The Dardan keels had never touched our shore!"
She spake, and burying in the couch her face:
"I shall die unavenged, but let me die,"
She said: "thus, thus with joy I take the road
To darkness. Let the cruel Dardan's eyes
Drink in the conflagration from the deep,
And my death-tokens haunt him on his way."   662
She had said; and, in the midst of words like these
Her folk beheld her sunk upon the sword,
And the blade reeking, and blood-dabbled hands.
Shrieks to the roof-top rise. Fame revels high
Through the stunned city. With laments and groans
And women's wail the palace rings, the sky
Resounds with their loud mourning. Even as if
With in-poured foes, all Carthage or old Tyre
Fell headlong, while the flames roll fiercely on
O'er towers of men and temples of the gods.
Half-dead to hear, and scared at breathless speed
With nail-torn features and fist-smitten breast,
Darts through the midst her sister, and calls loud
The dying one by name, "Was it then this,
Child of my sire?—would'st thou put fraud on me?—

This that yon pyre, these flames and altars meant?   *676*
What shall I weep for first, left desolate!
Dying, didst spurn to have thy sister near?
Thou should'st have bid me share thy doom, the same
Sword-pang, the self-same hour had found us both.
Nay, did I rear it with these hands, and call
Loud on our father's gods, ah! cruel, to be
Far off, and thou laid here? Thou hast destroyed,
Sister, thyself and me, the folk and sires
Of Sidon, and thy city. Let me lave
Her wounds with water, the last hovering breath
Catch haply on my lips." As thus she spake,
The lofty steps surmounted, she had clasped
Her dying sister to her bosom's warmth
With groans, the dark blood stanching with her robe. *687*
She, fain to lift her heavy eyes, sinks back
Swooning; the sword grides fixed within her breast.
Thrice, struggling, she uprose on elbow propped,
And thrice rolled backward on the couch, and sought
Light in the vault of heaven, with wandering eyes,
And, finding, groaned. Almighty Juno then,
Pitying her long pain, and hard-fought-for death,
Sent Iris from Olympus down to loose
Her struggling spirit and writhen limbs; for since
Neither by fate, nor as the wage of sin,
She dying lay, but woe-struck, ere her hour,
And fired with sudden frenzy, Proserpine
Not yet had reft her of the yellow lock,
Nor to the Stygian Orcus doomed her head.   *699*
So Iris, on her saffron wings through heaven,
Glides dewy down, trailing a thousand tints,
That shift against the sun, and, o'er her head
Standing: "This offering unto Dis I bear,
As bidden, and from thy body set thee free."
So spake she, and with right hand sheared the lock:
At once the warmth ebbed wholly, and therewith
Her life into the breezes sped away.   *705*

BOOK V

Meanwhile Aeneas upon the mid sea-way
Held steadfast with his fleet, and cut through waves
That scowled beneath the north wind, glancing oft
Back to the city-walls, now all aglow
With poor Elissa's funeral-flames. What cause
Has lit so fierce a fire, is hid from sight;
But outraged love's fierce anguish, and the thought
Of what a frantic woman can, lead on
The Teucrians' hearts to presages of woe.   7
   Soon as their galleys gained the open deep,
And now no longer land appeared, but lo!
Ocean on all sides, and on all sides heaven,
There stood a dark-blue storm-cloud o'er his head,
Laden with night and tempest, and the wave
Shuddered beneath the gloom. From the high poop
The very helmsman, Palinurus, cries:
"Alas! why have such clouds encircled heaven?   13
What next, O Father Neptune?" Having said,
Straightway he bids them trim the rigging taut,
And bend to their stout oars, and to the wind
Slants sail, and speaks: "High-souled Aeneas, even
Though Jupiter should pledge me on his word,
No hope were in me to fetch Italy
In such a sky. The winds veer round, and roar
Athwart, upgathering from the murky west,
And all the air is thickening into cloud.
Make head against it, or strive hard enow
We cannot. Since fortune betters us, be ours
To follow, and at her bidding shape our way.
Nor far thy brother Eryx' friendly shores
And ports Sicanian deem I, if the stars,
Erst noted, with due memory I retrace."   25
Then answered good Aeneas: "For my part I
Have long since seen the winds will have it so,
And that all vainly thou withstand'st them: turn
The vessels' course. Could there be any land
To me more welcome, or where gladlier I
Would beach the weary ships, than that which holds
My Dardan friend, Acestes, and laps round
In its embrace my sire Anchises' dust?"

This said, they make for harbour; and the gales,
Now favouring, stretch the canvas; swiftly rides
Their fleet upon the flood; and glad of heart
At length they steer into the well-known shore.   *34*

    But from a high far hill-top, marvelling
At their arrival, and the friendly barks,
Acestes speeds to meet them, bristling o'er
With javelins and a Libyan she-bear's fell.
Him to the river-god Crimisus erst
A Trojan mother bare: nor heedless now
Of his old lineage, their return he greets,
Gives them glad welcome of his rustic wealth,
And soothes their weariness with friendly cheer.   *41*

    When the next day-beam in the utmost east
Had put the stars to rout, from the whole shore
Aeneas calls a gathering of his friends,
And from a mounded hillock speaks: "Great sons
Of Dardanus, from heaven's high race derived,
A year's course, with its months accomplished, now
Is rounding to a close, since we in earth
My divine father's bones and relics hid,
And mourning altars consecrated. Now,
Or I misdeem, the day is here, which I
Shall ever hold—for so ye gods have willed—
Sacred to grief and honour without end.   *50*
This, were I passing 'mid Gaetulian shoals
An outcast, aye, or ta'en at unawares
In Argive waters, or Mycenae's town,
Still had I quit my yearly vows, and pomp
Of solemn ordinance, and with their gifts
Heaped high the altars. Now, beyond all hope,
Not undesigned nor all unwilled of heaven,
I take it, by my sire's own dust and bones
We stand, safe-wafted to the friendly port.
Up, then, and all glad homage let us pay!
Sue we for winds, and may he grant that I
May build a city, and offer year by year
These rites in temples hallowed to his name!   *60*
Two head of steers Acestes, sprung from Troy,
Gives every ship by tale: bid to the feast
The hearth-gods, not your sires' alone, but those
Our host Acestes worships. Furthermore,
If the ninth dawn bring kindly day to men,
And with her beams disclose the world, I then
Will contests for the Phrygian folk ordain:
First of the swift fleet; then—whoe'er excels

In speed of foot, or, dauntless in his strength,
Steps forth, a champion in the javelin-bout,
And light-winged arrows, or with raw-hide gloves
Bold to do battle—let them all appear,
And look for palms to be the victor's prize.
Now hush ye, all: with garlands bind the brow."   *71*
Thus spake he, and about his temples twined
His mother's myrtle. So does Helymus,
So, ripe of age, Acestes, so the lad
Ascanius, and the rest thereafter. He
Strode from the council to the tomb, thronged round
With many thousands, 'midst a mighty train.
Here, meet libation, on the ground he pours
Two goblets of pure wine, of fresh milk two,
Two of the blood of victims; and he flings
Bright flowers, and cries: "Hail, sacred sire, once
    more!
Hail, dust of him once rescued, but in vain,
And shade and spirit of my father! not
With thee was it vouchsafed to seek the bounds
And destined fields of Italy, nor yet
Ausonian Tiber, whatsoe'er it be."   *83*
He spake, and ceased, when from the shrine's recess
A slippery serpent trailed seven monstrous coils,
Plied seven times, fold on fold, and quietly
Twined round the tomb, and o'er the altars slid,
Whose back with dark blue spots was pied, his scales
Lit with the gleam of dappled gold; as when
The cloud-bow flings a thousand shifting tints
In the sun's eye. Aeneas at the sight
Stood wonder-struck: at last, with lengthy train
Gliding among the bowls and polished cups,
It tasted of the viands, and once more,
All harmless, sought the shelter of the tomb,
Leaving the altars it had lipped. Hereat
He to his father all the more renews
The interrupted rites, doubtful the while
Or genius of the spot to deem it, or
His sire's attendant spirit: two young sheep
He duly slaughters, and as many swine,
As many black-backed heifers, and poured forth
The wine-bowl, and on great Anchises' shade
Called, and the ghost let loose from Acheron.   *99*
His friends withal, as each had substance, bring
Glad gifts, and heap the altars, and slay steers.
Others in turn set cauldrons on, and, stretched

Along the greensward, lay live coals beneath
The spits, and roast the flesh.
                                    The expected day
Was come, the ninth dawn in a cloudless sky,
Drawn by the steeds of Phaëthon: report
And great Acestes' name the neighbouring folk
Had summoned; in blithe groups they thronged the
        shore
To see the children of Aeneas, some too
Prepared to join the contest. Full in sight,
And midmost of the ring, are first disposed
The prizes, sacred tripods, and green wreaths,
And palms to crown the victors, arms, and robes
With purple dyed, and talent-weights of gold
And silver: and from a hillock in the midst
The trumpet's note proclaims the sports begun.   *113*
For the first contest, matched with heavy oars,
Enter four vessels picked from all the fleet.
Mnestheus with keen crew drives swift Pristis on—
Mnestheus-of-Italy to be, from whom
Takes name the race of Memmius: Gyas next
The huge Chimaera's mighty bulk, in mass
A city, which the Dardan youth propel
With triple sweep, a threefold tier of oars
Rising together: on the Centaur's might
Sergestus, whence the Sergian house is named,
Cloanthus upon dark blue Scylla rides,
From whom thy race, Cluentius of Rome.   *123*
    Far seaward fronts the foaming shores a rock
Oft drowned and beaten by the billowy swell,
What time the wild north-westers hide the stars;
In calm it sleeps, reared on still waves, a plain,
And standing-ground to sunny seagulls dear.
Here a green ilex-goal Aeneas, as Prince,
Sets up for signal, that the crews might know
Whence to return and their long circuit bend.
Then lots they cast for places; and the chiefs
Themselves upon the poop shine forth afar,
Glorious in gold and purple; for the rest,
The crews are crowned with wreaths of poplar-spray,
And steeped in oil their naked shoulders shine.   *135*
They man the thwarts, arms stretched to oars, full
        stretch
Await the signal: drains each bounding heart
Quick-knocking fear, and the wild thirst for praise.
Then, when the shrill trump sounded, in a trice

All from their bounds leapt forward; a sea-shout
Strikes heaven; the floods foam, churned with
    indrawn arms.
Abreast they cleave the furrows; the whole main
    yawns
Convulsed with oars and triple-pointed beaks.
Not in such heady race the two-horsed cars,
Poured from the bounds, grip course and go, nor shake
Their billowy reins above such scouring teams
The drivers, hanging forward to the lash.   147
Then with applause of men, shouts, favouring cheers,
The whole grove rings: the pent shore rolls along,
And the hills, smitten, buffet back, the din.
Outspeeds the rest, and skims the forward wave,
'Mid crowd and tumult, Gyas: follows him
Cloanthus, lustier-oared, but the pine's weight
Retards him: next, and at like interval,
Pristis and Centaur strive for foremost place.   155
Now Pristis has it, and now the Centaur huge
Outstrips and overhauls her; and now both
Ride, beak and beak, together, and with long keel
Cleave the salt billows: by this they neared the rock,
And had the goal in grasp, when Gyas, now first,
And of the half-course victor, loudly hails
Menoetes, his ship's pilot: "Whither away
So far to starboard? hither steer, hug shore;
Let the oar graze the larboard cliff, and leave
The deep for others!" He said; Menoetes still,
Fearing blind rocks, steers off toward open sea:
"Whither away so wide? Make for the rocks,
Menoetes!" Gyas shouts and calls again;
And, glancing back, Cloanthus he beholds,
Now hard astern, holding the nearer course.   168
'Twixt Gyas' vessel and the roaring rocks
He to the left skims inward, suddenly
Passes his leader, leaves the goal behind,
And gains the safe smooth water. Then indeed
Grief in the young man's frame blazed fierce and
    high,
Nor did his cheeks lack tears, and heedless both
Of his own honour and his comrades' lives,
Laggard Menoetes sheer from the high poop
Into the sea he flings: himself instead
The tiller takes, pilot and captain too,
Cheers on his men, and shoreward turns the helm.
But from the sea-floor scarce at length cast up,

Menoetes, heavy now with age, and soaked
In his wet garments, to the cliff-top climbed,
And on the dry rock sat. The Teucrian folk
Laughed at him falling, swimming, and laugh now
To see the salt waves from his chest disgorged.   *182*
Here the two last, Sergestus, Mnestheus, feel
Glad hope within them kindle to outstrip
The lagging Gyas. Sergestus gains the lead
And nears the crag, yet overlaps he not
A whole keel's length, but part alone, and part
The jealous Pristis presses with her beak.
Then, through his vessel striding, 'midst the crew,
Mnestheus exhorts them: "Rise to the oar, now, now,
Comrades of Hector, whom in Troy's last hour
I chose to be my fellows; now put forth
That strength, that spirit, which erst ye showed
          amidst
Gaetulian quicksands, on the Ionian Sea,
And Malea's chasing waves. No more seek I,
Mnestheus, the foremost place, nor strive to win;   *194*
Yet oh!—but let them conquer, to whom thou,
Neptune, hast granted it. Count we it shame
Last to arrive! thus far, my countrymen,
Prevail ye, and ward off disgrace!" They bend
Forward, and strive their utmost: the brass poop
Quivers beneath their mighty strokes: the floor
Runs from beneath them: then thick panting shakes
Limbs and dry lips: the sweat flows out in streams.
A mere chance brought them the much-wished-for
          place;
For while Sergestus, mad at heart, drives close
In toward the rocks, and draws to dangerous ground,
Hapless, upon projecting reefs he stuck.   *204*
The cliffs were jarred; on a sharp crag the oars
Smote with a crash, and the prow struck and hung.
Up leap the crew loud-shouting, fast aground,
Bring iron-shod boat-hooks and sharp-pointed poles,
And from the billows pluck their broken oars.
Mnestheus exults, and, keener by success,
Scuds with swift oar-sweep, and a prayer to the winds,
Down the slope seas, and scours the open main.   *212*
As, from her cave roused suddenly, a dove,
Whose home and sweet brood lie in the crannied
          rock,
Flies fieldward borne, with clamorous pinion-clap
Scared from her cell; soon, gliding in calm air,

She skims the sky-way swift on moveless wing:
So Mnestheus, Pristis so, of her own will
Cleaves the last water, so mere speed of way
Carries her flying. And first he leaves behind
Sergestus, struggling on the lofty rock,
And in the shoals, calling in vain for aid,
And learning to make way with broken oars.
Then Gyas and his Chimaera vast of bulk
He overtakes: she yields, of helmsman reft.   224
And now, and close upon the goal, remains
Alone Cloanthus: him he makes for, him,
Striving with utmost strength, pursues. Ah! then
The shouts redouble; all goad him to the chase
With eager cheers: heaven echoes to their din.
These deem it shame, except they hold their own—
The glory they have won—would barter life
Itself for fame: those thrive upon success;
They can because they think they can; and so
Perchance even now they would have ta'en the prize,
Prow matched with prow, had not Cloanthus
    stretched
Clasped hands across the deep, and poured forth
    prayers,
Calling the gods to hear his vows. "Ye gods
That sway the main, over whose waves I run,
Gladly before your altars on this shore,
I, vow-beholden, will a white bull set,
Into the salt flood fling his entrails far,
And pour clear-flowing wine." He spake, and him
Under the deep waves all the Nereïd-band
Heard, and the choir of Phorcus, and with them
The maiden Panopea; and himself
The sire Portunus with his mighty hand
Pushed him upon his way. To shore she flies
Swifter than south wind or a wingèd shaft,
And now lies sheltered in the haven's depth.   243
Then, duly summoning all, Anchises' son
Proclaims Cloanthus victor by loud voice
Of herald, and with green bay-leaf binds his brow;
And to the crews three bullocks of their choice
He gives, and wine, and a great talent-weight
Of silver, to bear off, and to the chiefs
Themselves adds special honours—for the first
A gold-wrought scarf, twice round whose borders ran
Broad Meliboean purple, in winding wave.
Therein embroidered is the royal boy

[193]

On leafy Ida, as he tires the stag
With javelin and the chase, keen, like to one
Panting, whom Jove's swift armour-bearer snatched
Aloft from Ida with crook'd talons: see!
His aged guardians stretch vain hands on high,
And the hounds' baying goes fiercely up to heaven.　257
But to the hero who gat second place
In prowess, a corslet linked with polished hooks
Of gold twilled triple, which his own victor hand
Had from Demoleos on swift Simois' bank
Torn beneath lofty Troy, he gives to bear,
A glory and defence in battle. It
Scarce could the carls Phegeus and Sagaris,
Shoulder to shoulder, heave with all its folds;
But clad in it of yore Demoleos drave
Full speed the flying Trojans. The third prize
He makes twin brazen cauldrons, and cups wrought
Of cunning silver, rough with tracery-work.　267
And now, thus dowered, and glorying in their gifts,
Brow-bound with purple fillets, all went forth,
When, from the cruel rock with much ado
'Scaped hardly, oars lost, crippled of one tier,
'Mid laughter urging his inglorious bark,
Sergestus came. As oft at unawares
A serpent, caught upon the heaped highway,
Which or a brazen wheel hath crossed aslant,
Or heavy-smiting traveller left half dead
And mangled with a stone, now trying to flee
Twists his long body into coils, in vain,
Part still defiant, and, with fiery eyes,
Rearing aloft the hissing throat; but part
Maimed by the wound retards him, as he wreaths
Joint upon joint, self-knotted and convolved:
So oared, the ship came slowly labouring on,
Yet she spreads sail, and, full sail, enters port.　281
Aeneas with promised boon Sergestus dowers,
Glad for ship saved and rescued crew: to him
Is given a slave, skilled in Minerva's craft,
The Cretan Pholoë, twin boys at her breast.
　　Then good Aeneas, the race dispatched, moves on
Into a grassy plain, by sloping hills
Girdled with forest; and amidst the vale
There was an amphitheatre, whereto
The prince with many thousands strode, and sat
On a high mound, the centre of the throng.　290
Here in fleet foot-race whoso list to strive

He lures with prizes, sets the guerdon forth.
Teucrians, Sicanians, mixed, from all sides flock:
See! foremost Nisus and Euryalus!
Euryalus famed for beauty and fresh youth,
Nisus for the fair love he bore the boy.
Next followed, reared from Priam's noble stem,
Princely Diores: after him, together,
Salius and Patron, Acarnanian one,
One of Arcadia's blood, a Tegean born.   *299*
Then two Trinacrian comers, Helymus
And Panopes, to forest-life inured,
Comrades of old Acestes; many more
To boot, whom rumour doth in darkness hide.
Then in their midst Aeneas spake: "My words
Take now to heart, and lend me cheerful heed.
None of all here will I let giftless go.   *305*
Two Gnosian javelins bright with burnished steel,
And an axe silver-chased, I bid them bear;
Be this one meed to all. The foremost three
Shall receive prizes, and their heads be bound
With pale green olive. Let the first to wit,
As victor, have a horse with trappings proud;
The next an Amazonian quiver, filled
With Thracian arrows, which a broad gold belt
Circles, a smooth-gemmed buckle clasps; the third
Depart contented with this Argive helm."   *314*
This said, they take their stand, and suddenly,
The signal heard, catch at the course, and leave
The barriers, like a cloud poured forth, their eyes
Fixed on the finish. First draws ahead, darts far
Beyond all rivals Nisus, swifter he
Than wind or wings of lightning; next to him,
But next at a long distance, on his track
Comes Salius; then, some space between them left,
The third, Euryalus; Euryalus
Has Helymus behind him, close on whom
Flies, see! Diores, heel now grazing heel,
And shoulders jostling; and, were more space left,
He would slip past him, and leave doubt behind.   *326*
And now, the course nigh finished, with breath spent,
They neared the goal, when Nisus by ill luck
Slips in some blood chance-spilt upon the ground
From slaughtered steers, that soaked the greensward.
    Here
Just flushed with triumph, he could not keep his feet,
Tripped by the ground they trod on, but fell prone

Right in the foul dung and slain victims' gore.
Yet of Euryalus, yet of his heart's love
Not he forgetful! for in Salius' path
He cast him, rising through the slush, who, rolled
Over and over, on the thick soil lay.   336
Forth darts Euryalus, and the first place holds,
Winner by his friend's gift, and speeds him on
'Mid favouring shouts and tumult. Next to him
Comes following Helymus, and, now third prize,
Diores. But here Salius with loud shouts
Fills the whole concourse of the mighty ring
With gazing sires in front, reclaims the prize
Snatched from his hand by craft. Euryalus
Is strong in favour, and the grace of tears,
And worth, seen comelier in a lovely form.   344
Backs him Diores too with loud appeal,
Who, to a prize succeeding, has for naught
Gained the last guerdon, if the foremost place
Be given to Salius. Then Prince Aeneas:
"Your gifts remain assured you, boys, and none
Changes the order of the prize: let me
Pity my friend's unmerited mishap."
So saying, he gives to Salius the vast fell
Of a Gaetulian lion, with rough hair
Heavy, and claws of gold. Then Nisus: "If
Such be defeat's reward, and those that fell
Win pity of thee, what worthy recompense
Hast left for Nisus? The first crown was mine
By merit and exploit, had not the luck,
That frowned on Salius, frowned alike on me."   356
And with the word he shows his face and limbs
Smeared with wet filth. At him the gracious sire
Laughed, and a shield bade bring, the workmanship
Of Didymaon, by the Danai once
From Neptune's sacred portal torn. With this
He dowers the noble youth, a princely prize.
    Then, the race ended, and the gifts dispensed,
"Come now," he cries, "and if in any breast
Be courage and prompt heart, let him approach,
Bind on the gloves, and lift his arms." So saying,
He names a twofold guerdon for the fray,
A steer for the winner, garlanded with gold,
Sword and proud helm, the vanquished to appease.   367
No pause: at once in all his giant strength
Uplifts him Dares, and stands forth to view
'Mid murmurs of the crowd, he who alone

Would match with Paris, and at the tomb wherein
Lies mightiest Hector conquering Butes smote—
Who with his vast bulk bore him to the field,
Of the Bebrycian house of Amycus—
And stretched him dying upon the tawny sand.
Such was this Dares, who lifts high his head
First for the fray, displays his shoulders broad,
Launches his arms out, and spars right and left,
Lashing the air with buffets. Him to match
They seek another; but out of all that throng
No one durst face the champion, don the gloves. 379
So, deeming all men from the prize withdrew,
Promptly he plants him at Aeneas' feet,
Tarrying no more, then by the left horn grasps
The bull, and speaks: "O goddess-born, if none
Durst risk the fight, what end to waiting, say?
How long befits it I stand loitering here?
Bid me lead off the prize." The Dardans all,
Shouting with one voice, bade the promised boon
Be rendered to their champion. Hereupon
Acestes with stern words Entellus chides,
As he sat next him on the grassy couch: 388
"Entellus, once most valiant, but in vain,
Wilt thou such gifts see tamely borne away,
And strike no blow? Where now, we ask, that god,
Thy master, Eryx, idly vaunted? Where
The fame that filled Trinacria, and those spoils
Still hanging from thy roof-tree?" He replied:
"It is not that the love of fame is sped,
Nor fear hath cast out honour; but indeed
Chilled is my blood and dulled by sluggish eld,
And all my body's strength numbed and outworn. 396
If, which erst was, wherein yon braggart still
Boldly exults, if now that youth were mine,
I had not stayed for prize or noble steer
To lure me forward, nor heed I the gifts."
So saying, twin gauntlets of vast weights he hurls
Into the midst, wherewith keen Eryx wont
Advance his hand to battle, and bind his arms
With the tough hide. Astonied were all hearts;
So vast the seven huge ox-hides that lay stiff
With in-sewed lead and iron. More than all,
Dares himself stands dazed, and far recoils:
This way and that high-souled Anchises' son
Poises and turns the thongs' enormous folds.
Then the old man with deep-drawn accents spake: 409

"What then if one had seen the gloves and arms
Of Hercules himself, and the grim fight
Upon this very strand? Those weapons once
Thy brother Eryx wore: thou seest them yet
Blood-stained and brain-bespattered: he with these
Stood against great Alcides; to these I
Myself was used, while sounder blood gave strength,
Ere snowy age had sprinkled both my brows.
But if the Trojan Dares shun these arms
Of ours, and good Aeneas be set thereon,
Backed by Acestes' sanction, fight we fair.
I waive the hides of Eryx, calm thy dread,
And do thou doff the Trojan gloves." So saying,
He from his shoulder flings the twofold robe,
Bares his huge limb-joints, mighty bones and thews,
And stands gigantic in the arena's midst.   *423*
Then equal gloves the sire, Anchises' son,
Brought, and with like arms bound the hands of both.
Straining on tip-toe, each at once took stand,
And raised his arms undaunted high toward heaven.
Their towering heads far from the blow withdrawn,
Fist with fist mingling, they provoke the fray.
One nimbler-footed, and relying on youth,
One strong in bulk of body; but his slow knees
Totter and quake, and all his mighty frame
Heaves with a painful panting. Many a blow
The champions idly bandy, each with each,
Many they rain on hollow flank, and make
Loud music on their chests; round ear and brow
The quick fist plays, jaws crackle with hard blows.   *432*
Ponderous in the selfsame posture stands
Unmoved Entellus, with his body alone
And watchful eye shunning the strokes. The other—
As who with engines batters a tall town,
Or sits down armed before some mountain-hold—
Tries this approach and that, and, hovering round
Artful at every point, plies him in vain
With manifold assault. Entellus then,
With right hand threatening and uplifted high,
Rose to the blow: which the other with quick glance
Foresaw descending, and with nimble frame
Slipped out of reach and foiled it. All his strength
Entellus spent on air, and, self-impelled,
By his own heaviness, heavily to the earth
Fell with prodigious weight; so falls at times
On Erymanthus or on Ida's height

A hollow pine-tree by the roots up-torn.   *449*
Teucrians, Trinacrians, by one impulse urged,
Leap from their seats; a shout goes up to heaven;
And first Acestes hastes, and pityingly
Lifts from the earth his age-mate and his friend.
But he, nor checked nor daunted by the fall,
Returns yet keenlier to the fray; wrath goads
To violence: shame and conscious valour, too,
Kindle his strength; and all on fire he drives
Dares at headlong speed the whole course through,
Raining his buffets now with right, now left:
No stop, no respite: thick as hail, when clouds
Fall rattling on the roof, so pelt the blows
He showers on Dares, and with either hand
Pounds him and spins. Then Prince Aeneas brooke
Wrath go no further, nor Entellus yet
Rage on in bitterness of heart, but bade
The battle end, and rescued the spent strength
Of Dares, and thus speaks with soothing words: *464*
"Unhappy man! what craze hath caught thy soul?
Dost not perceive that here is alien strength,
Gods turned against thee? yield to heaven!" He spake,
And with the word broke off the fight; but him
Dragging faint knees, his head to either side
Lolling, and spitting from his mouth thick gore
And teeth with blood commingled, his true friends
Lead to the ships: the helmet and the sword,
When summoned, they receive, the palm and bull
Leave to Entellus. Then the victor speaks,
Elate with pride, and glorying in the bull:
"O goddess-born, and you, ye Teucrians, mark
Both what was once my body's youthful might,
And Dares from what death your rescue saves."   *476*
He spake, and fronting the steer's forehead full,
Which stood there, prize of battle, drew aback
His right hand, levelled the tough gloves, and straight
'Twixt either horn, up-towering to the blow,
Crushed the skull inward, and dashed out the brain;
On earth stretched lifeless, quivering, the bull falls.
Then with deep utterance spake he over it:
"This better life, for death of Dares due,
Eryx, I pay thee—with this triumph crowned,
The gauntlets and the boxer's art lay by."   *484*
    Forthwith Aeneas to the swift arrow-match
Invites who will, and sets the prizes forth;
Then from Serestus' ship with mighty hand

The mast uprears, and by a rope passed round
Suspends a fluttering dove from the tall top,
As target for their points. The men are met;
The thrown lot lies within a brazen helm,
And for first place outleaps, with favouring cheer,
The son of Hyrtacus, Hippocoön; next,
Late victor in the ship-race, Mnestheus comes,
Mnestheus now garlanded with olive green.   *494*
Eurytion was the third, brother to thee,
O most renownèd Pandarus, who of old,
Bidden the treaty to confound, wert first
To hurl thy dart amid the Achaean ranks.
Last in the helmet's depth Acestes lay,
Still bold of hand the tasks of youth to try.   *499*
Then, each for self, with sinewy might they bend
Their curving bows, pluck shaft from quiver; and first
The bolt of the son of Hyrtacus through heaven
Cleaves the fleet breezes from the whizzing string,
Arrives, and sticks in the mast-tree fair and full.
Quivered the mast, the bird clapped wings in fear,
And all the region rang with loud applause.
Next took his stand keen Mnestheus, bow drawn
      home,
High-pointing, with one level of shaft and eye;
He, luckless, the bird's self with bolt to strike
Skilled not, but cut the noose and hempen cord,
Foot-bound whereby to the tall mast she hung:
Into the south winds and black clouds she flew.   *512*
Then, bow long since held ready, and bolt on string,
With a quick prayer to his brother to hear his vows,
Eurytion marked the dove, now triumphing
In the free sky, and, as she clapped her wings
Under a dark cloud, pierced her. Dead she fell,
And left her life among the stars of heaven,
Down-trailing with the arrow in her side.
Acestes, the prize lost, alone remained,
Yet upward aimed his bolt into the air,
Showing an old sire's skill and sounding bow.   *521*
Here on their eyes a sudden portent falls,
To prove of mighty presage; the event
Taught them its vastness in the after-time,
And awful seers their omen sang too late.
For, on its flight amid the floating clouds,
The reed took fire, and traced a path in flame,
And into thin air burnt itself away;
As oft, from heaven unfixed, shoot flying stars,

And trail their locks behind them. All, aghast,
Stood rooted, and implored the gods of heaven,
Trinacrian folk and Teucrian: nor did great
Aeneas spurn the omen, but his arms
Cast about glad Acestes, whom he loads
With mighty gifts, thus speaking: "Take them, sire;
For by such tokens great Olympus' king
To thee no lot-drawn honour hath decreed.   534
From old Anchises' self this gift be thine,
A bowl embossed with figures, which of yore
Cisseus the Thracian as a noble gift
Gave to my sire Anchises, of his love
The record and the pledge to bear." This said,
He wreathes his temples with green bay, and hails
First, before all, Acestes victor, nor
Did kind Eurytion grudge the rank preferred,
Albeit he only struck the bird from heaven.
Next for the prize comes in who cut the cord,
Last with fleet arrow he that pierced the pine.   544
    But Prince Aeneas, ere the sports were sped,
Calls to his side Epytides, the squire
Who watched o'er young Iulus, and thus speaks
Into his faithful ear: "Hie thee, and bid
Ascanius, if his boyish band he now
Have ready, and his manœuvring troop arrayed,
Lead forth the squadron in his grandsire's name,
And show himself in arms." Such charge he gave,
And with his own voice bids the crowd withdraw,
Flooding the long course, and the field be cleared.   552
The boys ride in, before their fathers' eyes
Glittering on bridled horses in array,
By all Trinacria's chivalry and Troy's
Hailed with admiring murmurs as they go.
The locks of all a trim wreath duly binds,
Each bears two cornel spear-shafts tipped with steel,
Some polished quivers upon the shoulder; high
On breast, along the throat there runs a hoop
Pliant of twisted gold. The companies
Of horse are three; three chiefs ride to and fro,
And, following each, a band of twice six boys,
The troop trisected, with like leaders, shine.   562
One youthful squadron a child-Priam leads
To victory, and recalls his grandsire's name,
Thy glorious seed, Polites, soon to swell
The tribes of Italy; a Thracian steed
Bears him, with white spots dappled, that displays

White-stepping pasterns, and white-towering brow.
The next is Atys, from whom trace their line
The Latin Atii; the child Atys, loved
Of his boy-friend Iulus. Last appears,
In beauty before all, Iulus' self
On a Sidonian horse, fair Dido's gift,
Of her heart's love the record and the pledge.   572
The remnant ride Trinacrian steeds of old
Acestes. With a cheer the Dardan folk
Welcome the timid lads, and gaze with joy,
Tracing the features of their sires of old.
When the gay cavalcade had ridden the round
Of the whole concourse under their friends' eyes,
And all were ready, Epytides from far
Shouted the signal and cracked loud his whip.
They rushed apart symmetric, in three troops
With open ranks dividing, and once more
Wheel at the order, and charge point to point.
Then other onsets and retreats they try
In quarters opposite, and interweave
Circle with circle, each with each, and wake
The semblance of armed warfare, now expose
Their backs in flight, now point their levelled spears,
Now with peace plighted, as close comrades, ride.   587
As erst the labyrinth in lofty Crete
Had, as folk tell, a way with blind walls woven,
And a dark trap with thousand paths perplexed,
Whose maze unsearched and irretraceable
Might balk all clues for following, such the course
Wherein the Trojan boys their steps involve,
Weaving the sportive web of flight and fray:
As dolphins, swimming through the watery seas,
Carpathian cleave or Libyan, and make sport
Amid the waves. Such use of horsemanship,
Such games as these, Ascanius, as he girt
With walls his Alba Longa, first revived,
And trained the ancient Latins to the mode
Of his own boyhood with the youth of Troy;   599
The Albans taught their sons; from whom
        bequeathed
Majestic Rome received and kept alive
The ancestral rite: now, named from Troy, the lads
Are called the Trojan troop. Thus far were held
The games in honour of the sacred sire.
    Here Fortune changing first revoked her faith.
Whilst they with various pastime to the tomb

Render due rites, Saturnian Juno now
Sends Iris from on high to Ilium's fleet,
And breathes fair winds to waft her, rife with
    schemes,
Still of her ancient smart insatiate. She,
Speeding along her myriad-tinted bow,
Shoots down the swift track, maid beheld of none.   *610*
She views the mighty throng, and scans the shore
And sees the harbour void, the fleet forsook.
But far withdrawn upon a lonely beach
The Trojan dames wept for Anchises' loss,
And, weeping, all together eyed the deep.
Ah, what vast floods, what weary length of sea
Was still before them, with one voice they cry.
They crave a city, the travail of the main
Sick of enduring. So into their midst,
Well versed in harm, she flings her, doffs the face
And garb of goddess, becomes Beroë,
The agèd wife of Tmarian Doryclus,
Who once had lineage, and a name, and sons;
So 'mid the Dardan mothers makes her way.   *622*
"O hapless women, whom no Greek hand in war
Dragged 'neath your native walls to death," she cries,
"O race ill-starred, for what destruction, say,
Doth fate reserve ye? Since Troy's overthrow,
The seventh summer now wheels her course, the
    while,
Borne over seas and traversing all lands,
So many inhospitable rocks and climes,
We chase the still receding Italy
On the vast ocean, by its billows tossed.
Here are our brother Eryx' bounds, our host
Acestes: who forbids to cast up walls,
And give a city to our countrymen?   *631*
O fatherland, and household gods in vain
Snatched from the foeman, shall no city bear
Troy's name for ever? Nowhere shall I see
A Simois or a Xanthus, Hector's streams?
Nay up, and help me burn the ill-omened ships!
For in my sleep the seer Cassandra's shade
Appeared, methought, and offered blazing brands.
'Here look for Troy; here is your home,' quoth she.
The hour is ripe for action; prodigies
So mighty brook no tarriance. Lo ye, four
Altars to Neptune! and the god himself
Supplies the firebrand and the will." So saying,

She, snatching first the deadly flame, upreared
Aloft her right hand, brandished with main strength,
And threw it. Brain-wildered were the Trojan dames,
And heart-astonied. Then, of many, one
In years their eldest, Pyrgo, royal nurse
Of all those sons of Priam, cries, "See you not,
This is no Beroë, no Rhoeteïan wife
Of Doryclus, good mothers! Mark the signs
Of heavenly beauty, and the glowing eyes:
What breath about her! what a glance she hath!
What tone of voice, and stateliness of step!   649
Nay, I myself left Beroë only now,
Sick, chafing that she only in such rite
Should lack a part, nor to Anchises pay
The honours due to him." So spake she. But
The matrons, wavering at the first, 'gan eye
The ships with looks malign, halting between
Infatuate passion for their present land
And realms that called them with the voice of fate.
But on poised wings the goddess borne through
        heaven
Cut, flying, a mighty bow beneath the clouds.
Then, by the portent crazed, and frenzy-spurred,
All from their hearths' recesses, with one shout,
Snatch fire; some strip the altars, and fling on
Leaf, brushwood, bough. With loose rein Vulcan riots
O'er thwarts and oars and sterns of painted pine.   663
To Anchises' barrow and the circus-seats
Eumelus of the blazing fleet brings word.
Then glancing back they see the pitchy reek
Float in a cloud. And first Ascanius,
Then gaily leading his manœuvring troop,
Rode at full speed to the disordered camp,
Even as he was, nor can his breathless guards
Detain him. "What new frenzy is this?" he cries,
"Or whither now, say whither are ye bound,
My wretched countrywomen? 'Tis no foe,
No hostile camp of Argives, that ye burn,
But your own hopes. See, it is I, your own
Ascanius!" and before his feet he flung
The empty helmet, wherewith armed but now
He woke in sport the counterfeit of war.   674
At once Aeneas, at once the Teucrian train
Speed to the spot. But scattering o'er the beach,
This way and that the affrighted women fly,
Make for the woods by stealth, and wheresoe'er

The rocks are caverned: now they loathe the deed
And daylight, know their own with altered eye,
And Juno's power is shaken from their soul.
But not for that the conflagration's blaze
Slacks its resistless fury: the tow glows
Beneath the wet wood, spewing forth slow smoke;
The creeping heat devours the keels, a plague
That sinks through all the vessels' bulk, nor strength
Of men, nor showers of water can avail.   *684*
Then good Aeneas from off his shoulders rent
The raiment, and besought the gods for aid,
With outstretched hands: "Almighty Jupiter,
If all the Trojans, to a man, not yet
Thou hatest, if thy goodness of old time
Recks aught of human woes, grant that the flames
Now 'scape our fleet, O father, and pluck thou
The Teucrians' shrunken power from ruin. Else
Level thy thunderbolt, and what remains
Hurl down to death, if such be my desert,
And overwhelm us here with thy right hand."   *692*
Scarce had he spoken, when with outpoured showers
A black storm rages, uncontrollable;
Earth trembles to the thunder, hill and plain;
From the whole welkin a wild water-flood
Comes rushing, pitch-black from the thickening
      south;
The ships are filled, and over; the half-burnt
Timbers are soaked; till all the heat is quenched,
And, four keels lost, all else escape the plague.
But Prince Aeneas, stunned by the shrewd chance,
Shifted and turned the mighty load of care
Within his breast, now this way, and now that,
Whether to settle in Sicilian fields,
Heedless of fate, or grasp Italia's shore.   *703*
Then agèd Nautes, whom of all men most
Tritonian Pallas taught, and with much lore
Made famous—she it was declared to him
That which or heaven's high wrath portended or
Fate's course required—he thus bespake Aeneas
With comfortable words: "O goddess-born,
Pull or repel they, follow we the fates;
Betide what will, fortune in every phase
Is conquered but by bearing. Here thou hast
Acestes of the Dardan stock divine:
Him take, a willing yoke-fellow, to share
Thy counsels; unto him deliver those

Who are left shipless, or have weary grown
Both of thy fortunes and the great emprise.   *714*
Men full of years, and mothers wearied out
With ocean, and whate'er of weak thou hast,
Fearful of danger, choose, and in this land
Give ramparts to the weary ones. Their town,
Grant thou the name, Acesta shall be called."
   Fired by such words from his friend's agèd lips,
Now was his soul with care on care distraught.   *720*
And black night, chariot-lifted, held the sky,
When sudden lo! the likeness of his sire
Anchises seemed to glide from heaven, and speak
With such-like utterance: "Son, than life to me
Dearer, while life was mine—son, sorely tasked
By Ilium's destinies, hither I come
At Jove's command, who from thy fleet drave off
The fire, and hath at length ta'en pity on thee
Out of high heaven. Obey the goodly rede
Now given by agèd Nautes; men of choice,
The bravest hearts, lead on to Italy;
Hardy the race, and rude of life, which thou
In Latium must war down. First none the less
Approach the infernal halls of Dis, and through
Avernus' depth seek colloquy with me,
My son. For guilty Tartarus holds me not,
Nor the sad ghosts, but in Elysium
'Mid fair assemblies of the blest I dwell.
Thither with plenteous bloodshed of black kine
The Sibyl pure shall lead thee. Then shalt thou
Learn all thy kindred, and what walls are given.   *737*
And now farewell! dank night her midway course
Is wheeling, and the Orient's panting steeds
Breathe pitiless upon me." He had said,
And passed, like vapour, into empty air.
"Ah! whither hurrying, whither whirled away?"
Exclaims Aeneas, "whom fliest thou, or who
Bars thee from my embraces?" With that word
He wakes the embers and the slumbering fire,
And with pure meal and brimming censer pays
Honour to Troy's Lar and hoar Vesta's shrine.   *745*
Straight summons he his friends, Acestes first,
Of Jove's command and his dear sire's behest
Instructs them, and what purpose now stands fixed
Within his soul. None hinder the design,
Nor thwarts his word Acestes. They transfer
The matrons to their city, and set on shore

Who would, such souls as crave not high renown.
Themselves repair the thwarts, and shape afresh
The fire-gnawed ship-beams, and fit oars and ropes,
Few, but a pulse of manhood quick for war.
Aeneas meanwhile is marking with a plough
The city-boundaries, and assigning homes,
Bids here an Ilium, here a Troy to be.
Trojan Acestes, glorying in his realm,
Proclaims a court, and to the assembled sires
Gives laws. To Venus of Idalium then
Nigh to the stars, on Eryx' top, they found
A dwelling and Anchises' tomb endow
With priest and grove of widespread sanctity.   *761*

    Now the whole race nine days have wassail held,
And to the altars is due honour done:
Calm winds have laid the ocean, and once more
Auster with quickening breath invites to sea.
Uprises hark! along the winding shore
A mighty wail: clasped in each other's arms
They linger out the hours of night and day.
Now e'en the matrons, e'en the men, who late
Shuddered at ocean's face, scarce brooked its name,
Fain would set forth, bear all the toil of flight.
Them kind Aeneas soothes with friendly words,
And, weeping, to Acestes' care consigns,
His kinsman. Then to Eryx he bids slay
Three heifers, and a ewe lamb to the storms,
And duly loose the moorings. He himself,
Bound with trim olive-leaves about his head,
Stands high upon the prow, and holds a bowl,
Into the salt waves flings the entrails far,
And pours clear-flowing wine. Rising astern,
A breeze escorts them on their way. The crews
With emulous oar-strokes sweep the ocean plain.   *778*

    Venus meanwhile, to cares a prey, thus pleads
With Neptune, and pours out her heart's complaint:
"Juno's fell wrath and heart insatiable
Constrain me, Neptune, stoop to every prayer.
No lapse of time, no goodness can assuage,
Nor Jove's command, nor fate itself, avail
To break and tame her. With outrageous hate
'Twas not enough from 'midst the Phrygian folk
To eat away their city, and drag them on
Through every retribution: what remains,
The very dust and bones of perished Troy,
She persecutes. Let her own heart resolve

The causes of such madness. Thou thyself
Art witness, on the Libyan waves but now
What sudden coil she raised—mixed all the seas
With heaven, upon the storms of Aeolus
Vainly relying, and dared it in thy realm.   *792*
See, too, Troy's matrons goading into crime,
Their ships she hath burnt foully, forcing them,
With minished fleet, upon an unknown shore
To leave their comrades. Those that yet remain—
Let them, I pray thee of thy goodness, spread
Safe sail across the billows; let them reach
Laurentian Tiber, lawful if my suit,
If there the walls by destiny assigned."   *798*
      Then Saturn's son, the lord of the deep sea,
Made answer: "Cytherea, 'tis full meet
Thou trust this realm of mine, that gave thee birth;
And I have earned it: often have I quelled
Such wrath and fury both of sea and sky,
Nor less on land, Xanthus and Simoïs
Attest, hath thine Aeneas been my care.
What time Achilles, the disheartened hosts
Of Troy pursuing, dashed them on their walls,
And many thousands did to death, till groaned
The choked-up rivers, nor could Xanthus find
A passage, and roll out to sea, then I
Seeing Aeneas with brave Peleus' son
Ill-matched alike in strength and aid from heaven,
In a cloud's hollow caught him, though full fain
From their foundation to cast down the walls
Of perjured Troy, that mine own hands had built.   *811*
Now too within me the same purpose holds;
Away with fear! unscathed he shall arrive
The Avernian havens, goal of thy desire;
One only shall there be, thou'lt seek in vain
Upon the flood, one life for many given."
So soothing with his words the goddess' heart
To gladness, the Sire yokes his steeds with gold,
Fastens to their wild mouths the foaming bit,
And, through his hands out-slackening all the reins,
Skims light the sea-top in his azure car.   *819*
Down sink the waves; the swelling water-floor
Beneath his thunderous wheel is levelled smooth;
The clouds fly routed through the vast of air.
Then to attend him came shapes manifold,
Monsters enormous, Glaucus' agèd choir,
Palaemon son of Ino, and the swift

[208]

Tritons, and Phorcus with his whole array;
Thetis upon the left, and Melite,
And maiden Panopea, and Nisaeë,
Spio, Thalia, and Cymodoce.   *826*
Then lo! through Prince Aeneas' tortured soul
Thrills the sweet solace of returning joy;
Quickly he bids each mast be reared, each sail
Stretched on the yardarms. All made taut the sheet
Together, with one accord, now left, now right,
Slackening the canvas; all together turn
And turn again the lofty sail-yard horns;
The winds they wait for, bear the fleet along.
First, before all, leading the dense array,
Was Palinurus, others after him
Bidden to shape their course. Now dewy night
Had well-nigh reached the mid-way goal of heaven;
In slumber calm the crews relaxed their limbs
Beneath the oars, on the hard benches stretched,
When Sleep slid lightly from the stars on high,
Parted the dusky air, and cleft the gloom,
Thee, Palinurus, seeking, and for thee
Fraught with a fatal dream, though innocent.
There on the high stern sat the god, and, like
To Phorbas, pours this utterance from his lips: *842*
"O Palinurus, son of Iasus,
See, of its own will ocean wafts the fleet;
The gales breathe equably; the hour is given
To slumber. Bow the head, and steal from toil
The weary eyes. Myself awhile will take
Thy task upon me." With scarce lifted look,
To him speaks Palinurus: "Bid'st thou me
Mark not the sea's smooth face and tranquil waves?
Put faith in such a monster? Wherefore trust
Aeneas to the false breezes, tempt again
The oft-rued treachery of a smiling sky?"   *851*
Such words he spake, and clutched and clung, nor
        aught
Let go the tiller, and held his upward eyes
Still fixed upon the stars: when lo! the god
O'er either temple shakes a bough besprent
With Lethe-dew, and drugged with Stygian power,
That loosed his swimming eyes, reluctant. Scarce
Had the first stealth of unexpected sleep
Slackened his limbs, when, bending from above,
It hurled him headlong, half the stern torn off,
Rudder and all, into the weltering waves,

With many a cry to friends that could not aid.   *859*
But into empty air the vision's self
Soared on the wing. Nathless the fleet unscathed
Speeds on its journey, and rides undismayed
In Father Neptune's promise. And now it neared
The Siren-crags, found perilous of old,
Whitened with bones of many, while the rocks
With ceaseless surge were booming hoarse afar.
Soon as the Prince perceived his vessel drift
Aimless for lack of helmsman, he himself
Over the midnight wave, with many a groan,
Steered her, sore shaken by his friend's mischance:
"O all too trustful of the smiling face
Of sky and ocean, on an unknown shore,
And naked, Palinurus, thou wilt lie."   *871*

BOOK VI

Weeping he spake, and gave his fleet the rein,
And to Euboean Cumae's shore at length
Glides smoothly in. They turn prows seaward; then
The anchors' tooth 'gan grip the vessels fast;
The round sterns rim the beach. Outleaps amain
The war-host on Hesperia's strand; some search
For seeds of fire hid deep in veins of flint;
Some scour the wild beasts' tangled forest-lairs,
Or point to new-found streams. But good Aeneas
Makes for the hill-top, where aloft sits throned
Apollo, and a cavern vast, the far
Lone haunt of the dread Sibyl, into whom
The Delian bard his mighty mind and soul
Breathes, and unlocks the future. Even now
'Neath Trivia's grove and golden roof they come.   *13*
    Daedalus, flying from Minos' realm, 'tis said,
Dared on swift wings to trust him to the sky,
Upon his uncouth journey floated forth
Toward the chill Bears, and stood light-poised at last
On the Chalcidian hill. Here first to earth
Restored, he dedicated to thy name,
Phoebus, the oarage of his wings, and built
A giant temple. On the doors behold!
The murder of Androgeos; therewithal
The sons of Cecrops, bidden, alas! to pay
For yearly ransom, seven of their sons' lives:
The urn stands, and the lots are drawn. Uptowers
From Ocean, fronting it, the Gnosian land: *23*
Here her fell love o' the bull, Pasiphaë
Mated by cunning, and, that mongrel-birth,
The Minotaur, a twy-formed offspring, stands,
Record of monstrous passion; here was that
Laborious dwelling with the wandering maze,
Inextricable, but that Daedalus,
Pitying the princess' mighty passion, solved
Himself the riddle of its winding paths,
Guiding blind footsteps with a thread. Thou too
In such a work hadst borne a mighty part,
Had grief allowed, O Icarus. Thy fall
Twice had he sought in gold to fashion, twice

[211]

The father's hands dropped. Aye, and still their eyes
O'er all would have been ranging, had not now
Come from his quest Achates, and with him,
Priestess of Phoebus and of Trivia,
Deiphobe, Glaucus' child, who therewithal
Thus hails the king: "Such shows a time like this
Demands not: better were it now to slay
Seven bullocks from the unbroken herd, and ewes
Picked duly of like number." Having thus
Addressed Aeneas—nor were the heroes slack
To do her sacred bidding—the priestess now
Summons the Teucrians into the high fane.   *41*

    The mighty face of the Euboean rock
Is scooped into a cavern, whither lead
A hundred wide ways, and a hundred gates;
Aye, and therefrom as many voices rush,
The answers of the Sibyl. They had gained
The threshold, when the maid exclaims: " 'Tis time
To ask the oracles; lo! the god, the god!"
Before the doors thus speaking, suddenly
Nor countenance, nor hue, nor braided locks
Stayed in one fashion: but her bosom heaves,
Her heart swells wild with frenzy; and more vast
She seems, nor mortal rings her voice, when now
Touched by the nearer breath of deity.
"So slack to vows and prayers," she cries, "so slack,
Trojan Aeneas? for the mighty mouths
Of the awed temple will not ope till then."
So spake she, and was mute. A shudder chill
Ran through the Teucrians' hardy frames, the while
Their king from his heart's deepest pours forth
      prayer.   *55*
"O Phoebus, who the heavy woes of Troy
Hast always pitied, who erst the Dardan shaft
And hand of Paris didst guide against the bulk
Of the son of Aeacus, at thy bidding I
Pierced all those seas that roam round mighty shores,
The far-withdrawn Massylian tribes, and fields
That skirt their quicksands, till at length we grasp
The flying shores of Italy: thus far
Let Troy's ill fate have followed her. Ye too
May justly spare the race of Pergamus,
Gods all and goddesses, to whom Ilium
And the vast Dardan fame was an offence.
And thou most holy seer, who dost foreknow
The future, grant—I do but ask the realm

Owed to my destiny—that Teucria's sons
May rest in Latium with their wandering gods,
And storm-tossed Trojan deities. Then I
To Phoebus and to Trivia will uprear
A shrine of solid marble, and holy days
In name of Phoebus. And thee too awaits
In our new realm a mighty sanctuary.   71
For there thine oracles and mystic dooms,
Spoke to my people, will I set, and choose
Men, and ordain them thine, O gracious one.
Only to leaves commit not thou thy strains,
Lest they fly scattered, sport of whirling winds;
Chant them with thine own lips, I pray." He made
An end of speaking. But the seer, not yet
Patient of Phoebus, in the cavern storms
Immeasurably, if haply from her breast
She may shake off the mighty god; but he
So much the rather plies her raving mouth,
Tames her wild heart, and moulds her to his might.   80
And now the temple's hundred monster-gates
Ope of themselves, and through the air convey
The answers of the Sibyl: "O thou that hast
Outborne at length the sea's vast perils, know
Yet worse on shore await thee. True, the sons
Of Dardanus to Lavinium's realm shall come;
Of this care ease thy bosom; yet shall it not
Rejoice them of their coming. War, grim war,
And Tiber foaming high with blood, I see.   87
Simois and Xanthus and a Dorian camp
There shalt thou lack not; yea, for Latium
Even now a new Achilles hath been found,
Himself too goddess-born. Nor anywhere
Shall Juno from the Teucrians hold her hand,
While, suppliant in thy need through Italy,
What race, what city, shalt thou leave unsued?
Once more is cause of all the Teucrians' woe
An alien bride, once more a foreign bed.
Yield not to ills, but face them boldlier thou,
Even as thy fortune suffers thee. The first
Pathway to safety, little as thou deem'st,
Shall from a Grecian town appear." In such
Words from the shrine doth Cumae's Sibyl chant
Her awful riddles, and echo through the cave,
In darkness shrouding truth; so shakes the reins
Apollo in her raving mouth, and plies
Deep in her breast the goad. Soon as had ebbed

Her frenzy, and the frantic lips were still,
The hero speaks—Aeneas: "No phase of toil
To me, O maid, strange or unlooked for comes.   *104*
All things have I forecast, and in my mind
Traversed ere seen. One boon I beg: since this
Is called the portal of the infernal king,
And the dark pool of Acheron's overflow,
Let me to my dear sire's own presence pass;
Teach thou the way, and ope the sacred gates.
Him I through flames and thousand following darts
Rescued upon these shoulders, and bore safe
From midst the foemen: he, my wayfellow,
Endured with me all seas, all threats of sky
And ocean, weak of body, beyond the lot
And strength of age. Moreover he it was
Charged and implored me with this suppliant suit
Thy threshold to approach. Both son and sire
Pity, I pray thee, of thy grace; for thou
Canst all things, nor for naught hath Hecate
Made thee the mistress of Avernian groves.   *118*
If Orpheus could recall his loved one's shade,
Armed but with Thracian harp and tuneful strings,
If Pollux, dying in turn, redeemed his brother,
Trod and retrod the way so oft—why speak
Of mighty Theseus, of Alcides why?
My lineage also is from Jove in heaven."
So spake he praying, and clasped the altar; then
The seer brake silence: "Sprung from blood of gods,
Trojan Anchises' son, easy the road
Down to Avernus: night and day the door
Of gloomy Dis stands open; but thy steps
Back to retrace, emerge to upper air,
This is the task, the labour this. Some few,
Favoured and loved of Jupiter, or borne
By their own glowing virtue to the sky,
Sons of the gods, attained it. All between
Is forest-clothed, and with black-gliding coil
Cocytus winds about it. But if thou
So yearn'st at heart, if such thy longing, twice
To stem the Stygian pool, twice view the gloom
Of Tartarus; and it please thee to give play
To a mad quest, hear what must first be done.
Hid in a tree's dark shade there lurks a bough,
Gold both in leaf and limber twig, and called
Sacred to nether Juno. All the grove
Hides it, by obscure valleys closed in gloom.   *139*

But none may probe the vaults of earth or ere
He pluck the gold-tressed sapling from the tree.
This to be brought as her peculiar gift
Fair Proserpine ordained. The first torn off,
Fails not a second, gold no less, whose spray
Sprouts of the selfsame ore. So with thine eyes
Search deep, and, duly finding, with thy hand
Pluck it, for freely at a touch 'twill yield,
If thou art called of fate: not, otherwise,
By any force wilt thou prevail to win,
Or with hard steel to tear it. Furthermore
The breathless corse of one that was thy friend
Still lies—alas! thou know'st not—and with death
Taints the whole fleet, while on our threshold here
Thou hoverest, seeking counsel. Him first bear
To his own place, and hide in tomb, and bring
Black cattle in expiation, before all: *153*
So shalt thou see at last the Stygian groves,
And realms unfooted by the quick." She spake,
And with closed lips was silent.
                           But Aeneas
With downcast eyes and gloomy brow strides on,
Quitting the cave, alone with his own heart
Revolving hidden issues. At his side
Goes true Achates, with like load of care
Planting his footsteps. Many a thought they wove
In varying converse—of what lifeless friend
The priestess spake, what corse for burial. So
At length arrived, on the dry beach they see
Misenus, snatched by an untimely death,
Misenus, son of Aeolus, than whom
None more renowned with clarion's clang to rouse
Heroes, and fire the war-god with his blast.   *165*
Great Hector he had served, at Hector's side,
Famous alike for trumpet and for spear,
Would join the fray: whom when Achilles quelled
And robbed of life, he, bravest of the brave,
Had ta'en Aeneas the Dardan for his lord,
Following no meaner destiny. But then,
While with his hollow shell he thrills the main,
Madman, and challenges the gods to match
His music, Triton, if the tale be true,
Seized him, in jealousy, and under sea
Plunged in a moment amid foaming rocks.
So all around they clamoured with loud cries,
And, foremost, good Aeneas. Then with speed

The Sibyl's bidding they dispatch with tears,
A funeral-altar toiling to upbuild
Of heapèd boughs, and rear it to the sky.   *178*
Into an ancient forest forth they fare,
The wild beasts' lofty cover. Down go the pines,
Loud rings the ilex to the smiting axe,
And ash-trees and the splintering heart of oak
Are cleft with wedges: from the hills they roll
Huge mountain-ashes down. Aeneas, no less
Foremost amid such toil, cheers on his friends,
And girds him with like weapons. Then alone
With his sad heart he ponders, gazing o'er
The boundless forest, and thus prays aloud: *186*
"If now that golden branch upon the tree
Might to our eyes in this vast grove appear!
Since all too truly spake the prophetess
Of thee, alas! Misenus." Scarce had he
Uttered the word, when, as it happed, twin doves
Under his very eyes from heaven came flying,
And light on the green sod. The mighty chief,
His mother's birds discerning, prays with joy:
"Oh! be my guides, if any path there be,
And steer your airy course into the grove,
Where the rich bough o'ershades the fertile ground.
And our perplexity forsake not thou,
O goddess-mother." So saying, he stops to mark
What signs they bring, their course bend whither-
        ward.   *198*
They, feeding, still fly forward just so far
As the pursuer's eye might bear in sight.
Then, having gained Avernus' poisonous jaws,
Swiftly they mount, and, gliding through clear air,
Perch both, and settle upon the wished-for tree,
Flashed through whose boughs the gold's contrasting
        gleam.
As mistletoe, when winter chills the woods,
Bursts into new leaf, sown on alien tree,
And, saffron-berried, clips the tapering trunk,
Such was the seeming of that leafy gold
On the dark ilex; so in the light breeze
Rustled the foil. Aeneas instantly
Seizes and rives it from its lingering hold
With hungry clutch, and bears it 'neath the roof
Of the prophetic Sibyl.   *211*
                        Nor less meanwhile
The Teucrians on the shore Misenus wept,

Paying the last dues to the thankless dust.
First, rich with pine-brands, of hewn timber vast,
A pyre they raise, with dark leaves wreathe the sides,
Plant funeral-cypresses in front, above
Deck it with gleaming arms. Some set to heat
Water, and cauldrons heaving on the flame,
And wash the death-cold body, and anoint,
And make loud moaning. Then the wept-for limbs
Upon the couch they lay, and over them
Cast purple robes, the well-known raiment: some,
Sad service, bowed them to the heavy bier,
And, eyes averted, their ancestral wont,
Applied the torch and held. The heaped gifts blaze—
Frankincense, viands, and bowls of streaming oil.   225
When sank the embers, and the flame was stilled,
The remnant of the thirsty dust they drench
With wine, and Corynaeus gathered up,
And in a brazen casket hid, the bones.
He with pure water, too, thrice paced the round
Of comrades, with the light dew sprinkling them
From bough of fruitful olive, and purified
The heroes, and spake out the latest words.
But good Aeneas, for tomb, a mighty mound
Heaps o'er the dead, and his own arms, both oar
And trumpet, 'neath a skyey mount, which now
From him is called Misenus, and preserves
From age to age his everlasting name.   235
   This done, with speed he girds him to fulfil
The Sibyl's bidding: a deep cave there was
With huge gape monstrous, jaggèd, and hemmed in
By the dark mere and forest's gloom, o'er which
Nothing that flies could wing a scathless way,
Such breath from the black jaws outpouring sped
Into the vault of heaven (from whence the Greeks
Have called the place Aornos). And here first
The priestess ranges four black-bodied bulls,
Pours wine upon their brows, and 'twixt the horns
Plucking as first-fruit throws the topmost tuft
Into the sacred flames, calling aloud
On Hecate, queen both in heaven and hell.   247
Others set knives beneath them, and in bowls
Catch the warm blood. Aeneas a black-fleeced lamb,
Unto the mother of the Eumenides
And her great sister, with his own sword strikes,
A barren heifer, O Proserpine, to thee,
Then to the Stygian king inaugurates

Altars by night, and casts upon the fire
Whole carcasses of bulls, pouring fat oil
Upon the blazing entrails. But behold!
Hard upon dawn and sunrise, 'neath their feet
The ground 'gan rumble, and a-quaking fell
The forest-ridges, and through the gloom there
    seemed
Dogs howling, as the goddess drew anigh.
"Hence, hence, unhallowed ones!" the priestess
    shrieks;
"From the whole grove avaunt! and thou, Aeneas,
Set forth upon the road, pluck sword from sheath;
Now need'st thou all thy courage and a stout heart."   *261*
Thus far she spake, and like a fury plunged
Into the cave's mouth: he, no falterer, keeps
Pace with the steps of his advancing guide.

    Gods of the spirit-realm, and voiceless shades,
And Chaos and Phlegethon, vast tracts of night
And silence, grant me, what mine ear hath heard
To utter, and, with your fiat, to unfold
Things whelmed in darkness and the under-world.
    On strode they blindly through the gloom, beneath
The solitary night, through the void halls
And ghostly realms of Dis: as men may walk
The wood-way 'neath a coy moon's grudging light,
When Jupiter with shade hath curtained heaven,
And black night of her colour robs the world.   *272*
Fronting the portal, even in Orcus' jaws,
Grief and avenging Cares have made their bed;
And pale Diseases house, and dolorous Eld,
And Fear and Famine, counsellor of crime,
And loathly Want, shapes terrible to view,
And Death and Travail, and, Death's own brother,
    Sleep,
And the soul's guilty joys, and murderous War
Full on the threshold, and the iron cells
Of the Eumenides, and mad Discord, who
With blood-stained fillet wreaths her snaky locks.   *281*
    Spreads in the midst her boughs and agèd arms
An elm, huge, shadowy, where vain dreams, 'tis said,
Are wont to roost them, under every leaf
Close-clinging: and many a monster-form beside
Of various beasts—Centaurs against the door
Are stalled, and twy-formed Scyllas, and Briareus,
He of the hundred hands, and Lerna's brute
Horribly hissing, Chimaera armed with flames,

Gorgons and Harpies, and the shadowy shape
Three-bodied. Here, in a tremor of sudden fear,
Grasped at his sword Aeneas, and with bare edge
Opposed their coming, and, but for warning word
From his wise comrade that they were but thin
Unbodied lives, 'neath hollow shows of form
Flitting, upon them he would rush, and cleave
Shadows in twain with ineffectual sword.   *294*
    Hence runs a road to the Tartarean waves
Of Acheron leading, where his eddying gulf,
Seething with mud and a wild whirlpool, boils,
Into Cocytus belching all his sand.
These floods and waters a grim ferryman
Guards, of fell squalor, Charon, on whose chin
Lies a thick grizzle, all untrimmed; his eyes
Are orbs of staring fire, and by a knot
Hangs from his shoulders a soiled garb. Himself
Plies with a pole his craft, and tends the sails,
Freighting with dead the dusky barge; now old,
But with the age of godhead hale and green.
Toward him the whole crowd rushing floods the
     bank;
Matrons and men, and great heroic frames
Done with life's service, boys, unwedded girls,
Youths placed on pyre before their father's eyes: *308*
Countless as forest-leaves that fluttering fall
In the first chill of autumn, or as birds
Flock countless shoreward from the weltering deep,
When the chill year, now chasing over-sea,
Drives them to sunny lands. There stood they praying
Each to be first o'erferried, and stretched forth
Their hands with yearning for the further shore.
But the sour boatman takes now these, now those,
And others from the strand thrusts far aloof.
Aeneas, sore startled by the tumult, cries:
"Say, maid, what means this thronging to the stream? *318*
What seek the spirits? or by what law quit these
The brink, skim those the leaden oar-swept tide?"
Briefly to him the aged priestess spake:
"Anchises' son, sure offspring of the gods,
Cocytus' deep pools and the Stygian marsh
Here thou discernest, by whose power the gods
Fear to swear falsely; helpless, tombless all
This crowd, which thou behold'st; yon ferryman
Is Charon; those that cross have found a grave.
But o'er the dread banks and hoarse-sounding flood

Waft them he may not, till their bones have rest.　　*328*
A hundred years about these shores they flit
And wander, then at length, their ban removed
The longed-for pools revisit." Anchises' son
Halted, and stayed his steps, revolving much,
And pitying from his heart their cruel fate.
There—woful forms, and lacking death's last due—
Leucaspis and Orontes he espies,
Chief of the Lycian fleet, whom both, from Troy
Borne over squally seas, the South o'erwhelmed,
Winding in watery shroud both craft and crew.　　*336*
　Lo! there the helmsman Palinurus went,
Who late, star-gazing on their Libyan voyage,
Pitched from the stern had fallen amid the sea:
Whom, when at length the sorrowing face he knew
Through the thick gloom, he first addressed: "What
　　god,
O Palinurus, snatched thee from our sight,
And in mid ocean plunged thee? Tell me who:
For, ne'er till then found faithless, in this one
Presage Apollo fooled my mind, who sang
That scathless over sea thou shouldst arrive
Ausonia's bounds. Is this his promised word?"　　*346*
But he: "Nor Phoebus' tripod failed thee aught,
My chief, Anchises' son, nor any god
Plunged me in ocean: for behold! while I
Clave to the tiller, as my charge was, and steered,
Hurled headlong, I tore off, with mighty force,
And dragged it with me. By the rough waves I swear
No terror seized me for myself so much
As for thy ship, lest now, of tackle shorn,
Dashed from beneath her master, she should fail
Amid such mounting billows. Three wintry nights
Over the boundless ocean-plains the South
With fury drave me: scarce, the fourth dawn, high
On a wave's crest I sighted Italy.　　*357*
By inches I swam shoreward; safety now
Was in my grasp; had not the savage folk,
As heavy with soaked weed my fingers' clutch
Caught at the ruggèd mountain-heads, with sword
Assailed and for a prize misdeemed me. Now
The wave holds, and winds toss me on the beach.
But by the pleasant light and air of heaven,
And by thy sire, I pray thee, by thy hopes
In young Iulus, pluck me from these ills,
O thou unconquered! Either, for thou canst,

Cast earth on me, reseeking Velia's port,
Or, if there be a way, if any way
Thy goddess-mother show thee—for not all
Unwarranted of heaven, methinks, wouldst thou
Stem these vast waters, and the Stygian mere—
Grant to my tears thy hand, and bear me o'er
The billows with thee, that at least in death
I may find quiet resting." Thus he spake,
And thus the prophetess began: "From whence.
O Palinurus, sprang this wild desire?   373
Shalt thou unburied view the Stygian waves,
And the stern river of the Eumenides,
Or tread the bank unbidden? Cease to hope
That heaven's fixed doom can be unbent by prayer:
But, thy hard lot to solace, hear and heed:
For lo! the border townsfolk far and near,
Goaded by heavenly portents, shall appease
Thy dust, and build a tomb, and to the tomb
Pay yearly offerings; and the place shall bear
The name of Palinurus evermore."
These words allayed his pain, and drove the grief
Awhile from his sad bosom; and he takes
Joy in the land that is to bear his name.   383
    So they pursue the path, and near the stream.
But at that point, when from the Stygian wave
The boatman saw them through the silent wood
Moving, and striding toward the bank, he thus
Accosts them, and upbraids withal: "Whoe'er
Thou art, that to our river comest in arms,
Stand, and say why thou comest, and check thy step.
This is the place of shades, Sleep, slumberous Night;
The quick on Stygian barge I may not bear.
Nor was it to my joy that erst I took
And sped Alcides on the watery way,
Nor Theseus and Peirithous, albeit
Both god-begotten and of unconquered strength.   394
He the Tartarean warder sought to enchain
Before the king's own throne, and cowering dragged;
These from the bride-chamber of Dis essayed
His queen to ravish." Whereunto replied
Briefly the priestess of Amphrysus: "Here
Is no such trickery: cease to storm: these arms
Mean not offence: let the huge gatekeeper
With ceaseless baying scare the bloodless ghosts;
Guard Proserpine her uncle's doors from stain:
Lo! here, renowned for goodness as for arms,

Trojan Aeneas to the nether shades
Of Erebus descends, to seek his sire.   404
If thee such goodness moves not to behold,
At least this bough"—the bough which lay within
Her robe disclosing—"canst thou not ignore."
Then ebbed the swelling tide of his heart's wrath,
Nor further spake he. At the awful gift
Wondering, the doom-wand, hid from sight so long,
He turns the dark-blue barge, and nears the shore.
Then other spirits, which on the long thwarts sat,
Thrust forth, he clears the benches, and on board
Takes vast Aeneas; groaned beneath his weight
The seamy craft, and through its chinks let in
The marsh-wave freely. Safe across the stream
Both prince and priestess he unships at last
On grey-green sedges and unsightly mire!   416
    These are the realms huge Cerberus makes ring
With his three-throated baying—a monstrous bulk
Stretched in the cave's mouth fronting them. To him,
Seeing his neck now bristling with its snakes,
A bait the priestess throws, with honey drugged
And medicated meal. His triple maw
With ravenous hunger opening, from her hand
He caught it, and, his monster-length relaxed,
Lies prone, spread huge o'er all the cavern-floor.
The warder sunk in sleep, Aeneas takes
The entrance, and quits swift the water's rim,
Renavigable never.   425
                    Forthwith are heard
Voices of mighty wailing, and the cry
Of infant souls upon the threshold's brink,
Whom, dowerless of sweet life, torn from the breast,
A dark day quelled and plunged in bitter death.
Next them were those by false charge doomed to die:
Not that their places without lot or judge
Are dealt them: Minos, as inquisitor,
Handles the urn, the silent council calls,
And learns the story of their lives and crimes.
And next have place the unhappy souls, who wrought
Their own end, guiltless, and flung life away,
Loathing the sunlight. Ah! how fain were these
Now in the upper air to bide both want
And hardship! Fate forbids: the unlovely swamp
Binds with its sullen wave, while pens them fast
Styx, with her ninefold barrier poured between.   439
Not far from hence, on every side outstretched,

Are shown the Mourning Fields: such name they bear.
Here, whom fell love with cruel wasting gnawed
Close walks conceal, and myrtle-groves embower:
Their pangs even death removes not. There he sees
Phaedra, and Procris, Eriphyle sad,
Showing the wounds her ruthless son had dealt,
Evadne, and Pasiphaë, and with these
Laodamia, and once man, now maid,
Caeneus, by fate to his old shape restored.
And, among these, Phoenician Dido roamed,
Fresh from her wound, within the mighty grove:
Whom when the Trojan hero stood anigh,
And knew, though dim through darkness—as a man
Sees when the month is young, or thinks he sees,
The moon through clouds arising—the tears fell,
And with sweet words of love he greeted her: *455*
"Unhappy Dido, was the tale then true,
Brought to mine ears, that thou wert quenched in
 death,
And with the sword hadst sought the end of all?
Alas! was I thy doomsman? By the stars
I swear, and by the gods above, and by
Whate'er is sacred in the under-world,
Right loth, O queen, was I to quit thy shore.
But heaven's decrees, which now to walk the shades,
Tracts rough with squalor, and abysmal night,
Compel, then drave me with their high behests:
Nor could I think that I should bring thee dole
So deep by my departure: stay thy step:
Withdraw not from my gaze: whom fliest thou?—this
Of all my greetings doomed to be the last!" *466*
Aeneas with such words 'mid welling tears
Her fiery soul, fierce-glancing, sought to soothe.
She held her looks aloof, eyes fixed on earth,
And at his proffered speech changed face no more
Than hard flint stood she, or Marpesian rock.
At length she whirled away, and frowning sought
The green gloom, where Sychaeus her first lord
Echoes her grief, and gives her love for love.
Nathless Aeneas, stunned by her sad fate,
Follows with pitying tears her steps afar. *476*
 From hence he girds him to the appointed path.
And now the utmost fields they gain, where those
War-famous dwell apart. Here Tydeus, here
Parthenopaeus meets him, famed in arms,
And the pale spectre of Adrastus; here,

Much wept by those on earth, and fallen in war,
The Dardan chiefs, whom all in long array
He groaned beholding—Glaucus, Medon, there,
Thersilochus, Antenor's children three,
And Polyphetes, Ceres' priest, and, yet
Grasping the car, Idaeus, yet his arms.   *485*
Thronging, the souls press round him, right and left;
Nor does one look suffice them: still they love
To linger, pace beside him, and inquire
His cause of coming. But the Danaan lords,
And Agamemnon's cohorts, when they spied
The hero's armour gleaming through the shade,
Quake with vast fear: some, turning, fled, as erst
They sought the ships; some lift a meagre voice:
The would-be war-cry mocks their gaping mouths.   *493*
    Aye, and the son of Priam here he saw,
Deiphobus—sore mangled all his frame,
Face and both hands rent cruelly, his ears
From the maimed temples shorn, and nostrils lopped
With shameful butchery. Nay, scarce knew he him,
Cowering and cloaking his rough chastisement,
Then in the oft-heard accents hailed him first:
"Deiphobus, thou warrior dread, and sprung
From Teucer's lofty line, who listed, say,
To wreak such cruel vengeance, or who thus
Had power upon thee? To mine ears it came
On that last night of all, that, wearied out
With endless slaughter of Pelasgians, thou
Hadst on an heap of mingled carnage fallen.   *504*
Then I myself on the Rhoetean shore
Upreared an empty tomb, and with loud voice
Thrice called upon thy spirit: thy name and arms
Still mark the spot: thee, friend, I could not see,
Nor lay, ere parting, in our native earth."
Whereto the son of Priam: "In naught hast thou
Failed me, O friend, but to Deiphobus
And to the dead man's shade hast quitted all.
But fate and the pernicious guilt of that
Laconian woman plunged me in this woe:
These tokens are by her bequeathed. For how
That latest night in treacherous joys we spent
Thou knowest, must even remember all too well.   *514*
When o'er the lofty citadel of Troy
Leapt at a bound the doom-fraught horse, and bare
Armed soldiery within its labouring womb,
She feigned a solemn dance, and, leading round

The Phrygian dames with Bacchic revelling-cries,
Held in their midst herself a mighty torch,
And called the Danai from the fortress-height.
Then I with trouble spent, weighed down with sleep,
Was holden of our ill-starred bridal bower,
Lying with deep sweet slumber overwhelmed,
Deep as the calm of death. My peerless wife
Meanwhile all arms from out the palace moves—
The true sword first from 'neath my pillow filched—
Calls Menelaus in, throws wide the door,
Hoping forsooth that to her lover this
Would prove a mighty boon, and so be quenched
The fame of old offences. Why delay?
They burst into my chamber: joins their crew,
Prompter of crimes, the son of Aeolus.
Ye gods, like measure to the Greeks repay,
If with pure lips revenge I claim. But come,
Tell me in turn what chance brings hither thee,
A living man: by ocean-wanderings led,
Or at the hest of heaven? What fortune, say,
Spurs thee to seek the sad, unsunned abodes,
Regions of Chaos?" In this interchange
Of talk, Aurora in her rosy car
Had crossed the mid pole on her path through
    heaven;   *536*
And haply all the allotted time they thus
Had wasted, but the Sibyl at his side
Spake a brief warning word: "Night comes apace,
Aeneas, and we with weeping wear the hours.
This is the spot where splits the road in twain:
The right leads to the giant walls of Dis,
Our way to Elysium: but the left wreaks doom
On sinners, and to guilty Tartarus sends."
Deiphobus made answer: "Be not wroth,
Great priestess; I will hence, fill up the tale,
To darkness get me back. Our glory, go,
Go, entertain a happier fate." Thus far
He spake, and, speaking, turned his steps away.   *547*
   Aeneas looks swiftly back, and 'neath a rock
Sees leftward a wide fort, with triple wall
Girded: and round it a fierce torrent goes
Of billowy fire, Tartarean Phlegethon,
Who hurls the rocks in thunder: full in front
A vast gate, columns of solid adamant!
So that no might of man, nay, not the hosts
Of heaven avail to shatter it in war.

An iron tower stands skyward, where enthroned,
Girt with a gory robe, Tisiphone
Guards sleeplessly the threshold, night and day. *556*
Hence groans are heard, and sound of cruel stripes
And clank of iron, and trailing chains. Aeneas
Stopped, and stood rooted, by the din dismayed.
"What shapes of crime are here, O maiden, say;
With what pains visited? What cry so swells
To heaven?" Then thus the prophetess began:
"Famed Teucrian leader, no pure foot may tread
The accursèd floor: but Hecate herself,
What time she set me o'er the Avernian groves,
Taught me the punishments of heaven, and led
Through all its precincts. Here—an iron reign—
Rules Gnosian Rhadamanthus, of dark crimes
Both punisher and judge, from guilty lips
Extorting whatso' any upon earth,
Exulting in the empty cheat, hath left
Of sins inexpiate till the hour of death. *569*
Straightway Tisiphone, armed with vengeful scourge,
Swinges and spurns the guilty, in her left
Brandishing snakes, and summoning the ranks
Of her fell sisters; then the awful gates
Open at last upon harsh-grinding hinge.
Seest thou what warder sits before the door?
What grim shape guards the threshold? But within,
Monster of fifty throats black-yawning, keeps
Ward a yet fiercer Hydra. Therewithal
Lo! Tartarus' self, that opes sheer down, and strikes
Into the nether darkness, twice so far
As to Olympus' skyey top and heaven
The eye scans upward. Here that ancient brood
Of earth, the Titan children, where the bolt
Felled them, lie wallowing in the deep abyss. *581*
Here too beheld I, bodies of vast bulk,
The twin sons of Aloëus, who essayed
With rude hands to tear ope the mighty heaven,
And hurl Jove downward from his throne on high.
Aye, and I saw Salmoneus suffering still
The cruel doom that fell while aping yet
Jove's fire and thunders of Olympus: he,
Drawn by four horses, and with waving torch,
Through the Greek tribes and 'midst of Elis town
In triumph rode and claimed the rank of gods,
Madman! the clouds' incomparable bolt
With brass to mock and tramp of hoofèd steeds! *591*

But through thick clouds the Sire Omnipotent
Let loose a shaft—no brand or smoky glare
Of pine-torch he—that with its mighty wind
Down drave him headlong: there too Tityos,
Nursling of Earth, all-mother, might be seen,
Whose bulk o'er nine whole acres stretched, the while
A crook-beak'd monstrous vulture, gnawing still
The imperishable liver and entrails rife
With anguish, digs for dainties, housing deep
Within his bosom, and no respite gives
To the requickened fibres. Why tell o'er
The Lapithae, Ixion, Peirithous,
On whom a black crag, ever like to slip,
Frowns and seems falling? the high festal couch
Shines golden-propped; the feast before their eyes
Is spread with royal splendour; hard at hand
The eldest of the Furies, couched, forbids
Their fingers touch the board, and up she starts
With torch high-lifted and loud-thundering mouth.   *607*
Those who their brethren loathed while life endured,
Or smote a parent, or for client knit
The mesh of fraud, or over treasures found
Brooded alone, nor meted to their kin—
The mightiest number these—or who were slain
For loves adulterous, or to rebel arms
Clave, and feared not with masters to break faith,
Prisoned, await their doom. Seek not to learn
What doom, what phase or fate, hath whelmed them.
    Some
Roll a vast stone, or racked on wheel-spokes hang;
Sits hapless Theseus and for ay will sit;
And Phlegyas, wretchedest of men, warns all,
And with loud voice bears witness through the
    shades;   *619*
'Be taught, learn justice, and spurn not the gods.'
One sold for gain his country, on her neck
Planted a mighty tyrant, for a bribe
Made laws and unmade; one his daughter's bed
Assailed, banned nuptials; all some monstrous guilt
Have dared, and of their daring reaped the joy.
Not though a hundred tongues, a hundred mouths
Were mine, a voice of iron, would these avail
To sum in gross and single all the crimes,
No, nor their penalties rehearse by name."   *627*
    So Phoebus' agèd priestess, and anon
"Up! seize the path, fulfil the attempted task,

Speed we our steps," she cried; "I see the walls
Reared by the Cyclops' forges, and the gate,
With arch confronting, where they bid us lay
The appointed tribute." She had said, and through
Dim ways they, striding side by side, snatch up
The intervening space, and near the doors.
Aeneas then takes the entrance, on his limbs
Sprinkles fresh water, and makes fast the bough
Full in the gateway. This at last performed,
The goddess' dues accomplished, they arrived
The happy region and green pleasaunces
Of the blest woodlands, the abode of joy.   *639*
An ampler ether with purpureal light
Clothes here the plain; another sun than ours,
And other stars they know. Some ply their limbs
Upon the grassy wrestling-ground, and strive
In sport, and grapple on the tawny sand;
Some, footing, beat the dance, and chant the lay.
Here too the Thracian priest, with trailing robe,
Makes eloquent the seven divided notes
To match their measures, and, with fingers now,
And now with comb of ivory, strikes them. Here
Are Teucer's ancient stock, a glorious line,
The high-souled heroes born in happier years,
Ilus, Assaracus, and Dardanus,
Founder of Troy. He marvels to behold
Their arms and ghostly chariots from afar.   *651*
The spears stand fixed in earth; their steeds, unyoked,
Roam grazing o'er the plain. What pride had each,
Alive, in arms and chariot, or what pains
To pasture his sleek steeds, the same no less
Attends them still, now hid beneath the earth.
Lo! some he sees to right hand and to left
Feasting along the greensward, or in choir
Chanting a joyous paean, 'mid a grove
Of perfumed bay, whence risen Eridanus
Rolls wide through forests of the upper world.
Here is the band of those who suffered wounds,
Fighting for country, or, while life remained,
Were priests and pure, or holy bards that spake
Things worthy Phoebus, or who sweetened life
With new-found arts, earning by service wrought
Of some to be remembered—these are all
With snow-white fillet bound about the brow.   *665*
Whom, pouring round, the Sibyl thus addressed,
Musaeus before all, for midmost he

Of that vast multitude their upward gaze
O'ertops with towering shoulders: "Happy shades,
And thou, of bards the best, what region, say,
What haunt, now holds Anchises? for his sake
Have we come hither, and crossed the mighty floods
Of Erebus." To her the hero thus
Brief answer made: "No fixed abode is here;
In shadowy groves we dwell, and make our home
The slope of banks, or freshet-quickened mead;
But, tends your heart's wish thither, mount this ridge:
Soon will I set you on an easy track."
He spake and strode before, and from above
Shows them the shining levels; then they quit
The mountain-summits.   678
              Prince Anchises now
Deep in a green dell lay with busy thought
The souls there pent surveying, thence to pass
Up to the light of heaven, and, as it chanced,
Was telling o'er the tale of all his kin,
The well-loved offspring of his seed to be,
Their fates, their fortunes, characters, and deeds.
But when advancing towards him o'er the sward
He saw Aeneas, both eager palms he stretched,
And his cheeks ran with tears, and from his lips
This utterance fell: "And art thou come at last,
And has the love long looked for by thy sire
Conquered the toilsome road? May I behold
Thy face, my son, and hear the well-known voice
And answer? So indeed with pondering heart
I deemed that it would be, counting the days;
Nor did my longing cheat me. O'er what lands,
What vast seas, art thou borne to my embrace,
Tossed by what perils, O my son! What fears
Had I lest Libya's realm should prove thy bane!"   694
But he: "It was thy mournful shade, my sire,
Aye thine, so oft appearing, drave me toward
These portals. Our ships ride the Tuscan main.
Give, father, give me thy right hand to clasp,
Nor from my arms withdraw thee." Thus he spake,
Bathing his face, the while, with floods of tears.
Thrice, as he stood, his arms he sought to cast
About his neck; and thrice the baffled hands
Closed upon nothing, and a form that fled,
Like to light breezes, one with wingèd sleep.   702
    Meanwhile Aeneas within the vale's recess
Spies a sequestered grove, wood-whispering brakes,

And therewith Lethe river, that flows by
The dwellings of repose. Here, round about,
Nations and peoples without number flew;
Even as in cloudless summer, when the bees
Settling on meadow-flowers, now this, now that,
Stream o'er the milk-white lilies, all the plain
Hums with their buzzing. At the sudden sight
Aeneas starts, and witless asks the cause,
And what those floods afar, and who be they
That throng the banks in multitude so vast.
Then Prince Anchises: "Souls, to whom are owed
By fate new bodies; they by Lethe's stream
Drink heedless draughts of long forgetfulness.   715
These to tell o'er and show thee face to face
Long have I yearned, and count my seed to be,
That thou the rather may'st my joy partake
In Italy new-found." "And must we deem,
Some spirits, father, heavenward mount from hence,
And to their sluggish bodies back return?
Holds them so fond a longing for the light,
Unhappy souls?" "I will even tell thee, son,"
Replies Anchises, "nor prolong thy doubt,"
And all in order point by point reveals.   723
    "Know first that heaven, the earth, the watery
        plains,
The moon's bright orb, and Titan's starry sphere—
These doth a spirit inly feed; a mind,
Its limbs pervading, stirs the whole mass through,
And with the vast frame mingles. Hence arise
Mankind, and beastkind, wingèd life, and what
The sea bears monstrous 'neath his marble floor.
Of fiery vigour, heavenly source, those germs,
Save as impaired by flesh corruptible,
Dulled with frames earthy, and limbs prone to
        death.
Hence they desire, and fear, and grieve, and joy,
Nor light of heaven can they discern, shut fast
In the blind darkness of their prison-house.   734
Nay, nor when life with its last beam departs,
Doth every ill, or all the body's plagues,
Ah! hapless, leave them wholly; many a blot
Must, long ingrained there, cling in wondrous wise.
Therefore, by sorrow schooled, of their old ills
They pay the punishment: some hang exposed
To the void winds; some have the dye of guilt
Purged in vast whirlpool, or burnt out with fire.

Each his own weird we suffer—and then are sent
To range Elysium, and, some few, possess
Those happy fields—suffer, till lapse of time,
Now run full circle, shall eradicate
Each inbred blemish, and leave naught behind
But sense aethereal and pure spirit-fire.   747
These, having whirled a thousand years away,
Are in a vast throng summoned all by God
To Lethe's stream, that, memory lost, they may
Heaven's vault revisit, and a wish beget
Into the body to return once more."
    Anchises ceased, and drawing thence his son
And eke the Sibyl into the mid press
And murmuring throng, takes stand upon a mound
Whence in long line he might peruse them all,
Full face, and learn their features, as they came.   755
    "Come now, the Dardan offspring, and their fame
Hereafter following, from Italian stock
What seed awaits thee, spirits of renown,
Heirs of our name, I will unfold in words,
Thy fortunes teach thee. Yonder, whom thou seest,
A youth, and leaning on a headless spear,
Nearest to light hath drawn a place; he first
From the mixed strain of Italy shall rise
Into the air of heaven, an Alban name,
Silvius, thy youngest offspring, whom, late-born,
Child of old age, thy wife Lavinia
Shall in the forest rear to be a king
And sire of kings, from whom our race shall rule
In Alba Longa. Procas next to him,
Glory of Trojan race, and Capys too,
And Numitor, and, second of thy name,
Silvius Aeneas, excellent alike
In goodness and in arms, if ever he
Come to his Alban kingdom. Lo! what men!
What might, see, in their bearing! and their brows
With civic oak o'ershadowed! These for thee
Nomentum, Gabii, and Fidenae's town,
These towered Collatium on the hills shall rear,
Pometia, and the fort of Inuus,
Bola, and Cora. Those shall then be names,
Now nameless lands. Aye, and the son of Mars
Shall join him to his grandsire—Romulus,
Reared by his mother Ilia from thy blood,
Assaracus. Seest how the twin plumes stand
Upon his crest, and how his sire even now

By his own token marks him for a god?   *780*
Lo! 'neath his auspices yon glorious Rome
Shall bound, my son, her empire with the world,
Her pride with heaven, and with encircling wall
Clasp to her single heart the sevenfold hills,
Blest in a breed of heroes: even as when
The Berecyntian mother in her car
Rides through the Phrygian cities, turret-crowned,
Glad in her brood of godhead, as she clasps
A hundred children's children, dwellers all
In heaven, and tenants of the heights above.
Both eyes turn hither now, this race behold,
Thine own, the Romans. Here is Caesar, here
The whole line of Iulus, that shall pass
One day beneath the mighty pole of heaven.   *790*
This, this the man so oft foretold to thee,
Caesar Augustus, a god's son, who shall
The golden age rebuild through Latian fields
Once ruled by Saturn, and push far his sway
O'er Garamantians and the tribes of Ind,
A land that lies beyond the stars, beyond
The year's path and the sun's, where, prop of heaven,
Atlas upon his shoulder turns the pole,
Studded with burning constellations. See!
Even now, against his coming, Caspian realms
At the gods' omens shudder; aye, and plains
Maeotic and the mouths of sevenfold Nile
Quake and are troubled. Not Alcides even
Traversed so much of earth, I trow, albeit
The brazen-footed hind he pierced, and stilled
The Erymanthian groves, and with his bow
Affrighted Lerna; nor who steers his car
With reins of vine-leaf, Liber, as he guides
From Nysa's lofty crest his tiger-team.   *805*
And still by prowess to spread wide our power
Doubt we, and doth fear hinder us to tread
Ausonia's land? But who is he afar
With olive-boughs conspicuous, in his hand
Vessels of sacrifice? I recognize
The locks and hoar beard of the Roman king,
Who shall the rising city base on law,
From lowly Cures and a land of need
Launched on a mighty empire. Next in turn
Comes Tullus, who shall break his country's peace,
And stir ease-sunken warriors to the fray,
And ranks disused to triumphs; and hard on him

Ancus, o'erboastful, and too much even now
Caught by the breath of the vain multitude.   *816*
Wouldst see the Tarquin kings too, the proud soul
Of Brutus the avenger, and the rods
Of power retrieved? He first, with consul's sway,
Shall the stern axes wield, and his own sons,
New strife upstirring, for fair freedom's sake,
Bid to their doom, unhappy one! Howe'er
Censured in after time, his country's love
And boundless thirst for honour shall prevail.
The Decii and the Drusi too behold
Far off, Torquatus cruel with his axe,
Camillus bringing home the standards. Those
Whom yonder glittering in like arms thou seest,
Of one heart now and while in darkness penned,
Let but their eyes attain the light, alas!
Each against each, what wars will they provoke,
What stricken fields and carnage! From the Alps'
Heaped barriers and Monoecus' citadel
The sire descending, while his daughter's lord
Confronts him with the armies of the East!   *831*
Make not a home within your hearts, my sons,
For strifes so cruel, nor the broad thews she bred
Bend at your country's bosom. And thou first
Forbear, who from Olympus dost derive;
Fling from thine hand the weapons, O my blood!
He yonder to the Capitol on high
Shall drive his victor chariot, triumphing
O'er Corinth, for Achaean slaughter famed.
He Argos and Mycenae shall uproot,
City of Agamemnon, and the heir
Of Aeacus himself, from war-renowned
Achilles sprung, his ancestors of Troy
Avenging and Minerva's outraged shrine.   *840*
Who thee, great Cato, would to silence leave,
Or thee, O Cossus? who the Gracchan clan,
Or the two Scipios, thunderbolts of war,
The bane of Libya, or Fabricius
Puissant in poverty, or, Serranus, thee,
Sowing amid the furrow? I am spent,
And whither whirl ye me, O Fabii?
Thou art that Maximus, our mightiest, who
Alone by loitering dost the State restore.
Others the breathing brass shall softlier mould,
I doubt not, draw the lineaments of life
From marble, at the bar plead better, trace

[233]

With rod the courses of the sky, or tell
The rise of stars: remember, Roman, thou,
To rule the nations as their master: these
Thine arts shall be, to engraft the law of peace,
Forbear the conquered, and war down the proud."   *853*
  So Prince Anchises in their wondering ears
Spake, and yet further: "How Marcellus strides,
Look you, conspicuous with the splendid spoils,
Triumphant, and o'ertowering all men! he
Shall stay Rome's empire, when invasion's storm
Beats fiercely, ride the Carthaginian down,
Aye, and the rebel Gaul, and dedicate
To Sire Quirinus the thrice-taken spoils."
And here Aeneas, for at his side he saw
A youth of peerless form in radiant arms
Pacing, but with unjoyful brow, and glance
Dejected: "Who is he, my sire, who thus
Attends the hero as he steps? A son,
Or later offspring of his mighty race?   *864*
What buzzing crowds about them! his own mould
How mighty! but black night around his head
With harsh gloom hovers." Prince Anchises then
With brimming tears began: "Seek not, my son,
To know thy kin's vast sorrow; him to earth
Fate shall but show, nor grant a longer stay.
Too potent in your eyes, O gods, had seemed
The Roman stock, were such gifts given to keep.
What wail of heroes shall that field of Mars
Waft to his mighty city! what funeral-train
Shalt thou behold, O Tiber, as thy stream
Flows by the new-made tomb! No boy e'er bred
Of Ilian race shall to such height of hope
Uplift his Latian sires, nor e'er the soil
Of Romulus so boast her of a son.   *877*
Mourn for his goodness, for his old-world faith,
His hand in war unconquered! Man to man,
None could have grappled him unscathed, on foot
Strode he against the foeman, or with spur
Goaded the red flanks of his foaming steed.
O boy, our sorrow, if any way thou couldst
Burst the harsh bonds that doom thee, thou shalt be
Marcellus. Bring me lilies with full hands,
The bright flowers let me strew, these gifts at least
Heap o'er his shade, and the vain tribute pay."   *885*
  So here and there, through the whole realm of mist,
In its broad fields they roam, surveying all.

And when Anchises had from end to end
Guided his son, and fired his soul with love
Of future fame, thereafter he makes known
What wars must next be waged, and teaches him
Of tribes Laurentian, and Latinus' town,
And how to shun or suffer every toil.   *892*
There are twin gates of Sleep, whereof the one
Of horn is rumoured, and real spirits thereby
Win easy outlet; and one finished fair
Of gleaming ivory, but false dreams are thence
Sent by the Manes to the world above.
There with these words Anchises, following forth
His son and eke the Sibyl, sees them pass
Out at the ivory gate: the hero speeds
Fleetward, returning to his friends, then steers
Straight for Caieta's port along the shore;
The prows drop anchor; the sterns press the beach.   *901*

BOOK VII

Thou too, Caieta, dying, a deathless fame,
Nurse of Aeneas, to our shores hast given;
And still thy glory guards thy place of rest,
And the name marks, if such renown be aught,
Thy bones in great Hesperia. But, the rites
Of death paid duly, and a funeral mound
Reared, good Aeneas, now the deep was stilled,
Sails on his journey, and leaves port behind.   7
The gales breathe on into the night; the moon
White-orbed their course denies not; all the deep
Glitters beneath her quivering beam. From hence
Next skirted are the shores of Circe's land,
Where the rich daughter of the Sun makes ring
With ceaseless singing her unfooted groves,
And in proud hall burns odorous cedar-wood
For light in darkness, with shrill-whirring comb
Crossing the subtle web. From hence are heard
The growls and wrath of lions, against their chains
Rebellious, roaring late into the night,
And bristly swine, and bears within their pens
Raging, and howling of huge wolfish forms,
Whom Circe, goddess fell, with drugs of power,
Stripped of man's likeness, had arrayed in hides
And features bestial. Which so monstrous change
Lest the good Trojans suffer, into port
Once wafted, or draw nigh the dreadful shore,
With favouring breezes Neptune filled their sails,
Sped flying, and bore them past the seething shoals.   24
   Now 'gan the sea with ruddy beams to blush,
And in high heaven the dawn on roseate car
Shone saffron-tinted, when down dropped the breeze,
And every breath of wind sank suddenly,
And on the slow smooth surface toil their oars.
Thereat Aeneas from out the deep descries
A mighty grove before him; cleaving it,
Lo! Tiber's pleasant stream in hurrying swirls,
And yellow with much sand, bursts forth to sea.
Around, above, were birds of various plume,
Haunters of bank and river-bed, that charmed
The air with song, and fluttered through the grove.

[236]

He bids the crew shift course, and shoreward steer,
And, blithe of heart, enters the shady stream.   *36*
   Now aid me, Erato; what kings had sway,
What exploits marked the time, how stood the weal
Of ancient Latium, when the outland host
First beached their galleys on Ausonia's shore,
I will unfold, and of the opening strife
Recall the prelude. Do thou teach thy bard,
Thou goddess. I will tell of grisly wars,
Tell of embattled hosts, kings to their death
By fury driven, and the Tyrrhenian ranks,
And all Hesperia gathered under arms.
A mightier roll of exploit opens up
Before me, and a mightier task I try.   *44*
   O'er fields and cities lulled in lasting peace
Reigned King Latinus yet, now full of years;
Son he to Faunus and Laurentum's nymph
Marica, saith the legend. Faunus' sire
Was Picus; from thy loins, O Saturn, he
Claims lineage; of his blood first founder thou.
Son and male heir the king had none, cut off
By doom of heaven in youth's first dawn. His home
And stately palace one sole daughter kept,
Now ripe for husband, of full age to wed.
From Latium's breadth, Ausonia's utmost bounds,
Came many a wooer; before all who came,
Turnus the goodliest, mighty by descent
From sires and grandsires, whom as son to clasp
The royal consort yearned with keen desire:
But heaven with many a fearful sign forbad.   *58*
There was a laurel in the secluded depth
Midmost the palace-court, of sacred leaf,
And cherished many a year with awe, which King
Latinus, finding, as he laid, folk say,
The citadel's foundation, had himself
To Phoebus dedicated, and from thence
Gave to his settlers their Laurentian name.
Upon its topmost point a cloud of bees,
Wondrous to tell, with mighty buzzing borne
Across the clear air, settled, foot with foot
Linked fast together, and from the leafy bough
Hung there, a sudden swarm. Forthwith the seer:
"A foreign hero I descry," quoth he,
"Hither approaching, and a host that seek
The selfsame quarter by the selfsame way,
And lord it in the topmost citadel."   *70*

[237]

Moreover, while the altar with pure torch
She kindles, and beside her father stands,
The maid Lavinia in her flowing locks,
O horror! seemed to catch the flame, and all
Her head-gear to let burn with crackling fire—
Ablaze her queenly tresses, and ablaze
The jewelled splendour of her coronal—
Till, wrapped in a dun glare of smoky light,
She spread the fire-god all the palace through.
Fearful in sooth and wondrous to behold
That sight was rumoured: for herself, they sang,
Should be renowned in fortune and in fame;
But to her folk it boded mighty war.   *80*
Vexed by such portents, to the oracle
Of Faunus, his prophetic sire, the king
Betakes him, and consults the grove 'neath high
Albunea, that, of woods the mightiest,
Rings with her haunted well, and through the gloom
Breathes forth a deadly vapour. Hence the tribes
Of Italy and all the Oenotrian land
In doubt seek answers. Hither when the priest
His gifts hath borne, on fleeces of slain sheep
Stretched him 'neath hush of night, and sought
        repose,
Full many a phantom flitting he discerns
In wondrous wise, and divers voices hears,
Enjoys communion with the gods, and holds
Converse with Acheron in Avernus' depth.   *91*
Here King Latinus, too, then suing himself
For answers, with a hundred woolly sheep
Did sacrifice, and propped upon their hides
And outspread fells was lying, when suddenly
A voice gave utterance from the forest-depth:
"Seek not in Latin wedlock to unite
Thy daughter, O mine offspring, nor put faith
In bridal bowers made ready; sons from far
Approach, whose blood must bear our name to
        heaven,
And whose posterity, where the circling sun
Views either ocean, shall the whole world see
Move 'neath their feet obedient." Such response
Of his sire Faunus, and such warning given
Beneath the hush of night, within his lips
Latinus locks not; but Fame flitting wide
Had through the Ausonian cities borne the tale,
When now the children of Laomedon

Made fast their galleys to the grassy bank.   *106*
   Aeneas and his chief captains, with fair-faced
Iulus, stretch their limbs beneath the boughs
Of a tall tree, and set the banquet on,
And 'neath the viands along the sward lay cakes
Of sacrificial meal—great Jupiter
So bade them—and with country fruits pile high
The wheaten floor. All else, it chanced, consumed,
When, driven by lack of food, they turned to munch
The thin flour-fare, with hand and venturous teeth
Invade the circle of the fateful crust,
Nor from the out-pressed squares refrain them; "Ha!
Eat we our tables too?" Iulus cries
Jesting, and adds no more. That utterance heard
First set a term to trouble; and at once
Catching it, as it left the lip, his sire
Checked him, astounded at the sign from heaven.   *119*
Then, "Hail, O land, from destiny my due,
And ye, Troy's faithful hearth-gods," he exclaimed,
"Here is our home, and this our country; yea,
My sire Anchises—I recall it now—
Bequeathed me these dark words of destiny:
'When wafted to an unknown shore, my son,
Hunger compels thee, as food fails, to eat
Thy tables, then remember, look to find
A home, way-wearied; thy first dwellings then
Found, and entrench them with a rampart.' This,
This was that hunger that till last remained,
To mark destruction's utmost. Wherefore come,
Blithely explore we, with first ray of dawn,
What is this place, or what folk dwell therein,
And where the nation's city, in divers ways
Forth faring from the harbour. Now to Jove
Bowls of libation pour ye, and with prayers
Call on my sire Anchises, and set fresh
The wine-cup on the board." So saying he binds
With leafy branch his temples, and adores
The Genius of the spot, and, first of gods,
Earth, and the nymphs and streams unknown as yet:
Then Night too, and the rising Signs of Night,
And Ida's Jove invokes, and in due course
The Phrygian Mother, and his parents twain
In heaven and Erebus. Then from the height
The Almighty Sire thrice thundered clear, and shook
And from the sky with his own hand displayed
A cloud resplendent with bright shafts of gold.   *143*

[239]

Here through the Trojan ranks swift rumour spreads,
The day has come their destined walls to found.
Eagerly they renew the feast, and cheered
By the great sign from heaven, set on the bowls,
And crown the wine-cups. Soon as next day's dawn
'Gan earth with light to sprinkle, scattering wide,
They explore the Nation's city, bounds, and coast;
These are the waters of Numicius' fount,
This Tiber stream; here the brave Latins dwell.   *151*
Then chose Anchises' son from every rank
A hundred envoys, bidding them repair
To the king's stately ramparts, all decked out
With boughs of Pallas, bear the hero gifts,
And for the Teucrians claim his clemency.
They tarry not, but at his bidding speed,
Borne with swift strides along. Himself marks out
The ramparts with low trench, prepares a site,
And the first dwelling camp-wise girds about
There on the shore, with battlements and mound.   *159*
And now the warriors, all their journey done,
Beheld the Latin towers and roofs arise,
And to the wall draw near. Before the town
Boys, see, and youths in manhood's opening bloom,
Ply horsemanship, and tame amid the dust
Their chariot-teams, or stretch the eager bow,
Or the tough javelin hurl with strength of arm,
Or challenge to the race and boxing bout;
When, spurring forward, lo! a messenger,
Who to the agèd monarch's ear brings word
Of mighty men in uncouth garb at hand.
Into the palace he bids summon them,
And midmost sits on his ancestral throne.   *169*
The stately pile, gigantic, reared aloft
On hundred columns in the city's top,
Once palace of Laurentian Picus, stood,
Awful with groves and olden sanctity.
Here 'twas auspicious that kings first receive
The sceptre, and uplift the rods of power.
This temple was their senate-house, and this
Their holy feast-hall: here the elders wont,
After ram slain, at the long boards to sit.
Aye, and the forms of their forefathers, ranged
A-row of ancient cedar, Italus,
Father Sabinus, planter of the vine,
In semblance holding still a curvèd hook,
And hoary-headed Saturn, and the shape

Of two-faced Janus, in the entry stood,
And other kings primaeval, and who else
Fighting for country had borne wounds in war.   *182*
And on the sacred doors great store of arms,
As captive chariots, curvèd axes, hung,
And helmet-crests, and massy bars of gates,
Javelins, and shields, and beaks from vessels torn.
Himself too, with Quirinal augur-staff,
And scanty toga girt, was seated there,
And in his left hand held the sacred shield,
Picus, of steeds the tamer, whom his bride
Circe, love-maddened, smote with golden rod,
With drugs transformed into a bird, and flecked
His wings with colours. Such the shrine wherein
Latinus, sitting on his father's seat,
Summoned the Teucrians to his presence-hall,
And hailed them, entered, with these words of peace: *194*
"O sons of Dardanus—for not to us
Unknown your race and city, and we have heard
Of your sea-faring hither—what seek ye? say
What cause, what need, hath borne your barks so far
O'er the blue billows to Ausonia's strand?
Whether track lost, or tempest-driven—such hap
As sailors suffer oft on the high sea—
Ye have passed between our river banks, and safe
In haven ride, shun not our welcoming,
And know the Latins are of Saturn's seed,
A race made righteous by no bond of law,
But of their own free will refraining them,
And by the fashion of their ancient god.   *204*
And I indeed, though dim with years the tale,
Still mind me of the Auruncan elders saying
How from these fields sprang Dardanus, from hence
To Phrygian Ida's cities won his way,
And Thracian Samos, now named Samothrace.
Hence from the Tuscan house of Corythus
Forth fared the hero: now upon a throne
In the gold palace of the starry sky
He sits, and swells the altar-roll of heaven."   *211*
   He spake, and Ilioneus took up the word:
"King, peerless son of Faunus, nor wave driven
Hath louring storm compelled us to your coast,
Nor star or shore from the right course beguiled:
Of purpose sail we all with willing hearts
To this your city, outcasts from a realm,
Erewhile the mightiest which the sun beheld

In his far journey from the ends of heaven.   218
From Jove our lineage springs; in Jove for sire
Exult the Dardan youth; our king himself
Is of Jove's lofty line, Aeneas of Troy,
Who to thy doors hath sent us. What wild storm,
Poured forth from fierce Mycenae, swept the plains
Of Ida, by what destinies impelled
Europe met Asia, and world clashed with world,
Even he hath heard whom earth's remotest bound
Withdraws by ocean's baffled rim, or whom
The zone of the sun's fury, that lies stretched
Midmost the four zones, severs from his kind.   227
Forth from that deluge over the wide waste
Of waters borne, we for our country's gods
Crave a scant home, a harmless gift of coast,
And air and water, free alike to all.
No blot upon your kingdom shall we be,
Nor light your fame be bruited, nor the grace
Of deed so noble perish; nor shall e'er
Ausonia's sons repent them to have clasped
Troy to their bosom. By the fates I swear
Of lord Aeneas, and by the strong right hand,
Whether in troth or arms and battle tried:
Full many a race and nation—scorn us not
That we come proffering garlands in our hands
And prayers upon our lips—have wooed and willed
To knit us to themselves; but heaven's decrees
With their high mandate drave us to seek out
No land but yours. From hence sprang Dardanus;
Hither Apollo bids us back, and goads
Toward Tuscan Tiber and the sacred pools
Of fount Numicius with his high behests.   242
Some slender offerings of his former state
Beside he gives thee, from the flames of Troy
A remnant rescued. With this gold his sire
Anchises at the altar poured the wine:
This was the gear of Priam, when, as wont,
Unto the assembled nations he gave law—
Sceptre, to wit, and sacred diadem,
And robes, the handiwork of Ilian dames."   248
   As thus spake Ilioneus, Latinus held
His face set firmly in one downward stare,
And to the earth cleaves motionless, his eyes
Rolling intently. Nor doth broidered robe
Of purple, no, nor Priam's sceptre stir
The king so deeply, as in thought he broods

Upon his daughter's bridal troth and bower,
And ponders in heart's core the oracle
Of ancient Faunus. This then is the man,
That traveller from an outland home, and son
By fate predicted, summoned with like sway
To share his kingdom; he, whose race should prove
In valour peerless, destined by their might
To hold the universe in fee. At length
Joyful he cries: "Heaven prosper our intent,
And its own presage! granted be thy suit,
O Trojan! nor spurn I the gifts. While reigns
Latinus, a rich land's fertility
Lack shall ye never, nor the wealth of Troy.   262
Let but Aeneas, if his heart so yearn
To us-ward, if for hospitable ties
Impatient, and the name of fellowship,
Himself draw near, nor shrink before the gaze
Of friendly faces. Of my terms of peace
This shall be part, your prince's hand to press.
Ye now in turn this message bear from me
Back to your king. A maiden child have I,
Whom with a lord of our own race to wed
Nor oracles from out my father's shrine
Nor many a prodigy from heaven permits.
Sons from an outland country are to come—
So chant they Latium's destiny—whose blood
Must raise our name to heaven. That this is he
By fate demanded I both deem, and, if
My mind of truth aught presage, him adopt."   273
So saying, the sire from out his whole array
Picks chosen steeds: three hundred stood there sleek
In lofty stalls: these bids he straight be led
Wing-footed forth, for every Teucrian one,
With purple and with broidered housings decked;
Droop to their chests gold necklets; trapped with
      gold,
Red-gold the bits between their champing teeth;
But for Aeneas, for their absent king,
Car and twin coursers of celestial strain,
With nostrils snorting fire, sprung from the stock
Of those which subtle Circe to her sire
Raised, and by stealthy mating mixed the breed.
So dowered, so greeted by the king, Troy's sons,
Towering on steed, hie homeward and bring peace.   285
    But from Inachian Argos, as she came,
Lo! the fierce spouse of Jove her airy voyage

Was holding when, from heaven far off as lies
Sicilian Pachynus, she espied
Aeneas rejoicing, and the Dardan fleet.
Even now she sees them building homes, even now,
Their barks abandoned, trusting to the shore.
Stabbed with sharp agony she stopped, and then,
Shaking her head, this heart-wrung utterance
    poured:
"Ah! loathèd stock, ah! Phrygian destinies
At odds with ours! upon Sigeum's plain
Say could they perish, or, when captive ta'en,
Be captured? did the flames of Troy burn up
Her warriors? through armed hosts, through fire, they
    have found
An outlet. But my deity belike
At length lies spent; or, surfeited with hate,
I have turned me to my rest: nay, even when hurled
From home and country, o'er the billows I
Relentless spared not to pursue them still,
And bar the exiles' path on every main.   300
Upon the Teucrians have been spent the powers
Of sky and ocean. What did Syrtes, say,
Or Scylla, or Charybdis' weltering waste
Avail me? In the Tiber's wished-for bed
They shroud them, careless of the main and me.
Mars on the monstrous Lapithaean brood
Could ruin wreak; the Sire of gods himself
To Dian's wrath old Calydon consigned—
For what desert of sin so heinous doomed
Or Lapithae or Calydon? But I,
Jove's mighty consort, who have deigned to leave
Nothing undared—ah! wretched, to all shifts
Have turned me—by Aeneas am subdued.
Well, if my deity lack might enow,
I'd spurn not to ask aid from whencesoe'er;
If powerless to bend heaven, I'll stir up hell.   312
'Twill not be mine to bar him from the throne
Of Latium—be it so; and Lavinia stands
Immutably his fate-appointed bride:
Yet stay the hour, heap hindrances on hopes
So mighty—this I may, and extirpate
Of either prince the people: at such cost
Of their own kin let son with sire unite!
O maid, with Trojan and Rutulian blood
Shalt thou be dowered, and for thy brideswoman
Bellona waits thee. Nor did Cisseus' child

Alone of women travail with a brand,
And bring forth nuptial fires; nay, Venus too
Hath the like offspring—a new Paris—borne,
A bale-torch to the towers of Troy re-risen." *322*

So saying, she dropped to earth, an awful form,
And from the dwelling of the sisters dread,
Even from the nether darkness, summons forth
Baneful Allecto, to whom dolorous wars,
Wraths, treacheries, and disastrous feuds, are dear.
Loathed even by Pluto, who begat her, loathed
By her own hellish sisters, is the pest;
So many her changing shapes, so fierce her forms,
So thick she bristles with black-sprouting snakes.
Her Juno thus with goading words bespoke:
"Grant me this service, this thy proper task,
O Night-born maiden, lest mine honour fail,
Or fame fall shattered, and the sons of Troy
With marriage-bonds be able to win o'er
Latinus, or Italia's bounds beset. *334*
Thou canst arm brothers of one mind for strife,
With hate wreck houses, on the homes of men
Fling scourge and funeral-torch; a thousand names
To thee belong, a thousand arts of ill.
Stir thy rife bosom, snap the cords of peace,
Sow battle's rancorous seed; let all at once
Desire, demand, and clutch the tools of war."

Forthwith Allecto, steeped in Gorgon-bane,
To Latium first repairs, and the proud halls
Of the Laurentian monarch, and besets
Amata's silent bower, who, as she mused
Upon the coming of the Teucrian lords,
And Turnus' bridal troth, was seething hot
With all a woman's grief, a woman's ire. *345*
At her the goddess from her steely locks
A serpent hurls, and in her bosom plants
Hard by the heart; that, maddened with the pest,
She may the whole house in confusion whelm.
'Twixt robe and ivory bosom in it creeps,
Glides without touch, and maddens unaware,
Its vipery breath instilling: the great snake
Becomes the twisted gold about her throat,
Becomes the hanging head-band, wreathes her hair,
And o'er her body winds its slippery way.
Now, while the first contagion creeping in
With clammy poison penetrates her sense,
And wraps her bones in fire, ere yet the soul

Through all her bosom's depth had caught the flame,
Mildly she spoke, in mother's wonted wise,
Over her daughter shedding many a tear,
And at the Phrygian bridal: "Is it then
To Teucrian exiles that Lavinia's hand,
Good father, must be given? Hast thou no touch
Of pity for thy daughter and thyself?   360
None for her mother, whom, with the first north
    wind,
Yon faithless rover will leave desolate,
Flying o'er ocean with his maiden-prey?
Was it not thus the Phrygian shepherd thrid
His way to Lacedaemon, and from thence
Bore Leda's Helen to the towns of Troy?
What of thy plighted word? Where now the love
Of old time for thy people, the right hand
So oft to Turnus, to thy kinsman, given?
If from a foreign race must needs be sought
A son for Latium, and that purpose hold,
And thy sire Faunus' word upon thee weigh,
Then I deem foreign every land self-ruled
That from our sway lies severed, and that thus
The gods declare it. Aye, for Turnus too,
If back to its first fount his line be traced,
From Inachas and sire Acrisius sprang,
And mid Mycenae."   372
           When, with words like these
Making vain trial, she sees Latinus still
Withstand her, and the serpent's raging bane
Deep in her very heart has sunk, and now
Pervades her wholly, then the unhappy queen,
Goaded by monstrous horrors, unrestrained
Storms, like a thing possessed, from end to end
Of the broad city. As at times a top
Scuds 'neath the twisted whip-cord, which boys drive
In a great circle round some empty hall,
Intent upon their sport; it, lash-impelled,
Careers in curvèd courses; o'er it gape
The silly youthful throng, and still admire
The whirling box-wood; their blows lend it life:
She at no tardier speed is onward borne
Through midst of cities and impetuous tribes.   384
Nay, to the forest, under feignèd spell
Of Bacchic power, essaying mightier crime,
Launched on a mightier madness, forth she flies,
And hides her daughter on the wooded heights,

To rob the Teucrians of their bride, and stay
The nuptial torches, wildly clamouring
"Evoë Bacchus!" shrieking "Thou alone
Art worthy of the maid, in that she wields
For thee the pliant wand, thee celebrates
In dances, trims the sacred lock for thee."   *391*
The rumour flies, and lo! the matrons all,
A sudden frenzy kindling in their breasts,
The self-same passion at one moment drives
To seek new dwellings. They have left their homes,
Bared necks and tresses to the breeze; but some
With quivering shrieks fill heaven, and clad in skins
Bear wands of vine-wood. Midmost, all aglow,
Herself uplifts a blazing pine, and chants
The marriage-song of Turnus and her child,
Rolling a blood-shot eye, and sudden shouts
Fiercely: "Ho! Latian mothers, wheresoe'er,
Hearken! If any kindness yet survive
For poor Amata in your loving hearts,
Pricks you compunction for a mother's right,
Loose from your locks the wreaths, take up with me
The revel." So 'mid forest depths, amid
The wild beasts' lonely covert, far and wide
With Bacchic goad Allecto drives the queen.   *405*
When the first rage seemed whetted to her will,
Latinus' counsel to confusion turned,
And all his house, forthwith on murky wing
Floats the grim goddess to the city walls
Of the bold Rutule, which fair Danaë
For her Acrisian settlers, as folk tell,
Founded, borne shoreward by the furious South.
By men of old the place was Ardea called;
And Ardea still her mighty name retains,
Though fallen in fortune. Here in his high halls
Turnus at murk midnight deep slumber drew.   *414*
Allecto doffs grim face and fury-form,
Shifts to an old wife's semblance, and ploughs up
Her baleful brow with wrinkles: hoary locks
She dons and fillet, then, twining therewithal
An olive-sprig, takes shape as Calybe,
The priestess old of Juno and her shrine,
And with these words confronts the warrior's sight:
"Turnus, wilt suffer to see all thy toils
Poured out in vain, the crown that is thine own
Signed o'er to Dardan settlers? Lo! the king
Denies thee bride alike and blood-bought dower;

And for his throne is sought an outland heir.   *424*
Go now, face thankless perils, jeers for pay;
Go, tread the Etruscan armies down, protect
With peace the Latins. Such the very words
Saturn's almighty daughter, self-revealed,
Bade utter in thine ear, when thou should'st be
Lapped in the hush of night. Uprouse thee then,
And blithely bid thy warriors arm and march
Forth from the gates to battle, and burn up
These that have moored them in our river fair,
The Phrygian captains and their painted keels.
The mighty power of heaven commands it. Yea,
Let King Latinus' self, an he demur
To yield thee bridal and his oath obey,
Now taste and prove the power of Turnus armed."   *434*
   Then, jeering at the prophetess, thus oped
The youth his lips in answer: "Of a fleet
Arrived in Tiber's water-way the tale
Hath not escaped my hearing, as thou deem'st.
Fashion me no such terrors: not of us
Unmindful is queen Juno; but thyself
Old age, good mother, quelled with slow decay,
Of truth waxed barren, vexeth with vain cares,
And fools thee, prophetess, 'mid warring kings
With empty fear. Thy task it is to guard
God's images and altars; wars and peace
Leave men to manage, by whom wars are waged."   *444*
   Allecto at such words blazed out in wrath.
But in mid utterance a swift shudder seized
The warrior's limbs; his eyes grew stony-stiff;
So thick with myriad serpents hissed the fiend,
So vast her form expanded. Rolling then
Her fiery eyes, as he lay faltering there,
Searching what more to say, she spurned him back,
Reared from her locks twin serpents, cracked her
    whips,
And with wild utterance added: "It is I,
Look you, whom, quelled with slow decay, old age,
Of truth waxed barren, fools 'mid warring kings
With empty fear! Turn thee and look on these.
From the dread Sisters' dwelling am I come,
And in my hand I carry wars and death."   *455*
So saying, a torch she hurled at him, and fixed
The fire-brand all a-smoke with murky light
Deep in his breast. Vast terror brake his sleep,
And a sweat bursting forth bathed all his frame,

Body and bone. For arms he wildly shouts,
Ransacks for arms both couch and castle; then
Lust of the sword and frenzy of cruel war
Storm high within him, wrath to boot: as, when
With mighty roar a faggot-fire is heaped
Under a seething cauldron's sides, up-dance
With heat the waters; the pent flood within
Rages and reeks and surges high with foam;
Nor can the wave now hold itself; anon
Flies the dark vapour to the void. He then
Calls on his captains, outraging fair peace,
To march on King Latinus; bids all arms
Be ready, to compass Italy and thrust
The foeman from the land: himself for both,
Teucrian and Latin too, would sole suffice.   470
When thus he had said, called heaven to hear his
    vows,
Rutule cheers Rutule eagerly to the fray:
One the rare charm of youth and beauty moves,
One his ancestral royalties, and one
His deed-renownèd hand.
                      While Turnus thus
With breath of valour fills each Rutule breast,
Allecto hies on Stygian wing to seek
The Teucrians, marking, with a new device,
The spot where fair Iulus on the bank
Snares the wild quarry, or on foot pursues.   478
Here flings upon his hounds the maid of hell
A sudden fury, and with the well-known scent
Infects their nostrils for the stag's hot chase—
First source of ill, which set the rustic heart
Afire for war. A stag of matchless mould
There was, and spreading antlers, from its dam
Stolen and nourished up by Tyrrheus' sons
And their sire Tyrrheus, of the royal herds
Ruler, and ranger of the wide domain.
Their sister Silvia with all tenderness
Had tamed it to obedience, and would deck
Its antlers and with pliant wreaths entwine,
Comb the wild thing, and in pure water lave.   489
Trained to her hand, and at the master's board
Familiar, it would wander in the woods,
And of itself again, how late soe'er,
Home to the well-known threshold wend its way.
Now wandering wide, Iulus' ravening hounds
Amid their hunt aroused it, as down stream

It chanced to float, or on the grassy bank
The heat allayed. Ascanius, too, himself
Fired with the love of peerless praise, bent bow
And levelled shaft, nor swerved his hand for lack
Of a god guiding; and with loud whirr, driven
Through belly and through flank, the bolt sped
    home.   *499*
But to the well-known roof for shelter fled
The stricken beast, into the homestead crept
Moaning, and, blood-bedabbled, with loud plaint,
As supplicating aid, filled all the house.
First sister Silvia, smiting hand on arm,
Cries out for help, and summons the stout hinds.
They, for within the silent forest yet
Lurks the fell pest, ere looked for, are at hand,
One with fire-hardened stake for weapon, one
With heavily knotted club: what every hand
First groping found, wrath makes a tool of war.
Tyrrheus, just cleaving, as it chanced, an oak
With wedges' force split four-wise, gripped an axe,
And breathing out fierce rage, cheers on the band.   *510*
But from her watch-tower the grim goddess now,
Seizing the hour for mischief, to the stall's
High roof repairs, and from its summit winds
A pastoral point of war, on wreathèd horn
Straining the hellish note: from end to end
Shuddered the whole grove, and the forest-depths
Re-echoed: heard it Trivia's lake afar,
Heard it Nar's river, white with sulphurous wave,
And Velia's springs; and mothers at the sound
Trembled, and clasped their children to their breasts. *518*
Then, hurrying at the call, the signal-blast
By the dread trumpet given, from every side
The dauntless husbandmen snatch arms and rush
Together: nor less the Trojan youth pour forth
Aid for Ascanius through the open gates.
The ranks are set: no more in rustic strife
Is plied the knotty club or fire-seared stake;
Nay, but with two-edged steel they fight it out,
While the dark harvest bristles far and wide
With naked sword-blades, and the flash of brass
Sun-fretted darts its radiance to the clouds: *527*
As, when a wave beneath the rising gale
'Gins whiten, the sea slowly heaves, and rears
Its billows higher, then from the lowest deep
Mounts in one mass to heaven. And hereupon

First of the foremost by a whizzing shaft
Young Almo is struck down, once eldest-born
Of Tyrrheus; for the wound within his throat
Lodged, and choked up the channel of moist speech
And the thin life with blood. Around him fell
Full many a warrior-form, and with them old
Galaesus, as for peace he interposed;
Erewhile of all men the most upright he,
And wealthiest in Ausonian soil. For him
Five bleating flocks, five herds, from pasture came,
And with a hundred ploughs he turned the sod.   539

    While on a doubtful field so sways the fight,
The goddess, proved no weaker than her word,
Thus having dipt the war in blood and oped
With death the onset, quits Hesperia's land,
Wheels through the sky-way, and to Juno thus
Speaks in proud tone triumphant: "At thy suit
See discord ripened into dolorous war!
Bid them knit friendship or strike treaty now!
I, who have sprinkled with Ausonian blood
The Teucrians, will add this beside—so be
Thy will assured to me—draw neighbouring towns
With rumours to the fray, and fire their hearts
With the mad war-god's lust, from far and near
To aid them. I will sow the land with arms."   551
Juno replies: "Enough of fears and plots;
Firm stand the grounds of quarrel; in armed fight
Man grapples man; the weapons chance supplied
Reek with fresh blood to-day. Such nuptial rite,
Such bridal let them hold—the peerless seed
Of Venus and great Latium's king. That thou
With freer foot should'st roam the air of heaven,
The mighty Sire, lord of Olympus' height,
Would suffer not; give place; what further toil
May hap, myself will cope with." Such the words
Saturnia spake. But the other rears aloft
Her serpent-hissing pinions, quits the vault
Of heaven, and homeward to Cocytus hies.   562
There is a spot midmost of Italy
Beneath tall mountains, famous, and renowned
In many a land, Amsanctus-vale; 'tis hemmed
On this side and on that by wooded walls
Dark with dense foliage; and amidst it boils
And swirls among the rocks with broken roar
A torrent. Here is shown an awful cave,
Outlet of cruel Dis; and a vast chasm,

Where up bursts Acheron, opes its noisome jaws;
Thereinto plunged the Fury, loathèd power,
And lightened earth and heaven. 571
                              Nor less meanwhile
Sets Queen Saturnia to the work of war
Her consummating hand. From field to town
Rush the whole shepherd-rout, bear home their slain—
Young Almo, and Galaesus' mangled face—
Conjure the gods, and on Latinus call.
Turnus is there, 'mid fierce death-kindled cries
Redoubling terror: "Teucrians called to reign—
A Phrygian shoot engrafted—he himself
Spurned from the door!" Then they, whose matrons
        still,
Blinded by Bacchus, foot the pathless groves
In dance—for mighty is Amata's name—
Muster from all sides, and importune war. 582
Straight, one and all, in spite of signs, in spite
Of dooms from heaven, by some thwart power
        beguiled,
Clamour for cursèd strife. With emulous zeal
Round King Latinus' palace-gates they swarm.
He like an unmoved ocean-cliff withstands—
An ocean-cliff, which, when a great crash falls,
And multitudinous billows bark around,
Holds steadfast by sheer bulk: in vain the crags
And foamy rocks roar round it; and the weed,
Dashed on its bases, is washed idly back. 590
But when no power to quell their blind resolve
Is given, and at fierce Juno's beck goes all,
Then, heaven and the void air invoking oft,
"Ah! broken," cried the sire, "by fate are we,
And driven before the tempest! Ye yourselves
Will with your impious blood atone for this,
Fond wretches! Thee, O Turnus, thee the crime
And its dread reckoning shall await; and thou
Wilt sue to heaven too late for prayers to aid.
My rest is won, and, hard on harbour's verge,
'Tis but a happy death I miss." Therewith
He ceased to speak, within his palace doors
Immured him, and let go the reins of power. 600
    There was a wonted rite in Latium's realm
Hesperian, holy held from age to age
By Alba's cities, as to-day by Rome,
Earth's mightiest, when they rouse the god of war
To battle, whether against Getic foes

Intent to launch amain the dolorous fray,
Or Arabs, or Hyrcanians, or to march
On India's sons, or track the morning-star,
And from the Parthian their lost standards claim.
There are twin gates of War—so named and known—
By holy fear and terror of fell Mars
Made venerable: a hundred brazen bolts
Constrain them, and the eternal strength of iron,
Nor Janus on the threshold slacks his guard.   *610*
Here, be the fathers' will on battle bent,
The Consul in Quirinal robe arrayed
And Gabine cincture, the harsh-griding valves
Himself unbars, himself invokes the fray,
Then all the war-host follow, and with one throat
The brazen clarions blare their hoarse assent.
Now too on this wise was Latinus bidden
War to proclaim against the sons of Troy,
Unclose the sullen portals. From their touch
The sire recoiled, turned from the loathèd task
Shrinking, and shrouded him in eyeless gloom.
Then, gliding from on high, the queen of heaven
With her own hand the lingering portals pushed,
And Saturn's daughter upon back-swung hinge
Asunder burst the iron-bound gates of war.   *622*
Ausonia, erst supine, immovable,
Anon takes fire. Some gird them o'er the plain
To march afoot; some, mounted on tall steeds,
Storm through a cloud of dust; all shout for arms.
Some furbish with rich lard the buckler smooth,
The javelin bright, or on the whetstone wear
Their axes to an edge: with joy they thrill
To advance the standard, hear the trumpet bray.   *628*
Five mighty cities set their anvils up
To fashion arms anew—Atina strong,
Proud Tibur, Ardea, and Crustumeri,
And turret-crowned Antemnae. For head-gear
Helmets they hollow, and for the boss of shields
Bend wicker-plait; some corslets beat from brass,
Smooth greaves from pliant silver. Even to this
The pride of share and hook, to this hath fallen
All passion for the plough: their fathers' swords
I' the furnace they re-temper. And now sounds
The clarion, speeds the watchword for the war.
One in hot haste plucks helm from house-wall; one
Couples his snorting coursers to the yoke,
In shield and hauberk triple-twilled with gold

Arrays him, and girds trusty sword on thigh.   *640*
   Now, Muses, ope the gates of Helicon
And wake the song—what kings were roused to war,
What hosts behind them following filled the plain;
Bloomed with what heroes, with what armour burned,
Even then the nursing soil of Italy:
For, being maids immortal, ye both mind
And can recount them: scarcely to our ears
Floats through the ages a thin breath of fame.
   First to the field, despiser of the gods,
Speeds fierce Mezentius from the Tyrrhene coast,
And arms his ranks for battle; hard by him
Lausus his son, than whom no goodlier man,
Save Turnus of Laurentum. At his back
Lausus, steed-tamer, beast-destroyer, leads
His thousand from Agylla's town—in vain;
Worthy of happier service as a son,
And other than Mezentius for his sire.   *654*
Behind them on the grassy sward displays
His palm-crowned chariot and victorious steeds
A hero, sprung from Hercules the fair,
Fair Aventinus: on his shield he bears
A hundred serpents, his ancestral sign,
The snake-encircled Hydra. Him by stealth
The priestess Rhea on wood-clothed Aventine,
Woman with god commingling, bare to light,
When the Tirynthian victor, Geryon quelled,
Arrived the fields Laurentian, and there bathed
His kine Iberian in the Tuscan stream.
Javelins and cruel pikes they wield for war,
And with smooth-polished dart Sabellian fight.
Himself, swinging a lion's monstrous fell
Shaggy with fearful bristles, o'er his head
Flung with its flashing teeth, thus strode on foot
Into the palace, grisly-rough, the garb
Of Hercules about his shoulders clasped.   *669*
   Then brethren twain from Tibur's hold, a folk
Called from their brother's name Tiburtus, come,
Catillus and keen Coras, Argive youths.
First of the foremost, on they press, where darts
Throng thickest: as when from some tall
     mountain-top
Descend two cloud-born Centaurs, Homole
Or snow-capped Othrys quitting with swift stride;
The mighty forest as they go gives place,
And with loud crash the thickets yield them way.   *677*

Nor lacked the founder of Praeneste's town,
King sprung from Vulcan 'mid the pasturing herds,
And by the fireside found, as every age
Hath deemed him—Caeculus. A rustic band
Spread wide attends him, those that dwell on steep
Praeneste's height, or Gabian Juno's fields,
Chill Anio, or the stream-dewed Hernic rocks;
Whom rich Anagnia nurtures, or whom thou,
Sire Amasenus. Arms they have not all,
Nor shield, nor sounding chariot. The more part
Sling bullets of blue lead. Some javelins twain
Brandish in hand, with tawny wolfskin cap
For head-gear: the left foot bare-soled they plant;
The other a raw bull's-hide sandal sheathes.   690

    Messapus, the steed-tamer, Neptune's child,
Whom none with fire, nor yet with steel, may quell,
Tribes long inert and ranks to battle strange
Calls suddenly to arms, grasps sword once more.
These have Fescennine warriors in their host,
And Aequi of Falerium; these hold high
Soracte and Flavinian fields, the lake
And hill of Ciminus, and Capena's groves.
In measured time they march and chant their king:
As snow-white swans that, through the liquid clouds
From food returning, utter forth their full
Long-throated strains. The stream and Asia's fen
Afar ring smitten. Nor had one deemed them there
A mail-clad army blent in vast array,
But rather of hoarse birds an airy cloud,
That from the deep mid-ocean shoreward ply.   705

    Lo! Clausus of old Sabine blood, who leads
A mighty host, himself a host in might!
From whom the Claudian tribe and clan to-day,
Since Rome was with the Sabine shared, spreads
    wide
Through Latium: and along with them the vast
Cohort of Amiternum and old-world
Quirites, all Eretum's folk, and they
Of olive-rife Mutusca; men who throng
Nomentum's city and the Rosean plain
Hard by Velinus; who the rugged rocks
Of Tetrica, and mount Severus hold,
Casperia's town, and Forali, and where flows
Himella's stream; who drink of Tiber's wave
And Fabaris, or whom chilly Nursia sends,
With Horta's squadrons and the Latian tribes,

[255]

And they whom Allia, evil-boding name,
Parts with dividing current: numberless
As billows that on Libya's sea-floor roll,
When fierce Orion sets in wintry wave,
Or thick as clustering corn-ears, that beneath
The young sun ripen, or on Hermus' plain,
Or Lycia's yellowing fields. Their bucklers clang,
And the earth quakes for terror as they tread. 722
    Halaesus next, of Agamemnon's stock,
Foe to the name of Troy, yokes steed to car,
And whirls a thousand warlike tribes along
To fight for Turnus, men who till with hoe
The wine-blest Massic region, or sent forth
From their high hills by the Auruncan sires,
Or Sidicine low-dwellers hard at hand;
Comers from Cales, and who dwell beside
Volturnus' shoaly river, and with these
The rough Saticulan, and the Oscan band;
Smooth-polished clubs for missiles, 'tis their wont
With a tough thong to fit them; the left arm
A leathern target shields; curv'd swords they bear
For close encounter. 732
              Nor must thou depart
Unhonoured of our song, O Oebalus,
Whom, as folk tell, the nymph Sebethis bare
To Telon, when now full of years he ruled
The Teleboic realm of Capreae.
But, with his sire's domain waxed ill-content,
Even then the son was curbing 'neath his sway
The wide Sarrastian peoples, and the plains
By Sarnus washed, folk that in Rufrae dwell
And Batulum and Celemna's furrowed fields,
And those on whom the battlements look down
Of apple-boughed Abella. These were wont
In Teuton-wise long darts to hurl amain:
Peeled cork-tree bark for head-gear, their slight
    shields
Are glittering brass, and glittering brass their swords. 743
   And thee too, Ufens, from her mountain-perch
Nersae sent forth to battle, fame-renowned,
And fortunate in war, whose Aequian folk
On their stiff clods are rugged beyond all,
And to hard hunting in the woods inured.
In arms they task the furrow, and evermore
Amass new plunder, and by rapine live. 749
   Aye, and a priest of race Marruvian came,

His head with garland of rich olive dight,
By King Archippus sent, Umbro the brave,
Who on the viper's brood and water-snakes
Of baneful breath, with charm of voice and touch
Shed slumber, and assuaged their wrath, his craft
Their bites allaying. But stroke of Dardan spear
To heal he skilled not, nor his slumbrous charms
Availed against their wounds, nor herbs with care
Culled on the Marsian mountains. Wept for thee
Anguitia's grove, for thee the glassy wave
Of Fucinus, the crystal pools for thee.   760
 There Virbius to the war in beauty strode,
Son of Hippolytus, whom in flower of fame
His mother sent, Aricia; nursed he was
In groves Egerian round the humid shores,
Where Dian's rich and gracious altar stands.
Aye, for Hippolytus, so runs the tale,
By stepdame's treachery done to death, and torn
By his scared steeds, to glut a sire's revenge,
Returned to daylight and the air of heaven,
Called by the Healer's herbs and Dian's love.   769
Then, wroth that mortal should from shades of hell
Rise to the light of life, the Almighty Sire
With his own levin-bolt to Stygian wave
Thrust down the finder of such craft and cure,
The Phoebus-born. But Trivia of her grace
In a dim dwelling hides Hippolytus,
To nymph Egeria and her grove consigned,
Alone, obscure, in woods of Italy
With altered name, as Virbius, to live on.
Whence too, from Trivia's shrine and hallowed
  groves
Horn-hoofèd steeds are banished, for that they,
Frighted by ocean-monsters, on the shore
Flung car and warrior. But the son no less
His fiery steeds along the level plain
Was driving, and rushed charioted to war.   782
 Himself too Turnus, of surpassing mould,
Amid the foremost moving, arms in hand,
By a whole head o'ertops them; his proud helm,
Tressed with a triple plume, Chimaera bears,
Out-breathing from her jaws Aetnean fires,
The madlier raging with more baleful flames
As deeplier the red field with carnage ran.
But his smooth shield Io with lifted horns
In gold emblazoned, now with hair o'ergrown,

Now turned to heifer, a stupendous sign,
And Argus, the maid's warder, and therewith,
His flood outpouring from a graven urn,
Sire Inachus. Behind the hero comes
A cloud of footmen, and o'er all the plain
The shielded ranks are thickening, Argive men;
The Auruncan musters with the Rutule ranks;
And old Sicani, the Sacranian host
And gay-shielded Labici; who thy lawns,
O Tiber, and Numicius' sacred shore
Till, or with ploughshare tame the Rutule heights
And Circe's ridge; over whose fields enthroned
Rules Jove of Anxur, and Feronia sits
Rejoicing in her greenwood; where out-stretched
Lies the black marsh of Satura, and where
Along the valley-bottoms winds his way
Cold Ufens, till he plunges in the deep.   *802*

   To crown them comes Camilla, Volscian-bred,
Heading her horse-troop, squadrons bright with
     brass,
A warrior-maid, her woman's hands unused
To loom or basket of Minerva's wool,
But strong to bide the battle, and on foot
Out-race the breezes: she might even have sped
Over the unlopped harvest-blades, nor bruised
The tender ears in running, or have skimmed
Mid-ocean, poised upon the billow's swell,
Nor in the surges dipped her flying feet.
At her, astonied, youths and maidens all
From house and field throng gazing, as she goes,
Agape with wonder at the royal pomp
Of purple draped about her shoulders smooth,
Her tresses intertwined with clasp of gold,
To mark the Lycian quiver that she bears,
And pastoral wand of myrtle tipped with steel.   *817*

BOOK VIII

When Turnus from his citadel flung out
The flag of war, and hoarse the clarions blared,
When his bold steeds he roused, and clashed his arms,
Straight every heart is stirred; all Latium thrills,
Leagued in one wild uprising, and her sons
Rage madly. From all sides the warrior chiefs,
Messapus, Ufens, and Mezentius
The god-despiser, call their musters in,
And strip the wide fields of their husbandmen.   8
Then to the city of great Diomede,
To sue for succour, Venulus is sent
With tidings of a Teucrian host afoot
In Latium; that Aeneas, to their shores
Fleet-wafted, with his vanquished household-gods
Invades them, claims to be their destined king;
That to the Dardan lord cleaves many a tribe,
And louder and more loud through Latium's
        breadth
His name is rumoured: what he builds on these
Beginnings, to what outcome of the fray,
Should fortune follow at his back, aspires—
This must to Diomede more plain appear
Than to King Turnus, or the Latin king.   17
        So sets the tide through Latium. But the prince,
Laomedon's great son, beholding all,
Is rocked upon a mighty sea of cares;
Hither and thither his swift mind he parts,
Speeds it all ways, and sweeps the round of thought:
As when from water in a brazen vat
A flickering beam, shot by the mirrored sun
Or bright moon's image, flits from side to side
O'er all things, and at last up-mounting strikes
The fretted ceiling of the roof on high.   25
        'Twas night, and weary creatures, the world o'er,
Both bird and cattle-kind, deep slumber held;
When Prince Aeneas on the bank beneath
Heaven's chilly vault, and by the dolorous war
Heart-troubled, stretched him, and let sleep at last
Steal o'er his limbs. To him appeared the god
Of that fair spot, he of the pleasant stream,

Old Tiber, rising 'mid his poplar-leaves;
Veiled in a grey-green mantle of fine lawn,
With shadowy reeds about his locks, he thus
In words addressed him, and his grief allayed: *35*
  "O heaven-descended, thou who bring'st us back
Troy's city from the foeman, and preserv'st
Her towers for ever, on Laurentum's soil
And Latium's fields long-looked for, here for thee
Waits a sure dwelling—draw not back—and sure
Penates: nor be scared by threats of war:
All the gods' swelling anger has died out;
And now, lest these things to thine eyes appear
A dream's vain figment, thou shalt find anon,
Under the holm-oaks on the margin laid,
A mighty sow, with thirty head of swine
New-littered, white, stretched out along the ground,
White young about her udders; sign whereby
Ascanius in thrice ten returning years
Shall Alba found, of glorious name: I chant
No doubtful doom. Now, mark, the present need
How to dispatch and triumph o'er, in brief
Will I discover. Arcadians on this coast,
A race derived from Pallas, in the train
Of King Evander following, have a site
Chosen, and built a city on the hills,
From their sire Pallas Pallanteum called.   *54*
These with the Latins wage perpetual war;
These welcome to thy tents, and knit with bonds
Of friendship. I myself betwixt the banks
And straight up stream will lead thee. that thou may'st
The adverse current conquer, oar-impelled.
Up, goddess-born! and with first set of star
Do homage meet to Juno, and disarm
With suppliant vows her wrath, her threats; to me
Thou shalt pay conqueror's tribute. Lo! 'tis I,
Whom grazing here the banks with brimming flood,
And cleaving the rich cornland thou behold'st,
Blue Tiber, river best-beloved of heaven.   *64*
Here doth my watery mansion outlet find,
Life-source of lofty cities." Having said,
Into his deep pool plunged the river-god,
Seeking the bottom. Night and slumber left
Aeneas: he rises, and the Orient beam
Marks of the sun in heaven, then from the flood
Takes duly in the hollow of his hands
Water, and holds it, and pours forth to heaven

Such words as these: "O Nymphs, Laurentian
    Nymphs,
Whence rivers have their being, and thou too,
O Father Tiber, with thy hallowed flood,
Take to your care Aeneas and at length
From perils fend him. Whencesoe'er be fed
The pool that holds thee, pitier of our woes,
Where'er thou hast thy glorious outgoing,
Ever with offering, evermore with gifts,
By me shalt thou be graced, the hornèd flood,
Lord of Hesperian waters. Only grant
Thy presence, and with nearer token seal
The heavenly utterance." Thus he spake, and chose
From out his fleet twin biremes, fits their decks
With oarsmen, and equips with arms the crew.   *80*
But lo! a sudden portent strange to see!
White, of one colour with her milk-white young,
Along the wood, on the green bank lay stretched
A sow, conspicuous; which to thee, to thee,
O mightiest Juno, good Aeneas slays
In sacrifice, and at the altar sets,
With all her offspring. Through that livelong night
Tiber his swelling stream assuaged, and so,
With refluent effort halting, hushed his tide,
That, like still pool or quiet mere, he spread
A watery plain, whereon the oar might lack
All labour. So with favouring shout they speed
Upon the voyage begun: the tarred pine slides
Along the surface: wonder holds the waves,
Wonder the unaccustomed grove, to see
The shields of warriors gleaming bright afar,
And the gay vessels gliding on the stream.   *93*
They with their rowing wear out night and day,
Pass the long bends, are roofed with divers trees,
And cleave green forests on the glassy flood.
The fiery sun to heaven's mid cope had climbed,
When walls and citadel afar they spy,
And scattered house-roofs, which Rome's power
    to-day
Has matched with heaven, then but the needy realm
Swayed by Evander. Shoreward speedily
They turn their prows, and to the town draw nigh.   *101*
It chanced that day the Arcadian monarch paid
Due honour to Amphitryon's mighty son
And the high gods, within a grove that faced
The city. His son Pallas, hard at hand,

With all the chiefs and simple senate, brought
Incense, and warm blood at the altar smoked.
Soon, as they saw the lofty ships glide in,
Through the dark grove, and rest on silent oars,
Scared at the sudden vision, all leap up
And quit the board. But Pallas, undismayed,
Forbids break off the banquet, grasps a spear,
Speeds toward them, and from a far hillock cries:
"Warriors, what cause to try an unknown path
Constrains you? Whither fare ye? Of what race?
Sprung from what home? and bring ye peace or war?" *114*
Then Prince Aeneas from the lofty stern
Speaks, in his hand a peaceful olive-branch
Out-stretching: "These are Trojans whom ye see;
Darts deadly but to Latins, who have spurned
And forced us into flight with wanton war.
We seek Evander: bear this message back,
And say the flower of Dardan chiefs are come
Craving an armed alliance." At the sound
Of that great name Pallas stood thunderstruck:
"Whoe'er thou art, descend, and with my sire
Speak face to face, and enter the abode
Of hospitable hearth-gods." So, with grasp
Of welcome, to the chief's right hand he clave:
Forth through the grove they fare, and quit the
    stream.   *125*
  Then courteously Aeneas hails the king:
"Best of the sons of Greece, to whom I pray—
So wills it Fortune—and come proffering boughs
With fillet decked, I feared not for that thou
A Danaan leader art, Arcadian-born,
And from the twin Atridae's stem derived;
But my own worth, high auguries from heaven,
And our ancestral kinship, and thy fame
Spread through the world, have knit me to thy side,
And led me fain along the path of fate.
Dardanus, father of our Ilian town
And founder, to the Teucrians came of old,
Sprung from Electra the Atlantid, so
Greek legend saith; Electra was begot
Of mightiest Atlas, who up-shouldering bears
The orbs of heaven. Your sire is Mercury,
Whom Maia fair on chill Cyllene's top
Conceived and bore; but Maia, if tales heard
Win credence, from the selfsame Atlas sprung,
Atlas, who holds aloft the starry heaven:

So branches from one blood the line of both.   *142*
On this relying, no embassage I planned,
No artful first approaches: me myself,
Yea mine own person, have I brought, and come
A suppliant to your doors. The selfsame race,
The Daunian, persecutes ourselves, as thee,
With cruel warfare: if they drive us forth,
'Twere all as one, think they, beneath their yoke
To thrust Hesperia wholly, and possess
Both seas that wash her shores, above, below.   *149*
Take and return our friendship; we have hearts
Valiant for war, high courage, and a youth
In action tried." Aeneas ceased. The king
Long since the speaker's countenance and eyes
And his whole frame was scanning; then he makes
Brief answer: "Bravest of the sons of Troy,
Thus to receive, to recognize thee thus,
How fain am I! How I recall the words,
The voice, the features of thy sire, the great
Anchises! for I mind how Priam once,
Son of Laomedon, when he came to view
The realm of Hesione his sister, bound
For Salamis, passed thence and visited
Arcadia's chill borders. In those days
The down of early manhood clothed my cheeks;
And I admired the Teucrian lords, admired
Laomedon's great son, but high o'er all
Anchises towered. With youthful zeal I burned
To accost the hero, and clasp hand to hand.   *164*
Approaching, eagerly his steps I led
To Pheneus' city. He, departing thence,
A glorious quiver gave me, Lycian shafts,
A gold-embroidered scarf, and bridles twain
All golden, which my Pallas owns to-day.
Therefore the hand ye seek is joined with yours
In treaty, and when first to-morrow's dawn
Shall earth revisit, I will send you hence,
Glad of our succour, and with stores supply.
Meanwhile, since hither as my friends ye come,
This yearly rite, which to defer were sin,
Keep with us, of your grace, and learn even now
To grow familiar at your comrade's board."   *174*
    So saying, the viands and wine-cup, erst removed,
He bids set on afresh, with his own hand
Ranges the heroes on a grassy couch,
To a heaped cushion of rough lion's fell

Welcomes Aeneas, as most honoured guest,
And entertains him on a maple throne.
Then those appointed, with the altar-priest,
In emulous service bring roast flesh of steers,
Pile upon baskets Ceres' hand-wrought boon,
And serve the wine-cup. There Aeneas feasts,
With him the Trojans, upon long bull's chine
And sacrificial morsels. When at length
Hunger was ousted, lust of food appeased,
Spake King Evander: "These our solemn rites,
This wonted feast, this altar so divine,
No idle superstition, that knows not
The gods of old, hath ordered; as men saved
From deadly perils, O my Trojan guest,
These offerings pay we, and of right renew.   *189*
First look upon yon cliff-hung crag, and how
Huge blocks afar lie scattered, and void stands
The mountain-dwelling! Of down-tumbled rocks
How vast the havoc! Here was once a cave,
Deep-yawning inward, where, terrific shape,
Half-human Cacus dwelt, to the sun's rays
Impenetrable; and evermore the ground
Reeked with fresh blood, and to its tyrannous doors
Hung nailed men's faces, blanched with grim decay.
This monster's sire was Vulcan; his the flames
Dark-issuing from his mouth, as on he strode
In bulk gigantic. To us also time
Brought in due course, at our desire, the aid
And advent of a god. For hard at hand
Alcides, mightiest of avengers, stood,
Now glorying in the slaughter and the spoils
Of triple Geryon, as this way he drove
His giant bulls, triumphant, while the kine
Filled vale and river-side. But Cacus now,
In a brute-frenzy, not to leave undared
Or unattempted aught of crime or guile,
Four bulls of peerless beauty stole from stall,
With heifers of surpassing mould to match.   *208*
These by the tail, no forward track to leave,
Into his cavern, with back-pointing steps,
He haled, and hid them in the gloomy rock:
No footprint led the seeker to the cave.
Meanwhile, when his full herds Amphitryon's son
Would from their pasture shift, at point to go,
Bellowed the parting oxen; all the grove
O'erflows with their complaining, and the hills

Are clamorously forsaken. To that cry
One of the heifers from the cave's vast depth
Lowed in response, and from her prison foiled
The hope of Cacus. In Alcides' heart
Black-venomed wrath straight into fury blazed.
Seizing his arms and heavily-knotted club,
Full speed he hies him up the skyey steep.　　　*221*
Then first our folk beheld Cacus afeard,
And trouble in his eyes: away he speeds
Swifter than Eurus, his feet winged with fear,
And seeks the cave: soon as, shut fast within,
He had burst the chains, and let the vast rock fall,
Which hung there by his father's art and iron—
Propped firm and barricaded thus the door,
Lo! he of Tiryns, in a frenzy of wrath,
Was close upon him, to this side and that
Turning his eyes, as each approach he scanned,
And gnashing with his teeth. Thrice he surveys,
Boiling with anger, Aventine's whole hill,
Thrice tries in vain the rocky portal, thrice
Sinks wearied in the valley. A sharp peak
Stood there, with rocky sides up-rising sheer
Above the cave's back, far as sight could soar,
Fit dwelling for foul birds to build in. This,
As headlong from the ridge it leftward leaned
Over the river, from the right he shook
Straining against it, and up-wrenched, and tore
Loose from its lowest roots, then suddenly
Launched forth; and, as he launched it, bellowed loud
The mighty welkin, and asunder leapt
The river banks, and the affrighted stream
Flowed backward. But the cave and ample hall
Of Cacus lay discovered, bare to view,
With its dark hollows yawning to their depth:
As the rent earth should open wide her mouth,
Unlock the infernal dwellings and disclose
The pale realm hated of the gods, whereby
The vasty gulf should from above be seen,
And the ghosts tremble, as floods in the light.　　　*246*
Him, then, quick-caught by the unlooked-for glare,
Pent in his rock-cage, uttering uncouth roars,
Alcides from above plies home with darts,
Calls every arm to aid him, and bombards
With boughs and mighty mill-stones. He the while,
Escape none else remaining, from his jaws
Vomits a vast smoke, marvellous to tell,

Wraps in pitch darkness the whole den, and blots
All eyesight out, up-rolling from the abyss
One stifling night of blackness blent with fire.
This brooked not fierce Alcides: through the flames
With headlong bound he cast him, where the smoke
Was billowing densest, and the mighty cave
Boiled with black vapour. Cacus here he seized,
Still belching forth vain fires amid the gloom,
Locked limbs about him, and strangled as he clave,
Till his eyes started and his throat lacked blood.   261
Straight are the doors burst, the black den laid bare,
The stolen cattle and the theft forsworn
Shown to the eye of heaven; and by its feet
The huge mis-shapen carcass is dragged forth.
Men's souls cannot be sated, as they gaze
Upon the terrible eyes, face, bristling breast
Of the man-monster, and his fire-quenched throat.
Hence sprang this high observance; and with joy
Have younger generations kept the day:
Potitius, the first founder, and the house
Pinarian, keeper of the sacred rites
Of Hercules, erected in the grove
This altar, which shall evermore be called
Mightiest, and mightiest evermore shall be.   272
Up, then, O warriors! such high deeds to grace
Garland your locks, hold forth the cup in hand,
Call on our common god, and with good will
Pour ye the wine." He scarce had said, when lo!
About his locks the twy-hued poplar's twine,
Shade dear to Hercules, festooned and hung,
And his right hand the sacred beaker clasped.
Then on the board right quickly one and all
Make glad libation, and the gods adore.   279
    Evening meanwhile adown Olympus' slope
Draws nearer; and the priests, Potitius first,
Marched, as was wont, skin-clad and carrying fire.
They spread the board afresh, new dainties bring
For the new feast, and heap the altars high
With laden trenchers. Then come forth to sing
The Salii round the altar-glow, brow-bound
With sprays of poplar; here a band of youths,
Of elders there, commemorate in song
The fame and feats of Hercules; how first
With grip of hand he strangled the twin snakes,
The monsters of his step-mother; anon
Dashed peerless cities to the ground in war,

[266]

Troy and Oechalia: how hard toil on toil,
As King Eurystheus' vassal, he endured,
By cruel Juno's doom. "Unconquerable,
Thou didst the cloud-begotten and twy-formed
Hylaeus slay and Pholus with thy might,
Thou too the Cretan monster, and the vast
Lion that dwelt beneath the Nemean rock.   295
Trembled at thee the Stygian lake, at thee
Hell's warder, couched above his mumbled bones
In the blood-boultered cave: no bodily shape
E'er daunted thee, no, not Typhöeus' self,
Up-towering armed; nor round thee, shiftless caught,
Reared Lerna's worm its multitudinous head.
Hail, very child of Jove, to the high gods
An added glory! with propitious foot
To us and thine own rites draw kindly nigh."
Such themes in song they celebrate, and crown
All with the cave of Cacus, and himself
Out-panting blasts of fire. To their loud din
The whole grove echoes and the hills resound.   305
    Then, sacrifice done duly, one and all
Turn city-ward. The king, o'ercrept with age,
Moved onward, keeping ever at his side
Aeneas and his son, with various talk
Lightening the way. Aeneas on all around
Casts quick admiring eyes; spot after spot
Enthralls him; and with rapture he inquires
And learns the legends of the men of old.
Then, founder of Rome's fortress on the height,
Spake King Evander: "In these woodlands once
Dwelt native Fauns and Nymphs, a race of men
From tree-stocks sprung and stubborn hearts of oak,
Who had no rule, no art of life, nor knew
To yoke the steer, heap wealth, or husband it,
But fed on branches and rough hunting-fare.   318
Then from Olympus' height first Saturn came,
Flying the arms of Jove, from his lost realm
An exile. He the untutored race, broadcast
Among the mountain-tops, together brought,
And gave them laws, and chose for the land's name
Latium, since there safe-hidden he had lain.
Under his sceptre were the golden years
Men tell of, in such peace he ruled the folk;
Till a worse age and duller-hued crept in
Little by little, and wild rage of war,
And lust of having. Then the Ausonian host

And tribes Sicanian came; and many a time
The land of Saturn cast her name away;
Then kings arose, and with his monstrous bulk
Fierce Thybris, from whom we of Italy
Have since called Tiber's river, when Albula
Lost its true olden name. Myself, from home
Outcast and exile, to the utmost bounds
Of ocean questing, the resistless might
Of Fortune and inevitable Fate
Here planted, by my mother's dread behest,
The Nymph Carmentis, driven, and by the word
And warrant of Apollo's voice divine."   *336*
He said, and passing thence the altar shows
And gate Carmental, name by Rome of yore
In honour of the Nymph Carmentis given,
That prophetess of sooth, who first foretold
The future greatness of the Aeneadae
And Pallanteum's glory. Next he shows
A vast grove which brave Romulus made serve
For sanctuary, and 'neath the chill rock's depth
Lupercal, by Parrhasian custom called
Of Pan Lycaean. And he shows the grove
Of sacred Argiletum, and invokes
The spot to witness, and recounts the death
Of his guest Argus. Hence he leads them on
To the Tarpeian Rock, the Capitol,
Gay-golden, now, but whilom bristling rough
With woodland thickets. Its dread awe made quake
Even then the fearful rustics; aye, even then
They shuddered at the forest and the rock.   *350*
"This grove," said he, "this hill with leafy crown
Is a god's dwelling, but what god's, unknown.
Arcadia's folk believe they oft have seen
Jove's very hand the darkening aegis shake,
And summon up the storm-cloud. Here again
Two cities seest thou with dismantled walls,
Relics and records of the men of old:
One fort Sire Janus, and one Saturn, built—
This called Saturnia, that Janiculum."
So parleying they drew nigh the roof where dwelt
Thrifty Evander, and saw cattle stray
Lowing within Rome's Forum and superb
Carinae. When to his abode they came,
"These doors," said he, "Alcides' conquering feet
Once entered; him this palace hath contained.   *363*
Dare to spurn riches, O my guest, and shape

Thyself, too, worthy godship, and approach
All undisdainful of our humble hoard."
He spake, and 'neath the roof-tree's narrow slope
Led great Aeneas, and set him on a couch
Of strewn leaves, and a Libyan she-bear's fell.
   Night falls, and clasps the earth with dusky wings.
But Venus, mother-like, with no vain fear
Scared, and disturbed by the Laurentians' threats
And rude up-rising, thus to Vulcan speaks,
And in her golden nuptial bower begins,
Breathing the love-tones of immortal lips: 372
"While Argive kings were ravaging with war
Troy's doomèd towers, and ramparts soon to sink
In hostile flames, no succour I, nor arms
Craved of thine art or power; nor, dearest lord,
Thee or thy travail would I tax for naught,
Deep though my debt to Priam's sons, and oft
Though my tears mourned Aeneas' sore distress.
Now, by Jove's sovereign word, his foot stands firm
Upon the Rutule shore: I therefore now
Come suing, and of the godhead I adore
Crave boon of arms, a mother for her son.
Thee Nereus' daughter, thee Tithonus' bride,
Could with their tears unbend. See what a league
Of nations, see what cities with closed gates
Now whet the sword, to uproot me and mine."   386
The goddess ceased, and with the soft embrace
Of snowy arms about his body wound
Fondled him, as he faltered. Quick he caught
The wonted fire; the old heat pierced his heart,
Ran through his melting frame: as oftentimes
A fiery rift, burst by the thunder-clap,
Runs quivering down the cloud, with flash of light.
This saw his spouse, and at her guile rejoiced
In conscious beauty. Then thus spake the God
Enthralled by love immortal: "Wherefore seek
Afar for pretexts? Whither then hath fled
Thy faith in me, my goddess? Nay, hadst thou
So yearned of yore, even then I had not sinned
To arm the Teucrians; nor the Almighty Sire,
Nor Fate forbad it, that for ten years yet
Troy-towers should stand, and Priam's life endure.   399
And now, if war thou hast in hand to wage,
If such thy purpose, lo! what pains so-e'er
My craft can offer, what from ore of iron
Or molten electrum may be wrought, so far

As fire and air may stead thee—cease to pray,
Mistrustful of thy power." So saying, he gave
The embrace she longed for, on her bosom sank,
And wooed calm slumber to o'er-glide his limbs.

Soon as the first repose had banished sleep,
Hard on the half-way course of driven night,
What time a woman, forced to eke out life
With distaff and Minerva's slender toil,
Stirs up the embers of her slumbering fire,
To labour adding night, and by the glare
Plies hard her handmaids o'er the tedious task,
That she may keep her husband's couch from stain
And rear her infant sons, not otherwise,
Nor than that hour more slothful, from soft bed
Rose to his anvil-work the lord of fire.   *415*

There is an isle hard by Sicania's coast
That rises, and Aeolian Lipare,
With smoking rocks precipitous, where beneath
Thunders a cave, and Aetna's vaults, scooped out
By Cyclopean forges; the strong strokes
Of anvils to the ear bring echoing groans;
Hisses the steel ore through its hollow depths,
And from its furnaces pants fire—the home
Of Vulcan, and Vulcania the land's name.
Then hither from heaven's height the lord of fire
Descends. In their vast cave the Cyclops-brood
Were forging iron, Brontes and Steropes,
And naked-limbed Pyracmon. By their hands
Shaped, and e'en now part-burnished, was a bolt
Such as the Sire from heaven's wide cope to earth
Hurls many a time; part yet unfinished lay.   *428*
Three shafts of writhen shower, of watery cloud
Three, had they fused together, three of red
Flame and of wingèd south-wind, and were now
Mingling terrific flashes with the work,
And din, and dread, and wrath's pursuing fires.
Elsewhere a chariot and swift-flying wheels
For Mars were they dispatching, wherewithal
He rouseth men and cities, and eagerly
With serpent-scales of gold were burnishing
The terrible aegis, stormy Pallas' arm,
Snakes intertwined, and on the goddess' breast
The Gorgon's self, throat-severed, and with eyes
Rolling. "Away with all!" he cried. "Take hence,
Aetnean Cyclopes, your unfinished tasks,
And hither hark ye: armour must be made

For a bold warrior. Now is need of strength,
Now of deft hands, and all your master-skill: *442*
Spurn loitering!" There he ceased: they swiftly all
Bent to the task, like share to each assigned.
Flows brass in torrents, and flows ore of gold;
Melts in huge furnace the wound-working steel.
A mighty shield they shape, sole to withstand
All weapons of the Latins, welding it
Orb upon orb clenched sevenfold. Some, the while,
Working the windy bellows, in and out
Let the blasts drive; some dip i' the water-trough
The sputtering brass: groans with their anvils' weight
The cave-floor. They alternately in time
With giant strength uplift their arms, and turn
The massy metal with the forceps' grip.   *453*
    While on Aeolian shores the Lemnian sire
Speeds on the work, Evander the kind dawn
And matin-songs of birds beneath the eaves
Rouse from his lowly dwelling. The old man
Rises, and with a tunic clothes his limbs,
And binds Tyrrhenian sandals round his feet;
Then, fast to side and shoulder buckling on
A Tegean sword, flings back the panther's hide
Low-drooping on his left: and therewithal
Twain watch-dogs from the lofty threshold go
Before him, and their master's steps attend.
Toward the secluded chamber of his guest
Aeneas fared the hero, of their talk
Mindful, and his own promised boon. Nor less
Meanwhile Aeneas was astir betimes;
Beside him strode Achates, by the king
Pallas his son. Encountering they clasp hands,
Then, seated in the palace-midst, at length
Enjoy free converse. First the king began: *469*
"O mightiest leader of the Teucrian host,
Who living, ne'er will I confess the realm
And power of Troy defeated,—scant enow,
To match a name so famous, are our means
Of warlike aid: on one side hems us in
The Tuscan river, on one the Rutule foe
Presses, and thunders round our wall in arms;
But mighty tribes, a camp with kingdoms rich
With thee to knit I purpose—safety shown
By chance unlooked for. At the call of Fate
Hither thou wendest. Not far distant lies
A peopled city, reared of ancient stone,

Agylla, where the war-famed Lydian race
Once had their home upon the Etruscan heights.   *480*
Full many a year it flourished, and then passed
'Neath the proud sceptre and fierce iron sway
Of king Mezentius. Why the tale repeat—
His impious butcheries and mad tiger-deeds?
Hoard them, ye gods, on his own head to fall,
And on his children's! Nay, he would even link
Dead corpses to the quick, hand locked to hand,
And mouth to mouth—grim torment—and so steeped
In the rank moisture of that vile embrace
By lingering death destroy them. But at length,
Sick of his frantic raging, his own folk
Hie them to arms, close king and palace round,
Cut down the guards, and at the roof fling fire.   *491*
He, 'mid the carnage, safe to Rutule soil
Flies, and finds shelter with the friendly host
Of Turnus. All Etruria hereupon
Hath risen in righteous fury, and reclaims
Her king for vengeance. Of these thousands I
Will make thee chief, Aeneas: for their ships
O'er all the shore throng clamouring, and bid march
To battle, whom their agèd seer restrains,
Thus chanting doom: 'Maeonia's chosen hearts,
Prime flower and pith of a brave race of old,
Whom righteous anger hurls upon the foe,
Fired with just wrath against Mezentius, none
Italian-born so proud a race may tame;   *502*
Choose outland leaders.' Then the Etruscan host,
By the gods' warning frighted, on yon plain
Reposed them. Tarchon to myself hath sent
Envoys, with crown and sceptre of the realm,
The signs of empire to my charge commits,
Bids join the camp, assume the Etruscan sway.   *507*
But me the numbing frost of time-worn eld,
And strength past exploit, grudge the high command.
My son I had urged, but that his mother's blood
Blent him a Sabine and half native here.
Thou who in years and lineage both alike
Of Fate art favoured, whom the heavens demand,
Go forth, most valiant leader of the sons
Of Troy and Italy. Aye, and with thee
Pallas, my comfort and life's hope, I'll send;
Thy scholar, let him learn to brook the field
And the stern work of war, thy deeds behold,
And thee from youth's first opening years admire.   *517*

Arcadian horse two hundred, our picked strength
Of manhood, I will give him, and the like
Pallas in his own name shall give to thee."
    Scarce had he said: Aeneas, Anchises' son,
And true Achates, with eyes earthward bent,
On many a peril mournfully 'gan muse,
When lo! the Cytherean from clear skies
Gave signal: for, unlooked for, out of heaven
Came quivering flash and thunder-peal, and all
Seemed sudden to reel round them, and anon
A Tyrrhene trumpet-clang through heaven to blare.
Upward they glance; again and yet again
Crashed the vast din; then, canopied in cloud
Amid a stormless region of clear air,
Lo! the red gleam and thunderous shock of arms.   *529*
Others stood heart-amazed, but in that sound
Troy's hero knew his heavenly mother's pledge.
Then, "Seek not, O my host, seek not," he cried,
"What fate the portent bodes; 'tis I am called
From heaven. This sign the goddess who me bare
Foretold, should war assail us, she would send,
And wafted through the air from Vulcan bring
Armour to aid me. What vast carnage now
Hangs o'er the doomed Laurentines! What a price,
O Turnus, shalt thou pay me! 'Neath thy tide
How many shields, helms, bodies of the brave
Wilt roll, O father Tiber! Let them call
Their armies out, and snap the cords of peace!"   *540*
    So saying, he gat him from his lofty seat,
And first with fire to Hercules awakes
The slumbering altars, and with joy draws nigh
The Lar of yesterday, and hearth-gods small.
Alike Evander and Troy's youth alike
Slay duly chosen victims. To the ships
Then hies the hero, and re-seeks the crews,
And of their number culls the flower of war
To follow him afield; the remnant left
Ride on the downward stream, and idly float
With favouring current, to return and tell
Ascanius of their fortunes and his sire.
To Teucria's sons for Tyrrhene borders bound
Chargers are given; a steed of choice they lead
Forth for Aeneas, in tawny lion's skin
Housed wholly, that gleamed out with claws of gold. *553*
    Noised through the little town swift rumour flies
That to the palace of the Tyrrhene king

Horsemen are speeding. Mothers then for fear
Their vows redouble; more close on peril treads
Panic, and larger looms the shape of war.
Then to his son's right hand, at point to go,
Fast clings Evander, and insatiate weeps.
"Ah! would but Jupiter," he cries, "give back
The years departed, and the man I was
When close beneath Praeneste I mowed down
The foremost ranks, kindled the heapèd shields
Victorious, and to nether darkness hurled
With this right hand king Erulus! to him,
Her son, Feronia at his birth had given—
Fearful to tell—a triple life to live,
Thrice to bear arms, thrice o'er to be in death
Down-stricken: yet him of all his lives that day
This right hand robbed, and stripped of arms to
    match.   *567*
Ne'er from thy dear embrace had I been torn,
As now, my son; nor on this neighbour-head
With armèd insult had Mezentius dealt
Carnage so cruel, nor of so many sons
Bereaved my city. But O, ye powers above,
And Jupiter, prime potentate of heaven,
Pity, I you beseech, Arcadia's king,
And hear a father's prayer: 'If your dread wills,
If Fate, keep whole my Pallas, if life be
Once more to see and meet him, then for life
I beg, all burdens can with patience bear.   *577*
But, if some dire mischance thou threatenest, now,
Now, Fortune, let me snap life's cruel thread,
While sorrow masks her meaning, while hope hangs
Uncertain of the future, while I hold
Thee, boy beloved, my late and lone delight,
Clasped thus, nor heavier tidings wound mine ear.' "
Such final farewell words the sire outpoured,
Then swooned, and by his serfs was borne within.   *584*
   Now had the horse-troop through the open gates
Issued: Aeneas at their head with true
Achates came; then other lords of Troy.
Pallas himself midmost the column rode,
With scarf and inwrought arms conspicuous seen:
As when the dawn-star, washed in ocean's wave,
Dearer to Venus than all stellar fires,
Uplifts in heaven his sacred head and melts
The darkness. Mothers on the ramparts stand
Trembling, and following with their eyes afar

The dust-cloud, and the squadrons bright with brass. *593*
They through the brushwood, where the journey's
    end
Lay nearest, move in arms: a shout goes up,
And in formed column, hark! the four-foot tramp
Of galloping horse-hoofs shakes the crumbling plain.
There is a vast grove near cold Caere's stream,
Wide-worshipped with ancestral awe; a cirque
Of hollow hills enfolds it, with black pine
Girdling the forest. 'Twas dedicate, folk tell,
Both grove and feast-day, to Silvanus, god
Of field and flock, by the Pelasgians old,
Who erst within the Italian borders dwelt. *602*
Not far from hence, camped in a sheltered spot,
Were Tarchon and the Etruscans; all their host
From the high hill-top might be seen outspread
Along the tented fields. Hither repair
Aeneas and his chosen warrior train,
And for tired limbs and horses find repose.
    But Venus, the white goddess, gifts in hand,
Now through the clouds of heaven drew near, and
    when
Her son she spied in the lone vale afar,
By the cool stream sequestered, with such words
Hailing, she flashed her presence on his sight: *611*
"Lo! by my lord's skill perfected, I bring
The promised boon, that thou not shrink, my son,
Or proud Laurentians or keen Turnus' self
To bid to battle." Cytherea spake,
And sought her son's embrace: the gleaming arms
Beneath a fronting oak she set. He, glad
Of the divine gift and deep honour done,
Gazes insatiate, and from point to point
Lets his eyes wander, and admires, and turns
'Twixt hand and arm the terrible-crested helm
Out-darting fires, and the death-dealing sword,
And stiff brass-tempered corslet, blood-red, huge,
As when a dark-blue cloud from the sun's rays
Takes fire, and gleams afar; then the smooth greaves—
Electrum and twice-smelted gold—the spear
And inexpressible fabric of the shield. *625*
There had the fire-lord, skilled in prophet-lore,
Nor witless of the future, wrought the tale
Of Italy, the triumph-roll of Rome,
There all the kindred of the race to be,
Sprung from Ascanius, and the wars they waged,

One after one; thereon too he had wrought
The parent-wolf in the green cave of Mars
Lying outstretched; around her teats the twins
Hung playing, and to their mother set their lips
Undaunted; she, with shapely neck bent back,
Fondles by turns, and moulds them with her tongue.   *634*
Nor far from hence he had portrayed withal
Rome, and the Sabine maidens' lawless rape
In the thronged seats at the great Circus-games,
And a new war up-starting, as the sons
Of Romulus with agèd Tatius closed
And his stern Cures. Next, the strife allayed,
Lo! these two kings were standing armed before
Jove's altar, cup in hand, as each with each
They knit firm treaty o'er a slaughtered swine.
Hard by, the four-horse cars swift-driven had torn
Mettus in twain—thou should'st have kept thine
          oath,
    O Alban!—through the brake the liar's limbs
Tullus is haling; the splashed thorns drip blood.   *645*
Here too Porsenna, bidding them take back
The banished Tarquin, with a mighty siege
Hemmed in the city, while Aeneas' sons
Rushed on the sword for freedom. You might see
Wrath's semblance, aye, and menace in his face,
That Cocles should so dare break down the bridge,
And Cloelia, with snapped fetters, swim the flood.
There on the top of the Tarpeian hold,
Manlius, before the temple standing guard,
Held the high Capitol, the royal roof
New-bristling with the thatch of Romulus.   *654*
And here, in gilded colonnades, the goose
Fluttered in silver, shrieking that the Gauls
Were at the gate! and lo! the Gauls were near
Among the brushwood, hard upon the height,
Shielded by darkness and night's cloudy boon.
Of gold their locks, and golden their attire;
They glitter in striped cloaks, their milk-white necks
Circled with gold; two Alpine javelins each
They brandish, and long bucklers guard their limbs.   *662*
And here the dancing Salii he had forged,
And bare Luperci, the wool-tufted caps,
And shields that fell from heaven: and through the
          streets
Chaste matrons the high pomp on cushioned cars
Were leading. Far from hence hereto he adds

The halls Tartarean, lofty doors of Dis,
And dooms of sin, and, on the sheer rock poised,
Thee, Catiline, by Fury-faces scared,
And in sequestered seats the good—to them
Cato dispensing justice. Thereamidst
Rolled wide the semblance of the swelling main
Golden, but with hoar billows foamed the blue;
And dolphins of bright silver, circling round,
Swept ocean with their tails, and cleft the tide.   *674*
And fleets of brass i' the centre could be seen,
The battle-lines of Actium; you might mark
Leucate all a-glow with war's array,
And billows gleaming gold. Here to the strife
Caesar Augustus leading forth the host
Of Italy, with fathers and with folk,
The hearth-gods and the mighty gods of heaven,
Stands on the lofty stern; from his bright brows
Shoot two-fold fires, and his ancestral star
Dawns overhead. Elsewhere Agrippa towers,
Leading the line with winds and gods to aid;
Bright gleam his temples—proud device of war—
Beaked with the naval crown. Antonius here
With host barbaric and with motley arms,
Triumphant from the peoples of the dawn
And the Red Sea, brings Aegypt in his train,
The Orient's strength, and utmost Bactria,
Followed, O shame! by his Aegyptian bride.   *688*
Lo! all rush on together; the whole deep foams,
With in-drawn oars and triple beaks up-torn.
Seaward they press; thou'dst deem the Cyclades
Up-rooted swam the main, or mountains tall
Crashed against mountains, with such monstrous
    weight
The warriors mass them on the tower-crowned poops.
Hurled from the hand are showers of flaming tow
And wing'd steel missiles: with new carnage blush
The fields of Neptune. In their midst the queen
With native timbrel cheers her ranks, nor sees
As yet the twin snakes threatening from the rear.   *697*
Barking Anubis and strange bodied gods
Of every kindred, against Neptune ranged
And Venus and Minerva, poise their darts.
Storms Mavors in the battle's midst, embossed
In iron, with the fell Furies from on high;
And, in rent robe rejoicing, Discord stalks,
Bellona at her heels with blood-stained scourge.

Actian Apollo saw, and from above
His bow was bending: at whose terror all
Aegypt and Ind, with Arabs, every man,
And all the sons of Saba, turned and fled.   *706*
The queen herself to gales that heard her cry
Seemed spreading canvas, and now, now in act
To slip the loosened sheet. The lord of fire
Had fashioned her pale-faced with coming death
Amid the fray, borne on by wave and wind;
And opposite, in all his mighty bulk
Mourns Nilus, and throws open fold on fold,
With wide-spread vesture welcoming the rout
To his blue lap and watery fastnesses.   *713*
But Caesar, here in triple triumph borne
Within Rome's ramparts, to Italia's gods
Was dedicating through the city's breadth
Three hundred mighty fanes, his deathless vow;
With gladness, games, and shouting the streets rang.
In all the fanes were matron-bands, in all
Were blazing altars; at each altar-foot
Slain bullocks strewed the ground. The hero's self,
On fire-bright Phoebus' snowy threshold throned,
Tells o'er and hangs above those haughty gates,
The gifts of nations. In long pomp wind on
The vanquished peoples, manifold of speech,
As in the fashion of their garb and gear.   *723*
Here Mulciber the nomad race had formed,
And ungirt Africans, the Leleges
And Cares, and Gelonian arrow-men;
There went Euphrates now with humbler wave,
And, utmost of mankind, the Morini,
The hornèd Rhine, and Dahae unsubdued,
And proud Araxes chafing to be bridged.
Such marvels sees the hero on Vulcan's shield,
His mother's gift, and glorying in the signs
Of things he knows not, high on shoulder heaves
The fame and fortunes of his sons to be.   *731*

BOOK IX

Now while elsewhere afar these things are done,
Saturnian Juno hath to Turnus bold
Sent Iris out of heaven. It chanced that then
Turnus amidst his sire Pilumnus' grove
Sat in the sacred dell; to whom, as thus,
The child of Thaumas spake with rosy lip:
"That which no god had dared at thy desire
To pledge thee, Turnus, lo! the circling hour
Hath brought unbidden. Town, fleet, and comrades
    left,
Aeneas hies him to Evander's seat
And sceptre of the Palatine; nay, more,
To the utmost towns of Corythus hath pierced,
And gathers in armed bands the rustic folk
Of Lydia. Palter not; now, now's the time
To call for steeds and chariot; stop for naught,
But instant fall on their disordered camp."   *13*
She spake, and, on poised pinions reared aloft,
Cut flying a mighty bow beneath the clouds.
The warrior knew her, and, both hands upraised,
With such-like words her flying form pursued:
"Who sped thee, Iris, ornament of heaven,
Adown the cloud-way earthward to my side?
From whence this sudden splendour of the sky?
I see the pole part midway, and the stars
Roving the vault. I follow the great sign,
Whoe'er thou art, my summoner to arms."
So saying, he gat him to the stream, from off
Its eddying face drew water, to the gods
Breathed many a prayer, and burdened heaven with
    vows.   *24*
    And now his war-host through the open plain
Moved onward in its might; no lack of steeds,
No lack of broidered raiment and of gold.
The vanward ranks Messapus sways, the rear
The warrior-sons of Tyrrheus; midmost rides
Turnus, their captain: as with seven still streams
Ganges in silence rising high, or Nile,
When his rich river ebbs from off the plain,
And now hath sunk within his bed. Anon

[279]

The Teucrians a black cloud of sudden dust
See gather, and darkness rise upon the plain.
First from a fronting mound Caïcus cries: *35*
"What mass of pitchy gloom, my countrymen,
Rolls onward? Speed to arms, bring weapons, mount
The walls! The foeman is upon us, ho!"
With clamorous shouts the Teucrians through all gates
Plunge in, and fill the ramparts. For even thus
Aeneas, warrior peerless, ere he went
Had charged them, if that aught meanwhile should
  hap,
Nor venture to draw out the ranks of war,
Nor trust the plain, but keep the camp alone,
And sheltering bulwark of the walls. So now,
Though shame and anger point them to the field,
The gates they bar, his bidding do, and armed
Within their hollow towers await the foe.   *46*
Turnus, whose swift advance his tardier troop
Had distanced, with a score of chosen horse
Behind him, stands, ere looked for, at the gate;
Borne on a Thracian steed of dappled white,
A gold helm guards him decked with ruddy plume.
"Friends, is there any will first upon the foe
With me?"—he cries, "now mark you": and a spear
Whirling he casts, as prelude of the fray,
And, towering high, careers along the plain.   *53*
His men catch up the challenge clamorously,
And with terrific war-cries follow: much
They marvel at the Teucrians' laggard hearts,
That a fair field they face not, nor abide
The battle-shock like men, but hug the camp.
Hither and thither stormily he rides
Scanning the ramparts, and, where way is none,
Questing for entrance. As a wolf, that lies
In wait for some full sheep-fold, at the doors
Stands howling, buffeted of wind and rain
At midnight; safe beneath their mother's sides
The lambs bleat loudly; he, with savage wrath
Insatiate, rages out of reach, spurred on
By the long-gathering frantic lust of food,
And droughty jaws unbloodied: even so
The Rutule's wrath takes fire, as on their walls
And camp he gazes: in his iron frame
Burns indignation—by what art essay
An entrance? from behind their ramparts how
Drive forth the Teucrians, pour them on the plain?   *68*

The fleet, which close beside the camp lay snug,
Hedged round with earth-works and the river-wave,
On this he falls, to his exulting mates
Cries out for fire, and grasps, himself on flame,
A blazing pine-torch. Then to work they fall,
Spurred on by Turnus' presence; the whole troop
Arm them with murky brands: the hearths are
    stripped;
The reeking torch sends up a pitchy glare,
And Vulcan wafts the sooty lees to heaven.   76
    What god, O Muses, from the Teucrians turned
So vast a conflagration? from their decks
Who dashed the fire? It is an old-world faith,
But famed for ever. What time Aeneas first,
On Phrygian Ida fashioning his fleet,
To the high seas addressed him, in such wise
The Berecynthian mother of the gods
Spake to Almighty Jove: "Grant, son, the boon
Which thy dear mother for Olympus quelled
Now craves of thee. A pine-forest had I
Beloved for many a year, a grove that crowned
The hill-top, whither offerings would be brought,
Dark with black pitch-trees and with maple-boles:
These, when a fleet he lacked, full fain I gave
Unto the Dardan youth: now anxious fear
Disquiets and torments me. Loose my dread,
And let a parent's prayers prevail, that these
Nor voyage may break, nor whirlwind overwhelm;
So speed them from my mountains to have sprung."   92
To whom her son, who wheels the starry worlds:
"Whither would'st bid the Fates? for these thy barks
What seek'st thou, Mother? Shall ships of mortal
    build
Win rights immortal, or Aeneas roam
Through changeful perils, unassailed by change?
What god may boast such plenitude of power?
Nay, but when, service o'er, they one day reach
Their bourne, Ausonia's haven, such as then
Have 'scaped the waves, and borne the Dardan chief
To shores Laurentian, these will I divest
Of mortal mould, and bid be goddesses
Of the great deep, as Doto, Nereus' child,
And Galatea, who breast the foaming sea."
He spake, and by his Stygian brother's stream,
Banks that with pitch and a black whirlpool boil,
Nodded assent, and with the nod set all

Olympus quaking.
    So the promised day
Had come, the Fates their destined hours fulfilled,
When Turnus' outrage the great Mother warned
To drive the fire-brands from her sacred ships.
Here a strange light first flashed upon their eyes,
And from the Dawn a vast cloud seemed to speed
Athwart the sky, with Ida's choirs. Then fell
An awful utterance through the air, that filled
Both Trojan ranks and Rutule: "Trouble not,
Ye Teucrians, to defend my ships, nor arm
Your hands with weapons; Turnus shall have power
To burn the seas up, ere yon sacred pines.
And go ye free, go, Ocean-goddesses;
The Mother bids you." And the barks forthwith
Rend each her cable from the bank, dip beaks,
And dive like dolphins to the watery depth;
Then one and all—stupendous prodigy—
As maiden-forms emerge, and stem the main. *122*
 Astounded were the Rutules; terror fell
Even on Messapus and his plunging steeds;
Tiber himself, hoarse-murmuring, stays his flood,
And from the deep recoils. But not for that
Quailed the bold heart of Turnus; nay, with words
He roused their spirit, and spared not even to chide:
"These portents threat the Trojans; aye, from them
Great Jove himself hath reft their wonted aid;
They bide not Rutule darts and fires. So then
The seas are trackless to the Teucrians, flight
Denied them, and one half the world cut off;
As for the mainland, in our grasp it lies;
So many thousands—tribes of Italy—
For battle stand. The bodeful dooms of heaven,
Howe'er the Phrygians vaunt them, fright not me: *134*
Enough to Fate and Venus hath been given,
That Troy has touched Ausonia's fertile shore.
I too have counter-fates, to smite nor spare
The accursèd stock that balks me of my bride;
Not Atreus' sons alone that pang can pierce,
Nor but Mycenae's city rise in arms. *139*
'But suffering once suffices'? Yes, had once
To sin sufficed them, hating from their hearts
Well nigh all woman-kind. And these to trust
Their screening rampart, by a hindering trench
Emboldened, a poor span 'twixt death and them!
Why, saw they not Troy-walls, by Neptune's hand

Up-builded, sink in flame? But which of you,
My chosen hearts, makes ready to hew down
The rampart at sword's point, and rush with me
Upon their fluttered camp? No need have I
Of arms from Vulcan, or a thousand keels,
To face the Teucrians. Let Etruria now
Band all her sons to aid them. They need fear
No darkness, no Palladium's coward theft,
Or sentries slaughtered on the fortress-height.
Nor will we shroud us in a horse's womb
Out of men's eyes. In the broad light of day
We are purposed to ring round their walls with fire.   *153*
I trow they shall not say they have to do
With Danaan and Pelasgic chivalry,
Whom Hector till the tenth year baffled. Now,
Day's better part o'erpast, for what remains,
Refresh you, warriors, heartened by success,
And deem, so doing, ye fit you for the fray."   *158*
Meanwhile Messapus to blockade the gates
Hath charge with sentry-pickets, and surround
The works with watch-fires. Twice seven Rutule chiefs
Are chosen with soldiery to keep the walls;
Each has a hundred warriors in his train,
Gay with red helmet-plumes and glittering gold.
They speed apart, and shift the alternate watch,
Or, stretched on greensward, let the wine have way,
And tilt the brazen bowls. The fires burn bright;
The guard with games the sleepless night prolong.   *167*
    This spy the Trojans from the rampart's height,
As armed they man the summit; in trembling haste
They try the gates, yoke bridge and tower, bring darts.
Mnestheus and keen Serestus goad them on,
Whom Prince Aeneas, should mischance demand,
Set to control the host and guide the war.
Parting the peril, the whole band by turn,
Each at his post, keep watch along the walls.   *176*
    Nisus, keen warrior, held the gate, the son
Of Hyrtacus, whom in Aeneas' train
Ida the huntress sent; quick-handed he
With spear, and light-winged arrows; beside him
Euryalus, than whom no comelier youth
Clave to Aeneas, or donned Trojan arms—
Whose smooth boy-face showed faint the budding
        man.
These had one heart between them: side by side
They wont to rush on battle; and now too

Each with like charge was posted at the gate.   *183*
Quoth Nisus: "Is't the gods thus fire our hearts,
Or maketh each his wild desire a god,
Euryalus? My heart's long since afret
On war to launch me, or some great essay,
With stagnant ease ill-satisfied. Thou seest
What confidence in fortune holds the foe:
Few gleam their lights and far; themselves lie prone,
In sleep and wine dissolved; all's hushed around.
Mark further what I muse of, in my mind
What purpose rises. 'Tis the cry of all,
Both folk and fathers, that we summon back
Aeneas, send messengers with tidings sure.   *193*
If what I ask they promise thee—myself
The deed's own fame suffices—'neath yon mound
Methinks my feet would guide me to the walls
And fort of Pallanteum." Euryalus,
Thrilled and transfixed with mighty love of praise,
Thus at the word his glowing friend bespeaks:
"Nisus, dost shun to knit me to thy side
In high exploit? Or should I let thee go
To face such perils singly? 'Twas not thus
My sire Opheltes, to war's work inured,
'Mid Argive terrors and the woes of Troy
Trained me and reared; nor at thy side have I
So borne me, since I followed to the field
High-souled Aeneas and his utmost fate.
Here, here's a soul that scorns the sunlight, deems
That fame thou striv'st for cheaply bought with life." *206*
Then Nisus: "No such fear of thee had I,
Nor just it were; nay, so may mighty Jove,
Or whoso on these things bends favouring eye,
Restore me to thy side in triumph. But if—
As oft in such adventure thou behold'st—
Some chance or god should hurry me to harm,
I would that thou survive me. At thine age
It is more meet to live. O, be there one
To lay me, snatched or ransomed from the fray,
In earth, or, if some wonted hap forbid,
Pay funeral offerings to my absent dust,
And grace me with a tomb! Nor let me bring
Such grief on that sad mother, who, alone
Of many mothers, dared follow thee, her boy,
And hath no heart for great Acestes' town."   *218*
But he: "Thou weavest empty pleas in vain,
Nor doth my purpose alter or give way.

Speed we betimes!" He spake, and roused the watch,
Who to their charge succeed, then quits his post,
And, step by step with Nisus, seeks the prince.
   All creatures else on earth were easing care
With slumber, and their hearts forgot to ache.
The foremost Teucrian lords, their flower of war,
Were kingdom's weal debating—what to do,
Who to Aeneas should the tidings bear.   *228*
Leaning on their long spears, and shield on arm,
Midmost the camp in a clear space they stood.
Then Nisus and with him Euryalus
In eager haste crave audience: what they urged
Was weighty, and would recompense delay.
Iulus first to their impatient suit
Gave audience, and bade Nisus speak; then thus
The son of Hyrtacus: "O sons of Troy,
Hearken with kindly heed, nor let the worth
Of what we offer by our years be weighed.
Dissolved in wine and sleep, the Rutuli
Keep silence: our own eyes have marked a spot
For stratagem left open, where yon gate
Lets in or out upon the seaward side.   *237*
Their line of fires is broken, and black smoke
Goes up to heaven. Let us but use the chance
To seek Aeneas and Pallanteum's fort,
Soon will ye see us here at hand with spoils,
After great slaughter done. Nor will the way
We go beguile us: down the valleys dim,
Assiduous in the chase, we have seen gleam
The city, and all the river-windings know."
Aletes hereupon, with years o'erweighed
And ripe of wisdom, spake: "Gods of our sires,
Whose power divine still watches over Troy,
Howbeit, ye think not a full end to make
Of all the Teucrians, in that ye vouchsafe
Our youth such valour and heart-steadfastness."
So saying, the shoulders and right hands of both
Embraced he, and bathed all his face with tears.   *251*
"What guerdon, heroes, of your glorious deeds
Can I deem worthy to be paid you? First
Heaven and your own hearts will the best bestow;
Then good Aeneas, what else remains anon
Will yield you, and Ascanius, whose fresh youth
Service so noble never can forget."
"Nay I," breaks in Ascanius, "whose sole hope
Of safety hangs upon my sire's return,

By the great hearth-gods, Nisus, thee adjure,
The guardian spirit of Assaracus,
And hoary Vesta's shrine; whate'er I have
Of faith or fortune in your laps I lay:
Bring back my sire, restore him to my sight:
He here again, grief is not. Goblets twain
Silver-wrought, rough with tracery, will I give,
Ta'en by my sire, what time he smote and quelled
Arisba, and twin tripods, and of gold
Two mighty talents, and a bowl of yore,
Sidonian Dido's gift. But if our lot
Be to take Italy, to win and wield
A conqueror's sceptre, and mete out the spoil—
Thou sawest the war-steed whereon Turnus rode
In arms, all golden—none but that, with shield
And ruddy plume, O Nisus, will I pluck
Forth from the lot, thine even from this day.   *271*
Matrons twice six beside of choicest form
My sire will give thee, and men-captives eke,
All with their armour, and of land, to boot,
What King Latinus hath for his domain.
But thee, thrice honoured youth, whose age my own
Doth in the race press closer, from this hour
To my whole heart I take, betide what may,
And clasp thee for my comrade. Without thee,
For mine own lot no glory shall be wooed;
Come peace or war, to thee, both deed and word,
Be all my heart unbosomed." Answered then
Euryalus: "From such bold venture me
No time shall prove degenerate, let but Fate
Be kind, not cruel. But all gifts beyond,
One boon I beg: I have a mother sprung
From Priam's ancient race, whom Ilian land
Held not, poor soul, nor king Acestes' town
From faring forth with me. Her now I leave
Unwitting of this peril, whatsoe'er,
Aye, and ungreeted—Night and thy right hand
My witness be—for that I may not brook
A parent's weeping. But do thou, I pray,
Comfort her need and aid her loneliness.   *289*
Let me bear hence this hope of thee: hereby
Into all dangers I shall boldlier go."
Touched to the heart, the Dardans wept, and fair
Iulus before all, whose soul was wrung
With likeness of the love he bore his sire.
Then thus he speaks: "Assure thee of all done

That thy great exploit merits: for she shall be
As my own mother, lacking but the name
Crëusa; nor slight honour waits the womb
That bore so nobly. Let what fortune may
Be the deed's sequel, by this head I vow,
As oft my sire was wont, whate'er to thee
I promise, prosperously returned, the same
Shall for thy mother and thy kin abide."   302
Weeping he spake, and from his shoulder doffs
A gilded sword, which erst Lycaon of Crete
Wrought with rare skill, and fitted for the hand
With ivory sheath. A shaggy lion's hide
Mnestheus to Nisus gives; Aletes true
Makes interchange of helmets. Thus arrayed
Onward they move, whom all the band of chiefs,
Both young and old, escorting to the gates,
Follow with vows. And fair Iulus too,
Armed with man's thought and spirit beyond his
        years,
Full many a message to his sire bade bear.
But one and all the rude winds rend amain,
And to the clouds consign them unfulfilled.   313
    Thence issuing forth, they cross the trench, and seek
Through shades of night the foeman's camp—yet first
To be the death of many. In drunken sleep
Stretched on the greensward scattered forms they see,
Cars tilted on the beach, 'twixt wheels and reins
Their masters, and with these one litter of arms
And wine. First spake the son of Hyrtacus:
"Now for a bold stroke! now, Euryalus,
The deed itself invites; here lies our way.
Watch thou, and keep wide outlook, lest some hand
Should from behind assail us: here will I
Deal havoc, and by a broad lane lead thee on."   323
He spake, then checks his utterance, and lets drive
At haughty Rhamnes, who, it chanced, high-propped
On heapèd carpets, the full-chested breath
Of sleep was heaving—king himself, and seer,
Best-loved of kingly Turnus; but no whit
His seer-craft might avail to ward off doom.
Three of his folk hard by, at random laid
Among their weapons, he takes unaware,
And the armour-bearer, aye, and charioteer,
Of Remus, close beside his horses caught,
And with the sword shears through their lolling
        necks;   331

Then from their lord himself he lops the head,
And leaves the red trunk gurgling; with black gore
Reek couch and greensward. Lamyrus withal,
Lamus, and young Serranus, who that night
Had played full long, and in his beauty's pride
Lay there limb-vanquished by the o'erpotent god—
Ah! happier had he played a night-long bout,
Nor made an end till morn!—such havoc as when
An unfed lion, ravaging amid
Full sheep-folds—for mad famine goads him on—
Mangles and rends the mild flock mute with fear,
And roars with blood-stained mouth. Nor less mean-
    while
The slaughter of Euryalus; he too
Rages like fire, and, as they blocked his path,
Falls on a vast and nameless crowd, and slays
Fadus, Herbesus, Rhoetus, Abaris,
Or ere they knew it. Rhoetus awake saw all,
But crouched in fear behind a mighty bowl;   *346*
Full in whose breast, as up he rose, the youth
At arm's length, to the hilt, his sword-blade plunged,
And steeped in death withdrew it. He pours forth
The red life, dying, and blood-mingled wine;
The other on his dark errand hotly hies.
Now was he making for Messapus' train,
Where the last gleams of dying fire, and steeds
Tethered a-row, and grazing, he beheld,
When Nisus briefly—for he saw him borne
Beyond all bounds with lust of carnage—cried:
"Forbear we now; the unfriendly dawn draws nigh.   *355*
We have drunk full deep of vengeance, through the
    foe
Hewed out a passage." Many a trophy fair—
Men's arms of solid silver wrought, and bowls,
And sumptuous coverlets, they leave behind.
Euryalus the trappings tears away
And gold-bossed belt of Rhamnes, which of yore
Right wealthy Caedicus sent as a gift
To Remulus of Tibur, when from far
For friend he sought him: to his grandson's hand
Dying he left them, by the Rutule host
After his death in war and battle won.
These he tears off, and on his shoulders brave
Binds, but in vain, then dons Messapus' helm
Well-fitted, plume-adorned. So forth from camp
They pass, and make for safety.   *366*

But meanwhile
Horsemen, sent forward from the Latin town,
While halts the main host on the plain arrayed,
Came bringing answers for King Turnus' ear,
Three hundred, shield-men all, by Volscens led.
Even now they approach the camp, and near the wall,
When at some distance they descry the twain
Rounding the path to leftward; and the helm
In glimmer of night betrayed Euryalus
Unheedful, and flashed back the opposing ray:
Nor seen for naught. Cries Volscens from his troop: 375
"Stand, warriors; wherefore thus afoot? and say
Who are ye that go armed, and whither fare?"
Naught urge they in reply, but speed amain
Into the woods, and trust them to the night.
The horsemen interpose, bar right and left
The well-known crossways, and with sentinels
Fringe every outlet. The wood bristled wide
With brambles and dark ilex, every way
Choked with impenetrable thorns; the path
Through the dim forest-tracks gleamed brokenly.   383
Euryalus by darkness of the boughs
Perplexed, and spoil-encumbered, is by fear
Fooled of his bearings. Nisus wins clear off:
And now, all heedless, he had passed the foe,
And region, afterward from Alba's name
Hight Alban—then the lofty cattle-stalls
Of King Latinus—when he stopped, looked back
For his lost friend, in vain. "Euryalus,
Unhappy one! where have I left thee? how
Follow, and unthrid all the tangled path
Of treacherous woodland?" Therewith, questing back,
His footsteps he retraces, roaming on
Through the hushed brakes. He hears the horses'
     tread,
Hears the loud din and signals of pursuit.   394
Nor long the time till to his ear a shout
Comes, and he sees Euryalus, whom trapped
By the false ground and darkness, and confused
By sudden onslaught, the whole band even now
Hale onward, struggling valiantly, in vain.
What can he do? Say, with what force, what arms
A rescue dare? Or should he rush on doom
Amid the sword-blades, and precipitate
Through wounds a glorious death? Quick drawing
     back

His arm, and brandishing a spear, he looks
Up to the moon in heaven, and prays aloud: *403*
"Thou, goddess, thou, Latona's child, be near
To aid my effort, glory of the stars
And guardian of the groves; if Hyrtacus
My sire hath ever to thine altars brought
Gifts for my sake, if any I myself
Have added from the chase, and in thy dome
Hung them, or fastened to thy sacred roof,
Let me confound this banded mass, and guide
My darts through air." He spake, and hurls the steel
With his whole body's strength. The flying spear
Sunders the shades of night, meets the turned back
Of Sulmo, and there snaps, the splintered shaft
Riving his heart: he, spouting from his breast
The hot life-stream, rolls over, chilled in death,
And long gasps heave his palpitating sides.   *415*
All eyes look every way. He thereupon
The keenlier poises, see! a second dart
Aimed from the ear-tip. While they hesitate,
Through Tagus' either temple sped the spear
Hissing, and clave warm in the piercèd brain.
Volscens storms fiercely, but can nowhere spy
The wielder of the weapon, nor whereon
To launch his fury. "Thou at least," he cried,
"Shalt with thy life-blood pay the debt of both,"
And so drew sword, and on Euryalus
Was rushing. Then indeed, with terror mad,
Nisus shrieks wildly, nor can shroud himself
Longer in darkness, or such anguish bear: *426*
"Here, here am I, the doer, on me, on me
Turn all your steel, O Rutules! Mine the fault,
Mine only: he nor dared, nor could have done it;
This heaven, these stars, be witness, that know all!
He only loved his hapless friend too well."
So spake he; but the sword, with strength driven
    home,
Has pierced the ribs, and rends the snowy breast.
Euryalus rolls in death; the blood runs o'er
His beauteous limbs, and on his shoulder sinks
The faint neck: as a bright flower, by the plough
Shorn through, droops dying, or poppies weary-
    necked,
By a chance shower o'er-weighted, bow the head.   *437*
But Nisus leaps amidst them, seeks through all
Volscens alone, for none but Volscens stays.

The foe, massed round him close on either side,
Beat him aback. Nathless he presses on,
And whirls his lightning blade, till, plunging it
Full in the shouting Rutule's face, he reft,
Dying, the foeman's life, then, pierced with wounds,
Flung him upon his lifeless friend, and there
At last lay pillowed calm in death's repose.
　　Ah! happy pair! if aught my verse avail,
No lapse of hours from time's recording page
Shall e'er erase you, while Aeneas' house
Dwells on the Capitol's unshaken rock,
And the great Roman sire holds sovereignty. 　　　449
　　The conquering Rutules, masters of the spoil
And plunder, now with tears the breathless corse
Of Volscens bear to camp; nor in the camp
Less wild their grief for Rhamnes lifeless found,
And all those chiefs in one fell carnage slain
With Numa and Serranus. A great throng
Makes for the dead and dying, where all reeked fresh
With slaughter, and the full streams foamed with
　　　blood.
One with another, they recognize the spoil,
Messapus' gleaming helm and trophies fair,
That cost such sweat of battle to win back. 　　　458
　　Now, rising from Tithonus' saffron bed,
Young Dawn was sprinkling with new beams the
　　　world;
In floods the sunlight, and lays all things bare,
When Turnus, girt in his own warlike arms,
Summons to arms his men, and every chief
Musters for battle his brass-mailed array,
And with a thousand rumours whets their wrath.
Aye, and on upraised spear-points, piteous sight!
They fix, and follow with loud shouts, the heads
Of Nisus and Euryalus. But Troy's sons
Unflinching on the ramparts' leftward side
Have set their line of battle—for the right
Is girded by the river—and there guard
The yawning trench, and on the lofty towers
Stand sorrowing, moved to see on spear-heads borne
Those warrior-faces, known, alas! too well,
And dripping with dark gore. 　　　472
　　　　　　　　　Winged Fame the while
Speeds with the tidings through the affrighted town,
And to the mother of Euryalus
Comes floating in at ear. Then, hapless one!

Warmth left her frame of a sudden; from both hands
Dashed was the shuttle, and all her task unwound.
Forth flies the ill-fated dame with woman's shrieks,
Rent locks, and madly for the ramparts makes
And foremost fighters, heedless she of men,
Heedless of danger and of darts, then fills
The heaven with lamentations: "Is it thus,
Euryalus, I see thee? and could'st thou,
Late refuge of mine age, so leave me lone?
Ah! cruel; and on such perilous errand sent,
Might thy poor mother bid thee no farewell?   484
Alas! in a strange land thou liest, a prey
To Latin dogs and vultures! Nor have I,
Thy mother, led thy funeral-pomp, or closed
Thine eyes, or washed thy wounds, or with the robe
Thee covered, which I toiled at, night and day,
Easing an old wife's sorrow with the loom.
Say, whither can I follow, or what land now
Holds thy dismembered frame and mangled corse?
Son, bring'st me back no more of thee than this?
Is't this I followed over land and main?   492
If ye have men's hearts, pierce me, upon me
Heave all your shafts, O Rutules; with the sword
Me first devour: or thou, great Sire of gods,
Have pity, and with thy bolt to Tartarus' depth
Hurl this detested head, since sunder else
Life's cruel yoke I may not." With her sobs
All hearts were torn; a moan of anguish passed
From rank to rank, their valour numbed and crushed
For battle. As thus she fed the flame of woe,
Idaeus and Actor, bidden of Ilioneus
And tear-dissolved Iulus, in their arms
Caught her, and bore within.   502
                             But hark! the trump
Its terrible note of clanging brass afar
Has uttered; a shout follows, and the sky
Reverberates. The Volscians side by side
Urge the shield-tortoise onward, fain to fill
The trench, and rend the rampart. Other some
Quest for an entrance, and with scaling-gear
To mount the wall, there where the line was scant,
And the gapped circle, sparselier manned, showed
   thin
The Teucrian host with motley missile-showers
Meet who assail them, and stout push of pole,
Taught by long warfare to defend their walls.   511

[292]

Stones too of deadly weight they roll, in hope
The roofèd ranks to shatter, though fain are these
All shocks to bear'neath that impervious shell.
Yet fail they now: for where yon mighty swarm
Threatens, up-roll the Teucrians and heave o'er
A monstrous mass, which on the Rutules wrought
Wide havoc, and brake their coverlet of mail.
No longer the bold Rutules care to wage
A blindfold war, but from the rampart strive
With darts to thrust them. Otherwhere, grim sight,
Mezentius, brandishing a Tuscan pine,
Hurls smoky fire-brands; while Messapus, see!
Tamer of horses, Neptune's child, tears down
The rampart, and cries "Ladders to the wall!"   524

    O Calliope, inspire me, thou and thine,
To sing what havoc, what deaths upon that day
Dealt Turnus with the sword, what warrior's life
Sped each to Orcus; and unroll with me
The mighty margins of the scroll of war.

    There was a tower that strained the upward gaze,
With gangways high, on site of vantage set,
Which all of Italy strove amain to storm,
And toiled their utmost to o'er-topple: this
The Trojans were defending, armed with stones,
And through the loop-holes hurled their darts in
    showers.   534
Turnus first flung a blazing torch, and drave
Into its flank the fire, which, swollen with wind,
Caught board and beam, and clung there and
    devoured.
Wild panic reigns within, and vain essay
To shun disaster. While they huddle close,
Back-settling to the side which lacks the bane,
Suddenly, over-weighed, down fell the tower,
And all the welkin thundered with the crash.   541
Half-dead to earth they come, the monster-mass
Behind them, pierced alike by their own darts,
And with hard splinters through the breast impaled.
Scarce one alone, Helenor, and with him
Lycus, escaped; Helenor in youth's prime,
Whom slave Licymnia erst had secretly
Borne to Maeonia's king, and sent to Troy
In arms forbidden, with bare sword light-arrayed
And blank shield nameless. Soon as he beheld
About him Turnus' thousands, with the ranks
Of Latium standing on this side and that,

As a wild beast that, by the huntsmen's ring
Hemmed closely, storms against the darts, and leaps,
Eyes open, upon death, and with a bound
Springs on the spear-points, even so the youth
Midmost the foemen rushed on doom, and, where
He saw the darts throng thickest, aimed his way.   555
But Lycus, with his feet far doughtier, thrids
Through foes and darts his flight, and gains the wall,
Fain to clutch coping and reach comrades' hands.
Whom Turnus, following both with foot and spear,
Thus taunts in triumph: "Fool, thought'st thou to escape
My grasp?" so seized him as he clung, and tore
Down with a mighty fragment of the wall: 562
As when, with hare or snowy-bodied swan
Gripped in his hookèd talons, soars aloft
Jove's armour-bearer, or as wolf of Mars
Snatches a lamb from fold, with bleat on bleat
Sought by its mother. From every side ascends
The war-shout; on they press, and from the mound
Fill in the trenches. Others at the roofs
Fling blazing brands. With a huge mass of rock,
Torn from a mountain, Ilioneus strikes down
Lucetius, as with fire in hand he drew
Anigh the gate; Liger Emathion,
Asilas Corynaeus, with javelin that,
This skilled with sly-winged arrow from afar.
Caeneus Ortygius, Turnus Caeneus, quells,
Fresh from his victory; Turnus Itys too
And Clonius, Dioxippus, Promolus,
And Sagaris, and Idas, as he stood
In forefront of the bulwarks; Capys slays
Privernus. Him Themilla's glancing spear
At first had grazed, who, madly dropping shield,
Laid hand on hurt: on flew the wingèd shaft,
Pinned to left side his palm, probed deep, and tore
With murderous breach the passages of breath.   580
The son of Arcens stood in splendid arms
With needle-broidered scarf superbly dight
Of dark Iberian dye, for beauty famed,
Whom his sire Arcens to the field had sent,
Reared in his mother's grove anigh the streams
Symaethian, where Palicus' altar stands,
Gift-dowered and gracious: flinging spears aside,
Mezentius with strained thong the whizzing sling
Thrice whirled about his head, with molten ball

Cleft the mid-forehead of the opposing foe,
And stretched him all his length upon the sand.   *589*
  Then first, 'tis said, Ascanius his swift shaft
Levelled in war, till now but wont to fright
The flying quarry, and with his hand laid low
The brave Numanus, surnamed Remulus,
To Turnus' younger sister late-allied
In wedlock. He before the vanward ranks
Strode, shouting words meet and unmeet to tell,
And swollen at heart with his new royalty,
Stalked vainly, clamouring loud: "Ah! blush ye not,
Twice captured Phrygians, yet again to be
Cooped within rampart by the leaguer's ring,
And thus to wall off death? Lo! these the men
Who claim our wives at the sword's point! What god,
What madness, say, drove you to Italy?   *601*
Not here the Atridae, nor Ulysses here
Tongue-trickster. Hardy and of a hardy stock,
Down to the river our very babes we bring,
And brace them with the water's cruel cold.
Our boys hunt tireless, and wear out the woods,
Their sport to rein the steed, stretch shaft on bow.
Patient of toil, to need inured, our youth
Tame earth with mattocks, or shake towns with war.
No age of life but with hard steel is worn;
With spear reversed our bullocks' flanks we goad;
Nor sluggish eld doth our hearts' strength impair,
Or warp our vigour: on white locks we press
The helmet-rim, and evermore delight
To mass new plunder and by rapine live.   *613*
Yours are embroidered robes of saffron tint,
Or gleaming purple; sloth is your delight;
Ye love to revel in the dance, and wear
Sleeved tunics and stringed turbans. Phrygians ye,
Women, indeed, not men; go, range the heights
Of Dindymus, where to practised touch the pipe
Utters its twofold note. The timbrels, hark!
The Idaean mother's Berecynthian flute
Calls you: leave arms to men, and quit the sword."   *620*
  Such wordy boasting and loud-threatening taunts
Ascanius brooked not: on the horse-hair string
He stretched a shaft, confronting him, and drew
His arms apart, and stood, first praying to Jove
With suppliant vows: "Almighty Jupiter,
Smile on my bold essay. I to thy shrine
Will yearly offerings bring, and set a steer

Brow-gilded at thine altar, dazzling white,
His head borne level with his dam's, now meet
To butt with horn and spurn with hoof the soil."   629
The Father heard, and from a clear sky-space
Thundered upon the left; at once the bow
Twanged with its deadly freight. The shaft drawn
    home
Flew whistling grim, and borne through Remulus'
    head
Cleft with steel barb the hollows of his brow.
"Go then, with haughty words at valour mock!
The twice-ta'en Phrygians to the Rutules send
This answer back." Thus far Ascanius spake;
The Teucrians cheer responsive, shout for joy,
And mount in soul to heaven. It chanced that then
Long-haired Apollo from a tract of sky
Was glancing downward on the Ausonian host,
And city, cloud-enthroned, and thus addressed
Iulus, as he triumphed: "Good luck have thou
Of thy new valour, boy! So men mount heaven,
O god-descended, sire of gods to be.
Rightly shall all wars, doomed to rise, sink down
Beneath the offspring of Assaracus.   643
Troy cannot hold thee." With that word he shoots
From heaven on high, disparts the breathing gales,
And seeks Ascanius. Then his form he shifts
To that of agèd Butes, who erewhile
Was armour-bearer to the Dardan chief
Anchises, and true warder of the gate;
Thereafter charged by the lad's sire to guard
Ascanius. Onward then Apollo strode,
Like the old man in all, both voice and hue,
As in white locks, and fiercely-clashing arms;
Then thus to fiery-souled Iulus spake: 652
"Child of Aeneas, enough that by thy shafts
Numanus unavenged hath bit the dust;
This thy first praise doth great Apollo grant,
Nor grudges arms that emulate his own.
Cease, boy, from further warfare." Thus began,
But in mid utterance left the eyes of men,
Apollo, and into empty air afar
Vanished from sight. The Dardan princes knew
The god, and his divine artillery,
And heard the quiver rattling as he flew.   660
Ascanius, eager for the fray, they check
With Phoebus' word of power; themselves once more

Fill up the battle-ranks, and cast their lives
Into the yawning peril. A shout runs
From tower to tower, the whole wall's length; they
    stretch
Their eager bows, and whirl the javelin-thong.
Earth is all strewn with missiles; shield and helm
Ring hollow to their blows; fierce swells the fight;
Thick as a shower that, rising from the west,
Beneath the watery kid-stars whips the ground,
Or heavy as hail that headlong pelts the sea,
When, rough with southern blasts, the sky-god whirls
His watery storm, and bursts the clouds in heaven.   *671*
    Pandarus and Bitias, from Alcanor sprung
Of Ida, whom Iaera, forest-nymph,
Reared in the grove of Jupiter, now men
Tall as their native pines or mountain peaks,
Throw wide a portal to their charge consigned
By the chief's word, and, on their arms relying,
Bid enter free the foemen through the walls.
Themselves within, to right hand and to left,
Take stand before the bulwarks, armed in iron,
While the plumes flutter on their towering heads.
Even as on either side some river's flow,
On Padus' banks, or by sweet Athesis,
Twin oak-trees soar aloft, and rear to heaven
Their unshorn heads, with nodding crest sublime.   *682*
In burst the Rutules, when the approach they see
Wide open. Quercens and Aquicolus,
In glorious arms, and Tmarus, rash of heart,
And Haemon, son of Mavors, there and then,
With all their squadrons routed, turned aback,
Or on the very threshold laid life down.
Then wrath waxed fiercer in their battling souls;
And now the Trojans to the selfsame spot
Gather in swarms, to close encounter come,
Nor fear to launch into the open.   *690*
               Word
Is to Prince Turnus brought, as far aloof
He stormed and wrought confusion, that the foe
Seethe with fresh slaughter, and throw wide their
    gates.
His hand he stays, and, wildly raging, speeds
Toward those proud brethren at the Dardan gate.
And first Antiphates, as offering first,
Born of a Theban mother, and bastard son
To great Sarpedon, his launched javelin smites.

Flies through the buxom air the Italian shaft
Of cornel-wood, and, in the gullet lodged,
Ran deep into his breast; the black wound's chasm
Gives forth a foaming tide, and in his lung
The fixèd steel grows warm. Then Erymas
And Merops he lays low with might of hand;
Aphidnus then, then Bitias, fiery-eyed
And furious-hearted—not with javelin stroke,
For to no javelin had he yielded breath;
But, hissing loud, a whirled Phalaric spear
Sped like a thunderbolt; nor bull-hides twain,
Nor trusty corslet's double links of gold
Could stay it: the limbs gigantic fall in a heap,
Earth groans, and his huge shield clangs over him.   709
So on Euboean Baiae's shore at times
Tumbles a stony mass, which, welded first
In mighty blocks, men cast into the sea;
So headlong it trails havoc, and, far down,
Dashed on the shallows, finds its sunken bed.
The billows boil, dark sand comes silting up;
Then Prochyta's foundations at the sound
Quake, and Inarimë's rough bed of pain,
Piled o'er Typhöeus by Jove's sovereign word.   716

　　Now Mars, the lord of battle, lent new strength
And valour to the Latins, deep in heart
Turning his eager goads; and Flight withal
Among the Teucrians and dark Fear he sent.
From every side, now scope for fight is given,
They swarm; the war-god leaps into their soul.
When Pandarus sees his brother's outstretched corse,
How fortune sits, and what chance wields the day,
By a mighty effort on its turning hinge
He swings the gate back with stout shoulder-push,
Leaves many a friend amid the cruel fray
Shut out from camp, but others, in hot haste
Retreating, with himself shuts safely in.
Madman! to see not midmost of the rout
Burst in the Rutule monarch—yea, wantonly
Within their walls to impound him, as it were
Some monstrous tiger among helpless herds.   730
At once strange light flashed from the hero's eyes;
His arms rang terribly; his helmet-crest
Quivered blood-red, and from his shield he darts
Quick gleams of lightning. Suddenly dismayed,
The sons of Troy know well that hated form
And limbs gigantic. Then huge Pandarus

Springs from their midst, and for his brother's death
Red-hot with wrath bespeaks him: "This is not
Amata's bridal palace, nor Ardea now
Holds Turnus fast within his native walls;
'Tis the foe's camp thou seest, all exit barred."   *739*
To him spake Turnus, smiling, calm at heart:
"Begin, if thou hast manhood, and fall on.
Word shalt thou bear to Priam that here too
Thou found'st Achilles." He had said; the foe,
With main strength heaving, hurled a ruggèd spear,
Knotty with untrimmed bark; the breezes took it;
Saturnian Juno from its course made swerve
The coming wound; the spear sticks in the gate.
"Not so this weapon, my right hand wields amain,
Shalt thou escape; for no such falterer here
Aims wound or weapon." So saying, he rises high
To his uplifted sword, and with the blade
Full betwixt either temple, a grisly stroke,
Cleft him through forehead and through beardless
    cheeks.   *751*
A loud crash followed; earth reels with the vast
    weight;
Rolled in a heap, with his brain-spattered arms,
The limbs fell dying; in equal halves the head
This way and that from either shoulder hung.
Wild panic seized the Trojans, and they fled:
And had the victor now ta'en instant thought
To burst the gate-bolts and let in his friends,
That day the war had ended, and the race.   *759*
But rage impelled him, and mad lust of blood
Like fire upon the foe. First Phaleris
He overtakes, and Gyges, 'neath the knee
Slitting his sinews. Plucking forth the spears
From these, he hurls them on the fliers' backs;
Juno lends strength and courage. Next he sends
Halys to join them, and, through shield transfixed,
Phegeus; then, all unwitting, on the wall
Still kindling war, Alcander, Halius,
Noëmon, Prytanis. As Lynceus strides
Forward, calls up his comrades, with one strong
Bright sword-sweep from the rampart on the right
He takes him; severed by a single stroke
At arm's length, head and helm lay rolled afar.
Then Amycus, of woodland beasts the scourge,
Than whom none happier-handed to anoint
Darts, and envenom steel, and Aeolus' son,

Clytius, and Cretheus, to the Muses dear—
Cretheus, the Muses' mate. who ever loved
Song and the lyre, and to stretch note on string,
And steeds and arms and battles ever sang.   *777*

   At length the Teucrian leaders hear the tale
Of their friends' slaughter, and together meet,
Mnestheus and keen Serestus; they discern
Friends flying wide, the foe within their gates.
Then Mnestheus: "Whither next, whither," he cries,
"Urge ye your flight? what other walls remain,
What ramparts beyond these? Shall it be told
That one man, O my countrymen, and he
Hemmed by your circling lines, wrought unavenged
Such carnage through the camp, to Orcus hurled
So many of our bravest? Coward souls,
Your wretched country and her ancient gods,
And great Aeneas—do these no pity stir,
No shame?" By such words kindled, they take heart
And halt in dense array. Then foot by foot
'Gan Turnus from the conflict to withdraw,
Make for the river, and wave-encircled side.   *790*
At this the Teucrians with a mighty shout
Press keenlier on, and form one solid mass:
As when a crowd with threatening spears beset
Some savage lion, he, terrified, yet fierce
And angry-eyed, recoils; valour and wrath
Forbid him turn aback, nor yet, though fain,
Through darts and huntsmen can he force his way;
So now doth Turnus doubtfully withdraw
No hurrying steps; wrath surges in his soul.   *798*
Aye, and even then upon the foemen's midst
Twice had he rushed, twice turned their ranks to rout
Along the wall; but the whole host from camp
In hot haste rally and unite, nor durst
Saturnian Juno lend him strength enow
To match them; for now Jupiter from heaven
Sent air-borne Iris with no mild behests
Charged for his sister, except Turnus quit
The Teucrians' lofty ramparts. So nor shield
Nor good right hand avails him to stand firm,
On every side with pelting darts o'erpowered.
Clatters the helm about his hollow brow
With ceaseless din; the solid plates of brass
By stones are split, the crest dashed from his head;
Such strokes the boss may bear not; spear on spear
Trojans, and Mnestheus' self with lightning-hand,

Launch thick upon him. Then o'er all his frame
The sweat flows, pouring—and no space to breathe—
Its grimy torrent; a sick panting shakes
The o'er-wearied limbs. At length, with headlong
    bound,
Armed at all points he plunged into the flood.
Its tawny eddies took him, as he came,
Up-bore with buoyant waters, cleansed of blood,
And sent him back rejoicing to his friends.   *818*

BOOK X

Now is thrown wide the almighty house of heaven,
And lo! the Sire of gods and King of men
Summons a council to his starry court,
Whence from on high he doth all lands of earth,
The Dardan camp, and Latium's folk behold.
Within the double-gated hall they sit:
Himself breaks silence: "Mighty sons of heaven,
Why is your purpose turned aback? or why
So strive with rancorous hearts? That Italy
With Troy should clash in onset I forbade;
What is this feud, defiant of my ban?
What terror hath seduced or these, or those,
To rush on battle, and provoke the sword?   *10*
War's rightful hour—forestall it not—will come,
What time fierce Carthage on Rome's heights shall
    hurl
Mighty destruction and the opened Alps:
Then hate for hate, then rapine shall have sway:
But now give o'er, and cheerfully confirm
The peace decreed." Thus Jupiter in brief:
Not briefly golden Venus makes reply:
"O Sire, O sovereign power eterne of men
And all things—for what else is left us yet
To pray to?—dost thou mark how insolent
The Rutules? and how Turnus, chariot-borne,
Vaunts him in mid career, and speeds amain
Flushed with war's triumph? Their close walls no
    more
Now shield the Teucrians: nay, within their gates,
Even on the mounded ramparts, hand to hand
They grapple, and all the trench o'erflows with blood. *24*
Aeneas is unaware, far off. Wilt thou
Ne'er yield us respite from the leaguer's ring?
Over the walls of new-born Troy once more
A foe is hovering, and once more a host;
And from Aetolian Arpi, as of old,
Up-springs against the Teucrians Tydeus' son.
My wounds, methinks, await me yet, and I,
Thine offspring, but delay some mortal spear.
If unapproved and all unwilled of thee

The Trojans have sought Italy, that sin
Let them atone, nor speed them with thine aid:
But, if obedient unto call on call
From Heaven and Hades, how can any now
Reverse thy bidding, and write fate anew?   35
Why call to mind the fleet on Eryx' shore
Burnt up with fire? Why of the lord of storms
And his mad blasts roused from Aeolia, tell,
Or Iris sped from heaven? now too she stirs—
Tract unattempted yet—the shades below;
And, on the upper world launched suddenly,
Allecto riots through the Italian towns.
Of empire naught I reck; that hope was ours
While Fortune stood: win whom thou wouldst have
     win.   43
If realm be none which thy relentless spouse
Can spare the Teucrians, by Troy's overthrow
And smoking ruins, O Sire, I thee conjure,
Suffer me pluck Ascanius from the fray
Scathless; my grandson—suffer him to live.
Aeneas on unknown waters may be tossed,
And follow fortune, whatso path she point:
Let me this life avail to shield, and filch
From war's dread peril. Amathus is mine,
Mine lofty Paphos and Cythera's isle,
And fair Idalia's home: there let him pass
His days unarmed, inglorious. With proud sway
Bid Carthage curb Ausonia; naught from thence
Shall balk the Tyrian cities. To have 'scaped
The plague of war what boots him, to have fled
Clean through the Argive fires, and drained so oft
Dangers of sea and desert, while Troy's sons
Seek Latium's shore and Pergamus re-risen?   58
Were it not better to have sat them down
Amid their land's last ashes, and the soil
Where once was Troy? Ah! hapless, give them back
Xanthus and Simois; let the Teucrians, Sire,
Unroll afresh the tale of Ilium's woe."
    Then royal Juno, by fierce frenzy spurred:
"Why my deep silence driv'st thou me to break,
And vent abroad in words a hidden pain?
Aeneas hath any man or god compelled
To fly to arms, and launch him as a foe
On king Latinus? At the call of fate
He sought the shores of Italy; so be it;   67
Urged by Cassandra's raving; was it we

Bade him quit camp, trust to the winds his life,
To a boy's guidance commit walls and war,
Stir treason in Etruria's peaceful folk?
What god, what cruel tyranny of ours,
Impelled him to his bane? say, where in this
Was Juno's hand, or Iris sent from heaven?
'Tis shame for Italy's sons to gird with fire
Your new-born Troy, and on his native soil
Turnus set foot, from old Pilumnus sprung,
Venilia for his mother, Nymph divine: 76
What for the Trojans then with smoking brands
To fall on Latium, crush beneath the yoke,
Ravage and plunder lands that knew them not,
Pick wives at will, tear bride from lover's breast—
Hands craving peace, and vessels lined with war?
Thou canst Aeneas from Greek hands filch away,
Mist and void air present them for a man,
Into as many nymphs canst turn their fleet:
That we to Rutules too some aid should bring—
Counts it for crime? Aeneas is unaware,
Far off, thou sayest; far off and unaware
Let him remain. Paphos, Idalium,
Are thine, and tall Cythera: why provoke
Fierce bosoms, and a town that teems with war?   87
Think you 'tis I who labour to o'erthrow
The crumbling power of Phrygia? I, or he
Who on the hapless Trojans first drew down
The Achaean onslaught? Wherefore, say, to arms
Did Europe rise, and Asia with a rape
The cords of peace unravel? Did I lead
The adulterous Dardan to storm Sparta's hold,
I find him weapons, or fan war with love?
Fears for thy children had become thee then:
Now, all belated, and with baseless plaints
Rising, thou flingest thy fierce taunts in vain."   95
   So pleaded Juno, and the assembled gods
Murmured approval with divided voice;
As rising blasts that, in the forest caught,
Murmur, and, rolling a dull roar along,
Bode storm to sailors. Then the almighty Sire,
Prime potentate, brake silence; as he speaks,
Hushed is the gods' high palace, and the earth
From her base trembles; the deep vault is still;
The winds are dropped; the sea smoothes flat his
      floor.   103
"Hear then, and graft within your heart, my words.

[304]

Ausonian, Teucrian, since no league may join,
Nor your own jars have end, howe'er to-day
Thrive either, cleave what path of hope he will,
Or Trojan, or Rutulian, shall by me
Be deemed alike indifferent, whether now
The destinies of Italy, or Troy's
Own baneful error and ill counsel, hold
Her camp beleaguered: nor herefrom loose I
The Rutules. Each shall his own sowing reap—
Or toil or triumph: Jupiter is king
Alike for all. The fates will find a way."
He spake, and by his Stygian brother's stream,
Banks that with pitch and a black whirlpool boil,
Nodded assent, and with the nod made all
Olympus tremble. Here their parle had end.
Then Jupiter from off his golden throne
Rises, escorted to his palace-doors
By all the companies of heaven.   *117*
                    Meanwhile
At every gate the Rutules press around
To deal red death, and ring the walls with flame.
But fast within their palisades are penned
Aeneas' leaguered host: no hope of flight.
Forlorn upon the lofty towers they stand
In vain, and with a scant ring crown the walls:
The first rank Asius, son of Imbrasus,
And Hicetaon's son Thymoetes, then
The twain Assaraci, and Thymbris old
And Castor: brothers of Sarpedon both,
Clarus and Themon at their side are ranged
From lofty Lycia. Straining his full bulk,
Lyrnesian Acmon bears a monstrous rock,
No mean part of a mountain; lesser-thewed
He nor than Clytius, from whose loins he sprang,
Nor his own brother Mnestheus. Some with darts
Strive to ward off the foemen, some with stones,
Or hurl the fire-brand, or fit shaft to string.   *131*
Midmost the press, for Venus' care most meet,
Behold! the Dardan boy, his comely head
Uncovered, glitters like a gem that cleaves
The red gold round it, to deck head or throat,
Or as gleams ivory, cunningly inlaid
In boxwood or Orician terebinth:
The milk-white neck his showery locks receives
Up-gathered in a ring of pliant gold.
Thee too, O Ismarus, the great-hearted folk

Saw aim the wound, and arm the reed with bane,
High-born of house Maeonian, where men till
Rich furrows by Pactolus washed with gold.   *142*
There too was Mnestheus, whom his late renown
In routing Turnus from the rampart's height
Exalts to heaven, and Capys there, from whom
The great Campanian city draws her name.
   These in the grip of stubborn war had closed:
Aeneas was cleaving now the midnight sea.
For, from Evander parted, and arrived
The Etruscan camp, soon as he meets the king,
And to the king relates his race and name,
Boon asked or offered, and reveals what arms
Mezentius wins to aid him, and therewith
The unbridled heart of Turnus—warning him
How mutable things human, and with pleas
Mingling entreaties—without more ado
Tarchon joins forces, and strikes treaty: then
Fate-free, the Lydian folk at heaven's behest
Beneath an alien's banner leap aboard.
The good ship of Aeneas leads the van,
The Phrygian lions yoked beneath her prow;   *157*
O'er them hangs Ida, a boon sight to see
For Teucrian exiles. Great Aeneas here
Sits and revolves in his own heart the while
War's changeful issues; to his leftward side
Cleaves Pallas, and now asks him of the stars—
The road-way of dark night—anon of all
His jeopardies endured by land and sea.
   Now open Helicon, ye goddesses,
And wake the strain, what hero-company,
Following Aeneas from the Etruscan strand,
Array the decks for war, and ride the deep.   *165*
   First, in his brass-beaked Tiger, Massicus
Cleaves the sea-billows, beneath whom are ranged
A thousand warriors, from walled Clusium come,
And Cosae's city; arrow-men are they,
Girt with light quiver and death-bearing bow.
With him grim Abas, his whole band aflame
With glorious arms, Apollo gilded bright
Upon the stern. Six hundred of her sons
Had Populonia lent him, proved in war,
But Ilva's isle three hundred, whose rich womb
Teems with the Chalybes' unexhausted mines.   *174*
Third, that interpreter 'twixt gods and men,
Asilus comes, obedient to whose will

Are victims' entrails, and the stars of heaven,
And tongues of birds, and bodeful lightning-fires.
A thousand speeds he on in close array,
And with spears bristling, to his banner bid
By Pisa, city of Alphean birth,
On soil Etruscan. Follows in their wake
Thrice beauteous Astyr, Astyr on his steed
And gay-wrought arms relying; along with him—
All of one heart to follow—hundreds three
From Caere's home, or who in Minio's fields
And ancient Pyrgi dwell, and fever-fraught
Graviscae.   *184*

        No, nor thee must I pass o'er,
Liguria's bravest chieftain, Cinyras,
Or thee, Cupavo, with thy scanty train,
Springs from whose crest the plumage of a swan;
Love your reproach,—for cognizance ye bear
Your father's form. For Cycnus, as folk tell,
Bemoaning his loved Phaethon—what time
Amid those sisters' shadowy poplar-leaves
He sings, with music solacing love's woe—
Donned downy feathers for the snows of age,
Left earth behind, and starward soared in song.
The son, embarked with all his warlike peers,
Urges with oars the mighty Centaur on;
Who leans above the flood, and menaces
With monstrous rock the billows, towering high,
And furrows with long keel the watery deep.   *197*

    Summons a war-host from his native shores
Great Ocnus too, from Manto, prophetess,
Sprung, and the Tuscan river, who to thee
Gave walls, O Mantua, and his mother's name,
Mantua now rich in noble sires, but not
All of one stock; a threefold race are they,
Four several States in each; o'er all the States
Herself the head, her strength of Tuscan blood.
Hence too Mezentius arms to his own bane
Five hundred, whom the form of Mincius, crowned
With grey-green rushes, sire Benacus' child,
Was seaward leading in their pine of war.   *206*
Aulestes labouring onward smites the flood
With hundred tree-stems rising to the stroke;
The sea-floor is up-churned, the waters foam.
Him monstrous Triton bears, and with his shell
Frights the blue billows; downward to the flank
His shaggy front shows human, as he swims;

Ends in a fish the belly; 'neath his waist
Half bestial the wave gurgles as it foams.
　　Such was the tale of chosen chiefs who came
In thrice ten vessels to the aid of Troy,
Cleaving with brass the fields of brine.　　　　　*214*
　　　　　　　　　　　And now
Kind Phoebe, daylight from the sky withdrawn,
Smote mid-Olympus with night-wandering car:
Aeneas, for care denied his limbs repose,
Sole sitting, guides the helm and tends the sails;
When a fair band of once his way-fellows
See! meet him in mid course: the nymphs, whom kind
Cybebe bade have worship of the sea,
And turned to nymphs from vessels, toward him
　　　　swam,
Cleaving the floods together, each and all
That had as brazen prows stood moored to shore.　　*223*
Their king they know from far, with solemn dance
Surround him; but their skilfullest of speech,
Cymodocea, following in his wake,
Grasps with her right the stern, shoots shoulder-high,
And with her left hand oars the silent wave.
Then thus she accosts him, though he knew not her:
"Wakest thou, son of heaven, Aeneas? Wake
And slack the sail-sheets. Lo! thy fleet are we,
Pine-trees of Ida from his sacred crest,
Now ocean-nymphs. When us the Rutule false
With sword and fire urged headlong, we thy bonds
Unwilling snapped, and seek thee o'er the main.
The mighty Mother, pitying, this our form
Re-wrought, and gave us to be goddesses,
And under ocean all our days to spend.　　　　　*235*
But young Ascanius wall and trench confine
'Mid Latium's darts and bristling front of war.
The Arcadian horse and stout Etruscan stand
Even now together at the appointed spot.
With interposing host to block their path,
And bar from camp, is Turnus' set resolve.　　　*240*
Up then! at earliest dawn bid rouse to arms
Thy friends, and take the shield, the lord of fire
Gave thee himself, of adamantine might,
And edged the rims with gold. To-morrow's sun,
If vain my words thou deem not, shall descry
Vast heaps of Rutule slaughter." She had said,
And with her right hand pushed the lofty stern
At parting, nowise witless of the way

Swifter than javelin, or wind-wingèd shaft,
It skims along the waves; thereat the rest
Quicken their course. The Trojan prince himself,
Son of Anchises, stands amazed, yet takes
Heart from the omen; then, with eyes upturned
To the high vault of heaven, he briefly prays: *251*
"Kind queen of Ida, mother of the gods,
Whom Dindymus, and cities turret-crowned,
And lions coupled to thy rein, delight,
Be thou my guide in battle, and this sign
Bring to fair issue, and with favouring foot
Attend the Phrygians, goddess." There he ceased.
Meanwhile returning dawn sped round apace,
To broad day ripening, and had banished night: *257*
First to his comrades he gives charge that all
Obey the signal, brace their hearts to war,
And fit them for the fray. And now he holds
The Teucrian host and his own camp in sight,
Upon the high poop standing: suddenly
On his left arm the blazing shield he rears.
The Dardans from the wall raise shouts to heaven;
Hope comes to heighten wrath; their darts they
     shower;
As cranes from Strymon under murky clouds
Give signal, and skim clamorously the air,
And scud before the south with trailing cry.
But to the Rutule prince right marvellous,
And to Ausonia's captains, seemed the thing,
Till, looking back, the vessels' stems they spy
Turned shoreward, the whole main one moving fleet. *269*
Blazes yon helm-top; from the crest above
Spouts fire; the gold boss belches floods of flame:
As on a clear night glows the baleful glare
Of blood-red comets, or as Sirius' heat,
Fraught with disease and drought for suffering men,
Rises, and saddens heaven with light malign.
   Yet bates not gallant Turnus his bold hope
To seize the shore and beat the invaders back.   *277*
"Here is the hap ye prayed for, sword in hand
To shatter them. The war-god's very self
Is in the hands of heroes. Now let each
Of wife and home be mindful, now recall
The great deeds and the glories of your sires.
Up! let us meet them at the brink, while yet
Confused and tottering, as their feet touch land.
Fortune befriends the bold." So saying, he mused

Inly whom best to lead against the foe,
Or to whose charge the leaguered walls confide.   *286*
   Meanwhile, with gangways from each lofty stern
Aeneas unships his comrades. Many wait
The slack sea's ebb, and hazard a bold leap
Into the shallows; some with aid of oars.
Tarchon espies a beach where shoals nor pant,
Nor roars the broken billow, but unchecked
Ocean glides onward with advancing tide—
Anon steers thither, and calls upon his men: *293*
"Now, chosen crews, bend to your sturdy oars,
Lift and bear in the barks; cleave with their beaks
This hostile land, and let the keel's sheer weight
Plough its own furrow. In such a roadstead I
Shrink not from shipwreck, once we clutch the
    shore."
So Tarchon spake, and all his mates at once
Rise on their oar-blades, and to Latium's plain
Bear in the foaming vessels, till their beaks
Now grip the dry, and every keel anon
Lies safely bedded; but not, Tarchon, thine:
For, dashed amid the shallows, while she hangs
Upon a treacherous ridge, long poised in doubt,
And wearies out the waves, she splits, and casts
Her crew among the billows; broken oars
And floating thwarts entangle them, their feet
The while dragged backward by the water's ebb.   *307*
   No laggard sloth checks Turnus; swift he hurls
His whole line at the Teucrians, on the beach
Halts, and confronts them. Then the trumpets sound.
First leapt Aeneas on the rustic ranks—
Fair augury of fight—and trampled down
The Latins, and slew Theron, mightiest-thewed,
Who dared assault Aeneas. The sword driven
Through links of brass, through tunic stiff with gold,
Drank of his gaping side. And next he strikes
Lichas, once ripped from his dead mother's womb,
And sacred to thee, Phoebus, as a babe
Suffered to 'scape the perils of the steel.
And rugged Cisseus, and huge Gyas, too,
While levelling with their clubs the ranks hard by,
He smote to death; no whit might these bestead
The arms of Hercules, or their stout hands,
And sire Melampus, erst Alcides' mate,
Long as earth yielded him his travails sore.
While Pharus, see! flings deedless words abroad,

The hero brandishes and plants a spear
Full in his bawling mouth. Thou, Cydon, too,
In luckless quest of Clytius, thy new joy,
The young down yellowing on his cheek, hadst lain
Stretched 'neath the Dardan's hand, a piteous sight,
Heedless of youthful loves, thy life-long care,
Had not thy brethren, a close-banded throng,
Offspring of Phorcus, crossed the foeman's path,
Their number seven, and seven the darts they fling:
From shield and helmet some bound idly back,
Some, by kind Venus turned aside, his limbs
Graze merely. Then Aeneas thus bespeaks
Trusty Achates: "Bring me store of darts;
None of all those shall my right hand for naught
Launch at the Rutules, which on Ilium's plain
In Grecian flesh stood planted." Therewithal
A mighty spear he grasps and hurls; it flew,
And shattering through the brass of Maeon's shield,
Cleaves plate alike and breast. To his brother's aid
Up comes Alcanor, props him, as he falls,
With right hand brotherly; but through his arm
The spear, sped onward, wins its bloody way,
And from his shoulder by the sinews, lo!
The hand hung dying. Then, from his brother's corse
Snatching the weapon, Numitor assails
Aeneas, yet might not strike him full, and grazed
Tall-limbed Achates on the thigh. Thereat
Clausus of Cures, in his youthful frame
Trusting, drew near, and with a javelin-cast
Smote Dryops 'neath the chin, and, urging home
The tough shaft, pierced his throat, and in mid-
    speech
Reft life and voice; his forehead strikes the earth,
And from his lips he vomits out thick gore.   *349*
Three, too, from Thrace, of Boreas' lofty line,
And three, by their sire Idas sent to war,
And Ismarus their country, he lays low
By divers deaths. Halaesus to the fray
Hastes with the bands Auruncan, and up-speeds
Messapus, child of Neptune, steed-renowned.
Now these, now those, strive to fling back the foe,
And on Ausonia's very verge contend.
As in the vast of air when wrangling winds
Rise to do battle, matched in wrath and might,
None to the other yields, wind, cloud, or sea,
Long sways the combat, all stand locked in strife:

So Trojan ranks and Latin, each with each
Clash; foot to foot clings, and man crowds on man.　361
　　But yonder, where a torrent far and wide
Had sent rocks rolling and torn bush from bank,
When Pallas his Arcadians saw, unused
To foot encounter, fly the hot pursuit
Of Latium—for the rough ground counselled them
Their steeds to abandon—now with prayers, and now
With taunting words, sole refuge in his strait,
He fires their courage: "Whither fly ye, friends?
By your brave deeds, by Chief Evander's name
And his triumphant wars—aye, by the hope
That springs in me to match my sire's renown—
Trust not to flight. It is the sword must cleave
Through foes our passage. Where yon warrior-throng
Press thickest, your proud country calls you back,
Pallas to lead you. No gods bear us down;
Mortals by mortals are we driven, who yet
Boast lives and hands as many. Behold! the deep
With its vast bar confines us, and land fails
For flight: shall ocean be our aim, or Troy?"　378
So saying, he dashed amid the hostile press.
First meets him Lagus, led by fates malign,
Whom, tugging at a huge and ponderous stone,
With javelin hurled he pierces, where the spine
'Twixt ribs and ribs made severance, and plucks back
His weapon whence it clave amid the bones.
Yet Hisbo from above surprised him not,
Though surely hoping; for, as on he rushed,
Blinded with rage for his friend's bitter fate,
Pallas forestalls him, in his swollen lung
Plunging the sword-blade. Next on Sthenius
He hurls him, and Anchemolus, derived
From Rhoetus' ancient stem, who dared defile
His step-dame's bridal chamber. And ye, too,
Twin sons of Daucus, on the Rutule plain
Fell, Thymber and Larides, wearing both
One likeness, e'en to your own parents' eyes
A sweet insoluble perplexity.　392
But bitter difference now hath Pallas wrought
Betwixt ye; for thy head the Evandrian sword
Hath shorn, O Thymber, and thy lopped right hand
Gropes for its lord, Larides, and half-quick
The fingers quiver, and clutch the sword anew.
Fired by the hero's chiding, and at sight
Of his resplendent deeds, 'twixt rage and shame

The Arcadians steel their hearts to face the foe.
Then Pallas pierces Rhoeteus as he sped
Past in his chariot. Respite and delay
Thus much gat Ilus: for at Ilus he
Had aimed a doughty javelin from afar;
But Rhoeteus, intercepting it midway,
From thee, right noble Teuthras, as he fled,
And from thy brother Tyres, rolled from car,
Hammers with dying heel the Rutule plain.   *404*
As, at his wish, when summer winds have risen,
Some shepherd fires the forest here and there;
All in a moment the mid spaces catch,
And o'er the wide plains in unbroken line
Sweeps the grim-flickering edge of Vulcan's war—
He, perched triumphant, marks the revelling flame
So all thy comrades wax in valour one,
And glad thee, Pallas. But to meet them moves
Halaesus, brave in onset, the whole man
Behind his shield up-gathered, and hews down
Ladon and Pheres and Demodocus;   *413*
Strymonius' right hand, raised against his throat,
With flashing blade he shears, then smites with a rock
The face of Thoas, and batters in the bones,
Blood mixed with brain. Halaesus in the woods
Had by his prophet-sire been hid; when now
The old man's eyes failed and were glazed in death,
Fates claim their own, and to Evander's darts
Devote the son. At him now Pallas aimed,
First praying thus: "O father Tiber, grant
Now to this weapon, which I poise for fight,
A prosperous way through stout Halaesus' heart;
So shall thine oak his arms and spoils possess."   *423*
This heard the god; Halaesus, while he shields
Imaon, to the Arcadian dart lays bare
His luckless breast. But Lausus, of the fight
Main champion, brooks not that his ranks be scared
By all the hero's slaughter: at their head
Encountering he slays Abas, a tough knot
And barrier of the battle. Then goes down
Arcadia's manhood, down the Etruscans go,
And ye, whose frames defied the slaughtering Greeks,
O Teucrians! Matched in leaders, as in might,
Host rushes upon host. The rearward ranks
Close up and crowd the battle, hand and spear
Wedged beyond wielding. Here is Pallas, see,
Pressing and straining, there, confronting him,

Lausus, in age his equal, both alike
Peerless in beauty, but by fortune's ban
Doomed to no home-return. Yet were they not
Suffered by great Olympus' lord to close
In conflict; each beneath a mightier foe
Waits his impending destiny.   *438*
                              Meanwhile
His gracious sister now bids Turnus bring
Relief to Lausus; and on flying car
He cleaves the ranks between them. When his friends
He spied, "Ho now! cease fighting; I alone
Go to meet Pallas! Pallas is my due,
Mine only: fain were I his sire himself
Stood here to see." So spake he, and his friends
Withdrew them from the space proclaimed. But
     when
The Rutules had made room, the noble youth,
Much marvelling at the haughty mandate, stares
Amazed at Turnus, over the vast frame
Lets roll his eyes, and with fierce glance afar
Scans him at every point, then, speech for speech,
Makes answer to the monarch: "Now shall I
Be praised as winner of the splendid spoils,
Or for a famous death; and either fate
My sire can face. Away with threats." So saying,
He strides into the arena's midst. About
The Arcadian's heart-strings the blood curdles cold.   *452*
Turnus has leapt from chariot, and on foot
Prepares for close encounter. As a lion,
That from his lofty outlook hath espied
A bull far off, erect upon the plain
Brooding on battle, flies upon the prey,
Even such the look of Turnus as he came.
But Pallas, when he deemed the foe would be
Now within spear-cast, hastens to begin,
So some kind hap might help the bold essay
Of ill-matched powers: then thus to the great heaven
He cries: "By my sire's welcome, and the board
Whereto thou cam'st a stranger, I thee pray,
Alcides, aid me in my vast emprise.   *461*
Let him behold me from his limbs yet quick
Strip off the blood-stained arms, and Turnus' eyes,
Dying, endure a conqueror." The youth's prayer
Alcides heard, and, stifling a deep groan
Within his heart, shed unavailing tears.
Then with kind words the Sire bespake his son:

"Each hath his term appointed; brief the span
Of all men's life, and irretrievable;
But by great feats to lengthen fame, here lies
The task of valour. 'Neath Troy's lofty walls
Fell many a god-begotten; nay, with them
Perished Sarpedon, mine own offspring. Aye,
And Turnus his fates summon, now arrived
The goal of age allotted." Thus he spake,
And from the Rutule plain his eyes withdrew.   *473*
But Pallas launches with main strength a spear,
And plucks from hollow sheath his flashing sword.
On flew the shaft, and, where the shoulder-plates
Rose to their highest, lit, and forced its way
Through the shield's edges, and glanced off at length
Even from the mighty frame of Turnus. Then
Turnus, long poising a steel-pointed spear,
Hurls it at Pallas, crying, "Look you now
Whether my dart pierce deeper." He had said,
But crashing through the centre of the shield—
Iron upon iron welded, brass on brass,
Wound all about with bull's hide manifold—
With quivering impact the point tore, and pierced
The corslet's barrier and the mighty breast.
He plucks the warm dart from the wound in vain;   *486*
Outburst one way the life-blood and the life;
Prone on the wound he sinks, and over him
Loud clanged his armour, as the dying lips,
Blood-dabbled, smote upon the foeman's soil.
Then, standing o'er him, Turnus spake and said:
"Arcadians, heed, and to Evander's ear
Bear this my message: say that, in such plight
As he hath earned him, I send Pallas home.
What grace a grave, what solace burial hath,
Freely I grant. Right dearly will he rue
His welcome of Aeneas." Thus he spake,
And with his left foot pressed the lifeless corse,
Seizing the belt's vast burden, with the crime
Engraved there—in one nuptial night a band
Of youths slain foully, and the bride-bower drenched
In blood; which Clonus, son of Eurytus,
Had traced upon thick gold: but of the prize
Turnus now boasts him, glorying in the spoil.   *500*
Ah! mind of man, to fate and coming doom
Blind, and that knows no bridle, when elate
With prosperous fortune! there shall come a time
When Turnus fain at a great price would buy

Pallas back scathless, and will yon proud spoils
Loathe, and the day he won them. But his friends
With many a groan and tear throng round and set
Pallas on shield, and bear him from the fray.
O grief and mighty glory to thy sire
Anon returning! This one day begins
And ends alike thy warfare; none the less
Huge heaps of Rutule dead thou leav'st behind.   509
    Now no mere rumour of so dear a loss,
But weightier witness to Aeneas hies;
His friends but a bare span from death, 'tis time
Troy's routed ranks to succour. With the sword
He reaps what's nearest, and through serried foes,
Like fire, a wide path hews him, thee to seek,
Turnus, exulting in new deeds of blood.
Pallas, Evander—on his very eyes
Flashed the whole scene, the board whereto he came
Then first, a stranger, and the pledged right hands.
Four warriors hereupon from Sulmo sprung,
As many reared by Ufens, he takes quick,
To slay as offerings to the shade, and drench
The blazing funeral-pyre with captive blood.   520
Next from afar at Magus he had aimed
A deadly spear. But he comes crouching up
Slily, while o'er him the shaft quivering flew,
Then clasped the hero's knees, and suppliant spake:
"By thy sire's soul, I pray thee, by thy hopes
Ripening with young Iulus, spare my life
For son and sire. A stately house have I,
Where talent-weights of silver fair-embossed
Lie buried deep, and massy gold is mine,
Wrought and unwrought. Nor hinges hereupon
The Teucrians' triumph, nor one life alone
Can work so vast a difference." He had said.
To whom Aeneas thus spake in answer: "All
Thy boasted store of silver and of gold
Save for thy sons. Such trafficking in arms
Turnus fore-cancelled in that hour when he
Smote Pallas dead. So deems among the shades
My sire Anchises, and Iulus so."   534
He spake, and with his left hand grasped the helm,
And bending the neck backward, as he prayed,
Plunged in his sword-blade to the hilt. Hard by
The son of Haemon, priest of Phoebus, stood,
And Trivia, chapleted about the brow
With sacred fillet-bands, from head to heel

One splendour of white raiment, glittering arms.
Him then he meets, and drives adown the plain,
Stands o'er him slipped and fallen, and slaughters
 him,
And in vast darkness whelms. The warrior's arms,
Up-gathered, Serestus shoulders and bears off,
Trophy to thee, Gradivus, lord of war.   *542*
Now Caeculus, from the stock of Vulcan sprung,
And Umbro who from Marsian mountains came,
Repair the battle-ranks. Against them storms
The Dardan. With the sword he had lopped off
Anxur's left arm, and, with the arm, his shield's
Whole circle; the man had uttered some big boast,
And thought with deed to match it, and belike
Was even exalting his proud soul to heaven
With promise of hoar eld and length of days;   *549*
When, in bright arms exulting, Tarquitus,
Whom Dryope the nymph erewhile had borne
To woodland Faunus, crossed his fiery path.
He, drawing back his spear, pins fast in one
The corslet and huge burden of his shield;
Then, as he vainly prays, with many a word
Still ripe for utterance, hurled to earth his head,
And, rolling in the dust the yet warm trunk,
In bitter mood spake o'er it: "Now lie there,
Redoubted warrior! no kind mother's hand
In earth shall hide thee, or heap above thy limbs
Ancestral soil: but to the ravenous birds
Shalt thou be left, or gulf shall drown and wave
Bear thee, and hungry fishes lip thy wounds."   *560*
Antaeus next and Lucas, foremost ranks
Of Turnus, he o'ertakes, and Numa brave,
And tawny Camers, noble Volscens' son,
Richest in land of all Ausonia's folk,
Who ruled in hushed Amyclae. Even as when
Aegeon, fabled of a hundred arms,
A hundred hands, and from whose fifty mouths
And breasts blazed fire, against the bolts of Jove
Clashed on like shields as many, as many swords
Drew; so Aeneas over the wild plain
Rages his fill victoriously, when once
His blade waxed warm. Nay see! he moves to meet
Niphaeus' four-horse team and threatening front.   *571*
Soon as they saw him striding with huge steps,
And fiercely muttering, the steeds wheeled for
 fear,

Rushed backward, and flung forth their lord, and
    whirled
The chariot shore-ward. Lucagus meanwhile
With twain white war-steeds dashed amid the throng,
He and his brother Liger; Liger reins
And guides the horses; Lucagus waves fierce
His circling sword-blade. Their so fiery rage
Aeneas brooked not, but upon them rushed,
Towering conspicuous with opposing spear. 579
To whom spake Liger: "Here dost thou behold
Nor Diomede's coursers, nor Achilles' car,
Nor Phrygia's plain: the last of war and life
Now on this soil awaits thee." Such wild words
Fly from mad Liger's lips. But not in words
Troy's hero shapes his answer; at the foe
A dart he launches; and when Lucagus
Low-leaning, as to smite them, with the steel
His team had chidden, and now, left foot advanced,
Plants him for battle, through the nether rims
Of his bright buckler entering, the spear pierced
His groin to leftward: tumbled from the car
Dying, he rolls upon the plain. To whom
In bitter accents good Aeneas spake: 591
"Thy chariot, Lucagus, no coward flight
Of steeds betrayed, nor foe-flung shadows vain
Turned backward; leaping from the wheels, thyself
The car forsak'st." So saying, he caught the team.
Down from the chariot, stretching helpless hands,
Slid too the unhappy brother: "By thyself,
And by the twain who framed thee that thou art,
Great Trojan, leave me life, and to my plaint
Lend pitying ear." Yet more he would have prayed,
When thus Aeneas: "Not such the words erewhile
Thou uttered'st. Die, nor brother be divorced
From brother." Thereat with the sword's point his
    breast
He cleaves, and lets the life-breath from its lair. 601
Thus through the plain the Dardan chief dealt death,
Raging like torrent-wave or black typhoon.
At length the young Ascanius and his host
Break forth, quit camp, and foil the leaguer's ring.
  Meanwhile to Juno thus high Jove begins:
"O sister mine and sweetest wife in one,
'Tis Venus, as thou deemed'st—nor errs aught
Thy judgement—who upholds the power of Troy,
Not warrior's right hand, throbbing for the fray,

Nor fiery soul that can all danger dare."   610
Quoth Juno meekly: "Wherefore, fairest lord,
Vex a sick heart, of thy stern words afear'd?
Had but my love that power it boasted once,
And still should boast, I had not asked in vain
Of thine omnipotence to grant me this—
Leave to filch Turnus from the fight, and keep
Unscathed for Daunus, for his sire. But now
Even let him perish, and with that loyal blood
Pay forfeit to the Teucrians. He nathless
Draws from the stock of heaven his name, and springs
Fourth from Pilumnus; and his lavish hand
Hath oft thy threshold heaped with bounteous gifts." 620
Briefly to her spake high Olympus' lord:
"If but from present death reprieve be asked,
And respite for the warrior, ere he fall,
And thou perceiv'st I rule it so, bear hence
Away, pluck Turnus from the impending fate;
Such scope is mine to pleasure thee. But if
There lurk beneath thy prayer some ampler boon,
As deeming that the war's whole course may shift
And suffer change, thou feed'st an empty hope."
And Juno answered weeping: "What and if
Thy heart vouchsafed me what thy lips deny,
And pledged this loan of Turnus' life to last?   629
Now, some dread end awaits him innocent,
Or I drift void of truth. Yet O to be
By false fear cheated, and that thou, who canst,
Wouldst bend thy course to better!" Having said,
Forthwith she darted from the welkin's height,
And trailing storm through heaven, and girt in cloud,
Sought Ilium's army and Laurentum's camp.
Then out of hollow mist the goddess shapes
A shade, thin, void of strength, in semblance like
Aeneas—a monstrous marvel to behold—
Decks it with Dardan gear, and counterfeits
The shield, the horse-plume of the godlike head,
Gives unreal words, gives sound devoid of soul,
And mocks the very motions of his stride;
Like phantoms that, folk say, flit after death,
Or visions that befool the slumbering sense.   642
Now in the van of battle stalks the shade
Exulting, with its weapons goads the foe,
With shouts defies him. Turnus rushes on't,
And hurls from far a hissing spear; the shape
Wheels and retires. But Turnus, when he deemed

Aeneas fled back, and with bewildered soul
Drank the delusive hope, cries "Whither fly'st,
Aeneas? Quit not thy plighted bridal-bower:
The soil, thou hast crossed the waterways to find,
This hand shall yield thee." With such clamorous
    shouts
He follows, and brandishes his naked blade,
Nor marks the light winds bear his boast away.   652
Fast by a tall rock's base there chanced to stand
A vessel with steps set and gangway geared,
Which King Osinius bare from Clusium's coast.
Hither the mock Aeneas hurrying fled,
And plunged for shelter; nor at slacker speed
Turnus pursues, treads all that stays him down,
Clears the high bridge, and scarce had touched the
    prow,
Ere Saturn's daughter rends the rope, and speeds
O'er back-rolled billows the shore-sundered ship.   660
Aeneas meanwhile defies a vanished foe,
And many a warrior-frame that crossed his path
Sends death-ward. For no further shelter then
Seeks the light phantom, but took wing aloft,
And with a dark cloud mingled: the rough blast
Meanwhile bears Turnus through the billows' midst.
Blind to the cause, unthankful for escape,
Backward he gazes, and lifts high his voice
With hands up-clasped to heaven: "Almighty Sire,
Hast deemed me worthy of reproach so deep,
To pay such forfeit doomed me? Whither bound?
Whence came I hither? What flight, and in such guise,
Wafts me from shore? Shall I again behold
Laurentum's camp and bulwarks? What of those
Brave hearts, the followers of my sword and me?   672
Whom one and all—ah! horror!—I have left
To nameless butchery, yea, can see them now
Rank-scattered, and hear groaning as they fall?
What must I do? What land now deep enough
Can gape to hide me? Rather do ye winds
Take pity, and drive the ship on reef, on rock—
I, Turnus, from my heart implore—or cast
On cruel quicksands, where no Rutule foot,
Nor rumour that knows all, may track me out."   679
So saying, his soul rocks this way, and rocks that,
Whether upon his sword, so deep the shame,
Madly to hurl him, and 'twixt rib and rib
Drive the stern blade, or plunge amid the seas,

So swimming gain the curvèd beach, and fall
Once more upon the Teucrians. Either way
Thrice he essayed; thrice, pitiful of heart,
Great Juno checked and held him. The ship skims
Cleaving the deep, and, sped by tide and wave,
To his sire Daunus' ancient town is borne.   *688*

   Fiery Mezentius now by Jove's behest
Takes up the battle, and falls upon Troy's host
Amidst their triumph. The Etruscan ranks
Rally together, and on him alone,
Alone on him, with gathered fury press,
And showering missiles. Even as a rock,
That juts far out into the mighty main,
Bare to wind's brunt, a target for the sea,
All stress, all menace both of sky and deep
Outfaces, fixed abiding; so to earth
He strikes down Hebrus, Dolichaon's son,
And Latagus, and Palmus as he fled;
But Latagus full in face and mouth surprised
With a huge fragment of hill-rock he smote;
Hamstrung and helpless he let Palmus sprawl,
And gave the arms to Lausus, on his back
To wear them, in his helm to fix the crest:
Phrygian Euanthes too, and Mimas, whom,
Once friend of Paris and his peer in age,
Theano bare to Amycus his sire,
The selfsame night that Cisseus' royal child
Teemed with a firebrand, and gave Paris birth.
Paris within his father's city lies,
Mimas, unknown, Laurentum's coast doth keep.   *706*
Lo! as a mighty boar, by sharp-toothed hounds
Driven from the mountain-heights, which many a
     year
Pine-fruitful Vesulus hath sheltering held,
Many Laurentum's marsh-land, pastured fair
Within her reedy jungle, he, once come
Amid the meshes, halts with angry grunt,
And bristles up his shoulders; none durst rage
Against him, or draw nearer; at safe range
With darts and shouts they harass him from far;
He, dauntless, slowly to this side and that
Turns with teeth gnashing, and shakes off the spears:
So, of all those who burned with righteous wrath
Against Mezentius, none durst draw the sword
And close in onset, but with deafening shouts
And far-sped shafts assail him. There had come

From the ancient bounds of Corythus a Greek,
Acron, who, leaving half-done marriage rites,
Had fled away; him seeing from afar
Amid the ranks deal havoc, gay with plumes,
And in the purple of his plighted bride—
As oft-times, ranging the deep forest-lairs,
An unfed lion, by mad hunger urged,
If haply he hath spied a fleet-foot goat,
Or towering-antlered stag, exults and opes
His monstrous jaws, uprears his mane, and hangs
Over the rent flesh, couching; the foul gore
Drenches his cruel mouth—so eagerly
Upon the foemen's mass Mezentius leaps.   729
Down goes the hapless Acron, with his heels
Hammers the dark earth, dying, and stains red
The splintered spear-shaft. He too deigned not smite
Orodes flying, nor deal him a blind blow
With javelin-cast, but meets him face to face,
And man to man encounters, by no stealth
Filching the vantage, but sheer force of arms.
Then, on the prostrate foe with foot and spear
Pressing, he spake: "Here tall Orodes lies,
My men, no paltry portion of the war."
His comrades after him glad paean raise.   738
With ebbing breath the other: "Whoe'er thou art,
Not unavenged I fall, nor long shalt thou
Enjoy thy victory; for thee, too, like fates
Are watching; the same fields thou soon shalt press."
To whom Mezentius, with wrath-mingled smile:
"Now die; the Sire of gods and King of men
Shall look to me." So saying, he drew the spear
From out the hero's body; stern repose
And iron slumber on his eyelids press,
And their orbs close in everlasting night.   746
Caedicus then cuts down Alcathous;
Sacrator slays Hydaspes; Rapo's sword
Falls on Parthenius and the knotty strength
Of Orses; Clonius by Messapus dies
With Lycaonian Ericetes, one
Stretched prone by stumbling of his reinless steed,
One foot to foot confronting him. Forth stood
Agis the Lycian too, whom Valerus
Nathless, naught lacking of ancestral worth,
Smote to the dust; then Thronius by the hand
Of Salius; Salius by Nealces falls,
For javelin and far-stealing arrow famed.   754

Fell Mavors now was meting forth to each
Like dole and mutual death; both equally
Victors, both vanquished, slew and fell, nor thought
Of flight had either. In Jove's hall the gods
Of these and those the fruitless rage lament,
And that poor mortals should such toils endure.
Venus on one side gazes, and on one
Saturnian Juno. Pale Tisiphone
Raves on amid their thousands on the plain.
But now Mezentius, shaking his huge spear,
Into the field strides stormily; and lo!
Vast as Orion when he cleaves a path,
Wading through middle Nereus' mightiest pools,
And with his shoulder tops the waves, or when,
Bearing an aged ash from mountain-height,
He stalks on earth, and hides his head in cloud—
So strode Mezentius onward, vast in arms.   768
Aeneas adown the line of battle spies,
And moves to meet him. He his noble foe
Dauntless abides, and plants his ponderous bulk;
Then, measuring with his eyes a spear-throw's space:
"Now let my right hand's godhead and the dart
I poise for flight bestead me! Here I vow
To make thee, Lausus, thee, a living man,
Arrayed in spoils torn from the robber's corse,
My trophy of Aeneas." He had said,
And hurled from hand a hissing spear; it flew,
And glanced from off the shield, and pierced afar
Noble Antores betwixt side and loin—
Antores, friend of Hercules, who, sent
From Argos, to Evander clave, and found
Beneath Italian walls a home. But ah!
Smit by another's wound he lies, and looks
On heaven, and, dying, of his dear Argos dreams.   782
Then good Aeneas hurls a spear; it sped
Right through the hollow disk of threefold brass,
Through layers of linen, and the inwoven work
Of triple bull's hide, and lodged low i' the groin,
But pushed not home its passage. Swiftly then
Aeneas drew sword, rejoicing to behold
The Tuscan's blood, forth plucks it from his thigh,
And hotly presses on the staggering foe.
Lausus for love of his dear sire groaned deep
At sight of it, and tears rolled o'er his face.   790
Nor here thy piteous doom, thy matchless deeds,
If length of time e'er make believable

Such exploit, nor thyself, brave youth, right meet
To be remembered, will I leave unsung.
He, thus defenceless and sore hampered, now
Was back retiring, trailing from his shield
The foeman's dart; forth leapt the youth, and thrust
Betwixt their points, and, as Aeneas' right hand
Now rose to strike, ran in beneath his sword,
And, hindering, stayed the striker. Loud his folk
Cheer him, and follow with their eyes, until
The sire, son-shielded, might win safe retreat,
And hurl their javelins, and bear back the foe
With darts from far. Aeneas storms with rage,
And keeps shield-covered. As, when with boisterous
    hail
The clouds fall headlong, plough-folk, every one,
And country hinds fly scattered from the fields,
And cowers the wayfarer in some safe hold,
Or river-bank, or high o'er-arching rock,
While rain still pelts the earth, that they may task
The daylight with returning sunshine: so
Aeneas, o'erwhelmed with countless darts, endures
The war-cloud, till it growl itself away,
Still chiding Lausus, threatening Lausus: "Why
Rush upon death, and overdare thy strength?   *811*
Love fools thee into rashness." Not the less
Madly he riots, till in the Dardan chief
Fierce wrath rose headier, and the sister-Fates
Lausus' last threads up-gather; for now drives
Aeneas his strong sword through the stripling's
    frame
Till the whole blade is buried. His light shield,
Frail arms for one so threatening, the point pierced,
And pierced the tunic which of pliant gold
His mother wove him, and blood filled his breast;
Then life, regretful, on its airy way
Fled to the shades, and left the body lone.   *820*
But when he saw the dying look and face,
The face so wondrous pale, Anchises' son
Uttered a deep groan, pitying him, and stretched
His right hand forth as in his soul there rose
The likeness of the love he bore his sire.
"Poor boy! what guerdon for thy glorious deeds—
Say what, to match that mighty heart of thine,
Shall good Aeneas yield thee? Those thine arms,
Wherein thou gloried'st, keep them; and thyself,
If such a care may touch thee, to the shades

And ashes of thy fathers I restore.   *828*
Unhappy! yet for thy sad end some balm
Be this: by great Aeneas thou art slain."
Then hails he his attendants, chiding them
For loiterers, and uplifts their lord from earth,
Where he lay dabbling his trim locks with blood.
   Meanwhile the sire by Tiber's stream now
      staunched
His wounds with water, and for ease lay propped
Against a tree-trunk. On the boughs apart
Hangs the brass helmet, and his ponderous arms
Rest on the meadow-sward. About him stand
His flower of war; he panting and in pain
Foments his neck, and lets the flowing beard
O'erspread his bosom, many a time inquires
Of Lausus, and oft sends to call him back,
And bear the lad his sorrowing sire's command.   *840*
But Lausus, laid on shield, a lifeless corse,
His friends in tears were bearing—mighty soul
Quelled by a mighty wound. The father's heart,
Ill-boding, recognized their wail afar.
With showers of dust his hoary locks he soils,
And spreads both hands to heaven, and clasps his
      arms
About the corse. "Did then such joy of life
Possess me, O my son, that in my stead
I suffered thee, even thee whom I begat,
To meet the foeman's stroke? Am I, thy sire,
Saved through thy wounds, and living by thy death?
Ah! to my sorrow now at last I know
What exile is! now is the wound pushed home.   *850*
Yea, and I too with infamy, my son,
Thy name have spotted, by men's hate of me
Thrust from the throne and sceptre of my sires!
To mine own country and my people's spite
I should have paid the forfeit, by all deaths
Freely have yielded up this guilty life.
Now I live on, from men and light of day
Not yet departing; but depart I will."
So saying, at once upon his wounded thigh
He raised him, and, albeit from the deep wound
His force flagged somewhat, with no downcast air
Called for his war-steed. This was ay his pride,
And this his solace; hereon he was wont
From all his wars to ride victorious home.
The sorrowing creature now he thus bespeaks: *860*

"We have lived long, O Rhaebus, if aught long
Pertain to mortals. Or to-day shalt thou
Bear back in triumph the bloody spoils and head
Of yon Aeneas, and be of Lausus' pangs
My co-avenger, or, if all force fail
Our path to open, shalt beside me lie:
No, nor wilt thou, methinks, my bravest, deign
Brook stranger's bidding, or a Teucrian lord."
He said, and, mounted on his willing back,
As ever wont, bestrode him, and both hands
Charged with keen javelins, his head bright with
    brass,
Shaggy with horse-hair plume. So galloping
He dashed amidst them. In one single heart
Upsurges a vast tide of shame and grief
With fury mingled; and thrice o'er he called
With mighty voice "Aeneas!" Well, I trow,
Aeneas knew it, and prayed a jubilant prayer: *874*
"May the great Sire of gods so bring to pass,
So lord Apollo! fall on, begin the fray!"
Thus much he spake, and with his threatening spear
Moved on to meet him. But the other cried:
"Reft of my son, why thinkest thou, fierce man,
To fright me now? sole way was this whereby
To work my ruin. I shudder not at death,
No, nor spare any of thy gods. Now cease;
I come to die, but bring thee first these gifts."
He spake, and hurled a dart against the foe,   *882*
Then yet another and another plants,
In a wide circle wheeling; but the boss
Of gold bides all. Thrice round the watchful foe
Rode he in rings to leftward, from his hand
Launching the javelins; thrice the Trojan prince
Bears round with him upon his brazen targe
A dense spear-forest. Then wearying to prolong
Delays so many, so many darts to pluck,
And by the unequal conflict sore bestead,
Much inly pondering, forth at last he springs,
And in betwixt the war-steed's hollow brows
Hurls his spear mightily. The beast reared up,
Lashed with his hooves the air, his rider flung,
Then, following him, head downward, pinned to earth
And with his shoulder pressed the fallen man.   *894*
Trojan and Latin shouts set heaven ablaze.
Up speeds Aeneas, and plucks sword from sheath,
Then o'er him: "Where is bold Mezentius now,

And all his heart's wild violence?" Unto whom
The Etruscan, as up-glancing he drew in
A draught of heaven, and to himself returned:
"Why, bitter foe, dost taunt and threaten death?
In slaying is no sin; nor with such thought
Came I to battle, nor did my Lausus so
Pledge terms betwixt us. This alone I crave,
By whatso grace to fallen foes may be:
Let earth my body hide. Girt round am I
With bitter hate of my own folk, I wot.
Fend me from this their rage, and with my son
Grant fellowship in burial." So he spake,
Welcomed the sword to his expectant throat,
And o'er his arms let pour life's ruddy tide.   *908*

BOOK XI

Meanwhile Aurora rising left the sea;
Aeneas, though stress of grief bade yield the hour
To burial of his friends, with mind by death
Bewildered, to the gods at earliest dawn
His victor-vows was paying. A mighty oak,
Lopped bare of branches, on a mound he plants,
And decks in gleaming armour torn from Prince
Mezentius—trophy to thy praise, great King
Of battle. The hero's plume, still dripping blood,
And splintered spears he hangs there, the cuirass
Twice six times smitten and pierced through and
    through,
And on the left hand binds the brazen shield,
And hangs the ivory sword about its neck.   11
Then his rejoicing friends—for the whole band
Of chiefs thronged close about him—he exhorts,
Thus breaking silence: "The main work o' the war
Has been achieved, my heroes; for the rest,
Let every fear be banished: lo! ye see
The spoils and first-fruits of the tyrant king;
And here, my handiwork, Mezentius stands.
Now lies our path to Latium's king and town.
Arm you in spirit; in hope forestall the fray;
That when the gods give signal to pluck hence
Our standards, and lead forth the host from camp,
No pause impede you, caught at unawares,
Nor faltering purpose, born of fear, retard.   21
Meanwhile our comrades, that unburied lie,
Commit we to the earth—sole honour left
In depths of Acheron. Aye, go forth," he said,
"With farewell tribute grace the peerless souls
Who with their life-blood this our country won,
And to Evander's sorrowing city first
Be Pallas sent, whom, lacking naught of man,
The dark day reft, and plunged in bitter doom."   28
    Weeping he spake, and to the tent retraced
His steps, where Pallas' lifeless corse was laid,
Watched by Acoetes old, who bare the arms
Once of Evander the Parrhasian, now
In less auspicious hour was faring forth,

Of his loved foster-child the appointed friend.
And all the attendant train and Trojan throng
Stood round, with Ilian women, their locks loosed
In wonted wise for sorrow; but when Aeneas
Within the high doors entered, they uplift
A mighty wail to heaven, and beat their breasts,
And all the royal place resounds with shriek
Of sorrow. He likewise, when the pillowed head
And face of Pallas snowy-white he saw,
And marked the Ausonian spear-head's gaping
        wound
On his smooth breast, spake with o'er-welling tears: *41*
"Poor boy, did fortune, when so blithe she came,
Envy me thee, that thou shouldst never look
Upon my realm, or home in triumph ride?
Not such my parting promise touching thee
Made to thy sire Evander, when he clasped
And sped me forth to win a mighty realm,
And, fearful, warned me that right brave the foe,
Stubborn the race, we strove with. And now he,
With empty hope fooled utterly, belike
Is proffering vows, and heaping high with gifts
The altars; we, the while, a lifeless corse,
That owes no more to any god in heaven,
Escort with sorrow's ineffectual pomp.   *54*
Unhappy, thou that wilt behold thy son
Slain piteously! Is this the home-return,
The expected triumph? This my solemn pledge?
Yet here no recreant, scarred, with shameful wounds,
Shalt see, Evander, nor a son so saved
That thou, his sire, for dreaded death shalt pray.
Ah me! Ausonia, what a tower of help
Here art thou reft of, and, Iulus, thou!"   *58*
    So, having wept his fill, he bids them lift
The hapless corse, and picks a thousand men
From his whole host, and sends them to escort
The farewell pomp, and with the father's tears
Their own commingle—for so vast a grief
Scant solace, yet to that sad father due.
Others of arbute-boughs and oaken shoots
In haste plait hurdle-wise a pliant bier,
And the heaped bed with leafy covering shroud.   *66*
High on the rustic litter him they lay;
Even as a flower by maiden's finger culled,
Or violet mild, or drooping hyacinth,
Ere yet the lustre or the loveliness

Hath from its form departed; mother Earth
Feeds it no longer, nor with strength supplies.
Then garments twain, with gold and purple stiff,
Aeneas bare forth, which, ravished with the toil,
Sidonian Dido erst with her own hands
Had wrought, and shot the web with subtle gold.   75
One of these twain—grief's latest rite—he wraps
About the dead, and with its covering veils
The fire-doomed tresses, and heaps high withal
Full many a prize from the Laurentian fray,
Bidding the booty in long line be borne.
Steeds too he adds, and darts, from foemen reft:
And captives he had bound, hands lashed behind,
To send as offerings to the shade, and, slain,
Dash with their blood the fire. The chiefs them-
        selves
He bids bear tree-trunks clad with hostile arms,
And foemen's titles to be fixed thereon.   84
Hapless Acoetes, overworn with age,
Is onward led, now marring with clench'd fists
His bosom, now with nails his face, and falls
Forward, and casts his length upon the ground.
The car too, bathed in Rutule blood, they lead.
Behind, the war-horse Aethon, trappings doffed,
Goes weeping, and the big drops wet his face.
Others bear spear and helmet; for all else
Turnus, as victor, holds. Then, sad array,
Follow the Teucrians and Etruscans all,
And men of Arcady with arms reversed.   93
But when the long procession of his friends
Had wholly passed, Aeneas, groaning deep,
Stopped, and spake further: "Unto other tears
We by the same grim destinies of war
Are summoned hence. I bid thee hail! for aye,
O mightiest Pallas, and for aye farewell."
No more he spake, but to the lofty walls
Turned him, and campward bent his steps.

                                And now
From Latium's town came envoys, olive-wreathed,
Craving his clemency: the dead, which lay
Sword-scattered o'er the plain, would he give back,
And suffer 'neath an earthen mound to pass;
With vanquished folk and bodies void of breath
There is no warring; let him spare whom once
He hailed as hosts, and fathers of his bride.   105
Aeneas, for such a prayer he might not spurn,

Grants courteously the boon, and adds these words
Moreover: "Latins, say what hard mishap
Hath wound you in so vast a web of war
That thus ye fly our friendship? Do ye ask
Peace for the dead, by chance of battle quelled?
Fain would I grant it to the living too.
Nor came I, had not fate assigned me here
A place wherein to settle, nor any war
Wage I against your folk: it was the king
Left our alliance, and made choice to lean
On Turnus' sword for succour. 'Twere more meet
Had Turnus faced the death ye mourn to-day.　　　*115*
If with armed force he thinks to fight it out,
And drive the Teucrians forth, beseemed him well
To meet me man to man, and spear to spear:
He should have lived whose life was granted him
Of heaven or his right hand. Now hie ye hence,
And 'neath your hapless comrades pile the fire."
Aeneas had spoken. They stood wonder-hushed,
Eyes fixed and faces in one mutual stare.　　　*121*
Then, old in years, and still with slanderous spite
Armed against youthful Turnus, Drances thus
Makes answer: "O mighty in fame, in arms
Yet mightier, Trojan hero, by what praise
Can I exalt thee to the sky? Or should
Thy soul's uprightness, or thy toils in war
Win first my wonder? We indeed thy words
Will to our native town bear blithely back,
And knit thee fast, so fortune find a way,
To Latium's king. Let Turnus for himself
Go seek confederates. Nay, 'twill please us well
The destined ramparts of thy walls to rear,
And on our shoulders heave the stones of Troy."　　　*131*
He had said; and all his comrades with one mouth
Murmured assent. For twice six days a truce
They plighted, and, with peace to interpose,
Teucrians and Latins o'er the wooded heights
Roamed without scathe together. The tall ash
Rings to the two-edged steel; sky-piercing pines
They topple o'er, and still with wedges cleave
Tough heart-of-oak and scented cedar-bole,
And freight with mountain-ash the groaning wains.　　*138*
　　And now was wingèd Fame, the harbinger
Of woe so vast, filling Evander's ears,
Evander's home and city—she, who late
Of Pallas' triumph o'er the Latins told.

Out-streaming to the gates, Arcadia's sons
Grasp each a funeral-torch, their ancient wont.
Bright gleams the road with a long line of fire
That parts the fields afar. The Phrygian band,
Moving to meet them, joins the weeping train.
Soon as the matrons saw them pass the wall,
With shrieks they set the sorrowing town ablaze.
As for Evander then—no force avails
To stay him; but he thrusts amid the throng,
And, when the bier was set, on Pallas' form
Casts him, and clings to it with groans and tears.
Scarce loosed by sorrow, words at length win way: *151*
"Not such the pledge thou gavest to thy sire,
My Pallas, warily to put thy faith
In the fell god of battles. Well I wist
How potent was the new-born pride in arms,
And a first onset's all-entrancing spell. *158*
Ah! bitter first-fruit of youth's flower! and harsh
Prelude of neighbour war! and vows and prayers
No god gave ear to! and thou, holiest wife,
And happy in thy death, that spared thee not
To see this sorrow! But, by living, I
Have overshot my doom, to linger on
A son-surviving sire. Troy's friendly arms
Would I had followed! would the Rutule darts
Had overwhelmed me! So should I have given
This life of mine, and I, not Pallas here,
Been thus with funeral-pomp borne homeward! Yet
You would I blame not, Teucrians, nor our league
And right hands clasped in friendship: long ago
The lot ye deal me to mine age was owed.
But if untimely doom was o'er my son
Impending, 'twill rejoice me that he smote
His Volscian thousands, ere himself was slain,
Leading the Teucrians into Latium. Nay,
Nor other funeral could I deem thy due,
Pallas, than good Aeneas hath devised,
And the great Phrygians, and the Tyrrhene lords,
And all the host Tyrrhenian. Trophies great
They bring of whom thy right hand did to death;
And thou too, Turnus, a huge trunk in arms
Wert standing now, had age and strength of years
Been matched between ye. But why, evil-starred,
Stay I the Teucrians from the onset? Go,
Bear heedfully this message to your king:
That I, bereft of Pallas, still drag on

This hated life, thy right hand is the cause,
Which, well thou seest, to son alike and sire
Owes Turnus. Yea, for fortune and exploit
No room is left thee else. The joys of life
I ask not; 'tis forbid me: but to bear
My son these tidings in the shades below."   *181*

   Meanwhile the Dawn her kindly light had reared
For suffering men, renewing task and toil.
Now Prince Aeneas, now Tarchon, have set up
Their funeral-pyres along the winding shore.
Hither bare each the bodies of their kin,
With rite ancestral; from the murky flames,
Lit under, the high vault in vaporous gloom
Is muffled. Thrice about the blazing piles,
Girt in bright arms, the course they ran, thrice o'er
Compassed on steeds the mournful fires of death,
With loud lamentings. Their tears rain on earth,
And rain on armour. Up to heaven is borne
Shouting of men, and clarion-blare. Anon
Others take spoil from slaughtered Latins torn,
And heap it on the fire—helms, goodly swords,
Bridles, and glowing wheels; but others bring
Gifts to the dead familiar, their own shields
And luckless weapons. Many a steer around
To death falls stricken; and bristly swine and sheep,
From all the country ravished, they let bleed
Above the flame. Then over the wide shore
They watch their comrades burning, and keep ward
O'er the charred embers, nor can tear them thence,
Till dewy night now turns the face of heaven,
Studded with glittering stars.   *202*
                Nor less, the while,
The hapless Latins, far remote, have reared
Innumerable pyres: of many slain
Some in the delvèd earth they lay, some lift
And carry to the neighbouring fields, or send
Home to the city: what remains, one vast
And indistinguishable slaughter-heap,
They burn untold, unhonoured. Then far and wide
Flare the void fields, thick-sown with rival-fires.
Thrice dawn had driven chill darkness from the sky,
When sadly from the pyres they rake and heap
The ashes up, and undistinguished bones,
And warm above them pile the mounded earth.   *212*
But now in homes of rich Latinus' town
Is the chief uproar, and the mightiest share

Of long-drawn lamentation. Mothers here
With their son's brides forlorn, here cherished hearts
Of sorrowing sisters, boys of sires bereft,
Curse the fell war and Turnus' bridal troth.
Him they bid arm, with his own single sword
Fight out the quarrel, who for himself demands
The realm of Italy, honours of a prince.   *219*
Fierce Drances fans the fire, bears testimony
Turnus alone is challenged, he alone
Called to do battle. Many a voice withal
In various counter-strain for Turnus pleads;
The queen's great name o'ershadows him, the praise
Of many a well-earned triumph is his stay.
    Amid this stir and fiery tumult, lo!
From Diomede's great city, to crown all,
The envoys bring sad answer: all their toils
For naught were lavished; naught have gifts, or
    gold,
Or strenuous prayers availed them; other arms
Must Latium look to, or with terms of peace
Approach Troy's monarch. 'Neath that load of woe
Sinks King Latinus. That Aeneas is here,
Fate-borne at heaven's clear bidding, the god's wrath
Warns him, and those new graves before his eyes.   *233*
Therefore a mighty council of his chiefs,
By royal mandate summoned, he convenes
Within his lofty portals. They have flocked
Together, and all along the crowded ways
Stream toward the palace. In the midst is set,
Eldest in years, and first in sceptred sway,
With joyless brow, Latinus. Hereupon
The envoys from the Aetolian town returned
He bids declare their tidings, point by point
Demands full answer. Then on every tongue
Fell silence, and obedient to his word
Thus Venulus begins: *242*
          "O citizens,
We have seen Diomede and the Argive camp,
And overpassed all perils of the way,
And touched the hand whereby fell Ilium's realm.
He walled Argyripa was founding, named
From his own nation, in the new-won fields
Of Iapygian Garganus. So,
When we had entered, and gat leave to speak,
Our gifts we proffer, name and race declare,
Who our invaders, for what cause we come

To Arpi. Having heard us, he replied
Thus with unruffled brow: 'O happy race
Of Saturn's realm, Ausonian folk of old,
What chance disturbs your quiet, and lures you on
To challenge wars ye know not? We, whoe'er
Outraged the fields of Ilium with the sword—
I waive all sufferings 'neath her lofty walls
In battle drained, the warriors that lie whelmed
In yonder Simois—have, the wide world through,
Paid, one and all, the forfeit of our crime
In untold pangs, a remnant Priam's self
Might pity. Let Minerva's gloomy star
Bear witness, and the Euboean crags, and thou,
Caphereus the avenger. From that field
Wide-scattered, Menelaus, Atreus' son,
Far as to Proteus' pillars exiled dwells;
Ulysses hath the Aetnean Cyclops seen.   263
Why of the realm of Neoptolemus
Tell, or Idomeneus' uprooted home,
Or Locrians dwelling on the Libyan shore?
Even he, the great Achaeans' chief himself,
Lord of Mycenae, on the threshold's edge
Fell by the hand of his accursèd wife;
For conquered Asia crouched a paramour.
To think that heaven hath grudged me to return
Home to my country's altars, and behold
The wife I long for, and fair Calydon!
Nay, sight-appalling signs pursue me still,
And my old comrades, lost to me, as birds
Now wing the vault, or roam the rivers—ah!
That such dire torment on my folk should fall!—
And fill the rocks with lamentable cries.   274
Naught else had I to look for from that hour
When with infatuate weapon I assailed
Celestial frames, and outraged with a wound
The hand of Venus. Nay, constrain me not
To such encounters. With the sons of Troy,
Since Pergama fell down, no war I wage,
Nor with delight mind me of ancient ills.   280
The gifts ye bring me from your native shores
Bear rather to Aeneas. We have faced
The rude edge of his weapons, hand to hand
Have grappled with him: trust me, who have tried,
How huge he rises to the shield, how swings
The whirlwind of his spear. Had Ida's land
Borne twain beside, such heroes, Troy herself

Had stormed the gates of Inachus, and Greece,
With doom reversed, were wailing. All the time
We lingered 'neath the walls of stubborn Troy,
'Twas Hector and Aeneas by whose might
Checked was Greek victory, and for ten years' space
Fell backward. Both renowned for valour, both
Matchless for martial exploit, this man bare
The palm for goodness. Hand to hand with him
Unite in friendship, by what means ye may,
But see your weapons shun the shock of his.'   *293*
Thou hast heard the monarch's answer, gracious sire,
And what he counsels for this mighty war."

    Scarce ceased the envoys, ere tumultuously
From mouth to mouth of the Ausonians ran
A various hubbub; as, when rocks impede
Some rushing river, from the imprisoned flood
A dull roar rises, and the neighbour-banks
Chafe loud with plashing waters. Soon as hearts
Beat calm again, and busy tongues were still,
First calling upon heaven, from his high throne
The King brake silence: "Well could I have wished,
Latins, and better had it been, ere now
To have determined of our kingdom's weal,
Nor at such hour to bid you to debate,
While foemen sit before the walls. A war
Disastrous wage we, O my countrymen,
With the gods' offspring and a hero-race
Invincible, who tire not of the fight,
No, nor when vanquished can let go the sword.   *307*
Hope in Aetolia's confederate arms,
If aught ye had, resign it. His own hope
Is every man: but this how frail ye see;
All else, in what wide ruin overthrown,
Needs but the witness of your eyes and hands.
Nor blame I any; what utmost valour could,
We have compassed, with the realm's whole strength
    have striven.   *313*
Now mark; the upshot of my wavering thoughts
I will unfold, and—give me your good heed—
Teach briefly. Bordering on the Tuscan stream
An ancient tract have I, stretched westward far
Past the Sicanian borders: tilled it is
By Rutules and Auruncans, who with plough
Task the stiff hills, and on the roughest slopes
Graze cattle. Let all this region, with its belt
Of lofty pine-clad highland, be made o'er

[336]

To Teucrian friendship; and just terms of peace
Name we, and summon them to share our realm.   322
Here let them settle, if this be their desire,
And build them ramparts. But, if other bounds,
Another folk than ours, they list to win,
Are free to quit our borders,—twice ten ships
Of oak Italian frame we, ay, or more,
If they can man them; by the water's edge
Lies wood enow; their number and their size
Themselves shall teach us; be it ours to give
Brass, hands, and shipmen's tackle. Furthermore,
For word hereof, and warrant of our league,
I will, a hundred Latins, noblest-born,
Make embassage, and proffer boughs of peace,
And bear them presents—talent-weights of gold,
And ivory, and a chair and robe of state,
Our royal emblems. Freely before all
Give counsel, and uphold the weary state."   335
    Then Drances, foe inveterate, whom the fame
Of Turnus aye with sidelong envy stirred
And stung to bitterness, lavish of wealth,
Tongue-valiant, but a frosty hand for war,
At council-board no vain adviser held,
In faction strong,—his mother's proud descent
Ennobling whom an obscure sire begat—
Drances at length uprising, with these words,
Heightens and heaps their wrath: 342
                       "Obscure to none
Nor needing voice of ours, O gracious sire,
The theme that thou debatest. One and all
Whereto the State's weal tendeth own they know,
Yet dare but mutter. Let him now concede
Untrammelled speech, and his blown pride abate,
Through whose disastrous leading, froward mien—
Ay, I will speak it, though with arms and death
He menace me—so many stars of war
Have we seen set, and the whole city plunged
In mourning, while the Trojan camp he braves,
Counting on flight, and scares the heaven with arms.   351
Yet one to all those gifts thou badest send
Or promise to the Dardans—add but one,
Thrice gracious king, and let no blusterer's wrath
O'ersway thee not to give thy daughter, sire,
In meet espousal to a peerless son,
And on this treaty set a lasting seal.
But if such terror hold us, heart and mind,

Himself conjure we, sue his grace to yield,
And their inalienable right resign
To ruler and to realm. Why hurl so oft
These hapless folk into the jaws of peril,
O fount and well-spring of our Latium's ills?　361
No safety is in war: 'tis peace we all
Crave of thee, Turnus, and, with peace, her one
Inviolable pledge. I first, whom thou
Feign'st for thy foe, nor reck I so to be,
Sue suppliant-wise. Have pity of thine own;
Abate thy pride, and, vanquished, quit the field.
Enough of routs and slaughters have we seen,
Vast tracts have left to desolation. Else,
If glory stir thee, if such hardihood
Thou nurse within thy breast, so hug to heart
A palace for thy bridal dower, be bold,
And launch thee fearless on the opposing foe.　370
Must we, that Turnus to his arms may take
A royal bride, as paltry lives forsooth,
A herd unwept, unburied, strew the plain?
Thou too, if there be in thee aught of force,
Aught of the war-god of thy sires, confront
And face thy challenger."

　　　　　　As thus he spake
Out blazed the fury of Turnus; loud he groaned,
And from his bosom's depth these words broke way:　377
"Lavish, I wot, is aye thy wealth of tongue,
Drances, when war demandeth hands, and when
The sires are summoned, there the first art thou.
Nathless naught need we fill our court with words,
Which, big albeit, fly from thee safe enow,
While the wall-rampart keeps the foe at bay,
Nor blood yet drowns the trenches. Ay, let peal
The wordy thunder; 'tis thy wont of old;
And charge me, Drances, thou, with cowardice,
Seeing thy hand hath reared such slaughter-heaps
Of Teucrians, and set all the fields ablaze
With trophies. What the pulse of valour can,
Yet may'st thou prove: nor far methinks to seek,
But round our very ramparts swarm the foe.
We march to meet them: wherefore hold'st aback?
Or will the war-god ever make his home
But in that windy tongue, those flying feet?　391
What, vanquished? I? Will any, thou foul liar,
Flout me as vanquished justly, who beholds
Tiber still swelling o'er with Ilian blood,

Evander's whole house by the roots laid low,
And his Arcadians stripped of arms? Not such
Did Bitias prove me, and huge Pandarus,
Nor whom, a thousand in a single day,
My victor-arm to nether Tartarus hurled,
Penned and shut fast within the foeman's wall.   *398*
'No safety in war?' Such brainless bodings keep
For thine own fortune, and the Dardan's head.
Ay, cease not with gross panic to whelm all
In wide confusion, laud to heaven the might
Of a twice-conquered nation, and decry
Latinus' arms beside it. Now, forsooth,
The Myrmidonian lords and Tydeus' son
Tremble before the Phrygian host, now, too,
Achilles of Larissa; and Aufidus
From Hadria's waves flees backward. Or, again,
When feigns the schemer's villainy to cower
Before my chiding, and with terror whets
The sting of calumny! Nay, such a life—
Cease to be troubled—by this hand of mine
Ne'er shalt thou forfeit; let it with thee dwell,
Of that thy breast fit denizen. Now, sire,
To thee and thy great counsels I return.   *410*
If in our arms thou rest no further hope,
If we so friendless are, and, routed once,
Are utterly o'erthrown, and fortune foiled
Hath no retrieval, pray we then for peace,
And reach out helpless hands. But ah! if aught
Were ours of wonted valour, him would I
Deem before all men of his travail blest,
Peerless of soul, who, such a sight to shun,
Fell once for all, and bit the dust, in death.
But if means yet be ours, a host for war
Unminished, and Italia's towns and tribes
Remain to aid us; if with outpoured blood
Troy bought her triumph—for their own dead have
          they,
And the like tempest swept o'er all—why thus
Inglorious faint we on the threshold's edge?
Why quake our limbs before the trumpet-call?   *424*
Time, and the shifting toil of changeful days,
Hath many a lot repaired; and many a man
Wave after wave of fortune hath by turns
Played with, and planted on firm ground again.
The Aetolian—Arpi—will not succour us:
Yet will Messapus, and Tolumnius blest,

And all those chiefs by many a nation sent;
Nor will scant fame attend the chosen flower
Of Latium and Laurentum's land. Ours, too,
Camilla, from the Volscians' peerless stem,
Heading her horse-troop, squadrons bright with
    brass.   433
But if the Teucrian lords bid me alone
Do battle, and ye would have it so, and I
Stand here the hinderer of your common good,
Why, Victory hath not from these hands of mine
Shrunk with such loathing, that for hope so high
I should draw back from any bold essay.
Dauntless will I confront him, though he match
Even great Achilles, and don arms like his,
Wrought by the hand of Vulcan. Lo! to you
And my bride's sire, Latinus, I devote
My life—I, Turnus, of the brave of old
Second to none in valour. Me alone
Aeneas summons? Let him, I implore,
Nor Drances rather, if heaven's wrath be here,
With his life pay the forfeit, nor, if here
Prowess and honour, bear the palm away!"   444
  So of dark issues held they hot debate:
Aeneas meanwhile moved on from camp to field.
Lo! one with tidings, amid uproar wild,
Speeds through the palace, and with mighty dread
Fills all the city, that for battle dight
Teucrian and Tyrrhene host are marching down
From Tiber's river o'er all the plain. At once
Confusion and heart-shaking seize the crowd,
And wrath, roused in them with no gentle stings.
With quivering hands they clutch at arms; for arms
Clamour their youth; the sires to weeping fall
And mournful mutterings. Now from every side
Rises to heaven a loud discordant din;
Even as in some tall grove when flocks of birds
Have settled, or on Padusa's fishy stream
Swans hoarsely cry athwart the clamorous pools.   458
"Ay, crowd to council, citizens," Turnus cries,
Seizing the moment, "and sit praising peace,
While they rush armed on empire." No word more
He uttered, but, up-starting, swiftly flung
From out the lofty hall. "Thou, Volusus,
Bid arm the Volscian cohorts," he exclaimed,
"And lead the Rutules on. Messapus, thou,
And Coras with thy brother, array the horse,

And o'er the wide plain spread them. Some secure
Each access to the town, and man the towers;
The rest, where I shall bid, fall on with me."   467
At once a wild rush to the wall begins
From every quarter. Sire Latinus too
Quits council, and breaks off his high designs,
By the dark hour dismayed; and oft his heart
Upbraids him that he freely welcomed not
Dardan Aeneas to the adopted rank
Of citizen and son. Before the gates
Others dig trenches, or heave stakes and stones
On shoulder. The hoarse clarion for the fray
Gives bloody signal. Then in motley ring
Boys, see, and matrons gird the ramparts, all
To one last effort summoned. Furthermore,
Up to the temple that crowns Pallas' height,
Thronged with a company of dames, the queen
Rides onward, bringing gifts, and at her side
The maid Lavinia, source of all that woe,
Her comely eyes cast earthward. Entering in,
The matrons fill the holy place with smoke
Of incense, and send forth a mournful cry
From the high portal: "O mighty in arms,
And mistress of the sword, Tritonian maid,
Break with thy might the Phrygian robber's spear,
Himself cast prone on earth, and spurn him low
Beneath our lofty gates." Turnus the while
With emulous fury arms him for the fray.   486
Even now, the ruddy breastplate donned, he stood
Bristling with brazen scales; his legs he had sheathed
In golden cuishes, and, bare-browed as yet,
But battle-blade on thigh, all golden shone,
As down he hies him from the fortress-height
Exulting, and in hope forestalls the foe:
As with snapped tether free at length, a horse
Breaks stall, and, launched upon the open plain,
Or seeks the herds and pastures of the mares,
Or, wont to plunge him in the well-known stream,
Darts forth, and, rearing his proud crest on high,
Neighs for mere wantonness; the tossing mane
Plays over neck and shoulder. Him to meet,
Backed by her Volscian host, Camilla sped,
And hard beside the gateway leapt from horse,
Queen as she was, whom following, all the band
Glide from their steeds to earth. Then thus she spake: 501
"Turnus, if aught self-trust beseem the brave,

I dare and pledge me here Troy's troop to face,
And sole against the Tyrrhene horsemen ride.
Let me first prove the perils of the fray:
Tarry thou here on foot beside the wall,
And guard the ramparts." Whereunto replied
Turnus, his eyes on the dread maiden fixed,
"O maiden, glory of Italy, what thanks
Can I or hope to utter or repay?
But since thy spirit doth all price out-soar,
Share now the task with me. Aeneas, 'tis said—
And scouts sent forth confirm the tale—hath pushed
Forward, relentless still, his light-armed horse,
To scour the plain; himself, mounting the ridge,
Draws cityward by the lone mountain-heights.   514
In the wood's hollow track a sleight of war
I purpose—to beset with armèd men
The thoroughfare of the mountain gorge. Do thou
Meet and do battle with the Etruscan horse;
Valiant Messapus at thy side will be,
With Latium's squadron and Tiburtus' band;
Take thou too on thyself a leader's sway."
So saying, Messapus and the federate chiefs
Cheered with like words to battle, he moves to meet
The foe. There is a vale that curves and bends,
Well framed for stratagems and wiles of war,
Hemmed in on either side by wooded walls
Impenetrably dark. Hereinto leads
A narrow footpath, and a strait ravine
Churlish of access. Over it there lies
High on the watch-towers of the mountain-top
A broad expanse unlooked for, safe retreat
To charge from right and left-ward, or take stand
Upon the ridge, and roll down mighty rocks.   529
Hither the warrior, thridding well-known ways,
Hies him, has seized the spot, and sat him down
Within the treacherous forest.

                        But meanwhile
Latona's daughter in the halls of heaven
Addressed fleet Opis, of the sacred band
Of maids that be her fellows, and poured forth
These sorrowing words: "Lo! to the cruel war
Goes forth Camilla, maiden, and in vain
Girds on these arms of ours, though dear to me
Beyond all others. Nor soothly is that love,
Thou knowest, new-born to Dian, nor her heart
Touched with a sudden charm. When Metabus,

Now driven through hate of his tyrannic sway
Forth from his realm, Privernum's ancient hold
Was leaving, through the battle's press he bore
His babe in flight, to share his banishment,
And named her from her mother, in altered wise,
Camilla for Casmilla. To the long
Lone forest-heights he sped, still carrying her
Before him on his bosom. From all sides
Fierce darts beset him, and in circling swarms
Hovered the Volscian soldiery, when lo!
Athwart his flight full Amasenus' flood
Foamed with o'er-brimming banks; so wild a storm
Had burst the clouds of heaven. Here, fain to swim,
Love for the babe withholds him, and he quakes
For his dear burden. Pondering every way,
Hardly at last this swift resolve took root: 551
A huge spear, which the warrior's stalwart hand
Bare, of hard-knotted and fire-seasoned oak—
To this he lashed his daughter, swathed in bark
Of the wild cork, and midmost of the shaft
Bound her for throwing, and then, with mighty hand
Poising it, cried to heaven: 'O gracious Maid,
Child of Latona, hauntress of the grove,
I vow this babe thy servant, I her sire;
Thy weapon first she grasps, and from her foe
Flies through the air, thy suppliant. For thine own,
Goddess, receive her, I implore, who now
Is to the random breezes given.' He spake,
Drew back his arm, and strongly wheeled the spear,
And threw it: the waves roared; over the swift stream
Flies poor Camilla on the hurtling dart.   563
But Metabus, by a mighty band the while
Pressed closelier, plunges, and in triumph plucks
His gift to Trivia from the grassy bank,
Javelin and maid together. Him thenceforth
Nor homes of men, nor city-walls received;
Nor had his wild heart brooked it, but he led
A life of shepherds on the lonely hills.
Here in the brakes, amid rough forest-dens,
Reared he his daughter upon wild mare's milk,
Squeezing the teats into her tender lips.   572
Soon as the baby-feet their earliest steps
Had planted, with sharp javelin's weight he armed
Her hands, and from the tiny shoulder hung
Shafts and a bow. For gold to deck her hair,
And for long-trailing robe, a tiger's spoils

Hung from her head adown the back. Even then
With tender hand she launched her puny darts,
And, whirling round her head the smooth-thonged
    sling,
Struck crane Strymonian, or white swan, to earth.
Her many a mother through the Tyrrhene towns
Sought for their sons, but vainly. Well content
To mate alone with Dian, she cherishes
A lifelong passion for the hunter's darts
And maidenhood unsullied. Would she had ne'er,
Caught up by such a wave of war, essayed
To brave in fight the Teucrians! so were she
Still dear, and of my maiden band to-day.   *586*
But come, since harsh fate dogs her hard at heel,
Glide, nymph, from heaven, and Latium's borders
    seek,
Where now begins the dark ill-omened fray,
Take these, and pluck from quiver a vengeful shaft.
Herewith, whoe'er with wound her sacred flesh—
Or Trojan or Italian—shall profane,
Let him like quittance pay me blood for blood.
Thereafter I in hollow cloud will bear
Her hapless corse for burial, and, of arms
All undespoiled, to her own land restore."
She spake, but the other down the light air sped
Hurtling, her form in a black whirlwind swathed.   *596*
    Meanwhile the Trojan host draw nigh the walls,
The Etruscan chiefs and all their horse-array,
Told into ordered troops. The war-steed neighs,
Paws the wide plain and with the tight-drawn curb
Fights, as he faces to this side and that:
Then bristles the wide plain with iron spears,
And the field blazes with their brandished blades.
Nor less Messapus, Latium's swift-foot sons,
And Coras with his brother, and the light troop
Of maid Camilla, show forth upon the plain,
Confronting them; with back-drawn hands afar
They couch the spear, or shake the quivering lance; *606*
And fiery-fierce now grows the tramp of men,
Neighing of steeds. By this had either host
Paused within spear-cast: then, with sudden shout,
Forward they burst, cheer on their maddened steeds,
And all together, from all sides, pour forth
Darts thick as snowflakes, that obscure the sky.
At once Tyrrhenus and Aconteus keen
Rush each on each with spears that meet amain,

And first deal thunderous downfall, either steed
Shock-shattered with the brunt of breast to breast.
Aconteus, like a levin-bolt flung forth,
Or ponderous engine-stone, is hurled afar
Headlong, and scatters to the winds his life.   *617*
Straight all is disarray; the Latins turn,
Set shield to back, and for the ramparts ride.
Troy gives them chase; Asilas leads the van.
And now the gates they near, when once again
The Latins lift the war-shout, and wheel round
Their chargers' supple necks. The victors fly,
And with loose bridle gallop fast and far.
As when, with alternating ebb and flow,
The advancing sea now rushes to the beach,
Shoots o'er the crags in torrent foam, and bathes
With curvèd billow all the sandy bourne,
Now, with swift ebb, retreats, and sucking back
The shingle, leaves the beach with gliding shoal.   *628*
Twice o'er the Tuscans to their ramparts drive
The Rutules headlong, and twice o'er look back
Routed, and sling behind their covering shields.
But when, for the third onset charging home,
Army gripped army, and man singled man,
Then were there dying groans, and deep in blood
Roll arms and bodies and death-wounded steeds,
Mingled with slaughtered men; the fight swells fierce.
Orsilochus at the steed of Remulus—
Himself he feared to face—a javelin hurled,
And left the steel beneath its ear, whereat
The stricken brute rears furiously, and flings
In air his fore-legs, with uplifted breast,
Sustaining not the wound. Tumbled to earth,
His rider rolled. Catillus hurls from horse
Iollas, and, of giant heart to match
His giant arms and frame, Herminius:
Bare-headed he with tawny locks, bare too
His shoulders; nor wounds daunt him, such a front
He offers to all weapons. The spear sped,
And, quivering through the mighty shoulder-joints,
Pinned, and bowed double all his bulk with pain.   *645*
Dark blood flows wide, as with the sword they slay,
Fighting, or seek through wounds a glorious death.
    But midst the slaughter, like an Amazon,
One breast for battle bared, and quiver-girt,
Rages Camilla, and now thick and fast
Showers from her hand tough javelins, and now grips

The doughty war-axe with unwearying grasp,
While from her shoulder clangs the golden bow,
The arms of Dian. Nay, if forced to fly,
And backward beaten, with bow turned she aims
Retreating arrows. Round about her throng
The comrades of her choice, Larina, maid,
And Tulla, and Tarpeia brandishing
An axe of bronze, Italia's daughters; whom
Godlike Camilla for her own glory chose,
And as good helpers both in peace and war: *658*
Like Thracian Amazons, when Thermodon's flood
Shakes to their tramp, as in gay arms they ride
To battle, or round Hippolyte, or when
Penthesilea, child of Mars, from war
Comes charioted, and all the woman-host
With loud tumultuous shouting madly prance,
Armed with their moony shields. Whom first, whom
    last,
Fierce maiden, didst thou dash to earth? What tale
Of warrior-forms stretch dying in the dust?   *665*
Eunëus first, from Clytius sprung, whose breast,
Confronting and left bare, she pierces through
With her long pine-shaft. Vomiting forth streams
Of blood, he falls, and bites the gory dust,
And, dying, writhes upon his wound; anon
Liris, and o'er him Pegasus, of whom
One thrown in act to gather up the reins,
His steed stabbed under him, one hurrying up
With unarmed hand to aid him as he falls,
Meet headlong death together. Then to these
She adds Amastrus, son of Hippotas,
And, leaning forward, plies with spear from far
Tereus, Harpalycus, Demophoön,
And Chromis; yea, for every shaft that sped,
Hurled from the maiden's hand, some Phrygian fell.
In uncouth arms on Iapygian steed,
Afar rides hunter Ornytus; a hide
Stripped from a bullock swathes his shoulders broad,
Turned warrior now; a wolf's huge-gaping mouth
For head-gear—jaws and flashing teeth; his hands
Armed with rude hunting-blade: so through the ranks
He moves, and by a whole head tops them all.   *683*
Him now she caught—amid the battle's rout
Light task enow—and speared, and over him
Cried in fierce scorn: "O Tuscan, didst thou deem
'Twas forest-game thou huntedst? Lo! the day

Is come that shall your people's vaunts refute
With woman's darts. Yet to thy father's shades
No mean renown goes with thee, to have fallen
Slain by Camilla's spear." Orsilochus
And Butes next, in bulk Troy's mightiest twain:
But Butes from behind she stabbed, where gleamed
The neck 'twixt helm and hauberk, as he rode,
And the light shield from his left shoulder hung: 693
Orsilochus she flies, and, heading off
In a wide sweep, wheels inward, and so foils,
Pursuing the pursuer. Then at length,
Up-towering higher, through basnet and through
     bone
With strokes redoubled the strong axe she drives
For all his supplicating cries: the wound
Spatters his face with the hot brain. Here happed
Upon her path, and at the sudden sight
Hung terrified aback, the warrior-son
Of Aunus, dweller upon Apennine,
Not meanest of Ligurians, while the Fates
Allowed his lies. He, seeing he could not shun
The fray by flight, nor turn aside the queen
Now hard at heel, with subtle craft and wile
Essaying to ply trickery, thus begins:
"What glory is it, woman as thou art,
To trust in a steed's strength? Give o'er escape,
Dare close with me on equal ground, and come
Gird thee to fight on foot; full soon shalt know
To whom vain boasting bringeth bane." He spake;
She, stung to fury, and with the bitter smart
Burning, her charger to a comrade gave,
And in like arms stood fronting him on foot,
With bare blade dauntless, and unblazoned shield.   711
But, deeming guile had won, away darts he,
Turns bridle in hot haste, rides off, and goads
His galloper to full speed with armèd heel.
"Thou, false Ligurian, puffed with empty pride,
Thy slippery native tricks hast played in vain;
Ay, nor shall treachery win thee scathless way
To juggler Aunus." Thus the maiden cries,
And swift as fire, with lightning steps, afoot
Passes the steed, confronts him, grasps the rein,
Grapples, and wreaks red vengeance on the foe:
Lightly as when a hawk, that bodeful bird,
Winging from some tall crag, o'ertakes a dove
High in the cloud, and, clutched within his gripe,

Mangles her body with hooked feet, the while
Blood and rent feathers flutter from the sky.   724
    But with no eyeless watch the Sire of men
And gods hereon from high Olympus' top
Sat gazing. To the ruthless fight he goads
Tyrrhenian Tarchon, with no gentle stings
Pricks him to fury. So, 'mid weltering heaps,
Ranks wavering, rides he, with this cry or that
Kindles the troops, and, calling each by name,
Rallies the runaways to fight. "What fear,
O never to be shamed, O laggards still!
What coward sloth hath seized your Tuscan hearts?   733
Routs and makes rabble of such ranks as these
A woman? Say why then wield we sword, or grasp
These idle darts? To love naught slack are ye
And nightly bouts, or, when the wry-necked fife
Of Bacchus hath the dance proclaimed, to look
For revel and wine-cup on the loaded board—
Your joy, your passion this—till favouring seer
Announce the sacred feast, and victim fat
To the tall groves invite you." Thus he spake,
And, courting his own death, amid the press
Spurs, and at Venulus like a whirlwind drives,
Hales him from horse, and in a foeman's grip
Clasped to his breast bears off at furious speed.   744
A shout goes up to heaven; all Latin eyes
Upon them turn. Like fire along the plain,
Bearing both man and armour, Tarchon flies;
Then from the foe's spear snapping off the head,
Gropes for a vulnerable point, to deal
A death-blow. The other from his throat the while,
Struggling, wards off the wound, force baffling force: 750
As when a golden eagle, soaring high,
Swoops and bears off a serpent in his clutch,
Foot-fastened in its folds, with claws that cling;
But the maimed snake writhes tortuous, coil on coil,
Pricks scales erect, and hisses with its mouth,
High-towering; none the less with hookèd beak
He plies his struggling victim, all the while
Scourging the air with pinion-strokes: e'en so
Tarchon from Tibur's battle-ranks bears off
His prize in triumph. Maeonia's sons rush on
Following their chief's example and success.
Then Arruns, ripe for doom, wheels, dart in hand,
Round swift Camilla, and, with many a wile
Preventing, tries what chance may best bestead.

Where'er the maid spurs furious'mid the ranks,
There up comes Arruns, silent scours her track—
Where'er triumphant from the foe retires,
Thither turns he his swift and furtive rein.
Now this approach, now that, he traverses,
Circling on all sides, and relentless shakes
His deadly javelin. Chloreus, as it chanced,
Sacred to Cybele, and erewhile her priest,
In Phrygian arms shone glorious from afar,
Urging his foamy steed, its saddle-cloth
A fell with brass scales feathered, clasped with gold.   *771*
In foreign purple darkly dight he rode,
Launching Gortynian shafts from Lycian bow;
Gold hung the bow from shoulder, gold the casque
On the diviner's head; a saffron scarf
Rustling with gauzy waves he had bound up
Into a knot with tawny gold, and wore
Needle-wrought tunic and barbaric hose.
Him now the maid, or fain to fix on shrine
Arms Trojan, or to flaunt in captive gold,
From all the mêlée singling, huntress-like,
Chased blindly, and through the ranks all reckless
     burned
With woman's love of booty and of spoil;
When Arruns from his ambush seized at last
The moment, and let speed his javelin, thus
Imploring heaven: "Apollo, chief of gods,
And guardian of Soracte's sacred height,
Whom we of all men honour, for whom is fed
The glow of heapèd pine, while'midst the fire
Thy votaries we, by holy zeal up-borne,
In the live embers deep our footprints press,
Grant, Sire, that this foul shame, for thou canst all,
Be by my darts abolished. I desire
Nor arms, nor trophies of the maid's defeat,
Nor any spoil; what else my hand has wrought
Shall win me glory: let but this dread pest
Fall'neath my weapon, I will get me back
Inglorious to the cities of my sires."   *793*
Apollo heard, and inwardly vouchsafed
Half the fulfilment of his prayer, but half
To the fleet winds he scattered. To lay low
Camilla with swift stroke of death—thus far
Yields he his asking; that his stately home
Should see him back return, he granted not;
The wild winds changed his utterance into air.

[349]

So, when the spear sped hurtling, launched through
    heaven,
Their eager thoughts and eyes the Volscians all
Turned toward the queen. She only nor of breeze
Nor hurtling sound nor sky-borne weapon weened;
Till, buried in her protruding breast, the spear
Clave, deeply driven, and drank her maiden blood.   *804*
Her scared troop hurry round her, and sustain
Their sinking mistress. Fearful beyond all
Flies Arruns, terror mingling with his joy;
Nor longer dares he on his lance rely,
Nor face the maidens' weapons. And as the wolf,
Ere hostile darts can follow, plunges straight
By pathless ways into the mountain heights,
If shepherd he hath slain, or mighty bull,
And, 'ware of his bold deed, with slackened tail
Clapped quivering 'neath his belly, seeks the woods;
So Arruns whirled from men's eyes madly, plunged,
Content with flight, amid the warrior throng.   *815*
She plucks the dart with dying hand; but deep
Betwixt the rib-bones sticks the embedded steel.
Bloodless she droops; droop too her death-chilled
    eyes;
The once bright colour from her face has ebbed.
Then thus with failing breath to Acca, one
Of her companions, spake she, who alone
Of all Camilla's maiden-band had been
Friend of her bosom, and partner of her cares:
"Acca, my sister," in such wise she spake,
"I can no more; even now the bitter wound
Quells me, and all around grows dim and dark.
Fly, bear to Turnus this my latest word: *825*
Bid him bear up the battle, and ward off
The Trojans from the wall. And now—farewell."
So saying, she dropped the reins, all helplessly
Gliding to earth. Then, cold and colder grown,
Slowly she slipped the body's bonds, let fall
The neck now nerveless, and death-ravished head,
Dropping her war-gear; and the spirit passed
Moaning indignant to the shades below.
Then boundless uproar surging heavenward strikes
The golden stars; around Camilla fallen
The fight grows bloodier; in one dense array
On rush the Teucrian host, the Tyrrhene chiefs,
And, flanking all, Evander's Arcad horse.   *835*
    But Opis, Trivia's sentinel, long since,

Throned on the mountain-height, sits undismayed
Watching the conflict. When amid the din
Of raging warriors far away she spied
Camilla by death's bitter doom fordone,
She groaned, and thus with heart-drawn utterance
    spake:
"Dearly, too dearly, maid, hast thou atoned
Thine armed defiance of the sons of Troy,
Nor aught availed thee in green solitudes
To have served Dian, or on shoulder borne
The quiver of our craft. Yet hath thy queen
Not left thee, even in death's extremity,
Bare of all honour, nor shall this thine end
Be noised not through the world, nor thou endure
An unavengèd name. For whosoe'er
With desecrating wound hath pierced thy flesh,
The well-earned forfeit with his life shall pay."
'Neath a tall mountain stood the giant tomb
Of King Dercennus, the Laurentine old,
Of mounded earth, and roofed with ilex dark: *851*
Here first the lovely goddess with swift spring
Plants her, and from the lofty rising-ground
Spies Arruns. When in flashing armour bright
She marked him vainly swelling, "Why," she cries,
"Swerv'st thou aside? Turn hither, and draw nigh
To meet thy doom, and for Camilla take
Due guerdon. Must such as thou by Dian's darts
Perish?" She spake, and, like a Thracian maid,
Forth from gilt quiver plucked a wingèd shaft,
Stretched it on bow to strike him, and drew far,
Until, the bent tips meeting, and both hands
Now level, with her left the point she touched,
Her bosom with the bow-string in her right.
Forthwith the shaft's hiss and the hurtling air
Heard Arruns, and the selfsame moment felt
The barb within his body. Him, gasping out
Life's latest groan, his comrades leave to lie
Forgotten in the plain's unnoted dust;
Opis to high Olympus wings her way.   *867*
    First flies, of queen bereft, Camilla's troop
Of light-armed horse; the Rutules break and fly;
Flies keen Atinas; captains scattered far
And cohorts leaderless for shelter make,
And, backward turning, for the ramparts ride.
Nor any can with darts sustain the rush
Of the death-dealing Teucrians, or make stand

Against them; but their unstrung bows they cast
On fainting shoulders, and the four-foot tramp
Of galloping horse-hooves shakes the crumbling plain.
Rolls toward the ramparts a black storm of dust,
And on the watch-towers mothers beat their breasts,
And raise a woman's wail aloft to heaven.   *878*
Who through the open gates dash first, on these
The foe press madly, mingling with the rout;
Nor 'scape they piteous slaughter, but thrust through
Even on the threshold, with their native walls
And sheltering homes around, gasp out their lives.
Some close the gates, and dare not to their friends
Open, or let them pass, for all their prayers,
Within the ramparts; and anon begins
Most piteous carnage, as these guard with swords
The portal, those upon the sword-points rush.   *886*
Shut out before their weeping parents' eyes,
Into the trenches some are headlong hurled
By the wild rout; some, spurring at full speed,
With battering force tilt blindly at the gates
And their stout barriers. At the conflict's height
The very mothers from the walls—true love
Of country points them—when their eyes beheld
Camilla, shower down darts with trembling hand;
With stout oak-truncheons and fire-hardened stakes
Hotly they strive to ape the strength of steel,
And foremost for their ramparts burn to die.   *895*
    Meanwhile amid the wood fills Turnus' ear
The terrible tale, and fraught with dire amaze
Comes Acca's word; the Volscian ranks are quelled,
Camilla fallen; the foe rush fiercely on,
And with triumphant arms have swept the field;
Now to the ramparts spreads the panic. He,
Raging—so rules it Jove's relentless will—
Quits his hill-ambush, the rough wood forsakes.
Scarce had he passed from sight, and gained the plain,
Ere Prince Aeneas enters the void glen,
And tops the ridge, and quits the forest-gloom.   *905*
So swiftly both with all their war-array
March town-ward, nor far parted each from each;
And lo! Aeneas at once beheld the plain
Smoking with dust afar, and therewithal
Laurentum's host; and Turnus was aware
Of fell Aeneas armed for fight, and heard
The approach of tramping feet and neighing steeds.
And straight in shock of battle would they clash,

But ruddy Phoebus in the Iberian flood
Now dips his tired team, and with ebbing day
Bids night return. Before the city-walls
They bivouac, and entrench the ramparts round.   *915*

BOOK XII

When Turnus saw the Latins had waxed faint,
Crushed by the war's reverse, his promise now
Claimed for fulfilment, all eyes turned on him,
With wrath implacable he burns, and rears
Aloft his courage. As lo! on Punic plains
A lion, his breast by hunters wounded sore,
At last to battle stirs him, with fierce joy
Shakes from his neck the shaggy mane, and snaps
The robber's rooted weapon, undismayed,
Roaring with blood-stained mouth; not otherwise,
Once fired, the rage of Turnus swells apace:
Then thus the king accosts he, and begins
With blustering speech: "In Turnus is no stop;
Yon dastards of Aeneas have no plea
Their bond to cancel, or their vows recant: 12
I go to meet him. Bring the holy rites,
Sire, and rehearse the treaty. Or will I
To Tartarus hurl this Dardan runagate
From Asia—let the Latins sit and see—
With my sole arm our common shame rebut;
Or let him hold us as his thralls of war,
And take to bride Lavinia."

                    With calm breast
Answered Latinus: "Peerless-hearted youth,
The loftier mounts thy valour, the more meet
That I stint naught of counsel, weigh with fear
All issues. Thine is thy sire Daunus' realm,
And many a war-won city; nor lack I
Latinus gold or the goodwill to give.   23
In Latium's and Laurentum's realm are yet
Maids, nor of race to shame thee. Let me strip
The ungentle utterance bare of all disguise;
And thou in soul absorb it: unto none,
Who heretofore came wooing, might I wed
My daughter; so sang gods alike and men.
Won o'er by love of thee, won o'er by claim
Of kinship, and my sorrowing consort's tears,
I brake all fetters, plucked from her true lord
The plighted bride, and flew to impious arms.   31
Thenceforth what perils, what wars pursue me still,

Turnus, thou seest, yea, and what mighty toils
Thyself art first to suffer. On stricken field
Twice conquered, scarce within our walls we guard
The hopes of Italy; Tiber-waves are yet
Warm with our blood, the wide plain white with
    bones.
Why drift I back so oft? What madness turns
My purpose? If, the light of Turnus quenched,
I stand prepared to welcome them as friends,
Why rather, while he lives, not stay the strife?   39
What will thy Rutule kinsmen say, what all
In Italy beside them, if to death—
Fortune refute the word!—I thee betray,
Seeking our daughter and alliance? Mark
War's shifting chances; pity thine old sire,
Whom now his native Ardea far aloof
Holds sorrowing." With such words he bends no whit
The fury of Turnus; it but mounts the more,
Grown worse with healing. When his lips at length
Gat utterance, he begins: "Prithee, good sire,
The load of care, that for my sake thou hast,
Lay for my sake aside, and suffer me
To pledge my life for honour. Our hand too
Can scatter darts, and wield no weakling sword;
When we too strike, blood follows. Nowise near
Will be his goddess-mother with a cloud
To shield the recreant, woman-like, and hide
Her form in empty shadows."   53
                        But the queen,
At these new terms of battle sore dismayed,
Stood weeping, and, as one resolved to die,
Clave to her fiery son. "By these my tears,
O Turnus, and if aught still touch thy heart
Of reverence for Amata—thou art now
Sole hope and solace of my sad old age;
Latinus' honour and imperial sway
Rest in thy keeping; upon thee alone
Leans all our tottering house—one boon I beg,
Forbear to fight the Teucrians. In yon strife
What doom soe'er awaits thee, waits no less,
Turnus, for me: the selfsame hour will I
Quit the loathed light, nor with a captive's eyes
Look on Aeneas as my daughter's lord."   63
Lavinia heard her mother's voice with cheek
Flaming and tear-suffused; for a deep flush
Kindled and o'er her burning features ran:

Even as if Indian ivory one should stain
With blood-red purple, or as lilies white
Blush with the blended rose; such hues o'er-spread
The maiden's features. He, with love distraught,
Fastens his eyes upon the maid. He burns
The more for battle, and briefly thus bespeaks
Amata: "Follow me not with tears, I pray,
Or with these dark forebodings to the war's
Grim strife, O mother; for Turnus is not free
To bid death tarry. Idmon, do thou bear
This message—nowise welcome—from my lips
To Phrygia's tyrant: soon as morrow's dawn
With crimson chariot-wheel shall flush the sky,
Let him not Teucrian against Rutule lead;
Rest Rutule arms and Teucrian; that we twain
With our own blood may set a term to strife,
And on that field Lavinia's hand be won."   80
   So saying, he swiftly gat him home, and there
Calls for his steeds, and views them with delight
Snorting before him, which, a glorious gift,
Erst to Pilumnus Orithyia gave,
To out-vie snows in whiteness, winds in speed.
Around them, bustling, stand the charioteers,
Clap with their hollow hands the sounding chests,
And comb the manèd necks. A corslet then
He binds about his shoulders, stiff with gold
And pale-hued orichalc, and to his use
Fits sword and shield, and red-plumed helmet-spikes;
Sword, which the lord of fire himself had forged
For his sire Daunus, and had dipped white-hot
In Stygian water. Last, a mighty spear,
As it stood propped against a column vast
Amid the hall, Auruncan Actor's spoil,
Strongly he seized, and shook the quivering shaft,
Crying aloud: "O spear, that never yet
Hast balked my bidding, now the hour is come;
Thee mightiest Actor once, now Turnus wields;
Grant me with doughty hand on earth to stretch
The effeminate Phrygian, shatter and rend ope
His corslet, and defile with dust the locks
Curled with hot iron, and reeking-moist with myrrh." 100
So raves he, fury-driven; from all his face
Shoot fiery sparks; his eager eyes flash flame:
As when a bull, against some battle-bout
Uplifts a fearful bellowing, and for proof
Flings wrath into his horns, and butts against

A tree-trunk, and provokes the air with blows,
Or, scattering sand, makes prelude of the fray.
   Aeneas no less, girt in his mother's gear,
Now fiercely whets the war-god in his heart,
And kindles into wrath, right glad the while
That thus, truce proffered, shall the strife be stayed.
Then comforts he his comrades, soothes the fear
Of sad Iulus, teaching them of fate,
And unto King Latinus bids return
Sure answer, and the terms of peace declare.   *112*
   Scarce was the next dawn sprinkling with new ray
The mountain-tops, what time from Ocean's deep
Up-spring the sun-steeds, and breathe forth the light
Through lifted nostrils, when both Rutule folk
And Teucrian 'neath their mighty city-walls
Make ready and mete out the battle-ground,
And hearths and grassy altars thereamidst
Rear to their common gods. Others the while
Bring freshet-wave and fire, girt apron-wise,
Brow-bound with vervain. The Ausonian host
Move onward, and in ranks close-banded pour
Through the thronged portals. Here in unlike arms
Speeds all the Trojan and Tyrrhenian host,
Even as at war's stern bidding, ranged in mail.
Amid their thousands to and fro the chiefs
Hover, in pride of purple and of gold,
Mnestheus, of old Assaracus the seed,
And stout Asilas, and, from Neptune sprung,
Messapus the steed-tamer. Either host,
At trumpet-call to its own ground retire,
Fix spears in earth, and lay their shields aslant.
Then eager-thronging matrons, a mixed crowd
Of folk defenceless and infirm old men,
Fill all the towers and house-roofs; other some
Hard by the lofty portals stand at gaze.   *133*
   But Juno from the hill, hight Alban now,
Then nameless, without fame or glory, peered
Forth on the plain, and either host beheld,
Laurentine, Trojan, and Latinus' town.
Straightway to Turnus' sister thus she spake—
Goddess to goddess—who hath power o'er pools
And sounding streams; such honour had high Jove,
The King of heaven, for theft of maidenhead
With hallowing hand assigned her: "Nymph," she
    cried,
"Glory of rivers, to my heart most dear,

Whoe'er to high-souled Jove's unthankful bed
Of Latin maids have mounted, thee, thou knowest,
O'er all have I preferred, for thee with joy
Found part and place in heaven: now learn thy grief,
Juturna, that thou blame not me. So far
As Fortune seemed to suffer, Fate allow
Good hap to Latium, I have guarded well
Thy town and Turnus: now I see him rush
Ill-matched upon his fate, and lo! the hour
Of destiny draws near, and force malign.   *150*
This fight, this treaty, never can mine eyes
Endure to look on. For thy brother thou,
If aught thou durst of more effectual aid,
On! it becomes thee. Happier days belike
Shall follow misery." Ere she ceased, the tears
Burst from Juturna's eyes, and with her hand
Thrice, four times o'er, she smote her lovely breast.
"No time for tears," Saturnian Juno cries:
"Hie thee with speed, thy brother snatch from death,
If any way thou mayest, or else wake war,
Dash from their hands the plighted peace: 'tis I
Bid brave it." And, so warned, she left her there
Doubting, wit-wildered by the baleful blow.   *160*
    Meanwhile the kings ride forth, Latinus first,
Mighty of stature, on a four-horse car,
About whose temples gleam twelve golden rays,
Badge of the Sun, his grandsire: Turnus next
With snow-white pair comes charioted, his hand
Twin javelins brandishing, broad-tipped with steel.
Then Prince Aeneas, of Rome's stem the root,
Blazing with starry shield, celestial arms,
And at his side Ascanius, of great Rome
The after-hope, move onward from the camp;
While pure-robed priest a two-year sheep unshorn,
With offspring of a bristly boar hath brought,
And by the blazing altars set the beasts.   *171*
They, with eyes turned toward the rising sun,
Scatter salt meal from hand, and graze with knife
The foreheads of the victims, and pour wine
Upon the altars. Drawing then his sword,
Thus good Aeneas prays: "Now may the Sun
Attest my utterance, and this land for which
I have essayed such mighty toils to bear,
The Sire omnipotent, and his consort thou,
Saturnia, goddess, now at last, I pray,
More favourable; and Mavors the renowned,

Who dost all wars with power paternal sway;   *180*
And Floods I call, and Fountains, and what Awe
Dwells in high heaven, what gods in the blue sea:
If victory to Ausonian Turnus hap,
We vanquished will depart—so stands the bond—
Hence to Evander's town; Iulus then
Shall quit the soil, nor e'er in after-time,
Armed for new war, Aeneas' sons return,
Or vex this kingdom with invasion. But,
If victory will the battle to our hand—
As I deem rather, and so seal it heaven!—
Nor shall Italian at my bidding bow
To Teucrian, nor list I to reign; let both,
Unconquered, beneath equal laws unite
In everlasting bonds of amity.   *191*
My gods I'll give them, and my sacred things;
The sword Latinus, as my sire, must sway,
And, as my sire, the daily round of State:
For me the Teucrians shall build walls, my town
Be named from fair Lavinia." So spake first
Aeneas, and after him Latinus thus,
Eyes raised to heaven, and right hand star-ward
     stretched:
"Now by the self-same Earth, Sea, Stars, I swear,
Aeneas, and by Latona's double brood,
And two-faced Janus, and the might of gods
Infernal, and relentless Pluto's shrine;   *199*
Let the Sire hear, who doth on treaties set
His seal of thunder. I these altars touch,
The flames and powers betwixt us I adjure:
No lapse of time shall break for Italy
This covenant of peace, betide what may,
Nor any force me from my purpose turn;
Nay, not though earth into the waves be washed
In one blind deluge, and the vault of heaven
Poured into Tartarus: as this sceptre here"--
For sceptre in right hand he chanced to wield—
"Shall never into light-leaved twigs expand,
Or shady spray, since in the greenwood once,
Lopped from the parent-stem, beneath the axe
It shed both boughs and foliage; erst a tree,
Now by the craftsman's handiwork made o'er
Bound in fair brass, for Latin sires to hold."   *211*
So spake they, pledging mutual vows of peace,
Amid the gazing lords, then solemnly
Let bleed the sacred victims o'er the flame,

[359]

And flay the flesh yet quivering, and anon
With laden trenchers heap the altars high.
  But long ere this to Rutule eyes ill-matched
Appears the conflict, and their bosoms heave
With manifold emotion more and more,
As closelier seen the odds of strength they scan.   218
Swells their disquietude withal to mark
How softly Turnus to the altar stepped,
His lowly reverent mien, his downcast eyes,
The wasted cheek, the youthful form so wan.
But when Juturna, when his sister, saw
Whispers wax rife, the crowd with wavering hearts
Irresolute, amid the ranks in form
Like unto Camers—who, of hero-strain,
Was from a sire of peerless valour sprung,
Himself no laggard warrior—'mid the ranks
She plunges, and, well witting of the task,
Scatters wide rumour, and bespeaks them thus: 228
"Blush ye not, Rutules, thus to jeopardize
One life for all, and all so valiant? Say
In numbers are we over-matched, or might?
Trojans, Arcadians, these are all they boast,
See! and the fate-led bands Etruria's wrath
Hurled upon Turnus. Every second man
Grappled we them, scarce each should find a foe.
He doubtless, winged with glory, to the gods,
Gods to whose altars he devotes his life,
Shall soar, ride living on the lips of men;
We, reft of home, to haughty lords must bow,
Who thus sit idly, cumberers of the field."   237
Fired by such words, now more and more up-blazed
The warriors' purpose, and from rank to rank
Speeds on the murmur; even Laurentum's sons,
Even Latium's folk are changed. Who late for rest
From battle, and safety for their fortune, sighed,
Now wish for arms, implore the league undone,
And pity Turnus and his cruel fate.
Hereto another and a mightier spell
Juturna adds, and shows a sign in heaven,
Than which no cause, more potent to confound,
Fooled omen-wise the hearts of Italy.   246
For as in ruddy sky Jove's tawny bird
Flew chasing water-fowl, a clamorous rout
In wing-borne column, suddenly he swooped
Down on the stream, and seized a lordly swan
Ruthless in taloned gripe. Italia's folk

Gave eager heed, as all the birds at once
Wheeled screaming, wondrous to behold! and hid
The heaven with wings, and in a serried cloud
Urge through the air their foe, till, overborne
By the sheer weight of onset, he gave o'er,
Into the flood let fall his loosened prey,
And vanished amid cloudy depths of heaven.   256
The Rutules hail the omen with a shout.
And free their hands for battle; and first out-spoke
Augur Tolumnius: "This, ay this it was,
So oft my prayers desired: I greet the call,
And own the gods herein; follow my lead,
Even mine, and seize the sword, ye miserable,
Whom yon rapacious stranger frights with war,
Like silly birds, and rudely ravages
Your borders. He will turn, trim sail, and fly
Far o'er the deep. With one heart close your ranks,
And fight for rescue of your ravished king."   265
He spake, and, dashing forward, hurled his lance
Full at the foe; the hurtling cornel hissed,
And cleft the air, and erred not. Hard upon,
Rose a vast shout; through all the welded ranks
Confusion ran, and hearts beat fiery-fast.
As sped the spear, right in its onward track
Stood grouped nine goodly brethren, borne alike
Of one true Tuscan mother to her lord
Gylippus of Arcadia. One of these,
Where the sewn belt pressed midmost of his bulk
Hard on the belly, and the ribs' edges felt
The buckle's bite—a youth of peerless form
In glittering armour—through the flank it pierced,
And on the dun sand stretched him. At the sight
His brethren, a bold band, now fired with grief,
Some drawing sword, some snatching darts to hurl,
Rush blindly onward. The Laurentine ranks
Dash forth to meet them; from the opposers' side
Trojans, Agyllines, and Arcadia's host
Girt in gay arms, one turbid torrent pour,
All, each, on fire to let the sword decide.   282
They have stripped the altars; a thick javelin-storm
Scours all the sky; the steel sleet drives apace.
The bowls, the hearths, they hale away: fast flies
Latinus, and bears off his baffled gods,
Leaving the league undone. Some harness cars,
Some hurl to horse, and with drawn swords are there.
Messapus, eager to confound the league,

Spurs at and scares Aulestes, Tuscan king,
Dight with the kingly diadem; but he,
Luckless, leaps backward, strikes the altar-stone
Behind him, and rolls head and shoulders o'er   288
Up speeds Messapus fiery-swift, with spear
Huge as a beam, and towering upon steed
Deals him, for all his prayers, one deadly blow
Downward, and cries: "He hath it: here behold
A nobler victim to the high gods given!"
Italia's folk throng round him, and despoil
The yet warm body. Then Corynaeus snatched
A charred brand from the altar, and therewith,
As Ebysus rode up and sought to strike,
Dashed in his face the flame; his mighty beard
Blazed brightly, and sent forth a burning stench.
Following, he clutches in left hand the locks
Of his dazed foe, with push of bended knee
Pins him to earth, and buries the stark blade
Deep in his side. As shepherd Alsus rushed
Through showering darts along the battle's front,
Lo! Podalirius with bare blade pursues
And overhangs him; whom with axe swung back
Full in his face, he cleft from brow to chin
Drenching his armour with wide-spattered gore.   308
Stern rest and iron slumber seal his eyes,
And their orbs close in everlasting night.

   But good Aeneas, stretching forth his hand
Unarmed the while, bare-headed, with loud shouts
Cried ever to his men: "Why storm ye forth?
Whence springs this sudden quarrel? O curb your ire!
The league is stricken, and all its laws allowed;
I only may do battle; balk me not,
And have no fear: this hand shall consummate
The treaty; by these rites is Turnus mine."   317
As thus he spake, even in mid utterance, lo!
Wing-borne against him glides a whizzing shaft,
Launched by what hand, who steered its stormy
      speed,
Knows no man, nor what power, or chance, or god,
Glory so boundless to the Rutule brought;
The fame of that high deed lay locked from sight,
And none e'er boasted of Aeneas' wound.
When Turnus marked Aeneas quit the host,
The chiefs dismayed, with sudden hope he fires,
Anon cries out for horses and for arms,
Springs proudly on the car, and grasps the reins.

In swift career full many a mighty form
He gives to death, or tumbles them half-slain,
Crushes whole ranks beneath his car, or plucks
Spear after spear, and hurls them on the fliers.   *330*
As when at furious speed, anigh the banks
Of Hebrus' icy wave, blood-dabbled Mars
Clangs on his shield, and, rousing war, lets loose
His raging steeds; they scour the open plain
Swifter than south or west wind; utmost Thrace
Groans with their hoof-beat; all around him rush
Dark-frowning Fear and Wraths and Treacheries,
The god's attendant train: so eager goads
Turnus his smoking steeds amid the fray,
Trampling the foe slain piteously; each hoof
At furious speed spirts showers of ruddy dew,
And 'neath their tread the sand is caked with gore.   *340*
Now Sthenelus to slaughter hath he given,
And Thamyrus and Pholus, this and this
Encountering close, that other from afar;
From far both Glaucus too and Lades, sons
Of Imbrasus, whom Imbrasus himself
In Lycia reared, and with like arms arrayed
To fight as footmen, or out-ride the winds.
Elsewhere Eumedes hies him to the fray,
The war-famed son of ancient Dolon he,
His grandsire's name, his sire's own doughty deeds
Renewing, who erst, upon the Danaan camp,
To creep and make espial, for wage dared ask
Pelides' chariot; with far other wage
Dowered for his daring by great Tydeus' son,
He to Achilles' team no more aspires.   *352*
Him Turnus eyeing afar on open plain,
First with light dart through length of air pursues,
Then checks the twin yoked steeds, and leaps from car
To find him fallen half-lifeless, on his neck
Plants foot, and wrests from his right hand the sword,
And in his throat dyes deep the glittering blade,
And thus withal speaks over him: "Lie there,
Trojan, and measure those Hesperian fields
Thou cam'st to fight for: lo! such meed they win,
So found their walls, who dare me to the fray."
Next with hurled spear, to bear him company,
He sends Asbutes, Chloreus, Sybaris,
Dares, Thersilochus, and Thymoetes, flung
Prone from the neck of his unruly steed.   *364*
And as when Thracian Boreas with his blast

Roars o'er the deep Aegean, and pursues
Its billows to the shore, where swoop the winds,
The clouds scud fast through heaven, so yield the ranks
To Turnus, where he cleaves a path, and all
Their battle is swept backwards; his own speed
Impels him, and the breeze his chariot breasts
Tosses his flying plume. Such fierce assault
And stormy arrogance Phegeus might not brook;
He crossed the car's path, grasped and wrenched
    aside
The mouths o' the mad steeds foaming at the bit: *373*
So dragged, and hanging to the yoke, the broad
Spear-head uncovered found him, and its thrust
Broke ope the corslet's double-woven mail,
And tasted of his body. He nathless,
Shield set before him, facing still the foe,
From his bare blade sought succour, when the wheel
And onward-hurrying axle prone to earth
Smote him, and Turnus, stooping, with his sword
'Twixt helmet-edge and corslet's topmost rim
Lopped off his head, and left the trunk to lie.   *382*
    While Turnus thus triumphant o'er the plain
Deals havoc, Mnestheus and Achates true,
Ascanius at their side, in camp have set
Aeneas, now bleeding, every second step
Propped on his long spear. He, in rage of soul,
Striving to pluck forth barb and splintered shaft,
Calls for what aid lies nearest: let them cleave
With a broad battle-blade, probe deep, the wound
Where the barb lurks, and send him back to war.   *390*
And now Iapis, son of Iasus,
Dear before all to Phoebus, draws anigh,
Whom erst Apollo, by keen love subdued,
With his own arts and gifts—prophetic lore,
The lyre, and arrows swift—was fain to bless.
He, to protract his sire's appointed span
Now nigh to death, the power of herbs to know,
The healer's skill, chose rather, and to ply
A silent art, inglorious. Chafing sore,
Propped on his mighty spear, 'mid a vast throng
Of warriors, with Iulus grieving nigh,
Untroubled by their tears, Aeneas stood.
The agèd sire, his garb Paeonian-wise
Flung back and girt about him, with deft hand,
And Phoebus' herbs of power, makes much ado
Vainly, with vain endeavour at the shaft

Pulls, or with biting pincer grips the barb.   *404*
Fortune no clue, no aid his patron-god
Apollo lends him; and now fiercer grows
The alarm of battle, and more nigh the bane.
They see the heaven up-stand in solid dust;
On come the horsemen, and amid their camp
Javelins fall thick and fast. A dismal shout
Is borne to heaven of those that fight and fall
'Neath the stern war-god's hand. Then, mother-like,
Smit to the heart by her son's cruel pain,
Venus from Cretan Ida culls a stalk
Of dittany, with downy leaves thick-fledged,
And purple flower; the wild goats know it well,
When wingèd arrows have fastened in their side.   *415*
This bare she down, veiled in a mantling mist,
And tinges therewithal fresh water, poured
In bright-brimmed vessel, darkly drugging it,
And sprinkles life-juice from ambrosia bled,
And sweet-breathed panacea. With that lymph,
Unwitting, old Iapis bathed the wound;
When lo! from out the limbs all pain hath passed,
All gush of blood in the deep wound is stayed;
And at a touch the arrow unimpelled
Out-falling, his old strength returns anew.   *424*
"Arms for the hero, quick! Why tarry ye?"
Loud cries Iapis, and first fires their wrath
Against the foe. "Man's power and master-craft
Work not such issues, nor doth hand of mine
Save thee, Aeneas; some mightier one, some god
Is operant here, and unto mightier deeds
Restores thee." Ravenous for the fray meanwhile
He, right and left, had sheathed his legs in gold,
Spurning all checks, and brandishing his spear.
When shield to side, corslet to back were braced,
About Ascanius his mailed arms he flung,
And lightly kissed him through the helm, and said
"O boy, learn valour and true toil from me,
Fortune from others. Now shall my right hand
Shield thee in fight, and lead where high rewards
Await the winning: hereafter look that thou,
When ripening years have made thee perfect man,
Be mindful, and the exemplars of thy race
Recalling, let Aeneas for thy sire,
Hector thine uncle, be thy spurs to fame."   *440*
    So having said, forth from the gate he strode
Gigantic, shaking his portentous spear:

Antheus and Mnestheus therewithal rush on
With serried column; from the abandoned camp
Streams the whole host. Then all the plain is blent
In one blind dust-cloud; the affrighted earth
Trembles beneath their foot-tread. Turnus saw
From an opposing height, as on they came;
The Ausonians saw, and through their inmost bones
Ran a chill shudder: instant before all
The Latin host Juturna heard the sound,
Knew it, and fled in terror. He speeds on,
Hurrying his dark line o'er the open plain.
As, when with bursting squall a hurricane
Drives landward o'er mid-ocean, hapless hinds
Shudder, afar foreboding; it will bring
Downfall to trees, destruction to the crops,
Whelm all in one wide havoc; the winds fly
Bearing its sound before it to the beach: *455*
So the Rhoeteian chief his war-host speeds
Full on the foe; in wedges dense they close,
Massed at his side. Thymbraeus smites with sword
Osiris huge, Mnestheus Arcetius;
Achates hews in sunder Epulo,
And Gyas Ufens; falls Tolumnius too,
The Augur, who had first hurled hostile dart.
The cry mounts heaven, and Rutules, chased in turn,
Their backs with flight dust-mantled, scour the plain. *463*
Himself, nor deigns he strike to death who fled,
Nor follow up who met him, foot to foot,
Or wielding javelins: Turnus, him alone,
He tracks, still circling through the battle's night,
Bids him alone to combat. Hereupon
With fear heart-stricken, Juturna, the man-maid,
Flings forth Metiscus, Turnus' charioteer,
From 'twixt the reins, and leaves him far behind
Fallen from the pole, so leaps into his seat,
And, grasping, guides herself the wavy thongs,
Metiscus' voice, form, arms, assuming all.   *472*
Even as a black swift through the mansion flits
Of some rich lord, and skims the lofty hall
With circling pinion, for her noisy brood
Some tiny morsels gleaning, and now whirrs
Adown the empty corridors, and now
Round the moist fish-ponds; with like course to hers,
Juturna through the thickest foemen drives,
Careering o'er the field with flying car.
Now here, now there, her brother she displays

In triumph, yet suffers not in fight to close,
But whirls far off away. Aeneas no less
To meet him thrids the winding maze of war,
And tracks his steps, and through the sundered ranks
With mighty voice defies him. Oft as he
Spied out the foe, and strove afoot to match
The flying hooves, so oft Juturna wheeled
And turned the chariot. Ah! what can he do?
Tossed vainly on a restless tide, and called
Now this, now that way by conflicting cares!
At him Messapus, for his left hand chanced
To hold two supple javelins tipped with steel,
Up-speeding lightly, levelled and let fly
One with unerring aim. Aeneas stopped,
Huddled behind his shield, and on one knee
Sank; yet the swift spear took his helmet-top,
And smote away the crest-plume. Then up-surged
His ire, and, by their treachery constrained,
While steeds and chariot whirl away from sight,
Jove and the altars of their outraged league
Invoking oft to witness, 'mid the ranks
He bursts, and, terrible in victorious strength,
At last awakens indiscriminate
Grim carnage, and lets loose the reins of wrath.   *499*
    What god may now in song for me tell o'er
The tale of horrors, diverse forms of death,
And fall of chieftains, whom o'er all the plain
Now Turnus, now the Trojan hero, drives?
Was it thy will, great Jove, that folk with folk,
To everlasting peace ordained, should rush
So furiously together? Aeneas meets
Sucro the Rutule—and that fight first checked
The Teucrian onset—but, not long detained,
Takes him in flank, and, by death's quickest way,
Through ribs and breast-work drives his reeking
        blade.   *508*
Amycus and Diores, brothers twain,
Turnus unhorses, and confronts on foot;
One, still approaching, with long lance he strikes,
And one with sword-blade; the lopped heads of both
He bears, blood-dripping, fastened to his car.
Talos and Tanais and Cethegus brave,
Three at one rush, that other sends to death,
And sad Onites, Echionian name,
Offspring of Peridia. This strikes down
The brethren sent from Lycian land, and fields

Loved of Apollo, and, loathing war in vain,
Youthful Menoetes the Arcadian, who
By Lerna's fishy stream had erst his craft
And full poor home, nor cares of greatness knew,
Whose father needs must hire the land he sowed.   520
As when two fires from points opposing fall
On a dry forest and brakes of rustling bay,
Or as, down-tumbling from the mountain-heights,
Roar foamy rivers, and, swept seaward, strew
Each its own path with ruin: so, swift as they,
Aeneas and Turnus through the battle rush;
Now, now wrath boils within them, and nigh burst
The indomitable hearts; now with main strength
They hurl them upon wounds. Murranus, still
Mouthing of sires and grandsires, names of yore—
A whole line downward traced through Latium's kings—
Aeneas with whirl of a huge craggy rock
Dashed headlong from his car, and stretched on earth;
So lying 'neath reins and yoke, the rolling wheels
Dragged him, and with quick hoof-beat o'er his head
Trod the swift steeds, unmindful of their lord.   534
The other met Hyllus, as he rushed along
Immeasurably exulting in his pride,
And at his gold-bound temples hurls a dart;
Pierced helm and brain the weapon, and there stuck.
Nor could thine arm from Turnus win thee free,
Cretheus, of Greeks the bravest, nor his gods
Shield their Cupencus, as Aeneas drew nigh;
His bosom meets the invading bolt, nor aught
'Steads the doomed wretch his brazen buckler's stay.
Thee too Laurentum's plain, O Aeolus,
Saw perish, and spread thy bulk on earth; thou fall'st,
Whom Argive armies, nor Achilles' self,
Wrecker of Priam's realm, availed to slay.   545
Here was thy bourne of death; 'neath Ida's hill
Thy stately home; thy stately home where lies
Lyrnesus, in Laurentum's soil thy tomb.
Yea, the whole lines, now turning—Latins all,
All Dardans, Mnestheus and Serestus keen,
Messapus, steed-subduer, Asilas bold,
The Tuscan ranks, Evander's Arcad horse—
Strain each to do man's uttermost; no pause,
No respite, but one giant tug of war.   553
    Now from his beauteous mother was the thought
Borne on Aeneas to draw nigh the walls,
Upon the city launch his host amain,

And with swift slaughter Latium's folk confound.
As through the ranks from point to point he roves,
Still tracking Turnus with wide-circling eye,
He marks the city from all that conflict free,
At ease and unmolested. Fires his heart
Forthwith the vision of a mightier fray;
Mnestheus, Sergestus, and Serestus bold,
His chiefs, he summons, and plants him on a mound,
Where all the remnant of the Teucrian host
Throng dense around, but loosed not hold of shield
Or javelin. Midmost on the hillock's height
Erect he cries: "Let naught my bidding stay—
Jove with us stands—nor yet be any man,
That sudden seem the call, more slack to go.   566
To-day this city, the cause of war, itself
Latinus' seat of sovereignty, will I—
Except they take my bridle in their mouth,
Confess a conqueror's bidding—topple o'er,
And level with the dust her smoking towers.
Am I to wait, forsooth, till Turnus choose
To bide our onset, and, once beaten, brook
The fight's renewal? Here stands the head and front,
O countrymen, of this accursèd war.
Bring torches quick! with tongues of fire reclaim
The treaty." He had said, when all, as one,
With emulous hearts, wedge-welded, on the walls
In dense array bear down, and in a trice
Lo! ladders, and the flash of sudden fire!   576
Some, scattering for the gates, who front them slay;
Some hurl the steel, and darken heaven with darts;
Aeneas, his right hand toward the rampart raised,
Chides with loud voice Latinus, in their van,
Bids heaven attest him forced again to fight,
The folk of Italy twice o'er his foes,
And snapped the second treaty. Strife up-springs
Betwixt the fluttered townsmen; some bid ope
The city-gates, let in the Dardans, yea,
Would to the ramparts hale their very king;
Others bring arms, and haste to man the walls: 586
As, when some shepherd hath a swarm of bees
Tracked to their hiding in the caverned crag,
With smarting smoke he fills it; they, within,
Scared for their safety, through the waxen camp
Dart wildly, and with loud buzzings whet their wrath;
The black stench rolls from cell to cell; anon
Is heard a hum, rock-stifled, and smoke soars

Into the void of air. *592*
        This further fate
Befell the war-worn Latins, and with grief
Shook the whole city to its base. The queen,
When from her towers she sees the approaching foe,
Her walls assailed, fire to the house-roofs fly,
No Rutule host, no sign of Turnus near
In arms to meet them, deems, unhappy soul,
Her champion quenched in onset, and, distraught
With sudden agony, shrieks against herself,
As cause and guilty source of all their woe;
Then in a frenzy of anguish uttering
Mad words a many, resolved to die, she grasps
And rends her purple raiment, and knits fast
To the high beam a noose of hideous death. *603*
Whose woful end when Latium's women knew
Lavinia first, her daughter, with rude clutch
Tore flower-like locks and vermeil cheek, then
The rest around her throng, one frenzied rout;
Rings the wide palace with their wail. From hence
Through the whole city the dark tidings spread;
Hearts sink; Latinus with rent raiment goes,
Stunned by his consort's fate, the city's doom,
Soiling his white hair with unsightly dust. *613*
    But Turnus, battling on the plain's last verge,
Still drives the minished stragglers, more and more
Slackening the while, and ever less and less
Exulting in his steeds' victorious course.
Blent with blind terrors came the wind-borne cry,
And from the city smote his straining ears
Sound of confusion, and no joyful hum.
"Ah me! what mighty anguish shakes the walls?
What shrill cry from the city speeds afar?" *621*
So saying, half frantic he draws rein, and halts.
To whom his sister, wearing still the form
Of charioteer Metiscus, as she swayed
Steeds, reins, and chariot, thus gives counter-word:
"This way pursue we yet the sons of Troy,
Turnus, where quickest victory clears a path;
Others there are may strike for house and home.
Aeneas falls hotly on Italia's folk,
And spreads the broil of battle; hurl we too
Fierce havoc on the Teucrians: nor in fame,
Nor tale of dead, shalt thou come worse away." *630*
"Sister, long since I knew thee," Turnus cried,
"Who first by stratagem didst mar the league,

And plunge into the fight; and vainly now
Wouldst cloak thy godhead. But by whom wert sent
From high Olympus, such sore toils to bear?
Was it thy brother's piteous death to see?
For what can I? What pledge of safety yet
Doth Fortune yield me? Nay, these very eyes
Saw perish, and with my name upon his lips,
Murranus, dearest-left of all my friends,
Mighty, and vanquished by a mighty wound.   *640*
Fell ill-starred Ufens, not to see my shame;
His corse, his arms, are now the Teucrians' spoil.
And shall I suffer—that alone was left—
Our home's upheaval? nor with blows rebut
The taunts of Drances? Shall I fly?—this land
See Turnus play the runagate? Is death
A lot so grievous? O ye Powers of hell,
Befriend me, for heaven's face is turned away.
To you, a stainless shade, will I descend,
Witless of that foul wrong, nor ever yet
Degenerate from my mighty sires of old."   *649*
    Scarce had he said when through the foemen's
        midst
Lo! Saces, borne upon a foamy steed,
Comes rushing, full in face an arrow-wound,
By name conjuring Turnus as he flies:
"Turnus, in thee is our last hope of life;
Have pity on thine own. Aeneas in arms
Lightens and thunders, threatening to hurl down,
Raze utterly, the tall Italian towers;
Even now their firebrands to the house-roofs fly.
On thee their looks, their eyes, the Latins bend;
The King himself, Latinus, muttering, doubts
Whom to call son, to whose alliance turn.
Aye, and the queen, thine ever staunchest friend,
Self-slain, hath fled in terror from the light.   *660*
Messapus, keen Atinas, at the gates
Are our sole props of battle. Around these
The serried lines throng close, and with bare blades
Bristles the iron harvest: thou the while
Whirlest thy chariot o'er an empty plain."
Wildered with manifold imaginings
Stood Turnus, mutely gazing; in one heart
Seethe boundless shame, and madness mixed with
    grief,
And frenzy-goaded love, and conscious worth.
Soon as, the darkness from his heart dispelled,

Light dawned afresh, toward the walls he bent
His burning eyeballs stormily, and glanced
Back from his chariot on the mighty town;
When lo! a spire of wreathèd flame, rolled on
From floor to floor, went wavering up to heaven,
And clasped the tower, the tower which his own hand
Of welded beams had reared, and under it
Set wheels, and from aloft high gangways hung.   675
"Now, sister, now Fate masters us; forbear
To hold me loitering; follow me where heaven
And cruel fortune call. Resolved am I
To grapple with Aeneas, resolved to bear
The utmost of death's bitterness; no more
Shalt see me shamed, my sister. Thus far first
Suffer the madman to give madness way."
He spake, and swiftly leapt from car to plain,
And dashed through foes, through javelins, and there
          left
His sister sorrowing, and at furious speed
Cleaves the mid battle-ranks. As when a crag
From mountain-top shoots headlong, torn away
By the wind's blast—whether with stormy shower
Washed free, or loosened by slow lapse of years—
With mighty rush relentless the mass swings
Down the abyss, and riots o'er the plain,
Men, flocks, and forests rolled along with it;
So rushes Turnus through the scattered ranks
On to the city-walls, where streams the earth
Deepest with torrent-gore, and sings the wind
With missiles, and there beckons with his hand,
And with loud voice begins: "Rutules, forbear,
And hold your darts, ye Latins; mine to-day
The award of Fortune, whatsoe'er it be.
Let me—'tis meeter—for your broken troth
Sole penance pay, my sword alone decide."   695
The mid ranks part asunder and make room.
    But Prince Aeneas, hearing Turnus' name,
Forsakes the wall, forsakes the lofty towers,
Spurns all delay, breaks off all enterprise,
Exultant, and clangs terribly his arms:
Vast as mount Athos, or as Eryx vast;
Old Apennine no vaster, when he roars
Through all his quivering holm-oaks, and aloft
With snowy crest soars jubilant to heaven.   703
Now Rutules, Trojans, and Italians all
Turn emulous eyes—who held the lofty towers,

Nor less who battered at the walls below—
And shield from shoulder drop. Latinus even
Stood all amazed those mighty ones to see,
Born in far distant climes, met man to man,
To try the sword's arbitrament. But they,
Soon as the plain gave open space, dart forth,
Hurl from afar their spears, and with loud clang
Of brazen bucklers dash into the fray.   712
Earth groans, and thick and fast the sword-strokes
    shower,
Valour with chance commingling. Even as when
On mighty Sila or Taburnus' top
Two bulls for fierce encounter each on each
Rush, brow to brow; the affrighted keepers fly;
The herd stands hushed in fear; the heifers muse
Which of the twain shall lord it o'er the grove,
Which all the kine must follow; they mix amain
Blow upon blow, and gore with butting horns;
Blood streams o'er neck and shoulder; all the grove
Rebellows with the roar: not otherwise
Trojan Aeneas and the Daunian chief
Clash shields together; the vast din fills heaven.   724
Two scales at equipoise in his own hand
Holds Jupiter, and sets therein of both
The diverse destinies—whom travail dooms,
Whose weight with death sinks downward. Hereupon
Forth Turnus darts, nor dreaming of mishap
Rears his whole height to the uplifted sword,
And strikes. Trojans and Latins all a-quake
Cry out; both armies stand at eager gaze.
But snaps the treacherous weapon, in mid stroke
Failing its fiery master, except flight
Befriend him. Swifter than the wind he flies
At sight of a strange hilt in swordless hand.   734
Folk say when first the harnessed battle-car
He mounted, his sire's sword in headlong haste
Then left behind him, he caught up the brand
Of charioteer Metiscus; and, while yet
The straggling Teucrians turned their backs in flight,
Long time it served him; but with Vulcan's arms
Of a god's making matched, the mortal blade
Like brittle ice fell shivered at a stroke—
Mere splinters glittering on the tawny sand.
So Turnus madly scours the plain in flight,
And hither, thither, weaves a wayward maze;
For round him closed the Teucrians' ring, and here

Spreads a waste fen, here girdling ramparts tower.   *745*
  Nor less Aeneas, though, hindered by the wound,
His knees oft fail him, and their speed deny,
Pursues and hotly presses, stride by stride,
The panting foe: as, when a hound of chase
Lights on a stag hemmed in by river-bend,
Or hedged about with scare of crimson plumes,
With foot and clamorous tongue it plies him; he,
Or of the toils, or the steep bank afeared,
Darts here, darts there, a thousand ways; but close
Clings the keen Umbrian open-mouthed, and seems
Now, now to clutch him, and, as though he clutched,
Snaps with his jaws, and baffled bites the air.   *755*
Ah! then a shout uprises; marge and mere
Re-echo round; all heaven roars back the din.
He flying upbraids the while, calls, each by name,
The Rutules, clamouring for the sword he knew.
Aeneas in turn vows death and present doom,
Should one approach, and scares the tremblers more,
Threatening to dash their city to the dust,
And, wounded, still pursues him. Circles five
They measure in their course, as oft again
Unravel and retrace them; for not light
The prize they seek, nor trivial; the heart's blood
And very life of Turnus are at stake.   *765*
A bitter-leaved wild olive, as it chanced,
Sacred to Faunus, here had stood, a tree
Revered of old by seamen, where they wont,
Snatched from the billows, to set gifts, and hang
Their votive raiment to Laurentum's god.
But Teucrian hands indifferently had shorn
The sacred trunk away, thereby to win
Clear space for shock of battle. Here stood fixed
The lance of Aeneas; hither its own rush
Had driven, and in the tough root held it fast.   *774*
The son of Dardanus bent over it,
Fain by sheer strength to wrench the weapon free,
And follow up with spear, whom catch with speed
He could not. Then at last, with terror crazed,
Cried Turnus: "Pity me, O Faun, I pray,
And, kind earth, keep the weapon, if I still
Held dear your honours, which the Aeneadae
Have with foul war polluted." So he spake,
Nor to vain prayers invoked the aid of heaven.   *780*
For wrestling, lingering o'er the stubborn stem,
No strength availed Aeneas to prise ope

The knotty vice. While hard he tugs and strains,
Forth darts the Daunian goddess, changed once more
To charioteer Metiscus, and restores
Her brother the lost sword. Then Venus, wroth
At the nymph's chartered arrogance, drew near,
And from the deep root wrenched the weapon free.
So both elate, with arms and courage new,
He trusting to his sword, and he with spear
Impetuously up-towering, take their stand
Face to face, panting, in the lists of war.   790
    Meanwhile the Lord of heaven's almighty throne
To Juno speaks, as from a golden cloud
She marks the strife: "Say, what shall be the end,
O consort? or what yet remains to do?
Full well thou knowest, and dost thyself allow,
Heaven claims Aeneas a tutelary god,
Fate lifts him to the stars. What schem'st thou yet?
With what hope hang'st amid these chilly clouds?
A god by mortal wounded—was it meet?
Or—for what could Juturna without thee?—
In Turnus' hand to set the sword anew,
And re-invigorate the vanquished? Nay,
Give o'er at length, and bend thee to my prayers;
Let not such grief thy silent heart devour,
Nor bitter woes from thy sweet lips so oft
Return to vex me. Lo! the bound is reached;
To chase the Teucrians over land or wave
Thou hast had power, to kindle monstrous strife,
Mar a fair home, and mix the bridal song
With mourning: further venture I forbid."
Thus Jupiter; and thus with look demure
Replies Saturnia: "Even because thy will
Was known to me, great Jove, have I forsook
Turnus and earth, unwilling; else shouldst thou
Not see me thus on my lone airy seat,
Patient of foul or fair; but girt with fire
I on the battle's very verge had stood
Drawing the Teucrians on to deadly fray.   811
Juturna—I confess—I moved to aid
Her hapless brother, for his life's sake allowed
Scope to her daring; not to hurl the dart
Or bend the bow; I swear it by the source
Of Stygian wave inexorable, sole awe
Of binding power vouchsafed to gods above.
Well, now I yield, and, loathing, quit the strife.   818
One boon, withholden by no law of fate,

[375]

For Latium, for thy kindred's majesty,
I beg thee: when with happy bridal-rites
They pledge the peace—so be it—when now they knit
Their terms of treaty, bid them not put by
The native name of Latins, nor become
Trojans, or pass for Teucrians on men's lips,
Nor alien speech assume, nor altered garb.
Let Latium, and let Alban kings endure
For ages; be there still a Roman stock,
Strong with Italian valour. Troy is fallen,
And, name with nation, let the fallen lie."   828
The Author of mankind and all that is
Smiling made answer: "Jove's own sister thou,
And Saturn's other offspring, such wild waves
Of passion heav'st within thy bosom's depth!
But come, this unavailing wrath allay:
Thy suit I grant, and willing let thee win.
Ausonia's folk their native tongue shall keep
And customs; and, as now, their name shall be;
The Teucrians shall but in the mass be merged
And settle; I myself will add their rites
Of ceremonial worship, and make all
Of one tongue, Latins. Hence shall spring a race
Blent of Ausonian blood, whom thou shalt see
Outsoar mankind, outsoar the very gods,
In duty; nor shall any race beside
Pay thee like homage." Juno at the word
Assents, and with changed purpose, blithe at heart,
Anon withdraws from heaven, and quits the cloud.   842
    This done, the Sire, revolving in his heart
Yet more, bestirs him from her brother's aid
To part Juturna. There are monsters twain,
Yclept the Furies, at one selfsame birth
Born, with Megaera's hellish shape, of Night
That knows no seasons, and with serpent-coils
Wreathed each alike, and dowered with windy wings.
These at Jove's throne and on the threshold wait
Of the fierce monarch, and whet terror's edge
In suffering mortals, whensoe'er heaven's king
Launches disease and direful death, or scares
With war offending cities. One of these
Swiftly from heaven's cope Jupiter sent down,
And bade confront Juturna, for a sign.   854
She speeds, borne earthward on the hurrying blast.
As some cloud-piercing arrow, shot from string,
Which Parthian in fell venom-bane hath dipped—

Or Parthian or Cydonian—and launched forth,
A shaft past healing-power; with strident sound
It skims the rushing darkness, known of none;
So, journeying earthward, sped the child of Night.
When Ilium's host and Turnus' ranks she viewed,
Shrunk suddenly into a small bird's shape,
Which oft on tomb or lonely roof-top sits,
And nightly shrills a late ill-boding lay
Through darkness—in such altered guise the fiend
Flits shrieking, and still flits in Turnus' face,
Flapping his shield with pinion-strokes. A strange
And fearful numbness loosed his limbs; his hair
Stood stiff with horror, the voice stuck in his throat. *868*
But when from far the Fury's whistling wings
She knew, Juturna, hapless one, rent loose
Her tresses, and marred, sister-like, her face
With wounding nails, and with clenched hands her
  breast.
"How shall thy sister stead thee, Turnus, now?
What more avails my hardihood? Wherewith
May I prolong thy life-day, or how face
A pest so dire? Now, now I quit the field:
Fright not the trembler more, ye birds of bale;
I know your wing-beat and its deathful whirr;
The haughty mandates of imperious Jove
I miss not. Quits he thus my maiden loss?
Why dowered he me with life eternal? Why
Of mortal's lot bereaved me? I might else
Surely have ended all these miseries.
Trod the dark road at my poor brother's side. *881*
Immortal! I? could aught of all I have,
Brother, be sweet without thee? Ah! might Earth
Somewhere yawn deep enough to serve my need,
And hurl me—goddess—to the ghosts below!"
She ceased, her head in grey-green mantle wrapped,
Sore sighing, and plunged beneath her sacred pool.
 Aeneas pressed onward, brandishing his spear,
Huge, like a tree-trunk, and with wrathful heart
Made utterance: "What delays thee next? why still
So backward, Turnus? Not with speed of foot
Strive we, but in grim arms, and hand to hand.
Shift to all shapes, yea, muster all thou canst
Of craft or valour; pray now to wing aloft
The star-way, or in earth's pent hollows hide." *893*
He shook his head: "Thy fiery words, fierce man,
Affright me not; the gods and adverse Jove

Affright me." There he ceased, and, glancing round,
Spied a vast stone, an ancient stone and vast,
Which chanced to lie there, for a landmark pitched,
'Twixt rival fields to sever, on the plain.
Scarce could twice six, of such as earth in bulk
Now bears, upon their necks have heaved it; he
Caught with quick hand and hurled it on the foe,
High-towering, and at hero's utmost speed.
Yet knew he not himself, as on he rushed,
Or reared aloft and swung the mighty stone;
But his knees totter, his blood curdles cold:
Nor the stone's self, which through the void he
    whirled,
Sped to full distance, or brought home the blow.   *907*
Even as in dreams of night, when languorous sleep
Weighs down the eyelids, with vain wish we seem
Some eager course to ply, but helpless sink
Even in mid effort; and the tongue lacks power,
And the limbs' wonted strength besteads us not,
Nor voice nor utterance follows: even so,
Strain as his valour might, the goddess fell
Bars Turnus from fulfilment. Through his heart
Shift changeful phantasies; on Rutule host
And on the town he gazes, and with dread
Falters, and quails before the impending lance;
Nor whither 'scape, with what force meet the foe,
Nor car he sees, nor sister-charioteer.   *918*
Even as he faltered his death-bearing dart
Aeneas brandished, marking with his eye
The happy moment, then with all his bulk
Hurled it against him. Never stone so crashed,
Flung from the leaguer's engine, nor such roar
Burst with the fire-bolt. Like a black typhoon,
Laden with dire destruction, sped the spear,
And rending ope the warrior's corslet rims
And utmost circle of his sevenfold shield,
Right through the thigh rushed hurtling. At the blow
Turnus fell huge to earth on bended knee.   *927*
Upsurge the Rutules with one groan, and all
The mountain round rebellows, and far off
The forest-depths reverberate the cry.
Lowly, with up-cast eyes, a suppliant hand
Outstretching, "I have earned it," he exclaims,
"Nor deprecate my doom; thy fortune use.
If a sad father's yearning heart at all
Can touch thee, I implore—thou too hadst such

A sire, Anchises—upon Daunus old
Have pity, and me, or, if thou wilt, my corse,
Reft of the daylight, to mine own restore.
Thou art the victor; and Ausonia's folk
Have seen me stretch forth vanquished hands; 'tis
    thine
To wed Lavinia; further hate forgo."
Fierce in his arms, with rolling eyeballs, stood
Aeneas, and checked his hand; and more and more
The words 'gan work upon his faltering will,
When high on shoulder lo! the luckless belt
Lay bare, and with its well-known bosses gleamed
The girdle of young Pallas, whom erewhile
Turnus with wound had vanquished, and laid low,
And now on shoulder bore the fatal badge.
Soon as those relics—record of fierce grief—
His eyes drank in, with sudden frenzy fired,
And terrible in his wrath: "Wouldst thou go hence—
Tricked in my comrade's trophies 'scape my hand?
Thou art Pallas' victim; Pallas deals this blow,
And claims the forfeit of thy felon blood."   *949*
So saying, with fiery force he plunged the steel
Full in his bosom. Then the warrior's limbs
Grow chilled and slackened, and the spirit flies
Moaning indignant to the shades below.   *952*

PRINTED IN THE U.S.A.